DATE DUE

AP 7 '97			

DEMCO 38-296

THE NEW OXFORD BOOK OF
CANADIAN SHORT STORIES
IN ENGLISH

THE NEW OXFORD BOOK OF
CANADIAN SHORT STORIES
IN ENGLISH

SELECTED BY

MARGARET ATWOOD & ROBERT WEAVER

Toronto   Oxford   New York

OXFORD UNIVERSITY PRESS

1995

Oxford University Press, 70 Wynford Drive, Don Mills, Ontario M3C 1J9

Oxford New York Athens Auckland Bangkok Bombay
Calcutta Cape Town Dar es Salaam Delhi Florence Hong Kong Istanbul Karachi
Kuala Lumpur Madras Madrid Melbourne Mexico City Nairobi Paris
Singapore Taipei Tokyo Toronto

and associated companies in
Berlin Ibadan

Oxford is a trademark of Oxford University Press

Canadian Cataloguing in Publication Data

Main entry under title:

The new Oxford book of Canadian short stories in English

Includes bibliographical references and index.
ISBN 0-19-541025-4

1. Short stories, Canadian (English).* 2. Canadian
fiction (English) - 20th century.* I. Atwood, Margaret, 1939-
II. Weaver, Robert, 1921-

PS8319.N48 1995   C813'.010805   C95-932179-9
PR9197.32.N48 1995

Contents

～

Acknowledgements

CAROLINE ADDERSON. 'The Chmarnyk' is reprinted from *Bad Imaginings* by Caroline Adderson (The Porcupine's Quill, 1993).

MARGARET ATWOOD. 'True Trash' from *Wilderness Tips* by Margaret Atwood. Copyright © 1991 by O.W. Toad Limited. Used by permission of the Canadian Publishers, McClelland & Stewart, Toronto, Doubleday, a division of Bantam Doubleday Dell Publishing Group, Inc., and Bloomsbury, 1991.

SANDRA BIRDSELL. 'Flowers for Weddings and Funerals' from *Agassiz Stories* (Turnstone Press, 1982, 1987). © Sandra Birdsell. Reprinted by permission.

NEIL BISSOONDATH. 'Digging Up the Mountains' from *Digging Up the Mountains* by Neil Bissoondath, © 1985. Reprinted by permission of Macmillan Canada.

CLARK BLAISE. 'A Class of New Canadians' from *A North American Education* by Clark Blaise. Copyright © 1973 by Clark Blaise. Reprinted by permission of the author.

GEORGE BOWERING. 'The Hayfield' from *Protective Footwear* by George Bowering. Used by permission of the Canadian Publishers, McClelland & Stewart, Toronto.

DIONNE BRAND. 'Sans Souci' from *Sans Souci and Other Stories*. Copyright © 1989 by Dionne Brand. Reprinted by permission of Firebrand Books, Ithaca, New York.

BONNIE BURNARD. 'Deer Heart' from *Casino & Other Stories*. Copyright © 1994 by Bonnie Burnard. Published by HarperCollins Publishers Ltd. Reprinted with the permission of the author.

BARRY CALLAGHAN. 'The Black Queen' from *The Black Queen Stories*, © Barry Callaghan. Reprinted by permission of the author.

MORLEY CALLAGHAN. 'All the Years of Her Life' from *Morley Callaghan's Stories* by Morley Callaghan © 1959. Reprinted by permission of Macmillan Canada.

AUSTIN C. CLARKE. 'Griff!' from *When Women Rule* (1985) by Austin C. Clarke. Used by permission of the Canadian Publishers, McClelland & Stewart, Toronto and the author.

MATT COHEN. 'Trotsky's First Confessions' from *Lives of the Mind Slaves* by Matt Cohen, © 1994, Porcupine's Quill; reprinted by arrangement with Bella Pomer Agency Inc.

MARIAN ENGEL. 'Share and Share Alike' from *The Tattooed Woman* by Marian Engel. Copyright © The Estate of Marian Engel, 1985. Reprinted by permission of Penguin Books Canada Limited, and Virginia Barber Literary Agency Inc.

TIMOTHY FINDLEY. 'The Duel in Cluny Park' copyright © 1989 by Pebble Productions Ltd. This story was first published in *Toronto Life* magazine, and is reprinted by permission of the author.

CYNTHIA FLOOD. 'The Meaning of Marriage' from *My Father Took a Cake to France* by Cynthia Flood, copyright © 1992, Talon Books Ltd, Vancouver, BC.

MAVIS GALLANT. 'Scarves, Beads, Sandals', copyright © 1995 by Mavis Gallant. Reprinted by permission of Georges Borchardt, Inc. for the author. Originally published in *The New Yorker*.

HUGH GARNER. 'One-Two-Three Little Indians' from *Hugh Garner's Best Stories*. Used by permission of McGraw-Hill Ryerson Limited.

MARGARET GIBSON. 'Making It' is reprinted from *The Butterfly Ward* by permission of Oberon Press.

DOUGLAS GLOVER. 'Swain Corliss, Hero of Malcolm's Mills (Now Oakland, Ontario), November 6, 1814' reprinted from *A Guide to Animal Behaviour* by permission of Goose Lane Editions. Copyright © Douglas Glover, 1991.

KATHERINE GOVIER. 'Sociology', first published in *Fables of Brunswick Avenue*, Penguin Books of Canada. Reprinted by permission of the author.

BARBARA GOWDY. 'We So Seldom Look on Love' from *We So Seldom Look on Love* by Barbara Gowdy Copyright © 1992 by Barbara Gowdy. Reprinted by permission of Somerville House Books, HarperCollins Publishers Limited, and HarperCollins Publishers, Inc. This story first appeared in *Canadian Fiction Magazine*.

HUGH HOOD. 'Getting to Williamstown'. Copyright Hugh Hood. All rights reserved.

ISABEL HUGGAN. 'Celia Behind Me' is reprinted from *The Elizabeth Stories* by permission of Oberon Press.

JANICE KULYK KEEFER. 'Transfigurations' from *Transfigurations*, copyright © Janice Kulyk Keefer 1987. Reprinted by permission of the author.

THOMAS KING. 'One Good Story, That One' by Thomas King from *One Good Story, That One*, copyright 1993 by Dead Dog Cafe Productions Inc. Published in Canada by HarperCollins Publishers Ltd.

W.P. KINSELLA. 'Shoeless Joe Jackson Comes to Iowa' is reprinted from *Shoeless Joe Jackson Comes to Iowa* by permission of Oberon Press.

MARGARET LAURENCE. 'Mask of the Bear' from *A Bird in the House* by Margaret Laurence. © 1963 by Margaret Laurence. Used by permission of the Canadian Publishers, McClelland & Stewart, Toronto, New End Inc. and A.P. Watt Ltd on behalf of New End Inc.

NORMAN LEVINE. 'Something Happened Here' by Norman Levine, from *Something Happened Here*, published in Canada and the UK by Viking/Penguin. © Norman Levine 1991. Reprinted by arrangement with the author.

ALISTAIR MACLEOD. 'As Birds Bring Forth the Sun' from *As Birds Bring Forth the Sun* by Alistair MacLeod. Used by permission of the Canadian Publishers, McClelland & Stewart, Toronto.

JOYCE MARSHALL. 'The Old Woman' from *Any Time At All and Other Stories* by Joyce Marshall. Used by permission of the Canadian Publishers, McClelland & Stewart, Toronto.

JOHN METCALF. 'The Years in Exile' is reprinted by permission of the author.

ROHINTON MISTRY. 'The Ghost of Firozsha Baag' from *Tales from Firozsha Baag* by Rohinton Mistry. Used by permission of The Canadian Publishers, McClelland & Stewart, Toronto, Faber and Faber Ltd., and Lucinda Vardey Agency Ltd. 'The Ghost of Firozsha Baag' from *Swimming Lessons*. Copyright © 1987 by Rohinton Mistry. Reprinted by permission of Houghton Mifflin Co. All rights reserved.

ALICE MUNRO. 'The Jack Randa Hotel' from *Open Secrets* by Alice Munro. Copyright © 1994 by Alice Munro. Used by permission of the Canadian Publishers, McClelland & Stewart, Toronto and Alfred A. Knopf Inc. Published by Alfred A. Knopf, Inc. Reprinted by arrangement with the Virginia Barber Literary Agency. All rights reserved.

THOMAS H. RADDALL. 'The Wedding Gift' is reprinted with permission of the Governors of Dalhousie College and University.

JAMES REANEY. 'The Bully'. Used by permission of the author.

LEON ROOKE. 'The Woman Who Talked to Horses' from *Sing Me No Love Songs I'll Say You No Prayers* by Leon Rooke. Copyright © 1984 by Leon Rooke. First published by The Ecco Press in 1984. Reprinted by permission.

SINCLAIR ROSS. 'The Lamp at Noon' from *The Lamp at Noon* by Sinclair Ross. Used by permission of the Canadian Publishers, McClelland & Stewart, Toronto.

JANE RULE. 'The End of Summer' is reprinted with permission from *Inland Passage and Other Stories* by Jane Rule, published by Lester & Orpen Dennys. Copyright © 1985.

DIANE SCHOEMPERLEN. 'Red Plaid Shirt' © copyright Diane Schoemperlen 1989; reprinted by arrangement with Bella Pomer Agency Inc.

CAROL SHIELDS. 'Milk Bread Beer Ice' extracted from *The Orange Fish* by Carol Shields. Copyright © 1989 by Carol Shields. Reprinted by permission of Random House of Canada Limited and Viking Penguin, a division of Penguin Books USA Inc. Reprinted from *Various Miracles* by Carol Shields (London: Fourth Estate Ltd, 1994) by arrangement with Blake Friedmann.

LINDA SVENDSEN. 'White Shoulders' is reprinted by permission of the author and her agent, Robin Straus Agency, Inc., New York, and Farrar, Straus & Giroux, Inc. From *Marine Life* by Linda Svendsen, © 1992 by Linda Svendsen, published by HarperCollins Canada, Farrar, Straus & Giroux and Penguin Books in America. First published in *Saturday Night* Magazine.

AUDREY THOMAS. 'Bear Country' © Audrey G. Thomas, 1990. This story first appeared in the June, 1991 issue of *Saturday Night*.

W.D. VALGARDSON. 'God Is Not a Fish Inspector' is reprinted from *God Is Not a Fish Inspector* by permission of Oberon Press.

GUY VANDERHAEGHE. 'Dancing Bear' from *Man Descending* by Guy Vanderhaeghe © 1982. Reprinted by permission of Macmillan Canada.

BRONWEN WALLACE. 'For Puzzled in Wisconsin' from *People You'd Trust Your Life To* by Bronwen Wallace. Used by permission of the Canadian Publishers, McClelland & Stewart, Toronto and the Estate of Bronwen Wallace.

RUDY WIEBE. 'Where is the Voice Coming From?' by Rudy Wiebe from *River of Stone: Fictions and Memories*, copyright 1995 by Jackpine House Ltd. Published in Canada by Knopf Canada.

ETHEL WILSON. 'Haply the Soul of My Grandmother' from *Mrs. Golightly* by Ethel Wilson © 1961. Reprinted by permission of Macmillan Canada.

Every effort has been made to determine and contact copyright owners. In the case of any omissions, the publisher will be pleased to make suitable acknowledgement in future editions.

Introduction

By Margaret Atwood

The first edition of *The Oxford Book of Canadian Short Stories in English* appeared ten years ago, and included authors born from 1850 to 1951. So many stories of note have been written in the last decade, however, that for this second edition the editors have unfortunately had to make the decision—faced with constraints of space—to penalize the past in favour of the present. All but one of the story-writers in this collection were born in the twentieth century, and the emphasis is on stories written after the Second World War.

For the same reason—the recent astonishing proliferation of short fiction, in English, in Canada—it would be impossible to assume that this collection represents a 'canon' of any sort. Some of the stories may indeed by now be classics of a kind: Sinclair Ross's Depression story 'The Lamp at Noon'; or Joyce Marshall's haunting 'The Old Woman', which renders the Canadian North as malevolent female; or James Reaney's 'The Bully', one of the first examples of modern Southern Ontario Gothic, a mode that includes works by such novelists as Robertson Davies, Timothy Findley, Barbara Gowdy, Marian Engel, and Graeme Gibson. In other cases a writer—such as Margaret Laurence or Rudy Wiebe—may be better known as a novelist, but may also be an accomplished writer of stories: such ambidexterity is fairly common in Canada. In yet other cases it is the writer, not the individual story, that constitutes the classic: few would dispute the ascendancy in this form of Alice Munro and Mavis Gallant. But to worry unduly over such matters as canons and classics is to make a fool of oneself eventually, for a canon is merely an oft-duplicated list, and a classic is simply a work that is read, re-read, explored for meaning, and admired widely, over a sufficient period of time; and what one generation finds meaningful, the next may find puzzling, absurd, or even tedious. In any case, no classical claims are made for many of the stories in this collection, for the simple reason that they aren't old enough.

Some readers may find themselves wondering how this or that story got into this anthology, and why some other one was left out. Here then is the real truth about the process of selection. Having been morally coerced into saying we would do a second edition of this book (how were we coerced? 'So many new writers need to be considered . . .'), Robert Weaver and I set about the task, with the indispensable help of William Toye, who was the publisher's editor for the first edition and acted as goad, fellow-reader, and tie-breaker. Robert Weaver has read more short stories than you'd care to shake a stick at, and in the course of his career as executive producer of the Canadian Broadcasting Corporation's radio program *Anthology*, as editor of many other collections and of the literary magazine *The Tamarack Review*, and latterly as organizer of a CBC literary competition that attracts literally thousands of entries every year—and having, as a result, become a hard man to please—he has, in fact, shaken a stick at a good many of them. Over the course of his long anthological career, Bill Toye has read marginally fewer stories; but he reads them with great attention, and is noted for saying: 'Isn't there a shorter one we can use?' or, 'This will get us banned by some school board' (although I must add this was not a deterrent for him). I can't match the totals of the other two, but I have a childish longing to be amused, and am often diverted by novelty, so it is to my frivolous interests that you owe the peculiar stories in this book. I was also the one who said nervously, last time: 'How many women have we got?' This time I didn't say it, as it was no longer a thing I felt I had to fret over. The women are simply there. They write. They write well. No one, any longer, finds this freakish or surprising.

The first thing we did, over the wads of paper we had brought with us and the cups of tea we consumed to sharpen our wits, was to make a list of possible new writers, for which we all suggested names. We added this to the list of writers who were already in the book. Then we divided the entire list into three, and each of us went off to read the *oeuvre* of the writers on his or her list. We then got together again and exchanged opinions and stories. Some stories went in, others came out; over some we squabbled, over others we horse-traded; and there were many good stories that, to our distress, we could not include, either because the story was too long or because the book itself was too short. This collection, then, does not represent the taste of one, of two, or even of three people, but the taste of a sort of hybrid and mythical animal with—we hope—wings, legs, lungs, and gills; that is to say, the virtues of all three of us and the defects of none.

I must say also that we gave up some time ago trying to isolate the gene for 'Canadianness'. In a country thousands of miles wide and almost as tall, which covers terrain as diverse as the frozen Arctic, the Prairies, the West Coast rain forests, and the rocks of Newfoundland; in which fifty-two indigenous languages are spoken—none of which is English—and a hundred or so others are also in use; and which contains the most cosmopolitan city in the world, the erstwhile true-blue Toronto the Good—it's kind of difficult to pin such a thing down. If you write about Scotland, have you written a Scottish story? If a Scot comes to Canada—and many have—and writes a story about it, is that story Scottish or Canadian, or both? Does 'Canadian' mean a story about the country, or a story by one of its citizens, or something else entirely? This used to be a problem of self-definition peculiar to New World countries, but increasingly—as people move from here to there and back again, sometimes feeling more and more uneasy and uprooted every time—it's simply the state of the world. Canadians are no longer the only people who have a feeling of exile, or who consider themselves—in the words of Canadian poet P.K. Page—to be permanent tourists.

So some of the writers in this volume were born in Canada, others not; of the former group, some have set their stories outside the country, and of the latter some write from a perspective very much inside it. The adjective 'Canadian' may resemble nothing so much as a photograph of a spiral nebula: a dense cluster of bright specks at the middle, where you might say the object as a whole is more or less located, and then some other specks, further out, that revolve eccentrically in the same gravitational field. Some stories in this book could not be anything other than Canadian, and you know it as soon as you read them. With others, you have to blink, or peek at the author's biography. Some are born Canadian, some achieve Canadianness, and others have Canadianness thrust upon them. So let's just say that most of these folks have (or have had, or will have) their passports in order, and leave it at that.

Looking back at my Introduction to the first edition of this book, I find a confidence about the future of the story in Canada, and also about the future of the arts in Canada, and indeed about the future of Canada, that I am no longer able to feel. Many years of political division and wrangling have taken their toll; the Canadian identity, however defined, is under increasing siege from 'international' culture; and, perhaps fuelled by the under-the-table culture clauses in the Free Trade Agreement, the age of slash-and-burn—for arts funding in general and indeed for any kind of cultural programming—has arrived in earnest. Many Canadian publishers — both of books and of magazines—sense the rug being pulled out from under them, as both grant mechanisms and legal protections for their enterprises are demolished.

Despite the fact that Canada is more likely to be recognized abroad for its artistic achievements than for anything else, official support for these achievements is on the slide; and despite the fact that the cultural sector contributes more to the economy than do forest products, the politicians are playing to the cheap seats—those very same cheap seats that believe the making of a clothes peg is productive, but the making of a story is useless and self-indulgent. The 'market economy' is our new false god, one that it is considered sacrilegious to question; but not everything can be bought and sold, or assigned a true monetary value, and every human culture has always known that. We forget it at our peril. (Evening writing classes are of course stuffed with disillusioned businessfolk in search of their wandering souls, but that's another story.)

In conclusion one ought to crank out a Pollyanna note to keep hope alive—it's the usual thing on lifeboats adrift at sea—so here it is. Robert Weaver, Bill Toye, and I can all remember a time when there was no arts funding here worthy of the name, and when nothing that could be called 'money' could conceivably be made in Canada by writing. Back then—say, forty years ago—there was no funding for writing, because it was officially believed that there was no writing. Magazines and book-editing ran—even more than they do at present—on donated blood.

But those who wrote stories then wrote them anyway, because they wanted and needed to, and because they believed in the form itself, and in what it could say through them. As always, they began their writing lives in little magazines, which also did not make money and still don't. If the little magazines of this country all disappear because of political short-sightedness and the usual Canadian shoot-yourself-in-the-foot cultural death-wish, an important door for young writers will be closed; but it will be closed only temporarily, because the young writers will certainly open it again themselves.

So if this book is dedicated to anyone, it's to the writers—those who have made it this far within the improbable circumstances of this astonishing, puzzling, and often maddening country. It's for those whose stories are in this book, for those who preceded them, for those who have accompanied them on their journey—and, especially, for those young writers who haven't yet appeared.

ETHEL WILSON
(1888-1980)

Haply the Soul of My Grandmother

CLOWN: *What is the opinion of Pythagoras concerning wild fowl?*
MALVOLIO: *That the soul of our grandam might haply inhabit a bird.*
                                                    - TWELFTH NIGHT, Act IV, Scene ii.

'It is airless,' said Mrs Forrester.

'Yes, there is no air,' said the woman half beside her half in front of her.
The mouth of the tomb was no longer visible behind them, but there was
light. They stepped carefully downwards. Mrs Forrester looked behind her
at her husband. She was inexcusably nervous and wanted a look or a gleam
of reassurance from his face. But he did not appear to see her. He scruti-
nized the yellow walls which looked as if they were compounded with sandstone and clay. Marcus seemed to be looking for something, but there was
nothing on the yellowish walls not even the marks of pick and shovel.

Mrs Forrester had to watch her steps on the stairs of smoothed and worn
pounded sandstone or clay, so she turned again, looking downwards. It did
not matter whether she held her head up or down, there was no air. She
breathed, of course, but what she breathed was not air but some kind of
ancient vacuum. She supposed that this absence of air must affect the noses
and mouths and lungs of Marcus and of the woman from Cincinnati and the
guide and the soldier and that she need not consider herself to be special.
So. although she suffered from the airlessness and a kind of blind something, very old, dead, she knew that she must not give way to her impulse to
complain again, saying, 'I can't breathe! There is no air!' and certainly she
must not turn and stumble up the steps into the blazing heat as she wished
to do; neither must she faint. She had never experienced panic before, but
she recognized all this for near panic. She stiffened, controlled herself (she
thought), then relaxed, breathed the vacuum as naturally as possible, and
continued her way down into the earth from small light to small light. They
reached the first chamber which was partly boarded up.

Looking through the chinks of the planking they seemed to see a long
and deep depression which because of its shape indicated that, once, a body
had lain there, probably in a vast and ornate coffin so as to magnify the size
and great importance of its occupant. The empty depression spoke of a

removal of some long object which, Mrs Forrester knew, had lain there for thousands of years, hidden, sealed, alone, yet existing, in spite of the fact that generations of living men, know-alls, philosophers, scientists, slaves, ordinary people, kings, knew nothing about it. And then it had been suspected, and then discovered, and then taken away somewhere, and now there was only the depression which they saw. All that was mortal of a man or woman who had been all-powerful had laid there, accompanied by treasure hidden and sealed away by a generation from other generations (men do not trust their successors, and rightly) till only this great baked dried yellowish aridity of hills and valleys remained, which was called the Valley of the Kings. And somewhere in the valley were dead kings.

Peering between the boards and moving this way and that so as to obtain a better view, they saw that a frieze of figures ran round the walls above the level of the depression. The figures were all in profile, and although they were only two-dimensional, they had a look of intention and vigour which gave them life and great dignity. There was no corpulence; all were slim, wide of shoulder, narrow of hip. Mostly, Mrs Forrester thought, they walked very erect. They did not seem to stand, or, if they stood, they stood as if springing already into motion. She thought, peering, that they seemed to walk, all in profile and procession, towards some seated Being, it might be a man, or it might be sexless, or it might be a cat, or even a large bird, no doubt an ibis. The moving figures proceeded either with hieratic gesture or bearing objects. The colours, in which an ochreous sepia predominated, were faintly clear. The airlessness of the chamber nearly overwhelmed her again and she put out her hand to touch her husband's arm. There was not much to see, was there? between these planks, so they proceeded on downwards. The guide, who was unintelligible, went first. The soldier followed them.

If ever I get out of this, thought Mrs Forrester. The airlessness was only part of an ancientness, a strong persistence of the past into the now and beyond the now which terrified her. It was not the death of the place that so invaded her, although there was death; it was the long persistent life in which her bones and flesh and all the complex joys of her life and her machine-woven clothes and her lipstick that was so important to her were less than the bright armour of a beetle on which she could put her foot. Since all three of the visitors were silent in the tomb, it was impossible to know what the others felt. And anyway, one could not explain; and why explain (all this talk about 'feelings'!).

The farther down the steps they went the more the air seemed to expire, until at the foot of the steps it really died. Here was the great chamber of the great king, and a sarcophagus had been left there, instructively, perhaps, so that the public, who came either for pleasure or instruction, should be able to see the sort of sight which the almost intoxicated excavators had seen as they moved the earth and allowed in the desecrating air—or what passed for air.

Since Mrs Forrester was now occupied in avoiding falling down and thereby creating a small scene beside the sarcophagus which would annoy her and her husband very much indeed and would not help the lady from Cincinnati who had grown pale, none of the guide's talk was heard and no image of the sarcophagus or of the friezes or of the tomb itself remained in her mind. It was as a saved soul that she was aware of the general turning up towards the stairs, up towards the light, and she was not ashamed, now, to lay her hand upon her husband's arm, really for support, in going up the stairs.

They emerged into the sunlight which blinded them and the heat that beat up at them and bore down on them, and all but the two Egyptians fumbled for their dark glasses. The soldier rejoined his comrade at the mouth of the tomb, and the guide seemed to vanish around some cliff or crag. The two soldiers were unsoldierly in appearance although no doubt they would enjoy fighting anyone if it was necessary.

Marcus and Mrs Forrester and the lady from Cincinnati whose name was Sampson or Samson looked around for a bit of shade. The lion-coloured crags on their left did of course cast a shade, but it was the kind of shade which did not seem to be of much use to them, for they would have to climb onto farther low crags to avail themselves of the shade, and the sun was so cruel in the Valley of the Kings that no European or North American could make shift to move one step unless it was necessary.

'Where's that guide?' said Marcus irritably, of no one, because no one knew. The guide had gone, probably to wave on the motor car which should have been waiting to pick them up. Mrs. Forrester could picture him walking, running, gesticulating, garments flowing, making all kinds of gratuitous movements in the heat. We're differently made, she thought, it's all those centuries.

'I think,' said Mrs Sampson timidly, 'that this s-seems to be the best p-place.'

'Yes,' said Mrs Forrester who was feeling better though still too hot and starved for air, 'that's the best place. There's enough shade there for us all,' and they moved to sit down on some yellow rocks which were too hot for comfort. Nobody talked of the tomb which was far below the ground on their right.

Mrs Forrester spoke to her husband who did not answer. He looked morose. His dark eyes were concentrated in a frown and it was obvious that he did not want to talk to her or to anybody else. Oh dear, she thought. It's the tomb—he's never like that unless it's really something. They sat in silence, waiting for whatever should turn up. The two soliders smoked at some distance.

This is very uncomfortable, this heat, thought Mrs Forrester, and the tomb has affected us unpleasantly. She reflected on Lord Carnarvon who had sought with diligence, worked ardently, superintended excavation, urged on discovery, was bitten by an insect—or so they said—and had died. She thought of a co-worker of his who lay ill with some fever in the small clay-built house past which they had driven that morning. Why do they do those things, these men? Why do they do it? They do it because they have to; they come here to be uncomfortable and unlucky and for the greatest fulfilment of their lives; just as men climb mountains; just as Arctic and Antarctic explorers go to the polar regions to be uncomfortable and unlucky and for the greatest fulfilment of their lives. They have to. The thought of the Arctic gave her a pleasant feeling and she determined to life the pressure that seemed to have settled on all three of them which was partly tomb, no doubt, but chiefly the airlessness to which their lungs were not accustomed, and, of course, this heat.

She said with a sort of imbecile cheerfulness, 'How about an ice-cream cone?'

Mrs Sampson looked up at her with a pale smile and Marcus did not answer. No, she was not funny, and she subsided. Out of the rocks flew two great burnished-winged insects and attacked them like bombers. All three ducked and threw up their arms to protect their faces.

'Oh . . .' and 'oh . . .' cried the women and forgot about the heat while the two vicious bright-winged insects charged them, one here, one there, with a clattering hiss. Mrs Forrester did not know whether the insects had hit and bitten Marcus or Mrs Sampson. She had driven them away, she thought, and as she looked around and her companions looked up and around, she saw that the insects, which had swiftly retired, now dived down upon them again.

The car came round a corner and stopped before them. There was only the driver. The guide had departed and would no doubt greet them at the hotel with accusations and expostulations. They climbed into the car, the two women at the back and Marcus—still morose—in front with the driver. The car started. The visit to the tomb had not been a success, but at all events the two insects did not accompany them any farther.

They jolted along very fast in the dust which covered them and left a rolling column behind. At intervals the driver honked the horn because he liked doing it. In the empty desert he honked for pleasure. They had not yet reached the trail in the wide sown green belt that bordered the Nile.

The driver gave a last honk and drew up. As the dust settled, they saw, on their right, set back in the dead hills, a row of arches, not a colonnade but a row of similar arches separated laterally a little from each other and leading, evidently, into the hills. They must be tombs, or caves. These arches were black against the dusty yellow of the rock. Mrs. Forrester was forced to admit to herself that the row of arches into the hills was beautiful. There seemed to be about twenty or thirty arches, she estimated when she thought about it later.

There they sat.

'Well, what are we waiting for?' Marcus asked the driver.

The driver became voluble and then he turned to the women behind, as Marcus, who was impatient to get on, did not seem to co-operate.

'I think he has to w-wait a few minutes for someone who m-may be there. He has to pick someone up unless they've already gone,' said Mrs Sampson. 'He has to w-wait.'

The driver then signified that if they wished they could go up to the tombs within the arches. Without consultation together they all immediately said no. They sat back and waited. Can Marcus be ill? Mrs Forrester wondered. He is too quiet.

Someone stood at the side of the car, at Mrs Forrester's elbow. This was an aged bearded man clothed in a long ragged garment and a head-furnishing which was neither skull cap nor tarboosh. His face was mendicant but not crafty. He was too remote in being, Mrs. Forrester thought, but he was too close in space.

'Lady,' he said, 'I show you something' ('Go away,' said Mrs Forrester), and he produced a small object from the folds of his garment. He held it up, between finger and thumb, about a foot from Mrs Forrester's face.

The object on which the two women looked was a small human hand, cut off below the wrist. The little hand was wrapped in grave-clothes, and the small fingers emerged from the wrapping, neat, grey, precise. The fingers were close together, with what appeared to be nails or the places for nails upon them. A tatter of grave-clothes curled and fluttered down from the chopped-off wrist.

'Nice hand. Buy a little hand, lady. Very good very old very cheap. Nice mummy hand.'

'Oh g-go away!' cried Mrs Sampson, and both women averted their faces because they did not like looking at the small mummy's hand.

The aged man gave up, and moving on with the persistence of the East he held the little hand in front of Marcus.

'Buy a mummy hand, gentleman sir. Very old very nice very cheap, sir. Buy a little hand.'

Marcus did not even look at him.

'NIMSHI,' he roared. Marcus had been in Egypt in the last war.

He roared so loud that the mendicant started back. He rearranged his features into an expression of terror. He shambled clumsily away with a gait which was neither running nor walking, but both. Before him he held in the air the neat little hand, the little raped hand, with the tatter of grave-clothes fluttering behind it. The driver, for whom the incident held no interest, honked his horn, threw his hands about to indicate that he would wait no longer, and then drove on.

When they had taken their places in the boat with large sails which carried them across the Nile to the Luxor side, Mrs Forrester, completely aware of her husband's malaise but asking no questions, saw that this river and these banks and these tombs and temples and these strange agile people to whom she was alien and who were alien to her had not—at four o'clock in the afternoon—the charm that had surprised her in the lily green and pearly cool scene at six o'clock that morning. The sun was high and hot, the men were noisy, the Nile was just water, and she wished to get Marcus back to the hotel.

When they reached the hotel Marcus took off his outer clothes and lay on the bed.

'What is it, Marc?'

'Got a headache.'

It was plain to see, now, that he was ill. Mrs Forrester rang for cold bot- tled water for Marcus to drink and for ice for compresses. She rummaged in her toilet case and found that she had put in a thermometer as a sort of charm against disease. That was in Vancouver, and how brash, kind, happy, and desirable Vancouver seemed now. Marcus had a temperature of 104°.

There were windows on each side wall of the room. They were well screened and no flies could, one thought, get it; so, by having the windows open, the ghost of the breeze that blew off the Nile River entered and passed out of the room but did not touch Marcus. There was, however, one fly in the room, nearly as dangerous as a snake. Mrs Forrester took the ele- gant little ivory-handled fly switch that she had used in Cairo and, sitting beside her husband, flicked gently when the fly buzzed near him.

'Don't.'

'All right, dear,' she said with the maddening indulgence of the well to the sick. She went downstairs.

'Is that compartment still available on the Cairo train tonight?' she asked.

'*Si*, madame.'

'We will take it. My husband is not well.'

'Not well! That is unfortunate, madame,' said the official at the desk lan- guidly. 'I will arrange at once.'

It was clear that the management did not sympathize with illness and would prefer to get rid of sick travellers immediately.

Mrs Forrester went upstairs and changed the compress. She then went and sat by the window overlooking the Nile. She reflected again that this country, where insects carried curses in their wings, made her uneasy. It was too old and strange. She had said as much to Marcus who felt nothing of the kind. He liked the country. But then, she thought, I am far too susceptible to the power of the Place, and Marcus is more sensible; these things do not affect him in this way, and, anyway, he knows Egypt. However high the trees and mountains on her native British Columbia, they were native to her. However wide the prairies, she was part of them. However fey the moors of Devon, however ancient Glastonbury or London, they were part of her. Greece was young and she was at home there. The Parthenon in ruins of glory was fresh and fair. And Socrates, drinking the hemlock among his friends as the evening sun smote Hymettus . . . was that last week . . . was he indeed dead? But now . . . let us go away from here.

Below the window, between a low wall and the river, knots of men stood, chattering loudly—Egyptians, Arabs, Abyssinians, and an old man with two donkeys. The air was full of shouting. They never ceased. They shouted, they laughed, they slapped their thighs, they quarrelled. No one could sleep. The sickest man could not sleep in that bright hot loud afternoon. This was their pleasure, cheaper than eating, drinking, or lust. But she could do nothing. The uproar went on. She changed the compress, bending over the husband's dark face and closed eyes and withdrawn look.

It's odd (and she turned to the thought of this country which in spite of its brightness and darkness and vigour was fearful to her), that I am Canadian and am fair, and have my roots in that part of England which was ravaged and settled by blond Norsemen; and Marcus is Canadian and is dark, and before generations of being Canadian he was Irish, and before generations of being Irish—did the dark Phoenicians come?—and he finds no strangeness here and I do.

In the late evening Marcus walked weakly onto the Cairo train. The compartment was close, small, and grimy. The compressed heat of the evening was intense. They breathed dust. Mrs Forrester gently helped her husband on to the berth. He looked around.

'I can't sleep down here!' he said. 'You mustn't go up above in all this heat!' But he could do no other.

'I shan't go up,' she said consolingly. 'See!' and she took bedclothes from the upper berth and laid them on the floor beside his berth. 'I shall be cooler down here.' There she lay all night long, breathing a little stale air and grit which entered by a small grid at the bottom of the door. 'Oh . . . you sleeping on the floor . . . !' groaned Marcus.

And outside in the dark, she thought, as the train moved north, is that same country that in the early dawning looks so lovely. In the faint pearl of morning, peasants issue from huts far apart. The family—the father, the ox, the brother, the sons, the children, the women in trailing black, the dog, the asses—file to their work between the lines of pale green crops. There again is something hieratic, ageless, in their movements as they file singly one behind the other between the green crops, as the figures on the frieze had filed, one behind the other. Here and there in the morning stand the ibis, sacred, unmolested, among the delicate green. How beguiling was the unawareness, and the innocency. Then, in that morning hour, and only then, had she felt no fear of Egypt. This scene was universal and unutterably lovely. She . . .

'A LITTLE HAND,' said her husband loudly in the dark, and spoke strange words, and then was silent.

Yes, buy a little hand, sir, nice, cheap, very old. Buy a little hand. Whose hand?

When morning came Marcus woke and looked down in surprise.

'Whatever are you doing down there?' he asked in his ordinary voice.

'It was cooler,' said his wife. 'Did you sleep well?' and she scrambled up.

'Me? Sleep? Oy yes, I think I slept. But there was something . . . a hand . . . I seemed to dream about a hand . . . What hand? . . . Oh yes, that hand . . . I don't quite remember . . . in the tomb . . . you didn't seem to notice the lack of air in the tomb, did you . . . I felt something brushing us in there . . . brushing us all day . . . That was a heck of a day . . . Where's my tie?'

He stood up weakly. Without speaking, Mrs Forrester handed her husband his tie.

Marcus, whose was that little hand, she thought and would think . . . whose was it? . . . Did it ever know you . . . did you ever know that hand? . . . Whose hand was it, Marcus? . . . oh let us go away from here!

MORLEY CALLAGHAN
(1903-1990)

⌒

All the Years of Her Life

They were closing the drugstore, and Alfred Higgins, who had just taken off his white jacket, was putting on his coat and getting ready to go home. The little grey-haired man, Sam Carr, who owned the drugstore, was bending down behind the cash register, and when Alfred Higgins passed him, he looked up and said softly, 'Just a moment, Alfred. One moment before you go.'

The soft, confident, and quiet way in which Sam Carr spoke made Alfred start to button his coat nervously. He felt sure his face was white. Sam Carr usually said, 'Good night,' brusquely, without looking up. In the six months he had been working in the drugstore, Alfred had never heard his employer speak softly like that. His heart began to beat so loud it was hard for him to get his breath. 'What is it, Mr Carr?' he asked.

'Maybe you'd be good enough to take a few things out of your pocket and leave them here before you go," Sam Carr said.

'What things? What are you talking about?'

'You've got a compact and a lipstick and at least two tubes of toothpaste in your pockets, Alfred.'

'What do you mean? Do you think I'm crazy?' Alfred blustered. His face got red and he knew he looked fierce with indignation. But Sam Carr, standing by the door with his blue eyes shining brightly behind his glasses and his lips moving underneath his grey moustache, only nodded his head a few times, and then Alfred grew very frightened and he didn't know what to say. Slowly he raised his hand and dipped it into his pocket, and with his eyes never meeting Sam Carr's eyes, he took out the blue compact and the two tubes of toothpaste and a lipstick, and he laid them one by one on the counter.

'Petty thieving, eh, Alfred?' Sam Carr said. 'And maybe you'd be good enough to tell me how long this has been going on.'

'This is the first time I ever took anything.'

'So now you think you'll tell me a lie, eh? What kind of a sap do I look like, huh? I don't know what goes on in my own store, eh? I tell you you've been doing this pretty steady,' Sam Carr said as he went over and stood behind the cash register.

Ever since Alfred had left school he had been getting into trouble wherever he worked. He lived with his mother and his father, who was a printer. His two older brothers were married and his sister had got married last year, and it would have been all right for his parents now if Alfred had only been able to keep a job.

While Sam Carr smiled and stroked the side of his face very delicately with the tips of his fingers, Alfred began to feel that familiar terror growing in him that had been in him every time he had got into such trouble.

'I liked you,' Sam Carr was saying. 'I liked you and would have trusted you, and now look what I got to do.' While Alfred watched with his alert, frightened blue eyes, Sam Carr drummed with his fingers on the counter. 'I don't like to call a cop in point-blank,' he was saying as he looked very worried. 'You're a fool, and maybe I should call your father and tell him you're a fool. Maybe I should let them know I'm going to have you locked up.'

'My father's not at home. He's a printer. He works nights,' Alfred said.

'Who's at home?'

'My mother, I guess.'

'Then we'll see what she says.' Sam Carr went to the phone and dialed the number. Alfred was not so much ashamed, but there was that deep fright growing in him, and he blurted out arrogantly, like a strong, full-grown man, 'Just a minute. You don't need to draw anybody else in. You don't need to tell her.' He wanted to sound like a swaggering, big guy who could look after himself, yet the old, childish hope was in him, the longing that someone at home would come and help him. 'Yeah, that's right, he's in trouble,' Mr Carr was saying. 'Yeah, your boy works for me. You'd better come down in a hurry.' And when he was finished Mr Carr went over to the door and looked out at the street and watched the people passing in the late summer night. 'I'll keep my eye out for a cop,' was all he said.

Alfred knew how his mother would come rushing in; she would rush in with her eyes blazing, or maybe she would be crying, and she would push him away when he tried to talk to her, and make him feel her dreadful contempt; yet he longed that she might come before Mr Carr saw the cop on the beat passing the door.

While they waited—and it seemed a long time—they did not speak, and when at last they heard someone tapping on the closed door, Mr Carr, turning the latch, said crisply, 'Come in, Mrs Higgins.' He looked hard-faced and stern.

Mrs Higgins must have been going to bed when he telephoned, for her hair was tucked in loosely under her hat, and her hand at her throat held her light coat tight across her chest so her dress would not show. She came in, large and plump, with a little smile on her friendly face. Most of the store lights had been turned out and at first she did not see Alfred, who was standing in the shadow at the end of the counter. Yet as soon as she saw him she did not look as Alfred thought she would look; she smiled, her blue eyes never wavered, and with a calmness and dignity that made them forget that her clothes seemed to have been thrown on her, she put out her hand to Mr Carr and said politely, 'I'm Mrs Higgins. I'm Alfred's mother.'

Mr. Carr was a bit embarrassed by her lack of terror and her simplicity, and he hardly knew what to say to her, so she asked, 'Is Alfred in trouble?'

'He is. He's been taking things from the store. I caught him red-handed. Little things like compacts and toothpaste and lipsticks. Stuff he can sell easily,' the proprietor said.

As she listened, Mrs Higgins looked at Alfred sometimes and nodded her head sadly, and when Sam Carr had finished she said gravely, 'Is it so, Alfred?'

'Yes.'

'Why have you been doing it?'

'I been spending money, I guess.'

'On what?'

'Going around with the guys, I guess,' Alfred said.

Mrs. Higgins put out her hand and touched Sam Carr's arm with an understanding gentleness, and speaking as though afraid of disturbing him, she said, 'If you would only listen to me before doing anything.' Her simple earnestness made her shy; her humility made her falter and look away, but in a moment she was smiling gravely again, and she said with a kind of patient dignity, 'What did you intend to do, Mr Carr?'

'I was going to get a cop. That's what I ought to do.'

'Yes, I suppose so. It's not for me to say, because he's my son. Yet I sometimes think a little good advice is the best thing for a boy when he's at a certain period in his life,' she said.

Alfred couldn't understand his mother's quiet composure, for if they had been at home and someone had suggested that he was going to be arrested, he knew she would be in a rage and would cry out against him. Yet now she was standing there with that gentle, pleading smile on her face, saying, 'I wonder if you don't think it would be better just to let him come home with me. He looks a big fellow, doesn't he? It takes some of them a long time to get any sense,' and they both stared at Alfred, who shifted away with a bit of light shining for a moment on his thin face and the tiny pimples over his cheekbone.

But even while he was turning away uneasily Alfred was realizing that Mr Carr had become aware that his mother was really a fine woman; he knew that Sam Carr was puzzled by his mother, as if he had expected her to come in and plead with him tearfully, and instead he was being made to feel a bit ashamed by her vast tolerance. While there was only the sound of the mother's soft, assured voice in the store, Mr Carr began to nod his head encouragingly at her. Without being alarmed, while being just large and still and simple and hopeful, she was becoming dominant there in the dimly lit store. 'Of course, I don't want to be harsh,' Mr Carr was saying. 'I'll tel you what I'll do. I'll just fire him and let it go at that. How's that?' and he got up and shook hands with Mrs Higgins, bowing low to her in deep respect.

There was such warmth and gratitude in the way she said, 'I'll never for-get your kindness,' that Mr Carr began to feel warm and genial himself.

'Sorry we had to meet this way,' he said. 'But I'm glad I got in touch with you. Just wanted to do the right thing, that's all,' he said.

'It's better to meet like this than never, isn't it?' she said. Suddenly they clasped hands as if they liked each other, as if they had known each other a long time. 'Good night, sir,' she said.

'Good night, Mrs Higgins. I'm truly sorry,' he said.

The mother and son walked along the street together, and the mother was taking a long, firm stride as she looked ahead with her stern face full of worry. Alfred was afraid to speak to her, he was afraid of the silence that was between them, so he only looked ahead too, for the excitement and relief was still pretty strong in him; but in a little while, going along like that in silence made him terribly aware of the strength and the sternness in her; he began to wonder what she was thinking of as she stared ahead so grimly; she seemed to have forgotten that he walked beside her; so when they were pass-ing under the Sixth Avenue elevated and the rumble of the train seemed to break the silence, he said in his old, blustering way, 'Thank God it turned out like that. I certainly won't get in a jam like that again.'

'Be quiet. Don't speak to me. You've disgraced me again and again,' she said bitterly.

'That's the last time. That's all I'm saying.'

'Have the decency to be quiet,' she snapped. They kept on their way, looking straight ahead.

When they were at home and his mother took off her coat, Alfred was that she was really only half-dressed, and she made him feel afraid again when she said, without even looking at him, 'You're a bad lot. God forgive you. It's one thing after another and always has been. Why do you stand there so stupidly? Go to bed, why don't you?' When he was going, she said, 'I'm going to make myself a cup of tea. Mind, now, not a word about tonight to your father.'

While Alfred was undressing in his bedroom, he heard his mother mov-ing around the kitchen. She filled the kettle and put it on the stove. She moved a chair. And as he listened there was no shame in him, just wonder and a kind of admiration of her strength and repose. He could still see Sam Carr nodding his head encouragingly to her; he could hear her talking sim-ply and earnestly, and as he sat on his bed he felt a pride in her strength. 'She certainly was smooth,' he thought. 'Gee, I'd like to tell her she sound-ed swell.'

And at last he got up and went along to the kitchen, and when he was at the door he saw his mother pouring herself a cup of tea. He watched and he didn't move. Her face, as she sat there, was a frightened, broken face utterly unlike the face of the woman who had been so assured a little while ago in the drugstore. When she reached out and lifted the kettle to pour hot water into her cup, her hand trembled and the water splashed on the stove.

Leaning back in the chair, she sighed and lifted the cup to her lips, and her lips were groping loosely as if they would never reach the cup. She swallowed the hot tea gingerly, and then she straightened up in relief, though her hand holding the cup still trembled. She looked very old.

It seemed to Alfred that this was the way it had been every time he had been in trouble before, that this trembling had really been in her as she hurried out half-dressed to the drugstore. He understood why she had sat alone in the kitchen the night his young sister had kept repeating doggedly that she was getting married. Now he felt all that his mother had been thinking of as they walked along the street together a little while ago. He watched his mother, and he never spoke, but at that moment his youth seemed to be over; he knew all the years of her life by the way her hand trembled as she raised the cup to her lips. It seemed to him that this was the first time he had ever looked upon his mother.

Thomas H. Raddall
(1903-1994)

~

The Wedding Gift

Nova Scotia, in 1794. Winter. Snow on the ground. Two feet of it in the woods, less by the shore, except in drifts against Port Marriott's barns and fences; but enough to set sleigh bells ringing through the town, enough to require a multitude of paths and burrows from doors to streets, to carpet the wharves and the decks of the shipping, and to trim the ships' yards with tippets of ermine. Enough to require fires roaring in the town's chimneys, and blue wood smoke hanging low over the roof tops in the still December air. Enough to squeal under foot in the trodden places and to muffle the step everywhere else. Enough for the hunters, whose snowshoes now could overtake the floundering moose and caribou. Even enough for the always-complaining loggers, whose ox sleds now could haul their cut from every part of the woods. But not enough, not nearly enough snow for Miss Kezia Barnes, who was going to Bristol Creek to marry Mr Hathaway.

Kezia did not want to marry Mr Hathaway. Indeed she had told Mr and Mrs Barclay in a tearful voice that she didn't want to marry anybody. But Mr Barclay had taken snuff and said 'Ha! Humph!' in the severe tone he used when he was displeased; and Mrs Barclay had sniffed and said it was a very good match for her, and revolved the cold blue eyes in her fat moon face, and said Kezia must not be a little fool.

There were two ways of going to Bristol Creek. One was by sea, in one of the fishing sloops. But the preacher objected to that. He was a pallid young man lately sent out from England by Lady Huntingdon's Connexion, and seasick five weeks on the way. He held Mr Barclay in some awe, for Mr Barclay had the best pew in the meetinghouse and was the chief pillar of godliness in Port Marriott. But young Mr Mears was firm on this point. He would go by road, he said, or not at all. Mr Barclay had retorted 'Ha! Humph!' The road was twenty miles of horse path through the woods, now deep in snow. Also the path began at Harper's Farm on the far side of the harbour, and Harper had but one horse.

'I shall walk,' declared the preacher calmly, 'and the young woman can ride.'

Kezia had prayed for snow, storms of snow, to bury the trail and keep anyone from crossing the cape to Bristol Creek. But now they were setting out from Harper's Farm, with Harper's big brown horse, and all Kezia's prayers had gone for naught. Like any anxious lover, busy Mr Hathaway had sent Black Sam overland on foot to find out what delayed his wedding, and now Sam's day-old tracks marked for Kezia the road to marriage.

She was a meek little thing, as became an orphan brought up as house-help in the Barclay home; but now she looked at the preacher and saw how young and helpless he looked so far from his native Yorkshire, and how ill-clad for this bitter trans-Atlantic weather, and she spoke up.

'You'd better take my shawl, sir. I don't need it. I've got Miss Julia's old riding cloak. And we'll go ride-and-tie.'

'Ride and what?' murmured Mr Mears.

'I'll ride a mile or so, then I'll get down and tie the horse to a tree and walk on. When you come up to the horse, you mount and ride a mile or so, passing me on the way, and you tie him and walk on. Like that. Ride-and-tie, ride-and-tie. The horse gets a rest between.'

Young Mr Mears nodded and took the proffered shawl absently. It was a black thing that matched his sober broadcloth coat and smallclothes, his black woollen stockings and his round black hat. At Mr Barclay's suggestion he had borrowed a pair of moose-hide moccasins for the journey. As he walked a prayer-book in his coat-skirts bumped the back of his legs.

At the top of the ridge above Harper's pasture, where the narrow path led off through gloomy hemlock woods, Kezia paused for a last look back across the harbour. In the morning sunlight the white roofs of the little lonely town resembled a tidal wave flung up by the sea and frozen as it broke against the dark pine forest to the west. Kezia sighed, and young Mr Mears was surprised to see tears in her eyes.

She rode off ahead. The saddle was a man's, of course, awkward to ride modestly, woman-fashion. As soon as she was out of the preacher's sight she rucked her skirts and slid a leg over to the other stirrup. That was better. There was a pleasant sensation of freedom about it, too. For a moment she forgot that she was going to Bristol Creek, in finery second-hand from the Barclay girls, in a new linen shift and drawers that she had sewn herself in the light of the kitchen candles, in white cotton stockings and a bonnet and shoes from Mr Barclay's store, to marry Mr Hathaway.

The Barclays had done well for her from the time when, a skinny weeping creature of fourteen, she was taken into the Barclay household and, as Mrs Barclay so often said, 'treated more like one of my own than a bond-girl from the poorhouse'. She had first choice of the clothing cast off by Miss Julia and Miss Clara. She was permitted to sit in the same room, and learn what she could, when the schoolmaster came to give private lessons to the Barclay girls. She waited on table, of course, and helped in the kitchen, and made beds, and dusted and scrubbed. But then she had been taught to spin and to sew and to knit. And she was permitted, indeed encouraged, to sit with the Barclays in the meetinghouse, at the convenient end of the pew, where she could worship the Barclays' God and assist with the Barclay wraps at the beginning and end of the service. And now, to complete her rewards, she had been granted the hand of a rejected Barclay suitor.

Mr Hathaway was Barclay's agent at Bristol Creek, where he sold rum and gunpowder and corn meal and such things to the fishermen and hunters, and bought split cod—fresh, pickled or dry—and ran a small sawmill, and cut and shipped firewood by schooner to Port Marriott, and managed a farm, all for a salary of fifty pounds, Halifax currency, per year. Hathaway was a most capable fellow, Mr Barclay often acknowledged. But when after fifteen capable years he came seeking a wife, and cast a sheep's eye first at Miss Julia, and then at Miss Clara, Mrs Barclay observed with a sniff that Hathaway was looking a bit high.

So he was. The older daughter of Port Marriott's most prosperous merchant was even then receiving polite attentions from Mr Gamage, the new collector of customs, and a connection of the Halifax Gamages, as Mrs Barclay was fond of pointing out. And Miss Clara was going to Halifax in the spring to learn the gentle art of playing the pianoforte, and incidentally to display her charms to the naval and military young gentlemen who thronged the Halifax drawingrooms. The dear girls laughed behind their hands whenever long solemn Mr Hathaway came to town aboard one of the Barclay vessels and called at the big house under the elms. Mrs Barclay bridled at Hathaway's presumption, but shrewd Mr Barclay narrowed his little black eyes and took snuff and said 'Ha! Humph!'

It was plain to Mr Barclay than an emergency had arisen. Hathaway was a good man—in his place; and Hathaway must be kept content there, to go on making profit for Mr Barclay at a cost of only £50 a year. 'Twas a pity Hathaway couldn't satisfy himself with one of the fishermen's girls at the Creek, but there 'twas. If Hathaway had set his mind on a town miss, then a town miss he must have; but she must be the right kind, the sort who would content herself and Hathaway at Bristol Creek and not go nagging the man to remove and try his capabilities elsewhere. At once Mr Barclay thought of Kezia—dear little Kezzie. A colourless little creature but quiet and well-mannered and pious, and only twenty-two.

Mr Hathaway was nearly forty and far from handsome, and he had a rather cold, seeking way about him—useful in business of course—that rubbed women the wrong way. Privately Mr Barclay thought Hathaway lucky to get Kezia. But it was a nice match for the girl, better than anything she could have expected. He impressed that upon her and introduced the suitor from Bristol Creek. Mr Hathaway spent two or three evenings courting Kezia in the kitchen—Kezia in a quite good gown of Miss Clara's, gazing out at the November moon on the snow, murmuring now and again in the tones of someone in a rather dismal trance, while the kitchen help listened behind one door and the Barclay girls giggled behind another.

The decision, reached mainly by the Barclays, was that Mr Hathaway should come to Port Marriott aboard the packet schooner on December twenty-third, to be married in the Barclay parlour and then take his bride home for Christmas. But an unforeseen circumstance had changed all this. The circumstance was a ship, 'from Mogador in Barbary' as Mr Barclay wrote afterwards in the salvage claim, driven off her course by gales and wrecked at the very entrance to Bristol Creek. She was a valuable wreck, laden with such queer things as goatskins in pickle, almonds, wormseed, pomegranate skins and gum arabic, and capable Mr Hathaway had lost no time in salvage for the benefit of his employer.

As a result he could not come to Port Marriott for a wedding or anything else. A storm might blow up at any time and demolish this fat prize. He dispatched a note by Black Sam, urging Mr Barclay to send Kezia and the preacher by return. It was not the orthodox note of an impatient sweetheart, but it said that he had moved into his new house by the Creek and found it 'extream empty lacking a woman', and it suggested delicately that while his days were full, the nights were dull.

Kezia was no judge of distance. She rode for what she considered a reasonable time and then slid off and tied the brown horse to a maple tree beside the path. She had brought a couple of lamp wicks to tie about her shoes, to keep them from coming off in the snow, and she set out afoot in the big splayed tracks of Black Sam. The soft snow came almost to her knees in places and she lifted her skirts high. The path was no wider than the span of a man's arms, cut out with axes years before. She stumbled over a concealed stump from time to time, and the huckleberry bushes dragged at her cloak, but the effort warmed her. It had been cold, sitting on the horse with the wind blowing up her legs.

After a time the preacher overtook her, riding awkwardly and holding the reins in a nervous grip. The stirrups were too short for his long black-stockinged legs. He called out cheerfully as he passed, 'Are you all right, Miss?' She nodded, standing aside with her back to a tree. When he disappeared ahead, with a last flutter of black shawl tassels in the wind, she picked up her skirts and went on. The path climbed and dropped monotonously over a succession of wooded ridges. Here and there in a hollow she heard water running, and the creak of frosty poles underfoot, and knew she was crossing a small stream, and once the trail ran across a wide swamp on half-rotten corduroy, wind-swept and bare of snow.

She found the horse tethered clumsily not far ahead, and the tracks of the preacher going on. She had to lead the horse to a stump so she could mount, and when she passed Mr Mears again she called out, 'Please, sir, next time leave the horse by a stump or a rock so I can get on.' In his quaint old-country accent he murmured, 'I'm very sorry,' and gazed down at the snow. She forgot she was riding astride until she had passed him, and then she flushed, and gave the indignant horse a cut of the switch. Next time she remembered and swung her right leg back where it should be, and tucked the skirts modestly about her ankles; but young Mr Mears looked down at the snow anyway, and after that she did not trouble to shift when she overtook him.

The ridges became steeper, and the streams roared under the ice and snow in the swales. They emerged upon the high tableland between Port Marriott and Bristol Creek, a gusty wilderness of young hardwood scrub struggling up amongst the gray snags of an old forest fire, and now that they were out of the gloomy softwoods they could see a stretch of sky. It was blue-grey and forbidding, and the wind whistling up from the invisible sea felt raw on the cheek. At their next meeting Kezia said, 'It's going to snow.'

She had no knowledge of the trail but she guessed that they were not much more than half way across the cape. On this high barren the track was no longer straight and clear, it meandered amongst the meagre hardwood clumps where the path-makers had not bothered to cut, and only Black Sam's footprints really marked it for her unaccustomed eyes. The preacher nodded vaguely at her remark. The woods, like everything else about his chosen mission field, were new and very interesting, and he could not understand the alarm in her voice. He looked confidently at Black Sam's tracks.

Kezia tied the horse farther on and began her spell of walking. Her shoes were solid things, the kind of shoes Mr Barclay invoiced as 'a Common Strong sort, for women, Five Shillings'; but the snow worked into them and melted and saturated the leather. Her feet were numb every time she slid down from the horse and it took several minutes of stumbling through the snow to bring back an aching warmth. Beneath her arm she clutched the small bundle which contained all she had in the world—two flannel nightgowns, a shift of linen, three pairs of stout wool stockings—and of course Mr Barclay's wedding gift for Mr Hathaway.

Now as she plunged along she felt the first sting of snow on her face and, looking up, saw the stuff borne on the wind in small hard pellets that fell amongst the bare hardwoods and set up a whisper everywhere. When Mr Mears rode up to her the snow was thick in their faces, like flung salt.

'It's a nor-easter!' she cried up to him. She knew the meaning of snow from the sea. She had been born in a fishing village down the coast.

'Yes,' mumbled the preacher, and drew a fold of the shawl about his face. He disappeared. She struggled on, gasping, and after what seemed a tremendous journey came upon him standing alone and bewildered, looking off somewhere to the right.

'The horse!' he shouted. 'I got off him, and before I could fasten the reins some snow fell off a branch—startled him, you know—and he ran off, over that way.' He gestured with a mittened hand. 'I must fetch him back,' he added confusedly.

'No!' Kezia cried. 'Don't you try. You'd only get lost. So would I. Oh, dear! This is awful. We'll have to go on, the best we can.'

He was doubtful. The horse tracks looked very plain. But Kezia was looking at Black Sam's tracks, and tugging his arm. He gave in, and they struggled along for half an hour or so. Then the last trace of the old footprints vanished.

'What shall we do now?' the preacher asked, astonished.

'I don't know,' whispered Kezia, and leaned against a dead pine stub in an attitude of weariness and indifference that dismayed him.

'We must keep moving, my dear, mustn't we? I mean, we can't stay here.'

'Can't stay here,' she echoed.

'Down there—a hollow, I think. I see some hemlock trees, or are they pines?—I'm never quite sure. Shelter, anyway.'

'Shelter,' muttered Kezia.

He took her by the hand and like a pair of lost children they dragged their steps into the deep snow of the hollow. The trees were tall spruces, a thick bunch in a ravine, where they had escaped an old fire. A stream thundered amongst them somewhere. There was no wind in this place, only the fine snow whirling thickly down between the trees like a sediment from the storm overhead.

'Look!' cried Mr Mears. A hut loomed out of the whiteness before them, a small structure of moss-chinked logs with a roof of poles and birch-bark. It had an abandoned look. Long streamers of moss hung out between the logs. On the roof shreds of birch-bark wavered gently in the drifting snow. The door stood half open and a thin drift of snow lay along the split-pole floor. Instinctively Kezia went to the stone hearth. There were old ashes sodden with rain down the chimney and now frozen to a cake.

'Have you got flint and steel?' she asked. She saw in his eyes something dazed and forlorn. He shook his head, and she was filled with a sudden anger, not so much at him as at Mr Barclay and that—that Hathaway, and all the rest of mankind. They ruled the world and made such a sorry mess of it. In a small fury she began to rummage about the hut.

There was a crude bed of poles and brushwood by the fireplace—brushwood so old that only a few brown needles clung to the twigs. A rough bench whittled from a pine log, with round birch sticks for legs. A broken earthenware pot in a corner. In another some ash-wood frames such as trappers used for stretching skins. Nothing else. The single window was covered with a stretched moose-bladder, cracked and dry-rotten, but it still let in some daylight while keeping out the snow.

She scooped up the snow from the floor with her mittened hands, throwing it outside, and closed the door carefully, dropping the bar into place, as if she could shut out and bar the cold in such a fashion. The air inside was frigid. Their breath hung visible in the dim light from the window. Young Mr Mears dropped on his wet knees and began to pray in a loud voice. His face was pinched with cold and his teeth rattled as he prayed. He was a pitiable object.

'Prayers won't keep you warm,' said Kezia crossly.

He looked up, amazed at the change in her. She had seemed such a meek little thing. Kezia was surprised at herself, and surprisingly she went on, 'You'd far better take off those wet moccasins and stockings and shake out the snow of your clothes.' She set the example, vigorously shaking out her skirts and Miss Julia's cloak, and she turned her small back on him and took off her own shoes and stockings, and pulled on dry stockings from her bundle. She threw him a pair.

'Put those on.'

He looked at them and at his large feet, hopelessly.

'I'm afraid they wouldn't go on.'

She tossed him one of her flannel nightgowns. 'Then take off your stockings and wrap your feet and legs in that.'

He obeyed, in an embarrassed silence. She rolled her eyes upward, for his modesty's sake, and saw a bundle on one of the low rafters—the late owner's bedding, stowed away from mice. She stood on the bench and pulled down three bearskins, marred with bullet holes. A rank and musty smell arose in the cold. She considered the find gravely.

'You take them,' Mr Mears said gallantly. 'I shall be quite all right.'

'You'll be dead by morning, and so shall I,' she answered vigorously, if you don't do what I say. We've got to roll up in these.'

'Together?' he cried in horror.

'Of course! To keep each other warm. It's the only way.'

She spread the skins on the floor, hair uppermost, one overlapping another, and dragged the flustered young man down beside her, clutched him in her arms, and rolled with him, over, and over again, so that they became a single shapeless heap in the corner farthest from the draft between door and chimney.

'Put your arms around me,' commanded the new Kezia, and he obeyed.

'Now,' she said, 'you can pray. God helps those that help themselves.'

He prayed aloud for a long time, and privately called upon heaven to witness the purity of his thoughts in this strange and shocking situation. He said 'Amen' at last; and 'Amen', echoed Kezia, piously.

They lay silent a long time, breathing on each other's necks and hearing their own hearts—poor Mr Mears' fluttering in an agitated way, Kezia's steady as a clock. A delicious warmth crept over them. They relaxed in each other's arms. Outside, the storm hissed in the spruce tops and set up an occasional cold moan in the cracked clay chimney. The down-swirling snow brushed softly against the bladder pane.

'I'm warm now,' murmured Kezia. 'Are you?'

'Yes. How long must we stay here like this?'

'Till the storm's over, of course. Tomorrow, probably. Nor'easters usually blow themselves out in a day and a night, 'specially when they come up sharp, like this one. Are you hungry?'

'No.'

'Abigail—that's the black cook at Barclay's—gave me bread and cheese in a handkerchief. I've got it in my bundle. Mr Barclay thought we ought to reach Bristol Creek by supper time, but Nabby said I must have a bite to eat on the road. She's a good kind thing, old Nabby. Sure you're not hungry?'

'Quite. I feel somewhat fatigued but not hungry.'

'Then we'll eat the bread and cheese for breakfast. Have you got a watch?'

'No, I'm sorry. They cost such a lot of money. In Lady Huntingdon's Connexion we—'

'Oh well, it doesn't matter. It must be about four o'clock—the light's getting dim. Of course, the dark comes very quick in a snowstorm.'

'Dark,' echoed young Mr Mears drowsily. Kezia's hair, washed last night for the wedding journey, smelled pleasant so close to his face. It reminded him of something. He went to sleep dreaming of his mother, with his face snug in the curve of Kezia's neck and shoulder, and smiling, and muttering words that Kezia could not catch. After a time she kissed his cheek. It seemed a very natural thing to do.

Soon she was dozing herself, and dreaming, too; but her dreams were full of forbidding faces—Mr Barclay's, Mrs Barclay's, Mr Hathaway's; especially Mr Hathaway's. Out of a confused darkness Mr Hathaway's hard acquisitive gaze searched her shrinking flesh like a cold wind. Then she was shuddering by the kitchen fire at Barclay's, accepting Mr Hathaway's courtship and wishing she was dead. In the midst of that sickening wooing she wakened sharply.

It was quite dark in the hut. Mr Mears was breathing quietly against her throat. But there was a sound of heavy steps outside, muffled in the snow and somehow felt rather than heard. She shook the young man and he wakened with a start, clutching her convulsively.

'Sh-h-h!' she warned. 'Something's moving outside.' She felt him stiffen.

'Bears?' he whispered.

Silly! thought Kezia. People from the old country could think of nothing but bears in the woods. Besides, bears holed up in winter. A caribou, perhaps. More likely a moose. Caribou moved inland before this, to the wide mossy bogs up the river, away from the coastal storms. Again the sound.

'There!' hissed the preacher. Their hearts beat rapidly together.

'The door—you fastened it, didn't you?'

'Yes,' she said. Suddenly she knew.

'Unroll, quick!' she cried . . . 'No, not this way—your way.'

They unrolled, ludicrously, and the girl scrambled up and ran across the floor in her stockinged feet, and fumbled with the rotten door-bar. Mr Mears attempted to follow but he tripped over the nightgown still wound about his feet, and fell with a crash. He was up again in a moment, catching up the clumsy wooden bench for a weapon, his bare feet slapping on the icy floor. He tried to shoulder her aside, crying 'Stand back! Leave it to me!' and waving the bench uncertainly in the darkness.

She laughed excitedly. 'Silly!' she said. 'It's the horse.' She flung the door open. In the queer ghostly murk of a night filled with snow they beheld a large dark shape. The shape whinnied softly and thrust a long face into the doorway. Mr Mears dropped the bench, astonished.

'He got over his fright and followed us here somehow,' Kezia said, and laughed again. She put her arms about the snowy head and laid her face against it.

'Good horse! Oh, good, good horse!'

'What are you going to do?' the preacher murmured over her shoulder. After the warmth of their nest in the furs they were shivering in this icy atmosphere.

'Bring him in, of course. We can't leave him out in the storm.' She caught the bridle and urged the horse inside with expert clucking sounds. The animal hesitated, but fear of the storm and a desire for shelter and company decided him. In he came, tramping ponderously on the split-pole floor. The preacher closed and barred the door.

'And now?' he asked.

'Back to the furs. Quick! It's awful cold.'

Rolled in the furs once more, their arms went about each other instinctively, and the young man's face found the comfortable nook against Kezia's soft throat. But sleep was difficult after that. The horse whinnied gently from time to time, and stamped about the floor. The decayed poles crackled dangerously under his hoofs whenever he moved, and Kezia trembled, thinking he might break through and frighten himself, and flounder about till he tumbled the crazy hut about their heads. She called out to him 'Steady, boy! Steady!'

It was a long night. The pole floor made its irregularities felt through the thickness of fur; and because there seemed nowhere to put their arms but about each other the flesh became cramped, and spread its protest along the bones. They were stiff and sore when the first light of morning stained the window. They unrolled and stood up thankfully, and tramped up and down the floor, threshing their arms in a effort to fight off the gripping cold. Kezia undid her bundle in a corner and brought forth Nabby's bread and cheese, and they ate it sitting together on the edge of the brushwood bed with the skins about their shoulders. Outside the snow had ceased.

'We must set off at once,' the preacher said. 'Mr Hathaway will be anxious.'

Kezia was silent. She did not move, and he looked at her curiously. She appeared very fresh, considering the hardships of the previous day and the night. He passed a hand over his cheeks and thought how unclean he must appear in her eyes, with this stubble on his pale face.

'Mr Hathaway—' he began again.

'I'm not going to Mr Hathaway,' Kezia said quietly.

'But—the wedding!'

'There'll be no wedding. I don't want to marry Mr Hathaway. 'Twas Mr Hathaway's idea, and Mr and Mrs Barclay's. They wanted me to marry him.'

'What will the Barclays say, my dear?'

She shrugged. 'I've been their bond-girl ever since I was fourteen, but I'm not a slave like poor black Nabby, to be handed over, body and soul, whenever it suits.'

'Your soul belongs to God,' said Mr Mears devoutly.

'And my body belongs to me.'

He was a little shocked at this outspokenness but he said gently, 'Of course. To give oneself in marriage without true affection would be an offense in the sight of heaven. But what will Mr Hathaway say?'

'Well, to begin with, he'll ask where I spent the night, and I'll have to tell the truth. I'll have to say I bundled with you in a hut in the woods.'

'Bundled?'

'A custom the people brought with them from Connecticut when they came to settle in Nova Scotia. Poor folk still do it. Sweethearts, I mean. It saves fire and candles when you're courting on a winter evening. It's harmless—they keep their clothes on, you see, like you and me—but Mr Barclay and the other Methody people are terrible set against it. Mr Barclay got old Mr Mings—he's the Methody preacher that died last year—to make a sermon against it. Mr Mings said bundling was an invention of the devil.'

'Then if you go back to Mr Barclay—'

'He'll ask me the same question and I'll have to give him the same answer. I couldn't tell a lie, could I?' She turned a pair of round blue eyes and met his embarrassed gaze.

'No! No, you mustn't lie. Whatever shall we do?' he murmured in a dazed voice. Again she was silent, looking modestly down her small nose.

'It's so very strange,' he floundered. 'This country—there are so many things I don't know, so many things to learn. You—I—we shall have to tell the truth, of course. Doubtless I can find a place in the Lord's service somewhere else, but what about you, poor girl?'

'I heard say the people at Scrod Harbour want a preacher.'

'But—the tale would follow me, wouldn't it, my dear? This—er—bundling with a young woman?'

''Twouldn't matter if the young woman was your wife.'

'Eh?' His mouth fell open. He was like an astonished child, for all his preacher's clothes and the new beard on his jaws.

'I'm a good girl,' Kezia said, inspecting her foot. 'I can read and write, and know all the tunes in the psalter. And—and you need someone to look after your.'

He considered the truth of that. Then he murmured uncertainly, 'We'd be very poor, my dear. The Connexion gives some support, but of course—'

'I've always been poor,' Kezia said. She sat very still but her cold fingers writhed in her lap.

He did something then that made her want to cry. He took hold of her hands and bowed his head and kissed them.

'It's strange—I don't even know your name, my dear.'

'It's Kezia—Kezia Barnes.'

He said quietly 'You're a brave girl, Kezia Barnes, and I shall try to be a good husband to you. Shall we go?'

'Hadn't you better kiss me, first?' Kezia said faintly.

He put his lips awkwardly to hers; and then, as if the taste of her clean mouth itself provided strength and purpose, he kissed her again, and firmly. She threw her arms about his neck.

'Oh, Mr Mears!'

How little he knew about everything! He hadn't even known enough to wear two or three pairs of stockings inside those roomy moccasins, nor to carry a pair of dry ones. Yesterday's wet stockings were lying like sticks on the frosty floor. She showed him how to knead the hard-frozen moccasins into softness, and while he worked at the stiff leather she tore up one of her wedding bed-shirts and wound the flannel strips about his legs and feet. It looked very queer when she had finished, and they both laughed.

They were chilled to the bone when they set off, Kezia on the horse and the preacher walking ahead, holding the reins. When they regained the slope where they had lost the path, Kezia said, 'The sun rises somewhere between east and southeast, at this time of year. Keep it on your left shoulder a while. That will take us back towards Port Marriott.'

When they came to the green timber she told him to shift the sun to his left eye.

'Have you changed your mind?' he asked cheerfully. The exercise had warmed him.

'No, but the sun moves across the sky.'

'Ah! What a wise little head it is!'

They came over a ridge of mixed hemlock and hardwood and looked upon a long swale full of bare hackmatacks.

'Look!' the girl cried. The white slot of the axe path showed clearly in the trees at the foot of the swale, and again where it entered the dark mass of the pines beyond.

'Praise the Lord!' said Mr Mears.

When at last they stood in the trail, Kezia slid down from the horse.

'No!' Mr Mears protested.

'Ride-and-tie,' she said firmly. 'That's the way we came, and that's the way we'll go. Besides, I want to get warm.'

He climbed up clumsily and smiled down at her.

'What shall we do when we get to Port Marriott, my dear?'

'Get the New Light preacher to marry us, and catch the packet for Scrod Harbour.'

He nodded and gave a pull at his broad hat brim. She thought of everything. A splendid helpmeet for the world's wilderness. He saw it all very humbly now as a dispensation of Providence.

Kezia watched him out of sight. Then, swiftly, she undid her bundle and took out the thing that had lain there (and on her conscience) through the night—the tinderbox—Mr Barclay's wedding gift to Mr Hathaway. She flung it into the woods and walked on, skirts lifted, in the track of the horse, humming a psalm tune to the silent trees and the snow.

SINCLAIR ROSS
(1908)

The Lamp at Noon

A little before noon she lit the lamp. Demented wind fled keening past the house: a wail through the eaves that died every minute or two. Three days now without respite it had held. The dust was thickening to an impenetrable fog.

She lit the lamp, then for a long time stood at the window motionless. In dim, fitful outline the stable and oat granary still were visible; beyond, obscuring fields and landmarks, the lower of dust clouds made the farmyard seem an isolated acre, poised aloft above a sombre void. At each blast of wind it shook, as if to topple and spin hurtling with the dust-reel into space.

From the window she went to the door, opening it a little, and peering toward the stable again. He was not coming yet. As she watched there was a sudden rift overhead, and for a moment through the tattered clouds the sun raced like a wizened orange. It shed a soft, diffused light, dim and yellow as if it were the light from the lamp reaching out through the open door.

She closed the door, and going to the stove tried the potatoes with a fork. Her eyes all the while were fixed and wide with a curious immobility. It was the window. Standing at it, she had let her forehead press against the pane until the eyes were strained apart and rigid. Wide like that they had looked out of the deepening ruin of the storm. Now she could not close them.

The baby started to cry. He was lying in a homemade crib over which she had arranged a tent of muslin. Careful not to disturb the folds of it, she knelt and tried to still him, whispering huskily in a singsong voice that he must hush and go to sleep again. She would have like to rock him, to feel the comfort of his little body in her arms, but a fear obsessed her that in the dust-filled air he might contract pneumonia. There was dust sifting everywhere. Her own throat was parched with it. The table had been set less than ten minutes, and already a film was gathering on the dishes. The little cry continued, and with wincing, frightened lips she glanced around as if to find a corner where the air was less oppressive. But while the lips winced the eyes maintained their wide, immobile stare. 'Sleep,' she whispered again. 'It's too soon for you to be hungry. Daddy's coming for his dinner.'

He seemed a long time. Even the clock, still a few minutes off noon, could not dispel a foreboding sense that he was longer than he should be. She went to the door again—and then recoiled slowly to stand white and breathless in the middle of the room. She mustn't. He would only despise her if she ran to the stable looking for him. There was too much grim endurance in his nature ever to let him understand the fear and weakness of a woman. She must stay quiet and wait. Nothing was wrong. At noon he would come—and perhaps after dinner stay with her awhile.

Yesterday, and again at breakfast this morning, they had quarrelled bitterly. She wanted him now, the assurance of his strength and nearness, but he would stand aloof, wary, remembering the words she had flung at him in her anger, unable to understand it was only the dust and wind that had driven her.

Tense, she fixed her eyes upon the clock, listening. There were two winds: the wind in flight, and the wind that pursued. The one sought refuge in the eaves, whimpering, in fear; the other assailed it there, and shook the eaves apart to make it flee again. Once as she listened this first wind sprang inside the room, distraught like a bird that has felt the graze of talons on its wing; while furious the other wind shook the walls, and thudded tumbleweeds against the window till its quarry glanced away again in fright. But only to return—to return and quake among the feeble eaves, as if in all this dust-mad wilderness it knew no other sanctuary.

Then Paul came. At his step she hurried to the stove, intent upon the pots and frying-pan. 'The worst wind yet,' he ventured, hanging up his cap and smock. 'I had to light the lantern in the tool shed, too.'

They looked at each other, then away. She wanted to go to him, to feel his arms supporting her, to cry a little just that he might soothe her, but because his presence made the menace of wind seem less, she gripped herself and thought, 'I'm in the right. I won't give in. For his sake, too, I won't.'

He washed, hurriedly, so that a few dark welts of dust remained to indent upon his face a haggard strength. It was all she could see as she wiped the dishes and set the food before him: the strength, the grimness, the young Paul growing old and hard, buckled against a desert even grimmer than his will. 'Hungry?' she asked, touched to a twinge of pity she had not intended. 'There's dust in everything. It keeps coming faster than I can clean it up.'

He nodded. 'Tonight, though, you'll see it go down. This is the third day.'

She looked at him in silence a moment, and then as if to herself muttered broodingly, 'Until the next time. Until it starts again.'

There was a dark resentment in her voice now that boded another quarrel. He waited, his eyes on her dubiously as she mashed a potato with her fork. The lamp between them threw strong lights and shadows on their faces. Dust and drought, earth that betrayed alike his labour and his faith, to him the struggle had given sternness, an impassive courage. Beneath the whip of sand his youth had been effaced. Youth, zest, exuberance—there remained only a harsh and clenched virility that yet became him, that seemed at the cost of more engaging qualities to be fulfilment of his inmost and essential nature. Whereas to her the same debts and poverty had brought a plaintive indignation, a nervous dread of what was still to come. The eyes were hollowed, the lips pinched dry and colourless. It was the face of a woman that had aged without maturing, that had loved the little vanities of life, and lost them wistfully.

'I'm afraid, Paul,' she said suddenly. 'I can't stand it any longer. He cries all the time. You will go, Paul—say you will. We aren't living here—not really living—'

The pleading in her voice now, after its shrill bitterness yesterday, made him think that this was only another way to persuade him. He answered evenly, 'I told you this morning, Ellen; we keep on right where we are. At least I do. It's yourself you're thinking about, not the baby.'

This morning such an accusation would have stung her to rage; now, her voice swift and panting, she pressed on, 'Listen, Paul—I'm thinking of all of us—you, too. Look at the sky—what's happening. Are you blind? Thistles and tumbleweeds—it's a desert. You won't have a straw this fall. You won't be able to feed a cow or a chicken. Please, Paul, say we'll go away—'

'Go where?' His voice as he answered was still remote and even, inflexibly in unison with the narrowed eyes and the great hunch of muscle-knotted shoulder. 'Even as a desert it's better than sweeping out your father's store and running his errands. That's all I've got ahead of me if I do what you want.'

'And here—' she faltered. 'What's ahead of you here? At least we'll get enough to eat and wear when you're sweeping out his store. Look at it—look at it, you fool. Desert—the lamp lit at noon—'

'You'll see it come back. There's good wheat in it yet.'

'But in the meantime—year after year—can't you understand, Paul? We'll never get them back—'

He put down his knife and fork and leaned toward her across the table. 'I can't go, Ellen. Living off your people—charity—stop and think about it. This is where I belong. I can't do anything else.'

'Charity!' she repeated him, letting her voice rise in derision. 'And this—you call this independence! Borrowed money you can't even pay the interest on, seed from the government—grocery bills—doctor bills—'

'We'll have crops again,' he persisted. 'Good crops—the land will come back. It's worth waiting for.'

'And while we're waiting, Paul!' It was not anger now, but a kind of sob. 'Think of me—and him. It's not fair. We have our lives, too, to live.'

'And you think that going home to your family—taking your husband with you—'

'I don't care—anything would be better than this. Look at the air he's breathing. He cries all the time. For his sake, Paul. What's ahead of him here, even if you do get crops?'

He clenched his lips a minute, then, with his eyes hard and contemptuous, struck back, 'As much as in town, growing up a pauper. You're the one who wants to go, it's not for his sake. You think that in town you'd have a better time—not so much work—more clothes—'

'Maybe—' She dropped her head defencelessly. 'I'm young still. I like pretty things.'

There was silence now—a deep fastness of it enclosed by rushing wind and creaking walls. It seemed the yellow lamplight cast a hush upon them. Through the haze of dusty air the walls receded, dimmed, and came again. At last she raised her head and said listlessly, 'Go on—your dinner's getting cold. Don't sit and stare at me. I've said it all.'

The spent quietness in her voice was even harder to endure than her anger. It reproached him, against his will insisted that he see and understand her lot. To justify himself he tried, 'I was a poor man when you married me. You said you didn't mind. Farming's never been easy, and never will be.'

'I wouldn't mind the work or the skimping if there was something to look forward to. It's the hopelessness—going on—watching the land blow away.'

'The land's all right,' he repeated. 'The dry years won't last forever.'

'But it's not just dry years, Paul!' The little sob in her voice gave way suddenly to a ring of exasperation. 'Will you never see? It's the land itself—the soil. You've plowed and harrowed until there's not a root or fibre left to hold it down. That's why the soil drifts—that's why in a year or two there'll be nothing left but bare clay. If in the first place you farmers had taken care of your land—if you hadn't been so greedy for wheat every year—'

She had taught school before she married him, and of late in her anger there had been a kind of disdain, an attitude almost of condescension, as if she no longer looked upon the farmers as her equals. He sat still, his eyes fixed on the yellow lamp flame, and seeming to know her words had hurt him, she went on softly, 'I want to help you, Paul. That's why I won't sit quiet while you go on wasting your life. You're only thirty—you owe it to yourself as well as me.'

He sat staring at the lamp without answering, his mouth sullen. It seemed indifference now, as if he were ignoring her, and stung to anger again she cried, 'Do you ever think what my life is? Two rooms to live in—once a month to town, and nothing to spend when I get there. I'm still young—I wasn't—brought up this way.'

'You're a farmer's wife now. It doesn't matter what you used to be, or how you were brought up. You get enough to eat and wear. Just now that's all I can do. I'm not to blame that we've been dried out five years.'

'Enough to eat!' she laughed back shrilly. 'Enough salt pork—enough potatoes and eggs. And look—' Springing to the middle of the room she thrust out a foot for him to see the scuffed old slipper. 'When they're completely gone I suppose you'll tell me I can go barefoot—that I'm a farmer's wife—that it's not your fault we're dried out—'

'And what about these?' He pushed his chair away from the table now to let her see what he was wearing. 'Cowhide—hard as boards—but my feet are so calloused I don't feel them any more.'

Then he stood up, ashamed of having tried to match her hardships with his own. But frightened now as he reached for his smock she pressed close to him. 'Don't go yet. I brood and worry when I'm left alone. Please, Paul—you can't work on the land anyway.'

'And keep on like this? You start before I'm through the door. Week in and week out—I've troubles enough of my own.'

'Paul—please stay—' The eyes were glazed now, distended a little as if with the intensity of her dread and pleading. 'We won't quarrel any more. Hear it! I can't work—I just stand still and listen—'

The eyes frightened him, but responding to a kind of instinct that he must withstand her, that it was his self-respect and manhood against the fretful weakness of a woman, he answered unfeelingly, 'In here safe and quiet—you don't know how well off you are. If you were out in it—fighting it—swallowing it—'

'Sometimes, Paul, I wish I was. I'm so caged—if I could only break away and run. See—I stand like this all day. I can't relax. My throat's so tight it aches—'

With a jerk he freed his smock from her clutch. 'If I stay we'll only keep on all afternoon. Wait till tomorrow—we'll talk things over when the wind goes down.'

Then without meeting her eyes again he swung outside, and doubled low against the buffets of the wind, fought his way slowly toward the stable. There was a deep hollow calm within, a vast darkness engulfed beneath the tides of moaning wind. He stood breathless a moment, hushed almost to a stupor by the sudden extinction of the storm and the stillness that enfolded him. It was a long, far-reaching stillness. The first dim stalls and rafters led the way into cavern-like obscurity, into vaults and recesses that extended far beyond the stable walls. Nor in these first quiet moments did he forbid the illusion, the sense of release from a harsh, familiar world into one of peace and darkness. The contentious mood that his stand against Ellen had roused him to, his tenacity and clenched despair before the ravages of wind, it was ebbing now, losing itself in the cover of darkness. Ellen and the wheat seemed remote, unimportant. At a whinny from the bay mare, Bess, he went forward and into her stall. She seemed grateful for his presence, and thrust her nose deep between his arm and body. They stood a long time motionless, comforting and assuring each other.

For soon again the first deep sense of quiet and peace was shrunken to the battered shelter of the stable. Instead of release or escape from the assaulting wind, the walls were but a feeble stand against it. They creaked and sawed as if the fingers of a giant were tightening to collapse them; the empty loft sustained a pipelike cry that rose and fell but never ended. He saw the dust-black sky again, and his fields blown smooth with drifted soil.

But always, even while listening to the storm outside, he could feel the tense and apprehensive stillness of the stable. There was not a hoof that clumped or shifted, not a rub of halter against manger. And yet, though it had been a strange stable, he would have known, despite the darkness, that every stall was filled. They, too, were all listening.

From Bess he went to the big grey gelding, Prince. Prince was twenty years old, with rib-grooved sides, and high, protruding hipbones. Paul ran his hand over the ribs, and felt a sudden shame, a sting of fear that Ellen might be right in what she said. For wasn't it true—nine years a farmer now on his own land, and still he couldn't even feed his horses? What, then, could he hope to do for his wife and son?

There was much he planned. And so vivid was the future of his planning, so real and constant, that often the actual present was but half felt, but half endured. Its difficulties were lessened by a confidence in what lay beyond them. A new house—land for the boy—land and still more land—or education, whatever he might want.

But all the time was he only a blind and stubborn fool? Was Ellen right? Was he trampling on her life, and throwing away his own? The five years since he married her, were they to go on repeating themselves, five, ten, twenty, until all the brave future he looked forward to was but a stark and futile past?

She looked forward to no future. She had no faith or dream with which to make the dust and the poverty less real. He understood suddenly. He saw her face again as only a few minutes ago it had begged him not to leave her. The darkness round him now was as a slate on which her lonely terror limned itself. He went from Prince to the other horses, combing their manes and forelocks with his fingers, but always it was her face before him, its staring eyes and twisted suffering. 'See Paul—I stand like this all day. I just stand still—My throat's so tight it aches—'

And always the wind, the creak of walls, the wild lipless wailing through the loft. Until at last as he stood there, staring into the livid face before him, it seemed that this scream of wind was a cry from her parched and frantic lips. He knew it couldn't be, he knew that she was safe within the house, but still the wind persisted in a woman's cry. The cry of a woman with eyes like those what watched him through the dark. Eyes that were made now—lips that even as they cried still pleaded, 'See Paul—I stand like this all day. I just stand still—so caged! If I could only run!'

He saw her running, pulled and driven headlong by the wind, but when at last he returned to the house, compelled by his anxiety, she was walking quietly back and forth with the baby in her arms. Careful, despite his concern, not to reveal a fear or weakness that she might think capitulation to her wishes, he watched a moment through the window, and then he went off to the tool shed to mend harness. All afternoon he stitched and riveted. It was easier with the lantern lit and his hands occupied. There was a wind whining high past the tool shed too, but it was only wind. He remembered the arguments with which Ellen had tried to persuade him away from the farm, and one by one he defeated them. There would be rain again—next year or the next. Maybe in his ignorance he had farmed his land the wrong way, seeding wheat every year, working the soil till it was lifeless dust—but he would do better now. He would plant clover and alfalfa, breed cattle, acre by acre and year by year restore to his land its fibre and fertility. That was something to work for, a way to prove himself. It was ruthless wind, blackening the sky with his earth, but it was not his master. Out of his land it had made a wilderness. He now, out of the wilderness, would make a farm and home again.

Tonight he must talk with Ellen. Patiently, when the wind was down, and they were both quiet again. It was she who had told him to grow fibrous crops, who had called him an ignorant fool because he kept on with summer fallow and wheat. Now she might be gratified to find him acknowledging her wisdom. Perhaps she would begin to feel the power and steadfastness of the land, to take a pride in it, to understand that he was not a fool, but working for her future and their son's.

And already the wind was slackening. At four o'clock he could sense a lull. At five, straining his eyes from the tool shed doorway, he could make out a neighbour's building half a mile away. It was over—three days of blight and havoc like a scourge—three days so bitter and so long that for a moment he stood still, unseeing, his senses idle with a numbness of relief.

But only for a moment. Suddenly he emerged from the numbness: suddenly the fields before him struck his eyes to comprehension. They lay black, naked. Beaten and mounded smooth with dust as if a sea in gentle swell had turned to stone. And though he had tried to prepare himself for such a scene, though he had known since yesterday that not a blade would last the storm, still now, before the utter waste confronting him, he sickened and stood cold. Suddenly like the fields he was naked. Everything that had sheathed him a little from the realities of existence: vision and purpose, faith in the land, in the future, in himself—it was all rent now, stripped away. 'Desert,' he heard her voice begin to sob. 'Desert, you fool—the lamp lit at noon!'

In the stable again, measuring out their feed to the horses, he wondered what he would say to her tonight. For so deep were his instincts of loyalty to the land that still, even with the images of his betrayal stark upon his mind, his concern was how to withstand her, how to go on again and justify himself. It had not occurred to him yet that he might or should abandon the land. He had lived with it too long. Rather was his impulse still to defend it—as a man defends against the scorn of strangers even his most worthless kin.

He fed his horses, then waited. She too would be waiting, ready to cry at him, 'Look now—that crop that was to feed and clothe us! And you'll still keep on! You'll still say "Next year—there'll be rain next year"!'

But she was gone when he reached the house. The door was open, the lamp blown out, the crib empty. The dishes from their meal at noon were still on the table. She had perhaps begun to sweep, for the broom was lying in the middle of the floor. He tried to call, but a terror clamped upon his throat. In the wan, returning light it seemed that even the deserted kitchen was straining to whisper what it had seen. The tatters of the storm still whimpered through the eaves, and in their moaning told the desolation of the miles they had traversed. On tiptoe at last he crossed to the adjoining room; then at the threshold, without even a glance inside to satisfy himself that she was really gone, he wheeled again and plunged outside.

He ran a long time—distraught and headlong as a few hours ago he had seemed to watch her run—around the farmyard, a little distance into the pasture, back again blindly to the house to see whether she had returned—and then at a stumble down the road for help.

They joined him in the search, rode away for others, spread calling across the fields in the direction she might have been carried by the wind—but nearly two hours later it was himself who came upon her. Crouched down against a drift of sand as if for shelter, her hair in matted strands about her neck and face, the child clasped tightly in her arms.

The child was quite cold. It had been her arms, perhaps, too frantic to protect him, or the smother of dust upon his throat and lungs. 'Hold him,' she said as he knelt beside her. 'So—with his face away from the wind. Hold him until I tidy my hair.'

Her eyes were still wide in an immobile stare, but with her lips she smiled at him. For a long time he knelt transfixed, trying to speak to her, touching fearfully with his fingertips the dust-grimed cheeks and eyelids of the child. At last she said, 'I'll take him again. Such clumsy hands—you don't know how to hold a baby yet. See how his head falls forward on your arm.'

Yet it all seemed familiar—a confirmation of what he had known since noon. He gave her the child, then, gathering them up in his arms, struggled to his feet, and turned toward home.

It was evening now. Across the fields a few spent clouds of dust still shook and fled. Beyond, as if through smoke, the sunset smouldered like a distant fire.

He walked with a long dull stride, his eyes before him, heedless of her weight. Once he glanced down and with her eyes she was still smiling. 'Such strong arms, Paul—and I was so tired just carrying him. . . .'

He tried to answer, but it seemed that now the dusk was drawn apart in breathless waiting, a finger on its lips until they passed. 'You were right, Paul. . . .' Her voice came whispering, as if she too could feel the hush. 'You said tonight we'd see the storm go down. So still now, and a red sky—it means tomorrow will be fine.'

JOYCE MARSHALL
(1913)

∾

The Old Woman

He has changed, Molly thought, the instant she glimpsed her husband in the station at Montreal. He has changed. . . . The thought thudded hollowly through her mind, over and over during the long train-ride into northern Quebec.

It was more than the absence of uniform. His face seemed so still, and there was something about his mouth—a sort of slackness. And at times she would turn and find him looking at her, his eyes absorbed and watchful.

'I *am* glad to see you,' he kept saying. 'I thought you would never make it, Moll.'

'I know,' she said. 'But I had to wait till Mother was really well. . . . It *has* been a long three years, hasn't it?'

Apart from repeating his gladness at her arrival, he seemed to have little say. He was just strange with her, she tried to soothe herself. They had known each other less than a year when they married in England during the war, and he had left for Canada so soon without her. He must have found it hard to hold a picture of her, just as she had found it hard to hold a picture of him. As soon as they got home—whatever home might be in this strange romantic north to which the train was drawing them—he would be more nearly the Toddy she had known.

It was grey dawn faintly disturbed with pink when they left the train, the only passengers for this little town of Missawani, at the tip of Lake St John. The name on the greyed shingle reassured Molly a little. How often she had spelled out the strange syllables on letters to Toddy—the double s, the unexpected single n. Somewhere beyond this huddle of low wooden shacks, she knew, was the big Mason paper mill, and Toddy's power-house—one of several that supplied it with electricity—was more than thirty miles away. There was a road, Toddy had told her, but it was closed in winter.

A sullen youth waited behind the station with the dogs. Such beautiful dogs, black brindled with cream, their mouths spread wide in what seemed to Molly happy smiles of welcome. She put a hand towards the nose of the lead-dog, but he lunged and Toddy drew her back.

'They're brutes,' he told her. 'All of them wolfish brutes.'

It was a long strange journey over the snow, first through the pink-streaked grey, then into a sun that first dazzled and then inflamed the eyes.

Snow that was flung up coarse and stinging from the feet of the dogs, black brittle fir-trees, birches gleaming like white silk. No sound but the panting breath of the dogs, the dry leatherlike squeak of the snow under the sleigh's runners, and Toddy's rare French-spoken commands to the dogs.

At last he poked her back wordlessly and pointed a mittened hand over her shoulder. For an instant the picture seemed to hang suspended before Molly's eyes: the bare hill with the square red house at its top, the dam level with the top of the hill, the waterfall steaming down to a white swirl of rapids, the power-house like a squat grey cylinder at its foot.

'My old woman,' Toddy shouted, and she saw that he was pointing, not up the hill towards the house where they would live, but to the power-house below.

In England his habit of personalizing an electric generating plant had charmed her, fitting her picturesque notions of the Canadian north. But now she felt uneasiness prod her. It was such a sinister-looking building, and the sound of falling water was so loud and engulfing.

The kitchen of the red house had what Molly thought of as a 'poor' smell about it. Still, no one expected a man to be a good housewife. As soon as she could shut the door and get rid of the sound of that water, she told herself, it would be better. She looked quickly behind her, but Toddy had shut the door already. There must be a window open somewhere. It couldn't be possible that the waterfall was going to live with them in the house like this. It couldn't be possible.

'Cheerful sort of sound,' said Toddy.

Molly looked at him vaguely, half-hearing. A window somewhere—there must be a window she could close.

He showed her quickly over the house, which was fairly well furnished and comfortably heated by electricity. Then he turned to her almost apologetically.

I hope you won't mind if I go down right away,' he said. 'I'd like to see what kind of shape the old woman's got herself into while I've been away.'

He looked elated and eager, and she smiled at him.

'Go ahead,' she said, 'I'll be all right.'

After he had gone she unpacked her bags and went down to the living-room. It had a broad window, overlooking the power-house, the rapids, and a long snow-field disappearing into the black huddle of pine bush. Snow, she thought. I always thought snow was white, but it's blue. Blue and treacherous as steel. And fully for the first time she realized how cut off they were to be—cut off from town by thirty odd miles of snow and tangled bush and roadlessness.

She found a pail and mop and began to clean the kitchen. She would have it all fresh and nice by the time Toddy came back. She would have no time to look out into the almost instantly blinding glare of the snow. She might even be able to ignore the thundering of the water. She was going to have to spend a lot of time alone in this house. She would have to learn to keep busy.

Toddy did not come up till evening. The power-house was in very bad shape, he told her.

'Those French operators and assistants are a lazy bunch of bums. It's amazing how they can let things go to hell in just two days.'

Molly had set dinner on a little table in the living room. Toddy had wolfed his meal, his face preoccupied.

He *was* different. She hadn't just been imagining it. She had thought he would seem closer to her here, but he was more withdrawn than ever. For an instant she had a curious sense that none of this was real to him—not the dinner, nothing but the turbines and generators in the plant below.

Well, so you married this man, she told herself briskly, because you were thirty-eight and he looked nice in his officer's uniform. You followed him here because you were entranced with the idea of a strange and different place. So it is strange and different. And you have to start imagining things, just because your husband is a busy man who seems scarcely to notice that you are here.

'I'm going to make this place ever so much cosier,' she heard herself saying, in a voice so importunate she scarcely recognized it as her own.

'What—oh, yes—yes, fine. Make any changes you like.'

He finished eating and stood up.

'Well, I must be going back now.'

'Back?' He wasn't even apologizing this time, she realized dully. 'Won't your old woman give you an evening off—even when your wife has just come from the old country?'

'I've still things to do,' he said. 'You needn't be lonely. There's a radio—though I'm afraid the static's pretty bad on account of the plant. And I'll be only fifty feet away.'

It was a week before he considered the power-house in suitable shape to show her. He showed her around it proudly—the squat gleaming turbines lying like fat sleepers along the floor, one of the four dismantled so that he could explain the power-generator within, the gauges on the wall.

'It's very interesting, dear,' she said, trying to understand his love for these inanimates, his glowing delight in the meshing parts.

'Perhaps now she looks so slick,' she added, 'you won't have to give her so much of your time.'

'You'd be surprised how quickly she can go wrong,' said Toddy.

He continued to spend all his hours there, from eight in the morning until late at night, with only brief spaces for meals.

Molly worked vigorously about the house and soon it was cleaned and sparkling from top to bottom. After that it was harder to keep busy. She read all the books she had brought, even the ancient magazines she found about the house. She could not go out. It was impossible to do more than keep a path cleared down to the power-house. There were no skis or snow-shoes, and Toddy could not seem to find time to teach her to drive the dogs. There were no neighbours within miles, no telephone calls or visits from milkman or baker—only one of Toddy's sweepers coming in once a fortnight with supplies and mail from Missawani.

She looked forward almost wildly to these visits, for they meant a break as well as letters from home. The men all lived on the nearby concessions—'ranges' they were called here in northern Quebec—six or seven or eight miles away, driving back and forth to the power-house by dog-team. She tried to get them to tell her about their lives and their families, but they were taciturn, just barely polite, and she felt that they simply did not like this house of which she was a part.

She tried constantly to build up some sort of closeness between herself and Toddy. But he seemed only to become less talkative—he had always had a lot of cheerful small talk in England—and more absorbed in the power-house. He seemed to accept her presence as a fact which pleased him, but he had no companionship to spare for her.

'I wish,' she said to him one day, 'that you could go out with me soon and teach me to drive the dogs.'

'But where would you go?' he asked.

'Oh,' she said, 'around. Over the snow.'

'But I'm so busy,' he said. 'I'm sorry—but this is my work, and I'm so busy.'

As he spoke, she saw in his eyes again that look that had terrified her so the first day. Now she thought she recognized what it was. It was a watchful look, a powerful look, as if he were still in the presence of his machinery.

'But couldn't you take an afternoon? Those machines look as if they practically ran themselves. Couldn't you even take a Sunday, Toddy?'

'What if something went wrong while I was away?'

'Oh, Toddy, it can't need you every minute. I'm your wife and I need you too. You seemed so anxious for the time when I'd be able to come here. I can imagine how a person might get to hate being here alone, with the water always roaring and—'

Toddy's face became suddenly angry and wild.

'What do you mean?' he demanded.

'Just that you had three years here alone,' she began.

'I have never been bushed,' Toddy interrupted furiously. 'How dare you suggest that such a thing could ever happen to me? My God, apart from the war, I've lived in this country for twenty years.'

Bushed. The suggestion was his, and for a moment she allowed herself to think about it. She was familiar with the term. Toddy used it constantly about others who had come up north to live. He knew the country, but he had been away. And then he had returned alone to this place, where for so long every year the winter buried you, snow blinded you, the wind screamed up the hill at night, and the water thundered. . . .

'Toddy,' she said, afraid of the thought, putting it out of her mind, 'when spring comes, couldn't we get a cow or two. I *do* know about cattle—I wasn't in the Land Army all through the war for nothing. I think it would give me an interest.'

Toddy stared at her.

'Aren't you my wife?' he asked.

'Why yes—yes, of course.'

'Then how can you speak about needing an interest? Isn't there interest enough for you in simply being my wife?'

'But I'm—I'm left so much alone. You have your work, but I have so little to do.'

Toddy turned on his heel, preparing to go again to the power-house. At the door he glanced back over his shoulder, not speaking, merely watching her.

He doesn't want me to have an interest, thought Molly, her mind bruised with horror and fear. He looks at me watchfully, as if I were one of his machines. Perhaps that's what he wants me to be—a generator, quiet and docile, waiting for him here, moving only when he tells me to move.

And I am the sort of woman who must have work to do. If I don't, my mind will grow dim and misty. Already I can feel the long sweep of the snow trying to draw my thoughts out till they become diffused and vague. I can feel the sound of the water trying to crush and madden me.

After that, it seemed as if Toddy were trying to spend more time with her. Several times he sat and talked with her after dinner, telling her about the power-house and the catastrophes he had averted that day. But always his eyes would be turning to the window and the power-house showing grey and sullen against the snow.

'Oh, you can go down now, Toddy,' Molly would say. 'Obviously, that is where you wish to be.'

And then one day she found the work she wanted.

She looked up from her dishes to see Louis-Paul, one of the power-house oilers, standing in the doorway, snow leaking from his great felt boots on to the floor.

'Madame—' he said.

'Oh Louis, hello,' said Molly warmly, for she was friendlier with this slight fair youth than with any of Toddy's other workmen. They had long solemn conversations—she practising her French and he his English. 'But don't tell the Curé,' Louis would say. 'He does not like it if we speak English.'

'Did you come for my list?' Molly asked him. 'Are you going to town?'

'No, Madame, I have—how you say it?—I am today in big trouble. My Lucienne—'

'Oh, the baby—has your baby been born, Louis-Paul?'

'Yes, madame—'

With a hopeless gesture he relinquished his English. From his rapid desperate French, Molly learned that there was something that prevented

Lucienne from nursing her child, and none of the cows on any of the ranges were giving milk that winter.

'If you could come, madame, you might know—you might do something—'

His team of yellow dogs was tied at the kitchen stoop. Together Louis-Paul and Molly dashed across the snow to the house at the first range. Just a little bit of a house that Louis-Paul's father had built for him six years ago when he divided his thin-soiled farm and his timber-lots among his sons. Its roof was the warm grey of weathered wood, almost as deeply curved as the roof of a Chinese pagoda.

In the kitchen Lucienne's mother and sisters and aunts in all their black wept noisily, one of them holding the crying child. And in the bedroom the girl Lucienne was sobbing, because she realized that the presence of her relatives in their best black meant that her child could not be saved.

Molly looked at her for a moment—the swarthy broad cheeks, the narrow eyes, that showed a tinge of Indian blood.

'Would you be shy with me, Lucienne?' she asked. 'Too shy to take off your nightgown while I am here?'

'I would never be shy with you, madame,' said Lucienne.

Something hot came into Molly's throat as she eased the nightgown from the girl's shoulders and went into the kitchen for hot and cold water and a quantity of cloths.

Tenderly she bathed the heavy breasts with alternate hot and cold water, explaining that the nipples were inverted and that this should bring them into place. And before she left, Lucienne was holding the baby's dark head against her breast, weeping silently, the wailing in the kitchen had ceased, and Louis-Paul was fixing stiff portions of whisky blanc and home-made wine, passing the one wine-glass around and around the assembly.

Not until she was back at the red house, actually stamping the snow from her boots on the kitchen stoop, did Molly realize that it was long past the early dinner that Toddy liked. She went in quickly.

Toddy was standing in the middle of the room, his hands dangling with a peculiar slackness at his sides. He looked at her, and there was a great empty bewilderment on his face.

'You have been out?' he asked.

'Yes,' she said, elated still from her afternoon. 'I went over to Louis-Paul's with him. His wife's had her baby and—'

'He asked you?' said Toddy.

'Yes,' she said. 'He was desperate, poor lad, so I just had to offer to do what I could.'

He's afraid I'll go away, she thought. He must have come up here and found the stove cold and thought I had gone forever. The thought alternately reassured and chilled her. It was simple and ordinary for him to be anxious, but his expression was neither simple nor ordinary. Now that she had explained, he should not be staring at her still, his gaze thinned by surprise and fear.

'I'm sorry about dinner,' she said, 'but I'll hurry and fix something easy. You have a smoke and I'll tell you all about it.'

She told him but he would not join in her enthusiasms.

'Another French-Canadian brat,' he said. 'Molly, you're a fool.'

A few weeks later she realized she now had a place even in this barren land. Louis-Paul appeared again in the kitchen, less shy, for now she was his friend. His sister-in-law was having a baby and something was wrong. They would have taken her to Missawani, but there was every sign of a blizzard blowing up. Madame had been so good with Lucienne. Perhaps she could do something for Marie-Claire as well.

'I don't see how I could,' said Molly. 'I've helped bring little calves and pigs into the world, but never a baby—'

'She may die,' said Louis. 'They say the baby is placed wrong. They have given her blood of a newborn calf to drink, but still—'

'All right,' said Molly, 'I'll go.'

She set a cold meal for Toddy and propped a note against his plate. The thought of him nudged her mind guiltily during the dash over the snow to the little house. But that was absurd. She would be away only a few hours. Toddy would have to learn to accept an occasional absence. He was a little—well, selfish about her. He would have to learn.

With some help from an ancient grandmother, Molly delivered a child on the kitchen table of the little house. An old Cornish farm-hand had showed her once how to turn a calf that was breached. Much the same thing was involved now—deftness, daring, a strong hand timed to the bitter contractions of the girl on the table.

When she returned home late in the evening, she had not thought of Toddy for hours.

This time he was angry, mumbling, shakingly angry.

'Molly,' he shouted, 'you must put an end to this nonsensical—'

'But it's not nonsensical,' she said, serene still from this miracle of new life she had held across her hands. 'I brought a nice little boy into the world. He might never have been born except for me.'

'These women have been popping kids for years without you.'

'I know,' said Molly, 'but sometimes they lose them. And they're so—superstitious. I can help them, Toddy. I can.'

She paused, then spoke more gently.

'What is it, Toddy? Why don't you want me to go?'

The question caught him somehow, and his face, his whole expression became loosed, as if suddenly he did not understand his own rage.

'You're my wife,' he said. 'I want you here.'

'Well, cheer up,' she said, speaking lightly because his look had chilled her so. 'I am, usually.'

After that, no woman in any of the ranges ever had a baby without her husband's dogs whisking over the fields to the red house.

Molly now was famed for miles. She was good luck at a birth, and when something unexpected happened she could act with speed and ingenuity. She liked the people and felt that they liked her. Even the Curé, who hated the power-house and all it represented, bowed and passed the time of day when he and Molly met in a farm-house kitchen.

She sent away for government pamphlets and a handful of texts. Though it was true, as Toddy said, that these women had had babies without her, it pleased her that she was cutting down the percentage of early deaths.

Each of her errands meant a scene with Toddy. There was a struggle here, she felt, between her own need for life and work and what she tried to persuade herself was merely selfishness in him. In her new strength and happiness she felt that she ought to be able to draw Toddy into taking an interest in something beyond the power-house. But he would not be drawn.

Surely when the snows broke it would be possible. She would persuade him to take the old car in the barn and drive with her about the countryside. He was only a trifle bushed from the long winter. Though she had been shocked at first by the suggestion that he might be bushed, she found the hope edging into her mind more and more often now that it was nothing more.

And then one day it was Joe Blanchard's turn to come to get her. His wife was expecting her tenth child.

All day Molly was restless, going to the window to strain her eyes into the glare for a sight of Joe's sleigh and his tough yellow dogs winding out of the bush. Sunset came and she prepared dinner, and still he had not come.

Once she looked up from her plate and saw Toddy staring at her, his lips trembling in an odd small way.

'Is anything wrong?' she asked.

'No,' he said, 'nothing.'

'Toddy,' she said, gently, and under her gentleness afraid. 'I'll probably be going out tonight. I promised Joe Blanchard I'd help Mariette.'

Toddy looked at her, and his face blazed.

'No,' he shouted, 'by God—you will stay where you belong.'

'Why?' she asked, as she had before. 'Why don't you want me to go?'

He seemed to search through his mind for words.

'Because I won't have you going out at night with that ruffian—because, damn it, it's too dangerous.'

'Then you come too,' she said. 'You come with us.'

'Don't be a fool,' he said, 'How could I leave?'

'Well, stay home tonight,' she said. 'Stay here and—and rest. We'll decide what to do when Joe comes.'

'Rest—what do you mean?'

'I think you're—tired,' she said. 'I think you should stay home just one evening.'

Toddy scraped back his chair.

'Don't be a fool, Molly. Of course I can't stay. I can't.'

He walked to the door, then turned back to her.

'I shall find you here,' he said, 'when I return.'

The evening dragged between the two anxieties—between wondering when Joe would come and watching for Toddy's return.

Midnight came, and still neither Toddy nor Joe had come. Her anxiety grew. Toddy had never stayed this late before. It had been ten-thirty first, then eleven.

The sound of the back door opening sent her flying to the kitchen. Joe stood in the doorway, his broad face beaming.

'You ready, madame?'

Molly began to put on her heavy clothes, her snow-boots. Anxiety licked still in her mind. Past twelve o'clock and Toddy had not returned.

'Joe,' she said, 'you'll wait just a minute while I go down and tell my husband?'

Her feet slipped several times on the icy steps Toddy kept cut in the hillside. She felt a sudden terrible urgency. She must reassure herself of something. She didn't quite know what.

She pulled open the door of the power-house and was struck, as she had been before, by the way the thunder of the waterfall was suddenly replaced by a low even whine.

For an instant she did not see Toddy. Louis-Paul was propped in a straight chair dozing, across the room. Then she saw Toddy, his back, leaning towards one of the turbines. As she looked, he moved, with a curious scuttling speed, to one of the indicators on the wall. She saw the side of his face then, its expression totally absorbed, gloating.

'Toddy!' she called.

He turned, and for a long moment she felt that he did not know who she was. He did not speak.

'I didn't want you to worry,' she said. 'I'm going with Joe. If I shouldn't be back for breakfast—'

She stopped, for he did not seem to be listening.

'I probably *will* be back for breakfast,' she said.

He glared at her. He moved his lips as if to speak. Then his gaze broke and slid back to the bright indicator on the wall.

At that moment she understood. The struggle she had sensed without being able to give it a name had been between herself and the power-house. In an indistinct way Toddy had realized it when he said, 'I want you here.'

'Toddy!' she shouted.

He turned his back to her in a vague automatic way, and she saw that his face was quite empty except for a strange glitter that spread from his eyes over his face. He did not answer her.

For a moment she forgot that she was not alone with him, until a sound reminded her of Louis-Paul, awake now and standing by the door. And from the expression of sick shaking terror on his face she knew what the fear had been that she had never allowed herself to name.

'Oh Louis,' she said.

'Come madame,' he said. 'We can do nothing here. In the morning I will take you to Missawani. I will bring the doctor back.'

'But is he safe?' she asked. 'Will he—damage the machines perhaps?'

'Oh no. He would never hurt these machines. For years I watch him fall in love with her. Now she has him for herself.'

HUGH GARNER
(1913-1979)

〜

One-Two-Three Little Indians

After they had eaten, Big Tom pushed the cracked and dirty supper things to the back of the table and took the baby from its high chair carefully, so as not to spill the flotsam of bread crumbs and boiled potatoes from the chair to the floor.

He undressed the youngster, talking to it in the old dialect, trying to awaken its interest. All evening it had been listless and fretful by turns, but now it seemed to be soothed by the story of Po-chee-ah, and the Lynx, although it was too young to understand him as his voice slid awkwardly through the ageless folk-tale of his people.

For long minutes after the baby was asleep he talked on, letting the victorious words fill the small cabin so that they shut out the sounds of the Northern Ontario night: the buzz of mosquitoes, the far-off bark of a dog, the noise of the cars and transport trucks passing on the gravelled road.

The melodious hum of his voice was like a strong soporific, lulling him with the return of half-forgotten memories, strengthening him with the knowledge that once his people had been strong and brave, men with a nation of their own, encompassing a million miles of teeming forest, lake and tamarack swamp.

When he halted his monologue to place the baby in the big brass bed in the corner the sudden silence was loud in his ears, and he cringed a bit as the present suddenly caught up with the past.

He covered the baby with a corner of the church-donated patchwork quilt, and lit the kerosene lamp that stood on the mirrorless dressing table beside the stove. Taking a broom from a corner he swept the mealtime debris across the doorsill.

This done, he stood and watched the headlights of the cars run along the trees bordering the road, like a small boy's stick along a picket fence. From the direction of the trailer camp a hundred yards away came the sound of a car engine being gunned, and the halting note-tumbles of a clarinet from a tourist's radio. The soft summer smell of spruce needles and wood smoke blended with the evening dampness of the earth, and felt good in his nostrils, so that he filled his worn lungs until he began to cough. He spat the resinous phlegm into the weed-filled yard.

It had been this summer smell, and the feeling of freedom it gave, which had brought him back to the woods after three years in the mines during the war. But only part of him had come back, for the mining towns and the big money had done more than etch his lungs with silica: they had also brought him pain and distrust, and a wife who had learned to live in gaudy imitation of the boomtown life.

When his coughing attack subsided he peered along the path, hoping to catch a glimpse of his wife Mary returning from her work at the trailer camp. He was becoming worried about the baby, and her presence, while it might not make the baby well, would mean that there was someone else to share his fears. He could see nothing but the still blackness of the trees, their shadows interwoven in a sombre pattern across the mottled ground.

He re-entered the cabin and began washing the dishes, stopping once or twice to cover the moving form of the sleeping baby. He wondered if he could have transmitted his own wasting sickness to the lungs of his son. He stood for long minutes at the side of the bed, staring, trying to diagnose the child's restlessness into something other than what he feared.

His wife came in and placed some things on the table. He picked up a can of pork-and-beans she had bought and weighed it in the palm of his hand. 'The baby seems pretty sick,' he said.

She crossed the room, and looked at the sleeping child. 'I guess it's his teeth.'

He placed the pork-and-beans on the table again and walked over to his chair beside the empty stove. As he sat down he noticed for the first time that his wife was beginning to show her pregnancy. Her squat form had sunk lower, and almost filled the shapeless dress she wore. Her brown ankles were puffed above the broken-down heels of the dirty silver dancing pumps she was wearing.

'Is the trailer camp full?' he asked.

'Nearly. Two more Americans came about half an hour ago.'

'Was Billy Woodhen around?'

'I didn't see him, only Elsie,' she answered. 'A woman promised me a dress tomorrow if I scrub out her trailer.'

'Yeh.' He saw the happiness rise over her like a colour as she mentioned this. She was much younger than he was—twenty-two years against his thirty-nine—and her dark face had a fullness that is common to many Indian women. She was no longer pretty, and as he watched her he thought that wherever they went the squalor of their existence seemed to follow them.

'It's a silk dress,' Mary said, as though the repeated mention of it brought it nearer.

'A silk dress is no damn good around here. You should get some overalls,' he said, angered by her lack of shame in accepting the cast-off garments of the trailer women.

She seemed not to notice his anger. 'It'll do for the dances next winter.'

'A lot of dancing you'll do,' he said pointing to her swollen body. 'You'd better learn to stay around here and take care of the kid.'

She busied herself over the stove, lighting it with newspapers and kindling. 'I'm going to have some fun. You should have married a grandmother.'

He filled the kettle with water from an open pail near the door. The baby began to cough, and the mother turned it on its side in the bed. 'As soon as I draw my money from Cooper I'm going to get him some cough syrup from the store,' she said.

'It won't do any good. We should take him to the doctor in town tomorrow.'

'I can't. I've got to stay here and work.'

He knew the folly of trying to reason with her. She had her heart set on earning the silk dress the woman had promised.

After they had drunk their tea he blew out the light, and they took off some of their clothes and climbed over the baby into the bed. Long after his wife had fallen asleep he lay in the darkness listening to a ground moth beating its futile wings against the glass of the window.

They were awakened in the morning by the twittering of a small colony of tree sparrows who were feasting on the kitchen sweepings of the night before. Mary got up and went outside, returning a few minutes later carrying a handful of birch and poplar stovewood.

He waited until the beans were in the pan before rising and pulling on his pants. He stood in the doorway scratching his head and absorbing the sunlight through his bare feet upon the step.

The baby awoke while they were eating their breakfast.

'He don't look good,' Big Tom said as he dipped some brown sauce from his plate with a hunk of bread.

'He'll be all right later,' his wife insisted. She poured some crusted tinned milk from a tin into a cup and mixed it with water from the kettle.

Big Tom splashed his hands and face with cold water, and dried himself on a soiled shirt that lay over the back of a chair. 'When you going to the camp, this morning?'

'This afternoon,' Mary answered.

'I'll be back by then.'

He took up a small pile of woven baskets from a corner and hung the handles over his arm. From the warming shelf of the stove he pulled a bedraggled band of cloth, into which a large goose feather had been sewn. Carrying this in his hand he went outside and strode down the path toward the highway.

He ignored the chattering sauciness of a squirrel that hurtled up the green ladder of a tree beside him. Above the small noises of the woods could be heard the roar of a transport truck braking its way down the hill from the burnt-out sapling covered ridge to the north. The truck passed him as he reached the road, and he waved a desultory greeting to the driver, who answered with a short blare of the horn.

Placing the baskets in a pile on the shoulder of the road he adjusted the corduroy band on his head so that the feather stuck up at the rear. He knew that by so doing he became a part of the local colour, 'a real Indian with a feather'n everything,' and also that he sold more baskets while wearing it. In the time he had been living along the highway he had learned to give them what they expected.

The trailer residents were not yet awake, so he sat down on the wooden walk leading to the shower room, his baskets resting on the ground in a half circle behind him.

After a few minutes a small boy descended from the door of a trailer and stood staring at him. Then he leaned back inside the doorway and pointed in Big Tom's direction. In a moment a man's hand parted the heavy curtains on the window and a bed-mussed unshaven face stared out. The small boy climbed back inside.

A little later two women approached on the duckboard walk, one attired in a pair of buttock-pinching brown slacks, and the other wearing a blue chenille dressing gown. They circled him warily and entered the shower room. From inside came the buzz of whispered conversation and the louder noises of running water.

During the rest of the morning several people approached and stared at Big Tom and the baskets. He sold two small ones to an elderly woman. She seemed surprised when she asked him what tribe he belonged to, and instead of answering in a monosyllable he said, 'I belong to the Algonquins, Ma'am.' He also got rid of one of his big forty-five cent baskets to the mother of the small boy who had been the first one up earlier in the day.

A man took a series of photographs of him with an expensive-looking camera, pacing off the distance and being very careful in setting his lens openings and shutter speeds.

'I wish he'd look into the camera,' the man said loudly to a couple standing nearby, as if he were talking about an animal in a cage.

'You can't get any good picshus around here. Harold tried to get one of the five Dionney kids, but they wouldn't let him. The way they keep them quints hid you'd think they was made of china or somep'n,' a woman standing by said.

She glanced at her companion for confirmation.

'They want you to *buy* their picshus,' the man said. 'We was disappointed in 'em. They used to look cute before, when they was small, but now they're just five plain-looking kids.'

'Yeah. My Gawd, you'd never believe how homely they got, would you, Harold? An' everything's pure robbery in Callander. You know, Old Man Dionney's minting money up there. Runs his own soovenir stand.'

'That's durin' the day, when he's got time,' her husband said. The man with the camera, and the woman, laughed.

After lunch Big Tom watched Cooper prepare for his trip to North Bay. 'Is there anybody going fishing, Mr Cooper?' he asked.

The man took the radiator cap off the old truck he was inspecting, and peered inside.

'Mr Cooper!'

'Hey?' Cooper turned and looked at the Indian standing beside him, hands in pockets, his manner shy and deferential. He showed a vague irritation as though he sensed the overtone of servility in the Indian's attitude.

'Anybody going fishing?' Big Tom asked again.

'Seems to me Mr Staynor said he'd like to go,' Cooper answered. His voice was kind, with the amused kindness of a man talking to a child.

The big Indian remained standing where he was, saying nothing. His old second-hand army trousers drooped around his lean loins, and his plaid shirt was open at the throat, showing a grey high-water mark of dirt where his face washing began and ended.

'What's the matter?' Cooper asked. 'You seem pretty anxious to go today.'

'My kid's sick. I want to make enough to take him to the doctor.'

Cooper walked around the truck and opened one of the doors, rattling the handle in his hand as if it was stuck. 'You should stay home with it. Make it some pine-sap syrup. No need to worry, it's as healthy as a bear cub.'

Mrs Cooper came out of the house and eased her bulk into the truck cab. 'Where's Mary?' she asked.

'Up at the shack,' answered Big Tom.

'Tell her to scrub the washrooms before she does anything else. Mrs Anderson, in that trailer over there, wants her to do her floors.' She pointed across the lot to a large blue and white trailer parked behind a Buick.'I'll tell her,' he answered.

The Coopers drove between the whitewashed stones marking the entrance to the camp, and swung up the highway, leaving behind them a small cloud of dust from the pulverized gravel of the road.

Big Tom fetched Mary and the baby from the shack. He gave his wife Mrs Cooper's instructions, and she transferred the baby from her arms to his. The child was feverish, its breath noisy and fast.

'Keep him warm,' she said. 'He's been worse since we got up. I think he's got a touch of the 'flu.'

Big Tom placed his hand inside the old blanket and felt the baby's cheek. It was dry and burning to his palm. He adjusted the baby's small weight in his arm and walked across the camp and down the narrow path to the shore of the lake where the boats were moored.

A man sitting in the sternsheets of a new-painted skiff looked up and smiled at his approach. 'You coming out with me, Tom?' he asked.The Indian nodded.

'Are you bringing the papoose along?'

Big Tom winced at the word 'papoose', but he answered, 'He won't bother us. The wife is working this afternoon.'

'O.K. I thought maybe we'd go over to the other side of the lake today and try to get some of them big fellows at the creek mouth. Like to try?'

'Sure,' the Indian answered, placing the baby along the wide seat in the stern, and unshipping the oars.

He rowed silently for the best part of an hour, the sun beating through his shirt causing the sweat to trickle coldly down his back. At times his efforts at the oars caused a constriction in his chest, and he coughed and spat into the water.

When they reached the mouth of the creek across the lake, he let the oars drag and leaned over to look at the baby. It was sleeping restlessly, its lips slightly blue and its breath laboured and harsh. Mr Staynor was busy with his lines and tackle in the bow of the boat.

Tom picked the child up and felt its little body for sweat.

The baby's skin was bone dry. He picked up the bailing can from the boat bottom and dipped it over the side. With the tips of his fingers he brushed some of the cold water across the baby's forehead. The child woke up, looked at the strange surroundings, and smiled up at him.

He gave it a drink of water from the can. Feeling reassured now he placed the baby on the seat and went forward to help the man with his gear.

Mr Staynor fished for a half hour or so, catching some small fish and a large black bass, which writhed in the bottom of the boat. Big Tom watched its gills gasping its death throes, and noted the similarity between the struggles of the fish and those of the baby lying on the seat in the blanket.

He became frightened again after a time, and he turned to the man in the bow and said, 'We'll have to go pretty soon. I'm afraid my kid's pretty sick.'

'Eh! We've hardly started,' the man answered. 'Don't worry, there's not much wrong with the papoose.'

Big Tom lifted the child from the seat and cradled it in his arms. He opened the blanket, and shading the baby's face, allowed the warm sun to shine on its chest. He thought, if I could only get him to sweat; everything would be all right then.

He waited again as long as he dared, noting the blueness creeping over the baby's lips, before he placed the child again on the seat and addressed the man in the bow. 'I'm going back now. You'd better pull in your line.'

The man turned and felt his way along the boat. He stood over the Indian and parted the folds of the blanket, looking at the baby. 'My God, he is sick, Tom! You'd better get him to a doctor right away!' He stepped across the writhing fish to the bow and began pulling in the line. Then he busied himself with his tackle, stealing glances now and again at the Indian and the baby.

Big Tom turned the boat around, and with long straight pulls on the oars headed back across the lake. The man took the child in his arms and blew cooling drafts of air against its fevered face.

As soon as they reached the jetty below the tourist camp, Tom tied the boat's painter to a stump and took the child from the other man's arms.

Mr Staynor handed him the fee for a full afternoon's work. 'I'm sorry the youngster is sick, Tom,' he said. 'Don't play around. Get him up to the doctor in town right away. We'll try her again tomorrow afternoon.'

Big Tom thanked him. Then, carrying the baby and unmindful of the grasping hands of the undergrowth, he climbed the path through the trees. On reaching the parked cars and trailers he headed in the direction of the large blue and white one where his wife would be working.

When he knocked, the door opened and a woman said, 'Yes?' He recognized her as the one who had been standing nearby in the morning while his picture was being taken.

'Is my wife here?' he asked.

'Your wife. Oh, I know who you mean. No, she's gone. She went down the road in a car a few minutes ago.'

The camp was almost empty, most of the tourists having gone to the small bathing beach further down the lake. A car full of bathers was pulling away to go down to the beach. Big Tom hurried over and held up his hand until it stopped. 'Could you drive me to the doctor in town?' he asked. 'My baby seems pretty sick.'

There was a turning of heads within the car. A woman in the back seat began talking about the weather. The driver said, 'I'll see what I can do, Chief, after I take the girls to the beach.'

Big Tom sat down at the side of the driveway to wait. After a precious half hour had gone by and they did not return, he got to his feet and started up the highway in the direction of town.

His long legs pounded on the loose gravel of the road, his anger and terror giving strength to his stride. He noticed that the passengers in the few cars he met were pointing at him and laughing, and suddenly he realized that he was still wearing the feather in the band around his head. He reached up, pulled it off, and threw it in the ditch.

When a car or truck came up from behind him he would step off the road and raise his hand to beg a ride. After several passed without pausing he stopped this useless time-wasting gesture and strode ahead, impervious to the noise of their horns as they approached him.Now and again he placed his hand on the baby's face as he plodded along, reassuring himself that it was still alive. It had been hours since it had cried or shown any other signs of consciousness.

Once, he stepped off the road at a small bridge over a stream, and made a crude cup with his hands, tried to get the baby to drink. He succeeded only in making it cough, harshly, so that its tiny face became livid with its efforts to breathe.

It was impossible that the baby should die. Babies did not die like this, in their father's arms, on a highway that ran fifteen miles north through a small town, where there was a doctor and all the life-saving devices to prevent their deaths.

The sun fell low behind the trees and the swarms of black flies and mosquitoes began their nightly forage. He waved his hand above the fevered face of the baby, keeping them off, while at the same time trying to waft a little air into the child's tortured lungs.

But suddenly, with feelings as black as hell itself, he knew that the baby was dying. He had seen too much of it not to know, that the child was in an advanced stage of pneumonia. He stumbled along as fast as he could, his eyes devouring the darkening face of his son, while the hot tears ran from the corners of his eyes.

With nightfall he knew that it was too late. He looked up at the sky where the first stars were being drawn in silver on a burnished copper plate, and he cursed them, and cursed what made them possible.

To the north-west the clouds were piling up in preparation for a summer storm. Reluctantly he turned and headed back down the road in the direction he had come.

It was almost midnight before he felt his way along the path through the trees to his shack. It was hard to see anything in the teeming rain, and he let the water run from his shoulders in an unheeded stream, soaking the sodden bundle he still carried in his arms.

When he reached the shanty he opened the door and fell inside. He placed the body of his son on the bed in the corner. Then, groping around the newspaper-lined walls, he found some matches in a pocket of his mackinaw and lit the lamp. With a glance around the room he knew that his wife had not yet returned, so he placed the lamp on the table under the window and headed out again into the rain.

At the trailer camp he sat down on the rail fence near the entrance to wait. Some lights shone from the small windows of the trailers and from Cooper's house across the road. The illuminated sign said: COOPER'S TRAILER CAMP—Hot and Cold Running Water, Rest Rooms. FISHING AND BOATING— INDIAN GUIDES.

One by one, as he waited, the lights went out, until only the sign lit up a small area at the gate. He saw the car's headlights first, about a hundred yards down the road. When it pulled to a stop he heard some giggling, and Mary and another Indian girl, Elsie Woodhen, staggered out into the rain.

A man's voice shouted through the door, 'See you again, sweetheart. Don't forget next Saturday night.' The voice belonged to one of the French-Canadians who worked at a creosote camp across the lake.

Another male voice shouted, 'Wahoo!'

The girls clung to each other, laughing drunkenly, as the car pulled away.

They were not aware of Big Tom's approach until he grasped his wife by the hair and pulled her backwards to the ground. Elsie Woodhen screamed, and ran away in the direction of the Cooper house. Big Tom bent down as if he was going to strike at Mary's face with his fist. Then he changed his mind and let her go.

She stared into his eyes and saw what was there. Crawling to her feet and sobbing hysterically she left one of her silver shoes in the mud and limped along towards the shack.

Big Tom followed behind, all the anguish and frustration drained from him, so that there was nothing left to carry him into another day. Heedless now of the coughing that tore his chest apart, he pushed along in the rain, hurrying to join his wife in the vigil over their dead.

~

Scarves, Beads, Sandals

After three years, Mathilde and Theo Schurz were divorced, without a mean thought, and even Theo says she is better off now, married to Alain Poix. (Or 'Poids.' Or 'Poisse.' Theo may be speaking the truth when he says he can't keep in mind every facet of the essential Alain.) Mathilde moved in with Alain six months before the wedding, in order to become acquainted with domestic tedium and annoying habits, should they occur, and so avoid making the same mistake (marriage piled onto infatuation) twice. They rented, and are now gradually buying, a two-bedroom place on Rue Saint-Didier, in the Sixteenth Arrondissement. In every conceivable way it is distant from the dispiriting south fringe of Montparnasse, where Theo continues to reside, close to several of the city's grimmest hospitals, and always under some threat or other—eviction, plagues of mice, demolition of the whole cul-de-sac of sagging one-storey studios. If Theo had been attracted by her 'physical aspect'—Mathilde's new, severe term for beauty—Alain accepts her as a concerned and contributing partner, intellectually and spiritually. This is not her conclusion. It is her verdict.

Theo wonders about 'spirituality.' It sounds to him like a moist west wind, ready to veer at any minute, with soft alternations of sun and rain. Whatever Mathilde means, or wants to mean, even the idea of the partnership should keep her fully occupied. Nevertheless, she finds time to drive across Paris, nearly every Saturday afternoon, to see how Theo is getting along without her. (Where is Alain? In close liaison with a computer, she says.) She brings Theo flowering shrubs from the market on Île de la Cité, still hoping to enliven the blighted yard next to the studio, and food in covered dishes—whole, delicious meals, not Poix leftovers—and fresh news about Alain.

Recently, Alain was moved to a new office—a room divided in two, really, but on the same floor as the Minister and with part of an eighteenth-century fresco overhead. If Alain looks straight up, perhaps to ease a cramp in his neck, he can take in Apollo—just Apollo's head—watching Daphne turn into a laurel tree. Owing to the perspective of the work, Alain has the entire Daphne—roots, bark, and branches, and her small pink Enlightenment face peering through leaves. (The person next door has inherited Apollo's torso, dressed in Roman armour, with a short white skirt, and his legs and feet.) To Théo, from whom women manage to drift away, the situation might seem another connubial bad dream, but Alain interprets it as an allegory of free feminine choice. If he weren't so pressed with other work, he might write something along that line: an essay of about a hundred and fifty pages, published between soft white covers and containing almost as many coloured illustrations as there are pages of print; something a reader can absorb during a weekend and still attend to the perennial border on Sunday afternoon.

He envisions (so does Mathilde) a display on the 'recent nonfiction' table in a Saint-Germain-des-Prés bookshop, between stacks of something new about waste disposal and something new about Jung. Instead of writing the essay, Alain applies his trained mind and exacting higher education to shoring up French values against the Anglo-Saxon mud slide. On this particular Saturday, he is trying to batter into proper French one more untranslatable expression: 'airbag'. It was on television again the other day, this time spoken by a woman showing black-and-white industrial drawings. Alain would rather take the field against terms that have greater resonance, are more blatantly English, such as 'shallow' and 'bully' and 'wishful thinking', but no one, so far, has ever tried to use them in a commercial.

So Mathilde explains to Théo as she sorts his laundry, starts up the machine, puts clean sheets on the bed. She admires Théo, as an artist—it is what drew her to him in the first place—but since become Mme Poix she has tended to see him as unemployable. At an age when Théo was still carrying a portfolio of drawings up and down and around Rue de Seine, looking for a small but adventurous gallery to take him in, Alain has established a position in the cultural apparat. It may even survive the next elections: he is too valuable an asset to be swept out and told to find a job in the private sector. Actually, the private sector could ask nothing better. Everyone wants Alain. Publishers want him. Foreign universities want him. Even America is waiting, in spite of the uncompromising things he has said about the hegemony and how it encourages well-bred Europeans to eat pizza slices in the street.

Théo has never heard of anybody with symbolic imagery, or even half an image, on his office ceiling outlasting a change of government. The queue for space of that kind consists of one ravenous human resource after the other, pushing hard. As for the private sector, its cultural subdivisions are hard up for breathing room, in the dark, stalled between floors. Alain requires the clean horizons and rich oxygen flow of the governing class. Théo says none of this. He removes foil from bowls and dishes, to see what Mathilde wants him to have for dinner. What can a Théo understand about an Alain? Théo never votes. He has never registered, he forgets the right date. All at once the campaign is over. The next day familiar faces, foxy or benign, return to the news, described as untested but eager to learn. Elections are held in spring, perhaps to make one believe in growth, renewal. One rainy morning in May, sooner or later, Alain will have to stack his personal files, give up Apollo and Daphne, cross a Ministry courtyard on the first lap of a march into the private sector. Theo sees him stepping along cautiously, avoiding the worst of the puddles. Alain can always teach, Theo tells himself. It is what people say about aides and assistants they happen to know, as the astonishing results unfold on the screen.

Alain knows Theo, of course. Among his mixed feelings, Alain has no trouble finding the esteem due to a cultural bulwark: Theo and his work have entered the enclosed space known as 'time-honoured.' Alain even knows about the Poids and Poisse business, but does not hold it against Theo; according to Mathilde, one no longer can be sure when he is trying to show he has a sense of humour or when he is losing brain cells. He was at the wedding, correctly dressed, suit, collar, and tie, looking distinguished—something like Braque at the age of fifty, Alain said, but thinner, taller, blue-eyed, lighter hair, finer profile. By then they were at the reception, drinking champagne under a white marquee, wishing they could sit down. It was costing Mathilde's father the earth—the venue was a restaurant in the Bois de Boulogne—but he was so thankful to be rid of Theo as a son-in-law that he would have hired Versailles, if one could.

The slow, winding currents of the gathering had brought Theo, Alain, and Mathilde together. Theo with one finger pushed back a strayed lock of her hair; it was reddish gold, the shade of a persimmon. Perhaps he was measuring his loss and might even, at last, say something embarrassing and true. Actually, he was saying that Alain's description—blue-eyed, etc.—sounded more like Max Ernst. Alain backtracked, said it was Balthus he'd had in mind. Mathilde, though not Alain, was still troubled by Theo's wedding gift, a botched painting he had been tinkering with for years. She had been Mme Poix for a few hours, but still felt responsible for Theo's gaffes and imperfections. When he did not reply at once, she said she hoped he did not object to being told he was like Balthus. Balthus was the best-looking artist of the past hundred years, with the exception of Picasso.

Alain wondered what Picasso had to do with the conversation. Theo looked nothing like him: he came from Alsace. He, Alain, had never understood the way women preferred male genius incarnated as short, dark, and square-shaped. 'Like Celtic gnomes,' said Theo, just to fill in. Mathilde saw the roses in the restaurant garden through a blur which was not the mist of happiness. Alain had belittled her, on their wedding day, in the presence of her first husband. Her first husband had implied she was attracted to gnomes. She let her head droop. Her hair slid over her cheeks, but Theo, this time, left it alone. Both men looked elsewhere—Alain because tears were something new, Theo out of habit. The Minister stood close by, showing admirable elegance of manner—not haughty, not familiar; careful, kind, like the Archbishop of Paris at a humble sort of funeral, Theo said, thinking to cheer up Mathilde. Luckily, no one overheard. Her mood was beginning to draw attention. Many years before, around the time of the Algerian War, a relative of Alain's mother had married an aunt of the Minister. The outer rims of the family circles had quite definitely overlapped. It was the reason the Minister had come to the reception and why he had stayed, so far, more than half an hour.

Mathilde was right; Theo must be losing brain cells at a brisk rate now. First Celtic gnomes, then the Archbishop of Paris; and, of course, the tactless, stingy, offensive gift. Alain decided to smile, extending greetings to everyone. He was attempting to say, I am entirely happy on this significant June day. He was happy, but not entirely. Perhaps Mathilde was recalling her three years with Theo and telling herself nothing lasts. He wished Theo would do something considerate, such as disappear. A cluster of transparent molecules, the physical reminder of the artist T. Schurz, would dance in the sun, above the roses. Theo need not be dead—just gone.

'Do you remember, Theo, the day we got married,' said Mathilde, looking up at the wrong man, by accident intercepting the smile Alain was using to reassure the Minister and the others. 'Everybody kept saying we had made a mistake. We decided to find out how big a mistake it was, so in the evening we went to Montmartre and had our palms read. Theo was told he could have been an artist but was probably a merchant seaman. His left hand was full of little shipwrecks.' She may have been waiting for Alain to ask, 'What about you? What did your hand say?' In fact, he was thinking just about his own. In both palms he had lines that might be neat little roads, straight or curved, and a couple of spidery stars.

At first, Theo had said he would give them a painting. Waiting, they kept a whole wall bare. Alain supposed it would be one of the great recent works; Mathilde thought she knew better. Either Alain had forgotten about having carried off the artist's wife or he had decided it didn't matter to Theo. That aside, Theo and Theo's dealer were tight as straitjackets about his work. Mathilde owned nothing, not even a crumpled sketch saved from a dustbin. The dealer had taken much of the earlier work off the market, which did not mean Theo was allowed to give any away. He burned most of his discards and kept just a few unsaleable things in a shed. Speaking of his wedding gift, Theo said the word 'painting' just once and never again: he mentioned some engravings—falling rain or falling snow—or else a plain white tile he could dedicate and sign. Mathilde made a reference to the empty wall. A larger work, even unfinished, even slightly below Theo's dealer's exacting standards, would remind Mathilde of Theo for the rest of her life.

Five days later, the concierge at Rue Saint-Didier took possession of a large oil study of a nude with red hair—poppy red, not like Mathilde's—prone on a bed, her face concealed in pillows. Mathilde recognized the studio, as it had been before she moved in and cleaned it up. She remembered the two reproductions, torn out of books or catalogues, askew on the wall. One showed a pair of Etruscan figures, dancing face to face, the other a hermit in a landscape. When the bed became half Mathilde's, she took them down. She had wondered if Theo would mind, but he never noticed—at any rate, never opened an inquiry.

'Are you sure this thing is a Schurz?' said Alain. Nothing else bothered him. He wondered, at first, if Theo had found the picture at a junk sale and had signed it as a joke. The true gift, the one they were to cherish and display, would come along later, all the more to be admired because of the scare. But Theo never invented jokes; he blundered into them.

'I am not that woman,' Mathilde said. Of course not. Alain had never supposed she was. There was the crude red of the hair, the large backside, the dirty feet, and then the date—'1979'—firm and black in the usual place, to the right of 'T. Schurz'. At that time, Mathilde was still reading translations of Soviet poetry, in love with a teacher of Russian at her lycée, and had never heard of 'T. Schurz'. In saying this, Alain showed he remembered the story of her life. If she'd had a reason to forgive him, about anything, she would have absolved him on the spot; then he spoiled the moment by declaring that it made no difference. The model was not meant to be anyone in particular.

Mathilde thought of Emma, Theo's first long-term companion (twelve years), but by '79 Emma must have been back in Alsace, writing cookery books with a woman friend. Julita (six years) fit the date but had worn a thick yellow braid down her back. She was famous for having tried to strangle Theo, but her hands were too small—she could not get a grip. After the throttling incident, which had taken place in a restaurant, Julita had packed a few things, most of them Theo's, and moved to the north end of Paris, where she would not run into him. Emma left Theo a microwave oven, Julita a cast-iron cat, standing on its hind legs, holding a tray. She had stolen it from a stand at the flea market, Theo told Mathilde, but the story sounded unlikely: the cat was heavy to lift, let alone be fetched across a distance. Two people would have been needed; perhaps one had been Theo. Sometimes, even now, some old friend from the Julita era tells Theo that Julita is ill or hard up and that he ought to help her out. Theo will say he doesn't know where she is or else, yes, he will do it tomorrow. She is like art taken off the market now, neither here nor there. The cat is still in the yard, rising out of broken flowerpots, empty bottles. Julita had told Theo it was the one cat that would never run away. She hung its neck with some amber beads Emma had overlooked in her flight, then pocketed the amber and left him the naked cat.

When Mathilde was in love with Theo and jealous of women she had never met, she used to go to an Indian shop, in Montparnasse, where first Emma, then Julita had bought their flat sandals and white embroidered shifts and long gauzy skirts, black and pink and indigo. She imagined what it must have been like to live, dress, go to parties, quarrel, and make up with Theo in the seventies. Emma brushed her brown hair upside down, to create a great drifting mane. A woman in the Indian store did Julita's braid, just because she liked Julita. Mathilde bought a few things, skirts and sandals, but never wore them. They made her look alien, bedraggled, like the Romanian Gypsy women begging for coins along Rue de Rennes. She did not want to steal from a market or fight with Theo in bistros. She belonged to a generation of women who showed a lot of leg and kept life smooth, tight-fitting, close-woven. Theo was right: she was better off with Alain.

Still, she had the right to know something about the woman she had been offered as a gift. It was no good asking directly; Theo might say it was a journalist who came to tape his memoirs or the wife of a Lutheran dignitary or one of his nieces from Alsace. Instead, she asked him to speak to Alain; out of aesthetic curiosity, she said, Alain acquired the facts of art. Theo often did whatever a woman asked, unless it was important. Clearly, this was not. Alain took the call in his office; at that time, he still had a cubicle with a bricked-up window. Nobody recalled who had ordered the bricks or how long ago. He worked by the light of a neon fixture that flickered continually and made his eyes water. Summoned by an aide to the Minister, on propitious afternoons by the Minister himself (such summonses were more and more frequent), he descended two flights, using the staircase in order to avoid a giddy change from neon tube to the steadier glow of a chandelier. He brought with him only a modest amount of paperwork. He was expected to store everything in his head.

Theo told Alain straight out that he had used Julita for the pose. She slept much of the day and for that reason made an excellent model: was never tired, never hungry, never restless, never had to break off for a cigarette. The picture had not worked out and he had set it aside. Recently he had looked at it again and decided to alter Julita from the neck up. Alain though he had just been told something of consequence; he wanted to exchange revelations, let Theo know he had not enticed Mathilde away but had merely opened the net into which she could jump. She had grabbed Theo in her flight, perhaps to break the fall. But Alain held still; it would be unseemly to discuss Mathilde. Theo was simply there, like an older relative who has to be considered and mollified, though no one knows why. There was something flattering about having been offered an unwanted and unnecessary explanation; few artists would have bothered to make one. It was as though Theo had decided to take Alain seriously. Alain thanked him.

Unfortunately, the clarification had made the painting even less interesting than it looked. Until then, it had been a dud Schurz but an honest vision. The subject, a woman, entirely womanly, had been transfigured by Schurz's reactionary visual fallacy (though honest, if one accepted the way his mind worked) into a hefty platitude; still, it was art. Now, endowed with a name and, why not, an address, a telephone number, a social security number, and a personal history, Theo's universal statement dwindled to a footnote about Julita—second long-term companion of T. Schurz, first husband of Mathilde, future first wife of Alain Poix. A white tile with a date and a signature would have shown more tact and common sense.

All this Alain said to Mathilde that night, as they ate their dinner next to the empty wall. Mathilde said she was certain Theo had gone to considerable trouble to choose something he believed they would understand and appreciate and that would enhance their marriage. It was one of her first lies to Alain: Theo had gone out to the shed where he kept his shortfalls and made a final decision about a dead loss. Perhaps he guessed they would never hang it and so damage his reputation, although as a rule he never imagined future behaviour more than a few minutes away. Years ago, in a bistro on Rue Stanislas, he had drawn a portrait of Julita on the paper table-cloth, signed and dated it, torn it off, even made the edges neat. It was actually in her hands when he snatched it back, ripped it to shreds, and set the shreds on fire in an ashtray. It was then that Julita had tried to get him by the throat.

Yesterday, Friday, an April day, Theo was awakened by a hard beam of light trained on his face. There was a fainter light at the open door, where the stranger had entered easily. The time must have been around five o'clock. Theo could make out an outline, drawn in grey chalk: leather jacket, close-cropped head. (Foreign Legion deserter? Escaped prisoner? Neo-Nazi? Drugs?) He spoke a coarse, neutral, urban French—the old Paris accent was dying out—and told Theo that if he tried to move or call he, the intruder, might hurt him. He did not say how. They all watch the same programs, Theo told himself. He is young and he repeats what he has seen and heard. Theo had no intention of moving and there was no one to call. His thoughts were directed to the privy, in the yard. He hoped the young man would not take too long to discover there was nothing to steal, except a small amount of cash. He would have told him where to find it, but that might be classed as calling out. His checkbook was in a drawer of Emma's old desk, his bank card behind the snapshot of Mathilde, propped on the shelf above the sink. The checkbook was no good to the stranger, unless he forced Theo to sign all the checks. Theo heard him scuffing about, heard a drawer being pulled. He shut his eyes, opened them to see the face bent over him, the intent and watchful expression, like a lover's, and the raised arm and the flashlight (probably) wrapped in one of Mathilde's blue-and-white tea towels.

He came to in full daylight. His nose had bled all over the pillows, and the mattress was sodden. He got up and walked quite steadily, barefoot, over the stones and gravel of the yard; returning to the studio, he found some of yesterday's coffee still in the pot. He heated it up in a saucepan, poured in milk, drank, and kept it down. Only when that was done did he look in a mirror. He could hide his blackened eyes behind sunglasses but not the raw bruise on his forehead or his swollen nose. He dragged the mattress outside and spread it in the cold April sunlight. By four o'clock, Mathilde's announced arrival time—for it seemed to him today could be Saturday—the place was pretty well cleaned up, mattress back on the bed, soiled bed-clothes rolled up, pushed in a corner. He found a banquet-size table-cloth, probably something of Emma's, and drew it over the mattress. Only his cash had vanished; the checkbook and bank card lay on the floor. He had been attacked, for no reason, by a man he had never seen before and would be unable to recognize: his face had been neutral, like his voice. Theo turned on the radio and, from something said, discovered this was still Friday, the day before Mathilde's habitual visiting day. He had expected her to make the mattress dry in some magical and efficient, Mathilde-like way. He kept in the shed a couple of sleeping bags, for rare nights when the temperature fell below freezing. He got one of them out, gave it a shake, and spread it on top of the tablecloth. It would have to do for that night.

Today, Saturday, Mathilde brought a meal packed in a black-and-white bag from Fauchon: cooked asparagus, with the lemon-and-oil sauce in a jar, cold roast lamb, and a gratin of courgettes and tomatoes—all he has to do is turn on Emma's microwave—a Camembert, a round loaf of that moist and slightly sour bread, from the place on Rue du Cherche-Midi, which reminds Schurz of the bread of his childhood, a carton of thick cream, and a bowl of strawberries, washed and hulled. It is too early for French strawberries. These are from Spain, picked green, shipped palely pink, almost as hard as radishes, but they remind one that it is spring. Schurz barely notices seasons. He works indoors. If rain happens to drench the yard when he goes outside to the lavatory, he puts on the Alpine beret that was part of his uniform when he was eighteen and doing his military service.

Mathilde, moving out to live with Alain, took with her a picture of Theo from that period, wearing the beret and the thick laced-up boots and carrying the heavy skis that were standard issue. He skied and shot a rifle for eighteen months, even thought he might have made it a permanent career, if that was all there was to the Army. No one had yet fallen in love with him, except perhaps his mother. His life was simple then, has grown simpler now. The seasons mean nothing, except that green strawberries are followed by red. Weather means crossing the yard bareheaded or covered up.

Mathilde has noticed she is starting to think of him as 'Schurz'. It is what his old friends call Theo. This afternoon, she had found him looking particularly Schurz-like, sitting on a chair he had dragged outside, drinking tea out of a mug, with the string of the tea bag trailing. He had on an overcoat and the regimental beret. He did not turn to the gate when she opened it or get up to greet her or say a word. Mathilde had to walk all round him to see his face.

'My God, Schurz, what happened?'

'I tripped and fell in the dark and struck my head on the cat.'

'I wish you'd get rid of it,' she said.

She took the mug from his hands and went inside, to unpack his dinner and make fresh tea. The beret, having concealed none of the damage, was useless now. He removed it and hung it rakishly on the cat, on one ear. Mathilde returned with, first, a small folding garden table (her legacy), then with a tray and teacups and a teapot and a plate of sliced gingerbread, which she had brought him the week before. She poured his tea, put sugar in, stirred it, and handed him the cup.

She said, 'Theo, how long do you think you can go on living here, alone?' (It was so pathetic, she rehearsed, for Alain. Theo was like a child; he had made the most absurd attempt at covering up the damage, and instead of putting the mattress out to dry he had turned the wet side down and slept on top of it in a sleeping bag. Who was that famous writer who first showed signs of senility and incontinence on a bridge in Rome? I kept thinking of him. Schurz just sat there, like a guilty little boy. He caught syphilis when he was young and gave it to Emma; he said it was from a prostitute, in Montmartre, but I believe it was a married woman, the wife of the first collector to start buying his work. He can't stay there alone now. He simply can't. His checkbook and bank card were lying next to the trash bin. He must have been trying to throw them away.)

Her picture had been on the floor, too, the one taken the day she married Theo. Mathilde has a small cloud of red-gold hair and wears a short white dress and a jacket of the eighties, with shoulders so wide that her head seems unnaturally small, like a little ball of reddish fluff. Theo is next to her, not too close. He could be a relative or a family friend or even some old crony who heard the noise of the party and decided to drop in. The photograph is posed here, in the yard. One can see a table laden with bottles, and a cement-and-stucco structure—the privy, with the door shut, for a change—and a cold-water tap and a bucket lying on its side. You had to fill the bucket and take it in with you.

Schurz never tried to improve the place or make it more comfortable. His reason was, still is, that he might be evicted at any time. Any month, any day, the police and the bailiffs will arrive. He will be rushed off the premises, with just the cast-iron cat as a relic of his old life.

'I'll tell you what happened,' he said, showing her his mess of a face. 'Yesterday morning, while I was still asleep, a man broke in, stole some money, and hit me with something wrapped in a towel. It must have been his flashlight.'

(Oh, if you had heard him! she continued to prepare for Alain. A comic-strip story. The truth is he is starting to miss his footing and to do himself damage, and he pees in his sleep, like a baby. What kind of doctor do we need for him? What sort of specialist? A geriatrician? He's not really old, but there's been the syphilis, and he has always done confused and crazy things, like giving us that picture, when we really wanted a plain, pure tile.)

Schurz at this moment is thinking of food. He would like to be handed a plate of pork *ragoût* with noodles, swimming in gravy; but nobody makes that now. Or stewed eels in red wine, with the onions cooked soft. Or a cutlet of venison, browned in butter on both sides, with a purée of chestnuts. What he does not want is clear broth with a poached egg in it, or any sort of a salad. When he first came to Paris the cheapest meals were the heartiest. His mother had said, 'Send me a Paris hat,' not meaning it; though perhaps she did. His money, when he had any, went to supplies for his work or rent or things to eat.

Only old women wore hats now. There were hats in store windows, dusty windows, in narrow streets—black hats, for funerals and widows. But no widow under the age of sixty ever bought one. Young women wore hats at the end of summer, tilted straw things, that they tried on just for fun. When they took the hats off, their hair would spring loose. The face, freed of shadow, took on a different shape, seemed fuller, unmysterious, as bland as the moon. There was a vogue for bright scarves, around the straw hats, around the hair, wound around the neck along with strings of bright beads, loosely coiled—sand-coloured or coral or a hard kind of blue. The beads cast coloured reflections on the skin of a throat or on a scarf of a different shade, like a bead diluted in water. Schurz and his friends ate cheap meals in flaking courtyards and on terraces where the tables were enclosed in a hedge of brittle, unwatered shrubs. Late at night, the girls and young women would suddenly find that everything they had on was too tight. It was the effect of the warm end-of-summer night and the food and the red wine and the slow movement of the conversation. It slid without wavering from gossip to mean gossip to art to life-in-art to living without boundaries. A scarf would come uncoiled and hang on the back of a chair or a twig of the parched hedge; as it would hang, later, over the foot of someone's bed. Not often Schurz's (not often enough), because he lived in a hotel near the Café Mabillon, long before all those places were renovated and had elevators put in and were given a star in some of the guidebooks. A stiff fine had to be paid by any client caught with a late-night visitor. The police used to patrol small hotels and knock on doors just before morning, looking for French people in trouble with the law and for foreigners with fake passports and no residence permits. When they found an extra guest in the room, usually a frantic young woman trying to pull the sheet over her face, the hotelkeeper was fined, too, and the tenant thrown out a few hours later. It was not a question of sexual morality but just of rules.

When dinner was almost finished, the women would take off their glass beads and let them drop in a heap among the ashtrays and coffee cups and on top of the wine stains and scribbled drawings. Their high-heeled sandals were narrow and so tight that they had to keep their toes crossed; and at last they would slip them off, unobserved, using first one foot, then the other. Scarfless, shoeless, unbound, delivered, they waited for the last wine bottle to be emptied and the last of the coffee to be drunk or spilled before they decided what they specifically wanted or exactly refused. This was not like a memory to Theo but like part of the present time, something that unfolded gradually, revealing mysteries and satisfactions.

In the studio, behind him, Mathilde was making telephone calls. He heard her voice but not her words. On a late Saturday afternoon, she would be recording her messages on other people's machines: he supposed there must be one or two to doctors, and one for the service that sends vans and men to take cumbersome objects away, such as soiled mattresses. Several brief inquiries must has been needed before she could find Theo a hotel room, free tonight, at a price he would accept and on a street he would tolerate. The long unbroken monologue must have been for Alain, explaining that she would be much later than expected, and why. On Monday she would take Theo to the Bon Marché department store and make him buy a mattress, perhaps a whole new bed. Now here was a memory, a brief, plain stretch of the past: love apart, she had married him because she wanted to be Mme T. Schurz. She would not go on attending parties and gallery openings as Schurz's young friend. Nobody knew whether she was actually living with him or writing something on his work or tagging along for the evening. She did not have the look of a woman who would choose to settle for a studio that resembled a garage or, really, for Schurz. It turned out she could hardly wait to move in, scrape and wax whatever he had in the way of furniture, whitewash the walls. She trained climbing plants over the wire fence outside, even tried to grow lemon trees in terra-cotta tubs. The tubs are still there.

She came toward him now, carrying a bag she had packed so that he would have everything he needed at the hotel. 'Don't touch the bruise,' she said, gently, removing the hand full of small shipwrecks. The other thing she said today, which he is bound to recall later on, was 'You ought to start getting used to the idea of leaving this place. You know that it is going to be torn down.'

Well, it is true. At the entrance to the doomed and decaying little colony there is a poster, damaged by weather and vandals, on which one can still see a depiction of the structure that will cover the ruin, once it has finally be brought down: a handsome biscuit-coloured multipurpose urban complex comprising a library, a crèche, a couple of municipal offices, a screening room for projecting films about Bedouins or whales, a lounge where elderly people may spend the whole day playing board games, a theatre for amateur and professional performances, and four low-rent work units for painters, sculptors, poets, musicians, and photographers. (A waiting list of two thousand names was closed some years ago.) It seems to Theo that Julita was still around at the time when the poster was put up. The project keeps running into snags—aesthetic, political, mainly economic. One day the poster will have been his view of the future more than a third of his life.

Mathilde backed out of the cul-de-sac, taking care (he does not like being driven), and she said, 'Theo, we are near all these hospitals. If you think you should have an X-ray at once, we can go to an emergency service. I can't decide, because I really don't know how you got hurt.'

'Not now.' He wanted today to wind down. Mathilde, in her mind, seemed to have gone beyond dropping him at his hotel. He had agreed to something on Rue Delambre, behind the Coupole and the Dôme. She was on the far side of Paris, with Alain. As she drove on, she asked Theo if he could suggest suitable French for a few English expressions: 'divided attention' and 'hard-driven' and 'matchless perfection', the latter in one word.

'I hope no one steals my Alpine beret,' he said. 'I left it hanging on the cat.'

Those were the last words they exchanged today. It is how they said goodbye.

Something Happened Here

I felt at home soon as I got out of the Paris train and waited for a taxi out-side the railway station. I could hear the gulls but I couldn't see them because of the mist. But I could smell the sea. The driver brought me to a hotel along the front. It was a residential hotel beside other residential hotels with the menu in a glass case by the sidewalk. It had four storeys. Its front tall windows, with wooden shutters and small iron balconies, faced the sea. On the ground level was the hotel's dining-room. The front wall was all glass. And there was a man sitting alone by a table.

It looked a comfortable family hotel. The large wooden staircase belonged to an earlier time when it had been a family house. The woman who now owned and ran it liked porcelain. She had cups and saucers on large sideboards, on every landing, as well as grandfather clocks and old clocks without hands. They struck the hour at different times. There were fresh and not so fresh flowers in porcelain vases. There were large mirrors, in wooden frames, tilted against the wall, like paintings. There were china plates, china cups, and china teapots on top of anything that could hold them.

My room on the third floor didn't face the sea but a courtyard. I watched a short man in a chef's hat cutting vegetables into a pot. The room was spacious enough but it seemed over-furnished. It had a large double bed with a carving of two birds on the headboard. A tall wooden closet, a heavy wooden sideboard, a solid table, several chairs, a colour television, and a small fridge fully stocked with wine, brandy, champagne, mineral water and fruit juices. On the fridge was a pad and pencil to mark what one drank.

After I partly unpacked and washed I went down to the dining-room and was shown to a table by the glass wall next to the man sitting alone. He was smoking a cigarette and drinking coffee. He had on a fawn shirt with an open collar and a carefully tied black and white cravat at the neck. He also had fawn coloured trousers. He looked like Erich von Stroheim.

The proprietress came to take my order. She wobbled, coquettishly, on high heels. Medium height, a little plump, in her late forties or early fifties perhaps. She had a sense of style. She wore a different tailored dress every day I was there. A striking person. She had a white complexion and black hair. And looked in fine health. Her teeth were very good. There was a live-liness in her dark eyes. Every time I walked by the desk and the lounge she never seemed far away: doing accounts, dealing with the staff, talking to guests.

I gave her my order in English. I ordered a salad, an omelette, and a glass of *vin rosé*.

When she had gone the man at the next table said in a loud voice,

'Are you English or American?'

'Canadian.'

He began to talk in French.

Although I understood some of what he said I replied, 'I can't speak French well. I'm *English* Canadian.'

'I speak English,' he said. 'I had lessons in Paris at the Berlitz school. My English teacher, she was a pretty woman, said I was very good because I could use the word barbed-wire in a sentence. My name is Georges.'

I told him mine. But for some reason he called me Roman.

'Roman, what do you do?'

'I am a writer.'

'Come, join me,' he said. 'I like very much the work of Somerset Muffin and Heavelin Woof. Are you staying in this hotel?'

'Yes. I arrived a half-hour ago.'

'I live in the country. Since my wife is dead I come here once a week to eat. What do you write?

'Short stories,' I said, 'novels.'

'I read many books—but not novels. I read books of ideas. The conclusion I have come is that you can divide the people of the world. There are the sedentary. There are the nomads. The sedentary—they are registered. We know about them. The nomads—they leave no record.'

A young waiter, in a white double-breasted jacket, poured more coffee.

'Do you know Dieppe?'

'No, this is my first time here.'

'I will show you.'

And he did. When I finished eating he took me along the promenade. A brisk breeze was blowing but the sea remained hidden by mist. He brought me to narrow side-streets, main streets, and squares. He walked with a sense of urgency. A short, stocky man, very compact and dapper, with lively brown eyes and a determined looking head. He had a bit of a belly and his trousers were hitched high-up. He carried his valuables in a brown shoulder bag.

In a street for pedestrians only we were caught up in a crowd. It was market day. There were shops on both sides and stalls in the middle.

'Look, Roman, at the *wonderful* colours,' Georges said loudly of the glad-ioli, the asters, lilies, roses, geraniums. Then he admired the peaches, apricots, butter, tomatoes, carrots, the heaped strands of garlic and onions. He led me to a stand that had assorted cheese and large brown eggs, melons, leeks, and plums. And to another that had different sausages and salamis.

On one side he showed me live brown and white rabbits in hutches. And laughed when, directly opposite, brown and white rabbit skins were for sale. The street fascinated him. He stopped often and talked loudly to anyone whose face happened to interest him.

We had a Pernod at a table outside a café that had a mustard and orange façade. He lit a French cigarette. I, a Canadian cigarillo. The pleasure of the first puffs made us both silent. Nearly all the tables were occupied, shoppers were passing, and music came loudly from a record store.

I asked Georges, 'What do you think of Madame who runs the hotel?'

'*Très intelligente,*' he said and moved his hands slowly to indicate a large bosom. '*Et distinguée.*' He moved his hands to his backside to indicate large buttocks. And smiled.

He had a way of talking English which was a lot better, and more amusing, than my French.

He brought me inside an old church. He was relaxed until he faced the altar. He stiffened to attention, slid his left leg forward, as if he was a fencer, and solemnly made the sign of the cross. He remained in that position for several seconds looking like the figurehead at the prow of a ship. When he moved away he relaxed again. And pointed to a small statue of the Virgin with her arms open.

'Roman, the Virgin has opened her legs in welcome.'

I was feeling tired when we came out of the church. The train journey, the sightseeing, the conversation . . . but Georges walked on. He was heading for the docks. I said I would go back to the hotel as I had some letters to write.

'Of course,' he said, 'forgive me. You must be exhausted. Tomorrow, would you like to see where I live in the country? I will come for you after breakfast.

And he was there, as I came out of the hotel, at eight-thirty, sitting in a light blue Citroen, dressed in the same clothes.

'Did you sleep, Roman?'

'For eight hours.'

I could not see the sun because of the mist. But the surf, breaking on the pebbles, glistened. As he drove inland it began to brighten up. He drove fast and well. And he talked continually. Perhaps because he needed someone he could talk English to.

He said he had been an officer in the French navy. That in the last war he had been a naval architect in charge of submarines at their trials.

'I was at Brest, Cherbourg, Toulon, Marseille. MY daughter was born when I was stuck in submarine in the mud. My wife told me the nurse came to say, "The baby she is lovely. But the father—it is dead." ' And he laughed.

On a low hill, ahead, a large institution-like building with many windows and fire escapes.

'Lunatic asylum,' Georges said, 'full of patriots.'

The government, he said, had a publicity campaign for the French to drink more of their wine and appealed to their patriotism. After this whenever he mentioned anyone who liked to drink, Georges called him 'a patriot.' And if anyone looked more than that, '*Very* patriotic.'

The asylum was beside us. A cross on top. And all the top windows barred.

'When I was a boy . . . this place made big impression. Before a storm . . . the wind is blowing . . . and the people in lunatic asylum scream. I will never forget.'

He drove through empty villages, small towns. He stopped, walked me around, and did some shopping. I noticed that the elaborate war memorials, by the churches, were for the 1914-1918 war. The only acknowledgement of the Second World War was the occasional stone, suddenly appearing in the countryside, at the side of the road, that said three or four members of the Resistance had been shot at this spot.

'I have been to America,' Georges said. 'I like the Americans. But sometimes they are infantile. Nixon—dustbin. Carter—dustbin.'

He drove up a turning road by a small, broken, stone bridge that had rocks and uprooted trees on either side. 'There is a plateau,' he said, 'high up. It has many meadows. The water gathers there for many rivers. Once in a hundred years the water very quickly goes down from the plateau to the valley and turns over houses, bridges, trees. Last September a priest on the plateau telephone the Mayor and say the water looks dangerous. But the Mayor, a young man, say it is only an old man talking. Half-hour later the water come down and drown thirty people and took many houses. It was Sunday so many people were away from the houses otherwise more drown. All happen last September. In a half-hour. But it will not happen for another hundred years. And no one will be here who knows it. The young won't listen. They will, after some years, build houses in the same place. And it will happen all over again.'

In one of the large towns he stopped and showed me the cemetery where his family is buried. It was a vault, all stone, no grass around. Nor did any of the others have grass anywhere. On the stone was the vertical tablet with two rows of de Rostaings. The first was born in 1799. 'He was town architect.' A few names down. 'He had lace factory. . . . He build roads. . . . See how the names become larger as we come nearer today.'

'Will you be buried here?'

'No. My wife is Parisian. She is buried in Paris. I will lie with her.'

He continued on the main road, then turned off and drove on a dirt road. Then went slowly up a rough slope until he stopped, on the level, by the side of a converted farmhouse.

'We are here,' he said.

We were on a height. Below were trees and small fields—different shades of green, yellow and brown. Instead of fences or hedgerows, the fields had their borders in trees. And from this height the trees gave the landscape a 3-D look.

Georges introduced me to Marie-Jo, a fifteen-year-old schoolgirl from the next farm who did the cooking and cleaning during the summer. Short blonde hair, blue eyes, an easy smile. She was shy and tall for her age and walked with a slightly rounded back. While Marie-Jo barbecued salmon steaks at the far end of the porch, under an overhanging chimney, Georges walked me around. In front of the house, under a large elm, was a white table and white chairs. It was quiet. A light wind on the small leaves of the two near poplars. 'They say it will rain,' he said. And beside them a border of roses, geraniums, and lobelia.

We ate outside on a white tablecloth. I could hear people talking from the farm below. Further away someone was burning wood. The white smoke rose and thinned as it drifted slowly up. On top of the house was a small stone cross. A larger metal cross was embedded in the concrete of the front fence.

'I am Catholic,' Georges said. 'There are Protestants here too. My sister married a Jew. A Pole. From Bialystok.'

Marie-Joe brought a round wooden board with cow and goat cheeses on it. And Georges filled my glass with more red wine.

'When I was a young boy of seven we had great distilleries in my country. We hear the Russians are coming. We wait in the street. It is beginning to snow. But I do not want to go home. Many people wait for the Russians.

'Then they come. They look giants with fur hats and big boots and long overcoats. *Very* impressive.

'After a while—what happens? First the women. They say to Russian sol-diers—you want drink? They give them drink. A little later, in the street, you see the women wearing the Russian furs for—'

Georges indicated with his hands.

'Muffs,' I said.

'Yes, muffs, muffs. The women all have muffs.

'Then the French men give drink. Later, the French men you see in the street—they are wearing the Russian boots.

'The peasants—they *drowned* the Russians.'

Marie-Jo brought ripe peaches, large peaches, lovely colours, dark and light, red to crimson. They were juicy and delicious.

'How did your sister meet her husband?'

'At the Sorbonne. My sister always joking. He serious. I did not think they would stay together. When she go to Poland to meet his family we are wor-ried. We Catholic. They Jew. They have two children. Then the war. The Nazis. His is taken away. My mother, a tough woman, get priest and doctor to make fake certificate—say the two boys baptized. But my mother did not think that was enough. She tell me to take the boys to a farmer she know in the Auvergne. I take them. When I meet the farmer I begin to tell story. But the farmer just shake my hand. Say nothing. The children stay with him for the war.'

'What happened to the Polish Jew?'

'He died.'

We went to have coffee in the barn. The main room of the house. High ceiling with large windows and the original beams. To get to it from the inside you would go up some stairs. But you could walk to it from the garden by going up a grass slope. 'All farmers have this for the cattle to go up and down,' Georges said.

It was also his studio. On the walls were oil paintings by his uncle who was dead. Impressionist paintings of the landscape around here. 'They sell for 40,000 francs,' Georges said. 'I have about thirty good ones. Some in the flat in Paris, some in the flat in Cannes. A few here.' He also had his own paintings—on the wall, and one on an easel—like his uncle's but not as good.

Marie-Jo appeared with a jug full of coffee.

'I am working on a book,' he said. 'I have contract with Paris publisher. Eleven years—I am not finished. It will be traveller's dictionary of every place in the world that someone has written.'

We had coffee. He lit a cigarette and went over to his record player.

'Roman—have you heard the Japanese Noh?'

I answered no with a movement of my face.

'Very strange. Sounds like a cat . . . and a chain with bucket . . . and a man flogging his wife. I was twenty, a midshipman on cruiser. We visit Japan. Suddenly I was put there, for six hours, listening to this.'

He put a record on. 'This is the cat . . .' a single note vibrated . . . 'looking for another cat . . .' Georges was standing, talking with gestures. 'Now, the long chain with a bucket going down well . . . it needs oil. . . . This is a man flogging his wife. . . .'

He stopped the record.

'The Japanese they are different from the French. They believe the dead are with us all the time.'

He showed me a photograph of his wife, Colette.

She looked a determined woman, in her late forties. A strong jaw, thin lips, blonde hair pulled back on her head, light eyes.

'She had a beautiful voice,' George said. 'One of the things I like in people is the voice. If they have bad voice it is difficult for me to stay long with them.'

'How long is it since she died?'

'Three years.'

He must have thought of something else for he said abruptly, 'If you do not come into the world—then you cannot go.'

He took me for a walk through the countryside. There were all kinds of wild flowers I didn't know and butterflies and some, like the small black and white, I had not seen before either. But it was the trees that dominated. And I like trees. Probably because I have lived so long in Cornwall facing stone streets and stone terraces.

I wondered why Georges was not curious about my past. He appeared not interested in my personal life. Though I did give him bits of information.

'How long will you be in Dieppe?'

'Two, maybe three days more,' I said. 'I want to go to England, to a flat I have in Cornwall, and do some work.'

It was after nine, but still light, when we got back to Dieppe. 'I know a small place but good,' Georges said. And brought me to a restaurant opposite the docks called L'Espérance.

We were both tired and for a while didn't talk. I ordered marinated mackerel, a salad, and some chicken. And Georges ordered a half-melon, veal, and cheese. Also coffee and a bottle of red wine.

Two tables away a man and a woman, both plump , in their late fifties or early sixties, were eating with relish. The woman had a large whole tongue on her plate to start with, the man a tureen of soup. He tucked his napkin into his open-neck shirt. Then they both had fish, then meat with potatoes, then cheese, then a large dessert with whipped cream on top. . . . And all the time they were eating they didn't speak.

Beside them, going away towards the centre of the restaurant, were two young men. They were deaf and dumb. They were talking with their hands. They also mimed. When they saw us looking they included us in their conversation. One of the men looked Moroccan, with a black moustache on the top lip and down the side of his face. He was lean. And he mimed very quickly and well. He pointed at Georges' cigarette and at my cigarillo. And shook his head. He touched his chest and pretended he was coughing. And shook his head. He then showed himself swimming, the breast stroke. He was smiling. He showed us that he was also a long distance walker, getting up and staying in one place, he moved heel and toe, heel and toe, and that curious rotation of the hips.

'Roman,' Georges said loudly. 'The woman you see is fat. Her husband is fat. Look how they eat. Beside them two men, slim, young. They have to talk with their hands. They look happy—all the time the food comes—they are talking. But the two beside them—they do not talk at all—they concentrate on next bite. If I had movie camera—that is all you need. No words. No explanation. If I was young man, Roman, I would make films.'

As he drove me to the hotel, Georges could not forget the scene in the restaurant. On the hotel's front door there was a sign saying it was full.

'Tomorrow,' Georges said, 'I no see you.'

As tomorrow was Sunday I asked him if he was going to church.

'No, I do not like the clergy. The elm tree need spray. They get disease. I know a young man. He will do it. But I have to get him. And I go to see an old friend. He was an officer with me. He now alone in Rouen. We eat lunch on Sunday when I am here. Two old men. I see you the day after.'

And we shook hands.

Next morning I opened the large window of the room. The sun was out. It was warm. A blue sky. After breakfast I decided to go for a walk. I crossed the harbour by an iron bridge. And went up a steep narrow street of close-packed terraced houses. It looked working class. The houses were small, drab, unpainted. And the sidewalks were narrow and in need of repair. They had red and pink geranium petals that had fallen from the window boxes on the small balconies.

I passed an upright concrete church with a rounded top. It stood by itself, stark, against the skyline. I went through tall undergrowth and, when clear of it, I saw I was on top of cliffs. They were an impressive sight: white-gray, sheer, and at the bottom pebbles with the sea coming in.

I walked along for about an hour, on top of the cliffs, when I noticed the path becoming wider as it started to slope down. The cliffs here went back from the sea and left a small pebbled beach. People were on it.

I was looking at the dirt path, as I walked down, because it was uneven and steep when I saw a shrew, about two inches long, over another shrew lying on its side. The one on its side was flattened as if a roller had gone over it. I watched the head of the live shrew over the belly of the dead one—there didn't seem to be any movement. Then, for no reason, I whistled. The live shrew darted into the grass. And I saw the open half-eaten belly of the one on its side, a brilliant crimson. The colour was brighter than any meat I had seen at the butchers.

The small beach wasn't crowded. The surf gentle . . . the water sparkled . . . a family was playing boules. Someone was wind surfing across the length of the beach . . . going one way then turning the sail to go the other, and often falling in. A man in a T-shirt brought a dog, a terrier, on a leash. Then he let him go into the shallows. Under an umbrella a young woman was breast-feeding a baby. Nearer to the water a tall woman with white skin and red hair was lying on her back, topless. People were changing using large coloured towels . . . while the continual sound of the low surf as it came in breaking over the pebbles and sliding back.

I had brought a picnic: bread, a hard-boiled egg, cheese, tomatoes, a pear. And a can of cider to wash it down. After I had eaten I took off my shirt, shoes, socks, and lay down on the stones.

A loud noise woke me. It was two boys running over the stones between my head and the cliffs. I sat up. I didn't know how long I had been asleep. The surface of the water sparkled. The click of the boules was still going. From somewhere a dog was barking. The cliffs, a few yards behind me and on both sides, had light green streaks in the massive white grey. And high up, on the very top, a thin layer of grass.

The tide was coming in. I put on shirt, socks, and shoes, and walked over the pebbles to a paved slope that led from the beach to the road. I could now see a narrow opening between the cliffs. And as I walked up the slope the opening fanned out to show a suburb of houses with gardens, green lawns, and trees. As I came to the top of the paved slope I saw, across the road, on a stone, in French and English:

On this beach
Officers and Men of the
Royal Regiment of Canada
Died at Dawn 19 August 1942
Striving to Reach the Heights Beyond

You who are alive on this beach
remember that these men died far from home
that others here and everywhere might freely
enjoy life in God's mercy.

When I got back to the hotel the 'full' sign had been taken down. Madame greeted me with a smile.

'You have caught the sun. I have surprise for you.'

She soon re-appeared with a thin blonde girl of about twelve or thirteen.

'This is Jean. She is from Canada,' Madame said proudly. 'From Alberta.'

'Where from in Alberta?' I asked.

'Edmonton,' the girl replied in a quiet voice.

'How long will you be in Dieppe?'

'I live here. I got to school.'

'When were you in Edmonton?'

'Three weeks ago.'

'Is your father there?'

'No, he is somewhere else. He travels. I'm with my mother.'

'Can you speak French as well as you can English?'

'I can speak it better,' she said.

And she was glad to go off with Madame's only daughter, who was older and not as pretty, to roller-skate on the promenade.

'She is charming,' Madame said as we watched both girls run to get out.

'I went for a walk today, Madame,' I said, 'and came to the beach where in the war the Canadians—'

'*Ah.*' She interrupted and shook her head, then raised an arm, in distress or disbelief. She tried to find words—but couldn't.

'I have read many books about it,' she said quickly. 'Do you want to see the cemetery?'

'No,' I said.

That evening, while in the dining-room, I decided to leave tomorrow. For over three weeks I had been travelling in France. All inland, until Dieppe. It had been a fine holiday. I had not been to France before. But now I wanted to get back to the familiar. I was also impatient to get back to work. I had brought with me a large notebook but I had written nothing in it.

I said to Madame at the desk, 'I will be leaving tomorrow. Could you have my bill ready?'

'Of course,' she said, 'you will have it when you come down for breakfast.'

'It is a very comfortable hotel. Are you open all year?'

'In December we close.'

'Has it been a good season?'

'I think I go bankrupt,' she said loudly. 'Oil—up three times in two months. It is impossible to go on—' She held up a sheaf of bills.

'I will tell my friends,' I said.

'Is kind of you,' she said quietly. And gave me several brochures that said the hotel would be running a weekly cookery course in January and February of next year.

Late next morning, with my two cases in the lounge, I was having coffee and smoking a cigarillo, when Georges appeared. He saw the cases.

'Yes,' I said. 'I'm going today.'

'What time is your boat?'

'It goes in an hour.'

'I will take you.'

He insisted on carrying the cases to his car. Madame came hurrying away from people at the desk to shake my hand vigorously and hoped she would see me again.

While Georges was driving he gave me a card with his address in the country, in Cannes, and in Paris. And the dates he would be there. Then he gave me a large brown envelope. I took out what was in it—a small watercolour of Dieppe that he had painted. It showed the mustard and orange café with people sitting at the outside tables and others walking by. On the back he had written, 'For Roman, my new friend, Georges.'

'When I get to England,' I said, 'I will send you one of my books.'

'Thank you. I should like to improve my English. Perhaps I find in it something for my traveller's dictionary.'

At the ferry I persuaded Georges not to wait.

'Roman, I do not kiss the men.'

We shook hands.

I sat in a seat on deck, at the stern, facing Dieppe. The ferry turned slowly and I saw Dieppe turn as well. The vertical church with the rounded top, the cathedral, the square, the houses with the tall windows, and wooden shutters, and small iron balconies.

Then the ferry straightened out and we were in the open sea. After a while it altered course. And there were the cliffs where I had walked yesterday and the narrow opening. I kept watching the cliffs and the opening. And thought how scared they must have been coming in from the sea and seeing this.

The sun was warm, the sea calm. And when I next looked at the cliffs the opening had disappeared. All that was there was the white-grey stone sticking up. I thought of gravestones . . . close together on a slope. . . . You could see nothing else. Just gravestones. And they were gravestones with nothing on them . . . they were all blank.

On the loudspeaker the captain's voice said that coming up on the left was one of the world's largest tankers. People hurried to the rails with their cameras.

I went down to a lower deck and stood in the queue for the duty free.

MARGARET LAURENCE
(1926-1987)

∼

The Mask of the Bear

In winter my Grandfather Connor used to wear an enormous coat made out
of the pelt of a bear. So shaggy and coarse-furred was this coat, so unevenly
coloured in patches ranging from amber to near-black, and so vile-smelling
when it had become wet with snow, that it seemed to have belonged when it
was alive to some lonely and giant kodiak crankily roaming a high frozen
plateau, or an ancient grizzly scarred with battles in the sinister forests of the
north. In actuality, it had been an ordinary brown bear and it had come, sad
to say, from no more fabled a place than Galloping Mountain, only a hundred miles from Manawaka. The skin had once been given to my grandfather as payment, in the days when he was a blacksmith, before he became a
hardware merchant and developed the policy of cash only. He had had it
cobbled into a coat by the local shoemaker, and Grandmother Connor had
managed to sew in the lining. How long ago that was, no one could say for
sure, but my mother, the eldest of his family, said she could not remember
a time when he had not worn it. To me, at the age of ten and a half, this
meant it must be about a century old. The coat was so heavy that I could not
even lift it by myself. I never used to wonder how he could carry that phe-
nomenal weight himself, or why he would choose to, because it was obvious
that although he was old he was still an extraordinarily strong man, built to
shoulder weights.

Whenever I went into Simlow Ladies' Wear with my mother, and made
grotesque faces at myself in the long mirror while she tried on dresses,
Millie Christopherson who worked there would croon a phrase which made
me break into snickering until my mother, who was death on bad manners,
tapped anxiously at my shoulders with her slender, nervous hands. *It's you,
Mrs MacLeod*, Millie would say feelingly, *no kidding it's absolutely you*. I appro-
priated the phrase for my grandfather's winter coat. *It's you*, I would simper
nastily at him, although never, of course, aloud.

In my head I sometimes called him 'The Great Bear'. The name had
many associations other than his coat and his surliness. It was the way he
would stalk around the Brick House as though it were a cage, on Sundays,
impatient for the new week's beginning that would release him into the only
freedom he knew, the acts of work. It was the way he would take to the base-

ment whenever a man came to call upon Aunt Edna, which in those days was not often, because—as I had overheard my mother outlining in sighs to my father—most of the single men her age in Manawaka considered that the time she had spent working in Winnipeg had made more difference than it really had, and the situation wasn't helped by her flyaway manner (whatever that might mean). But if ever she was asked out to a movie, and the man was waiting and making stilted weather-chat with Grandmother Connor, Grandfather would prowl through the living room as though seeking a place of rest and not finding it, would stare fixedly without speaking, and would then descend the basement steps to the rocking chair which sat beside the furnace. Above ground, he would not have been found dead sitting in a rocking chair, which he considered a piece of furniture suitable only for the elderly, of whom he was never in his own eyes one. From his cave, however, the angry crunching of the wooden rockers against the cement floor would reverberate throughout the house, a kind of sub-verbal Esperanto, a disapproval which even the most obtuse person could not fail to comprehend.

In some unformulated way, I also associated the secret name with Great Bear Lake, which I had seen only on maps and which I imagined to be a deep vastness of black water, lying somewhere very far beyond our known prairies of tamed fields and barbed-wire fences, somewhere in the regions of jagged rock and eternal ice, where human voices would be drawn into a cold and shadowed stillness without leaving even a trace of warmth.

One Saturday afternoon in January, I was at the rink when my grandfather appeared unexpectedly. He was wearing his formidable coat, and to say he looked out of place among the skaters thronging around the edges of the ice would be putting it mildly. Embarrassed, I whizzed over to him.

'There you are, Vanessa—about time,' he said, as though he had been searching for me for hours. 'Get your skates off now, and come along. You're to come home with me for supper. You'll be staying the night at our place. Your dad's gone away out to Freehold, and your mother's gone with him. Fine time to pick for it. It's blowing up for a blizzard, if you ask me. They'll not get back for a couple of days, more than likely. Don't see why he don't just tell people to make their own way in to the hospital. Ewen's too easy-going. He'll not get a penny nor a word of thanks for it, you can bet your life on that.'

My father and Dr Cates used to take the country calls in turn. Often when my father went out in the winter, my mother would go with him, in case the old Nash got stuck in the snow and also to talk and thus prevent my father from going to sleep at the wheel, for falling snow has a hypnotic effect.

'What about Roddie?' I asked, for my brother was only a few months old.

'The old lady's keeping care of him,' Grandfather Connor replied abruptly.

The old lady meant my Grandmother MacLeod, who was actually a few years younger than Grandfather Connor. He always referred to her in this way, however, as a calculated insult, and here my sympathies were with him for once. He maintained, quite correctly, that she gave herself airs because her husband had been a doctor and now her son was one, and that she looked down on the Connors because they had come from famine Irish (although at least, thank God, Protestant). The two of them seldom met, except at Christmas, and never exchanged more than a few words. If they had ever really clashed, it would have been like a brontosaurus running headlong into a tyrannosaurus.

'Hurry along now,' he said, when I had taken off my skates and put on my snow boots. 'You've got to learn not to dawdle. You're an awful dawdler, Vanessa.'

I did not reply. Instead, when we left the rink I began to take exaggeratedly long strides. But he paid no attention to my attempt to reproach him with my speed. He walked beside me steadily and silently, wrapped in his great fur coat and his authority.

The Brick House was at the other end of town, so while I shuffled through the snow and pulled my navy wool scarf up around my nose against the steel cutting edge of the wind, I thought about the story I was setting down in a five-cent scribbler at nights in my room. I was much occupied by the themes of love and death, although my experience of both had so far been gained principally from the Bible, which I read in the same way as I read Eaton's Catalogue or the collected works of Rudyard Kipling—because I had to read something, and the family's finances in the thirties did not permit the purchase of enough volumes of *Doctor Doolittle* or the Oz books to keep me going.

For the love scenes, I gained useful material from The Song of Solomon. *Let him kiss me with the kisses of his mouth, for thy love is better than wine,* or *By night on my bed I sought him whom my soul loveth; I sought him but I found him not.* My interpretation was somewhat vague, and I was not helped to any appreciable extent by the explanatory bits in small print at the beginning of each chapter—*The church's love unto Christ. The church's fight and victory in temptation,* et cetera. These explanations did not puzzle me, though, for I assumed even then that they had simply been put there for the benefit of gentle and unworldly people such as my Grandmother Connor, so that they could read the Holy Writ without becoming upset. To me, the woman in The Song was some barbaric queen, beautiful and terrible, and I could imagine her, wearing a long robe of leopard skin and one or two heavy gold bracelets, pacing an alabaster courtyard and keening her unrequited love.

The heroine in my story (which took place in ancient Egypt—my ignorance of this era did not trouble me) was very like the woman in The Song of Solomon, except that mine had long wavy auburn hair, and when her beloved left her, the only thing she could bring herself to eat was an avocado, which seemed to me considerably more stylish and exotic than apples in lieu of love. Her young man was a gifted carver, who had been sent out into the desert by the cruel pharaoh (pharaohs were always cruel—of this I was positive) in order to carve a giant sphinx for the royal tomb. Should I have her die while he was away? Or would it be better if he perished out in the desert? Which of them did I like the least? With the characters whom I liked best, things always turned out right in the end. Yet the death scenes had an undeniable appeal, a sombre splendour, with (as it said in Ecclesiastes) the mourners going about the streets and all the daughters of music brought low. Both death and love seemed regrettably far from Manawaka and the snow, and my grandfather stamping his feet on the front porch of the Brick House and telling me to do the same or I'd be tracking the wet in all over the hardwood floor.

The house was too warm, almost stifling. Grandfather burned mainly birch in the furnace, although it cost twice as much as poplar, and now that he had retired from the hardware store, the furnace gave him something to do and he was forever stoking it. Grandmother Connor was in the dining room, her stout body in its brown rayon dress bending over the canary's cage.

'Hello, pet,' she greeted me. 'You should have heard Birdie just a minute ago—one of those real long trills. He's been moulting lately, and this is the first time he's sung in weeks.'

'Gee,' I said enthusiastically, for although I was not fond of canaries, I was extremely fond of my grandmother. 'That's swell. Maybe he'll do it again.'

'Messy things, them birds,' my grandfather commented. 'I can never see what you see in a fool thing like that, Agnes.'

My grandmother did not attempt to reply to this.

'Would you like a cup of tea, Timothy?' she asked.

'Nearly supper-time, ain't it?'

'Well, not for a little while yet.'

'It's away past five,' my grandfather said. 'What's Edna been doing with herself?'

'She's got the pot-roast in,' my grandmother answered, 'but it's not done yet.'

'You'd think a person could get a meal on time,' he said, 'considering she's got precious little else to do.'

I felt, as so often in the Brick House, that my lungs were in danger of exploding, that the pressure of silence would become too great to be borne. I wanted to point out, as I knew Grandmother Connor would never do, that it wasn't Aunt Edna's fault there were no jobs anywhere these days, and that, as my mother often said of her, she worked her fingers to the bone here so she wouldn't need to feel beholden to him for her keep, and that they would have had to get a hired girl if she hadn't been here, because Grandmother Connor couldn't look after a place this size any more. Also, that the dining-room clock said precisely ten minutes past five, and the evening meal in the Connor house was always at six o'clock on the dot. And—and—a thousand other arguments rose up and nearly choked me. But I did not say anything. I was not that stupid. Instead, I went out to the kitchen.

Aunt Edna was wearing her coral sweater and grey pleated skirt, and I thought she looked lovely, even with her apron on. I always thought she looked lovely, though, whatever she was wearing, but if ever I told her so, she would only laugh and say it was lucky she had a cheering section of one.

'Hello, kiddo,' she said. 'Do you want to sleep in my room tonight, or shall I make up the bed in the spare room?'

'In your room,' I said quickly, for this meant she would let me try out her lipstick and use some of her Jergens hand-lotion, and if I could stay awake until she came to bed, we would whisper after the light was out.

'How's *The Pillars of the Nation* coming along?' she asked.

That had been my epic on pioneer life. I had proceeded to the point in the story where the husband, coming back to the cabin one evening, discovered to his surprise that he was going to become a father. The way he ascertained this interesting fact was that he found his wife constructing a birch-bark cradle. Then came the discovery that Grandfather Connor had been a pioneer, and the story had lost its interest for me. If pioneers were like *that*, I had thought, my pen would be better employed elsewhere.

'I quit that one,' I replied laconically. 'I'm making up another—it's miles better. It's called *The Silver Sphinx*. I'll bet you can't guess what it's about.'

'The desert? Buried treasure? Murder mystery?'

I shook my head.

'Love,' I said.

'Good Glory,' Aunt Edna said, straight-faced. 'That sounds fascinating. Where do you get your ideas, Vanessa?'

I could not bring myself to say the Bible. I was afraid she might think this sounded funny.

'Oh, here and there,' I replied noncommittally. 'You know.'

She gave me an inquisitive glance, as though she meant to question me further, but just then the telephone rang, and I rushed to answer it, thinking it might be my mother or father phoning from Freehold. But it wasn't. It was a voice I didn't know, a man's.

'Is Edna Connor there?'

'Just a minute, please,' I cupped one hand over the mouthpiece fixed on the wall, and the other over the receiver.

'For you,' I hissed, grinning at her. 'A strange man!'

'Mercy,' Aunt Edna said ironically, 'these hordes of admirers will be the death of me yet. Probably Todd Jeffries from Burns' Electric about that busted lamp.'

Nevertheless, she hurried over. Then, as she listened, her face became startled, and something else which I could not fathom.

'Heavens, where are you?' she cried at last. 'At the station *here*? Oh Lord. Why didn't you write to say you were—well, sure I am, but—oh, never mind. No, you wait there. I'll come and meet you. You'd never find the house—'

I had never heard her talk this way before, rattlingly. Finally she hung up. Her face looked like a stranger's, and for some reason this hurt me.

'It's Jimmy Lorimer,' she said. 'He's at the C.P.R. station, He's coming here. Oh my God, I wish Beth were here.'

'Why?' I wished my mother were here, too, but I could not see what difference it made to Aunt Edna. I knew who Jimmy Lorimer was. He was a man Aunt Edna had gone around with when she was in Winnipeg. He had given her the Attar of Roses in an atomiser bottle with a green net-covered bulb—the scent she always sprayed around her room after she had had a cigarette there. Jimmy Lorimer had been invested with a remote glamour in my imagination, but all at once I felt I was going to hate him.

I realized that Aunt Edna was referring to what Grandfather Connor might do or say, and instantly I was ashamed for having felt churlishly disposed toward Jimmy Lorimer. Even if he was a cad, a heel, or a nitwit, I swore I would welcome him. I visualized him as having a flashy appearance, like a riverboat gambler in a movie I had seen once, a checkered suit, a slender oiled moustache, a diamond tie-pin, a dangerous leer. Never mind. Never mind if he was Lucifer himself.

'I'm glad he's coming,' I said staunchly.

Aunt Edna looked at me queerly, her mouth wavering as though she were about to smile. Then, quickly, she bent and hugged me, and I could feel her trembling. At this moment, Grandmother Connor came into the kitchen.

'You all right, pet?' she asked Aunt Edna. 'Nothing's the matter, is it?'

'Mother, that was an old friend of mine on the phone just now. Jimmy Lorimer. He's from Winnipeg. He's passing through Manawaka. Is it all right if he comes here for dinner?'

'Well, of course, dear,' Grandmother said. 'What a lucky thing we're having the pot-roast. There's plenty. Vanessa, pet, you run down to the fruit cellar and bring up a jar of strawberries, will you? Oh, and a small jar of chili-sauce. No, maybe the sweet mustard pickle would go better with the pot-roast. What do you think, Edna?'

She spoke as though this were the only important issue in the whole situation. But all the time her eyes were on Aunt Edna's face.

'Edna—' she said, with great effort, 'is he—is he a good man, Edna?'

Aunt Edna blinked and looked confused, as though she had been spoken to in some foreign language.

'Yes,' she replied.

'You're sure, pet?'

'Yes,' Aunt Edna repeated, a little more emphatically than before.

Grandmother Connor nodded, smiled reassuringly, and patted Aunt Edna lightly on the wrist.

'Well, that's fine, dear. I'll just tell Father. Everything will be all right, so don't you worry about a thing.'

When Grandmother had gone back to the living room, Aunt Edna began pulling on her black fur-topped overshoes. When she spoke, I didn't know whether it was to me or not.

'I didn't tell her a damn thing,' she said in a surprised tone. 'I wonder how she knows, or if she really does? *Good.* What a word. I wish I didn't know what she means when she says that. Or else that she knew what I mean when I say it. Glory, I wish Beth were here.'

I understood then that she was not speaking to me, and that what she had to say could not be spoken to me. I felt chilled by my childhood, unable to touch her because of the freezing burden of my inexperience. I was about to say something, anything, however mistaken, when my aunt said *Sh,* and we both listened to the talk from the living room.

'A friend of Edna's is coming for dinner, Timothy,' Grandmother was saying quietly. 'A young man from Winnipeg.'

A silence. Then, 'Winnipeg,' my grandfather exclaimed, making it sound as though Jimmy Lorimer were coming here straight from his harem in Casablanca.

'What's he do?' Grandfather demanded next.

'Edna didn't say.'

'I'm not surprised,' Grandfather said darkly. 'Well, I won't have her running around with that sort of fellow. She's got no more sense than a sparrow.'

'She's twenty-eight,' Grandmother said, almost apologetically. 'Anyway, this is just a friend.'

'Friend!' my grandfather said, annihilating the word. Then, not loudly, but with an odd vehemence, 'you don't know a blame thing about men, Agnes. You never have.'

Even I could think of several well-placed replies that my grandmother might have made, but she did not do so. She did not say anything. I looked at Aunt Edna, and saw that she had closed her eyes the way people do when they have a headache. Then we heard Grandmother's voice, speaking at last, not in her usual placid and unruffled way, but hesitantly.

'Timothy—please. Be nice to him. For my sake.'

For my sake. This was so unlike my grandmother that I was stunned. She was not a person who begged you to be kind for her sake, or even for God's sake. If you were kind, in my grandmother's view, it was for its own sake, and the judgement of whether you had done well or not was up to the Almighty. *Judge not, that ye be not judged*—this was her favourite admonition to me when I lost my temper with one of my friends. As a devout Baptist, she believed it was a sin to pray for anything for yourself. You ought to pray only for strength to bear whatever the Lord saw fit to send you, she thought. I was never able to follow this advice, for although I would often feel a sense of uneasiness over the tone of my prayers, I was the kind of person who prayed frantically—'Please, God, please, please *please* let Ross MacVey like me better than Mavis.' Grandmother Connor was not self-effacing in her lack of demands either upon God or upon her family. She merely believed that what happened to a person in this life was in Other Hands. Acceptance was at the heart of her. I don't think in her own eyes she ever lived in a state of bondage. To the rest of the family, thrashing furiously and uselessly in various snarled dilemmas, she must often have appeared to live in a state of perpetual grace, but I am certain she didn't think of it that way, either.

Grandfather Connor did not seem to have heard her.

'We won't get our dinner until all hours, I daresay,' he said.

But we got our dinner as soon as Aunt Edna had arrived back with Jimmy Lorimer, for she flew immediately out to the kitchen and before we knew it we were all sitting at the big circular table in the dining room.

Jimmy Lorimer was not at all what I had expected. Far from looking like a Mississippi gambler, he looked just like anybody else, any uncle or grown-up cousin, unexceptional in every way. He was neither overwhelmingly handsome nor interestingly ugly. He was okay to look at, but as I said to myself, feeling at the same time a twinge of betrayal towards Aunt Edna, he was nothing to write home about. He wore a brown suit and a green tie. The only thing about him which struck fire was that he had a joking manner similar to Aunt Edna's, but whereas I felt at ease with this quality in her, I could never feel comfortable with the laughter of strangers, being uncertain where an including laughter stopped and taunting began.

'You're from Winnipeg, eh?' Grandfather began. 'Well, I guess you fellows don't put much store in a town like Manawaka.'

Without waiting for affirmation or denial of this sentiment, he continued in an unbroken line.

'I got no patience with these people who think a small town is just nothing. You take a city, now. You could live in one of them places for twenty years, and you'd not get to know your next-door neighbour. Trouble comes along—who's going to give you a hand? Not a blamed soul.'

Grandfather Connor had never in his life lived in a city, so his first-hand knowledge of their ways was, to say the least, limited. As for trouble—the thought of my grandfather asking any soul in Manawaka to give aid and support to him in any way whatsoever was inconceivable. He would have died of starvation, physical or spiritual, rather than put himself in any man's debt by so much as a dime or a word.

'Hey, hold on a minute,' Jimmy Lorimer protested. 'I never said that about small towns. As a matter of fact, I grew up in one myself. I came from McConnell's Landing. Ever heard of it?'

'I heard of it all right,' Grandfather said brusquely, and no one could have told from his tone whether McConnell's Landing was a place of ill-repute or whether he simply felt his knowledge of geography was being doubted. 'Why'd you leave, then?'

Jimmy shrugged. 'Not much opportunity there. Had to seek my fortune, you know. Can't say I've found it, but I'm still looking.'

'Oh, you'll be a tycoon yet, no doubt,' Aunt Edna put in.

'You bet your life, kiddo,' Jimmy replied. 'You wait. Times'll change.'

I didn't like to hear him say 'kiddo'. It was Aunt Edna's word, the one she called me by. It didn't belong to him.

'Mercy, they can't change fast enough for me,' Aunt Edna said. 'I guess I haven't got your optimism, though.'

'Well, I haven't got it either,' he said, laughing, 'but keep it under your hat, eh?'

Grandfather Connor had listened to this exchange with some impatience. Now he turned to Jimmy once more.

'What's your line of work?'

'I'm with Reliable Loan Company right now, Mr. Connor, but I don't aim to stay there permanently. I'd like to have my own business. Cars are what I'm really interested in. But it's not so easy to start up these days.'

Grandfather Connor's normal opinions on social issues possessed such a high degree of clarity and were so frequently stated that they were well known even to me—all labour unions were composed of thugs and crooks; if people were unemployed it was due to their own laziness; if people were broke it was because they were not thrifty. Now, however, a look of intense and brooding sorrow came into his face, as he became all at once the champion of the poor and oppressed.

'Loan company!' he said. 'Them blood-suckers. They wouldn't pay no mind to how hard-up a man might be. Take everything he has, without batting an eye. By the Lord Harry, I never thought the day would come when I'd sit down to a meal alongside one of them fellows.'

Aunt Edna's face was rigid.

'Jimmy,' she said, 'Ignore him.'

Grandfather turned on her, and they stared at one another with a kind of inexpressible rage but neither of them spoke. I could not help feeling sorry for Jimmy Lorimer, who mumbled something about his train leaving and began eating hurriedly. Grandfather rose to his feet.

'I've had enough,' he said.

'Don't you want your dessert, Timothy?' Grandmother asked, as though it never occurred to her that he could be referring to anything other than the meal. It was only then that I realised that this was the first time she had spoken since we sat down at the table. Grandfather did not reply. He went down to the basement. Predictably, in a moment we could hear the wooden rockers of his chair thudding like retreating thunder. After dinner, Grandmother sat in the living room but did not get out the red cardigan she was knitting for me. She sat without doing anything, quite still, her hands folded in her lap.

'I'll let you off the dishes tonight, honey,' Aunt Edna said to me. 'Jimmy will help with them. You can try out my lipstick, if you like, only for Pete's sake wash it off before you come down again.'

I went upstairs, but I did not go to Aunt Edna's room. I went into the back bedroom to one of my listening posts. In the floor there was a round hole which had once been used for a stove-pipe leading up from the kitchen. Now it was covered with a piece of brown-painted tin full of small perforations which had apparently been noticed only by me.

'Where does he get his lines, Edna?' Jimmy was saying. 'He's like an old-time melodrama.'

'Yeh, I know.' Aunt Edna sounded annoyed. 'But let me say it, eh?'

'Sorry. Honest. Listen, can't you even—'

Scuffling sounds, then my aunt's nervous whisper.

'Not here, Jimmy. Please. You don't understand what they're—'

'I understand, all right. Why in God's name do you stay, Edna? Aren't you ever coming back? That's what I want to know.'

'With no job? Don't make me laugh.'

'I could help out, at first anyway—'

'Jimmy, don't talk like a lunatic. Do you really think I could?'

'Oh hell, I suppose not. Well, look at it this way. What if I wasn't cut out for the unattached life after all? What if the old leopard actually changed his spots, kiddo? What would you say to that?'

A pause, as though Aunt Edna were mulling over his words.

'That'll be the day,' she replied. 'I'll believe it when I see it.'

'Well, Jesus, lady,' he said. 'I'm not getting down on my knees. Tell me one thing, though—don't you miss me at all? Don't you miss—everything? C'mon now—don't you? Not even a little bit?

Another pause. She could not seem to make up her mind how to respond to the teasing quality of his voice.

'Yeh, I lie awake nights,' she said at last, sarcastically.

He laughed. 'Same old Edna. Want me to tell you something, kiddo? I think you're scared.'

'Scared?' she said scornfully. 'Me? That'll be the fair and frosty Friday.'

Although I spent so much of my life listening to conversations which I was not meant to overhear, all at once I felt, for the first time, sickened by what I was doing. I left my listening post and tiptoed into Aunt Edna's room. I wondered if someday I would be the one who was doing the talking, while another child would be doing the listening. This gave me an unpleasantly eerie feeling. I tried on Aunt Edna's lipstick and rouge, but my heart was not in it.

When I went downstairs again, Jimmy Lorimer was just leaving. Aunt Edna went to her room and closed the door. After a while she came out and asked me if I would mind sleeping in the spare bedroom that night after all, so that was what I did.

I woke in the middle of the night. When I sat up, feeling strange because I was not in my own bed at home, I saw through the window a glancing light on the snow. I got up and peered out, and there were the northern lights whirling across the top of the sky like lightning that never descended to earth. The yard of the Brick House looked huge, a white desert, and the pale gashing streaks of light pointed up the caverns and the hollowed places where the wind had sculptured the snow.

I could not stand being alone another second, so I walked in my bare feet along the hall. From Grandfather's room came the sound of grumbling snores, and from Grandmother's room no sound at all. I stopped beside the door of Aunt Edna's room. It seemed to me that she would not mind if I entered quietly, so as not to disturb her, and crawled in beside her. Maybe she would even waken and say, 'It's okay, kiddo—your dad phoned after you'd gone to sleep—they got back from Freehold all right.'

Then I heard her voice, and the held-in way she was crying, and the name she spoke, as though it hurt her to speak it even in a whisper.

Like some terrified poltergeist, I flitted back to the spare room and whipped into bed. I wanted only to forget that I had heard anything, but I knew I would not forget. There arose in my mind, mysteriously, the picture of a barbaric queen, someone who had lived a long time ago. I could not reconcile this image with the known face, nor could I disconnect it. I thought of my aunt, her sturdy laughter, the way she tore into the house-work, her hands and feet which she always disparagingly joked about, believing them to be clumsy. I thought of the story in the scribbler at home. I wanted to get home quickly, so I could destroy it.

Whenever Grandmother Connor was ill, she would not see any doctor except my father. She did not believe in surgery, for she thought it was tampering with the Divine Intention, and she was always afraid that Dr Cates would operate on her without her consent. She trusted my father implicitly, and when he went into the room where she lay propped up on pillows, she would say, 'Here's Ewen—now everything will be fine,' which both touched and alarmed my father, who said he hoped she wasn't putting her faith in a broken reed.

Late that winter, she became ill again. She did not go into hospital, so my mother, who had been a nurse, moved down to the Brick House to look after her. My brother and I were left in the adamant care of Grandmother MacLeod. Without my mother, our house seemed like a museum, full of dead and meaningless objects, vases and gilt-framed pictures and looming furniture, all of which had to be dusted and catered to, for reasons which everyone had forgotten. I was not allowed to see Grandmother Connor, but every day after school I went to the Brick House to see my mother. I always asked impatiently, 'When is Grandmother going to be better?' and my mother would reply, 'I don't know, dear. Soon, I hope.' But she did not sound very certain, and I imagined the leaden weeks going by like this, with her away, and Grandmother MacLeod poking her head into my bedroom doorway each morning and telling me to be sure to make my bed because a slovenly room meant a slovenly heart.

But the weeks did not go by like this. One afternoon when I arrived at the Brick House, Grandfather Connor was standing out on the front porch. I was startled, because he was not wearing his great bear coat. He wore no coat at all, only his dingy serge suit, although the day was fifteen below zero. The blown snow had sifted onto the porch and lay in thin drifts. He stood there by himself, his yellowish-white hair plumed by a wind which he seemed not to notice, his bony and still-handsome face not averted at all from the winter. He looked at me as I plodded up the path and the front steps.

'Vanessa, your grandmother's dead,' he said.

Then, as I gazed at him, unable to take in the significance of what he had said, he did a horrifying thing. He gathered me into the relentless grip of his arms. He bent low over me, and sobbed against the cold skin of my face.

I wanted only to get away, to get as far away as possible and never come back. I wanted desperately to see my mother, yet I felt I could not enter the house, not ever again. Then my mother opened the front door and stood there in the doorway, her slight body shivering. Grandfather released me, straightened, became again the carved face I had seen when I approached the house.

'Father,' my mother said. 'Come into the house. Please.'

'In a while, Beth,' he replied tonelessly. 'Never you mind.'

My mother held out her hands to me, and I ran to her. She closed the door and led me into the living room. We both cried, and yet I think I cried mainly because she did, and because I had been shocked by my grandfather. I still could not believe that anyone I cared about could really die.

Aunt Edna came into the living room. She hesitated, looking at my mother and me. Then she turned and went back to the kitchen, stumblingly. My mother's hands made hovering movements and she half rose from the chesterfield, then she held me closely again.

'It's worse for Edna,' she said. 'I've got you and Roddie, and your dad.'

I did not fully realise yet that Grandmother Connor would never move around this house again, preserving its uncertain peace somehow. Yet all at once I knew how it would be for Aunt Edna, without her, alone in the Brick House with Grandfather Connor. I had not known at all that a death would be like this, not only one's own pain, but the almost unbearable knowledge of that other pain which could not be reached nor lessened.

My mother and I went out to the kitchen, and the three of us sat around the oilcloth-covered table, scarcely talking but needing one another at least to be there. We heard the front door open, and Grandfather Connor came back into the house. He did not come out to the kitchen, though. He went, as though instinctively, to his old cavern. We heard him walking heavily down the basement steps.

'Edna—should we ask him if he wants to come and have some tea?' my mother said. 'I hate to see him going like that—there—'

Aunt Edna's face hardened.

'I don't want to see him, Beth,' she replied, forcing the words out. 'I can't. Not yet. All I'd be able to think of is how he was—with her.'

'Oh, honey, I know,' my mother said. 'But you mustn't let yourself dwell on that now.'

'The night Jimmy was here,' my aunt said distinctly, 'she asked Father to be nice, for her sake. For her sake, Beth. For the sake of all the years, if they'd meant anything at all. But he couldn't even do that. Not even that.'

Then she put her head down on the table and cried in a way I had never heard any person cry before, as though there were no end to it anywhere.

I was not allowed to attend Grandmother Connor's funeral, and for this I was profoundly grateful, for I had dreaded going. The day of the funeral, I stayed alone in the Brick House, waiting for the family to return. My Uncle Terence, who lived in Toronto, was the only one who had come from a distance. Uncle Will lived in Florida, and Aunt Florence was in England, both too far away. Aunt Edna and my mother were always criticizing Uncle Terence and also making excuses for him. He drank more than was good for him—this was one of the numerous fractured bones in the family skeleton which I was not supposed to know about. I was fond of him for the same reason I was fond of Grandfather's horse-trader brother, my Great-Uncle Dan—because he had gaiety and was publicly reckoned to be no good.

I sat in the dining room beside the gilt-boned cage that housed the canary. Yesterday, Aunt Edna, cleaning here, had said, 'What on earth are we going to do with the canary? Maybe we can find somebody who would like it.'

Grandfather Connor had immediately lit into her. 'Edna, your mother liked that bird, so it's staying, do you hear?'

When my mother and Aunt Edna went upstairs to have a cigarette, Aunt Edna had said, 'Well, it's dandy that he's so set on the bird now, isn't it? He might have considered that a few years earlier, if you ask me.'

'Try to be patient with him,' my mother had said. 'He's feeling it too.'

'I guess so,' Aunt Edna had said in a discouraged voice. 'I haven't got Mother's patience, that's all. Not with him, nor with any man.'

And I had been reminded then of the item I had seen not long before in the Winnipeg *Free Press*, on the social page, telling of the marriage of James Reilly Lorimer to Somebody-or-other. I had rushed to my mother with the paper in my hand, and she had said, 'I know, Vanessa. She knows, too. So let's not bring it up, eh?'

The canary, as usual, was not in a vocal mood, and I sat beside the cage dully, not caring, not even trying to prod the creature into song. I wondered if Grandmother Connor was at this very moment in heaven, that dubious place.

'She believed, Edna,' my mother had said defensively. 'What right have we to say it isn't so?'

'Oh, I know,' Aunt Edna had replied. 'But can you take it in, really, Beth?'

'No, not really. But you feel, with someone like her—it would be so awful if it didn't happen, after she'd thought like that for so long.'

'She wouldn't know,' Aunt Edna had pointed out.

'I guess that's what I can't accept,' my mother had said slowly. 'I still feel she must be somewhere.'

I wanted now to hold my own funeral service for my grandmother, in the presence only of the canary. I went to the bookcase where she kept her Bible, and looked up Ecclesiastes. I intended to read the part about the mourners going about the streets, and the silver cord loosed and the golden bowl broken, and the dust returning to the earth as it was and the spirit unto God who gave it. But I got stuck on the first few lines, because it seemed to me, frighteningly, that they were being spoken in my grandmother's mild voice—*Remember now thy Creator in the days of thy youth, while the evil days come not*—

Then, with a burst of opening doors, the family had returned from the funeral. While they were taking off their coats, I slammed the Bible shut and sneaked it back into the bookcase without anyone's having noticed.

Grandfather Connor walked over to me and placed his hands on my shoulders, and I could do nothing except endure his touch.

'Vanessa—' he said gruffly, and I had at the time no idea how much it cost him to speak at all, 'she was an angel. You remember that.'

Then he went down to the basement by himself. No one attempted to follow him, or to ask him to come and join the rest of us. Even I, in the confusion of my lack of years, realised that this would have been an impossibility. He was, in some way, untouchable. Whatever his grief was, he did not want us to look at it and we did not want to look at it either.

Uncle Terence went straight into the kitchen, brought out his pocket flask, and poured a hefty slug of whiskey for himself. He did the same for my mother and father and Aunt Edna.

'Oh Glory,' Aunt Edna said with a sigh, 'do I ever need this. All the same, I feel we shouldn't, right immediately afterwards. You know—considering how she always felt about it. Supposing Father comes up—'

'It's about time you quit thinking that way, Edna,' Uncle Terence said.

Aunt Edna felt in her purse for a cigarette. Uncle Terence reached over and lit it for her. Her hands were unsteady.

'You're telling me,' she said.

Uncle Terence gave me a quizzical and yet resigned look, and I knew then that my presence was placing a constraint upon them. When my father said he had to go back to the hospital, I used his departure to slip upstairs to my old post, the deserted stove-pipe hole. I could no longer eavesdrop with a clear conscience, but I justified it now by the fact that I had voluntarily removed myself from the kitchen, knowing they would not have told me to run along, not today.

'An angel,' Aunt Edna said bitterly. 'Did you hear what he said to Vanessa? It's a pity he never said as much to Mother once or twice, isn't it?'

'She knew how much he thought of her,' my mother said.

'Did she?' Aunt Edna said. 'I don't believe she ever knew he cared about her at all. I don't think I knew it myself, until I saw how her death hit him.'

'That's an awful thing to say!' my mother cried. 'Of course she knew, Edna.'

'How would she know,' Aunt Edna persisted, 'if he never let on?'

'How do you know he didn't?' my mother countered. 'When they were by themselves.'

'I don't know, of course,' Aunt Edna said. 'But I have my damn shrewd suspicions.'

'Did you ever know, Beth,' Uncle Terence enquired, pouring himself another drink, 'that she almost left him once? That was before you were born, Edna.'

'No,' my mother said incredulously. 'Surely not.'

'Yeh. Aunt Mattie told me. Apparently Father carried on for a while with some girl in Winnipeg, and Mother found out about it. She never told him she'd considered leaving him. She only told God and Aunt Mattie. The three of them thrashed it out together, I suppose. Too bad she never told him. It would've been a relief to him, no doubt, to see she wasn't all calm forgiveness.'

'How could he?' my mother said in a low voice. 'Oh Terence. How could he have done that? To Mother, of all people.'

'You know something, Beth?' Uncle Terence said. 'I think he honestly believed that about her being some kind of angel. She'd never have thought of herself like that, so I don't suppose it ever would have occurred to her that he did. But I have a notion that he felt all along she was far and away too good for him. Can you feature going to bed with an angel, honey? It doesn't bear thinking about.'

'Terence, you're drunk,' my mother said sharply. 'As usual.'

'Maybe so,' he admitted. Then he burst out, 'I only felt, Beth, that somebody might have said to Vanessa just now, *Look, baby, she was terrific and we thought the world of her, but let's not say angel, eh?* All this angel business gets us into really deep water, you know that?

'I don't see how you can talk like that, Terence,' my mother said, trying not to cry. 'Now all of a sudden everything was her fault. I just don't see how you can.'

'I'm not saying it was her fault,' Uncle Terence said wearily. 'That's not what I meant. Give me credit for one or two brains, Beth. I'm only saying it might have been rough for him, as well, that's all. How do any of us know what he's had to carry on his shoulders? Another person's virtues could be an awful weight to tote around. We all loved her. Whoever loved him? Who in hell could? Don't you think he knew that? Maybe he even thought sometimes it was no more than was coming to him.'

'Oh—' my mother said bleakly. 'That can't be so. That would be—oh, Terence, do you really think he might have thought that way?'

'I don't know any more than you do, Beth. I think he knew quite well that she had something he didn't, but I'd be willing to bet he always imagined it must be righteousness. It wasn't. It was—well, I guess it was tenderness, really. Unfair as you always are about him, Edna, I think you hit the nail on the head about one thing. I don't believe Mother ever realised he might have wanted her tenderness. Why should she? He could never show any of his own. All he could ever come out with was anger. Well, everybody to his own shield in this family. I guess I carry mine in my hip pocket. I don't know what yours is, Beth, but Edna's is more like his than you might think.'

'Oh yeh?' Aunt Edna said, her voice suddenly rough. 'What is it, then, if I may be so bold as to enquire?'

'Wisecracks, honey,' Uncle Terence replied, very gently. 'Just wisecracks.'

They stopped talking, and all I could hear was my aunt's uneven breathing, with no one saying a word. Then I could hear her blowing her nose.

'Mercy, I must look like the wreck of the Hesperus,' she said briskly. 'I'll bet I haven't got a speck of powder left on. Never mind. I'll repair the ravages later. What about putting the kettle on, Beth? Maybe I should go down and see if he'll have a cup of tea now.'

'Yes,' my mother said. 'That's a good idea. You do that, Edna.'

I heard my aunt's footsteps on the basement stairs as she went down into Grandfather Connor's solitary place.

Many years later, when Manawaka was far away from me, in miles and in time, I saw one day in a museum the Bear Mask of the Haida Indians. It was a weird mask. The features were ugly and yet powerful. The mouth was turned down in an expression of sullen rage. The eyes were empty caverns, revealing nothing. Yet as I looked, they seemed to draw my own eyes towards them, until I imagined I could see somewhere within that darkness a look which I knew, a lurking bewilderment. I remembered then that in the days before it became a museum piece, the mask had concealed a man.

JAMES REANEY
(1926)

~

The Bully

As a child I lived on a farm not far from a small town called Partridge. In the countryside about Partridge, thin roads of gravel and dust slide in and out among the hollows and hills. As roads go, they certainly aren't very brave, for quite often they round a hill instead of up it and even in the flattest places they will jog and hesitate absurdly. But then this latter tendency often comes from some blunder a surveying engineer made a hundred years ago. And although his mind has long ago dissolved, its forgetfulness still pushes the country people crooked where they might have gone straight.

Some of the farm-houses on these ill-planned roads are made of red brick and have large barns and great cement silos and soft large strawstacks behind them. And other farm-houses are not made of brick, but of frame and clapboard that gleam with the silver film unpainted wood attains after years of wild rain and shrill wind beating upon it. The house where I was born was such a place, and I remember that whenever it rained, from top to bottom the whole outside of the house would turn jet-black as if it were blushing in shame or anger.

Perhaps it blushed because of my father who was not a very good farmer. He was what is known as an afternoon farmer. He could never get out into the fields till about half-past eleven in the morning and he never seemed to be able to grow much of anything except buckwheat which as everyone knows is the lazy farmer's crop. If you could make a living out of playing checkers and talking, then my father would have made enough to send us all to college, but as it was he did make enough to keep us alive, to buy tea and coffee, cake and pie, boots and stockings, and a basket of peaches once every summer. So it's really hard to begrudge him a few games of checkers or a preference for talking instead of a preference for ploughing.

When I was six, my mother died of T.B. and I was brought up by my Aunt Coraline and by my two older sisters, Noreen and Kate. Noreen, the oldest of us, was a very husky, lively girl. She was really one of the liveliest girls I have ever seen. She rode every horse we had bare-back, sometimes not with a bridle at all but just by holding on to their manes. When she was fifteen, in a single day she wall-papered both our kitchen and our living-room. And when she was sixteen she helped my father draw in hay just like a hired man.

When she was twelve she used to tease me an awful lot. Sometimes when she had teased me too much, I would store away scraps of food for days, and then go off down the side-road with the strong idea in my head that I was not going to come back. But then Noreen and Kate would run after me with tears in their eyes and, having persuaded me to throw away my large collection of breakfast toast crusts and agree to come back, they would both promise never to tease me again. Although Kate, goodness knows, had no need to promise that for she was always kind, would never have thought of teasing me. Kate was rather like me in being shy and in being rather weak. Noreen's strength and boldness made her despise Kate and me, but she was like us in some ways. For instance Noreen had a strange way of feeding the hens. Each night she would sprinkle the grain out on the ground in the shape of a letter or some other pattern, so that when the hens ate the grain, they were forced to spell out Noreen's initials or to form a cross and a circle. There were just enough hens to make this rather an interesting game. Sometimes, I know, Noreen spelt out whole sentences in this way, a letter or two each night, and I often wondered to whom she was writing up in the skies.

Aunt Coraline, who brought me up, was most of the time sick in bed and as a result was rather pettish and ill-tempered. In the summer time, she would spend most of the day in her room making bouquets out of any flowers we could bring her; even dandelions, Shepherd's Purse, or Queen Anne's Lace. She was very skilful at putting letters of the alphabet into a bouquet, with two kinds of flowers, you know, one for the letters and one for the background. Aunt Coraline's room was filled with all sorts of jars and bottles containing bouquets, some of them very ancient so that her room smelt up a bit, especially in the hot weather. She was the only one of us who had a room to herself. My father slept in the kitchen. Aunt Coraline's days were devoted to the medicine-bottle and the pill-box, making designs in bouquets, telling us stories, and bringing us up; her nights were spent in trying to get to sleep and crying softly to herself.

When we were children we never were worked to death, but still we didn't play or read books all of the time. In the summer we picked strawberries, currants, and raspberries. Sometimes we picked wild berries into milkpails for money, but after we had picked our pails full, before we could get the berries to the woman who had commissioned them, the berries would settle down in the pails and of course the woman would refuse then to pay what she had promised because we hadn't brought her full pails. Sometimes our father made us pick potato beetles off the potato plants. We would tap the plants on one side with a shingle and hold out a tin can on the other side to catch the potato bugs as they fell. And we went for cows and caught plough-horses for our father.

Every Saturday night we children all took turns bathing in the dish-pan and on Sundays, after Sunday-school, we would all sit out on the lawn and drink the lemonade that my father would make in a big glass pitcher. The lemonade was always slightly green and sour like the moon when it's high up in a summer sky. While we were drinking the lemonade, we would listen to our victrola gramophone which Noreen would carry out of the house along with a collection of records. These were all very old, very thick records and their names were: *I Know Where the Flies Go, The Big Rock Candy Mountain, Hand Me Down My Walking Cane,* and a dialogue about some people in a boarding-house that went like this:

'Why can't you eat this soup?'

Various praising replies about the soup and its fine, fine qualities by all the fifteen members of the boarding-house. Then:

'So WHY can't you eat this soup?'

And the non-appreciative boarder replies:

'Because I ain't got a spoon.'

Even if no one laughed, and of course we always did, the Record Company had thoughtfully put in some laughter just to fill up the centre. Those Sunday afternoons are all gone now and if I had known I was never to spend any more like them, I would have spent them more slowly.

We began to grow up. Noreen did so gladly but Kate and I secretly hated to. We were much too weak to face things as they were. We were weak enough to prefer what we had been as children rather than what we saw people often grew up to be, people who worked all day at dull, senseless things and slept all night and worked all day and slept all night and so on until they died. I think Aunt Coraline must have felt the same when she was young and decided to solve the problem by being ill. Unfortunately for us, neither Kate nor I could quite bring ourselves to take this line. I don't know what Kate decided, but at the age of eleven I decided that school-teaching looked neither too boring nor too hard so a schoolteacher I would be. It was my one chance to escape what my father had fallen into. To become a teacher one had to go to high school five years and go one year to Normal School. Two miles away in the town of Partridge there actually stood a high school.

It was not until the summer after I had passed my Entrance Examination that I began to feel rather frightened of the new life ahead of me. That spring, Noreen had gone into town to work for a lady as a housemaid. At my request, she went to look at the high school. It was situated right next the jail, and Noreen wrote home that of the two places she'd much rather go to the jail, even although they had just made the gates of the jail three feet higher. Of that summer I particularly remember one sultry Sunday afternoon in August when I walked listlessly out to the mail-box and, leaning against it, looked down the road in the general direction of town. The road went on past our house and then up a hill and then not over the top of the hill for it went crooked a bit, wavered and disappeared, somehow, on the other side. Somewhere on that road stood a huge building which would swallow me up for five years. Why I had ever wanted to leave all the familiar things around me, I could hardly understand. Why people had to grow up and leave home I could not understand either. I looked first at the road and then into the dull sky as I wondered at this. I tried to imagine what the high school would really be like, but all I could see or feel was a strong tide emerging from it to sweep me into something that would give me a good shaking up.

Early every morning, I walked into high school with my lunch-box and my school-books under my arm. And I walked home again at night. I have none of the textbooks now that were used at that school, for I sold them when I left. And I can't remember very much about them except that the French book was fat and blue. One took fifteen subjects in all: Business Practice (in this you learned how to write out cheques and pay electric light bills, a knowledge that so far has been of no use to me); there was English, Geography, Mathematics, French, Spelling, History, Physical Training, Music, Art, Science (here one was taught how to light a Bunsen Burner) and there must have been other subjects for I'm sure there were fifteen of them. I never got used to high school. There were so many rooms, so many people, so many teachers. The teachers were watchful as heathen deities and it was painful to displease them. Almost immediately I became the object of everyone's disgust and rage. The Geography teacher growled at me, the English teacher stood me up in corners. The History teacher denounced me as an idiot. The French teacher cursed my accent. In Physical Training I fell off innumerable parallel-bars showing, as the instructor remarked, that I could not and never would co-ordinate my mind with my body. My platoon of the cadet corps discovered that the only way to make progress possible in drill was to place me deep in the centre of the ranks away from all key positions. In Manual Training I broke all sorts of precious saws and was soundly strapped for something I did to the iron-lathe. For no reason that I could see, the Art teacher went purple in the face at me, took me out into the hall and struck my defenceless hands with a leather thong. The French teacher once put me out into the hall, a far worse fate than that of being put in a corner, for the halls were hourly stalked by the principal in search of game; anyone found in the halls he took off with him to his office where he administered a little something calculated to keep the receiver out of the halls thereafter.

Frankly, I must have been, and I was, a simpleton, but I did the silly things I did mainly because everyone expected me to do them. Very slowly I began to be able to control myself and give at least some sort of right answer when questioned. Each night when I came home at first, Kate would ask me how I liked high school. I would reply as stoutly as I could that I was getting on all right. But gradually I did begin to get along not too badly and might have been a little happy if something not connected with my studies had not thrown me back into a deeper misery.

This new unhappiness had something to do with the place where those students who came from the country ate their lunch. This place was called a cafeteria and was divided into a girls' cafeteria and a boys' one. After about a month of coming to the boys' cafeteria to eat my lunch, I noticed that a certain young man (he couldn't be called a boy) always sat near me with his back to me at the next long table. The cafeteria was a basement room filled with three long tables and rows of wire-mended chairs. Now my lunch always included a small bottle of milk. The bottle had originally been a vinegar bottle and was very difficult to drink from unless you put your head away back and gulped it fast. One day when I had finished my sandwiches and was drinking my milk, he turned around and said quietly: 'Does baby like his bottle?'

I blushed and immediately stopped drinking. Then I waited until he would finish his lunch and go away. While I waited with downcast eyes and a face red with shame, I felt a furious rush of anger against Kate and Aunt Coraline for sending milk for my lunch in a vinegar bottle. Finally, I began to see that he had finished his lunch and was not going to leave until I did. I put the vinegar bottle back in my lunchbox and walked as quickly as I could out of the boys' cafeteria, upstairs to the classroom left open during the noon-hour so that the country people could study there. He followed me there and sat in the seat opposite me with what I managed to discover in the two times I looked at him, a derisive smile upon his face. He had heavy lips and he wore a dark green shirt. With him sitting beside me, I had no chance of ever getting the products of New Zealand and Australia off by heart and so I failed the Geography test we had that afternoon. Day after day he tormented me. He never hit me. He would always just stay close to me, commenting on how I ate my food or didn't drink my vinegar and once he pulled a chair from beneath me. Since our first meeting I never drank anything while he was near me. Between him and my friends the teachers, my life in first form at high school was a sort of Hell with too many tormenting fiends and not enough of me to go round so they could all get satisfaction. If I'd had the slightest spark of courage I'd have burnt the high school down at least.

At last, in the middle of November, I hit upon the plan of going over to the public library after I had eaten my lunch. Lots of other country students went there too. Most of them either giggled at magazines or hunted up art prints and photographs of classical sculpture on which they made obscene additions, or if more than usually clever, obscene comments. For over one happy week the Bully seemed to have lost me, for he did not appear at the library. Then I looked up from a dull book I was reading and there he was. He had my cap in his hand and would not give it back to me. How he had got hold of it I couldn't imagine. How I was to get it back from him, I couldn't imagine either. He must have given it back to me, I can't remember just how. Of course it wasn't the sort of hat anyone else wore, as you might expect. It was a toque, a red-and-white woollen one that Noreen used to wear. Every other boy at school wore a fedora or at least a helmet.

During the library period of my bullying he sat as close up against me as he could and whispered obscenities in my ear. After two weeks of this, being rather desperate, I did not go to the boys' cafeteria to eat my lunch but took my books and my lunch and went out into the streets. This was in early December and there was deep snow everywhere. I ran past the jail, down into the civic gardens, across the river, under a bridge, and down the other side of the river until I saw the town cemetery just ahead of me. It seemed fairly safe. I could eat my sandwiches under a tree and then keep warm by reading the inscriptions on gravestones and walking about.

The second day or the third, I discovered that the doors of the cemetery's mausoleum were open and that there were two benches inside where you can be buried in a marble pigeon-hole instead of the cold ground. To this place I came day after day, and I revelled in the morbid quiet of the place. I sat on one of the walnut benches and whispered irregular French verbs to myself or memorized the mineral resources of Turkey or the history of the Upper Canada Rebellion. All around and all above me dead citizens lay in their coffins, their rings flashing in the darkness, their finger-nails grown long like white thin carrots, and the hair of the dead men grown out long and wild to their shoulders. No one ever disturbed me. People's finger-nails and hair do keep on growing after they're dead, you know. Aunt Coraline read it in a book.

No one ever disturbed me at the mausoleum. The wind howled about that dismal place but no other voice howled. Only once I had some trouble in getting the heavy doors open when the factory whistles blew and it was time to start walking back to school. I usually arrived back at the school at twenty minutes after one. But one day the wind weakened the sound of the whistles and I arrived at school just at half-past one. If it had been allowed, I might have run in the girls' door and not been late. But it was not allowed and since the boys' door was at the other end of the building, by the time I had run to it, I was quite late and had to stay after four.

Just before Christmas they had an At Home at the school. The emphasis in pronouncing At Home is usually put on the AT. Everyone goes to the AT Home. The tickets are usually old tickets that weren't sold for the last year's operetta, cut in half. Noreen forced me to take her because she wanted to see what an AT Home was like. She did not mind that I could not dance. She only wanted to sip at second-hand what she supposed to be the delightful joys of higher education. We first went into the rooms where schoolwork was exhibited. Noreen kept expecting some of my work to be up and kept being disappointed. I was very nervous with a paint-brush so none of my drawings were up in the art display. At the writing exhibit none of my writing was up. I had failed to master the free-hand stroke, although away from the writing teacher I could draw beautiful writing that looked as if it had been done by the freest hand imaginable. At the Geography exhibit none of my charts of national resources had been pinned up. Noreen was heart-broken. I had learned not to care. For instance, almost everyone's window-stick got into the Manual Training show. Mine didn't because I had planed it down until it was about a quarter of an inch thick, and as the Manual Training teacher pointed out, it couldn't have held up a feather. But I didn't care.

Noreen and I went into the girls' gymnasium where we saw a short, brown-coloured movie that showed Dutch gardeners clipping hedges into shapes of geese and chickens, ducks and peacocks. The Dutch gardeners cut away with their shears so fast that the ducks and peacocks seemed fairly to leap out of the hedges at you. Noreen and I wondered how these gardeners were going to keep employed if they carved up things that fast. Then we went into the boys' gym where young men stripped almost naked and covered with gold paint pretended to be statues. After watching them for a while Noreen and I went up to the Assembly Hall where dancing was in progress and young girls hovered shyly at the edge of the floor. Some of these shy young girls were dressed in handmade evening gowns that seemed to be made out of very thin mosquito netting coated with icing sugar. Noreen had one of her employer's old dresses on. It was certainly an old dress, made about 1932 I guess, for it had a hunch-back sack of cloth flying out of the middle of the back. Noreen, I know, thought she looked extremely distinctive. I only thought she looked extremely extraordinary.

And she did so want to dance. So we went up to the third floor and there Noreen tried to teach me how to dance in one lesson, but it was no use. She asked me to introduce her to some of my friends who danced. I had no friends but there was one boy who borrowed everything I owned almost daily. Here was a chance for him to repay me if he could dance. We soon captured him, but although Noreen clung tightly to him for a good deal of the evening and although we led him to the mouth of the Assembly Hall, all the time proclaiming quite loudly how nice it must be to dance, he didn't ask Noreen for a dance. So we went down into the basement to the Domestic Science Room where punch was being served and thin cookies with silver beads in the middle of them. There was a great crowd of people in the Domestic Science Room and before we knew it, he had given us the slip. Then Noreen said, 'Where do you eat your lunch? Kate was telling me how she makes it every night for you.'

I replied that I ate in the boys' cafeteria.

'Oh, what's that? Come on. Show me.'

'It's not very interesting,' I said.

'But show me it. Show me it,' Noreen insisted stubbornly.

'It's down here,' I said.

We went past the furnace room.

'That's the furnace room, Noreen. There's the girls' cafeteria. Here's the—'

It was dark inside the boys' cafeteria and I felt along the wall just beside the door for a light button. I could hear someone climbing in one of the windows. Someone who didn't want to buy a ticket, I supposed. Probably someone who came here regularly at noon and thought of leaving a window open for himself. Before I could tell her not to, Noreen had found the light switch ahead of me and turned it on. The person climbing in the window turned out to be my friend the Bully. Like a wild animal he stared for a second at us and then jumped back through the window.

'Well, who on earth was that?' asked Noreen.

'I don't know,' I said, trembling all over.

'Don't tremble like a leaf!' said Noreen scornfully. 'Why you look and act exactly like you'd seen a ghost. What was so frightening about him?'

'Nothing,' I said, leaning against the wall and putting my hand to my forehead. 'Nothing.'

The Christmas holidays were haunted for me by my fear of what would happen at school when I went back there after New Year's. But I never complained to my father or Aunt Coraline. They would have been only too glad to hear me say that I didn't want to go back. I must somehow stick it until the spring and the end of first form at least. But I knew that before the spring came the Bully would track me down, and if I met him once again I knew it would be the end of me. I remember in those Christmas holidays that I went walking a lot with Kate over the fields that were dead white with snow. I wished then that we might always do that. I told Kate about my unhappiness at high school and it drew us closer together. If I had told Noreen she would only have called me a silly fool and made me hate her. But Kate was always more sympathetic towards me.

The first morning when I was back at school I found a note in my desk. All it said was this: *I want to see you eating where you should eat today, baby.* At noon I hid myself in the swarm of city students who were going home for lunch and arrived at the mausoleum by a round-about way. I couldn't get over the notion that someone was following me or watching me, which could easily have been true, since he had many friends.

I was just in the middle of eating my lunch. I was sitting on a bench in front of the Hon. Arthur P. Hingham's tomb. I saw the Bully trying to open the great doors to the mausoleum. But he couldn't seem to get them open. At last he did. All I can remember is seeing the advancing edge of the door before I toppled off the bench in a dead faint. By the time I came to it was half-past one so I started to walk home. My head ached violently as if someone had kicked it, which turned out to be the case, there being a red dent just below my left eye that turned blue after a few hours. On the way home that afternoon I had just reached a place in the road where you can see our house when I decided that I could not bear to go to high school any longer. So I went home and told them that I had been expelled for walking in through the girls' door instead of the boys' door. They never doubted that this was true, so little did they know of high schools and their rules. Noreen doubted me, but by the time she heard about my being expelled it was too late to send me back. Aunt Coraline cried a bit over it all; my father told me the whole thing showed that I really belonged on the farm. Only Kate realized how much school had meant to me and how desperately I had tried to adapt myself to it.

That night as I lay in bed, while outside a cold strong river of wind roared about the house shaking everything and rattling the dishes in the cupboard downstairs, that night I dreamt three dreams. I have never been able to discover what they meant.

First I dreamt that Noreen was the Bully and that I caught her washing off her disguise in the water-trough in the yard. Then I dreamt I saw the Bully make love to Kate and she hugging and kissing him. The last dream I had was the longest of all. I dreamt that just before dawn I crept out of the house and went through the yard. And all the letters Noreen had ever made out of grain there while she was feeding the chickens had all sprouted up into green letters of grass and wheat. Someone touched me on the shoulder and said sadly, *I haven't got a spoon,* but I ran away without answering across the fields into the bush. There was a round pond surrounded by a grove of young chokecherry trees. I pushed through these and came to the edge of the pond. There lay the Bully looking almost pitiful, his arms and legs bound with green ropes made out of nettles. He was drowned dead, half in the water and half out of it, but face up. And in the dim light of the dawn I knelt down and kissed him gently on the forehead.

HUGH HOOD
(1928)

~

Getting to Williamstown

'Many a green isle needs must be
In the deep wide sea of misery.'

Driving out of Montreal in the old days, it used to take me a couple of hours
to get off the island—they do it in forty-five minutes now—and by the time I
was up around the Ontario line I would decide to by-pass Cornwall, 'smelly
Cornwall,' the kids called it, rightly. How it stank, that town, of sulphur and
God knows what else! We got off the highway at Lancaster, jog right a hundred yards, jog left onto County Road 19, and away.

Mr Fessenden . . . Mr Fessenden?

There was a creek we followed upstream for miles, Raisin Creek, was it?
More than a creek, almost a river in places, but shallow. Broad but shallow,
like a lot of things, with trees bending over in the summer so they almost
formed an arch over the water. We always meant to stop and wade; we could
have done it easily. The children would have loved it but we had to get on.
Raisin Creek there, with the little bridges and culverts, and from time to
time in the distance to the south a view of the main line, and beyond the
glitter of the river. It seemed to be always sunny back then.

The road wound back and forth, not a modern highway, badly engi-
neered on the curves so that you couldn't go over forty without braking suddenly at every new curve. I taught the children what the highway signs
meant, a cross, a curved line to right or left, railroad tracks, intersections at
various angles. We were surrounded by rolling, beautifully cultivated fields
with the only interruption a few lines of maples bordering the farms, the
road and the river. The fields were expansive and rich, peaceful, ah, God!

I see it now, projected on my walls as though real. Five miles west of
Lancaster, about two-fifteen in the afternoon, we pass a gas-pump and a
refreshment stand, abandoned for the last few seasons. The pump has a
globe of opaque white glass for a head, with three red stars on it.
Underneath there is a transparent glass cylinder with gallonage calibrated
from zero to twenty, and below that the pump, with a long handle at the

side. As the attendant gives you gas, the level drops in the glass cylinder and the clean brilliant red fluid splashes and foams while the children watch fascinated. I pay him, and stand for a moment as he pumps gas back into his apparatus, until at last the cylinder is that beautiful red clear to the top, no nonsense about premium quality or tetraethyl.

Beside the abandoned gas-pump there's this old refreshment stand. In the late twenties somebody used it to sell pop and ice cream in the summer, and farm produce around harvest time. The shingled walls were green and the roof red; but now in 1934 the paint has flaked and peeled and I can just barely make out the colour. We made up stories about it; it was a little house or an enchanted castle. In truth the stand and pump sat there in overgrown grass, amid wildflowers, lonely and haunted.

Now we are coming to Williamstown; the trees are growing plentiful and the children need, they say, to stop. Deep, deep in the countryside. They can wet in the ditch at the roadside if they must, for there's no one to see or mind very much. But they hope for ice cream at the general store, so we don't stop by the side of the road. The trees thicken; bright sunlight glances on the green. I see it on these white walls.

The town lies tranquilly in a tiny valley beside the creek, in an island of green under the sun. We dip down in our Chrysler Airflow—there weren't big enough windows in that car; it was too experimental! Down we sail as the highway narrows and becomes King William Street, steep as we come into town, swooping toward a dangerously narrow bridge at the foot of the hill. As we descend, the foliage obscures the sun. We pass fields on our left, and on our right I have the sense, through the narrow windows of my Airflow, of a white building standing the width of a field from the edge of town, a building in a field that I have never really seen, but shining, always freshly painted, in the last sun before the shade trees crowd in on King William Street.

Careful turning onto the bridge. Cars cannot pass here but in twenty years I never had to dispute the passage with anyone, certainly not with a citizen of Williamstown. Once, I recall, I came to the bridge, going west into town, just as a farmer arrived, going east and homewards. He had a Model-T truck with a load of crated chickens; the crank stuck out of the face of the Model-T like a pipe. We smiled at one another and I backed off. When he drove past, he waved and nodded politely. Across the bridge we take a right, passing the few houses this side of the stores. This is where my heart stopped, every trip for fifteen years.

Just this side of the stores stands an old house that's for sale, has been ever since I've been driving through. It's yellow, or would be if the paint were restored; the porch sags somewhat. The windows are comprised of sixteen small leaded panes apiece; some are broken. It is a heavenly place. The backyard opens on fields, as do all the backyards in town, and the house will be maybe a hundred and thirty years old. There is a small lawn in front which someone cares for, perhaps the long-dead realtor whose bald sign penetrates the turf. Going by, I sigh and yearn. But for some reason, we never stopped just there. We proceed to the general store, grocery store, variety store, butcher shop, what would you call it?

Outside Williamstown the highway is paved, but in front of the cluster of stores, for whatever reason, the street is always dusty with a light haze hanging in the air. BUSTIN'S DRUGS: pharmacist's globes dim the window. DEVLIN'S HARDWARE: a display of C.C.M. bikes and a cream separator. In the window of the grocery store appear the name of the proprietor and the words SALADA TEA arranged in an arc, in white tin letters appliquéd to the glass in some mysterious way. Here we stop, taking no special care to park in this or that direction.

The kids have used the toilet here so often, at least six times a year, that the proprietor believes he knows us. He gives them extra large scoops of ice cream, dipping it from a cooler with big round holes in the top, and thick lids like gladiators' shields. Then he sprinkles orange and red and chocolate flakes of candy on top of the double-dips; this costs a nickel. He has a glittering and lethal meat slicer with which he cuts boiled ham and pork for picnic lunches, and a superb coffee grinder, and the place smells of spice and coffee. The showcases are bound in a beautiful walnut. I can't smell that smell. I can think of it but I can't recreate it. Later, perhaps.

'That's quite a car, Mister.'

'Yes, that's what they call streamlining. It came in this year.'

Into the dark hot car, then, and down King William Street westwards past the District Catholic School, just where the sidewalks end. It's three o'clock and we'll have to make up time if we're going to be in Maitland for dinner. The highway straightens and we get up to fifty, going straight west away from heaven.

Time for Mr Fessenden's injections.

But you couldn't get in and you couldn't get out, in those days. It took half a day to get to Williamstown and another three hours to Maitland, in all a seven-hour drive, a hundred and thirty miles, what with lunch in the car, stops for the toilet, occasional car-sickness. I dreamed of commuting, for it can't have been more than sixty-five miles from the city.

'I could go in by the day.'

'No you couldn't, Henry, you'd be exhausted. No, don't begin to explain it to me; there can't be any question of driving in and out of Montreal every day. Think of it! Your heart would never stand it.'

'But I'm a young man, Irma, and there's nothing wrong with my heart. I've just had my checkup and I'm fine, just fine. And only think of the peace in the winter, alone, a couple of feet of snow. Black dark and little lights in the parlour windows; there's a school, a good one I'm sure, and later on we could send them into Lancaster on a bus, or they could come with me.'

'And you seriously propose to bury me in that place with the children? Who would they play with?'

'I imagine there are children living there; there must be five hundred people in the place.'

'And what about me? What would I do for amusement, with the car gone all day? I'd go mad in a place like that.'

'It might be good for you, Irma.'

'What are you insinuating?'

'Oh, nothing, nothing. I love you, Irma.'

She would have a lightning switch of mood.

'I don't know how you put up with me, Henry, I'm such a mess.'

'Well, we all have faults, dear.'

'Yes, but think, Henry. No movies, no friends, no theatre.'

'We don't go to the theatre.'

'But we might sometime, and we *can* if we're desperate. No concerns, no public transit.'

'You don't need streetcars in a town that size; you can walk to church and the store. And I want to live there. It wouldn't be like this.'

'There's nothing wrong with this. You're doing splendidly. You have all your friends in the office and inside of two years you'll be a trust officer. You'd have to get up at five to drive into Montreal, and you wouldn't get home till nine, which exactly reverses your present hours. It would kill you.'

'I could make better time than that.'

'We don't have enough money to fix up that ruin.'

'Now that's not fair. You've never even been inside it.'

'Have you?'

'No. I've never been there but with you, driving through on the way to your mother's.'

'Henry, you have no idea what it costs to fix up a place in the country; that house looks good to you, seeing it for the first time from the outside; but it'll be full of dry rot and structural faults; there's no plumbing.'

'How do you know?'

'There's a little house in the backyard.'

'I didn't notice.'

'No, you wouldn't! I'm the one who'd have to nurse the children through typhoid.'

'I'll bet there isn't any more typhoid, per capita, in Williamstown than here.'

'We'll wait till they're a little older before we run the risk!'

She always closed a discussion by tabling the children's needs; we moved from the condition of my health to the children's needs and back. They were the poles of her dialectic. And about most points in the argument, she had fact and reason on her side. I *did* have friends in the office and almost nowhere else, and I *did* become a trust officer in charge of important port-folios, and I didn't have to go to war on account of the family and my pub-lic responsibilities as a trust officer. In Montreal, the public responsibilities of a financial officer are taken to be great and pressing.

'Mother, how can my friends come to an upstairs duplex? It was all right when I was small; I didn't understand. But look at the difference between us and the Lewises. It makes me so ashamed. Why can't we have a house like everybody else?'

'Sssshhh! Mustn't disturb your father, Frances. He's lying down before dinner.'

'He's always having his rest. What does he have to lie down for.'

'It's better, dear, when a man is middle-aged, for him to conserve his energy. Come into the dining-room.' Their steps recede.

'I want to have a skating party with coffee after.'

'Aren't some of the children young for coffee?'

'Oh, mother!'

'We can call it a coffee party anyway and no harm done. What sort of house do you think we should have, dear?'

'Mother, I want to live in the Town of Mount Royal!'

'So do I, dear!'

Oh thickening trees, oh shady sunlight, leaded panes and quiet dusty street.

There are no trees in the Town of Mount Royal; this is a fact. Here and there one finds a stunted shrub or two; but when they laid out the developments during, and just after, the war, they bulldozed down all the trees, a bad mistake that nobody seems to regret. Without noticing it, the citizens live on an arid plain where the grass yellows in May. If the land were clear prairie they would see this; but amidst the ranch houses the desert effect is half-obliterated. That you can't sit in your own backyard in July because of the glare seems to be taken for granted by all but me. It takes me an hour and a half to drive two miles to work, because of a bottleneck at a level crossing. In wintertime, it takes much longer.

'Everybody else has a television aerial.'

'Some people put them up without a set,' says Bunker.

'Oh, your father would never do that, would you, darling?'

'What is it, darling?'

'Frances and Bunker think we should have television.'

'Everybody on the street has it but us.'

'Then I'll order one today. I hadn't noticed. Are there good programs?'

'I believe it depends on your aerial, dear.'

'Ah, like the radio. I'll see about it this afternoon.' At this, the children—and wonderfully they aren't children any more—are silently pleased, as they should be. I've never denied them anything. Irma hugs me, and they observe us indulgently, gratified.

Yes, comatose, a terminal case, I'm afraid.

Terminal, that's what they said when Irma went and the house was empty, Frances married and living in Toronto, and Bunker in Maitland. He's a real

grandmother's boy, that one, looking after the store and the farm proper-
ties, and seeing about Irma's flowers now and then, something I couldn't do
myself from Montreal.

'That's quite a car, Mister.'

'Yes, that's a French car, a Citroen. Most comfortable car on the road, you
ought to try it sometime.'

I can go back and forth to Maitland in under three hours now, with 401
connected to the Metropolitan Highway and only one traffic light between
the Town of Mount Royal and Toronto. I don't have to have a fast car; the
Citroen isn't what you'd call a fast car. I just average a comfortable sixty
miles an hour and I'm there in no time. Why, Bunker might just as well have
been living with me, we've seen so much of each other, and he's been in to
see me . . . to see me here.

401 follows the river pretty much, about half a mile inland. You pick it up
at the Ontario border; you don't go into Lancaster, and naturally you don't
go anywhere near Williamstown. I haven't been through Williamstown since
before Irma died, I don't believe. Maybe I'll go, one of these days. But I've
been going out on 401, and for a while it's pretty country down by the locks
and the islands; every few minutes you can see the sunlight on the water. But
soon, northwest of Cornwall, the geography changes; you can't see the river
and the land is swamp. Scrub timber, marsh, cattails, and the occasional concession road running north into the scrub. There are probably plenty of
flies in there; but I've never stopped to see. Coming back down at night, it's
black as a yard up a stovepipe along 401; there isn't the traffic to justify a
superhighway through there but it had to go in because of Montreal and
Toronto. There are only the two gas stations between the border and
Maitland, and the province has to subsidize them, and the food is bad, especially the coffee.

Going along in my Citroen between the railroad tracks and the river, I
can always tell when we're passing Williamstown because I can see the
steeple of some church peeking up out of a clump of trees a few miles to my
right, a rectangular white tower with a pointed lead steeple on top; the town
must be five or six miles off the highway and one of the county roads con-
nects. One of these days I'll take the ramp, turn off north in my Citroen and
astonish the grocer, though the children won't be with me.

'You'd be better off to come and live in Maitland, Dad, where you'd be
near Mother.'

'Well, but Bunker, she's dead. I mean, I can't see that it matters where I
am, relative to where she is.'

'Haven't you got any feelings on the subject? After all, the DeVebers have
been established in Maitland almost a hundred and fifty years.
Grandmother used to tell me, and she showed me pictures.'

'I'm not a DeVeber. And I'm a Town of Mount Royal man, if there is such
a thing.'

'You don't like it in the Town, do you Dad? Think what that big house is costing to keep up, now we're all out of it. And maybe you'd enjoy helping me with the business; there's talk of a shopping plaza out by the 401 cloverleaf and I'm considering putting a store in there. Naturally there would have to be additional capital.'

'DeVeber capital, I hope.'

'Oh now, Dad, it would be a good investment. You could put in what you get for the house without liquidating any of your other holdings; that might be enough. What do you suppose the house is worth?'

How does he seem today, nurse?

Bunker has been in to see me right along; he drives down afternoons and has his supper in the city. Then he goes back after nine o'clock. He's attentive all right, and it's cheerful to have somebody here, although I can't work up the strength to discuss the house with him. Perhaps we'll sell. I never liked it, and it looks as if I may be here some time. No use having it standing empty and a tax charge. But I don't feel up to talking now. It wouldn't be good for me. I mean, I'm not well.

'Bunker, if you've brought me all this way on a false alarm, I'll kill you. You think you're the only one in the world with business to look after. Thursday night is Debbie's school play, and I haven't finished her costume. Tomorrow night Butler has tickets for the O'Keefe Centre, and you drag me to Montreal on a wild goose chase. Look at him, he's as comfortable as he could possibly be. They're doing every they can *for* him, not that there's much they can do, in his condition.'

'He'll hear you!'

'No, he won't. They've got him sedated. They have to because it's very painful at the end if they don't. I don't suppose he's felt a thing for days, poor Dad, but at least he isn't in any pain.'

'It's wonderful what they can do with drugs, these days.'

'Sometimes they don't help though. When I had Debbie, they had me doped right up and it still hurt like mad. I screamed my head off. But with this, it seems to work.'

'He's quiet enough, all right, poor old man. He was never the same, you know, after he lost Mother. He went right downhill, just as if he'd lost part of himself, and it isn't as if he were that old, either.'

'He's sixty-five, isn't he?'

'Sixty-six. He quit the Trust on his sixty-fifth birthday.'

'I remember. I guess they'll look after . . . uh . . . things, won't they?'

'Yes, they're the executors, with me.'

'With you?'

'If we're going to discuss this, let's whisper, Frances.'

'Why you, Mister Smartie, why not me? I'm older.'

'I'm a man.'

'I don't see it makes much difference. Anyway you're not that much of a man.'

'Frances!'

'Ah, I'm sorry, Bunker, I'll take that back. Who names the executors?

'Dad.'

'Why did he leave me off?'

'I have no idea; he probably thought it didn't matter. When you're making a will, you likely think all will be harmony and concord afterwards.'

'Just you try any tricks, Bunker Fessenden, and I'll harmony and concord you!'

'There'll be no tricks; the whole testament is as plain as day. The office wrote it up for us, and as far as succession duties go, it's a masterpiece. We get everything and the government gets nothing.'

'Nothing?'

'Practically. The minimum, and you can't do any better than that. The estate is divided equally between us. That's fair, isn't it?'

'I'm older. And I have Debbie.'

'But you've got a husband to look after you.'

'Hah!'

'Butler supports you, in spite of everything. Nobody supports me, and I've been thinking of getting married.'

'You?'

'Yes, me. That's a big house you know, and with grandmaw gone I'm all alone.'

Alone in a big house. Our house was the first California-redwood ranch in the Town of Mount Royal, with the refrigerator hung on the kitchen wall—too high to reach comfortably but very stylish. There's much glass, too much. When I wander through the house alone nights, with all the lights on, I'm always exposing myself accidentally to the curious stares of passersby. It's a house where you have to be careful how you quit bathroom or bedroom; there's always somebody looking at you from out on the sidewalk. The recreation room gives on the main street; it's the shape of a small bowling alley, with a tiled floor which gives your steps a curious dead ring. Walking back and forth in there at night, with a vast expanse of plate glass on one side of me, and the television and bar on the other, I'm unutterably solitary, like some aquatic creature in a tank, going purposelessly round and round. Now and then I throw darts at the wall; it must look very strange from outside, the brightness, the solitude, the aimless activity. It's a good thing we had that window in the recreation room, because that's how they found me.

Banging on the window, rap, rap, rap, reverberations in the sash.

Feet upstairs, then coming down.

Indistinct shapes beside me.

'You were right, Mary, it's Mr Fessenden, and he's sick.'

'Should we get mixed up in this?'
'We can't leave him here.'
'We can call the police and wait till they come.'
'I'll call them.'
'Don't touch anything, and be sure to get a release.'
Feet going away and then, later being carried gently.
'What's his trouble?'
'*Sais-pas.* Some kind of a deep coma.'
'No fractures, no hemorrhaging? Careful how we handle him; it might be anything.'
'What do you think?'
'Heart or malignancy.'
'Yes.'
'The tests will show.'
'Yes.'
'Off we go.'
What is this, this heavenly feeling of being carried, this lightness never felt before, lie back and float into the white room and the level bed, and afterwards the pictures flashed on the walls and now and then a voice or voices. Being carried, ah, ah.

Bunker lives in a stone house; they'll never find him when comes time; he'd better get married, start the whole thing off again in Maitland; but I won't come to the wedding. I'm going to take the ramp when I see that white rectangle, that leaden tower, in the sun above the trees five miles to the north. I see the sun on the walls now, and now coming through the walls. The trees bend over as we glide along beside the river; the walls open and fade and give on the county road and the rich cornfields, a line of trees in the distance and coming closer, lustrous in the sun.

Look after the Fessenden business, orderly!

Being carried along at the top of the hill and we swoop downwards as trees thicken, a green island, around us and here at the edge of town I see the white building gleaming in the sun under the soft sheen of the tower, one narrow field from town. Being carried gently in by men in white to the porch of the white building in the bright sun. Blaze of glory on leaves moving in the windows as these six bear me kindly up the aisle.

TIMOTHY FINDLEY
(1930)

~

The Duel in Cluny Park

The duel in Cluny Park took place just after dawn on a Sunday morning—December 16th, in 1979. That was the day when it also snowed for eighteen hours, nonstop. Two shots were fired—and only two, in spite of the fact that various people later were to claim that three or four had been heard. These phantom shots were more than likely echoes bouncing off the fieldstone walls that separated the park from various private gardens rising up behind the houses on Cluny Drive and Crescent Road.

Because of its shape, its size and its situation, Cluny Park was sometimes called the Pocket. Someone would ring you up on a clear, bright day and say, 'We're going to have a picnic down in the Pocket.' Then out would come the Embros hampers stuffed with pâté and salads and potted shrimp from David Wood and breads and brioche from Patachou and tall, cool bottles of frosted Riesling and sparking cider from the Liquor Board. Coloured blankets and tablecloths would be spread out wide on the ground and, if anyone looked down from the houses through the trees, the picnickers would be seen in their summer whites and wide-brimmed hats, raising their glasses to toast the sun. A lot of people miss that, now.

The park itself was little more than a bit of grass enclosed in a small ravine, the sides of which were steep enough in places to give the impression of peril. Standing, for instance, in Andrew and Hazel Cournoyer's grove of Japanese maples, you had the distinct sensation that one false step would send you tumbling all the way to the bottom. This, while not exactly reassuring, at least provided a view that was picturesque in a postcard sort of way. A postcard showing Edwardian revellers in one of those charming bucolic settings that seem to have passed forever, along with England.

To those who lived on its verges, Cluny Park was a private, pleasant and well-kept secret. Pleasant, at least, until that Sunday morning in December of 1979 when Mary Jane Powell and Bobby Finster fought their duel there and one of them was killed.

Andrew and Hazel Cournoyer were giving a black and white party to celebrate their tenth anniversary. *The anniversary,* as Hazel said in her telephoned invitations, *where everyone gives you something made of tin. . . .*

Bobby and Margot Finster were taking along a pair of tin snips—or shears (they had argued about the name)—in the hopes that everyone else would be giving something funny like old tin cans and the snips would come in handy. 'We can cut out rows of tin dolls,' Bobby said. Margot had wrapped the shears up in tinfoil, tied with a large black bow.

'Why do I keep on thinking December 15th is a date in history?' Margot said as she and Bobby were driving down through the twilight to Cluny Drive. It was Saturday night.

Bobby said: 'Because it is. December 15th was your mother's birthday.'

He smiled—and Margot smiled back.

'My mother isn't *history*,' she said.

'She is now,' said Bobby. 'Dead four years and mourned every minute of her absence.'

'Do you mean that?'

'Sure I do. Your mother was terrific. She was something to celebrate. Not many mothers are.'

'You make me nervous, talking like that.'

'Good heavens, why?'

'You're implying that, as mothers go, I may not be worth celebrating. . . .'

Margot turned away and looked out the window of the car—their very first Jaguar. Bobby looked over and took his hand from the wheel just long enough to give Margot's hair a brush with the backs of his fingers.

'You've got to forget it, M,' he said. 'You are one hell of a mother. Our kids adore you—and their adoration is real.'

'I know that. But. . . .' Margot looked down in her lap and found her evening bag. Silver—to go with her silver dress. She got out a packet of du Mauriers and lighted one.

'But nothing.' Bobby resettled his arm against his side, the fingers of his right hand grazing the wheel above his crotch. He was horny tonight. He could almost feel the heat rising up from where he sat. Something more than Margot—or the thought of Margot—was doing it; something about the red leather seats, the smells inside the car, including Margot's perfume; something about the boxer shorts he was wearing, the way they let his penis out through their open fly so it touched the wool of his trousers; the always sensuous irritation of evening clothes.

'You've got to stop thinking about it, M,' (was he talking to himself or to her?) 'now and forever—put it in the past. It's done. It was not your fault. Let's talk about, think about something else. Okay?'

'Okay.' She smiled. He was right. It hadn't been her fault. But it was all so wrong—so pointless; she would never get over that. The deaths of all children are pointless and wrong. Nothing anyone could say would ever give them credence or rightness.

They were driving down to Rosedale from Warren Road in Forest Hill and had reached the corner of St Clair and Yonge. Everywhere around them, the coloured lights in all the windows of all the shops and restaurants were proclaiming A MERRY CHRISTMAS AND A HAPPY NEW YEAR! Margot tried not to read them. The coloured lights in themselves were not problematical—but the message, the goddamned message. . . .

The goddamned message was like a goad. It was almost evil, somehow, as if every shop and restaurant owner and every window decorator in Toronto was out to taunt her with their goddamned messages of love, good cheer and hope.

If only it hadn't happened at Christmastime. . . .

She's dead. Sara Finster. Dead.

Climbed up over the kitchen sink to turn on the light—and had one hand on a running tap—just like that—aged five.

Five and would now have been seven.

Bobby shifted gear and looked at Margot again and said, 'Stop that right now, or we're going home.'

He meant it. He was angry.

'Yes, yes,' said Margot. 'I've stopped. I really have. . . .' She got out some Kleenex and blew her nose. 'It was just those bloody words done up in lights in all those windows.'

They drove in silence until they came to Inglewood Drive, where Bobby Finster turned the Jaguar towards the Mt Pleasant cutoff, heading south.

Just past the lip of the hill Margot said, 'There's a dead dog lying in the road back there.'

'I know,' said Bobby. 'I saw it.'

He kept on going.

'Why did they leave it lying there in the middle of the road like that? Why can't they move it over to the curb, at least?'

Bobby said nothing.

Then he said: 'All right. You win,' and he threw the car into reverse, spinning it backwards up the hill through all the downward spinning others.

Margot, alarmed, was afraid her remark about the dog being left on the road was going to drive them home—as if somehow, the dog on the road and the forbidden subject of Sara's death were inextricably connected.

'I only meant . . . ,' she began.

'Be quiet,' said Bobby.

They had reached the place where the dog was lying, caught in the streaming lights of the passing cars. It had snowed about an hour before, and the road was bright and wet and dangerous.

'Move him,' said Bobby, not unkindly, once he had drawn the Jaguar into the curb and shut off the motor. 'I'll wait here.'

Margot turned to him and beamed.

'Thank you,' she said. 'I knew I had married a god of mercy! I'll be as fast as I can.'

The traffic was intermittent, and as Margot left the car, the only thing approaching was one of those gigantic tractor-trailers with its pup in tow. It was shifting gears with a lot of violent wrenching and farting noises down at the bottom of the hill. Margot removed her cashmere shawl with its glass and silver passementerie and threw it back inside the car. Her shoes would be problematical because of their heels—but she dare not remove them for fear her stockings would be torn.

'You won't need your handbag, M,' said Bobby, and Margot threw that back into the car as well. She left the door open—an open door was a means of escape—and it also meant: *I'm coming back.*

She now had to wait for three cars to pass, each one of them veering at a different speed around the dog in its path—one of them honking loudly, angrily: *how dare this bloody dog lie down and die in front of my Volvo station wagon!*

Bobby was watching the tractor-trailer lumbering up by the opposite curb, its driver, still not seeing Margot, staring blankly through his windshield muttering something, maybe the words of a song. . . .

Margot strode out to where the dog was lying. She was relatively confident that she would not be hit in her silver dress. It acted as a great reflector.

Watching her, Bobby realized that here was one of the mysteries of Margot; her integrity showed itself in simple, almost childish ways: that dogs who had died should not be left like garbage on the road. And . . .

The dog wagged its tail.

It was alive.

Margot was bending over it—stupified. The dog looked back into her face and thumped its tail against the road three times.

Margot looked across at Bobby, waved her arm and Bobby waved back. *Get off the goddamned road, Margot.*

Two more cars went by, not even pausing. The tractor-trailer was disappearing up towards St Clair.

Margot reached down under the dog and hauled it up against her waist. Its body was cold and stiff and matted with bits of ice. It was a terrier, perhaps, though it was hard to tell; either an Irish terrier or a slightly mongrelized Airedale. It cried out once when she lifted it. Why was it so heavy, when it seemed so small? She tried to hold it firmly so it wouldn't bend, in case its back was broken, or its ribs. But, just as she got it over to the curb, its head lolled down and the weight became untenable. Blood spilled out of its mouth. It died.

Dear dog, she thought. *I'm sorry.*

Bobby leaned over and called through the open door.

'Okay?'

'It's dead,' said Margot—and laid it out on the ground.

'All right,' said Bobby. And then he said: 'Come on back, M. Get into the car. You've done your duty. We have to go.'

We have to go. We have to go, said Margot, in her mind, addressing the lifeless dog at her feet. *We have to go. To a goddamned party. I'm sorry. Your people will find you here when they come out looking, tomorrow.*

She started back to the car, but before she got inside she turned around and said, 'Goodbye.'

Sitting, warm again, next to Bobby as he turned the key and they started south, Margot closed her eyes. *He knew someone cared,* she thought. *Before he died, the dog knew someone cared.*

Bobby said, 'Are you all right?'

Margot said nothing. She wondered what Bobby could possibly mean.

Coming into the dip before the rise to Roxborough Drive, they saw another dog, this one alive. It was loping along beside the road, looking as if it knew where it was going.

There, thought Bobby. *That'll cheer her up.* 'Looks pretty happy to me,' he said.

Yes, Margot thought, *which is always when something dreadful happens. . . .* She did not say this out loud. Instead, she speculated about the guest list for the Cournoyers' party.

'The Powells are going to be there, sure as fate,' she said, making sure she was smiling when she said it. 'They're everywhere you go these days.'

'That's because Mary Jane is waiting to make his move. He doesn't dare give up a single opportunity. He even goes and sits in the sauna bath at the B and R—and waits. He hangs around the urinals at the Toronto Club. . . .'

'You're kidding!'

'Yes. I'm kidding. Not about the sauna—that much is true. Mary Jane knows that, one day, Brian Gossage and Gordon Perry are going to have to walk in there and he'll be waiting. But not by the urinals, no.'

'Why do they call him *Mary Jane?* I've never understood that,' said Margot.

'I don't think I do, either. His initials, though, are M.J. Stands for *something* Jackman. The M, I don't know.'

'I wondered if it had to do with marijuana.'

'Marijuana?'

'Don't you remember? They used to call marijuana *Mary Jane.* I wondered if that was why.'

'Somehow, I doubt it,' said Bobby. 'If Mary Jane Powell is getting off on drugs, it wouldn't be on marijuana.'

'You mean cocaine?'

'Oh, no. Much stronger than that, I think.'

'Heroin? Heavens!'

'No, Not heroin, either. *Money.*'

Bobby laughed.

'Ah, yes.' Margot settled back and pulled her cashmere closer round her shoulders. '*That* drug.'

'The best we have,' said Bobby, smiling.

Margot smiled back. 'Yeah,' she said. 'I kinda get off on money, myself.'

They were now on Crescent Road, where several of the houses sported coloured lights around their doors and strings of blue and white bulbs in the spruce and cedar trees or winking on and off along the bare, wet arms of magnolias.

'I always feel safe in here,' said Margot—meaning Rosedale.

Bobby didn't answer. He was watching a group of teenage carol singers moving along the sidewalk, coming in their direction. It was good, he thought, to see them there—the carrying on of old traditions was always a hopeful sign . . .

'Look at their faces,' said Margot. Her voice had gone white. She drew back further into the Jaguar, thinking—she did not know why—*I mustn't let them see me.*

Bobby looked. He still couldn't make out what had alarmed her.

'Put on your glasses!' said Margot, hoarse and whispering. 'Look.'

Bobby put on his glasses—steel-rimmed and cold. And while he did this, the Jaguar almost glided to a stop.

Their faces . . .

Holy shit.

The faces of the carol singers were covered with smooth brown leather masks. Helmets were fitted over their heads like skin—black leather helmets—brown leather faces. All that could be seen that was human were the whites of eyes and the shapes of mouths and nostrils, the mouths exhaling visible, pale grey bursts of breath.

The Jaguar was idling, it seemed of its own accord.

One of the singers stepped off the sidewalk onto the street and ran a leather hand along the side of the car.

Bobby flicked the door locks. *Click.* It sounded like a small explosion. The other singers were gathering, now, around the car, some of them pressing their faces close against the window glass.

'Don't say anything,' Bobby muttered. 'Don't say anything.'

They sat completely still—the way they might have sat through the final seconds in a theatre before the curtain rose. Margot wanted to close her eyes but couldn't.

'*God rest ye merry, gentlemen,*' the singers sang. '*Let nothing you dismay.*'

They sang it almost as a lullaby might have been sung, while they rocked the car gently side to side. And then they drew away—they even waved—and were gone.

Margot felt the car regain its power and saw the trees beside her move.

Bobby picked up speed, said nothing and turned the corner onto Cluny Drive.

They were there. Number thirty-six.

Margot sat still. There was blood on her silver dress.

Bobby got out and walked around the car. He was carrying the snips done up in foil and all the long black ribbons were hanging down towards the snow.

He opened the door.

'Come on,' he said. 'We're going inside to celebrate.'

The first thing Margot Finster heard when she reached the hall was her father's voice. This was not something she had expected, and she turned to Bobby with a look that was half alarm, and half chagrin. Before she could speak, however, Hazel Cournoyer was leaning in towards her, smelling of too much Opium and turning her red-red cheeks this way and that while making kiss-kiss noises and saying, 'We think it's so wonderful you could come. . . .' As if some circumstance unknown to Margot might have precluded her arrival.

'I need to go upstairs,' she said. 'Upstairs or into the kitchen. I've a stain on my dress and. . . .'

'Not in the kitchen!' said Hazel, overreacting, as always, to everything. 'The kitchen is just a mass of surprises! I wouldn't have you discover them for all the world, not till we're all at table together. Come upstairs. I'll help you. . . .'

They started across the hallway, which was wide and marbled and tricky to negotiate because of all the mirrors. Andrew and Hazel went through phases of manic collecting and Japanese lacquer had given way the previous summer to rococo mirrors.

'I thought I heard my father's voice,' said Margot, attempting nonchalance. 'I love your dress. I hadn't expected him to be here. Is something going on besides your anniversary?'

'No, of course not,' said Hazel. 'Yours is nice, too. It's just that Andrew wanted to spread the generations a little wider than usual. Says he gets sick of the same old healthy faces. . . . They make him feel inferior. We haven't been to Peebee once this season.'

'Well, it's a little early, yet,' said Margot. 'No one you'd really want to see arrives in Peebee till after New Year's, anyway.'

They were almost halfway up the stairs and Margot, preparing to negotiate the landing, turned and gazed back at the scene below them: Bobby adjusting his tie in one of the mirrors; Andrew Cournoyer crossing the black and white marble with Cybil Torrance and Peter Bongard, all of them laughing, Cybil tall in a long white dress, pale as an elegant Amazon. Alan Northey, nervous in a doorway, was fingering a glass of Perrier and listening to John Dai Bowen explain—for the hundredth time, no doubt—why Fabiana Holbach was God's best gift to fashion photography, in spite of the fact she hated having her picture taken. . . .

These were all people of Margot's generation—as Hazel was: the crop of the early fifties and mid-to-late forties—none of them older than thirty-five—all of them bound together by virtue of their schools and money and mutual inclinations to cluster at the foot of Bay Street, where their fathers' names were framed in mahogany and set in brass.

Alexander Peyton Wood.

There he was, in his dreadful brocade jacket, worn every Christmas and New Year's, his Chinese velvet pumps and his scarlet complexion—the tallest man and the thinnest in the world—with the reediest, most off-putting voice. Her father—looking up at her.

Margot turned away and continued to climb beyond the landing, out of sight.

Hazel, climbing beside her and reaching down to lift the silver folds of Margot's dress, was saying: 'What on earth is this? It looks like blood.'

'It is,' said Margot. She did not explain.

Everyone had done as they were told and across the hall from the sitting room where most of the guests had gathered before the fire, a table had been prepared to receive the gifts of tin. This was in the library, where the books stood up in unread rows that reached the ceiling. Guests, on occasion, perused the titles—but that was the extent of their attraction. The room was normally given over to games of trivia and bridge and, very often, to games of chance where the stakes were high and money changed hands without a thought about where it was going.

Money has no loyalties, Andrew Cournoyer had said, in one of his brighter moments. *You have to tie it down.* He was not, however, much in the habit of losing.

Andrew played his cards and dice with skill and the kind of concentration only professionals bring to games. He was dangerous in there, in the so-called library, whereas, beyond its walls, he was perceived only as Hazel's boyish husband—charming, but unassuming. People were always saying of him, *what does Andrew do?* because he was not the sort of man who could be identified by means of what he did. Whatever he did, he did as a dabbler. Andrew was never seen downtown except as a guest at other people's clubs. Whatever he did, it left no mark on him except the marks of ingratiation and availability: nervous eyes and a willing mouth. All of this changed when he stood inside the walls of number thirty-six Cluny Drive, inviting you in amongst the books for a game of seven-card stud or three-card monte.

Now, however, the library had been commandeered for the display of anniversary tin, which covered the length and depth of one whole table, twelve feet long. A tin cage with tin birds sitting amongst tin flowers sat in the middle of the table, surrounded by tin candlesticks, tin motorcars, tin cows and horses and a pear tree made of tin with boxes numbered from one to twelve beside it, each box containing one new day of Christmas, starting with a partridge made of tin and, buried at the bottom, twelve tin drummers drumming. Bobby and Margot Finster's snip-shears had been unpacked and added to this look—ribbons, tinfoil and all.

'Thank God this wasn't their fiftieth anniversary,' said Conrad Fastbinder, standing in the doorway looking in with grim amusement. 'I'd hate to think what twelve gold days of Christmas might have cost.'

Margot Finster and Claire Bongard were standing by the fire enjoying, as always, one another's company. In their final year together at Branksome

Hall, Claire had been head girl and Margot had been her confidante. Claire had always been immensely popular—nervously vital, talented, unpredictable. Now, in her adult life, the innocence of her appeal had failed to hold its own in the face of her increased demand that she be loved. A kind of chaos had come into her eyes. Even as she stood with you, she abandoned you and wandered off—afraid—into her own private world. Her left hand very often rose up under her chin where her fingers played with a chain that wasn't there.

She had married Peter Bongard at the age of seventeen. Rumour had it now that the Bongards were going their separate ways. At the Cournoyers' party, Peter had arrived with Cybil Torrance and Claire had arrived with someone she introduced to Margot Finster only as 'a man called Orenstein'.

'This is a man called Orenstein,' she'd said, and had sent him off to talk to Alan Northey.

Now, Claire was saying, 'Did you ever think, then—when we were girls—we would have to pay for our sins?'

Margot laughed. 'No,' she said. 'Sins? What sins?' Claire leaned against the mantelpiece and threw her cigarette into the flames. '*Sins*. You know. Just being who we are.'

Margot felt cold in spite of the fire. 'I don't understand what you mean,' she said. Claire turned partway around and nodded at the room with its clusters of chatting guests and its ebullient hosts. 'I mean that,' said Claire. 'Those people. Them and us—and who we are.'

'I never think about who we are at all,' said Margot, smiling at Bobby, who stood about ten feet away talking to John Dai Bowen and Fabiana Holbach. 'I like who we are and I don't know what you mean by *sin*.'

Claire blinked. She looked confused. Perhaps she had been inside her private world.

'You don't?' she said.

'No. I don't,' said Margot, still smiling. 'You're not a sinner, Claire. You've just had rotten luck, that's all.'

As soon as she'd said this, Margot wavered. She had seen her father watching her from across the room and something inside her fell to one side. A door came open inside and she had a view of what Claire meant—but only for an instant. The words *my father, my father* occurred to her. *Bang*! And the door slammed shut.

Claire said, 'I want a drink.'

'Me, too,' said Margot.

But just as they began to make their way across the room towards the barman, the doorbell rang.

Margot had been quite right.

It was Mary Jane Powell and a party of six.

'See who Mary Jane has with him,' said Claire.

'Your sister-in-law,' said Margot.

'Susan?'

'Yes.'

'Well, well,' said Claire. 'The son of a bitch deserves the bitch.'

Margot winced. Susan Bongard was someone she rather liked.

'On the other hand,' said Claire, 'the bitch does not deserve the son of a bitch. No one deserves the son of a bitch. He's a cannibal.'

'Yes,' said Margot. 'With that, I agree.'

But Margot was not concerned about Mary Jane Powell and Susan Bongard. She was concerned about the others who had come in with them. Brian Gossage and Gordon Perry. Again, she had been right. This was not a simple celebration of the Cournoyers' tenth anniversary. This was something else entirely.

They ate at two round tables for ten. Margot and Bobby were separated and Margot began to panic. It was not the fact of their separation that bothered her so much as the fact that Andrew's table, where Bobby was seated, was predominantly occupied by the group that had arrived with Mary Jane Powell and his brother, Tom. Apparently, Mary Jane Powell had sweated long enough in the B and R sauna to be there when Gossage and Perry at last arrived.

The seating arrangements had not been meant to work out this way, and all through the soup Hazel Cournoyer kept apologizing. 'I am so dreadfully distressed,' she said at least three times. 'I cannot abide the thought of a table made up entirely—well, almost entirely—of men. It means there will not be a single word of civilized conversation.'

'I absolutely agree with you,' said Tina Perry, who was small and tough and spent her life pursuing golf and tennis balls. She was wearing black, which showed off her tan and her hair, dyed honey blond. She was sitting next to Margot, whom she disliked intensely because she thought that Margot was responsible for Gordon Perry's infatuation with Bobby Finster. *Margot Finster is the kind of woman,* Tina Perry had once told Hazel Cournoyer, *who gets behind her husband and pushes him into places he does not belong.* Of course, there was not a word of truth in this, but there was nothing Margot could do but live with Tina's opinion. Gordon Perry, after all, was Bobby's mentor in the corporate world. The older man's affection for his protégé was almost that of a father for a son—and Bobby had neither objected to their relationship nor rejected the advancements it had brought him. *I would do anything for Gordon Perry,* Bobby had once declared in Margot's presence.

Margot had cringed at this enthusiasm—knowing as she did that Gordon Perry's affections could be dangerous. Long ago, he had made a leap in loyalties that had brought his best friend close to ruin, but nothing had ever been proved, nor could it be, because the leap had been made behind closed doors. This had been when Gordon Perry established his credentials with Alex Peyton Wood, back in the time when Margot was still a child and could only guess at the devastation caused when what her mother had called 'the knives' came out. The man who was nearly ruined had been her mother's brother—her beloved Uncle Terry, long since dead—and the ruin was completed when her mother died.

Bobby Finster had never believed this story. Gordon Perry was incapable, in Bobby's eyes, of anything that smelled of blood. Everyone knew that Uncle Terry's business failures had been brought about by his innate lack of business sense. *He was a charming, arrogant fool,* the story went, as Bobby told it, *who couldn't read the writing on the wall. . . .*

Now, as the shrimps in a ginger sauce were being served, Margot prayed those words would not, one day, be said about Bobby—who, himself, was an 'arrogant fool' where Gordon Perry was concerned. Not because Bobby could not, but because he would not read the writing on the walls—made every day more evident by Gordon Perry's restless shifting in Mary Jane Powell's direction.

Claire, who seemed increasingly ill at ease, had excused herself before the shrimp had arrived and had gone outside to 'get some fresh air and smoke a cigarette'. The man called Orenstein, who was sitting next to Margot, turned to her and said, 'You see that man over there—the one they call Mary Jane?'

Margot nodded, dreading what might be coming—some paean of manly praise, no doubt, a round of applause for the joys of climbing in Mary Jane's company up the ladder of success, larded with phrases like 'golden boy' and 'wunderkind'. . . .

'I nearly killed him once,' said Orenstein.

'You did?' said Margot—delighted and trying not to show it.

'Yes,' said the man called Orenstein, reaching out sadly for his glass of wine. 'He fucked my wife at a party back in 1975.'

'At a party,' said Margot.

'Yes, ma'am. A party. In Montreal.'

Orenstein took a long, slow pull at his wine and rolled the stem of the glass between his fingers.

Margot waited. But that was apparently all the man called Orenstein had to say. It was as if, in saying that Mary Jane Powell had fucked his wife at a party in Montreal, Mister Orenstein had told her the story of his life.

And, in his way, he had.

'If anyone wants to see the seventh wonder of the world,' said Claire, who had just returned from her breath of air, 'you had best come now and see it before it disappears.'

'What are you talking about?' said Hazel, verging on annoyance. She had just been about to call for removal of the shrimp and the serving of the grapefruit sorbet. 'I don't want to say,' said Claire, 'because I don't want to ruin the effect. How do I get to your terrace? Down these stairs?'

She was heading for the far end of the dining room, which faced the ravine at the back of the house.

Claire's mysterious invitation was sufficient excuse for half the guests to rise and follow her—and, once this exodus had been begun, the rest of the guests got up and made for the stairs.

'I don't know where we're going,' said Cybil Torrance. 'Does she really want us to go outside? I'm going to get my wrap. . . . '

'Bring mine,' said someone else.

'And mine!' said Tina Perry.

Margot had set her cashmere shawl on the back of her chair and, taking it, she also brought her glass of wine and started along the room.

On the way down the stairs, she put her free hand on Bobby's arm and whispered, 'I hope you're not in danger over there at that other table.'

'Me?'

'Yes, you. The lot of you look quite sinister.'

'Sinister!' Bobby was laughing.

'Yes. Like a swarm of deadly insects, my darling. What is going on?'

'A deal,' said Bobby.

'Dear God, no. With *them?*'

'Not to worry. I'm not involved. But it's quite exciting.'

'Sure,' said Margot. 'I'll bet.'

During their Edwardian phase, the Cournoyers had built a conservatory leading to the terrace which led, in its turn, to the hillside garden hanging over Cluny Park.

The conservatory was filled with nonexotic, relatively hardy flowering shrubs and miniature trees and groves of bamboo shoots in pots. A pool with goldfish pulled the eye towards one side, where wicker and wrought iron garden furniture provided a resting place beneath the branches of a lemon tree.

On arrival in the conservatory, it was evident the seventh wonder of the world could not be seen from there. The doors stood open leading to the terrace.

Margot drew her shawl around her shoulders before she walked out, and took a sip of wine.

Alex Peyton Wood was waiting just inside the doors to let her pass.

'Good evening, Father.'

'Margot.'

'It's been a while.'

'Yes.'

'Do I find you well?'

'You find me as you find me,' he said.

'And what does that mean?'

'Old,' said Peyton Wood.

Margot went through and they said no more. On the terrace, she wanted to stand with Bobby, but he was standing hands in pockets, over near the furthest edge against the darkness with Mary Jane and Gordon Perry and Brian

Gossage and Mary Jane's brother, Tom. Margot hung back and stood alone. Alex Peyton Wood went over. Everyone was looking at the sky.

'What is it? What?'

The sky was luminous back beyond the house, to the east. A colour that could only be described as smoky-orange infused the clouds of carbon compounds lying like a veil above the city. 'Fire,' somebody said.

'And a big one, too,' someone added.

'No, said Claire. 'It isn't fire. It's the seventh wonder of the world. Be patient. And be quiet. . . .'

Everyone stood on the terrace, each one staring upward—some with napkins, others with wine glasses, some in overcoats or furs, others with upturned collars or scarves or shawls, some standing absolutely still while others swayed from foot to foot in the cold with all their breaths making shorter and shorter bursts of white as they grew impatient. 'What?' 'What?' 'Where?'

And then it rose.

The seventh wonder of the world.

The moon.

It was red—almost as red as a blood orange is red when it is cut in half.

'Oh!'

'My!'

'Goodness!'

'Look at that . . . !'

Each voice was barely raised above a whisper.

'I swear you can see it moving,' said Susan Bongard.

'You can. You can see it moving,' said Fabiana Holbach.

'Oh, how beautiful . . . ,' said Andrew Cournoyer. 'I don't believe I'm seeing this.'

'And me without a camera,' said John Dai Bowen.

'*The night the moon was red*,' said Claire.

'Sort of like the night they murdered Caesar,' said Conrad Fastbinder.

'Good for you, Connie,' said Claire. 'There's always someone who brings it crashing down to earth.'

'I'm cold,' said Hazel.

'So am I,' said Tina Perry.

'To hell with this,' said Mary Jane Powell. 'I'm going inside.'

Mary Jane was halfway across the terrace when the singing started. It stopped him in his tracks.

Silent night, holy night,
All is calm,
All is bright. . . .

Margot shivered, thinking of the leather masks and helmets—thinking of Sara Finster, reaching out to turn on the light.

Bobby Finster turned away, perhaps because he was thinking of the leather faces, too. From the terrace, given the bare winter trees, he could see all the way to Cluny Park—spread out white and almost phosphorescent below them.

The moon rose up, immense, above the house and its light grew less and less red and more and more golden; copper; orange.

Andrew and Hazel Cournoyer and all their guests were silent—waiting for the song to end.

Sleep in heavenly peace,
Sleep in heavenly peace. . . .

It was done—and, lingering for one last look at the moon, they made their way inside across the stones and through the doors and under the trees and the frosted glass and up the stairs towards the remaining courses of the meal.

Alan Northey, who knew such things, was saying, as he left the terrace: 'The moon should not have been that colour. Not in this season. What we have seen is truly a phenomenon.'

Margot waited. Her left hand was fisted, her right hand held the wine glass close between her breasts.

Bobby came back from the edge and over the stones and stood beside her.

'Yes?' he said.

'I'm going home,' said Margot.

'You can't go home. We haven't eaten yet.'

'I've eaten all I can. I'm leaving.'

He knew she could not by any means be made or persuaded to stay. Something had caught her and wouldn't let go.

'I'm afraid,' she said. 'And I wish you'd come with me.'

'No, no. I can't,' he said. 'Impossible. But—here you take the car. . . .' He handed her the keys and kissed her on the mouth. She tasted of wine and salt. She did not kiss back. Her eyes were open. She took his hand in her fist—with the keys between his flesh and hers.

'Will you promise to come as soon as you can?

'I will.'

'I love you.'

'Yes. I love you, too.'

They went upstairs.

There would come a time in later years, as Claire's own story unfolded, when those who recalled these events would say of Andrew and Hazel Cournoyer's tenth anniversary party: *that was the night before the duel in Cluny Park; the night Claire Bongard came inside and told us she had seen the moon on fire.*

Everyone knows that someone else must always be made to take responsibility for what goes wrong. And so it was that Claire and the moon were blamed for the duel in Cluny Park. The others all said, *I don't remember. I wasn't there. I didn't see. What moon . . . ?*

Consequently, because she was the only one who truly wasn't there, the stories that Margot Finster was told about the duel in Cluny Park were made up of elements as disparate and incomplete as these:

If the moon had not turned red. . . .
If Claire had not come in and told us so. . . .
If Bobby Finster had sat at Hazel's table, not at Andrew's. . . .
If Mary Jane Powell had refrained from fucking Orenstein's wife. . . .
If Margot had paid attention when her father said: I'm old. . . .
If Margot had not gone home. . . .

But none of these things was the cause of the duel in Cluny Park. The cause was in the turning of a card.

Mary Jane Powell was a man both cautiously revered and hated. No one spoke ill of him, ever, to his face.

The golden colour of his skin, the impossible blue of his eyes, the width of his mouth, the breadth of his hands and the way he stood were magnets whose power could draw you in, no matter what your age or sex. When he spoke, he leaned in close so you could feel his breath and smell his hair. His voice was seldom raised—except in moments of utter jubilation, and these were rarely come upon in a life that was lived almost entirely on the verge of imminent collapse. He so rarely failed, on the other hand, that when he spoke of these imminent dangers no one could understand why he seemed so watchful always—always keyed and in gear—never for a moment seeming to be aware of fear.

But Mary Jane—whose given names were Mainwaring Jackman—had once encountered a wall he could neither scale nor demolish: his father. And this experience of coming up against an immovable object had left him wary forever after, certain that somewhere, sometime, another immovable object would loom in his path and he wanted to be ready for it.

Mary Jane's father, whose name was Sydney Powell, was Chairman and President of Dorchester Trust. He sat behind a polished length of barren table, showing the world he had no weapons but his will and his wits. Sitting there one day, when Mary Jane was twenty-one years old, Sydney Powell had rejected his son's proposal that he be his father's partner and, looking down forty storeys over Sherbrooke Street in Montreal, he had told his son, *I wouldn't have you seen in my company. No. I will not touch you with a ten-foot pole.*

Mary Jane had been astonished. Why had his father refused him?

Because, while Sydney Powell admired and even encouraged the killer instinct in both his sons and his daughter, he feared, from this son, the focus of that instinct.

He said, in a word, he was afraid of patricide. *I like it here, where I sit,* he told Mary Jane. *And I don't intend to share it with anyone. And especially not an assassin.*

Mary Jane often told this story, laughing as he did so. It was one of the tales he told at business lunches. *People should know who I am,* he liked to say.

And people did.

He was twenty-eight years old and on his way to the fourth of his millions.

The door to the library was closed. The men from Andrew's table had gone in there an hour ago and Tina Perry was raging in the living room about the fact that Hazel had still not managed to put her foot down.

'I'm going to buy you a large pair of boots,' she said. 'I shall come, if I must, and give you lessons. The men must not be allowed to do this to us. It is monstrous!'

'Do what?' said Claire.

'Ensconce themselves in that room. Are you aware of what they're doing in there?'

'Well, I doubt they're having sex, Tina,' said Claire.

'They are gambling away our fortunes!' Tina bellowed.

Hazel smiled. If that, indeed, was what the men were doing, then Andrew would probably do very well.

She wondered aloud if anyone would like more coffee.

'No,' said Tina. 'I'd like a double scotch—straight up.'

Half an hour later, or thereabouts, voices were raised beyond the library door and Hazel became alarmed. It wasn't like Andrew to permit such things. Furthermore, it wasn't like their friends to do them.

'What do you think it can be about?' said Cybil Torrance. The shouting had now gone on for over five minutes.

'For all we know,' said Hazel, 'it could be part of the game. There are such games, you know—where people shout as part of the proceedings. . . .'

'Prize fights, yes,' said Claire.

'Do you think we should go and break it up?' said Susan Bongard. 'I'm getting more than nervous.'

'No,' said Hazel. 'Please. Sit down.'

She refused to believe that anything like an argument—let alone a fight—could happen at one of her parties. Thank God Zena Cherry hadn't been invited. She'd have it in *The Globe and Mail* before the guests were halfway home.

'*Brian Gossage, Chairman and President of Amaken; Gordon Perry, Amaken's Executive Vice-Chairman; Robert Finster, President of Canwood and their spouses were involved in a verbal fracas the other night with Montreal's notorious gift to the business community, bad boy M.J. Powell. The fight took place at the home of Andrew Cournoyer, the noted collector, and his wife, Hazel. The cause, we are told, was. . . .*'

The door flew open at that very moment and Andrew came across the hall and into the living room pale as the snow that had just begun to fall outside.

'What is wrong?' asked Hazel, sitting down—prepared for the worst; perhaps the loss of all they owned, considering Andrew's state.

Andrew was coming straight toward her, reaching out for the brandy decanter which sat on the table just in front of her chair.

'What is it, Andrew? What?'

Tina intervened and grabbed him by the arm.

'Tell us what has happened!'

'There is going to be a duel,' said Andrew.

'A *duel?*' Claire burst out laughing.

No one else spoke.

Claire sat down. *This isn't funny, she thought. That moon. . . .*

'Will someone die?' Cybil asked.

Andrew turned around and walked away. He had arrangements to make.

Four hours later, when it was not quite three a.m., Bobby Finster and Claire Bongard were sitting in the conservatory drinking cognac beneath the lemon tree.

Bobby had accepted Andrew's offer of a Browning .38, the only handgun kept in the house. Mary Jane Powell had sent his brother Tom to fetch the Luger he had bought from a German acquaintance in 1973. These were the weapons. Bobby Finster hadn't fired a gun in more than a dozen years.

'I wish I could understand,' said Claire, 'why you feel you have to do this.'

'Honour.'

'Honour?'

'That's right. And please don't sneer.'

'I'm sorry,' said Claire. 'I didn't mean to sneer. I meant to laugh.'

'It has to be done, whatever you think.'

'Yes,' said Claire. 'I dare say.'

She looked at him. He was such a likeable man, with his boyish hair and hazel eyes behind those crazy glasses. 'Take them off,' she said to him, reaching over and removing them. 'You're so good-looking without them.'

'A lot of good it does me,' said Bobby, and he took the glasses back and settled them on his nose. 'Without them, I have to stand so near the mirror to see myself, I squish my nose on the glass.'

They both laughed lightly at that and then Claire took his hand and began to massage it between her own.

'I'll pay whatever losses there were,' she said, 'if you'd only call this off. I'm loaded with the stuff, you know. And you could pay me back if you want to, later on. Please don't do this, Bobby. It isn't fair to Margot. . . . '

'Margot will never know it happened,' said Bobby. 'Unless you tell her, of course.' He smiled.

'She'll know it happened if you're killed.'

'I won't be killed. There will be no killing.'

Claire let go of his hand and stood up.

'I won't believe you're that naïve,' she said. 'Are you saying you think he won't at least try to kill you?'

'I think he wouldn't dare.'

Claire was silent. Then she said, 'It's a pity, you know, that you're not a woman.'

'What the hell do you mean by that?'

'I mean that if you were a woman—and you had slept with M.J. Powell—you would know that he's a killer.'

Bobby looked up from under his tousled hair at Claire.

'You've slept with him?'

'Yes.'

She turned away.

Bobby ran his finger along his lip and was surprised to feel how dry it was.

'Killers always have a certain rhythm, Bobby. A way of fucking that gives them away.'

Bobby began to wish that Claire would stop. He did not know why, but his heart was beating somewhere in his ears and it frightened him.

He poured another drink and closed his eyes.

'I'm going to sleep,' he said. 'I'm going to sleep for half an hour.'

Claire turned around and told him not to worry. She would sit there with him and wake him up when it was time.

Everyone had decided to stay. It seemed the wisest thing to do—since each of them would need the other's protection once the duel had been fought and the outcome was known. Everyone must tell the same story—whatever happened.

Susan and Peter Bongard—both of them lawyers, the children of lawyers—and Cybil Torrance, the daughter of one of Ontario's Supreme Court judges, sat as if in conference at one of the round white tables in the dining room. The lights, on dimmers, had been lowered and all the reflections in the windows looked like golden optical illusions.

'What exactly happened?' said Cybil.

Peter said: 'Bobby caught Mary Jane cheating. Mary Jane denied it. Bobby wouldn't accept the denial. Mary Jane challenged him to a duel.'

Susan snorted—almost laughing. 'It sounds like a game that kids would play. You be Clint Eastwood and I'll be Robert Redford. . . .'

'Well,' said Peter, 'of course we all thought that Mary Jane had to be kidding. Now we know he doesn't. Kid.'

'You're damn well right he doesn't kid,' said Susan. 'I haven't learned much by going out with him—but that much I have learned.'

'What were they playing?' Cybil asked.

'They were playing three-card monte for Peyton Wood's Canwood stock. He was the banker—he put it on the table for one twenty-five a share. He was selling out, you see—in a way, he was selling out to the highest bidder. . . .'

'But Bobby Finster hasn't money like that,' said Susan.

'Bobby wasn't playing. Mary Jane and Gordon Perry were playing. They'd each bought in for half the stock. Whoever won the game would end up with Peyton Wood's controlling shares.

Cybil coughed and spluttered. She wanted, somehow, to cry, which baffled her. *But all that money—controlling interest—in a card game. . . .*

'Excuse me,' she said. And left the table.

She crossed the room and Peter and Susan were under the impression she had gone out into the hall—when, suddenly, she turned around and shouted at them: 'WHO ARE THOSE BASTARDS? WHY DOESN'T SOMEBODY KILL THEM?'

And then she ran out into the hall and up the stairs where she locked herself in one of the guest rooms.

Susan started to follow her, but Peter, who was thinking of marrying Cybil Torrance once he was divorced from Claire, said: 'No. Don't go. She wants to be alone. Her father has just discovered he hasn't half the money he thought he had and she's distressed. . . .'

A moment later, he explained to Susan: 'Clearly, there can be no doubt that Mary Jane cheated. I saw him do it, myself. I said nothing—ever the diplomat—but Bobby couldn't restrain himself, and there you have it. Finito.'

Susan looked at him.

'I wish you hadn't said that,' she said.

At about five-thirty a.m. they all assembled in the living room. All, that is, but Bobby Finster and Mary Jane Powell.

Alex Peyton Wood had agreed, because of his military background, to act as referee. The seconds had been appointed—and were now with their men in separate parts of the house. Mary Jane's seconds were his brother Tom and Brian Gossage. Bobby's seconds were Cybil Torrance, who had now regained her composure and was not the least bit angry any more, but calm and resolute. Cybil was joined, on Bobby's side, by the man called Orenstein—mostly because he wanted somehow, even symbolically—to pull the trigger on Mary Jane Powell.

'We must all go down together,' Alex Peyton Wood was saying in his reediest of voices. 'I believe it is best if all of us are witness to this event. That way, nothing can be distorted. We have chosen Cluny Park as the scene of our little adventure simply because it is there.' He smiled and took out a pair of darkly tinted glasses. 'Also, of course,' he added—once his glasses were in place and he looked the perfect linesman for a tennis match—'it is flat, it is self-contained, and it is private.'

And with that, he dispersed them all towards the rear of the house.

'Come along, gentlemen,' he called out to Bobby and to Mary Jane. 'The moment has arrived!'

When we were children, Claire was thinking, *Margot Peyton Wood and I would come down here to Cluny Park and smoke forbidden cigarettes and sit beneath these trees and read the dirty bits from* Peyton Place *and. . . .*

The path gave out before they had reached the bottom. Andrew had put up a chain link fence that was eight feet high and partly overgrown with wild Virginia creeper and deadly nightshade. A gate pushed outwards—difficult to open because of all the frozen fallen leaves that had blown against the fence.

Alex Peyton Wood was the first one through the gate once Andrew had kicked and pushed and shoved it open. Andrew stayed in place till everyone had passed.

No one spoke. It was like a silent film. Even Mary Jane was silenced. Claire was watching the back of his head where it rose above the collar of his great-coat. She was trying to remember what it had been like to love him. There had been so little time for love before she hated him—and she knew that this had been the way it was for all his women. Still, she had no pity for him now. There wasn't a chance in hell that he'd be killed.

The park gave off a rush of silence. Nothing moved but the falling snow and the sight of it was mesmerizing. Each of the figures standing against the backdrop of hillside trees was momentarily stilled as they might have been in one of John Dai Bowen's photographs.

Eighteen people in evening dress and snowflakes the size of quarters and here I am without my camera. . . .

'Gentlemen.'

Peyton Wood's voice was like a voice inside a tea cup—audible and crisp, but small. He wore his overcoat loosely around his shoulders and took his handkerchief out of his pocket in order to wipe his glasses. He beckoned to the seconds and asked them as a formality if they had made the appropriate attempts to dissuade the duellists from their chosen course of action. 'Yes. Yes. Yes,' he was told. And, 'Yes.' The four went back to their appointed places.

The distance between the two men was to be twenty paces when they fired. Each gun was loaded with a single clip—each clip containing a single bullet. One shot each and, whatever the outcome, that would be the end of it.

'Gentlemen, are you ready?'

'Yessir.'

'Yes.'

'Come forward please,' said Peyton Wood. 'I want you back to back where I have drawn this line.' He had drawn the line with his walking stick—and once Mary Jane and Bobby Finster were standing in their places, shoulders touching and their shirt sleeves grazing as they dropped their arms to their sides, Peyton Wood called out in a kindly way, as if to children at a summer picnic when the fireworks are about to start, 'Ladies and gentlemen—please clear the lines of fire . . . I thank you.'

Just before Peyton Wood began the count, Hazel Cournoyer and Fabiana Holbach, standing some ten or twelve feet apart, decided in the instant to raise the umbrellas they had snatched before they left the house. They were like two black, sudden flowers and Cybil Torrance closed her eyes. She held a deep belief in signs, and what this sign might mean was all too clear.

'I shall now commence the count,' said Peyton Wood. 'And *one. . . .*'

Bobby Finster wanted not to look like an awkward fool, but he felt like an awkward fool—with both arms tight against his sides and his knees locked tight against the jarring of the paces. . . .

'. . . *seven, eight, nine, ten. . . .*'

Alan Northey was thinking, *this will make the most interesting conversation piece when I get back home. Who will believe that I've been to a real live duel?*

'. . . *twelve, thirteen, fourteen, fifteen. . . .*'

Claire thought, *well—I have to watch this, don't I. For Margot's sake, if not for mine.*

An oak leaf fell from one of the trees and before it touched the ground, the count of twenty had been reached.

Somebody cried out, 'Don't!'

Bobby Finster raised his arm and, just as he was pulling his opponent up along his sights, a snowflake landed on his glasses, blinding him.

Someone started laughing wildly.

Bobby Finster fell down. Dead.

Later, much later that morning, someone was pushed, or jumped or fell from the Glen Road bridge. Male. Caucasian. Sandy hair. Hazel eyes. Five foot eleven. Wearing evening clothes.

That he had been shot was not immediately evident, due to the damage done to his head by the fall. This news came later, at the Coroner's. Several police went scrambling among the fallen leaves and branches beneath the bridge and, in due course, after perhaps an hour and fifteen minutes of diligent searching, one of them found the Luger with which the fatal shot had been fired.

On the Monday morning, the two men who lived at number one Beaumont Road, at the end of the bridge, were questioned about the previous day and one of them, dressed in a handsome bathrobe, said that—yes—there had definitely been a shot on the Sunday morning, but the man had concluded it was just a motorcar.

So this was the official rendering of Bobby Finster's death—and the one that Margot Finster had delivered to her door.

Stood on the bridge—etcetera—shot himself—etcetera—fell to his death—etcetera—all while of unsound mind.

That, barring Christmas, was how the decade ended. Two weeks and two days after Bobby Finster's death, the 1980s began.

ALICE MUNRO

(1931)

⌒

The Jack Randa Hotel

On the runway, in Honolulu, the plane loses speed, loses heart, falters and veers onto the grass, and bumps to a stop. A few yards it seems from the ocean. Inside, everybody laughs. First a hush, then the laugh. Gail laughed herself. Then there was a flurry of introductions all around. Beside Gail are Larry and Phyllis, from Spokane.

Larry and Phyllis are going to a tournament of Left-handed Golfers, in Fiji, as are many other couples on this plane. It is Larry who is the left-handed golfer—Phyllis is the wife going along to watch and cheer and have fun.

They sit on the plane—Gail and the Left-handed Golfers—and lunch is served in picnic boxes. No drinks. Dreadful heat. Jokey and confusing announcements are made from the cockpit. *Sorry about the problem. Nothing serious but it looks like it will keep us stewing here a while longer.* Phyllis has a terrible headache, which Larry tries to cure by applying finger-pressure points to her wrist and palm.

'It's not working,' Phyllis says. 'I could have been in New Orleans by now with Suzy.'

Larry says, 'Poor lamb.'

Gail catches the fierce glitter of diamond rings as Phyllis pulls her hand away. Wives have diamond rings and headaches, Gail thinks. They still do. The truly successful ones do. They have chubby husbands, left-handed golfers, bent on a lifelong course of appeasement.

Eventually the passengers who are not going to Fiji, but on to Sydney, are taken off the plane. They are led into the terminal and there deserted by their airline guide they wander about, retrieving their baggage and going through customs, trying to locate the airline that is supposed to honour their tickets. At one point, they are accosted by a welcoming committee from one of the Island's hotels, who will not stop singing Hawaiian songs and flinging garlands around their necks. But they find themselves on another plane at last. They eat and drink and sleep and the lines to the toilets lengthen and the aisles fill up with debris and the flight attendants hide in their cubbyholes chatting about children and boyfriends. Then comes the unsettling bright morning and the yellow-sanded coast of Australia far below, and the wrong time of day, and even the best-dressed, best-looking

passengers are haggard and unwilling, torpid, as from a long trip in steer-
age. And before they can leave the plane there is one more assault. Hairy
men in shorts swarm aboard and spray everything with insecticide.

'So maybe this is the way it will be getting into Heaven,' Gail imagines
herself saying to Will. 'People will fling flowers on you that you don't want,
and everybody will have headaches and be constipated and then you will
have to be sprayed for Earth germs.'

Her old habit, trying to think up clever and lighthearted things to say to
Will.

After Will went away, it seemed to Gail that her shop was filling up with
women. Not necessarily buying clothes. She didn't mind this. It was like the
long-ago days, before Will. Women were sitting around in ancient armchairs
beside Gail's ironing board and cutting table, behind the faded batik curtains, drinking coffee. Gail started grinding the coffee beans herself, as she
used to do. The dressmaker's dummy was soon draped with beads and had
a scattering of scandalous graffiti. Stories were told about men, usually
about men who had left. Lies and injustices and confrontations. Betrayals so
horrific—yet so trite—that you could only rock with laughter when you heard
them. Men made fatuous speeches (*I am sorry, but I no longer feel committed to
this marriage*). They offered to sell back to the wives cars and furniture that
the wives themselves had paid for. They capered about in self-satisfaction
because they had managed to impregnate some dewy dollop of womanhood
younger than their own children. They were fiendish and childish. What
could you do but give up on them? In all honour, in pride, and for your own
protection?

Gail's enjoyment of all this palled rather quickly. Too much coffee could
make your skin look livery. An underground quarrel developed among the
women when it turned out that one of them had placed an ad in the
Personal Column. Gail shifted from coffee with friends to drinks with
Cleata, Will's mother. As she did this, oddly enough her spirits grew more
sober. Some giddiness still showed in the notes she pinned to her door so
that she could get away early on summer afternoons. (Her clerk, Donalda,
was on her holidays, and it was too much trouble to hire anybody else.)

> *Gone to the Opera.*
> *Gone to the Funny Farm.*
> *Gone to stock up on the Sackcloth and Ashes.*

Actually these were not her own inventions, but things Will used to write
out and tape on her door in the early days when they wanted to go upstairs.
She heard that such flippancy was not appreciated by people who had driven some distance to buy a dress for a wedding, or girls on an expedition to
buy clothes for college. She did not care.

On Cleata's veranda Gail was soothed, she became vaguely hopeful. Like most serious drinkers, Cleata stuck to one drink—hers was Scotch—and seemed amused by variations. But she would make Gail a gin and tonic, a white rum and soda. She introduced her to tequila. 'This is Heaven,' Gail sometimes said, meaning not just the drink but the screened veranda and hedged back yard, the old house behind them with its shuttered windows, varnished floors, inconveniently high kitchen cupboards, and out-of-date flowered curtains. (Cleata despised decorating.) This was the house where Will, and Cleata too, had been born, and when Will first brought Gail into it, she had thought, This is how really civilized people live. The careless and propriety combined, the respect for old books and old dishes. The absurd things that Will and Cleata thought it natural to talk about. And the things she and Cleata didn't talk about—Will's present defection, the illness that has made Cleata's arms and legs look like varnished twigs within their deep tan, and has hollowed the cheeks framed by her looped-back white hair. She and Will have the same slightly monkeyish face, with dreamy, mocking dark eyes.

Instead, Cleata talked about the book she was reading, *The Anglo-Saxon Chronicle.* She said that the reason the Dark Ages were dark was not that we couldn't learn anything about them but that we could not remember anything we did learn, and that was because of the names.

'Caedwala,' she said. 'Egfrith. These are just not names on the tip of your tongue anymore.'

Gail was trying to remember which ages, or centuries, were dark. But her ignorance didn't embarrass her. Cleata was making fun of all that, anyway.

'Aelfflaed,' said Cleata, and spelled it out. 'What kind of a heroine is Aelfflaed?'

When Cleata wrote to Will, she probably wrote about Aelfflaed and Egfrith. Not about Gail. Not *Gail was here looking very pretty in some kind of silky grey summer-pajamas outfit. She was in good form, made various witty remarks. . . .* No more than she would say to Gail, 'I have my doubts about the love-birds. Reading between the lines, I can't help wondering if disillusionment isn't setting in. . . .'

When she met Will and Cleata, Gail thought they were like characters in a book. A son living with his mother, apparently contentedly, into middle age. Gail saw a life that was ceremonious and absurd and enviable, with at least the appearance of celibate grace and safety. She still sees some of that, though the truth is Will has not always lived at home, and he is neither celibate nor discreetly homosexual. He had been gone for years, into his own life—working for the National Film Board and the Canadian Broadcasting Corporation—and had given that up only recently, to come back to Walley and be a teacher. What made him give it up? This and that, he said. Machiavellis here and there. Empire-building. Exhaustion.

Gail came to Walley one summer in the seventies. The boyfriend she was with then was a boatbuilder, and she sold clothes that she made—capes with appliqués, shirts with billowing sleeves, long bright skirts. She got space in the back of the craft shop, when winter came on. She learned about import-ing ponchos and thick socks from Bolivia and Guatemala. She found local women to knit sweaters. One day Will stopped her on the street and asked her to help him with the costumes for the play he was putting on—*The Skin of Our Teeth*. Her boyfriend moved to Vancouver.

She told Will some things about herself early on, in case he should think that with her capable build and pink skin and wide gentle forehead she was exactly the kind of woman to start a family on. She told him that she had had a baby, and that when she and her boyfriend were moving some furni-ture in a borrowed van, from Thunder Bay to Toronto, carbon-monoxide fumes had leaked in, just enough to make them feel sick but enough to kill the baby, who was seven weeks old. After that Gail was sick—she had a pelvic inflammation. She decided she did not want to have another child and it would have been difficult anyway, so she had a hysterectomy.

Will admired her. He said so. He did not feel obliged to say, What a tragedy! He did not even obliquely suggest that the death was the result of choices Gail had made. He was entranced with her then. He thought her brave and generous and resourceful and gifted. The costumes she designed and made for him were perfect, miraculous. Gail thought that his view of her, of her life, showed a touching innocence. It seemed to her that far from being a free and generous spirit, she had often been anxious and desperate and had spent a lot of time doing laundry and worrying about money and feeling she owed so much to any man who took up with her. She did not think she was in love with Will then, but she liked his looks—his energetic body, so upright it seemed taller than it was, his flung-back head, shiny fore-head, springy ruff of greying hair. She liked to watch him at rehearsals, or just talking to his students. How skilled and intrepid he seemed as a direc-tor, how potent a personality as he walked the high-school halls or the streets of Walley. And then the slightly quaint, admiring feelings he had for her, his courtesy as a lover, the foreign pleasantness of his house and his life with Cleata—all this made Gail feel like somebody getting a unique welcome in a place where perhaps she did not truly have a right to be. That did not matter then—she had the upper hand.

So when did she stop having it? When he got used to sleeping with her when they moved in together, when they did so much work on the cottage by the river and it turned out that she was better at that kind of work than he was?

Was she a person who believed that somebody had to have the upper hand?

There came a time when just the tone of his voice, saying 'Your shoelace is undone' as she went ahead of him on a walk—just that—could fill her with despair, warning her that they had crossed over into a bleak country where his disappointment in her was boundless, his contempt impossible to chal-lenge. She would stumble eventually, break out in a rage—they would have days and nights of fierce hopelessness. Then the breakthrough, the sweet reunion, the jokes, and bewildered relief. So it went on in their life—she couldn't really understand it or tell if it was like anybody else's. But the peaceful periods seemed to be getting longer, the dangers retreating, and she had no inkling that he was waiting to meet somebody like this new person, Sandy, who would seem to him as alien and delightful as Gail herself had once been.

Will probably had no inkling of that, either.

He had never had much to say about Sandy—Sandra—who had come to Walley last year on an exchange program to see how drama was being taught in Canadian schools. He had said she was a young Turk. Then he had said she mightn't even have heard that expression. Very soon, there had developed some sort of electricity, or danger, around her name. Gail got some information from other sources. She heard that Sandy had challenged Will in front of his class. Sandy had said that the plays he wanted to do were 'not relevant'. Or maybe it was 'not revolutionary'.

'But he likes her,' one of his students said. 'Oh, yeah, he *really likes* her.'

Sandy didn't stay around long. She went on to observe the teaching of drama in the other schools. But she wrote to Will, and presumably he wrote back. For it turned out that they had fallen in love. Will and Sandy had fallen seriously in love, and at the end of the school year Will followed her to Australia.

Seriously in love. When Will told her that, Gail was smoking dope. She had taken it up again, because being around Will was making her so nervous.

'You mean it's not me?' Gail said. 'You mean I'm not the trouble?'

She was giddy with relief. She got into a bold and boisterous mood and bewildered Will into going to bed with her.

In the morning they tried to avoid being in the same room together. They agreed not to correspond. Perhaps later, Will said. Gail said, 'Suit yourself.'

But one day at Cleata's house Gail saw his writing on an envelope that had surely been left where she could see it. Cleata had left it—Cleata who never spoke one word about the fugitives. Gail wrote down the return address: 16 Eyre Rd, Toowong, Brisbane, Queensland, Australia.

It was when she saw Will's writing that she understood how useless everything had become to her. This bare-fronted pre-Victorian house in Walley, and the veranda, and the drinks, and the catalpa tree that she was always looking at, in Cleata's back yard. All the trees and streets in Walley, and the liberating views of the lake and the comfort of the shop. Useless cutouts, fakes and props. The real scene was hidden from her, in Australia.

That was why she found herself sitting on the plane beside the woman with the diamond rings. Her own hands have no rings on them, no polish on the nails—the skin is dry from all the work she does with cloth. She used to call the clothes she made 'handcrafted', until Will made her embarrassed about that description. She still doesn't quite see what was wrong.

She sold the shop—she sold it to Donalda, who had wanted to buy it for a long time. She took the money, and she got herself onto a flight to Australia and did not tell anyone where she was going. She lied, talking about a long holiday that would start off in England. Then somewhere in Greece for the winter, then who knows?

The night before she left, she did a transformation on herself. She cut off her heavy reddish-grey hair and put a dark-brown rinse on what was left of it. The colour that resulted was strange—a deep maroon, obviously artificial but rather too sombre for any attempt at glamour. She picked out from her shop—even though the contents no longer belonged to her—a dress of a kind she would never usually wear, a jacket-dress of dark-blue linen-look polyester with lightning stripes of red and yellow. She is tall, and broad in the hips, and she usually wears things that are loose and graceful. This outfit gives her chunky shoulders, and cuts her legs at an unflattering spot above the knees. What sort of woman did she think she was making herself into? The sort that a woman like Phyllis would play bridge with? If so, she has got it wrong. She has come out looking like somebody who has spent most of her life in uniform, at some worthy, poorly paid job (perhaps in a hospital cafeteria?), and now has spent too much money for a dashing dress that will turn out to be inappropriate and uncomfortable, on the holiday of her life.

That doesn't matter. It is a disguise.

In the airport washroom, on a new continent, she sees that the dark hair colouring, insufficiently rinsed out the night before, has mixed with her sweat and is trickling down her neck.

Gail has landed in Brisbane, still not used to what time of day it is and persecuted by so hot a sun. She is still wearing her horrid dress, but she has washed her hair so that the colour no longer runs.

She has taken a taxi. Tired as she is, she cannot settle, cannot rest until she has seen where they live. She has already bought a map and found Eyre Road. A short, curving street. She asks to be let out at the corner, where there is a little grocery store. This is the place where they buy their milk, most likely, or other things that they may have run out of. Detergent, aspirin, tampons.

The fact that Gail never met Sandy was of course an ominous thing. It must have meant that Will knew something very quickly. Later attempts to ferret out a description did not yield much. Tall rather than short. Thin rather than fat. Fair rather than dark. Gail had a mental picture of one of those long-legged, short-haired, energetic, and boyishly attractive girls. *Women.* But she wouldn't know Sandy if she ran into her.

Would anybody know Gail? With her dark glasses and her unlikely hair, she feels so altered as to be invisible. It's also the fact of being in a strange country that has transformed her. She's not tuned into it yet. Once she gets tuned in, she may not be able to do the bold things she can do now. She has to walk this street, look at the house, right away, or she may not be able to do it at all.

The road that the taxi climbed was steep, up from the brown river. Eyre Road runs along a ridge. There is no sidewalk, jut a dusty path. No one walking, no cars passing, no shade. Fences of boards or a kind of basket-weaving—wattles?—or in some cases high hedges covered with flowers. No, the flowers are really leaves of a purplish-pink or crimson colour. Trees unfamiliar to Gail are showing over the fence. They have tough-looking dusty foliage, scaly or stringy bark, a shabby ornamental air. An indifference or vague ill will about them, which she associated with the tropics. Walking on the path ahead of her are a pair of guinea hens, stately and preposterous.

The house where Will and Sandy live is hidden by a board fence, painted a pale green. Gail's heart shrinks—her heart is in a cruel clutch, to see that fence, that green.

The road is a dead end so she has to turn around. She walks past the house again. In the fence there are gates to let a car in and out. There is also a mail slot. She noticed one of these before in a fence in front of another house, and the reason she noticed it was that there was a magazine sticking out. So the mailbox is not very deep, and a hand, slipping in, might be able to find an envelope resting on its end. If the mail has not been taken out yet by a person in the house. And Gail does slip a hand in. She can't stop herself. She finds a letter there, just as she had thought it might be. She puts it into her purse.

She calls a taxi from the shop at the corner of the street. 'What part of the States are you from?' the man in the shop asks her.

'Texas,' she says. She has an idea that they would like you to be from Texas, and indeed the man lifts his eyebrows, whistles.

'I thought so,' he says.

It is Will's own writing on the envelope. Not a letter to Will, then, but a letter from him. A letter he has sent to Ms Catherine Thornaby, 491 Hawtre Street. Also in Brisbane. Another hand has scrawled across it 'Return to Sender, Died Sept. 13.' For a moment, in her disordered state of mind, Gail thinks that this means that Will has died.

She has got to calm down, collect herself, stay out of the sun for a bit.

Nevertheless, as soon as she has read the letter in her hotel room, and has tidied herself up, she takes another taxi, this time to Hawtre Street, and finds, as she expected, a sign in the window: 'Flat to let.'

But what is in the letter that Will has written Ms Catherine Thornaby, on Hawtre Street?

Dear Ms Thornaby,
    You do not know me, but I hope that once I have explained myself, we may meet and talk. I believe that I may be a Canadian cousin of yours, my grandfa-

*ther having come to Canada from Northumberland sometime in the 1870s about
the same time as a brother of his went to Australia. My grandfather's name was
William, like my own, his brother's name was Thomas. Of course I have no proof
that you are descended from this Thomas. I simply looked in the Brisbane phone
book and was delighted to find there a Thornaby spelled in the same way. I used
to think this family-tracing business was the silliest, most boring thing imaginable but now that I find myself doing it, I discover there is a strange excitement
about it. Perhaps it is my age—I am 56—that urges me to find connections. And I
have more time on my hands than I am used to. My wife is working with a theatre here which keeps her busy till all hours. She is a very bright and energetic
young woman. (She scolds me if I refer to any female over 18 as a girl and she is
all of 28!) I taught drama in a Canadian high school but I have not yet found
any work in Australia.*

Wife. He is trying to be respectable in the eyes of the possible cousin.

Dear Mr Thornaby,
    *The name we share may be a more common one than you suppose, though I
am at present its only representative in the Brisbane phone book. You may not
know that the name comes from Thorn Abbey, the ruins of which are still to be
seen in Northumberland. The spelling varies—Thornaby, Thornby, Thornabbey,
Thornabby. In the Middle Ages the name of the Lord of the Manor would be
taken as a surname by all the people working on the estate, including labourers,
blacksmiths, carpenters, etc. As a result there are many people scattered around
the world bearing a name that in the strict sense they have no right to. Only those
who can trace their descent from the family in the twelfth century are the true,
armigerous Thornabys. That is, they have the right to display the family coat of
arms. I am one of these Thornabys and since you do not mention anything about
the coat of arms and do not trace your ancestry back beyond this William I
assume that you are not. My grandfather's name was Jonathan.*

Gail writes this on an old portable typewriter that she has bought from
the secondhand shop down the street. By this time she is living at 491
Hawtre Street, in an apartment building called the Miramar. It is a two-
storey building covered with dingy cream stucco, with twisted pillars on
either side of a grilled entryway. It has a perfunctory Moorish or Spanish or
Californian air, like that of an old movie theatre. The manager told her that
the flat was very modern.
    'An elderly lady had it, but she had to go to the hospital. Then somebody
came when she died and got her effects out, but it still has the basic furniture that goes with the flat. What part of the States are you from?'
    Oklahoma, Gail said. Mrs Massie, from Oklahoma.
    The manager looks to be about seventy years old. He wears glasses that
magnify his eyes, and he walks quickly, but rather unsteadily, tilting forward.
He speaks of difficulties—the increase of the foreign element in the popula-

tion, which makes it hard to find good repairmen, the carelessness of certain tenants, the malicious acts of passersby who continually litter the grass. Gail asks if he had put in a notice yet to the Post Office. He says he has been intending to, but the lady did not receive hardly any mail. Except one letter came. It was a strange thing that it came right the day after she died. He sent it back.

'I'll do it,' Gail said. 'I'll tell the Post Office.'

'I'll have to sign it, though. Get me one of those forms they have and I'll sign it and you can give it in. I'd be obliged.'

The walls of the apartment are painted white—this must be what is modern about it. It has bamboo blinds, a tiny kitchen, a green sofa bed, a table, a dresser, and two chairs. On the wall one picture, which might have been a painting or a tinted photograph. A yellowish-green desert landscape, with rocks and bunches of sage and dim distant mountains. Gail is sure that she has seen this before.

She paid the rent in cash. She had to be busy for a while, buying sheets and towels and groceries, a few pots and dishes, the typewriter. She had to open a bank account, become a person living in the country, not a traveller. There are shops hardly a block away. A grocery store, a secondhand store, a drugstore, a tea shop. They are all humble establishments with strips of coloured paper hanging in the doorways, wooden awnings over the sidewalk in front. Their offerings are limited. The tea shop has only two tables, the secondhand store contains scarcely more than the tumbled-out accumulation of one ordinary house. The cereal boxes in the grocery store, the bottles of cough syrup and packets of pills in the drugstore are set out singly on the shelves, as if they were of special value or significance.

But she has found what she needs. In the secondhand store she found some loose flowered cotton dresses, a straw bag for her groceries. Now she looks like the other women she sees on the street. Housewives, middle-aged, with bare but pale arms and legs, shopping in the early morning or late afternoon. She bought a floppy straw hat too, to shade her face as the women do. Dim, soft, freckly, blinking faces.

Night comes suddenly around six o'clock and she must find occupation for the evenings. There is no television in the apartment. But a little beyond the shops there is a lending library, run by an old woman out of the front room of her house. This woman wears a hairnet and grey lisle stockings in spite of the heat. (Where, nowadays, can you find grey lisle stockings?) She has an undernourished body and colourless, tight, unsmiling lips. She is the person Gail calls to mind when she writes the letter from Catherine Thornaby. She thinks of this library woman by that name whenever she sees her, which is almost every day, because you are only allowed one book at a time and Gail usually reads a book a night. She thinks, There is Catherine Thornaby, dead and moved into a new existence a few blocks away.

All the business about armigerous and non-armigerous Thornabys came out of a book. Not one of the books that Gail is reading now but one she read in her youth. The hero was the non-armigerous but deserving heir to a great property. She cannot remember the title. She lived with people then who were always reading *Steppenwolf*, or *Dune*, or something by Kirshnamurti, and she read historical romances apologetically. She did not think Will would have read such a book or picked up this sort of information. And she is sure that he will have to reply, to tell Catherine off.

She waits, and reads the books from the lending library, which seem to come from an even earlier time than those romances she read twenty years ago. Some of them she took out of the public library in Winnipeg before she left home, and they seemed old-fashioned even then. *The Girl of the Limberlost. The Blue Castle. Maria Chapdelaine.* Such books remind her, naturally, of her life before Will. There was such a life and she could still salvage something from it, if she wanted to. She has a sister living in Winnipeg. She has an aunt there, in a nursing home, who still reads books in Russian. Gail's grandparents came from Russia, her parents could still speak Russian, her real name is not Gail, but Galya. She cut herself off from her family—or they cut her off—when she left home at eighteen to wander about the country, as you did in those days. First with friends, then with a boyfriend, then with another boyfriend. She strung beads and tie-dyed scarves and sold them on the street.

Dear Ms Thornaby,

I must thank you for enlightening me as to the important distinction between the armigerous and the non-armigerous Thornabys. I gather that you have a strong suspicion that I may turn out to be one of the latter. I beg your pardon—I had no intention of treading on such sacred ground or of wearing the Thornaby coat of arms on my T-shirt. We do not take much account of such things in my country and I did not think you did so in Australia, but I see that I am mistaken. Perhaps you are too far on in years to have noticed the change in values. It is quite different with me, since I have been in the teaching profession and am constantly brought up, as well, against the energetic arguments of a young wife.

My innocent intention was simply to get in touch with somebody in this country outside the theatrical-academic circle that my wife and I seem to be absorbed in. I have a mother in Canada, whom I miss. In fact your letter reminded me of her a little. She would be capable of writing such a letter for a joke but I doubt whether you are joking. It sounds like a case of Exalted Ancestry to me.

When he is offended and disturbed in a certain way—a way that is hard to predict and hard for most people to recognize—Will becomes heavily sarcastic. Irony deserts him. He flails about, and the effect is to make people embarrassed not for himself, as he intends, but for him. This happens seldom, usually when it happens it means that he feels deeply unappreciated. It means that he has even stopped appreciating himself.

So that is what happened. Gail thinks so. Sandy and her young friends with their stormy confidence, their crude righteousness might be making him miserable. His wit not taken notice of, his enthusiasm out-of-date. No way of making himself felt among them. His pride in being attached to Sandy going gradually sour.

She thinks so. He is shaky and unhappy and casting about to know somebody else. He has thought of family ties, here in this country of non-stop blooming and impudent bird life and searing days and suddenly clamped-down nights.

Dear Mr Thornaby,

Did you really expect me, just because I have the same surname as you, to fling open my door and put out the 'welcome mat'—as I think you say in America and that inevitably includes Canada? You may be looking for another mother here, but that hardly obliges me to be one. By the way you are quite wrong about my age—I am younger than you by several years, so do not picture me as an elderly spinster in a hairnet with grey lisle stockings. I know the world probably as well as you do. I travel a good deal, being a fashion buyer for a large store. So my ideas are not so out-of-date as you suppose.

You do not say whether your busy energetic young wife was to be part of this familial friendship. I am surprised you feel the need for other contacts. It seems I am always reading or hearing on the media about these 'May-December' relationships and how invigorating they are and how happily the men are settling down to domesticity and parenthood. (No mention of the 'trial runs' with women closer to their own age or mention of how those women are settling down to their lives of loneliness!) So perhaps you need to become a papa to give you a 'sense of family'!

Gail is surprised at how fluently she writes. She has always found it hard to write letters, and the results have been dull and sketchy, with many dashes and incomplete sentences and pleas of insufficient time. WHere has she got this fine nasty style—out of some book, like the armigerous nonsense? She goes out in the park to post her letter feeling bold and satisfied. But she wakes up early the next morning thinking that she has certainly gone too far. He will never answer that, she will never hear from him again.

She gets up and leaves the building, goes for a morning walk. The shops are still shut up, the broken venetian blinds are closed, as well as they can be, in the windows of the front-room library. She walks as far as the river, where there is a strip of park beside a hotel. Later in the day, she could not walk or sit there because the verandas of the hotel were always crowded with uproarious beer-drinkers, and the park was within their verbal or even bottle-throwing range. Now the verandas are empty, the doors are closed, and she walks in under the trees. The brown water of the river spreads sluggishly among the mangrove stumps. Birds are flying over the water, lighting on the hotel roof. They are not sea gulls, as she thought at first. They are smaller than gulls, and their bright white wings and breasts are touched with pink.

In the park two men are sitting—one on a bench, one in a wheelchair beside the bench. She recognizes them—they live in her building, and go for walks every day. Once, she held the grille open for them to pass through. She has seen them at the shops, and sitting at the table in the tearoom window. The man in the wheelchair looks quite old and ill. His face is puckered like old blistered paint. He wears dark glasses and a coal-black toupee and a black beret over that. He is all wrapped up in a blanket. Even later in the day, when the sun is hot—every time she has seen them—he has appeared wrapped in this plaid blanket. The man who pushes the wheelchair and who now sits on the bench is young enough to look like an overgrown boy. He is tall and large-limbed but not manly. A young giant, bewildered by his own extent. Strong but not athletic, with a stiffness, maybe of timidity, in his thick arms and legs and neck. Red hair not just on his head but on his bare arms and above the buttons of his shirt.

Gail halts in her walk past them, she says good morning. The young man answers almost inaudibly. It seems to be his habit to look out at the world with majestic indifference, but she thinks her greeting has given him a twitch of embarrassment or apprehension. Nevertheless, she speaks again, she says, 'What are those birds I see everywhere?'

'Galah birds,' the young man says, making it sound something like her childhood name. She is going to ask him to repeat it, when the old man bursts out what seems like a string of curses. The words are knotted and incomprehensible to her, because of the Australian accent on top of some European accent, but the concentrated viciousness is beyond any doubt. And these words are meant for her—he is leaning forward, in fact struggling to free himself from the straps that hold him in. He wants to leap at her, lunge at her, chase her out of sight. The young man makes no apology and does not take any notice of Gail but leans towards the old man and gently pushes him back, saying things to him which she cannot hear. She sees that there will be no explanation. She walks away.

For ten days, no letter. No word. She cannot think what to do. She walks every day—that is mostly what she does. The Miramar is only about a mile or so away from Will's street. She never walks in that street again or goes into the shop where she told the man that she was from Texas. She cannot imagine how she could have been so bold, the first day. She does walk in the streets nearby. Those streets all go along ridges. In between the ridges, which the houses cling to, there are steep-sided gullies full of birds and trees. Even as the sun grows hot, those birds are not quiet. Magpies keep up their disquieting conversation and sometimes emerge to make menacing flights at her light-coloured hat. The birds with the name like her own cry out foolishly as they rise and whirl about and subside into the leaves. She walks till she is dazed and sweaty and afraid of sunstroke. She shivers in the heat—most fearful, most desirous, of seeing Will's utterly familiar figure, that one rather small and jaunty, free-striding package, of all that could pain or appease her, in the world.

Dear Mr Thornaby

This is just a short note to beg your pardon if I was impolite and hasty in my replies to you, as I am sure I was. I have been under some stress lately, and have taken a leave of absence to recuperate. Under these circumstances one does not always behave as well as one would hope or see things as rationally. . . .

One day she walks past the hotel and the park. The verandas are clamorous with the afternoon drinking. All the trees in the park have come out in bloom. The flowers are a colour that she has seen and could not have imagined on trees before—a shade of silvery blue, or silvery purple, so delicate and beautiful that you would think it would shock everything into quietness, into contemplation, but apparently it has not.

When she gets back to the Miramar, she finds the young man with the red hair standing in the downstairs hall, outside the door of the apartment where he lives with the old man. From behind the closed apartment door come the sounds of a tirade.

The young man smiles at her, this time. She stops and they stand together, listening.

Gail says, 'If you would ever like a place to sit down while you're waiting, you know you're welcome to come upstairs.'

He shakes his head, still smiling as if this was a joke between them. She thinks she should say something else before she leaves him there, so she asks him about the trees in the park. 'Those trees beside the hotel,' she says. 'Where I saw you the other morning? They are all out in bloom now. What are they called?'

He says a word she cannot catch. She asks him to repeat it. 'Jack Randa,' he says. 'That's the Jack Randa Hotel.'

Dear Ms Thornaby,

I have been away and when I came back I found both your letters waiting for me. I opened them in the wrong order, though that really doesn't matter.

My mother has died. I have been 'home' to Canada for her funeral. It is cold there, autumn. Many things have changed. Why I should want to tell you this I simply do not know. We have certainly got off on the wrong track with each other. Even if I had not got your note of explanation after the first letter you wrote, I think I would have been glad in a peculiar way to get the first letter. I wrote you a very snippy and unpleasant letter and you wrote me back one of the same. The snippiness and unpleasantness and readiness to take offence seems somehow familiar to me. Ought I to risk your armigerous wrath by suggesting that we may be related after all?

I feel adrift here. I admire my wife and her theatre friends, with their zeal and directness and commitment, their hope of using their talents to create a better world. (I must say though that it often seems to me that the hope and zeal exceed the talents.) I cannot be one of them. I must say that they saw this before I did. It must be because I am woozy with jet lag after that horrendous flight that I can face up to this fact and that I write it down in a letter to someone like you who has her own troubles and quite correctly has indicated she doesn't want to be bothered with mine. I had better close, in fact, before I burden you with further claptrap from my psyche. I wouldn't blame you if you had stopped reading before you got this far. . . .

Gail lies on the sofa pressing this letter with both hands against her stomach. Many things are changed. He has been in Walley, then—he has been told how she sold the shop and started out on her great world trip. But wouldn't he have heard that anyway, from Cleata? Maybe not, Cleata was close-mouthed. And when she went into the hospital, just before Gail left, she said, 'I don't want to see or hear from anybody for a while or bother with letters. These treatments are bound to be a bit melodramatic.'

Cleata is dead.

Gail knew that Cleata would die, but somehow thought that everything would hold still, nothing could really happen there while she, Gail, remained here. Cleata is dead and Will is alone except for Sandy, and Sandy perhaps has stopped being of much use to him.

There is a knock on the door. Gail jumps up in a great disturbance, looking for a scarf to cover her hair. It is the manager, calling her false name.

'I just wanted to tell you I had somebody here asking questions. He asked me about Miss Thornaby and I said, Oh, she's dead. She's been dead for some time now. He said, Oh, has she? I said, Yes, she has, and he said, Well, that's strange.'

'Did he say why?' Gail says, 'Did he say why it was strange?'

'No. I said, She died in the hospital and I've got an American lady in the flat now. I forgot where you told me you came from. He sounded like an American himself, so it might've meant something to him. I said, There was a letter come for Miss Thornaby after she was dead, did you write that letter? I told him I sent it back. Yes, he said, I wrote it, but I never got it back. There must be some kind of mistake, he said.'

Gail says there must be. 'Like a mistaken identity,' she says.

'Yes. Like that.'

Dear Ms Thornaby,

It has come to my attention that you are dead. I know that life is strange, but I have never found it quite this strange before. Who are you and what is going on? It seems this rigamarole about the Thornabys must have been just that—a rigamarole. You must certainly be a person with time on your hands and a fantasizing turn of mind. I resent being taken in but I suppose I understand the temptation. I do think you owe me an explanation now as to whether or not my explanation is true and this is some joke. Or am I dealing with some 'fashion buyer' from beyond the grave? (Where did you get that touch or is it the truth?)

When Gail goes out to buy food, she uses the back door of the building, she takes a roundabout route to the shops. On her return by the same back-door route, she comes upon the young red-haired man standing between the dustbins. If he had not been so tall, you might have said that he was hidden there. She speaks to him but he doesn't answer. He looks at her through tears, as if the tears were nothing but a wavy glass, something usual.

'Is your father sick?' Gail says to him. She has decided that this must be the relationship, though the age gap seems greater than usual between father and son, and the two of them are quite unalike in looks, and the young man's patience and fidelity are so far beyond—nowadays they seem even contrary to—anything a son customarily shows. But they go beyond anything a hired attendant might show, as well.

'No,' the young man says, and though his expression stays calm, a drowning flush spreads over his face, under the delicate redhead's skin.

Lovers, Gail thinks. She is suddenly sure of it. She feels a shiver of sympathy, an odd gratification.

Lovers.

She goes down to her mailbox after dark and finds there another letter.

I might have thought that you were out of town on one of your fashion-buying jaunts but the manager tells me you have not been away since taking the flat, so I must suppose your 'leave of absence' continues. He tells me also that you are a brunette. I suppose we might exchange descriptions—and then, with trepidation, photographs—in the brutal manner of people meeting through newspaper ads. It seems that in my attempt to get to know you I am willing to make quite a fool of myself. Nothing new of course in that. . . .

Gail does not leave the apartment for two days. She does without milk, drinks her coffee black. What will she do when she runs out of coffee? She eats odd meals—tuna fish spread on crackers when she has no bread to make a sandwich, a dry end of cheese, a couple of mangos. She goes out into the upstairs hall of the Miramar—first opening the door a crack, testing the air for an occupant—and walks to the arched window that overlooks the street. And from long ago a feeling comes back to her—the feeling of watching a street, the visible bit of a street, where a car is expected to appear, or may appear, or may not appear. She even remembers now the cars themselves—a blue Austin mini, a maroon Chevrolet, a family station wagon. Cars in which she travelled short distances, illicitly and in a bold daze of consent. Long before Will.

She doesn't know what clothes Will will be wearing, or how his hair is cut, or if he will have some change in his walk or expression, some change appropriate to his life here. He cannot have changed more than she has. She has no mirror in the apartment except the little one on the bathroom cupboard, but even that can tell her how much thinner she has got and how the skin of her face has toughened. Instead of fading and wrinkling as fair skin often does in this climate, hers has got a look of dull canvas. It could be fixed up—she sees that. With the right kind of makeup a look of exotic sullenness could be managed. Her hair is more of a problem—the red shows at the roots, with shiny strands of grey. Nearly all the time she keeps it hidden by a scarf.

When the manager knocks on her door again, she has only a second or two of crazy expectation. He begins to call her name. 'Mrs Massie, Mrs Massie! Oh, I hoped you'd be in. I wondered if you could just come down and help me. It's the old bloke downstairs, he's fallen off the bed.'

He goes ahead of her down the stairs, holding to the railing and dropping each foot shakily, precipitately, onto the step below.

'His friend isn't there. I wondered. I didn't see him yesterday. I try and keep track of people but I don't like to interfere. I thought he probably would've come back in the night. I was sweeping out the foyer and I heard a thump and I went back in there—I wondered what was going on. Old bloke all by himself, on the floor.'

The apartment is no larger than Gail's, and laid out in the same way. It has curtains down over the bamboo blinds, which make it very dark. It smells of cigarettes and old cooking and some kind of pine-scented air freshener. The sofa bed has been pulled out, made into a double bed, and the old man is lying on the floor beside it, having dragged some of the bedclothes with him. His head without the toupee is smooth, like a dirty piece of soap. His eyes are half shut and a noise is coming from deep inside him like the noise of an engine hopelessly trying to turn over.

'Have you phoned the ambulance?' Gail says.

'If you could just pick up the one end of him,' the manager says. 'I have a bad back and I dread putting it out again.'

'Where is the phone?' says Gail. 'He may have had a stroke. He may have broken his hip. He'll have to go to the hospital.'

'Do you think so? His friend could lift him back and forth so easy. He had the strength. And now he's disappeared.'

Gail says, 'I'll phone.'

'Oh, no. Oh, no. I have the number written down over the phone in my office. I don't let any other person go in there.'

Left alone with the old man, who probably cannot hear her, Gail says, 'It's all right. It's all right. We're getting help for you.' Her voice sounds foolishly sociable. She leans down to pull the blanket up over his shoulder, and to her great surprise a hand flutters out, searches for and grabs her own. His hand is slight and bony, but warm enough, and dreadfully strong. 'I'm here, I'm here,' she says, and wonders if she is impersonating the red-haired young man, or some other young man, or woman, or even his mother.

The ambulance comes quickly, with its harrowing pulsing cry, and the ambulance men with the stretcher cart are soon in the room, the manager stumping after them, saying, '. . . couldn't be moved. Here is Mrs Massie came down to help in the emergency.'

While they are getting the old man onto the stretcher, Gail has to pull her hand away, and he begins to complain, or she thinks he does—that steady involuntary-sounding noise he is making acquires an extra *ah-unh-anh*. So she takes his hand again as soon as she can, and trots beside him as he is wheeled out. He has such a grip on her that she feels as if he is pulling her along.

'He was the owner of the Jacaranda Hotel,' the manager says. 'Years ago. He was.'

A few people are in the street, but nobody stops, nobody wants to be caught gawking. They want to see, they don't want to see.

'Shall I ride with him?' Gail says. 'He doesn't seem to want to let go of me.'

'It's up to you,' one of the ambulance men says, and she climbs in. (She is dragged in, really, by that clutching hand.) The ambulance man puts down a little seat for her, the doors are closed, the siren starts as they pull away.

Through the window in the back door then she sees Will. He is about a block away from the Miramar and walking towards it. He is wearing a light-coloured short-sleeved jacket and matching pants—probably a safari suit—and his hair has grown whiter or been bleached by the sun, but she knows him at once, she will always know him, as she does now, even trying to jump up from the seat, trying to pull her hand out of the old man's grasp.

'It's Will,' she says to the ambulance man. 'Oh, I'm sorry. It's my husband.'

'Well, he better not see you jumping out of a speeding ambulance,' the man says. Then he says, 'Oh-oh. What's happened here?' For the next minute or so he pays professional attention to the old man. Soon he straightens up and says, 'Gone.'

'He's still holding on to me,' says Gail. But she realizes as she says this that it isn't true. A moment ago he was holding on—with great force, it seemed, enough force to hold her back, when she would have sprung towards Will. Now it is she who is hanging on to him. His fingers are still warm.

When she gets back from the hospital, she finds a note that she is expecting.

Gail. I know it's you.

Hurry. Hurry. Her rent is paid. She must leave a note for the manager. She must take the money out of the bank, get herself to the airport, find a flight. Her clothes can stay behind—her humble pale-print dresses, her floppy hat. The last library book can remain on the table under the sagebrush picture. It can remain there, accumulating fines.

Otherwise, what will happen?

What she has surely wanted. What she is suddenly, as surely, driven to escape.

Gail, I know you're in there! I know you're there on the other side of the door.
Gail! Gail!

Talk to me, Gail. Answer me. I know you're there.

I can hear you. I can hear your heart beating through the key-hole and your stomach rumbling and your brain jumping up and down.

I can smell you through the keyhole. You. Gail.

Words most wished for can change. Something can happen to them, while you're waiting. *Love—need—forgive. Love—need—forever.* The sound of such words can become a din, a battering, a sound of hammers in the street. And all you can do is run away, so as not to honour them out of habit.

In the airport shop she sees a number of little boxes, made by Australian aborigines. They are round, and light as pennies. She picks out one that has a pattern of yellow dots, irregularly spaced on a dark-red ground. Against this is a swollen black figure—a turtle, maybe, with short splayed legs. Helpless on its back.

Gail is thinking, A present for Cleata. As if her whole time here had been a dream, something she could discard, going back to a chosen point, a beginning.

Not for Cleata. A present for Will?

A present for Will, then. Send it now? No, take it back to Canada, all the way back, send it from there.

The yellow dots flung out in that way remind Gail of something she saw last fall. She and Will saw it. They went for a walk on a sunny afternoon. They walked from their house by the river up the wooded bank, and there they came on a display that they had heard about but never seen before.

Hundreds, maybe thousands, of butterflies were hanging in the trees, resting before their long flight down the shore of Lake Huron and across Lake Erie, then on south to Mexico. They hung there like metal leaves, beaten gold—like flakes of gold tossed up and caught in the branches.

'Like the shower of gold in the Bible,' Gail said.

Will told her that she was confusing Jove and Jehovah.

On that day, Cleata had already begun to die and Will had already met Sandy. This dream had already begun—Gail's journey and her deceits, then the words she imagined—believed—that she heard shouted through the door.

Love —forgive

Love —forget

Love —forever

Hammers in the street.

What could you put in a box like that before you wrapped it up and sent it far away? A bead, a feather, a potent pill? Or a note, folded up tight, to about the size of a spitball.

Now it's up to you to follow me.

JANE RULE

(1931)

~

The End of Summer

Canchek arrived promptly at eight in the morning in what looked like a new work shirt and trousers, boots that had been carefully cleaned. Even his beard looked freshly laundered. So well covered by hair and cloth, his age was readable only in his eyes, young enough still for consternation and hope.

'Your holiday's done you good,' Judith Thornburn said.

'Got her pumped out?' he asked, ignoring her civility in a way she didn't mind. He was a man who didn't like wasting other people's money.

'Yes, they've just left. They couldn't see any cracks in it. Neither could I.'

'You looked in it yourself?' he asked, surprised.

'I wanted to know,' she answered.

Judith had been waiting for nealy a month to get this last of the summer problems solved before she closed the house for another year. There had been too many of them, a leaky skylight, a failed pump, and finally this seeping septic tank, whose pungent odours had driven her guests off the new back terrace with its lovely view. One man had dug down to it.

'It's cracked,' he told her. 'You'll probably have to get it replaced.'

When she called Canchek in urgent concern, he said, 'I'm going sailing for three weeks. She probably just needs patching. I'll do her when I get back.'

There was only one other man who could be called about such things, Thompson, but, once you'd had one work for you, the other wouldn't come back unless you made it clear that you were switching sides. Thompson was an older man, garrulous, who told the widows and grass widows he worked for, 'Don't go looking for trouble. Just don't put no paper down her, and don't clean your sinks with nothing to interfere with the natural process. These old places, they don't like to be disturbed any more than you do. Old plumbing is old plumbing.'

'He's a harmless old coot, and at least he's friendly,' those who sided with Thompson would say, and they'd add, 'And he'll take a neighbourly drink and he doesn't still live with his mother.'

Canchek wouldn't and Canchek did. Judith wasn't old enough yet, in her mid-thirties as Canchek was, to appreciate Thompson's vulgarity. And she was a person who liked to look for trouble, get to the bottom of it, and solve it. Canchek was her man even if she had to wait.

They walked around the house together, she carrying the trowel she had been using when he arrived.

'I thought I might lift some of the plants if you show me where you have to dig.'

'Don't know yet,' he said, flashing a light into the tank.

'It's odd,' she said. 'I even saw the cracks when we uncovered the outside, right about there, and I would have sworn they went right through. Fiberglass isn't that thick.'

Canchek blew out his breath harshly before he spoke. 'Not cracked,' he said, and then he walked down the sodden earth below the tank, 'but she's been leaking all right, for quite a while.'

'Is that why that plum tree looks so sick?'

'Lost two of my own apples just to run off. Probably.' He put a sympathetic hand on the trunk as he looked up to the blackened rather than turning leaves. 'They're only drawn to so much water. Not like a man.'

Even Canchek people said he was a dour, silent man, but good at what he did, hardworking and reliable. Perhaps that's why she valued these small attempts at conversation. They made her know that Canchek liked her, or at least didn't disapprove of her as she suspected he did a lot of people, even those who chose to be his particular customers. She didn't know why he did. She drank and smoked, both of which would probably be against his beliefs. Nobody seemed quite sure what sect it was he and his mother were the lonely representatives of. He was willing to drive a truck; he even did emergency work on Sunday, but his beard looked more like a religious than a personal choice. Judith knew so little about religious choices, she wasn't sure what anybody believed or was supposed to believe. She was not yet divorced, but the prospect seemed more and more likely. Surely Canchek wouldn't approve of that. He could easily have heard the gossip, if he listened to such things, about the Thornburn woman, out here most of the summer by herself. Husband bought her the place to get her out of the way, as so many of them did. A fancy car, a boat, whatever else she wanted or he wanted for her to show that she was well provided for. He didn't give her the one thing a man ought to give a woman: a child. Maybe, in a world increasingly both careless and frantic about money, Canchek liked her simply because the Thornburns were willing to pay the cost promptly of having things fixed.

'You can save the daisies,' he said, pointing. 'I'll save only some of the bulbs.' Did he notice her regret when he added, 'but bulbs just turn up, don't they?'

She wanted to save what flowers she could, but she also felt less guilty about asking him, or anyone, to do such an unpleasant job if she didn't flinch from it herself, and worked along with him.

'Funny thing,' Canchek said as he began to dig in the area she'd indicated. 'Man's the only animal that doesn't like his own smell.'

Judith heard the lines, 'And all is seared with trade; bleared, smeared with toil;/And wears man's smudge and shares man's smell.' Certainly Hopkins didn't like it.

It was warm enough, now that the early morning fog was burning off, for another workman to take off his shirt. Canchek would not. Judith had to imagine his shoulders, the muscles of his back. She was not so much attracted to him as curious. The skin on her husband's back already began to feel like the skin of a puppy which would grow into a large dog.

Judith supposed he still made love to her the way he still paid the bills, as a responsibility. He hadn't said anything about a divorce yet. When he first became involved with another woman and Judith confronted him, he said he expected her to be civilized about it. In front of him, she was. Alone her hysterical crying fits and destructive rages so humiliated her that he was the last person she'd subject to them. Judith hadn't even spoken to her close friends because her grief and her shame were both so boring and so predictable, as was her fantasy of being his mistress instead of his wife, the one he ran away to. This last summer, in fact, he was occasionally running away from his mistress to Judith or the quiet life she provided at what they called 'the cottage'. It was a good-sized house, set in some acres of woods, just across the road from the sea. His mistress was not being civilized, or she owned a vicious cat.

'At this point, my dear,' said a friend Judith hadn't confided in, 'they go back to their wives.'

Judith couldn't see why. There were no children for whose sake things should be done. For herself, he didn't any longer seem much of a prize for her good behaviour: 'Home is the sailor, home from the sea, and the hunter home from the hill.' She would never expel him from the world he had paid for, but she would not move out once he'd left either.

'Look,' Canchek said, 'This must be the crack you saw.'

She walked over and looked at the exposed curve of a badly damaged septic tank.

'That's it,' she agreed.

'Well, she's not yours. She's another one.'

'Really?'

'They must of broken this one putting her in, just smashed her up a bit more and put in this other one.'

'Why didn't they take the broken one out?'

'Couldn't be bothered maybe. These guys with machines won't get off them. Some of them don't even own a shovel.'

Canchek pulled great pieces of fibreglass out of the soil until he and she could have played at a giant jigsaw puzzle, but he was not interested in the wreckage. He wanted to find out what was leaking. As he dug, he occasionally grunted in discovery and disgust.

'There's no septic field here at all, nothing but some tile and mud. I'll have to get pipe.'

He had done enough work around the place for her to know he begrudged any purchase of new material if what was around could be used. Whether it belonged to the rich or the pensioned, money was money.

'We'll need some rocks,' he said, kicking about in the tall grass where cultivation ended.

'There's a pile over here,' she offered. 'They came out of the garden.'

He did not look up or acknowledge her offer, intent on his own search which seemed to her odd. Judith would not have looked for rocks like Easter eggs in the field grass.

Canchek grunted and sank down on his haunches, like a hunter checking prints and droppings, only the crest of his dark hair visible among the tassle tops. Then he stood up, shaking his head.

'You know, there's as sure a wrong way to do it as there is a right way. Look at this.'

Judith followed his path to where he stood, and there spreading out beside him was a sprawling pile of stones nearly uniform in size, hidden in the tall grass. She remembered having seen it in spring, matted over with last year's rot before new grass began to grow again.

'Why do they even dump it on the site if they don't intend to use it?' he asked himself and then gave his answer. 'They call in the inspector just before they're going to lay the pipe. He sees the trenches. He sees the pile of rock, says, 'Okay, boys, that's good.' And the minute he turns his back, they bulldoze the trenches and go home. What did I tell you? Not a shovel to their name!'

It was a long speech for Canchek. He walked over to the collapsed septic tank and dragged it over to his van.

'I'll take this to the dump on my way to get the pipe,' he said.

'You can fix it then?' she asked.

'Sure, today,' he answered and smiled at her slumping relief.

Judith had had her frugal lunch before Canchek returned, knowing he would have stopped for a man's lunch with his mother, a woman Judith had never met. Mrs Canchek spoke only enough English to call her son to the phone or say when he would be back. As far as Judith knew, she never left the place, a well-made log cabin in a clearing as neat and bare as a table top between meals. Canchek did their shopping. Occasionally Mrs Canchek could be seen behind the high deer fence around the vegetable garden, hoeing, drab kerchief around her head, skirts to the ground, a peasant in a painting. There were neither chickens nor dog to keep her company. The only sign of companionability was a bird feeder outside what was probably a kitchen window. No one was ever invited in.

Judith did not go out at once to greet him. She stayed at her own kitchen table and watched him work, shoveling new trenches away from the uncovered septic tank, like fingers stretching away from a palm, down hill. It was hot now, and, though the tank had been emptied, the soil he dug in must be putrid with clogging waste. Yet he was taking time, like a man not reckoning the hours, to sift what good bulbs he found and pile them for her to replant in the restored bed. As son to woman, obedient to her love of flowers, though there were none in his own beaten and swept yard. Was he, in fact, good to his mother? Or did he go home and sit sullen with the burden she was to him and let her bring him servile offerings?

The phone rang. Judith let it ring six times before she answered it.

'Outdoors, were you?' her husband asked, his dictating cheerfulness always freshly insulting her.

Judith wanted to answer truthfully, but instead said, 'I'm digging out the septic tank with Canchek.'

'My God, Judy, martyrdom doesn't have to go that far. Surely, the man is paid enough—if I recall the last bill correctly—to do it himself.'

'I wanted to save the bulbs,' she answered defensively.

'Buy more; buy a carload.'

Is there any point? Is there going to be a next year, she wanted to ask him, but she didn't.

'One of the reasons Canchek's so expensive is that he's too cheap to buy himself machinery. Is he out there with a shovel? I bet he is.'

'He says it's the only way to do it properly,' Judith answered.

'Once a shit shoveller, always a shit shoveller. Is he going to get it done by the week-end?'

'He said he'd be finished today.'

'Good. I'll be down then, tomorrow.'

'Driving?'

'No, I'm beat. I'll take the early train.'

He didn't ask her to meet him any more than he would ask to come down. At first, she had cancelled whatever other plans she had made either to go out, which he wouldn't want to do, or have friends in, because she didn't trust herself to keep up the façade with an attentive audience. Lately, she had not made week-end plans, a time she spent either in relieved loneliness or in nervous dread that this would be the last time. By now, she was equally afraid that he would decide to re-establish himself in their life or end it.

Canchek was now kneeling, replacing the terracotta tiles he had dug up. It would have been no use or terrible use to have had son, if not materially bound to her as Canchek was to his mother, still guilty to leave her as his father had done before him. People said it was harder for a man to leave when there were children. Was it? Sometimes Judith imagined her husband regretting his refusal to be a father, easier to leave her in children's distracting company than alone. But that allowed him some concern for her feelings. He didn't want to know she had any.

Canchek was now laying the long black perforated pipe along a trench, his feet planted on either side, walking backwards. She envied him a task to be absorbed in, then remembered the stench of it for a man whose only known pleasure was sailing, the freshening breeze taking him far out from shore until salt purified the odours of earth and the far horizon promised nothing, nothing at all.

He was standing at the back door.

'Have you got a bucket?' he asked.

His eyes were darker than they had been in the morning, as if they had absorbed the colour of earth. He had put on a sweat band. It pressed at his hairline, forcing his hair to stand up like a dark crop.

She found two buckets and went out with him to gather stones from the pile he had found. A wheelbarrow would have been more efficient, and there was one in the garden shed, but she did not want to think her husband's thoughts. A breeze had come up from shore with the faintest bite of autumn in it, cooling the afternoon, making their harvesting of rock easier. Sometimes he stopped to shovel dirt over the rock they had strewn, leaving her to haul by herself, and alone with her own job she felt more companionable with him, as if he accepted a simple partnership.

It was nearly six o'clock when they finished, the light nearly gone. She washed out the buckets while he collected scraps and tools.

'May I get you something?' Judith asked. 'Coffee? A cold drink?'

'Fill her up as soon as you can,' he said. 'I'll cover her up tomorrow, some time before dark.'

She nodded but waited, keeping the question between them.

'Her,' he said finally, nodding his head in a downward direction.

An apology, an excuse. Was that how her husband left his woman with that grunted female pronoun and a nod in the direction of the sea? Perhaps Canchek preferred a mother to a woman with more ambiguous needs and motives. Nothing bound him really but his acceptance of the bond.

'Thank you,' she said. 'I'm so glad it could be done.'

'There's always a way to do it right,' he said.

Canchek had not returned by the time Judith left to meet her husband's train. There was still an hour of daylight. To defend Canchek, she wanted him to have come and gone before she returned. For herself, she wanted him to be there when she got back, she couldn't say why. Canchek could not prevent anything from happening or make it happen, a dark figure in the dusk, shovelling.

'He doesn't look quite human,' her husband observed out the kitchen window, pouring himself a drink.

'He said yesterday, "Man's the only animal that doesn't like his own smell.' "

'What's that supposed to mean?' her husband asked.

'Just that, to him,' Judith answered.

'To you?' her husband asked, and she heard in his tone what she had been waiting for, hopefully, then dreadfully, for months.

'A reason for being civilized?' she suggested mildly.

He took a long drink and set the glass down. There wasn't a trace of sum-

mer in his face, of sea or earth. He was bleached with tiredness. She could-
n't offer him anything either. He had, in his own house, helped himself.

'I've appreciated it,' he said flatly.

The months' long fuse of her fury sputtered up toward an explosion right
behind her eyes. The second before it ignited, Canchek's fist on the back
door banged it out.

'She's done,' he said.

'Come have a drink,' Judith's husband suggested, humanly enough,
'after a stinking job like that.'

But Canchek had turned away quickly after his announcement and was
gone. Judith stood in the doorway, looking out at the buried tank, its now
secret fingers also properly rock-and-earth-covered, the surface carefully
raked to prepare for bulbs, the old ones Canchek had saved and the carload
her husband wanted her to buy. They would camouflage and be nourished
by man's 'smudge and smell', which Canchek, and perhaps all men, called
by the name of 'she', as they did ships which would bear them away. Judith
turned back to her husband.

'Thank you,' he said.

'You're welcome,' Judith answered, seeing him for the first time in
months as clearly as she saw Canchek, but this man was her husband, at
home.

AUSTIN C. CLARKE
(1932)

∽

Griff!

Griff was a black man from Barbados who sometimes denied he was black. Among black Americans who visited Toronto, he was black: 'Right on!' 'Peace and love, Brother!' and 'Power to the people!' would suddenly become his vocabulary. He had emigrated to Toronto from Britain, and as a result, thought of himself as a black Englishman. But he was blacker than most immigrants. In colour, that is. It must have been this double indemnity of being British and black that caused him to despise his blackness. To his friends, and his so-called friends, he flaunted his British experience, and the 'civilized' bearing that came with it; and he liked being referred to as a West Indian who had lived in London, for he was convinced that he had an edge, in breeding, over those West Indians who had come straight to Canada from the canefields in the islands. He had attended Ascot many times and he had seen the Queen in her box. He hated to be regarded as just black.

'Griff, but you're blasted black, man,' Clynn said once, at a party in his own home, 'and the sooner you realize that fact, the more rass-hole wiser you would be!' Clynn usually wasn't so honest, but that night he was drunk.

What bothered Griff along with his blackness was that most of his friends were 'getting through': cars and houses and 'swinging parties' every Friday night, and a yearly trip back home for Christmas and for Carnival. Griff didn't have a cent in the bank. 'And you don't even have *one* blasted child, neither!' Clynn told him that same night.

But Griff was the best-dressed man present. They all envied him for that. And nobody but his wife really knew how poor he was in pocket. Griff smiled at them from behind his dark-green dark glasses. His wife smiled too, covering her embarrassment for her husband. She never criticized him in public, by gesture or by attitude, and she said very little to him about his ways, in their incensed apartment. Nevertheless, she carried many burdens of fear and failure for her husband's apparent ambitionless attitudes. England had wiped some British manners on her, too. Deep down inside, Griff was saying to Clynn and the others, *godblindyougodblindyou!*

'Griffy, dear, pour your wife a Scotch, darling. I've decided to enjoy myself.' She was breathing as her yoga teacher had taught her to do.

And Griffy said, *godblindyougodblindyou!* again, to Clynn; poured his wife her drink, poured himself a large Scotch on the rocks, and vowed, *I am going to drink all your Scotch tonight, boy*! This was his only consolation. Clynn's words had become wounds. Griff grew so centred around his own problems that he did not, for one moment, consider any emotion coming from his wife. 'She's just a nice kid,' he told Clynn once, behind her back. He had draped his wife in an aura of sanctity; and he would become angry to the point of violence, and scare anybody, when he thought his friends' conversation had touched the cloud and virginity of sanctity in which he had clothed her: like taking her out on Friday and Saturday nights to the Cancer Calypso Club, in the entrails of the city, where pimps and doctors and lonely immigrants hustled women and brushed reputations in a brotherhood of illegal liquor. And if the Club got too crowded, Griff would feign a headache, and somehow make his wife feel the throbbing pain of his migraine, and would take her home in a taxi, and would recover miraculously on his way back along Sherbourne Street, and with the tact of a good barrister, would make tracks back to the Cancer and dance the rest of the limp-shirt night with a woman picked from among the lonely West Indian stags: his jacket let loose to the sweat and the freedom, his body sweet with the music rejoicing in the happy absence of his wife in the sweet presence of this woman.

But after these hiatuses of dance, free as the perspiration pouring down his face, his wife would be put to bed around midnight, high up in the elevator, high off the invisible hog of credit, high up on the Chargex Card, and Griff would be tense, for days. It was a tenseness which almost gripped his body in a paralysis, as it strangled the blood in his body when the payments of loans for furniture and for debts approached, and they always coincided with the approaching of his paycheque, already earmarked against its exact face value. In times of this kind of stress, like his anxiety at the racetrack, when the performance of a horse contradicted his knowledge of the Racing Form and left him broke, he would grumble, 'Money is *naught* all.'

Losing his money would cause him to ride on streetcars, and he hated any kind of public transportation. He seemed to realized his blackness more intensely; white people looking at him hard—questioning his presence, it seemed. It might be nothing more than the way his colour changed colour, going through a kaleidoscope of tints and shades under the varying ceiling lights of the streetcar. Griff never saw it this way. To him, it was staring. And his British breeding told him that to look at a person you didn't know (except she was a woman) was *infra dig*. *Infra dig* was the term he chose when he told Clynn about these incidents of people staring at him on the streetcars. The term formed itself on his broad thin lips, and he could never get the courage to spit it at the white people staring at him.

When he lost his money, his wife, after not having had dinner nor the money to buy food (the landlord locked the apartment door with a padlock one night while they were at a party), would smile in that half-censuring smile, a smile that told you she had been forced against the truth of her circumstances, to believe with him, that money was 'not all, at-all'. But left to herself, left to the ramblings of her mind and her aspirations and her fingers over the new broadloom in her girl-friend's home, where her hand clutched the tight sweating glass of Scotch on the rocks, her Scotch seeming to absorb her arriving unhappiness with the testimony of her friend's broadloom, or in Clynn's recreation room, which she called a 'den'; in her new sponge of happiness, fabricated like the house in her dreams, she would put her smile around her husband's losses, and in the embrace they would both feel higher than anybody present, because, 'Griffy, dear, you were the only one there with a Master of Arts.'

'I have more brains than *any one* there. They only coming-on strong. But I don't have to come on strong, uh mean, I don't *have* to come on strong, but . . .'

One day, at Greenwood Race Track, Griff put his hand into his pocket and pulled out five twenty-dollar bills, and put them on one race: he put three twenty-dollar bills on Number Six, on *the fucking nose—to win! Eh?* (he had been drinking earlier at the Pilot Tavern); and he also put two twenty-dollar bills on Number Six, *to show*. He had studied the Racing Form like a man studying his torts: he would put it into his pocket, take it out again, read it in the bathroom as he trimmed his moustache; he studied it on the sweet-smelling toilet bowl, he studied it as he might have studied laws in Britain; and when he spoke of his knowledge in the Racing Form, it was as if he had received his degrees in the Laws of Averages, and not in English Literature and Language.

And he 'gave' a horse to a stranger that same day at Greenwood. 'Buy Number Three, man. I read the Form for three days, taking notes. It *got* to be Number Three!' The man thanked him because he himself was no expert; and he spent five dollars (more than he had ever betted before) on Number Three, to *win*. 'I read the Form like a blasted book, man!' Griff told him. He slipped away to the wicket farthest away; and like a thief, he bought his own tickets: 'Number Six! Sixty on the nose! forty to show!' and to himself he said, smiling, 'Law o' averages, man, law of averages.'

Tearing up Number Six after the race, he said to the man who had looked for him to thank him, and who thanked him and shook his hand and smiled with him, 'I don't have to come on strong, man, I *mastered* that Form.' He looked across the field to the board at the price paid on Number Three, and then he said to the man, 'Lend me two dollars for the next race, man. I need a bet.'

The man gave him three two-dollar bills and told him, '*Any* time, pardner, any time! Keep the six dollars. Thank *you!*'

Griff was broke. Money is *naught* all, he was telling the same man who, seeing him waiting by the streetcar stop, had picked him up. Griff settled himself back into the soft leather of the new Riviera, going west, and said again to the man, 'Money is naught all! But I don't like to come on strong. Uh mean, you see how I mastered the *Form*, did you?'

'You damn right, boy!' the man said, adjusting the tone of the tape-deck. 'How you like my new car?'

The elevator was silent that evening, on the way up to the twenty-fifth floor; and he could not even lose his temper with it: 'This country is uncivilized—even the elevators—they make too much noise a man can't even think in them; this place only has money but it doesn't have any culture or breeding or style so everybody is grabbing for money money money.' The elevator that evening didn't make a comment. And neither did his wife: she had been waiting for him to come from work, straight, with the money untouched in his monthly paycheque. But Griff had studied the Racing Form thoroughly all week, and had worked out the laws and averages and notations in red felt-pin ink; had circles all the 'longshots' in green, and had moved through the 'donkeys' (the slow horses) with waves of blue lines; had had three 'sure ones' for that day; and had averaged his wins against heavy bets against his monthly salary, it was such a 'goddamn cinch'! He had developed a migraine headache immediately after lunch, sipped through the emergency exit at the side, holding his head in his hand, his head full of tips and cinches, and had caught the taxi which miraculously had been waiting there, with the meter ticking; had run through the entrance of the race-track, up the stairs, straight for the wicket to be on the Daily Double; had invested fifty dollars on a 'long shot' (worked out scientifically from his red-marked, green-and-blue wavy-line Form), and had placed 'two goddamn dollars' on the favourite—just to be sure!—and went into the clubhouse. The favourite won. Griff lost fifty dollars by the first race. But had had won two dollars on his two-dollar bet.

'I didn't want to come on strong,' he told the man who was then a stranger to him. The man could not understand what he was talking about: and he asked for no explanation. 'I didn't want to come on strong, but I worked out all the winners today, since ten o'clock last night. I *picked* them, man. I can pick them. But I was going for the 'long shot'. Hell, what is a little bread? Fifty dollars! Man, that isn't no bread, at all. If I put my hand in my pocket now, look . . . *this is* bread! . . . five *hundred* dollars. I can lose, man, I can afford to lose bread. Money don't mean anything to me, man, money is no *big* thing! . . . money is *naught* all.'

His wife remained sitting on the Scandinavian couch, which had the habit of whispering to them, once a month, 'Fifty-nine thirty-five owing on me!' in payments. She looked up at Griff as he gruffed through the door. She smiled. Her face did not change its form, or its feeling, but she smiled. Griff grew stiff at the smile. She got up from the couch. She brushed the anxiety of time from her waiting miniskirt ('My wife must dress well, and look *sharp*, even in the house!'), she tidied the already-tidy hairdo she had just got from Azans, and she went into the kitchen, which was now a wall separating Griff from her. Griff looked at the furniture, and wished he could sell it all in time for the races tomorrow afternoon: the new unpaid-for living-room couch, desk, matching executive chair, the table and matching chairs where they ate, desk pens thrown in, into the bargain the salesman swore he was giving them, ten Friday nights ago down Yonge Street, scatter rugs, Scandinavian-type settee with its matching chairs, like Denmark in the fall season, in style and design; he looked at the motto, CHRIST IS THE HEAD OF THIS HOME, which his wife had insisted upon taking as another 'bargain'; and he thought of how relaxed he felt driving in the man's new Riviera. He took the new Racing Form, folded in half and already notated, from his breast pocket, and sat on the edge of the bed, in the wisteria-smelling bedroom. His wife had been working, he said to himself, as he noticed he was sitting on his clean folded pyjamas. But he left them there and perused the handicaps and histories of the horses. The bundle buggy for shopping was rolling over the polished wood of the living-room floor. The hinges of the doors of the clothes cupboard in the hallway were talking. A clothes hanger dropped on the skating rink of the floor. The cupboard door was closed. The bundle buggy rolled down from its prop against the cupboard and jangled onto the hardboard ice. Griff looked up and saw a smooth brown, black-maned horse standing before him. It was his wife.

'Griffy, dear? I am ready.' She had cleaned out her pocketbook of old papers, useless personal and business cards accumulated over drinks and at parties; and she had made a budget of her month's allowance, allowing a place in the tidied wallet section for her husband's arrival. The horse in Griff's mind changed into a donkey. 'Clynn called. He's having a party tonight. Tennish. After the supermarket, I want to go round to the corner, to the cleaners' and stop off at the liquor store for a bottle of wine. My sisters're coming over for dinner, and they're bringing their boy-friends. I want to have a roast. Should I also buy you a bottle of Black-and-White, Griffy, dear?': *they're at post! they're off! . . . as they come into the backstretch, moving for the wire . . . it's Phil Kingston by two lengths, Crimson Admiral, third, True Willie . . . Phil Kingston, Crimson Admiral, True Willie . . .* but Griff had already moved downstairs, in the direction of the cashiers' wicket: 'Long-shot in your arse! Uh got it, this time, old man!' *True Willie is making a move. True Willie! . . . Phil Kingston now by one length, True Willie is coming on the outside! True Willie! It's True Willie!*

'It's almost time for the supermarket to close, Griff dear, and I won't like to be running about like a race horse, sweating and perspiring. I planned my housework and I tried to finish all my housework on time so I'll be fresh for when you came home. I took my time, too, doing my housework and I took a shower so I won't get excited by the time my sisters come and I didn't bother to go to my yoga class' *it's True Willie by a neck! True Willie! What a run, ladies and gentlemen! what a run! True Willie's the winner, and it's now official!* 'and I even made a promise to budget this month so we'll have some money for all these bills we have to pay. We have to pay these bills and we never seem to be paying them off and the rent's due in two days, no, today! oh, I forgot to tell you that the bank manager called about your loan, to say that' *it's True Willie, by a neck!*

Griff smashed all the furniture in the apartment in his mind, and then walked through the door. 'Oh Griffy, dear! Stooly called to say he's getting a lift to the races tomorrow and if you're going he wants you to . . .'

Griff was standing in the midst of a group of middle-aged West Indians, all of whom pretended through the amount of liquor they drank, and the 'gashes they lashed' that they were still young black studs.

'Man, when I entered that door, she knew better than to open her fucking mouth to me! To *me*? *Me*?' The listening red eyes understood the unspoken chastisement in his threatening voice. 'Godblindyou! she knew better than, *that*; me? if she'd only opened her fucking mouth, I would have . . .' They raised their glasses, all of them, to their mouths, not exactly at the same time, but sufficiently together, to make it a ritualistic harmony among men. 'As man!' Griff said, and then wet his lips. They would, each of them, have chastised their women in precisely the same way that Griff was boasting about disciplining his. But he never did. He could never even put his hand to his wife's mouth to stop her from talking. And she was not the kind of woman you would want to beat: she was much too delicate. The history of their marriage had coincided with her history of a woman's illness which had been kept silent among them; and its physical manifestation, in the form of a large scar that crawled halfway around her neck, darker in colour than the natural shade of her skin, had always, from the day of recovery after the operation, been covered by a neckline on each of her dresses. And this became her natural style and fashion in clothes. Sometimes, in more daring moods, she would wear a silk scarf to hide the scar. 'If my wife wasn't so blasted sickly, I would've put my hand in her arse, *many times!* I've thought o' putting my hand in her arse, after a bad day at the races!' He had even thought of doing something drastic about her smile and about his losses at the track and at poker. It was not clearly shaped in his mind: and at times, with this violent intent, he could not think of whom he would perform this drastic act on. After a bad day at the track, the thought of the drastic act, like a cloud over his thoughts, would beat him down and take its toll out of his slim body which itself seemed to refuse to bend under the great psychological pressure of losing, all the time. He had just lost one hundred dollars at Woodbine Race Track, when one evening as he entered Clynn's living-room, for the usual Friday night party of Scotch and West Indian peas and rice and chicken, which Clynn's Polish wife cooked and spoiled and learned how to cook as she spoiled the food, he had just had time to adjust his shoulders in the over-sized sports jacket, when he said, braggingly, 'I just dropped a hundred. At Woodbine.' He wet his lips and smiled.

'Dollars?' It was Clynn's voice, coming from the dark corner where he poured drinks. Clynn was a man who wouldn't lend his sister, nor his mother—if she was still alive—more than five dollars at one time.

'Money don't mean anything, man.'

'A *hundred* dollars?' Clynn suddenly thought of the amount of Scotch Griff had been drinking in his house.

'Money is *naught* all.'

'You're a blasted . . . boy, do you lose *just* for fun or wha'?' Clynn sputtered. 'Why the arse you don't become a *groom*, if you like racehorse so much? Or you's a . . . a *paffological* loser?'

'Uh mean, I don't like to come on strong, or anything, but, money is *naught* all . . .'

'Rass-hole put down my Scotch, then! You drinking my fucking Scotch!'

And it rested there. It rested there because Griff suddenly remembered he was among men who knew him: who knew his losses both in Britain and Canada. It rested there also, because Clynn and the others knew that his manner and attitude towards money, and his wife's expressionless smile, were perhaps lying expressions of a turbulent inner feeling of failure. 'He prob'ly got rass-hole ulcers, too'! Clynn said, and then spluttered into a laugh. Griff thought about it, and wondered whether he had indeed caused his wife to be changed into a different woman altogether. But he couldn't know that. Her smile covered a granite of silent and apparent contentment. He wondered whether he hated her, to the bone, and whether she hated him. He felt a spasm through his body as he thought of her hating him, and not knowing about it. For so many years living together, both here and in Britain; and she was always smiling. Her constancy and her cool exterior, her smiles, all made him wonder now, with the Scotch in his hand, about her undying devotion to him, her faithfulness, pure as the sheets in their sweet-smelling bedroom; he wondered whether 'I should throw my hand in her arse, *just* to see what she would do.' But Clynn had made up his own mind that she was, completely, destroyed inside: her guts, her spirit, her aspirations, her procreative mechanism, 'Hysterectomy all shot to pieces!' Clynn said cruelly, destroyed beyond repair, beneath the silent consolation and support which he saw her giving to her husband; at home among friends and relations, and in public among his sometimes silently criticizing friends. 'I don't mean to come on strong, but . . .'

'You really want to know what's wrong with Griff?' Clynn's sister, Princess, asked one day. 'He want a *stiff* lash in his backside! He don't know that he's gambling-'way his wife's life? He doesn't know that? Look, he don't have chick nor child! Wife working in a good job, for *decent* money, and they don't even live in a decent apartment that you could say, well, rent eating out his sal'ry. Don't own no record-player. *Nothing.* And all he doing is walking 'bout Toronto with his blasted head high in the air! He ain' know this is Northamerica? Christ, he don't even speak to poor people. He ain' have no motto-car, like some. Well, you tell me then, what the hell is Griff doing with thirteen-thousand Canadian dollars a year? Supporting race-horse? No, man, you can't tell me that, 'cause not even the *most* wutless o' Wessindians living in Toronto, could gamble-'way thirteen thousand dollars! Jesuschrist! that is twenty-six thousand back in Barbados! Think o' the land he could buy back home wid thirteen-thousand Canadian dollars. And spending it 'pon a race-horse? What the hell is a race-horse? *Thirteen thousand?* But lissen to me! one o' these mornings, that wife o' his going get up and tell him that she with-child, that she *pregnunt* . . .' ('She can't get pregnunt, though, Princess, 'cause she already had one o' them operations!') 'Anyhow, if his wife was a diff'rent person, she would 'ave walked-out on his arse *long ago*! Or else, break his two blasted hands! and she won't spend a *day* in jail!'

When Griff heard what Princess had said about him, he shrugged his shoulders and said, 'I don't have to come on strong, but if I was a different man, I would really show these West Indian women something . . .' He ran his thin, long, black fingers over the length of his old-fashioned slim tie, he shrugged the grey sports jacket that was a size too large, at the shoulders, into shape and place, wet his lips twice, and said, 'Grimme another Scotch, man.' While Clynn fixed the Scotch, he ran his thumb and index finger of his left hand down the razor edge of his dark brown trouser seams. He inhaled and tucked his shirt and tie neatly beneath the middle button of his sports jacket. He took the Scotch, which he liked to drink on the rocks, and he said, 'I don't have to come on strong, but I am going to tell you something . . .'

The next Friday night was the first day of fête in the long weekend. There hadn't been a long weekend in Canada for a long time. Everybody was tired of just going to work, coming home, watching CBC television, bad movies on the TV, and then going to bed. 'There ain' no action in this fucking town,' Clynn was saying for days, before the weekend appeared like raindrops on a farmer's dry-season head. And everybody agreed with him. It was so. Friday night was here, and the boys, their wives, their girl-friends, and their 'outside women' were noisy and drunk and happy. Some of the men were showing off their new bell-bottom trousers and broad leather belts worn under their bulging bellies, to make them look younger. The women, their heads shining like wet West Indian tar roads, the smell from the cosmetics and grease that went into their kinky hair and on their faces, to make them look sleek and smooth, all these smells and these women mixed with the cheap and domestic perfumes they used, whenever Avon called; and some women, wives who husbands 'were getting through', were wearing good-looking dresses, in style and fashion; others were still back home in their style, poured in against their wishes and the better judgement of their bulging bodies; backsides big, sometimes too big, breasts bigger, waists fading into the turbulence of middle age and their behinds, all poured against the shape of their noisy bodies, into evil-fitting, shiny material, made on sleepy nights after work, on a borrowed sewing machine. But everybody was happy. They had all forgotten now, through the flavour of the calypso and the peas and the rice, the fried chicken, the curry-chicken, that they were still living in a white man's country; and it didn't seem to bother them now, nor touch them now. Tonight, none of them would tell you that they hated Canada; that they wanted to go back home; that they were going 'to make a little money, first'; that they were only waiting till then; that they were going to go back before the 'blasted Canadian tourisses buy-up the blasted Caribbean';

they wouldn't tell you tonight that they all suffered some form of racial discrimination in Canada, and that that was to be expected, since 'there are certain things with this place that are not just right'; not tonight. Tonight, Friday night, was forgetting night. West Indian night. And they were at the Cancer Club to forget and to drink and to get drunk. To make plans for some strange woman's (or man's) body and bed, to spend 'some time' with a real West Indian 'thing', to eat her boiled mackerel and green bananas, which their wives and women had, in their ambitions to be 'decent' and Canadian, forgotten how to cook, and had left out of their diets, especially when Canadian friends were coming to dinner, because that kind of food was 'plain West Indian stupidness'. Tonight, they would forget and drink, forget and dance, and dance to forget.

'Oh-Jesus-Christ, Griff!' Stooly shouted, as if he was singing a calypso. He greeted Griff this way each time he came to the Club, and each time it was as if Stooly hadn't seen Griff in months, although they might have been together at the track the same afternoon. It was just the way Stooly was. 'Oh-Jesus-Christ, Griff!' he would shout, and then he would rush past Griff, ignoring him, and make straight for Griff's wife. He would wrap his arms round her slender body (once his left hand squeezed a nipple, and Griff saw, and said to himself, 'Uh mean, I won't like to come on strong about it, but . . .'; and did nothing about it), pulling up her new minidress above the length of decency, worn for the first time tonight, exposing the expensive lace which bordered the tip of her slip. The veins of her hidden age, visibly only at the back of her legs, would be exposed to Griff, who would stand and stare and feel 'funny', and feel, as another man inquired with his hands all over his wife's body, the blood and the passion and the love mix with the rum in his mouth. Sometimes, when in a passion of brandy, he would make love to his wife as if she was a different woman, as if she was no different from one of the lost women found after midnight on the crowded familiar floor of the Cancer.

'Haiii! How?' the wife would say, all the time her body was being crushed. She would say, 'Haiii! How?' every time it happened; and it happened every time; and every time it happened, Griff would stand and stare, and do nothing about it, because his memory of British breeding told him so; but he would feel mad and helpless afterwards, all night; and he would always want to kill Stooly, or kill his wife for doing it; but he always felt she was so fragile. He would want to kill Stooly more than he would want to kill his wife. But Stooly came from the same island as his wife. Griff would tell Clynn the next day, on the telephone, that he should have done something about it; but he 'didn't want to come on strong'. Apparently, he was not strong enough to rescue his wife from the rape of Stooly's arms, as he rubbed his body against hers, like a dog scratching its fleas against a tree.

Once, a complete stranger saw it happen. Griff had just ordered three drinks: one for his wife, one for himself, and one for Stooly, his friend. Griff looked at the man, and in an expansive mood (he had made the 'long shot' in the last race at Woodbine that afternoon), he asked the stranger, 'What're you drinking?'

'Rum, sah!'

'I am going to buy you a goddamn drink, just because I like you, man.'

The stranger did not change the mask on his face, but stood there, looking at Griff's dark-green lenses. Then he said, 'You isn' no blasted man at all, man!' He then looked behind: Stooly was still embracing Griff's wife. It looked as if he was feeling her up. The man took the drink from Griff, and said, 'You is no man, sah!'

Griff laughed; but no noise came out of his mouth. 'Man, that's all right. They went to school together in Trinidad.'

'In *my* books, you still ain' no fucking man, boy!' The stranger turned away from Griff: and when he got to the door of the dance floor, he said, 'Thanks for the drink, *boy.*'

The wife was standing beside Griff now, smiling as if she was a queen parading through admiring lines of subjects. She looked, as she smiled, like she was under the floodlights of some première performance she had prepared herself for a long time. She smiled, although no one in particular expected a smile from her. Her smiling went hand in hand with her new outfit. It had to be worn with a smile. It looked good, as usual, on her; and it probably understood that it could only continue to look good and express her personality if she continued smiling. At intervals, during the night, when you looked at her, it seemed as if she had taken the smile from her handbag, and had then powdered it onto her face. She could have taken it off any time, but she chose to wear it the whole night. 'Griffy, dear?' she said, although she wasn't asking him anything, or telling him anything, or even looking in his direction. 'Haiii! How?' she said to a man who brushed against her hips as he passed. The man looked suddenly frightened, because he wanted his advance to remain stealthy and masculine. When he passed back from the bar, with five glasses of cheap rum-and-Cokes in his hands, he walked far from her.

Griff was now leaning on the bar, facing the part-time barman, and talking about the results of the last race that day; his wife, her back to the bar, was looking at the men and the women, and smiling; when someone passed, who noticed her, and lingered in the recognition, she would say, 'Haiii! How?'

A large, black, badly dressed Jamaican (he was talking his way through the crowd) passed. He stared at her. She smiled. He put out his calloused construction hand, and with a little effort, he said, 'May I have this dance, gal?' Griff was still talking. But in his mind he wondered whether his wife would dance with the Jamaican. He became ashamed with himself for thinking about it. He went back to talking, and got into an argument with the part-time barman, Masher, over a certain horse that was running in the feature race the next day at Greenwood. Masher, ever watchful over the women, especially other men's, couldn't help notice that the calloused-hand Jamaican was holding on to Griff's wife's hand. With his shark-eyes he tried to get Griff's attention off horses and onto his wife. But Griff was too preoccupied. His wife placed her drink on the counter beside him, her left hand still in the paws of the Jamaican construction worker, whom nobody had seen before, and she said, 'Griffy, dear?' The man's hand on her manicured fingers had just come into his consciousness, when he wheeled around to give her her drink. He was upset. But he tried to be cool. It was the blackness of the Jamaican. And his size. Masher knew he was upset. The Jamaican reminded Griff of the 'Congo-man' in one of Sparrow's calypsos. Masher started to laugh in his spitting kee-kee laugh. And when Griff saw that everybody was laughing, and had seen the Congojamaican walk off with his wife, he too decided to laugh.

'It's all right, man,' he said, more than twice, to no one in particular, although he could have been consoling the Jamaicancongo man, or Masher, or the people nearby, or himself.

'I sorry, suh,' The Jamaican said. He smiled to show Griff that he was not a rough fellow. 'I am sorry, suh. I didn't know you was with the missis. I thought the missis was by-sheself, tonight, again, suh.'

'It's no *big* thing, man,' Griff said, turning back to talk to Masher, who by now had lost all interest in horses. Masher had had his eyes on Griff's wife, too. But Griff was worried by something new now: the man had said, '*by-sheself, tonight, again, suh*'; and that could mean only one thing: that his wife went places, like this very Club, when he wasn't with her; and he had never thought of this, and never even imagined her doing a thing like this; and he wasn't sure that it was not merely the bad grammar of the Jamaican, and not the accusation in that bad grammar, '*but language is a funny thing, a man could kill a person with language, and the accusation can't be comprehended outside of the structure of the language . . . wonder how you would parse this sentence, Clynn . . . a Jamaican fella told me last night, 'by-sheself, tonight, again, suh'; now, do you put any emphasis on the position of the adverb, more than the conditional phrase?*' Griff was already dozing off into the next day's dreams of action, thinking already of what he would tell Clynn about the accident: '*Which is the most important word in that fellow's sentence structure? "By-sheself", "again", or "tonight"?*'

'Never mind the fellow looks like a canecutter, he's still a brother,' Griff said to Masher, but he could have been talking into the future, the next day, to Clynn; or even to himself. 'I don't want to come on strong, but he's a brother.' The CBC television news that night dealt with the Black Power nationalism in the States. The Jamaican man and Griff's wife were now on the dance floor. Griff stole a glimpse at them, to make sure the man was not holding his wife in the same friendly way Stooly, who was a friend, would hold her. He thought he would be able to find the meaning of '*by-sheself*', '*again*', and '*tonight*' in the way the man held his wife. Had the Jamaican done so, Griff would have had to think even more seriously about the three words. But the Jamaican was about two hundred and fifty pounds of muscle and mackerel and green bananas. 'Some other fellow would have come on strong, just because a rough-looking chap like him, held on . . .'

'Man, Griff, you's a rass-hole idiot, man!' Masher said. He crept under the bar counter, came out, faced Griff, broke into his sneering laugh, and said, 'You's a rass-hole!' Griff laughed too, in his voiceless laugh. 'You ain' hear that man say, "*by-sheself*", "*tonight*", "*again*"? If I had a woman like that, I would kiss her arse, by-Christ, just for *looking* at a man like that Jamaikian-man!' Masher laughed some more, and walked away, singing the calypso the amateur band was trying to play: '*Oh Mister Walker, Uh come to see your daughter . . .*'

Griff wet his lips. His bottom lip disappeared inside his mouth, under his top lip; then he did the same thing with his top lip. He adjusted his dark glasses, and ran his right hand, with a cigarette in it, over his slim tie. His right hand was trembling. He shrugged his sports jacket into place and shape on his shoulders . . . '*Oh, Mister Walker, uh come to see ya daughterrrrr . . .*' He stood by himself in the crowd of West Indians at the door, and he seemed to be alone on a sun-setting beach back home. Only the waves of the calypsonian, and the rumbling of the congo drum, and the whispering, the loud whispering in the breakers of the people standing nearby, were with him. He was like the sea. He was like a man in the sea. He was a man at sea . . . '*tell she is the man from Sangre Grande . . .*'

The dance floor was suddenly crowded, jam-packed. Hands were going up in the air, and some under dresses, in exuberance after the music; the words in the calypso were tickling some appetites; he thought of his wife's appetite and of the Jamaican's, who could no longer be seen in the gloom of the thick number of black people; and tomorrow was races, and he had again mastered the Form. And Griff suddenly became terrified about his wife's safety and purity, and the three words came back to him: '*by-sheself*', '*tonight*', '*again*'. Out of the crowd, he could see Masher's big red eyes and his teeth, skinned in mocking laugh. Masher was singing the words of the calypso: '*Tell she I come for she . . .*' The music and the waves on the beach, when the sun went behind the happy afternoon, came up like a gigantic sea, swelling and roaring as it came to where he was standing in the wet white sand; and the people beside him, whispering like birds going home to branches and rooftops, some whispering, some humming like the sea, fishing for fish and supper and for happiness, no longer in sight against the blackening dusk . . . '*she know me well, I had she already! . . .*' Stooly walked in front of him, like the lightning that jigsawed over the rushing waves; and behind Stooly was a woman, noisy and Trinidadian, 'this part-tee can't done till morning come!' like an empty tin can tied to a motor car bumper. All of a sudden, the fishermen and the fishing boats were walking back to shore, climbing out of their boats, laden with catches, their legs wet up to their knees; and they walked with their boats up to the brink of the sand. In their hands were fish. Stooly still held the hand of a woman who laughed and talked loud, 'Fête for so!' She was like a barracuda. Masher, raucous and happy, and harmless, and a woman he didn't know, were walking like Siamese twins. One of his hands could not be seen. Out of the sea, now resting from the turbulent congo drumming of the waves in the calypso, came the Jamaicancongoman, and his wife.

'Thank you very much, suh' he said, handing Griff his wife's hand. With the other hand, she was pulling her miniskirt into place. 'She is a first class dancer, suh.'

'Don't have to come on *strong*, man.'

'If I may, some other time, I would like to . . .' the man said, smiling and wiping perspiration from his face with a red handkerchief. His voice was pleasant and it had an English accent hidden somewhere in it. But all the words Griff heard were 'I know she well, I had she already.' . . . '*by-sheself*', '*again*', '*tonight*' . . . and there were races tomorrow. His wife was smiling, smiling like the everlasting sea at calm.

'Haiii!' she said, and smiled some more. The Jamaicanman moved back into the sea for some more dancing and fish. The beach was still crowded; and in Griff's mind it was crowded, but there was no one but he standing among the broken forgotten pieces of fish: heads and tails, and empty glasses and cigarette butts, and some scales broken off in a bargain, or by chance, and the ripped-up tickets of wrong bets.

Masher appeared and said in his ear, 'If she was my wife, be-Christ, I tell you . . .' and he left the rest for the imagination.

Griff's wife's voice continued, 'Griffy, dear?'

Masher came back from the bar with a Coke for the woman he was with. When he got close to Griff, he said in his ear, 'Even if she was only just a screw like that one I have there . . . '

'Griffy, dear, let's go home, I am feeling . . ."

'. . . and if you was *something*,' Masher was now screaming down the stairs after them. Griff was thinking of the three little words which had brought such a great lump of weakness within the pit of his stomach.

'Masher seems very happy tonight, eh, Griffy, dear? I never quite saw Masher so happy.'

'. . . you, *boy*! you, *boy*! . . .'

'Masher, Haiii! How?'

'If it was mine,' Masher shouted, trying to hide the meaning of his message, 'if it was mine, and I had put only a two-dollar bet 'pon that horse, that horse that we was talking about, and, and that horse *behave*' so, well, I would have to *lash* that horse, till . . . *unnerstan?*'

'Griffy, dear? Masher really loves horses, doesn't he, eh?'

They were around the first corner, going down the last flight of stairs, holding the rails on the right-hand side. Griff realized that the stairs were smelling of stale urine, although he could not tell why. His wife put her arm round his waist. It was the first for the day. 'I had a *great* time, a real ball, a *lovely* time!' Griff said nothing. He was tired, but he was also tense inside; still he didn't have the strength or the courage, whichever it was he needed, to tell her how he felt, how she had humiliated him, in that peculiar West Indian way of looking at small matters, in front of all those people, he could not tell her how he felt each time he watched Stooly put his arms round her slender body; and how he felt when the strange Jamaican man, with his cluttered use of grammar broken beyond meaning and comprehending, had destroy something, like a dream, which he had had about her for all these fifteen years of marriage. He just couldn't talk to her. He wet his lips and ran his fingers over the slim tie. All she did (for he wanted to know that he was married to a woman who could, through all the years of living together, read his mind, so he won't have to talk) was smile. That goddamn smile, he cursed. The sports jacket shoulders were shrugged into place and shape.

'Griffy, dear? Didn't you enjoy yourself?' Her voice was like a flower, tender and caressing. The calypso band, upstairs, had just started up again. And the quiet waltz-like tune seemed to have been chosen to make him look foolish, behind his back. He could hear the scrambling of men and crabs trying to find dancing partners. He could imagine himself in the rush of fishermen after catches. He was thinking of getting his wife home quickly and coming back, to face Stooly and the Jamaican man; and he wished that if he did come back, that they would both be gone, so he won't have to come on strong; but he was thinking more of getting rid of his wife and coming back to dance and discuss the Racing Form; and tomorrow was races, again. He imagined the large rough Jamaican man searching for women again. He saw Stooly grabbing some woman's hand, some woman whom he had never seen before. But it was *his* Club. He saw Masher, his eyes bulging and his mouth wide open, red and white, in joy. And Griff found himself not knowing what to do with his hands. He took his hands out of his jacket pockets; and his wife, examining her minidress in the reflection of the glass in the street door they were approaching, and where they always waited for the taxicab to stop for them, removed her arm from his waist. Griff placed his hand on her shoulder, near the scar, and she shuddered a little, and then he placed both hands on her shoulders; and she straightened up, with her smile on her face, waiting for the kiss (he always kissed her like that), which would be fun, which was the only logical thing to do with his hands in that position around her neck, which would be fun and a little naughty for their ages like the old times in Britain; and his wife, expecting this reminder of happier nights in unhappy London, relaxed, unexcited, remembering both her doctor and her yoga teacher, and in the excitement of her usually unexcitable nature, relaxed a little, and was about to adjust her body to his, and lean her scarred neck just a little bit backward to make it easy for him, to get the blessing of his silent lips, (she remembered then that the Jamaican held her as if he was her husband) when she realized that Griff's hands had walked up from her shoulders, and were now caressing the hidden bracelet of the scar on her neck, hidden tonight by a paisley scarf. She shuddered in anticipation. He thought of Stooly, as she thought of the Jamaican, as he thought of Masher, as he squeezed, and of the races—tomorrow the first race goes at 1:45 P.M. And the more he squeezed the less he thought of other things, and the less those other things bothered him, and the less he thought of the bracelet of flesh under his fingers, the bracelet which had become visible, as his hands rumpled the neckline. He was not quite sure what he was doing, what he wanted to do; for he was a man who always insisted that he didn't like to come on strong, and to be standing up here in a grubby hallway killing his wife, would be coming on strong: he was not sure whether he was rapping his hands round her neck in a passionate embrace imitating the Jamaican, or whether he was merely kissing her.

But she was still smiling, the usual smile. He even expected her to say, 'Haiii! How?' But she didn't. She couldn't. He didn't know where his kiss began and ended; and he didn't know where his hands stopped squeezing her neck. He looked back up the stairs, and he wanted so desperately to go back up into the Club and show them, or talk to them, although he did not, at the moment, know exactly why, and what he would have done had he gone back into the Club. His wife's smile was still on her body. Her paisley scarf was falling down her bosom like a rich spatter of baby food, pumpkin and tomato sauce; and she was like a child, propped against a corner, in anticipation of its first step, toddling into movement. But there was no movement. The smile was there, and that was all. He was on the beach again, and he was looking down at a fish, into the eye of reflected lead, a fish left by a fisherman on the beach. He thought he saw the scales moving up and down, like small billows, but there was no movement. He had killed her. But he did not kill her smile. He wanted to kill her smile more than he wanted to kill his wife.

Griff wet his lips, and walked back up the stairs. His wife was standing against the wall by the door, and she looked as if she was dead, and at the same time she looked as if she was living. It must have been the smile. Griff thought he heard her whisper, 'Griffy, dear?' as he reached the door. Stooly, with his arm round a strange woman's body, took away his arm, and rushed to Griff, and screamed as if he was bellowing out a calypso line, 'Oh-Jesus-Christ-Griff!'

Masher heard the name called, and came laughing and shouting, 'Jesus-Christ, boy! You get rid o' the wife real quick, man! As man, *as man.*' Griff was wetting his lips again; he shrugged his sports jacket into place, and his mind wandered . . . 'show me the kiss-me-arse Racing Form, man. We going to the races tomorrow . . .'

MARIAN ENGEL
(1933-1985)

〜

Share and Share Alike

Happiness is a fragile thing, and alcohol, as I know from the house I grew up in, is dangerous to it. When, therefore, I started to drop in to the bar across the road from the office after work and drink with Max Brady, who was a good court reporter because he knew the system from the inside, I decided that there was something wrong with my life and I'd better fix it up quickly or I'd go the way of my rambunctious Aunt Edith and my father.

So I went home and confronted Jean-Louis; after a marathon talk, we agreed that we had married to spite our mothers and we could not now stand each other; that Caroline was a good kid who didn't deserve parents who went in for silent or boozy wars, and that I could have the use of our barn of a house until she was eighteen. He cleared his studio out of the top floor so I could rent it for enough to pay the taxes. It was a fairly amicable parting, though I admit I put away quite a lot of Scotch when Jean-Louis found a new woman to annoy his mother with almost immediately.

I was putting up a notice on the office bulletin board offering the flat for rent when Max's hollow voice sounded behind me. 'My wife Pol's looking for a place, too. You'd like her.'

'Why should I like her if you don't?'

'She's a woman of character like you. And Josie's about the age of your daughter.'

'Well, send her over and we'll try the girls out together.'

I liked Pol. She took the flat, and to give her her own bedroom we put Josie on the second floor next to Caroline. Since they were only children they ought not to have got on with each other, but they chose to combine not their egotism but their loneliness and became good friends for a couple of years.

I liked Pol, who was a bit older than me, more cynical, though she shouldn't have been, since I was a newspaper reporter and she was a social worker. She'd travelled more than me, and the years with Max had hardened her to circumstance; the years with Jean-Louis had only frightened me. He was an art director and his world was nothing when it wasn't glamorous. I wasn't good at glamour and I was glad to get out of it.

We lived like college room-mates, keeping each other company, keeping out of each other's hair as well. We didn't get involved in food issues, Pol paid her rent on time, we kept a timetable that left the girls covered and ourselves free more than either of us had been while we were married, and I look on Pol's first years as some of the best times we've had in this house.

We didn't agree on everything, and it showed in the men we trailed home (hiding large pairs of boots in order not to alarm the girls) during the busy, sexy seventies when everyone our age was loose and hunting. She picked up Central Europeans who looked vaguely as if they were in Canada feeding up for the next revolution somewhere else. I mothered rather innocent young men: I was a kind of transition between home and the big wide world. I told myself I was preparing for the change in values that Caroline's teen-age years would evince.

It wasn't always perfect. She had to forgive me for using tinned soup and peanut butter. I had to live with the smell of the earthy messes of roots and leaves she cooked. She grew leeks in the front flower beds which wouldn't have been a sin if one of the neighbours hadn't reported it to the housing inspector, who insisted on also coming in, and finding many expensive flaws in the house. I called her Central Europeans by the wrong names, until I decided to call them all Max and to tell them I was crazy.

I did small jobs on whatever newspapers were giving out work, suburban or urban. I never was ambitious. She quarrelled with her supervisors, borrowed money from someone, and went back to school. When Jean-Louis told me to raise her rent to cover the new wiring, I didn't have the heart.

But I did do something else. I met my friend Heather in the supermarket one day, and when she told me her new job was finding rooms for ex-mental patients, I told her that I had an empty room on the second floor. That was how we got Tom.

I thought he was fine. His social worker told me he was a bit withdrawn, and had no psychoses, only problems about keeping appointments and facing the world. He certainly, she said, would be no threat to the girls.

He was tall, and very pale and thin, like a piece of bleached horseradish. He was on drugs, which made him immobile and quiet. Caroline wasn't afraid of him; I guess Pol and Josie were away on some kind of holiday when I agreed to take him.

They came in late one night and there was no chance to tell them about him; not that I remember, anyway. Next morning he came down, walking stiffly and slowly like an automaton and I said, 'Pol, this is Tom. I've rented him the back room.'

She looked up at him. I could tell she didn't like what she saw. 'Where did you get him?' she asked.

'I'll tell you later.'

He looked at her. Then he hung his head and shuffled out the door.

'That friend of yours who finds places for patients, huh?'

'Yes, but he's very nice. And it's going to pay for the wiring.'

'Gwen, you idiot! The girls! The girls!'

'He's non-violent. He's got some kind of terrible background, but there's no psychosis. He just can't make decisions.'

'I don't like him'

'Well, why not?'

'I've been in the work for years, darn it. I should know. You're so innocent about people. He's going to be nothing but a problem.'

'He will be if you're negative.'

'Listen, I wanted to live in a nice house, not a zoo.'

'Your prejudices are showing.'

'Well, I'll tuck them away for now. But you just wait, Gwen Tennyson, just you wait.'

She always called me Gwen Tennyson when she thought I was being sentimental.

She was right, but not for good reasons. It wasn't the presence of Tom that changed things, it was Pol's attitude to Tom that changed things. The little girls got along with him fine, asked him to play Monopoly and Masterpiece with them, shared their television programs. But Pol had a kind of prurience that showed, and that shook me. 'What does he do when he's bad?' she asked.

I replied reluctantly that I'd been told that when he lost his grip he forgot to put his clothes on.

'For God's sake, Gwen.'

'Well, he hasn't yet.'

But I was worried about him. Whenever he saw Pol he drew into some corner of himself that was very far away.

And I watched her after that, liked her less. I felt that the way she stared at him was wrong; I felt she was expecting him to go mad again, and that he was weak and willing enough to offer her his madness. And I knew by the way she had begun to complain about my housekeeping, my fading crowd of young men, the neighbourhood, that she was annoyed to have to share the house with him. I wondered about Max and his drinking, though Max had a nature that had been dedicated to self-destruction from childhood, I knew. Still, there was something about Pol: she could make me misbehave, and she could get at Tom.

'It's my house, Pol,' I said a lot of times.

One Saturday morning Tom said he wasn't feeling very well. 'I got scared of Pol,' he said.

'You have to toughen up, Tom. There'll always be people who dislike your background.'

He went out, then, and from the front window I watched him trying to get up the courage to cross the road, putting a foot out again and again and again and withdrawing it. Josie looked at him and sighed, 'I wish Mom liked him. He's really nice, isn't he?'

'I wish he liked himself.'

Pol was going out with some gaunt man from Central Europe who liked to come and cook extraordinary goulashes in the big downstairs kitchen and didn't clean up very well afterwards. When I taxed her with this, she said, 'Well, you never use anything but a can opener. Why don't you move upstairs.'

'Pol, it's my house.'

Soon afterwards, I came home to find the police at the door and Pol screaming at Tom, who had no clothes on. I was pleased that the police were nice to him. 'We'll take him to the hospital,' they said. 'Don't worry, ma'am.' The little girls seemed unwounded, unoffended.

'Didn't I tell you,' Pol said. 'Now we can clean his room out and Max can live there.'

'I don't want Max to live there.'

'Why not, he's an old friend, isn't he?'

'You mean Max-Max, not your boyfriend?'

'Max, my ex-husband, Josie's benighted father. He's looking for a place.'

'I don't want him. He's a drunk.'

'How come you can have mental patients and not drunks? Josie needs her father.'

'Pol, it's my house.'

He came and had a good go at me. 'Gwennie, I need to be near the kid.'

'Max, I don't care if you're employed or unemployed, I don't want to live with you.'

'What's wrong with me? We've been buddies, Gwen, buddies.'

'You take too much joy in getting arrested. You drink too much.'

'Well, you like a drink, too.'

'I don't want you around, Max. You'll make trouble. I mean Pol has the odd friend, and it'll be hard to take.'

'Listen, I have the odd friend too, it won't mean a thing.'

I saw the house stacked up with bodies, and I said firmly and loudly again, 'It's my house, no.'

The upshot of this was that Pol took offence and dragged Josie out to an apartment in High Park where there was room for both Max and her lover. Then I took Josie back for a month while Pol recovered from the beating Max had administered because of the lover. I repainted the flat and rented it to library school students, and drove Josie and Pol to the airport to fly to England where Pol was to pursue her graduate studies. The seventies were over, and although Josie and Caroline clutched each other and cried at parting, Pol and I did not.

Then things changed. Caroline started high school and showed ominous signs of growing up on me. My young lovers grew up, too, and went off with girls their own age. My suburban newspapers folded one by one. I thought about a new career and decided that I was an ideal employee: I wanted an old-fashioned office job as dogsbody and telephone-answerer and mum.

I found one when an antique dealer on Queen Street advertised for a 'universal aunt'.

We've had our differences, Tibor and I. He doesn't admire pine furniture and he can't stand crazy quilts. He's critical of my attitude to furniture polishing. He thinks my bookkeeping is funny. On the other hand he likes my muscles, and the way I always know where things are (that's after years of 'Hey, Mum, where's my . . .?') He likes the way I get to the store on time, always ask him before I name a price, and treat customers with respect.

After my downy youngsters, Tibor is a delight. He is ten years older than I am and has been through hell and high water in terms of wars and revolutions, which he won't talk about, he calls himself an Austro-Hungarian and if that's what he wants to be it's all right with me. He's a good cook.

Mindful of Pol and her root-cookers, I asked him when I first went to work for him what his politics were. I explained that if this was a cell or something, I didn't want to be in it. 'If it's a cell, daughter,' he said, 'I'm a monk.'

He isn't one.

He came to the house first because I said I might have room to store a couple of Empire sofas for him. He and Caroline took to each other at once. 'He's just not like Dad,' she said. 'Not one bit. So I don't have to compare them, and that makes it easy,' she told me.

Slowly, he began replacing my Salvation Army furniture (Jean-Louis had taken most of the smart stuff, and I'd never earned enough or cared enough to replace it) with his antiques. Then he decided he'd better move into the house to take care of it. He rented his flat above the store to the young man who does his gilding and bookbinding.

Some mornings I wake up beside him and pinch myself because I'm so happy. Then he says, 'Don't pinch yourself. I'm here, and you're about to go downstairs and make tea. If we put that little Bokhara down, the bedroom will be warmer. I'm going to Sotheby's today, some new fool is getting rid of grandmother's Chippendale to replace it with distressed beech cut to look like pine and I don't think Rotenberg's going to bid on it. And I know a man who has just killed a goose: we shall eat tonight.'

Off he goes, off I go. Sometimes we meet for lunch in the neighbourhood, and once in one of the new, smart places that make us feel very old and dignified and worldly wise, we were waited on by Tom, who was happy to see me. When I explained that he had lived in the house, Tibor said, 'Well, why don't you invite him back now he's on lithium; if we rent a room we'll eat better than ever.'

So he did come back. He's fine, now. He can make decisions, he remembers to take his medication. He gets on with Caroline, and the house, which is very large, feels full and happy.

Happiness is a funny thing, like unpolluted air: you forget what it was like when it's gone. It's transparent and somehow silent.

A while ago, about five o'clock, I was home getting some potatoes ready for dinner because it was my turn to cook and Tibor's to close the store. The front hall was full of cartons of bric-a-brac from an auction, and when the doorbell rang I also had to squeeze past a large Regency bookcase Tibor had brought up from a sale in Boston. I peered through the glass panelling, and there was Pol, fatter and older.

'Hey, hi, when did you get back from England?'

'I just got off the plane. I came straight here. How are you, stranger?'

'I'm terrific. Where's Josie?'

'She's still there: Max's rich aunt is sending her to boarding school. Hey, what's all this, gone into the antique business?'

'Sort of. Come on in and I'll tell you about it.'

I got out a bottle of Tibor's Tokay and some crystal glasses he had brought home (there were only five in the lot) and poured us a drink. 'Now,' she said, 'let down your hair. But first, let me know where I'm going to sleep tonight.'

Let down your hair, Rapunzel, I thought. Let down your hair.

'There's a not-bad tourist home on Spadina.'

'Ah, come on Gwen, aren't we friends? Weren't we always? I'm just off a plane, you don't have to string me. What's wrong?'

'There isn't a bed in the place, Pol. There's half the school library on the top floor and I've got someone living with me.'

On cue, Tibor bounced in, beamed, sat down, shook hands, took a drink. Then Caroline came home. When she heard Tom on the stairs she put her hand over her mouth in dismay and rushed out to warn him. 'Tom's back,' I said to Pol. 'He's fine now. He's on lithium. I don't think you should cohabit: you've never liked each other.'

Pol shook her head. 'Gosh, every time, I think, there's one person I like, she's perfect, we get on fine; then you go and do it again: fill up your house with goons and mental patients and right wing pricks.'

'Right wing pricks?' asked Tibor.

'Where're you from, mister? What was your name in the States?'

'Pol . . .'

'Shut up, Gwen. You're so dumb you don't know this guy is . . . I'm at a loss for words.'

'I remember you,' Tibor said slowly. 'You used to go about with that little Alvarez before he committed suicide. Unlike Gwennyth, you dealt in other peoples' politics.'

'You mean to say you didn't?'

I felt the happiness not so much fading as swallowing itself. I said suddenly, 'Pol, get out.'

Tibor said, 'Gwen, I didn't mean to go that far.'

I could feel Tom vibrating on the step outside the door. He would need Caroline to help him cross the road. I said, 'Listen, Pol, we get on fine when there's no one else around, when you can decide who comes in and out of this house. But it's not that kind of house any more.'

'Are you saying it's *your* house again in that nauseating way?'

'It's not my house. Tibor bought it from Jean-Louis last year. Tell me about England. Josie didn't tell us whether you finished your degree or not.'

But she stood up and backed away. 'I don't like what you've turned into. I'd rather pay for a room in a hotel than stay where I'm not welcome.'

'I'm sorry, Pol. But we can't have Tom upset when he's doing so well.'

'Stop saying you're sorry. I'm going.' She stormed out through the hall, banging into the big bookcase. If she'd had an umbrella she'd have put it through the glass in its doors. 'Max is dead and you don't even care,' she said. 'I'm just off the plane, you turn me out . . .'

I let her go. Caroline watched her with narrowed brows. 'She doesn't have any luggage,' Caroline said.

'Max isn't dead.'

Tom drifted into the living-room on a sigh. 'I don't know why she upsets me,' he said.

'She reminds you of someone,' I said.

He thought. 'Marjorie. My sister Marjorie. She used to tell Dad I'd wet the bed when she couldn't get what she wanted.'

'It's just that there are people like that,' I said. 'Don't worry about her. They don't get power over you unless you let them.'

'And she did run the house, Mum,' Caroline put in. 'You did everything she told you.'

'I was a younger sister. Used to taking orders.'

'Not completely,' Tibor said with a laugh. Then he filled our two glasses again and raised his to the light. 'I congratulate you: you have developed at last a sense of evil. You are now grown up.'

I see her sometimes on the street, now, but if she sees me she puts her head down and slouches angrily past. I don't know what makes her feel so shabbily treated when she is not allowed to rule; I feel that she is eaten by some old anger. I wish she'd do something about it. I wish she'd learn to share our happiness.

Because we are happy, Tibor and Tom and Caroline and I. We're so happy that sometimes even Jean-Louis and his wife drop by for a drink and a piece of preserved goose and a joke, and we share this happiness with them carefully, spoon by spoon, in memory of other times when things were not so good.

~

The Woman Who Talked to Horses

'That's right,' she said, 'I talk to them. They will talk to me when they will talk to no one else.'

'But they *can* talk,' I said.

'Oh, sure.'

'To each other?'

'All the time.'

I looked over at the horses. They were in their stalls, eating hay, their rumps and hind legs about all I could see of them. They looked the same as they always had. I didn't believe they talked. I certainly didn't believe they would talk to her.

'What's your fee?' I asked.

She looked off at the horses, too, then glanced at me, then worked one toe into the ground and looked at that. She was wearing blue cloth shoes with thick white shoelaces—all very clean. Too clean. She looked clean all over. I didn't think she knew snot about horseflesh or about anything else. I figured she was a straight-out phoney.

'Your fee,' I said.

She had a little itch behind one ear. She scratched there.

'Before we go into my fee structure,' she said, 'we need to have a quiet discussion.'

Fee structures? Holy Christ.

I had a good mind to turn and walk away.

'You won't tell me your fee?'

She pawed the ground again and the hand again went up to get at that itch. I stared at that hand. She had long, slender fingers and white immaculate skin with hardly any fuzz on it, and wrists no thicker than my thumb. All very feminine. She wasn't wearing a ring; I noticed that. I had her figured by this time. She was another one of those frail, inhibited, emaciated females who knew nothing about the real world but like to think they could tell you about horses. One of those grim, pitiful creatures who was forever saying to themselves and to each other, *I can relate to horses.*

I'd had my share of that lot back when I had been boarding.

'I can't tell you my fee,' she said, 'until I know what you want of me and why you want it.'

I nearly laughed in her face. The whole business was stupid. I didn't know why I'd let myself get talked into calling her. I wished now that she'd just get in her car and go away, so I could go into the house and tell Sarah, 'Well, Sarah, you got any more of your dumb ideas? Let's hear them, Sarah.' Something like that. And watch her shrivel up. Watch her mew and sob and burn and hide away.

Christ, the time I was wasting. *All* the time I had wasted, listening to Sarah. Trying to take her seriously. Giving in when I knew it would prove a waste of time, all to keep a little peace in the house. To keep poor Sarah upright and not shrivelling.

I stared up at the house. Wondering if Sarah was watching. If she wasn't up there gritting her teeth, gnawing the woodwork, the broom in one hand, shoving hair out of her eyes with another, as she pressed her scared little face against a secret window. That was Sarah. Ever spying. The one way she had—so she'd tell it—of keeping her guard up.

'Mr Gaddis?' the woman said.

'Yes, what is it?'

'All I need to know is what trouble it is you are having. With your horses. Then we can talk price.'

'How about we talk *method*,' I said. '*Then* price. You going to go up and whisper sweet nothings in these horses' ears? Is that what I'm paying you for?'

The woman eyed me peculiarly. Her head tilted, her mouth a shade open. It wasn't dislike so much—though I knew she did. Nor was she making judgements. I didn't know what it was. A quiet distance. A watching.

Disapproval, too: that was there.

'I don't know what the trouble is,' I said. 'That's why I called you. I want to know what's going on. All I know is they've been acting funny lately.'

'Funny how?'

'It's hard to say. Standoffish, maybe.'

'Horses are like that. Can't horses have moods, Mr Gaddis?'

'Not on my time,' I said. 'They're not producing. You'd think the bastards had gone on vacation. Zombies, the lot of them.'

'I see,' the woman said.

Bull. She saw nothing.

I stared at her open throat. She had on this soft cottony blouse, tinted like old rose, with a wide, folded collar, and at her throat a gold necklace no thicker than a fish line.

She had on these black britches.

Up at the house Sarah had all the doors and windows shut up tight and outside not a hint of wind was stirring. Even the grass wasn't growing. It seemed to me all the life had gone out of that house. It looked dumb and impenetrable and cold.

'Sure they can have moods,' I said. 'And they do. All the time. But this time it's different. This time it's affecting me.'

She closed the blouse and held the hand at her throat.

'How do you mean?'

'I'm losing. I haven't had a horse in the running all year.'

'That could be bad luck. It could be that the other horses are better.'

'Could be but it isn't,' I said. 'These are good horses.'

She glanced up at the house. Then she went on to the roofline and from there up to the hills behind it. She wanted me to know she'd heard that story a thousand time before. Every owner thought he had good horses.

I thought to tell her I had a fortune tied up in these horses. That they were top dollar. Then I thought I had better not. You didn't talk fortune and top dollar when some nut was trying to get it from you. Especially a nut who imagined she could talk to horses.

'About fees,' she said. 'Naturally, if your horses that now are losing begin winning after I've had my chat with them, then my fee will be higher.'

'A chat!' I said. 'You're going to have a chat with them?'

'A serious discussion. Do you like that better?'

'I don't like any of it,' I said. You wouldn't be here if—' I stopped. I didn't see any point in raking up the family history.

'I didn't invited myself, Mr Gaddis. You invited me.'

She didn't say that with any anger. She was playing it very cool.

We both heard a door slam, and turned. Over at the back door of the house my wife stood, splashing out water from a white enamel pot. Then she swayed a little, standing there with her head bowed. Something must have told her we were looking. She glared our way, then flung her pot into the yard, and strutted back inside.

The woman beside me laughed.

I was pretty surprised myself. Sarah is prone to the odd explosion now and then—for reasons totally incomprehensible—but she'd never done anything like this before, not when someone else was around. Meek and long-suffering: that was the word for Sarah.

'I gather your wife dislikes that pot,' the woman said. She laughed again, a velvety, softly arching laugh. I wanted to tell her it was none of her business.

'Forget Sarah,' I said. 'A minute ago you were saying something about your fee structure and my hypothetical winnings.'

'Was I?'

For no reason at all this woman suddenly squatted down on her legs and began rooting through the thin grass with her long fingers. I couldn't make it out. I couldn't tell whether she was searching for rock or flower or clover, or for nothing at all. Maybe she had dropped a nickel. I had no idea what the hell she was doing. I moved a little closer. I was tempted to step on her hand. Her blouse ballooned out and I could see down her neckline to her breasts. She wasn't wearing any brassière.

Maybe that's why she was kneeling there.

She began speaking without lifting her head. 'Yes,' she said, 'I think that's fair. Obviously much more is involved, more work for me, if I am to talk to your horses, root out their troubles, and get them winning. On the other hand, if you simply want me to walk over to the stalls and ask how they're doing today— "How you making it, kid," that sort of thing—and then come back here and simply repeat to you what they said, well in that case my fee would be minimum. Thirty dollars, let's say. Is that what you want?'

My wife was standing at the back door again. She had this fixed, zombielike expression which altered even as I watched. The skin reddened, her lips twitched, and in a moment she was twitching all over.

Then she pitched a pillow out into the yard. One of our big bed-pillows with the green slipcover still on it. Then she retreated.

The horse lady, down on the grass, hadn't noticed.

I had got around so that my back was to the door. 'I was looking for something more solid,' I told her. 'Something tangible that I could act on. *Useful,* you know. Useful information. I *have heard* that you get good results.'

She stood up. She turned and silently regarded the pillow in the yard.

'But you want my services for free, is that it, Mr Gaddis?'

This made me mad. It was clear to me that this woman carried some sort of chip around on her shoulder. That she had no use for men. One of *those,* I thought.

'Now listen,' I said. 'George Gaddis pays for goods and services properly rendered, and he always has. He pays top dollar. But it's crazy for me to fork over hundreds of dollars just to watch you go over there for an hour or two and whisper into the ears of my horses.'

She stopped studying the pillow and looked across at the door. No one was at the door. Sarah had closed the screen door, then she'd closed the cedar door behind it. It was quiet as a tomb in there.

'I don't often whisper, Mr Gaddis,' she said. 'I speak distinctly and usually with some force, and if you'll allow me, most horses do the same.'

Haughty and reproving. She seemed to think I deserved this.

'Their powers of articulation are quite well-developed, Mr Gaddis. Perhaps more so than our own.'

'They *do* talk?'

She bristled. '*Yes, they talk!*'

She struck off, moving down towards the fence at a determined pace. She truly disliked me. There, she stood leaning up against the fence with her hands in her pockets. She had narrow shoulders and narrow bony hips that would fit in a cigar box. She was a woman all right, but she was too mean and skimpy for me.

'That filly I got from Quebec,' I said, 'she'd be speaking French, I suppose? *J'ai la mort dans mon â, J'ai la mort dans mon â, mon coeur se tend comme un lourd fardeau.*'

She spun and stared directly at me, her face burning. Mercy, one of the horses, plodded up to the fence and nuzzled her neck and shoulders. I wasn't impressed. Mercy was a dreamer. She liked people.

The woman strolled back, calm once more.

'We are getting nowhere,' she said, 'and my time is valuable. I did not drive out here to give you a free estimate, or to illustrate my capabilities, or to listen to your troubles. No, Mr Gaddis, the horses do not *talk* as such, not as we are talking, but they do think and develop their thoughts logically, except in dire cases. I am able, in a word, to read their minds.'

'ESP, you mean?'

'Something like that.' She fluttered a vague hand.

'You can guarantee this?'

'I do not give guarantees. I can swear to you that I shall talk to your horses, but the effectiveness with which you utilize the information I glean is clearly out of my hands.'

'All right,' I said. 'Suppose I employ you and make good use of your information, and my horses begin winning. What's your standard contract? How much do you get?'

'Normally, ten percent.'

'Good God! As much as that?'

'Yes. But in this instance I shall demand twenty-five.'

She shot that out. She wasn't negotiating any more.

'You're out of your mind,' I told her. 'You got a screw loose.'

'You are a difficult person to talk to,' she said. 'You are a distrusting person, a bullying one, and I should imagine your horses have picked up these traits or are responding to them. It will make my job that much more difficult.'

'Twenty-five *percent*!' I laughed. I still couldn't believe it. 'Hell, lady, you'd be costing me more than my trainer does!'

'Then let your trainer talk to your horses.'

It was my turn to walk down to the fence. Mercy saw me coming, and plodded away.

'I'll have to think about this,' I said. 'I don't know if any of it makes any sense.'

'You have my literature, sir,' she said. 'You have my testimonials. Call or not call, as you wish.'

She started over to her car, a low convertible, red and shining and new, which stood in my driveway with the top down. Very expensive. Just as she was.

'I'd much prefer you *didn't* call,' she said, stopping. 'I don't believe I like you. Your situation does not attract my interest.'

I waited until she got in the car.

'I don't suppose you like my horses *either*,' I said. 'I suppose you find *them* dull, too. I suppose you're one of those sanctified, scrubbed-out bitches who puts the dollar sign first. I don't suppose you care one crap about my horses' well-being.'

Go for the throat, I thought. Get them in the old jugular.

She wasn't offended. Her expression was placid, composed, even a little amused. I knew that look. It was the look Sarah had when she found me in something foolish. The look would last about two minutes, then she'd begin slamming doors.

She started the engine.

I stayed by the fence, close to laughter, waiting to see if this was a woman who knew how to drive a car.

She cut the engine. She stared a long time over at my house, her hands still up on the wheel, that same benign, watchful, untroubled look in her face. Then she turned in her seat and looked down at my fences and barn. All four horses had come out. Mercy had her nose between the lowest boards, trying to get at grass, but the other three had their necks out over the fence, looking at the woman in the car.

Something funny happened in the woman's eyes and in her whole face. She went soft. You could see it soaking through her, warming her flesh.

'Go on,' I said. 'Get out of here.'

She wasn't listening to me. She seemed, for the moment, unaware of my presence. She was attuned to something else. Her jaw dropped open—not prettily . . . she *was* a pretty woman—her brows went up, she grinned, and a second later her face broke out into a full-fledged smile. Then a good solid laugh.

She had a nice laugh. It was the only time since her arrival that I had liked her.

'What is it?' I asked.

'Your stallion,' she said. 'Egorinski, is that his name? He was telling me a joke. Not very flattering to you.'

Her eyes sparkled. She was genuinely enjoying herself. I looked over at Egor. The damned beast had his rear end turned to me. His head, too. He seemed to be laughing.

She got her car started again and slapped it up into first gear. 'I shall send you a bill for my time,' she said. 'Goodbye, Mr Gaddis.'

As she drove out, down the narrow, circling lane, throwing up dust behind her and over the white fence, I could still hear her laughing. I imagined I heard her—sportive now, cackling, giving full rein to her pleasure—even as she turned her spiffy car out onto the highway.

Sarah was at the yard pump. She'd picked up the enamel pot and was filling it with water. She was wearing her print work-dress, but for some reason she'd put back on the high heels she'd been wearing last night. She'd put on her lipstick. The little scratch on her forehead was still there. It had swollen some.

She'd brought out a blanket and dumped that out in the yard beside the pillow.

As I approached, she glanced up, severe and meaning business.

'Stay away,' she said. 'Don't touch me. Go on with whatever you were doing.'

I could see now wasn't the time. That the time hadn't come. That maybe it would be a long time before it did.

I went on down to the bar, scooted up the ladder, and sat on a bale of hay at the loft door. I looked out over the stables, over the fields, over the work-out track and the further pasture and out over all of the long valley. I looked at the grey ring of hills. I wondered what had gone wrong with my life. How I had become this bad person.

RUDY WIEBE
(1934)

Where Is the Voice Coming From?

The problem is to make the story.

One difficulty of this making may have been excellently stated by Teilhard de Chardin: 'We are continually inclined to isolate ourselves from the things and events which surround us . . . as though we were spectators, not elements, in what goes on.' Arnold Toynbee does venture, 'For all that we know, Reality is the undifferentiated unity of the mystical experience,' but that need not here be considered. This story ended long ago; it is one of finite acts, of orders, or elemental feelings and reactions, of obvious legal restrictions and requirements.

Presumably all the parts of the story are themselves available. A difficulty is that they are, as always, available only in bits and pieces. Though the acts themselves seem quite clear, some written reports of the acts contradict each other. As if these acts were, at one time, too well-known; as if the original nodule of each particular fact had from somewhere received non-factual accretions; or even more, as if, since the basic facts were so clear, perhaps there were a larger number of facts than any one reporter, or several, or even any reporter had ever attempted to record. About facts that are simply told by this mouth to that ear, of course, even less can be expected.

An affair seven-five years old should acquire some of the shiny transparency of an old man's skin. It should.

Sometimes it would seem that it would be enough—perhaps more than enough—to hear the names only. The grandfather One Arrow; the mother Spotted Calf; the father Sounding Sky; the wife (wives rather, but only one of them seems to have a name, though their fathers are Napaise, Kapahoo, Old Dust, The Rump)—the one wife named, of all things, Pale Face; the cousin Going-Up-To-Sky; the brother-in-law (again, of all things) Dublin. The names of the police sound very much alike; they all begin with Constable or Corporal or Sergeant, but here and there an Inspector, then a Superintendent and eventually all the resonance of an Assistant Commissioner echoes down. More. Herself: Victoria, by the Grace of God, etc., etc., QUEEN, defender of the Faith, etc., etc.; and witness 'Our Right Trusty and Right Well-beloved Cousin and Councillor the right Honourable Sir John Campbell Hamilton-Gordon, Earl of Aberdeen; Viscount

Formartine, Baron Haddo, Methlic, Tarves and Kellie in the Peerage of
Scotland; Viscount Gordon of Aberdeen, County of Aberdeen in the
Peerage of the United Kingdom; Baronet of Nova Scotia, Knight Grand
Cross of Our Most Distinguished Order of Saint Michael and Saint George,
etc., Governor General of Canada.' And of course himself: in the award
proclamation named 'Jean-Baptiste' but otherwise known only as Almighty
Voice.

But hearing cannot be enough; not even hearing all the thunder of A
Proclamation: 'Now Hear Ye that a reward of FIVE HUNDRED DOLLARS will be
paid to any person or persons who will give such information as will lead . .
. (etc., etc.) this Twentieth day of April, in the year of Our Lord one thousand eight hundred and ninety-six, and the Fifty-ninth year of Our Reign . . .'
etc. and etc.

Such hearing cannot be enough. The first item to be seen is the piece of
white bone. It is almost triangular, slightly convex—concave actually as it is
positioned at this moment with its corners slightly raised—graduating from
perhaps a strong eighth to a weak quarter of an inch in thickness, its scattered pore structure varying between larger and smaller on its polished, certainly shiny surface. Precision is difficult since the glass showcase is at least
thirteen inches deep and therefore an eye cannot be brought as close as the
minute inspection of such a small, though certainly quite adequate, sample
of skull would normally require. Also, because of the position it cannot be
determined whether the several hairs, well over a foot long, are still in some
manner attached to it or not.

The seven-pounder cannon can be seen standing almost shyly between
the showcase and the interior wall. Officially it is known as a gun, not a cannon, and clearly its bore is not large enough to admit a large man's first.
Even if it can be believed that this gun was used in the 1885 Rebellion and
that on the evening of Saturday, May 29, 1897 (while the nine-pounder, now
unidentified, was in the process of arriving with the police on the special
train from Regina), seven shells (all that were available in Prince Albert at
that time) from it were sent shrieking into the poplar bluffs as night fell,
clearly such shelling could not and would not disembowel the whole earth.
Its carriage is now nicely lacquered, the perhaps oak spokes of its petite
wheels (little higher than a knee) have been recently scraped, puttied and
varnished; the brilliant burnish of its brass breeching testifies with what
meticulous care charmen and women have used nationally advertised cleaners and restorers.

Though it can also be seen, even a careless glance reveals that the same
concern has not been expended on the one (of two) .44 calibre 1866 model
Winchesters apparently found at the last in the pit with Almighty Voice. It is
also preserved in a glass case; the number 1536735 is still, though barely, dis-
tinguishable on the brass cartridge section just below the brass saddle ring.
However, perhaps because the case was imperfectly sealed at one time
(though sealed enough not to warrant disturbance now), or because of sim-

ple neglect, the rifle is obviously spotted here and there with blotches of rust and the brass itself reveals discolorations almost like mildew. The rifle bore, the three long strands of hair themselves, actually bristle with clots of dust. It may be that this museum cannot afford to be as concerned as the other; conversely, the disfiguration may be something inherent in the items themselves.

The small building which was the police guardroom at Duck Lake, Saskatchewan Territory, in 1895 may also be seen. It had subsequently been moved from its original place and used to house small animals, chickens perhaps, or pigs—such as a woman might be expected to have under her responsibility. It is, of course, now perfectly empty, and clean so that the public may enter with no more discomfort than a bend under the doorway and a heavy encounter with disinfectant. The door-jamb has obviously been replaced; the bar network at one window is, however, said to be original; smooth still, very smooth. The logs inside have been smeared again and again with whitewash, perhaps paint, to an insistent point of identity-defying characterlessness. Within the small rectangular box of these logs not a sound can be heard from the streets of the, probably dead, town.

> *Hey Injun you'll get hung for stealing that steer*
> *Hey Injun for killing that government cow you'll*
> *get three weeks on the woodpile*
> *Hey Injun*

The place named Kinistino seems to have disappeared from the map but the Minnechinass Hills have not. Whether they have ever been on a map is doubtful but they will, of course, not disappear from the landscape as long as the grass grows and the rivers run. Contrary to general report and belief, the Canadian prairies are rarely, if ever, flat and the Minnechinass (spelled five different ways and translated sometimes as 'The Outside Hill,' sometimes as 'Beautiful Bare Hills') are dissimilar from any other of the numberless hills that everywhere block out the prairie horizon. They are bare; poplars lie tattered along their tops, almost black against the straw-pale grass and sharp green against the grey soil of the ploughing laid in half-mile rectangular blocks upon their western slopes. Poles holding various wires stick out of the fields, back down the bend of the valley; what was once a farmhouse is weathering into the cultivated earth. The poplar bluff where Almighty Voice made his stand has, of course, disappeared.

The policemen he shot and killed (not the ones he wounded, of course) are easily located. Six miles east, thirty-nine miles north in Prince Albert, the English cemetery. Sergeant Colin Campbell Colebrook, North West Mounted Police Registration Number 605, lies presumably under a gravestone there. His name is seventeenth in a very long 'list of non-commissioned officers and men who have died in the service since the inception of the force.' The date is October 29, 1895, and the cause of death is anonymous: 'Shot by escaping Indian prisoner near Prince Albert.' At the foot of this grave are two others: Constable John R. Kerr, No. 3040, and Corporal C. H. S. Hockin, No. 3106. Their cause of death on May 28, 1897, is even more anonymous, but the place is relatively precise: 'Shot by Indians at Min-etch-inass Hills, Prince Albert District.'

The gravestone, if he has one, of the fourth man Almighty Voice killed is more difficult to locate. Mr Ernest Grundy, postmaster at Duck Lake in 1897, apparently shut his window the afternoon of Friday, May 28, armed himself, rode east twenty miles, participated in the second charge into the bluff at about 6:30 p.m., and on the third sweep of that charge was shot dead at the edge of the pit. It would seem that he thereby contributed substantially not only to the Indians' bullet supply, but his clothing warmed them as well.

The burial place of Dublin and Going-Up-To-Sky is unknown, as is the grave of Almighty Voice. It is said that a Métis named Henry Smith lifted the latter's body from the pit in the bluff and gave it to Spotted Calf. The place of burial is not, of course, of ultimate significance. A gravestone is always less evidence than a triangular piece of skull, provided it is large enough.

Whatever further evidence there is to be gathered may rest on pictures. There are, presumably, almost numberless pictures of the policemen in the case, but the only one with direct bearing is one of Sergeant Colebrook who apparently insisted on advancing to complete an arrest after being warned three times that if he took another step he would be shot. The picture must have been taken before he joined the force; it reveals him a large-eared young man, hair brush-cut and ascot tie, his eyelids slightly drooping, almost hooded under thick brows. Unfortunately a picture of Constable R.C. Dickson, into whose charge Almighty Voice was apparently committed in that guardroom and who after Colebrook's death was convicted of negligence, sentenced to two months hard labour and discharged, does not seem to be available.

There are no pictures to be found of either Dublin (killed early by rifle fire) or Going-Up-To-Sky (killed in the pit), the two teen-age boys who gave their ultimate fealty to Almighty Voice. There is, however, one said to be of Almighty Voice, Junior. He may have been born to Pale Face during the year, two hundred and twenty-one days that his father was a fugitive. In the picture he is kneeling before what could be a tent, he wears striped denim overalls and displays twin babies whose sex cannot be determined from the double-laced dark bonnets they wear. In the supposed picture of Spotted Calf and Sounding Sky, Sounding Sky stands slightly before his wife; he wears a white shirt and a striped blanket folded over his left shoulder in such a manner that the arm in which he cradles a long rifle cannot be seen. His head is thrown back; the rim of his hat appears as a black half-moon above eyes that are pressed shut as if in profound concentration; above a mouth clenched thin in a downward curve. Spotted Calf wears a long dress, a sweater which could also be a man's dress coat, and a large fringed and embroidered shawl which would appear distinctly Doukhobor in origin if the scroll patterns on it were more irregular. Her head is small and turned slightly towards her husband so as to reveal her right ear. There is what can only be called a quizzical expression on her crumpled face; it may be she does not understand what is happening and that she would have asked a question, perhaps of her husband, perhaps of the photographers, perhaps even of anyone, anywhere in the world if such questioning were possible for a Cree woman.

There is one final picture. That is one of Almighty Voice himself. At least it is purported to be of Almighty Voice himself. In the Royal Canadian Mounted Police Museum on the Barracks Grounds just off Dewdney Avenue in Regina, Saskatchewan, it lies in the same showcase, as a matter of fact immediately beside that triangular piece of skull. Both are unequivocally labelled, and it must be assumed that a police force with a world-wide reputation would not label *such* evidence incorrectly. But here emerges an ultimate problem in making the story.

There are two official descriptions of Almighty Voice. The first reads: 'Height about five feet, ten inches, slight build, rather good looking, a sharp hooked nose with a remarkably flat point. Has a bullet scar on the left side of his face about 1 ½ inches long running from near corner of mouth towards ear. The scar cannot be noticed when his face is painted but otherwise is plain. Skin fair for an Indian.' The second description is on the Award Proclamation: 'About twenty-two years old, five feet, ten inches in height, weight about eleven stone, slightly erect, neat small feet and hands; complexion inclined to be fair, wavey dark hair to shoulders, large dark eyes, broad forehead, sharp features and parrot nose with flat tip, scar on left cheek running from mouth towards ear, feminine appearance.'

So run the descriptions that were, presumably, to identify a well-known fugitive in so precise a manner that an informant could collect five hundred dollars—a considerable sum when a police constable earned between one and two dollars a day. The nexus of the problems appears when these supposed official descriptions are compared to the supposed official picture. The man in the picture is standing on a small rug. The fingers of his left hand touch a curved Victorian settee, behind him a photographer's backdrop of scrolled patterns merges to vaguely paradisiacal trees and perhaps a sky. The moccasins he wears make it impossible to deduce whether his feet are 'neat small'. He may be five feet, ten inches tall, may weigh eleven stone, he certainly is 'rather good looking' and, though it is a frontal view, it may be that the point of his long and flaring nose could be 'remarkably flat'. The photograph is slightly over-illuminated and so the unpainted complexion could be 'inclined to be fair'; however, nothing can be seen of a scar, the hair is not wavy and shoulder-length but hangs almost to the waist in two thick straight braids worked through with beads, fur, ribbons and cords. The right hand that holds the corner of the blanket-like coat in position is large and, even in the high illumination, heavily veined. The neck is concealed under coiled beads and the forehead seems more low than 'broad'.

Perhaps, somehow, these picture details could be reconciled with the official description if the face as a whole were not so devastating.

On a cloth-backed sheet two feet by two and one-half feet in size, under the Great Seal of the Lion and the Unicorn, dignified by the names of the Deputy of the Minister of Justice, the Secretary of State, the Queen herself and all the heaped detail of her 'Right Trusty and Right Well-beloved Cousin', this description concludes: 'feminine appearance'. But the picture: any face of history, any believed face that the world acknowledges as *man*—Socrates, Jesus, Attila, Genghis Khan, Mahatma Gandhi, Joseph Stalin—no believed face is more *man* than this face. The mouth, the nose, the clenched brows, the eyes—the eyes are large, yes, and dark, but even in this watered-down reproduction of unending reproductions of that original, a steady look into those eyes cannot be endured. It is a face like an axe.

It is now evident that the de Chardin statement quoted at the beginning has relevance only as it prove itself inadequate to explain what has happened. At the same time, the inadequacy of Aristotle's much more famous statement becomes evident: 'The true difference [between the historian and the poet] is that one relates what *has* happened, the other what *may* happen.' These statements cannot explain the storymaker's activity since, despite the most rigid application of impersonal investigation, the elements of the story have now run me aground. If ever I could, I can no longer pretend to objective, omnipotent disinterestedness. I am no longer *spectator* of what *has* happened or what *may* happen: I am become *element* in what is happening at this very moment.

For it is, of course, I myself who cannot endure the shadows on that paper which are those eyes. It is I who stand beside this broken veranda post where two corner shingles have been torn away, where barbed wire tangles the dead weeds on the edge of this field. The bluff that sheltered Almighty Voice and his two friends has not disappeared from the slope of the Minnechinass, no more than the sound of Constable Dickson's voice in that guardhouse is silent. The sound of his speaking is there even if it has never been recorded in an official report:

> *hey injun you'll get*
> *hung*
> *for stealing that steer*
> *hey injun for killing that government*
> *cow you'll get three*
> *weeks on the woodpile hey injun*

The unknown contradictory words about an unprovable act that move a boy to defiance, an implacable Cree warrior long after the three-hundred-and-fifty-year war is ended, a war already lost the day the Cree watch Cartier hoist his guns ashore at Hochelaga and they begin the long retreat west; these words of incomprehension, of threatened incomprehensible law are there to be heard just as the unmoving tableau of the three-day siege is there to be seen on the slops of the Minnechinass. Sounding Sky is somewhere not there, under arrest, but Spotted Calf stands on a shoulder of the Hills a little to the left, her arms upraised to the setting sun. Her mouth is open. A horse rears, riderless, above the scrub willow at the edge of the bluff, smoke puffs, screams tangle in rifle barrage, there are wounds, somewhere. The bluff is so green this spring, it will not burn and the ragged line of seven police and two civilians is staggering through, faces twisted in rage, terror, and rifles sputter. Nothing moves. There is no sound of frogs in the night; twenty-seven policemen and five civilians stand in cordon at thirty-yard intervals and a body also lies in the shelter of a gully. Only a voice rises from the bluff:

> *We have fought well*
> *You have die like braves*
> *I have worked hard and am hungry*
> *Give me food*

but nothing moves. The bluff lies, a bright green island on the grassy slope surrounded by men hunched forward rigid over their long rifles, men clumped out of rifle-range, thirty-five men dressed as for fall hunting on a sharp spring day, a small gun positioned on a ridge above. A crow is falling out of the sky into the bluff, its feathers sprayed as by an explosion. The first gun and the second gun are in position, the beginning and end of the bristling surround of thirty-five Prince Albert Volunteers, thirteen civilians and fifty-six policemen in position relative to the bluff and relative to the unnumbered whites astride their horses, standing up in their carts, staring and pointing across the valley, in position relative to the bluff and the unnumbered Cree squatting silent along the higher ridges of the Hills, motionless mounds, faceless against the Sunday morning sunlight edging between and over them down along the tree tips, down into the shadows of the bluff. Nothing moves. Beside the second gun the red-coated officer has flung a handful of grass into the motionless air, almost to the rim of the red sun.

And there is a voice. It is an incredible voice that rises from among the young poplars ripped of their spring bark, from among the dead somewhere lying there, out of the arm-deep pit shorter than a man; a voice rises over the exploding smoke and thunder of guns that reel back in their positions, worked over, serviced by the grimed motionless men in bright coats and glinting buttons, a voice so high and clear, so unbelievably high and strong in its unending wordless cry.

The voice of 'Gitchie-Manitou Wayo'—interpreted as 'voice of the Great Spirit'—that is, the Almighty Voice. His death chant no less incredible in its beauty than in its incomprehensible happiness.

I say 'wordless cry' because that is the way it sounds to me. I could be more accurate if I had a reliable interpreter who would make a reliable interpretation. For I do not, of course, understand the Cree myself.

⌒

The Hayfield

The sun hangs in the sky, saying in a forceful whisper down through the air.
'yes . . . yes . . . yes', propelling it in beams, overpowering with great oldman
wisdom and domain, over men's signs in the park, saying 'NO: parking,
cycling, hunting, stopping, spitting, talking fishing, No.' Van Gogh's insane
sun, rings of solid orange paint around it, a D.H. Lawrence sun, growing
warm orange rings around the inside hearts of men, making them speak to
one another on the streets (warm enough for ya?), shirts open at the neck,
bespeaking chests of hair and skin, and the summer, a time to move across
the country, in the high grass along railway tracks, the country of fences a
long way from their people's houses, animals and men allowed to do many
things unseen by the cities along the tracks, the discarded cigarette package
in the same place for months, bleaching in the sun, never stepped on or
swept up. Park with no signs in it, a man can spit if he wants to, nobody to
say No, only the sun in the wide prairie sky, whispering yes through the air,
the warm lapping on a man's bare shoulders once he has discarded his shirt,
or at least stuffed it in his bag.

That was where Gordon set up his easel and little canvas-top stool. A man
wouldn't even have to bring paint if he could dip his long-handled brushes
in the colour of the yellow hay and blue horizon. Silly thing to think—a man
doesn't have to be a painter when you get right down to it, which Gordon
was finally doing this summer—not only on week-ends after marking papers
and preparing lectures. He opened the thermos and poured the cap full of
hot black coffee, completely in keeping here by the hayfield, cup held to the
mouth, under the shagbrow blue eyes squinting over the heat and the bright
yellow light waving off the hay in the wind. So he began to paint.

When out of the high grass appeared a strange-looking man. It was that
he was wearing the wrong kind of clothes: a corduroy suit, frumpy neutral-
coloured tie, off-white shirt, and in his mouth an old black briar pipe.
Gordon, dressed in dungarees and running shoes, looked up, smiled, and
continued to lay paint on the canvas, thick swabs of corn-yellow with deep
orange stripes, a tiger of a hayfield.

'I see you're a painter, too,' said the man in the corduroy suit, taking the
bowl of the pipe relaxed into his curved hand, coming closer to look pierc-

ingly at the canvas, expert fashion seen in movie shorts and colour adver-
tisements.

'Oh, are you a painter?' asked Gordon, squeezing horizon blue onto his
palette—an old dry painting.

'No, no,' corduroy suit said importantly. 'No, but I have looked at my
share of paintings. Pisarro, Tintoretto, Hogarth, eh, eh?'

'You like Hogarth?' said Gordon, politely, holding a dry brush. He hated
Hogarth, fat, ugly, pink cheeked, flat eyed.

'Well you know—Hogarth,' said the other. 'But don't let me disturb you,
go on, I'll rest myself.' He puffed at the empty black pipe.

Gordon, happy enough to settle for that, went on painting. Do your
painting in one sitting, he had decided. Don't come back to it, not even a
portrait. The hayfield was the hay of today, and so was Gordon. A test to do
the one painting despite roar of automobile and chomp of eating neighbours, even here in dry slope of railroad ridge between track and wire fence,
to paint the picture despite intrusion or weather. A man could paint a revolution this way, a violent act every day, thirty illustrations a month. Whereas
the hayfield offered another kind of instant, one that stretched out radially,
from the eye to the hole in eternity.

'Van Gogh,' said the man in the corduroy suit.

'What?'

'He would have loved that hayfield.'

'Oh, yes.'

'He went insane at the end,' said the man.

'Would you tell me your name, so I won't have to think of you as the man
in the corduroy suit?' asked Gordon, not good-naturedly, just with a kind of
necessity to meet the situation. He didn't like to carry that with him from
the city.

'Carmen Ethiopia,' said the man.

'My name's Gordon Featherall,' said Gordon.

'The name of a painter, something to conjure with. Monet, Tiepolo,
Brueghel—'

'Mr Ethiopia, would you mind if I just painted? I don't mind you being
here, and watching from a distance, but I haven't got time to talk and listen.
I've been promising myself this trip for a long time, and I don't want to
waste the sunlight. Okay?'

'Suits me, son. The temperament of the painter. Something to conjure
with, eh?' And Mr Ethiopia leaned back against the slope from the railroad
track, his teeth firm on the root of the pipe, his arms crossed over his chest
in the rural sun.

Gordon wrote MOLTO in orange paint on the top of the canvas, and painted slowly, letting his shoulders dip to the rhythm of the lines, the way it
always happened, his feet rocking from heel to toe under him, letting his
weight sink like a pear on the canvas stool. The hayfield didn't change, no
stroke on the canvas took anything away from the yellow miles in front.

Gordon thought about that and remembered a Japanese movie he'd seen, mediaeval poverty movie on the rainy gates of a southern Japan town, four men met in an old wooden shrine or church to wait out the rain, grim black and white picture, slanting rain of grey. In old rags of poorest mediaeval period three of the men began to take the building apart to make a fire and keep it going. The rain went on for days—the relics of the church came down piece by piece to feed the fire, then boards from the walls of the church; then the movie may have been over—Gordon remembered the fourth man who stood away from the fire and looked mournful as the church came into hands and fell into pyre, but he moved towards the fire eventually, staring mournfully at the flames, his arms crossed, hands on opposite shoulders in that skinny Japanese way; the movie probably was over but Gordon remembered the boards kept coming off till the church was gone, the rain put out the fire and the ashes lay in a soggy heap, the rain falling and falling, grey. . . .

He had been swabbing paint onto the canvas. Now he touched it lightly with a fine brush.

Lonely flute music reached his ear from the left. It was a lone soldier's flute in the middle of the vast empty land, long lone notes pinning a centre to the sunny day. With the flute noise nearing, the painting stopped. For a while he tried to groove the brush strokes to the music, but it was wrong, because the music was wrong for that place. It was Hindustan music, Old Testament music, like the bright wooden-looking colour prints of his old forgotten Bible, with picture of small David arms extended holding gigantic sword, foot on the giant unconscious and peaceful Goliath's chest, on the balance before the down! stroke!—in the Old Testament there were two possibilities for music, the long loud blare choruses of cornets as the walls of Jericho crashed in the sand, and the lonely soldier flute of shepherd David. Gordon imagined the later powerful king, escaping all alone from the blaring cornets of his palace, to walk into the desert and take the little flute out of a secret hanging fold in his investment—

The flute came very near, and stopped, in mid-phrase. Around from behind a tree appeared a modern shepherd, in one of those denim suits, tight-fitting pants, and a shoulder-hugging denim jacket. He was a young farm man, walking that way suggested years behind a plow, feet swinging along splayed, perfect for straddling a wide furrow, back slightly bent, for traces, arms swinging, shoulders lunging with each step, and the attitude that bespoke one-time big slicker of small town. The flute was nowhere in sight at first, but showed up protruding from the back pocket of the denims when he turned around to look behind him, at the imaginary straight furrow extending a track to the horizon.

'Howdy,' said Gordon, spitting over to one side in the conversational manner, and wondering why. 'You play a flute nice.'

Shucks, t'warn't nothin, he expected to hear, but Carmen Ethiopia opened his eyes and spoke first.

'Two artists! One walks into the lonely stretches of the wheat belt and is confronted with two artists in one spot,' he said, getting to his feet and taking off his corduroy jacket to shake the grass and dust from it.

The newcomer looked at Ethiopia warily, without saying anything, then turned and looked at Gordon's painting. He didn't look at Gordon. Instead he turned his head down while he intently rolled a cigarette from Old Chum tobacco.

'Welcome, my boy,' said Ethiopia. 'Would you consider giving a man a pinch of that tobacco? The jaws get pretty tired clamping on to an empty pipe.'

The newcomer finished rolling his cigarette and handed the tobacco to Ethiopia without saying anything. Gordon watched with simple admiration as the man crimped the ends of the cigarette and flipped one end between his lips, in the same motion picking a kitchen match out of his jacket pocket, bent wrist turning upward to thumb-scratch the match into flame, one puff drawing the flame into the end of the cigarette, the flip of the fingers and the match dying in flight away into a clump of couch-grass.

'Do you have a match?' asked Ethiopia, handing the tobacco back, shreds of it hanging over the edge of his pipe bowl. The man gave him one silently. Ethiopia looked for a rock to strike it on.

'It ain't that colour,' said the man, jutting his jaw to point at the hayfield with the cigarette in his mouth.

'No it's not. I'm not trying to make it the right colour,' said Gordon, wondering just what he could tell him, this man who has the previous and preemptive knowledge of the hayfield, much more than the portrait sitter who says 'No I don't look like that, you've got the eyes all wrong'; more, because his knowledge had required many moments in how many years, of looking out over miles of hayfields while taking a drag on a cigarette at the turn of the corner in his daily farm-section chores. Presumably.

'Impressionism,' said Mr Ethiopia, who was back with the pipe smoking now, the smoke blue, too pale. 'Renoir, Degas,' he added.

The newcomer had already learned, faster than Gordon, not to turn his head and look when Ethiopia said those things. They looked at one another for a moment. Whose turn to speak? For there was that—they both wanted to talk here, and in his sudden nervousness, the newcomer absently picked the flute out of his back pocket, lightly slapped the side of his leg with it.

'My name is Gordon Featherall,' said Gordon, finally, wondering if he should paint while he talked. He decided not to. There was the question of the colour.

'That hayfield there?' said the newcomer, pointing again with the cigarette.
'Yes—?'

'That's mine, my hayfield. Least it's going to be,' said the man. Then he took one backward step and leaned slightly to the side to look at the painting.

'It's pretty good,' he said.

'Thanks,' said Gordon. 'It's only the start.'

'Go ahead. Paint,' said the man.

Gordon fiddled with the paint on his palette, mixing the colours, blending. It would take a while to get paint to the picture.

'I wished I could of gone to painting school and learnt all the tricks,' said the newcomer. 'I always wanted to be an artist.'

'Why didn't you?' asked Gordon, mixing.

'I never even mentioned it to my old man. Hee! I can imagine what he would of said.'

I know what my old man said, or at least didn't say but thought, enough so I knew without him having to embarrass himself to say it. Gordon flattened the brush full of blue on the canvas, near the top.

The sun was moving over, to the west. There could have been a hand holding the sun, extended at arc of arm's reach, eventually down to flat west horizon. The sky was high, it was highest summer. Gordon painted. The newcomer blew gently on the flute, making low hollow tones, and as he did this, Gordon lined in the darker brown surface brown shadows under the brilliant crest of the hay. Ethiopia was gone, nowhere in sight on the flat land, some distance the other side of the railroad's ridge, then.

'You friend's gone,' said the newcomer.

'Mr Ethiopia,' said Gordon, not turning his face from the painting, absorbed now, though he knew it wasn't going at all well, still wanting to go on with it, do the one painting for the day. 'He appeared out of nowhere while I was painting.'

'What a pain in the ass he was.'

Gordon thought the newcomer would be looking to see what reaction he had, but the man was looking out at the hayfield.

'I believe you're right,' said Gordon.

'I guess he knew a lot about painting, though,' said the other.

'In a way.'

Because Mr Ethiopia was a man who was obliged to know something, that was why he popped up from behind the long grass in the first place, to be an observer, ambassador for the huddled union of men that is the city, where people are held together by the things they feel necessities to do for one another. One of the necessities was to know what the other people are doing, so that finally the people create a job that entails codifying the lives and habits of other people they would normally never meet, maybe never do.

Similarly for oneself. As he had thought earlier in the day, there is no necessity to be a painter, in relation with the hayfield, for instance. 'I wished I could of gone to painting school and learnt all the tricks,' the farm man had said. Farm boy, then. But what of obligation there? In the country.

'What are you going to do with it when you're finished?' asked the newcomer.

What indeed.

'Sometimes I keep them, in stacks in my painting room. Some I scrape the paint off when I'm short on canvas. Some I give to my friends, for favours, or nothing,' he said.

'Don't you ever sell them?'

'Not yet. Is that why you wanted to be a painter? To sell them?'

'I don't know. It don't matter anyway.'

The newcomer looked at the painting, as if sneaking a look at it. Or pretending he wasn't all that interested. Then he looked back at the hayfield. He put the flute in his back pocket, and touched his hands together, as in preparing for a long physical job, lifting a stove, or stacking a truckload of lumber.

'I wouldn't mind buying it off you,' he said.

As if that was the reason he'd put the flute in his back pocket, to hide it behind him, from both of them, so that he couldn't have to buy it with that.

'I mean I ain't got any money, but I was thinking, I mean from looking at you look at it. I could give you that there,' he said, waving at it.

'What?'

'I mean a piece of it. You know. A bale or something, when we cut it.'

Immediately Gordon thought: I want it. But what should he do with it? Eat it, maybe, when he lost his job in the fall. And on the other hand, what would that man do with the painting? Certainly he couldn't hang it in the house, what with the father there. In the barn was a strange notion, a painting of a hayfield hanging in a dark hay barn. . . .

'It isn't a very good painting,' said Gordon.

'That don't matter.'

'It's a bad painting,' said Gordon.

'Come on.'

'It's a deal,' said Gordon.

So he stood beside the easel, watching the man walk down the bare dust line that was the road to his house, walking crookedly over to one side, holding the big canvas from the other side, so the wet paint wouldn't hit his denim suit.

Gordon put the painting things away and sat for a while, finishing the rest of the coffee from the thermos. He looked out over the hayfield again, trying to see a portion that would pack into a bale. He threw out the dregs of the coffee in a swirl that caught the slanting sunlight, brown. And he started walking back, thinking, you do one painting a day, one sitting, and you don't come back to it. If you don't make it that day, you try again the next. There is no limitation on the chances you get. He took a last look at the hayfield in the slanting light and smiled. Then he went down out of sight, on the other side of the railroad ridge.

(1963; 1965)

W.P. KINSELLA
(1935)

⁓

Shoeless Joe Jackson Comes to Iowa

My father said he saw him years later playing in a tenth-rate commercial league in a textile town in Carolina, wearing shoes and an assumed name.

'He'd put on fifty pounds and the spring was gone from his step in the outfield, but he could still hit. Oh, how that man could hit. No one has ever been able to hit like Shoeless Joe.'

Three years ago at dusk on a spring evening, when the sky was a robin's-egg blue and the wind as soft as a day-old chick, I was sitting on the verandah of my farm home in eastern Iowa when a voice very clearly said to me, 'If you build it, he will come.'

The voice was that of a ballpark announcer. As he spoke, I instantly envisioned the finished product I knew I was being asked to conceive. I could see the dark, squarish speakers, like ancient sailors' hats, attached to aluminum-painted light standards that glowed down into a baseball field, my present position being directly behind home plate.

In reality, all anyone else could see out there in front of me was a tattered lawn of mostly dandelions and quack grass that petered out at the edge of a cornfield perhaps fifty yards from the house.

Anyone else was my wife Annie, my daughter Karin, a corn-coloured collie named Carmeletia Pope, and a cinnamon and white guinea pig named Junior who ate spaghetti and sang each time the fridge door opened. Karin and the dog were not quite two years old.

'If you build it, he will come,' the announcer repeated in scratchy Middle American, as if his voice had been recorded on an old 78-r.p.m. record.

A three-hour lecture or a 500-page guide book could not have given me clearer directions: Dimensions of ballparks jumped over and around me like fleas, cost figures for light standards and floodlights whirled around my head like the moths that dusted against the porch light above me.

That was all the instruction I ever received: two announcements and a vision of a baseball field. I sat on the verandah until the satiny dark was complete. A few curdly clouds striped the moon, and it became so silent I could hear my eyes blink.

Our house is one of those massive old farm homes, square as a biscuit box with a sagging verandah on three sides. The floor of the verandah slopes so that marbles, baseballs, tennis balls, and ball bearings all accumulate in a corner like a herd of cattle clustered with their backs to a storm. On the north verandah is a wooden porch swing where Annie and I sit on humid August nights, sip lemonade from teary glasses, and dream.

When I finally went to bed, and after Annie inched into my arms in that way she has, like a cat that you suddenly find sound asleep in your lap, I told her about the voice and I told her that I knew what it wanted me to do.

'Oh love,' she said, 'if it makes you happy you should do it,' and she found my lips with hers. I shivered involuntarily as her tongue touched mine.

Annie: She has never once called me crazy. Just before I started the first landscape work, as I stood looking out at the lawn and the cornfield, wondering how it could look so different in daylight, considering the notion of accepting it all as a dream and abandoning it, Annie appeared at my side and her arm circled my waist. She leaned against me and looked up, cocking her head like one of the red squirrels that scamper along the power lines from the highway to the house. 'Do it, love,' she said as I looked down at her, that slip of a girl with hair the colour of cayenne pepper and at least a million freckles on her face and arms, that girl who lives in blue jeans and T-shirts and at twenty-four could still pass for sixteen.

I thought back to when I first knew her. I came to Iowa to study. She was the child of my landlady. I heard her one afternoon outside my window as she told her girl friends, 'When I grow up I'm going to marry . . .' and she named me. The others were going to be nurses, teachers, pilots, or movie stars, but Annie chose me as her occupation. Eight years later we were married. I chose willingly, lovingly, to stay in Iowa. Eventually I rented this farm, then bought it, operating it one inch from bankruptcy. I don't seem meant to farm, but I want to be close to this precious land, for Annie and me to be able to say, 'This is ours.'

Now I stand ready to cut into the cornfield, to chisel away a piece of our livelihood to use as dream currency, and Annie says, 'Oh, love, if it makes you happy you should do it.' I carry her words in the back of my mind, stores the way a maiden aunt might wrap a brooch, a remembrance of a long-lost love. I understand how hard that was for her to say and how it got harder as the project advanced. How she must have told her family not to ask me about the baseball field I was building, because they stared at me dumb-eyed, a row of silent, thickset peasants with red faces. Not an imagination among them except to forecast the wrath of God that will fall on the heads of pagans such as I.

'If you build it, he will come.'

He, of course, was Shoeless Joe Jackson.

Joseph Jefferson (Shoeless Joe) Jackson
Born: Brandon Mills, South Carolina, July 16, 1887
Died: Greenville, South Carolina, December 5, 1951

In April 1945, Ty Cobb picked Shoeless Joe as the best left fielder of all time. A famous sportswriter once called Joe's glove 'the place where triples go to die.' He never learned to read or write. He created legends with a bat and a glove.

Was it really a voice I heard? Or was it perhaps something inside me making a statement that I did not hear with my ears but with my heart? Why should I want to follow this command? But as I ask, I already know the answer. I count the loves of my life: Annie, Karin, Iowa, Baseball. The great god Baseball.

My birthstone is a diamond. When asked, I say my astrological sign is hit and run, which draws a lot of blank stares here in Iowa where 50,000 people go to see the University of Iowa Hawkeyes football team while 500 regulars, including me, watch the baseball team perform.

My father, I've been told, talked baseball statistics to my mother's belly while waiting for me to be born.

My father: born, Glen Ullin, North Dakota, April 14, 1896. Another diamond birthstone. Never saw a professional baseball game until 1919 when he came back from World War I where he had been gassed at Passchendaele. He settled in Chicago, inhabited a room above a bar across from Comiskey Park, and quickly learned to live and die with the White Sox. Died a little when, as prohibitive favourites, they lost the 1919 World Series to Cincinnati, died a lot the next summer when eight members of the team were accused of throwing that World Series.

Before I knew what baseball was, I knew of Connie Mack, John McGraw, Grover Cleveland Alexander, Ty Cobb, Babe Ruth, Tris Speaker, Tinker-to-Evers-to-Chance, and, of course, Shoeless Joe Jackson. My father loved underdogs, cheered for the Brooklyn Dodgers and the hapless St. Louis Browns, loathed the Yankees—an inherited trait, I believe—and insisted that Shoeless Joe was innocent, a victim of big business and crooked gamblers.

That first night, immediately after the voice and the vision, I did nothing except sip my lemonade a little faster and rattle the ice cubes in my glass. The vision of the baseball park lingered—swimming, swaying, seeming to be made of red steam, though perhaps it was only the sunset. And there was a vision within the vision: one of Shoeless Joe Jackson playing left field. Shoeless Joe Jackson who last played major league baseball in 1920 and was suspended for life, along with seven of his compatriots, by Commissioner Kenesaw Mountain Landis, for his part in throwing the 1919 World Series.

Instead of nursery rhymes, I was raised on the story of the Black Sox Scandal, and instead of Tom Thumb or Rumpelstiltskin, I grew up hearing of the eight disgraced ballplayers: Weaver, Cicotte, Risberg, Felsch, Gandil, Williams, McMullin, and always, Shoeless Joe Jackson.

'He hit .375 against the Reds in the 1919 World Series and played errorless ball,' my father would say, scratching his head in wonder. 'Twelve hits in an eight-game series. And *they* suspended *him*,' Father would cry. Shoeless

Joe became a symbol of the tyranny of the powerful over the powerless. The name Kenesaw Mountain Landis became synonymous with the Devil.

Building a baseball field is more work than you might imagine. I laid out a whole field, but it was there in spirit only. It was really only left field that concerned me. Home plate was made from pieces of cracked two-by-four embedded in the earth. The pitcher's rubber rocked like a cradle when I stood on it. The bases were stray blocks of wood, unanchored. There was no backstop or grandstand, only one shaky bleacher beyond the left-field wall. There was a left-field wall, but only about fifty feet of it, twelve feet high, stained dark green and braced from the rear. And the left-field grass. My intuition told me that it was the grass that was important. It took me three seasons to hone that grass to its proper texture, to its proper colour. I made trips to Minneapolis and one or two other cities where the stadiums still have natural-grass infields and outfields. I would arrive hours before a game and watch the groundskeepers groom the field like a prize animal, then stay after the game when in the cool of the night the same groundsmen appeared with hoses, hoes, and rakes, and patched the grasses like medics attending to wounded soldiers.

I pretended to be building a Little League ballfield and asked their secrets and sometimes was told. I took interest in the total operation; they wouldn't understand if I told them I was building only a left field.

Three seasons I've spent seeding, watering, fussing, praying, coddling that field like a sick child. Now it glows parrot-green, cool as mint, soft as moss, lying there like a cashmere blanket. I've begun watching it in the evenings, sitting on the rickety bleacher just beyond the fence. A bleacher I constructed for an audience of one.

My father played some baseball, Class B teams in Florida and California. I found his statistics in a dusty minor-league record book. In Florida he played for a team called the Angels and, according to his records, was a bet-ter-than-average catcher. He claimed to have visited all forty-eight states and every major-league ballpark before, at forty, he married and settled down in Montana, a two-day drive from the nearest major-league team. I tried to play, but ground balls bounced off my chest and fly balls dropped between my hands. I might have been a fair designated hitter, but the rule was too late in coming.

There is the story of the urchin who, tugging at Shoeless Joe Jackson's sleeve as he emerged from a Chicago courthouse, said, 'Say it ain't so, Joe.'

Jackson's reply reportedly was, 'I'm afraid it is, kid.'

When he comes, I won't put him on the spot by asking. The less said the better. It is likely that he did accept money from gamblers. But throw the Series? Never! Shoeless Joe Jackson led both teams in hitting in that 1919 Series. It was the circumstances. The circumstances. The players were paid peasant salaries while the owners became rich. The infamous Ten Day Clause, which voided contracts, could end any player's career without com-pensation, pension, or even a ticket home.

The second spring, on a toothachy May evening, a covering of black clouds lumbered off westward like ghosts of buffalo, and the sky became the cold colour of a silver coin. The forecast was for frost.

The left-field grass was like green angora, soft as a baby's cheek. In my mind I could see it dull and crisp, bleached by frost, and my chest tightened.

But I used a trick a groundskeeper in Minneapolis had taught me, saying he learned it from grape farmers in California. I carried out a hose, and, making the spray so fine it was scarcely more than fog, I sprayed the soft, shaggy spring grass all that chilled night. My hands ached and my face became wet and cold, but, as I watched, the spray froze on the grass, enclosing each blade in a gossamer-crystal coating of ice. A covering that served like a coat of armour to dispel the real frost that was set like a weasel upon killing in the night. I seemed to stand taller than ever before as the sun rose, turning the ice 'to eye-dazzling droplets, each a prism, making the field an orgy of rainbows.

Annie and Karin were at breakfast when I came in, the bacon and coffee smells and their laughter pulling me like a magnet.

'Did it work, love?' Annie asked, and I knew she knew by the look on my face that it had. And Karin, clapping her hands and complaining of how cold my face was when she kissed me, loved every second of it.

'And how did he get a name like Shoeless Joe?' I would ask my father, knowing the story full well but wanting to hear it again. And no matter how many times I heard it, I would still picture the lithe ballplayer, his great bare feet white as baseballs sinking into the outfield grass as he sprinted for a line drive. Then, after the catch, his toes gripping the grass like claws, he would brace and throw to the infield.

'It wasn't the least bit romantic,' my dad would say. 'When he was still in the minor leagues he bought a new pair of spikes and they hurt his feet. About the sixth inning he took them off and played the outfield in just his socks. The other players kidded him, called him Shoeless Joe, and the name stuck for all time.'

It was hard for me to imagine that a sore-footed young outfielder taking off his shoes one afternoon not long after the turn of the century could generate a legend.

I came to Iowa to study, one of the thousands of faceless students who pass through large universities, but I fell in love with the state. Fell in love with the land, the people, the sky, the cornfields, and Annie. Couldn't find work in my field, took what I could get. For years, I bathed each morning, frosted my cheeks with Aqua Velva, donned a three-piece suit and snap-brim hat, and, feeling like Superman emerging from a telephone booth, set forth to save the world from a lack of life insurance. I loathed the job so much that I did it quickly, urgently, almost violently. It was Annie who got me to rent the farm. It was Annie who got me to buy it. I operate it the way a child fits together his first puzzle—awkwardly, slowly, but, when a piece slips into the proper slot, with pride and relief and joy.

I built the field and waited, and waited, and waited.

'It will happen, honey,' Annie would say when I stood shaking my head at my folly. People looked at me. I must have had a nickname in town. But I could feel the magic building like a gathering storm. It felt as if small animals were scurrying through my veins. I knew it was going to happen soon.

One night I watch Annie looking out the window. She is soft as a butterfly, Annie is, with an evil grin and a tongue that travels at the speed of light. Her jeans are painted to her body, and her pointy little nipples poke at the front of a black T-shirt that has the single word RAH! emblazoned in waspish yellow capitals. Her red hair is short and curly. She has the green eyes of a cat.

Annie understands, though it is me she understands and not always what is happening. She attends ballgames with me and squeezes my arm when there's a hit, but her heart isn't in it and she would just as soon be at home. She loses interest if the score isn't close, or the weather's not warm, or the pace isn't fast enough. To me it is baseball, and that is all that matters. It is the game that's important—the tension, the strategy, the ballet of the fielders, the angle of the bat.

'There's someone on your lawn,' Annie says to me, staring out into the orange-tinted dusk. 'I can't see him clearly, but I can tell someone is there.' She was quite right, at least about it being *my* lawn, although it is not in the strictest sense of the word a lawn; it is a *left field*.

I have been more restless than usual this night. I have sensed the magic drawing closer, hovering somewhere out in the night like a zeppelin, silky and silent, floating like the moon until the time is right.

Annie peeks through the drapes. 'There *is* a man out there; I can see his silhouette. He's wearing a baseball uniform, an old-fashioned one.'

'It's Shoeless Joe Jackson,' I say. My heart sounds like someone flicking a balloon with his index finger.

'Oh,' she says. Annie stays very calm in emergencies. She Band-Aids bleeding fingers and toes, and patches the plumbing with gum and good wishes. Staying calm makes her able to live with me. The French have the right words for Annie—she has a good heart.

'Is he the Jackson on TV? The one you yell 'Drop it, Jackson' at?'

Annie's sense of baseball history is not highly developed.

'No, that's Reggie. This is Shoeless Joe Jackson. He hasn't played major-league baseball since 1920.'

'Well, Ray, aren't you going to go out and chase him off your lawn, or something?'

Yes. What am I going to do? I wish someone else understood. Perhaps my daughter will. She has an evil grin and bewitching eyes and loves to climb into my lap and watch television baseball with me. There is a magic about her.

'I think I'll go upstairs and read for a while,' Annie says. 'Why don't you invite Shoeless Jack in for coffee?' I feel the greatest tenderness toward her then, something akin to the rush of love I felt the first time I held my daughter in my arms. Annie senses that magic is about to happen. She knows she is not part of it. My impulse is to pull her to me as she walks by, the denim of her thighs making a tiny music. But I don't. She will be waiting for me.

As I step out onto the verandah, I can hear the steady drone of the crowd, like bees humming on a white afternoon, and the voices of the vendors, like crows cawing.

A ground mist, like wisps of gauze, snakes in slow circular motions just above the grass.

'The grass is soft as a child's breath,' I say to the moonlight. On the porch wall I find the switch, and the single battery of floodlights I have erected behind the left-field fence sputters to life. 'I've tended it like I would my own baby. It has been powdered and lotioned and loved. It is ready.'

Moonlight butters the whole Iowa night. Clover and corn smells are thick as syrup. I experience a tingling like the tiniest of electric wires touching the back of my neck, sending warm sensations through me. Then, as the lights flare, a scar against the blue-black sky, I see Shoeless Joe Jackson standing out in left field. His feet spread wide, body bent forward from the waist, hands on hips, he waits. I hear the sharp crack of the bat, and Shoeless Joe drifts effortlessly a few steps to his left, raises his right hand to signal for the ball, camps under it for a second or two, catches it, at the same time transferring it to his throwing hand, and fires it to the infield.

I make my way to left field, walking in the darkness far outside the third-base line, behind where the third-base stands would be. I climb up on the wobbly bleacher behind the fence. I can look right down at Shoeless Joe. He fields a single on one hop and pegs the ball to third.

'How does it play?' I holler down.

'The ball bounces true,' he replies.

'I know.' I am smiling with pride, and my heart thumps mightily against my ribs. 'I've hit a thousand line drives and as many grounders. It's true as a felt-top table.'

'It is,' says Shoeless Joe. 'It is true.'

I lean back and watch the game. From where I sit the scene is as complete as in any of the major-league baseball parks I have ever visited: the two teams, the stands, the fans, the lights, the vendors, the scoreboard. The only difference is that I sit alone in the left-field bleacher and the only player who seems to have substance is Shoeless Joe Jackson. When Joe's team is at bat, the left fielder below me is transparent, as if he were made of vapour. He performs mechanically but seems not to have facial features. We do not converse.

A great amphitheatre of grandstand looms dark against the sky, the park is surrounded by decks of floodlights making it brighter than day, the crowd buzzes, the vendors hawk their wares, and I cannot keep the promise I made myself not to ask Shoeless Joe Jackson about his suspension and what it means to him.

While the pitcher warms up for the third inning we talk.

'It must have been . . . It must have been like . . .' But I can't find the words.

'Like having a part of me amputated, slick and smooth and painless.' Joe looks up at me and his dark eyes seem about to burst with the pain of it. 'A friend of mine used to tell about the war, how him and a buddy was running across a field when a piece of shrapnel took his friend's head off, and how the friend ran, headless, for several strides before he fell. I'm told that old men wake in the night and scratch itchy legs that have been dust for fifty years. That was me. Years and years later, I'd wake in the night with the smell of the ballpark in my nose and the cool of the grass on my feet. The thrill of the grass . . .'

How I wish my father could be here with me. If he'd lasted just a few months longer, he could have watched our grainy black-and-white TV as Bill Mazeroski homered in the bottom of the ninth to beat Yankees 10-9. We would have joined hands and danced around the kitchen like madmen. 'The Yankees lose so seldom you have to celebrate every single time,' he used to say. We were always going to go to a major-league baseball game, he and I. But the time was never right, the money always needed for something else. One of the last days of his life, late in the night while I sat with him because the pain wouldn't let him sleep, the radio picked up a static-y station broadcasting a White Sox game. We hunched over the radio and cheered them on, but they lost. Dad told the story of the Black Sox Scandal for the last time. Told of seeing two of those World Series games, told of the way Shoeless Joe Jackson hit, told the dimensions of Comiskey Park, and how, during the series, the mobsters in striped suits sat in the box seats with their colourful women, watching the game and perhaps making plans to go out later and kill a rival.

'You must go,' Dad said. 'I've been in all sixteen major-league parks. I want you to do it too. The summers belong to somebody else now, have for a long time.' I nodded agreement.

'Hell, you know what I mean,' he said, shaking his head. I did indeed.

'I loved the game,' Shoeless Joe went on. 'I'd have played for food money. I'd have played free and worked for food. It was the game, the parks, the smells, the sounds. Have you ever held a bat or a baseball to your face? The varnish, the leather. And it was the crowd, the excitement of them rising as one when the ball was hit deep. The sound was like a chorus. Then there was the chug-a-lug of the tin lizzies in the parking lots, and the hotels with their brass spittoons in the lobbies and brass beds in the rooms. It makes me tingle all over like a kid on his way to his first double-header, just to talk about it.'

The year after Annie and I were married, the year we first rented this farm, I dug Annie's garden for her; dug it by hand, stepping a spade into the soft black soil, ruining my salesman's hands. After I finished, it rained, an Iowa spring rain as soft as spray from a warm hose. The clods of earth I had dug seemed to melt until the garden levelled out, looking like a patch of black ocean. It was near noon on a gentle Sunday when I walked out to that garden. The soil was soft and my shoes disappeared as I plodded until I was near the centre. There I knelt, the soil cool on my knees. I looked up at the low grey sky; the rain had stopped and the only sound was the surrounding trees dripping fragrantly. Suddenly I thrust my hands wrist-deep into the snuffy-black earth. The air was pure. All around me the clean smell of earth and water. Keeping my hands buried I stirred the earth with my fingers and knew I loved Iowa as much as a man could love a piece of earth.

When I came back to the house Annie stopped me at the door, made me wait on the verandah and then hosed me down as if I were a door with too many handprints on it, while I tried to explain my epiphany. It is very difficult to describe an experience of religious significance while you are being sprayed with a garden hose by a laughing, loving woman.

'What happened to the sun?' Shoeless Joe says to me, waving his hand toward the banks of floodlights that surround the park.

'Only stadium in the big leagues that doesn't have them is Wrigley Field,' I say. 'The owners found that more people could attend night games. They even play the World Series at night now.'

Joe purses his lips, considering.

'It's harder to see the ball, especially at the plate.'

'When there are breaks, they usually go against the ballplayers, right? But I notice you're three-for-three so far,' I add, looking down at his uniform, the only identifying marks a large S with an O in the top crook, an X in the bottom, and an American flag with forty-eight stars on his left sleeve near the elbow.

Joe grins. 'I'd play for the Devil's own team just for the touch of a baseball. Hell, I'd play in the dark if I had to.'

I want to ask about that day in December 1951. If he'd lived another few years things might have been different. There was a move afoot to have his record cleared, but it died with him. I wanted to ask, but my instinct told me not to. There are things it is better not to know.

It is one of those nights when the sky is close enough to touch, so close that looking up is like seeing my own eyes reflected in a rain barrel. I sit in the bleacher just outside the left-field fence. I clutch in my hand a hot dog with mustard, onions, and green relish. The voice of the crowd roars in my ears. Chords of 'The Star-Spangled Banner' and 'Take Me Out to the Ballgame' float across the field. A Coke bottle is propped against my thigh, squat, greenish, the ice-cream-haired elf grinning conspiratorially from the cap.

Below me in left field, Shoeless Joe Jackson glides over the plush velvet grass, silent as a jungle cat. He prowls and paces, crouches ready to spring as, nearly 300 feet away, the ball is pitched. At the sound of the bat he wafts in whatever direction is required, as if he were on ball bearings.

Then the intrusive sound of a slamming screen door reaches me, and I blink and start. I recognize it as the sound of the door to my house, and, looking into the distance, I can see a shape that I know is my daughter, toddling down the back steps. Perhaps the lights or the crowd have awakened her and she has somehow eluded Annie. I judge the distance to the steps. I am just to the inside of the foul pole, which is exactly 330 feet from home plate. I tense. Karin will surely be drawn to the lights and the emerald dazzle of the infield. If she touches anything, I fear it will all disappear, perhaps forever. Then, as if she senses my discomfort, she stumbles away from the lights, walking in the ragged fringe of darkness well outside the third-base line. She trails a blanket behind her, one tiny first rubbing a sleepy eye. She is barefoot and wears a white flannelette nightgown covered in an explosion of daisies.

She climbs up the bleacher, alternating a knee and a foot on each step, and crawls into my lap silently, like a kitten. I hold her close and wrap the blanket around her feet. The play goes on; her innocence has not disturbed the balance. 'What is it?' She asks shyly, her eyes indicating she means all that she sees.

'Just watch the left fielder,' I say. 'He'll tell you all you ever need to know about a baseball game. Watch his feet as the pitcher accepts the sign and gets ready to pitch. A good left fielder knows what pitch is coming, and he can tell from the angle of the bat where the ball is going to be hit, and, if he's good, how hard.'

I look down at Karin. She cocks one green eye at me, wrinkling her nose, then snuggles into my chest, the index finger of her right hand tracing tiny circles around her nose.

The crack of the bat is sharp as the yelp of a kicked cur. Shoeless Joe whirls, takes five loping strides directly toward us, turns again, reaches up, and the ball smacks into his glove. The final batter dawdles in the on-deck circle.

'Can I come back again?' Joe asks.

'I built this left field for you. It's yours any time you want to use it. They play one hundred and sixty-two games a season now.'

'There are others,' he says. 'If you were to finish the infield, why, old Chick Gandil could play first base, and we'd have the Swede at shortstop and Buck Weaver at third.' I can feel his excitement rising. 'We could stick McMullin in second, and Eddie Cicotte and Lefty Williams would like to pitch again. Do you think you could finish centre field? It would mean a lot to Happy Felsch.'

'Consider it done,' I say, hardly thinking of the time, the money, the back-breaking labour it would entail. 'Consider it done,' I say again, then stop suddenly as an idea creeps into my brain like a runner inching off first base.

'I know a catcher,' I say. 'He never made the majors, but in his prime he was good. Really good. Played Class B ball in Florida and California . . .

'We could give him a try,' says Shoeless Joe. 'You give us a place to play and we'll look at your catcher.'

I swear the stars have moved in close enough to eavesdrop as I sit in this single rickety bleacher that I built with my unskilled hands, looking down at Shoeless Joe Jackson. A breath of clover travels on the summer wind. Behind me, just yards away, brook water plashes softly in the darkness, a frog shrills, fireflies dazzle the night like red pepper. A petal falls.

'God what an outfield,' he says. 'What a left field.' He looks up at me and I look down at him. 'This must be heaven,' he says.

'No. It's Iowa,' I reply automatically. But then I feel the night rubbing softly against my face like cherry blossoms; look at the sleeping girl-child in my arms, her small hand curled around one of my fingers; think of the fierce warmth of the woman waiting for me in the house; inhale the fresh-cut grass smell that seems locked in the air like permanent incense; and listen to the drone of the crowd, as below me Shoeless Joe Jackson tenses, watching the angle of the distant bat for a clue as to where the ball will be hit.

'I think you're right, Joe,' I say, but softly enough not to disturb his concentration.

CAROL SHIELDS
(1935)

~

Milk Bread Beer Ice

'What's the different between a gully and a gulch?' Barbara Cormin asks her husband, Peter Cormin, as they speed south on the Interstate. These are the first words to pass between them in over an hour, this laconic, idle, unhopefully offered, trivia-contoured question.

Peter Cormin, driving a cautious sixty miles an hour through a drizzle of rain, makes no replay, and Barbara, from long experience, expects none. Her question concerning the difference between gullies and gulches floats out of her mouth like a smoker's lazy exhalation and is instantly subsumed by the hum of the engine. Two minutes pass. Five minutes. Barbara's thoughts skip to different geological features, the curious wind-lashed forms she sees through the car window, and those others whose names she vaguely remembers from a compulsory geology course taken years earlier—arroyos, cirques, terminal moraines. She has no idea now what these exotic relics might look like, but imagines them to be so brutal and arresting as to be instantly recognizable should they materialize on the landscape. Please let them materialize, she prays to the grooved door of the glove compartment. Let something, *anything*, materialize.

This is their fifth day on the road. Four motels, interchangeable, with tawny, fire-retardant carpeting, are all that have intervened. This morning, Day Five, they drive through a strong brown and yellow landscape, ferociously eroded, and it cheers Barbara a little to gaze out at this scene of novelty after seventeen hundred miles of green hills and ponds and calm, staring cattle. 'I really should keep a dictionary in the car,' she says to Peter, another languid exhalation.

The car, with its new-car smell, seems to hold both complaint and accord this morning. And silence. Barbara sits looking out at the rain, wondering about the origin of the word drizzle—a likeable enough word, she thinks, when you aren't actually being drizzled upon. Probably onomatopoetic. Drizzling clouds. Drizzled syrup on pancakes. She thrashes around in her head for the French equivalent: *bruine*, she thinks, or is that the word for fog? 'I hate not knowing things,' she says aloud to Peter. Musing. And arranging her body for the next five minutes.

At age fifty-three she is a restless traveller, forever shifting from haunch to haunch, tugging her blue cotton skirt smooth, examining its weave, sighing and stretching and fiddling in a disapproving way with the car radio. All she gets is country music. Or shouting call-in shows, heavy with sarcasm and whining indignation. Or nasal evangelists. Yesterday she and Peter listened briefly to someone preaching about the seven Fs of Christian love, the first F being, to her amazement, the fear of God, the *feah of Gawd.* Today, because of the rain, there's nothing on the radio but ratchety static. She and Peter have brought along a box of tapes, Bach and Handel and Vivaldi, that she methodically plays and replays, always expecting diversion and always forgetting she is someone who doesn't know what to do with music. She listens but doesn't hear. What she likes are words. *Drizzle,* she repeats to herself, *bruiner.* But how to conjugate it?

In the back seat are her maps and travel guides, a bundle of slippery brochures, a book called *Place Names of Texas* and another called *Texas Wildlife.* Her reference shelf. Her sanity cupboard. She can't remember how she acquired the habit of looking up facts; out of some nursery certitude, probably, connecting virtue with an active, inquiring mind. *People must never stop learning;* once Barbara had believed fervently in this embarrassing cliché, was the first in line for night-school classes, tuned in regularly with perhaps a dozen others to solemn radio talks on existentialism, Monday nights, seven to eight. And she has, too, her weekly French conversation group, now in its fourteenth year but soon to disband.

Her brain is always heating up; inappropriately, whimsically. She rather despises herself for it, and wishes, when she goes on vacation, that she could submerge herself in scenery or fantasy as other people seemed to do, her husband Peter in particular, or so she suspects. She would never risk saying to him, 'A penny for your thoughts', nor would he ever say such a thing to her. He believes such 'openers' are ill-bred intrusions. He told her as much, soon after they were married, lying above her on the living-room floor in their first apartment with the oval braided rug beneath them pushing up its round cushiony ribs. 'What are you thinking?' she had asked, and watched his eyes go cold.

The rain increases, little checks against the car window, and Barbara curls her legs up under her, something she seldom does—since it makes her feel like a woman trying too hard to be whimsical—and busies herself looking up Waco, Texas, in her guidebook. There it is: population figures, rainfall statistics, a naïve but jaunty potted history. Why at her age does she feel compelled to know such things? What is all this shrewdness working itself up for? Waco, she learns, is pronounced with a long A sound, which is disappointing. She prefers—who wouldn't?—the comic splat of wham, pow, whacko. Waco, Texas. The city rises and collapses in the rainy distance.

Leaning forward, she changes the tape. Its absolute, neat plastic corners remind her of the nature of real things, and snapping it into place gives her more satisfaction than listening to the music. A click, a short silence, and then the violins stirring themselves like iced-tea spoons, like ferns on a breezy hillside. Side two. She stares out the window, watchful for the least variation. A water tower holds her eye for a full sixty seconds, a silver thimble on stilts. *Château d'eau,* she murmurs to herself. Tower of Water. Tower of Babel.

Almost all her conversations are with herself.

Imprisoned now for five long days in the passenger seat of a brand new Oldsmobile Cutlass, Barbara thinks of herself as a castaway. Her real life has been left behind in Toronto. She and Peter are en route to Houston to attend an estate auction of a late client of Peter's, a man who ended his life not long ago with a pistol shot. For the sake of the passage, admittedly only two weeks, she has surrendered those routines that make her feel busy and purposeful. (With another woman she runs an establishment on Queen Street called the Ungift Shop; she also reads to the blind and keeps up her French.) Given the confining nature of her life, she has surprising freedoms at her disposal.

We should have flown is the phrase she is constantly on the point of uttering. Driving had been Peter's idea; she can't now remember his reasons; two reasons he gave, but what were they?

He has a craning look when he drives, immensely responsible. And a way of signalling when he passes, letting his thumb wing out sideways on the lever, a deft and lovely motion. She is struck by the beauty of it, also its absurdity, a little dwarfish, unconscious salute, and silent.

There is too much sorrowful sharing in marriage, Barbara thinks. When added up, it kills words. Games have to be invented; theatre. Out loud she says, like an imitation of a gawking person, 'I wonder what those little red flowers are.' (Turning, reaching for her wildlife book.) 'We don't have those in Ontario. Or do we?'

The mention of the red flowers comes after another long silence.

Then Peter says, not unkindly, not even impatiently, 'A gully's deeper, I think.'

'Deeper?' says Barbara in her dream voice. She is straining her eyes to read a billboard poised high on a yellow bluff. IF YOU SMOKE PLEASE TRY CARLETONS. The word *please*, it's shocking. So!—the tobacco industry has decided to get polite. Backed into a corner, attacked on all sides, they're hitting hard with wheedling courtesies, *please.* Last week Barbara watched a TV documentary on lung cancer and saw a set of succulent pink lungs turning into what looked like slices of burnt toast.

'Deeper than a gulch.'

'Oh,' says Barbara.

'Unless I've got it the wrong way around.'

'It's slang anyway, I think.'

'What?'

'Gully. Gulch. They're not real words, are they? They sound, you know, regional. Cowboy lingo.'

Peter takes a long banked curve. On and on it goes, ninety degrees or more, but finely graded. His hands on the wheel are scarcely required to move. Clean, thick hands, they might be carved out of twin bars of soap. Ivory soap, carbolic. He smiles faintly, but in a way that shuts Barbara out. On and on. Rain falls all around them—*il pleut*—on the windshield and on the twisted landforms and collecting along the roadway in ditches. 'Could be,' Peter says.

'Does that look brighter up ahead to you?' Barbara says wildly, anxious now to keep the conversation going. She puts away the tape, sits up straight, pats her hair, and readies herself for the little fates and accidents a conversation can provide.

Conversation?

Inside her head a quizzing eyebrow shoots up. These idle questions and observations? This dilatory response? This disobliging exchange between herself and her husband of thirty-three years, which is as random and broken as the geological rubble she dully observes from the car window, and about which Peter can scarcely trouble himself to comment? This sludge of gummed phrases? Conversation?

It could be worse, thinks Barbara, always anxious to be fair, and calling to mind real and imaginary couples sitting silent in coffee shops, whole meals consumed and paid for with not a single word exchanged. Or stunned-looking husbands and wives at home in their vacuumed living rooms, neatly dressed and conquered utterly by the background hum of furnaces and air-conditioning units. And after that, what?—a desperate slide into hippo grunts and night coughing, slack, sponge-soft lips and toothless dread—that word *mute* multiplied to the thousandth power. Death.

An opportunity to break in the new car was what Peter has said—now she remembered.

Barbara met Peter in 1955 at a silver auction in Quebec City. He was an apprentice then, learning the business. He struck her first as being very quiet. He stared and stared at an antique coffee service, either assessing its value or awestruck by its beauty—she didn't know which. Later he grew talkative. Then silent. Then eloquent. Secretive. Verbose. Introspective. Gregarious. A whole colony of choices appeared to rest in his larynx. She never knew what to expect. One minute they were on trustworthy ground, feeding each other intimacies, and the next minute they were capsized, adrift and dumb.

'Some things can't be put into words,' a leaner, nervous, younger Peter Cormin once said.

'Marriage can be defined as a lifelong conversation,' said an elderly, sentimental, slightly literary aunt of Barbara's, meaning to be kind.

Barbara at twenty had felt the chill press of rhetorical echo: *a religious vocation is one of continuous prayer, a human life is one unbroken thought.* Frightening. She knew better, though, than to trust what was cogently expressed. Even as a young woman she was forever tripping over abandoned proverbs. She counted on nothing, but hoped for everything.

Breaking in the new car. But did people still break in cars? She hadn't heard the term used for years. Donkey's years. Whatever that meant.

A younger, thinner, more devious Barbara put planning into her conversations. There was breakfast talk and dinner talk and lively hurried telephone chatter in between. She often cast herself in the role of *ingénue,* allowing her husband Peter space for commentary and suggestions. It was Barbara who put her head to one side, posed questions and prettily waited. It was part of their early shared mythology that he was sometimes arrogant to the point of unkindness, and that she was sensitive and put upon, an injured consciousness flayed by husbandly imperative. But neither of them had the ability to sustain their roles for long.

She learned certain tricks of subversions, how with one word or phrase she could bring about disorder and then reassurance. It excited her. It was like flying in a flimsy aircraft and looking at the suddenly vertical horizon, then bringing everything level once more.

'You've changed,' one of her conversations began.

'Everyone changes.'

'For better or worse?'

'Better, I think.'

'You think?'

'I know.'

'You say things differently. You intellectualize.'

'Maybe that's my nature.'

'It didn't use to be.'

'I've changed, people do change.'

'That's just what I said.'

'I wish you wouldn't—'

'What?'

'Point things out. Do you always have to point things out?'

'I can't help it.'

'You could stop yourself.'

'That wouldn't be me.'

Once they went to a restaurant to celebrate the birth of their second son. The restaurant was inexpensive and the food only moderately good. After coffee, after glasses of recklessly ordered brandy, Peter slipped away to the telephone. A business call, he said to Barbara. He would only be a minute or two. From where she saw she could see him behind the glass door of the phone booth, his uplifted arm, his patient explanation, and his glance at his watch—then his face reshaped itself into furrows of explosive laughter.

She had been filled with a comradely envy for his momentary connection, and surprised by her lack of curiosity, how little she cared who was on the other end of the line, a client or a lover, it didn't matter. A conversation was in progress. Words were being mainlined straight into Peter's ear, and the overflow of his conversation travelled across the dull white tablecloths and reached her too, filling her emptiness, or part of it.

Between the two of them they have accumulated a minor treasury of anecdotes beginning with 'Remember when we—' and this literature of remembrance sometimes traps them into smugness. And, occasionally, when primed by a solid period of calm, they are propelled into the blue-tinged pre-history of that epoch before they met.

'When I was in Denver that time—'

'I never knew you were in Denver.'

'My mother took me there once . . .'

'You never told me your mother took you to . . .'

But Barbara is tenderly protective of her beginnings. She is also, oddly, protective of Peter's. Eruptions from this particular and most cherished layer of time are precious and dangerous; retrieval betrays it, smudges it.

'There's something wrong,' Barbara said to Peter some years ago, 'and I don't know how to tell you.'

They were standing in a public garden near their house, walking between beds of tulips.

'You don't love me,' he guessed, amazing her, and himself.

'I love you but not enough.'

'What is enough?' he cried and reached out for the cotton sleeve of her dress.

A marriage counsellor booked them for twelve sessions. Each session lasted two hours, twenty-four hours in all. During those twenty-four hours they released into the mild air of the marriage counsellor's office millions of words. Their longest conversation. The polished floor, the walls, the perforated ceiling tile drank in the unstoppable flow. Barbara Cormin wept and shouted. Peter Cormin moaned, retreated, put his head on his arms. The histories they separately recounted were as detailed as the thick soft novels people carry with them to the beach in the summer. Every story elicited a counter-story, until the accumulated weight of blame and blemish had squeezed them dry. 'What are we doing?' Peter Cormin said, moving the back of his hand across and across his mouth. Barbara thought back to the day she had stood by the sunlit tulip bed and said, 'Something's wrong', and wondered now what had possessed her. A hunger for words, was that all? She asked the marriage counsellor for a glass of cold water. She feared what lay ahead. A long fall into silence. An expensive drowning.

But they were surprisingly happy for quite some time after, speaking to each other kindly, with a highly specific strategy, little pieces moved on a chess board. What had been tricky territory before was strewn with shame. Barbara was prepared now to admit that marriage was, at best, a flawed and gappy narrative. Occasionally some confidence would wobble forward and one of them, Barbara or Peter, might look up cunningly, ready to measure the moment and retreat or advance. They worked around the reserves of each other's inattention the way a pen-and-ink artist learns to use the reserve of white space.

'Why?' Barbara asked Peter.

'Why what?'

'Why did he do it? Shoot himself.'

'No one knows for sure.'

'There's always a note. Wasn't there a note?'

'Yes. But very short.'

'Saying?'

'He was lonely.'

'That's what he said, that he was lonely?'

'More or less.'

'What exactly did he say?'

'That there was no one he could talk to.'

'He had a family, didn't he? And business associates. He had you, he's known you for years. He could have picked up the phone.'

'Talking isn't just words.'

'What?'

Barbara sees herself as someone always waiting for the next conversation, the way a drunk is forever thinking ahead to the next drink.

But she discounts the conversation of Eros which seems to her to be learned not from life, but from films or trashy novels whose authors have in turn learned it from other secondary and substandard sources. Where bodies collide most gloriously, language melts—who said that? Someone or other. Barbara imagines that listening at the bedroom keyholes of even the most richly articulate would be to hear only the murmurous inanities of *True Romance*. ('I adore your golden breasts,' he whispered gruffly. 'You give me intense pleasure,' she deeply sighed.) But these conversations actually take place. She knows they do. The words are pronounced. The sighing and whispering happen. *Just the two of us, this paradise.*

'We can break in the car,' Peter said to her back in Toronto, 'and have a few days together, just the two of us.'

Very late on Day Five they leave the Interstate and strike off on a narrow asphalt road in search of a motel. The cessation of highway noise is stunningly sudden, like swimming away in a dream from the noises of one's own body. Peter holds his head to one side, judging the car's performance, the motor's renewed, slower throb and the faint adhesive tick of the tires rolling on the hot road.

The towns they pass through are poor, but have seen better days. Sidewalks leading up to lovely old houses have crumbled along their edges, and the houses themselves have begun to deteriorate; many are for sale; dark shaggy cottonwoods bend down their branches to meet the graceful pitch of the roofs. Everywhere in these little towns there are boarded-up railway stations, high schools, laundries, cafés, plumbing supply stores, filling stations. And almost everywhere, it seems, the commercial centre has shrunk to a single, blinking, all-purpose, twenty-four-hour outlet at the end of town—pathetically, but precisely named: the Mini-Mart, the Superette, the Quik-Stop. These new buildings are of single-storey slab construction in pale brick or cement block, and are minimally landscaped. One or two gas pumps sit out in front, and above them is a sign, most often homemade, saying MILK ICE BREAD BEER.

'Milk ice bread beer', murmurs the exhausted Barbara, giving the phrase a heaving tune. She is diverted by the thought of these four purposeful commodities traded to a diminished and deprived public. 'The four elements.'

In the very next town, up and down over a series of dark hills, they find a subtly altered version: BEER ICE BREAD MILK. 'Priorities,' says Peter, reading the sign aloud, making an ironic chant of it.

Further along the road they come upon BREAD BEER MILK ICE. Later still, the rescrambled BEER MILK ICE BREAD.

Before they arrive, finally, at a motel with air-conditioning, a restaurant, and decent beds—no easy matter in a depressed agricultural region—they have seen many such signs and in all possible variations. Cryptic messages, they seem designed to comfort and confuse Peter and Barbara Cormin with loops of flawed recognition and to deliver them to a congenial late-evening punchiness. As the signs pop up along the highway, they take it in turn, with a rhythmic spell and counter-spell, to read the words aloud. Milk bread beer ice. Ice bread milk beer.

This marks the real death of words, thinks Barbara, these homely products reduced to husks, their true sense drained purely away. Ice beer bread milk. Rumblings in the throats, syllables strung on an old clothesline, electronic buzzing.

But, surprisingly, the short unadorned sounds, for a few minutes, with daylight fading and dying in the wide sky, take on expanded meaning. Another, lesser world is brought forward, distorted and freshly provisioned. She loves it—its weather and depth, its exact chambers, its lost circuits, its covered pleasures, its submerged pattern of communication.

AUDREY THOMAS
(1935)

❧

Bear Country

Last year Wilma took French at the YMCA downtown because it was right next door to where she worked part time as a secretary in the English department at Concordia. She is a performance artist in real life (that's what she always says, when asked) with a small but energetic company called Les Jours Sans et Les Jours Avec.

She is the newest member of the company, most of whom are at least functionally bilingual; she moved here from Vancouver Island just over a year ago. Last October she heard one male professor say to another that the air in Canada was putrid with feminism. She went home and wrote a skit based on the Pollution Scoreboard at the McGill metro. Instead of indicating levels of dust, sulphur dioxide, and carbon monoxide, the scoreboard at the back of the stage showed levels of feminism for that day. (Since the real sign is in French she created her sign in French as well, complete with the *bon* and *mauvais* at the bottom, anything over fifty being bad.) When she consults her dictionary she is surprised to discover that *féminisme* is a masculine word. This is not important to the skit but it gives her pause. Perhaps all words ending in *isme* are masculine in French? The skit involved a metro car, full of men and women, with a stewardess on board, just like in an airplane. The stewardess explains that if the levels of feminism get too high masks will automatically drop from the ceiling and they must breathe normally blah blah blah. Everything is said in both French and English. The train passes the McGill metro again and again. (This is done with blackouts and sound and the voice of the unseen conductor—a female voice—repeating '*prochain arrêt*, McGill.') The level goes above fifty on the board, the masks drop down as the men—most of them—clutch at their throats and gasp for breath, while the women—most of them—carry on reading or chatting or just waiting quietly to get to their destination. It was a very short piece, maybe ten minutes, and the first part ended in the dark with a voice (male) saying, 'Soon there were days when it wasn't safe for men to go out at all.'

In the second part of the skit, Mulroney (in mask) and Bush (in mask) are having an emergency summit to discuss the problem. Mrs Bush (without mask) is saying, 'But I thought it was Acid Rain.' 'Avid Ray?' say the men, from behind their masks.

The audience loved it; they thought it was hilarious. She called the piece 'Acceptable Levels' and she was mentioned in *The Mirror* and a few other places as a talent to watch. Very few of the people she worked with had attended the performance, which ran for three nights—even though she had put up posters announcing the event. The professor who had made the original remark looked at her strangely once or twice but she just smiled sweetly and continued filing applications for graduate studies.

Now—since last December—she doubted whether that man would have made such a remark out loud, in a more or less public place. He might have thought it but he wouldn't have said it out loud. *Putrid* with feminism! It was the use of the word putrid that scared her—something rotten and stinking, like a decayed tooth or a gangrenous leg: something poisonous and foul. Get rid of it quick.

This was an intelligent man, a good teacher—or so she had heard—respected in his field. He had a tendency towards marrying his students but in that he was hardly unique. Wilma had been a student not so long ago; she knew the pull of an attractive, knowledgeable older man, someone who leaned across the table at the Faculty Club and said, without the least trace of embarrassment: 'You look just like a Burne-Jones painting, did you know that?' (Or a Renoir or an Ingres, whatever.) Wilma never fell for it but only because she wanted to make a work of art, not be one. To be loved (or desired) by your mentor was pretty flattering, although she had found out in her senior year that Mentor was really Athena in disguise.

So she didn't lose her job over the pollution piece and she could have gone back to the 'Y'. She had enjoyed the class, and the teacher, a young man, was very interested in feminism. He had even shown them an NFB film, in French, about a woman who was raped. It was called *Scream Your Head Off* or something like that, and in the discussion that followed he said that men and boys were raped too—that he had been raped by an uncle when he was ten. Wilma wanted to ask him how that had affected his life, but the time was up. That was December 5. The next time the class met the discussion was about the massacre. 'I'm afraid,' Wilma said, '*J'ai peur.*' (In her dictionary she saw that blood was masculine, *le sang*, but wound was feminine, *la blessure*.)

In the spring, mostly to cheer herself up, Wilma concocted a much lighter piece, called 'Salad Days', about the Yuppie obsession with just the right cooking ingredients—sun-dried tomatoes, *crème fraîche*, balsamic vinegar, *coulis* of this or that. She devoured gourmet magazines and put on seven pounds doing research, because reading about food, especially looking at the pictures, made her so hungry she would rush out to the *dépanneur* and buy junk food—chips or ice cream or nasty little cakes in cellophane packages. She herself played the extra-virgin, as in extra-virgin olive oil, the only kind worth using in your Yuppie salad dressing. In the skit she is a kind of Mediterranean wallflower, over-protected by her parents and scorned by the village boys. She is never asked to dance, not even in the group dances, until one day an entrepreneur comes along and invents the idea of extra-virgin olive oil. From then on it is she who controls the olive groves, and young girls fight to be her attendants. Needless to say the sexual life of the young men comes to a virtual halt.

This piece was an even bigger success than the pollution skit (*pollution*, a feminine noun) and led to a scholarship at the Banff summer school of the arts. Now she is back in Montreal and she and her new friend, Annie, a painter she met at Banff, have decided they will go together to evening classes at the Université de Montréal. Annie comes from Nova Scotia and has been in Montreal for five years, but she graduated from Concordia and has an anglophone boyfriend; she feels she hasn't made much progress with her French. She dresses almost completely in black and wears bright red lipstick and yet, to Wilma, she seems to radiate a playful innocence. She zips around town on her bike (Wilma, who rode a bike in Victoria, decided long ago that she would never ride a bike in this mad traffic) but from where they both live the trip to UDM is a long way, so they arrange to meet at the Edouard Montpetit station and take the #51 bus to the university. Everyone on the bus appears to be speaking French except for them and they tell one another that not only will they probably get better teaching at UDM, they will hear French in the corridors and cafeteria. When Annie says 'cafeteria' Wilma asks if it makes her at all nervous to think they'll be taking classes, at night, at the university. Annie says that as a matter of fact she hadn't thought she was nervous but once they got on the bus she couldn't help thinking about it. 'I've never even been there,' Wilma says. 'I meant to go when I first arrived—just because I wanted to explore the whole city—but I never got around to Outremont and the university. Then, after the massacre' (*massacre*, a masculine noun in French) 'I felt as though it would be spying.'

Annie said she went for the vigil. Wilma had left for her holiday in Victoria—the trip was her parents' Christmas present—the day after the shooting so she hadn't even been present at that.

They got lost trying to find the place where they were to register and were half an hour late, as a consequence, for the placement exam. At first the professor wasn't going to let them in, but when Wilma said, waving the receipt, '*Mais nous avons déjà payé,*' he relented. But they would have to start in the middle; it was far too late to begin at the beginning. A notice on the blackboard said they should report to a building on Outremont Avenue on the following Monday and they would be assigned to their appropriate level. The questions were all multiple choice; neither of them had any idea how well or badly they had done.

Late Monday afternoon—Wilma was working at home—the phone rang and a voice, speaking rapid French, told her that the location for her class had been changed and she was to report to room B1.4 on the sixth floor of the Ecole Polytechnique. Wilma's heart began to pound. She asked the woman to repeat the message.

'How do I get there?' Wilma said, in French.

'You take the metro to the Université de Montréal or the *autobus* #51 and then you mount.'

Had the woman really said *mount?* Wilma dialled Annie's number, left a message on her machine, and told herself she was being ridiculous. She and Annie would be together and there would be others as well. If they dropped out just because the room had been changed to the Ecole Polytechnique then Marc Lépine had won—or they had lost.

Wilma had read in the paper that the enrolment of women in engineering faculties was up all over Canada, even here in Montreal. It was no good being frightened.

But when Annie called she said she had received no such message. She'd call the university and check. When she phoned Wilma back she said, 'You did too well on your test; you're in a higher level than I am, so we won't be going to the same place.'

'I don't want to go up there alone,' Wilma said.

'I don't blame you,' Annie said. 'Maybe you can talk to your teacher.'

Annie got off the bus way before Wilma—who asked a boy sitting next to her where was the best place to get off—and then Wilma stood, uncertainly, wondering just how she got to the top of the mountain. When she first arrived in Montreal, she had laughed that this hill was called 'the mountain' but now, at 6:15 on a September evening, it seemed to loom up above her in a threatening way. ('Mount Real,' she thought to herself. 'Come on, Wilma, don't just stand there.')

Several students gave her directions but it took quite a while to actually reach the classroom and she was only just on time. She had to go in an entrance, up a steep moving sidewalk, around to the left, out a door, around to the right, across a road, and then up a set of steep wooden steps (she counted forty-one) to the Ecole Polytechnique itself. It was still daylight but Wilma wondered what those steps would be like in winter. It seemed to her they were badly lit, with bushes on both sides. Had Marc Lépine gone up and down those steps, in and out of buildings, gathering his dark resolve to kill the feminists who dared to climb the mountain? There did not seem to be any security men around even now; people passed freely in and out of the main doors, up the steps and into the body of the building. By the time she reached the class she was so tense her shoulders hurt. As she went along corridors and passed by the cafeteria, she thought, 'Is this the way he went; did he shoot someone just here?'

The teacher was young and very pretty. When she asked if anyone had had trouble finding the room Wilma expected someone to speak up and say that they were afraid to come here. There were complaints but they all centred around how awkward it was to get there, how long it took. The teacher said she might be able to change the venue but she doubted it. She smiled: in any event, they had the best view of Montreal. Tonight they would witness a grand *coucher du soleil.* The sun was setting as she spoke; it glittered like a new penny or the bottom or a copper pan. Wilma looked at the clock. By

December it would be dark long before this. She imagined the students on that night, the last night before exams, listening to their professor (*professeur, m.*) or maybe day-dreaming a little about what they were going to do during their *vacances*. In the winter night the windows would act as mirrors; the teacher and the students would have an identical teacher and students sitting next to them in the windows. Perhaps someone saw him in the window first, saw and couldn't quite take it in, a guy with a gun, a rifle (*revolver, pistolet, fusil, canon, m. m. m. m.*) in camouflage clothes. Wha? What! *Quoi! Seigneur!*

When Wilma was in grade eight she took her first French class. She still remembers a paragraph she had to memorize.

J'entre dans la salle de classe. Je regarde autour de moi. Je vois les élèves et le professeur. Je dis bonjour au professeur. Je prends ma place.

Now she said this to herself, but saw the man with the rifle acting out the sentences.

J'entre dans la salle de classe. (The man comes in; he carries his rifle in front of him, his finger on the trigger. The garbage bag is outside in the hall.)

Je regarde autour de moi.

(He looks around.)

Je vois les élèves et le professeur.

Je dis. . . .

(He shouts. 'You're all fucking feminists'—what was that in French?)

Maudites féministes! But she has forgotten something; he made the men leave, first.

Je prends ma place.

The teacher has been calling Wilma's name. Now she laughs, '*Est-ce que vous êtes une rêveuse*, Wilma?'

'*Oui*,' Wilma says, '*toujours*.' Out the window the sun has burst and stained the sky with lovely colour: pinks, golds. The sky looks, to Wilma, like the inside of a shell. She has heard that the more dust there is in the air, the more pollution, the better the sunset.

At Banff last summer, with some help from others in her workshop, Wilma put on a performance piece called 'Bear Country'. She got the idea from a brochure she picked up in the tourist office down in the town. It said on the front YOU ARE IN BEAR COUNTRY and was full of advice and warnings. (Plus a few facts that astonished Wilma, such as the fact menstruating women have to be very careful where bears are concerned.) Because she has begun to enjoy playing around with the two official languages she reads the whole thing religiously in both French and English. When she sees that the French word for bear is '*ours*' she begins to have an idea. What comes forth is a feminist piece, of course. She can't seem to get away from that. It's funny but not funny and it requires audience participation.

A group of women stand on the stage wearing bear bells, which they ring loudly to let the bears know that they are coming. A tape in the background is playing 'The Teddy Bears' Picnic'. Wilma is dressed in a bear suit and she stands over with the men. (The men and women have been asked to sit on separate sides and on each seat Wilma has placed a short script.) At first the men are reluctant to join in—a lot of them don't take Wilma very seriously as an artist but, because the final performances are open to everyone, they've come along out of curiosity. Wilma is carrying her bear head under her arm as she explains how the piece will go, that it's antiphonal and she wants each side to really belt out its part. She puts on the bear's head and nods to the women to begin.

Over the ridiculous sound of the bear bells the women say, more or less in unison, 'We are in Bear Country.'

'This country is ours,' say the men.

ALISTAIR MACLEOD
(1936)

~

As Birds Bring Forth the Sun

Once there was a family with a highland name who lived beside the sea. And the man had a dog of which he was very fond. She was large and grey, a sort of staghound from another time. And if she jumped up to lick his face, which she loved to do, her paws would jolt against his shoulders with such force that she would come close to knocking him down and he would be forced to take two or three backward steps before he could regain his balance. And he himself was not a small man, being slightly over six feet and perhaps one hundred and eighty pounds.

She had been left, when a pup, at the family's gate in a small handmade box and no one knew where she had come from or that she would eventually grow to such a size. Once, while still a small pup, she had been run over by the steel wheel of a horse-drawn cart which was hauling kelp from the shore to be used as fertilizer. It was in October and the rain had been falling for some weeks and the ground was soft. When the wheel of the cart passed over her, it sunk her body into the wet earth as well as crushing some of her ribs; and apparently the silhouette of her small crushed body was visible in the earth after the man lifted her to his chest while she yelped and screamed. He ran his fingers along her broken bones, ignoring the blood and urine which fell upon his shirt, trying to soothe her bulging eyes and her scrabbling front paws and her desperately licking tongue.

The more practical members of his family, who had seen run-over dogs before, suggested that her neck be broken by his strong hands or that he grasp her by the hind legs and swing her head against a rock, thus putting an end to her misery. but he would not do it.

Instead, he fashioned a small box and lined it with woollen remnants from a sheep's fleece and one of his old and frayed shirts. He placed her within the box and placed the box behind the stove and then he warmed some milk in a small saucepan and sweetened it with sugar. And he held open her small and trembling jaws with his left hand while spooning the sweetened milk with his right, ignoring the needle-like sharpness of her small teeth. She lay in the box most of the remaining fall and into the early winter, watching everything with her large brown eyes.

Although some members of the family complained about her presence and the odour from the box and the waste of time she involved, they gradually adjusted to her; and as the weeks passed by, it became evident that her ribs were knitting together in some form or other and that she was recovering with the resilience of the young. It also became evident that she would grow to a tremendous size, as she outgrew one box and then another and the grey hair began to feather from her huge front paws. In the spring she was outside almost all of the time and followed the man everywhere; and when she came inside during the following months, she had grown so large that she would no longer fit into her accustomed place behind the stove and was forced to lie beside it. She was never given a name but was referred to in Gaelic as *cù mòr glas*, the big grey dog.

By the time she came into her first heat, she had grown to a tremendous height, and although her signs and her odour attracted many panting and highly aroused suitors, none was big enough to mount her and the frenzy of their disappointment and the longing of her unfulfilment were more than the man could stand. He went, so the story goes, to a place where he knew there was a big dog. A dog not as big as she was, but still a big dog, and he brought him home with him. And at the proper time he took the *cù mòr glas* and the big dog down to the sea where he knew there was a hollow in the rock which appeared only at low tide. He took some sacking to provide footing for the male dog and he placed the *cù mòr glas* in the hollow of the rock and knelt beside her and steadied her with his left arm under her throat and helped position the male dog above her and guided his blood-engorged penis. He was a man used to working with the breeding of animals, with the guiding of rams and bulls and stallions and often with the funky smell of animal semen heavy on his large and gentle hands.

The winter that followed was a cold one and ice formed on the sea and frequent squalls and blizzards obliterated the offshore islands and caused the people to stay near their fires much of the time, mending clothes and nets and harness and waiting for the change in season. The *cù mòr glas* grew heavier and even more large until there was hardly room for her around the stove or even under the table. And then one morning, when it seemed that spring was about to break, she was gone.

The man and even his family, who had become more involved than they cared to admit, waited for her but she did not come. And as the frenzy of spring wore on, they busied themselves with readying their land and their fishing gear and all of the things that so desperately required their attention. And then they were into summer and fall and winter and another spring which saw the birth of the man and his wife's twelfth child. And then it was summer again.

That summer the man and two of his teenaged sons were pulling their herring nets about two miles offshore when the wind began to blow off the land and the water began to roughen. They became afraid that they could not make it safely back to shore, so they pulled in behind one of the offshore islands, knowing that they would be sheltered there and planning to outwait the storm. As the prow of their boat approached the gravelly shore, they heard a sound above them, and looking up they saw the *cù mòr glas* silhouetted on the brow of the hill which was the small island's highest point.

'*M'eudal cù mòr glas*' shouted the man in his happiness—*m'eudal* meaning something like dear or darling; and as he shouted, he jumped over the side of his boat into the waist-deep water, struggling for footing on the rolling gravel as he waded eagerly and awkwardly towards her and the shore. At the same time, the *cù mòr glas* came hurtling down towards him in a shower of small rocks dislodged by her feet; and just as he was emerging from the water, she met him as she used to, rearing up on her hind legs and placing her huge front paws on his shoulders while extending her eager tongue.

The weight and speed of her momentum met him as he tried to hold his balance on the sloping angle and the water rolling gravel beneath his feet, and he staggered backwards and lost his footing and fell beneath her force. And in that instant again, as the story goes, there appeared over the brow of the hill six more huge grey dogs hurtling down towards the gravelled strand. They had never seen him before; and seeing him stretched prone beneath their mother, they misunderstood, like so many armies, the intention of their leader.

They fell upon him in a fury, slashing his face and tearing aside his lower jaw and ripping out his throat, crazed with blood-lust or duty or perhaps starvation. The *cù mòr glas* turned on them in her own savagery, slashing and snarling and, it seemed, crazed by their mistake; driving them bloodied and yelping before her, back over the brow of the hill where they vanished from sight but could still be heard screaming in the distance. It all took perhaps little more than a minute.

The man's two sons, who were still in the boat and had witnessed it all, ran sobbing through the salt water to where their mauled and mangled father lay; but there was little they could do other than hold his warm and bloodied hands for a few brief moments. Although his eyes 'lived' for a small fraction of time, he could not speak to them because his face and throat had been torn away, and of course there was nothing they could do except to hold and be held tightly until that too slipped away and his eyes glazed over and they could no longer feel his hands holding theirs. The storm increased and they could not get home and so they were forced to spend the night huddled beside their father's body. They were afraid to try to carry the body to the rocking boat because he was so heavy and they were afraid that they might lose even what little of him remained and they were afraid also, huddled on the rocks, that the dogs might return. But they did not return at all and there was no sound from them, no sound at all, only the moaning of the wind and the washing of the water on the rocks.

In the morning they debated whether they should try to take his body with them or whether they should leave it and return in the company of older and wiser men. But they were afraid to leave it unattended and felt that the time needed to cover it with protective rocks would be better spent in trying to get across to their home shore. For a while they debated as to whether one should go in the boat and the other remain on the island, but each was afraid to be alone and so in the end they managed to drag and carry and almost float him towards the bobbing boat. They lay him face-down and covered him with what clothes there were and set off across the still-rolling sea. Those who waited on the shore missed the large presence of the man within the boat and some of them waded into the water and others rowed out in skiffs, attempting to hear the tearful messages called out across the rolling waves.

The *cù mòr glas* and her six young dogs were never seen again, or perhaps I should say they were never seen again in the same way. After some weeks, a group of men circled the island tentatively in their boats but they saw no sign. They went again and then again but found nothing. A year later, and grown much braver, they beached their boats and walked the island care-fully, looking into the small sea caves and the hollows at the base of the wind-ripped trees, thinking perhaps that if they did not find the dogs, they might at least find their whitened bones; but again they discovered nothing.

The *cù mòr glas*, though, was supposed to be sighted here and there for a number of years. Seen on a hill in one region or silhouetted on a ridge in another or loping across the valleys or glens in the early morning or the shadowy evening. Always in the area of the half perceived. For a while she became rather like the Loch Ness Monster or the Sasquatch on a smaller scale. Seen but not recorded. Seen when there were no cameras. Seen but never taken.

The mystery of where she went became entangled with the mystery of whence she came. There was increased speculation about the handmade box in which she had been found and much theorizing as to the individual or individuals who might have left it. People went to look for the box but could not find it. It was felt she might have been part of a *buidseachd* or evil spell cast on the man by some mysterious enemy. But no one could go much farther than that. All of his caring for her was recounted over and over again and nobody missed any of the ironies.

What seemed literally known was that she had crossed the winter ice to have her pups and had been unable to get back. No one could remember ever seeing her swim; and in the early months at least, she could not have taken her young pups with her.

The large and gentle man with the smell of animal semen often heavy on his hands was my great-great-great-grandfather, and it may be argued that he died because he was too good at breeding animals or that he cared too much about their fulfilment and well-being. He was no longer there for his own child of the spring who, in turn, became my great-great-grandfather, and he was perhaps too much there in the memory of his older sons who saw him fall beneath the ambiguous force of the *cù mòr glas*. The youngest boy in the boat was haunted and tormented by the awfulness of what he had seen. He would wake at night screaming that he had seen the *cù mòr glas a'b-*

hàis, the big grey dog of death, and his screams filled the house and the ears and minds of the listeners, bringing home again and again the consequences of their loss. One morning, after a night in which he saw the *cù mòr glas a'bhàis* so vividly that his sheets were drenched with sweat, he walked to the high cliff which faced the island and there he cut his throat with a fish knife and fell into the sea.

The other brother lived to be forty, but, again so the story goes, he found himself in a Glasgow pub one night, perhaps looking for answers, deep and sodden with the whiskey which had become his anaesthetic. In the half darkness he saw a large, grey-haired man sitting by himself against the wall and mumbled something to him. Some say he saw the *cù mòr glas a'bhàis* or uttered the name. And perhaps the man heard the phrase through ears equally affected by drink and felt he was being called a dog or a son of a bitch or something of that nature. They rose to meet one another and struggled outside into the cobble-stoned passageway behind the pub where, most improbably, there were supposed to be six other large, grey-haired men who beat him to death on the cobblestones, smashing his bloodied head into the stone again and again before vanishing and leaving him to die with his face turned to the sky. The *cù mòr glas a'bhàis* had come again, said his family, as they tried to piece the tale together.

This is how the *cù mòr glas a'bhàis* came into our lives, and it is obvious that all of this happened a long, long time ago. Yet with succeeding generations it seemed the spectre had somehow come to stay and that it had become *ours*—not in the manner of an unwanted skeleton in the closet from a family's ancient past but more in the manner of something close to a genetic possibility. In the deaths of each generation, the grey dog was seen by some—by women who were to die in childbirth; by soldiers who went forth to the many wars but did not return; by those who went forth to feuds or dangerous love affairs; by those who answered mysterious midnight messages; by those who swerved on the highway to avoid the real or imagined grey dog and ended in masses of crumpled steel. And by one professional athlete who, in addition to his ritualized athletic superstitions, carried another fear or belief as well. Many of the man's descendants moved like careful hemophiliacs, fearing that they carried unwanted possibilities deep within them. And others, while they laughed, were like members of families in which there is a recurrence over the generations of repeated cancer or the diabetes which comes to those beyond middle age. The feeling of those who may say little to others but who may say often and quietly to themselves, 'It has not happened to me,' while adding always the cautionary '*yet*'.

I am thinking all of this now as the October rain falls on the city of Toronto and the pleasant, white-clad nurses pad confidently in and out of my father's room. He lies quietly amidst the whiteness, his head and shoulders elevated so that he is in that hospital position of being neither quite prone nor yet sitting. His hair is white upon his pillow and he breathes softly and sometimes unevenly, although it is difficult ever to be sure.

My five grey-haired brothers and I take turns beside his bedside, holding his heavy hands in ours and feeling their response, hoping ambiguously that he will speak to us, although we know that it may tire him. And trying to read his life and ours into his eyes when they are open. He has been with us for a long time, well into our middle age. Unlike those boys in that boat of so long ago, we did not see him taken from us in our youth. And unlike their youngest brother who, in turn, became our great-great-grandfather, we did not grow into a world in which there was no father's touch. We have been lucky to have this large and gentle man so deep into our lives.

No one in this hospital has mentioned the *cù mòr glas a'bhàis*. Yet as my mother said ten years ago, before slipping into her own death as quietly as a grownup child who leaves or enters her parents' house in the early hours, 'It is hard to *not* know what you do know.'

Even those who are most sceptical, like my oldest brother who has driven here from Montreal, betray themselves by their nervous actions. 'I avoided the Greyhound bus stations in both Montreal and Toronto,' he smiled upon his arrival, and then added, 'Just in case.'

He did not realize how ill our father was and has smiled little since then. I watch him turning the diamond ring upon his finger, knowing that he hopes he will not hear the Gaelic he knows too well. Not having the luxury, as he once said, of some who live in Montreal and are able to pretend they do not understand the 'other' language. You cannot *not* know what you do know.

Sitting here, taking turns holding the hands of the man who gave us life, we are afraid for him and for ourselves. We are afraid of what he may see and we are afraid to hear the phrase born of the vision. We are aware that it may become confused with what the doctors call 'the will to live' and we are aware that some beliefs are what others would dismiss as 'garbage'. We are aware that there are men who believe the earth is flat and that the birds bring forth the sun.

Bound here in our own peculiar mortality, we do not wish to see or see others see that which signifies life's demise. We do not want to hear the voice of our father, as did those other sons, calling down his own particular death upon him.

We would shut our eyes and plug our ears, even as we know such actions to be of no avail. Open still and fearful to the grey hair rising on our necks if and when we hear the scrabble of the paws and the scratching at the door.

BARRY CALLAGHAN
(1937)

The Black Queen

Hughes and McCrae were fastidious men who took pride in their old colonial house, the clean simple lines and stucco walls and the painted pale blue picket fence. They were surrounded by houses converted into small warehouses, trucking yards where houses had been torn down, and along the street, a school filled with foreign children, but they didn't mind. It gave them an embattled sense of holding on to something important, a tattered remnant of good taste in an area of waste overrun by rootless olive-skinned children.

McCrae wore his hair a little too long now that he was going grey, and while Hughes with his clipped moustache seemed to be a serious man intent only on his work, which was costume design, McCrae wore Cuban heels and lacquered his nails. When they'd met ten years ago Hughes had said, 'You keep walking around like that and you'll need a body to keep you from getting poked in the eye.' McCrae did all the cooking and drove the car.

But they were not getting along these days. Hughes blamed his bursitis but they were both silently unsettled by how old they had suddenly become, how loose in the thighs, and their feet, when they were showering in the morning, seemed bonier, the toes longer, the nails yellow and hard, and what they wanted was tenderness, to be able to yield almost tearfully, full of a pity for themselves that would not be belittled or laughed at, and when they stood alone in their separate bedrooms they wanted that tenderness from each other, but when they were having their bedtime tea in the kitchen, as they had done for years using lovely green and white Limoges cups, if one touched the other's hand then suddenly they both withdrew into an unspoken, smiling aloofness, as if some line of privacy had been crossed. Neither could bear their thinning wrists and the little pouches of darkening flesh under the chin. They spoke of being with younger people and even joked slyly about bringing a young man home, but that seemed such a betrayal of everything that they had believed had set them apart from others, everything they believed had kept them together, that they sulked and nettled away at each other, and though nothing had apparently changed in their lives, they were always on edge, Hughes more than McCrae.

One of their pleasures was collecting stamps, rare and mint-perfect, with no creases or smudges on the gum. Their collection, carefully mounted in a leatherbound blue book with seven little plastic windows per page, was worth several thousand dollars. They had passed many pleasant evenings together on the Directoire settee arranging the old ochre- and carmine-coloured stamps. They agreed there was something almost sensual about holding a perfectly preserved piece of the past, unsullied, as if everything didn't have to change, didn't have to end up swamped by decline and decay. They disapproved of the new stamps and dismissed them as crude and wouldn't have them in their book. The pages for the recent years remained empty and they liked that; the emptiness was their statement about themselves and their values, and Hughes, holding a stamp into the light between his tweezers, would say, 'None of that rough trade for us.'

One afternoon they went down to the philatelic shops around Adelaide and Richmond streets and saw a stamp they had been after for a long time, a large and elegant black stamp of Queen Victoria in her widow's weeds. It was rare and expensive, a dead-letter stamp from the turn of the century. They stood side by side over the glass counter-case, admiring it, their hands spread on the glass, but when McCrae, the overhead fluorescent light catching his lacquered nails, said, 'Well, I certainly would like that little black sweetheart,' the owner, who had sold stamps to them for several years, looked up and smirked, and Hughes suddenly snorted, 'You old queen, I mean why don't you just quit wearing those goddamn Cuban heels, eh? I mean why not?' He walked out leaving McCrae embarrassed and hurt and when the owner said, 'So what was wrong?' McCrae cried, 'Screw you,' and strutted out.

Through the rest of the week they were deferential around the house, offering each other every consideration, trying to avoid any squabble before Mother's Day at the end of the week when they were going to hold their annual supper for friends, three other male couples. Over the years it had always been an elegant, slightly mocking evening that often ended bittersweetly and left them feeling close, comforting each other.

McCrae, wearing a white linen shirt with starch in the cuffs and mother-of-pearl cuff links, worked all Sunday afternoon in the kitchen and through the window he could see the crab-apple tree in bloom and he thought how in previous years he would have begun planning to put down some jelly in the old pressed glass jars they kept in the cellar, but instead, head down, he went on stuffing and tying the pork loin roast. Then in the early evening he heard Hughes at the door, and there was laughter from the front room and someone cried out, 'What do you do with an elephant who has three balls on him . . . you don't know, silly, well you walk him and pitch to the giraffe,' and there were howls of laughter and the clinking of glasses. It had been the same every year, eight men sitting down to a fine supper with expensive wines, the table set with their best silver under the antique carved wooden candelabra.

Having prepared all the raw vegetables, the cauliflower and carrots, the avocados and finger-sized miniature corns-on-the-cob, and placed porcelain bowls of homemade dip in the centre of a pewter tray, McCrae stared at his reflection for a moment in the window over the kitchen sink and then he took a plastic slipcase out of the knives and forks drawer. The case contained the dead-letter stamp. He licked it all over and pasted it on his forehead and then slipped on the jacket of his charcoal-brown crushed velvet suit, took hold of the tray, and stepped out into the front room.

The other men, sitting in a circle around the coffee table, looked up and one of them giggled. Hughes cried, 'Oh my God.' McCrae, as if nothing was the matter, said, 'My dears, time for the crudités.' He was in his silk stocking feet, and as he passed the tray he winked at Hughes who sat staring at the black queen.

JOHN METCALF
(1938)

The Years in Exile

Although it is comfortable, I do not like this chair. I do not like its aluminum and plastic. The aluminum corrodes leaving a roughness on the arms and legs like white rust or fungus. I liked the chairs stacked in the summer house when I was ten, deck-chairs made of striped canvas and wood. But I am an old man; I am allowed to be crotchety.

By the side of my chair in the border are some blue and white petunias. They remind me, though the shade is different, of my youngest grandson's blue and white running shoes, Adidas I believe he calls them. They are one of this year's fads. He wears them to classes at the so-called college he attends. But I must not get excited.

It is one of her days. The voice of the vacuum cleaner is heard in the land. But I should not complain. I have my room, my personal things, the few books I still care to have about me. Before moving here, life was becoming difficult; the long hill up to the shopping centre for supplies I neither wished to cook nor eat, sheets, the silence broken only by the hum and shudder of the fridge.

Strange that this daughter of my first marriage, a child of whom I saw so little, should be the one who urged this home upon me. Or not so strange perhaps. I am old enough to know that we do not know what needs compel us.

The cartons were mentioned again this morning, those in my room and those in the basement. She calls them 'clutter', and perhaps she is right. The papers are promised to Queen's University but I cannot bring myself to sort through years of manuscript and letters from dead friends. Much of the order of things I couldn't remember and it is a task which smacks too much of some finality.

I am supposed to be resting today for this evening a man is coming to interview me for some literary journal or review. Or was it a thesis? I forget. They come quite often, young men with tape-recorders and note books. They talk of my novels and stories, ascribe influences I have never read, read criticism to me. I nod and comment if I understand them. I am not an intellectual; I am not even particularly intelligent. I am content to sit in my aluminum chair and stare at the weeping-willow tree in the next-door garden.

I have lived in Canada for sixty-one years covered now with honours yet in my reveries the last half century fades, the books, the marriages, the children, and the friends. I find myself dwelling more and more on my childhood years in England, the years when I was nine and ten. My mind is full of pictures.

My sleeplessness, the insistence of the pictures, are familiar signs. Were I younger, I would be making notes and outlines, drinking midnight coffee. But I will not write again. I am too old and tire too easily; I no longer have the strength to face the struggle with language, the loneliness, the certainty of failure.

I remember my own grandfather. I wonder if I seem to Mary and her children as remote as he appeared to me, talking to himself, conducting barely audible arguments in two voices, dozing, his crossed leg constantly jiggling, the dottle from his dead pipe falling down his cardigan front.

I remember the bone-handled clasp-knife, its blade a thin hook from years of sharpening. I can see his old hands slicing the rope of black twist into tiny discs, rubbing them, funnelling the prepared tobacco from the newspaper on his lap into his wooden box which stood on the mantelpiece. The mantelpiece had a velvet fringe along its edge with little velvet bobbles hanging down at two-inch intervals. I can see his old hands replacing the gauze mantle in the gas lamp, the white-yellow incandescence of the light.

Many might dismiss such meaningless particulars of memory.

I know that I am lost in silence hours on end dwelling on another time now more real to me than this chair, more real than the sunshine filtering through the fawn and green of the willow tree.

Summerfield, Hengistbury Head, Christchurch, with their rivers, the Avon and the Stour, and always central in my dream and reverie, the spoiled mansion, Fortnell House. Were I younger, I would attempt to frame its insistence.

Fortnell House.

A short story could not encompass it; it has the weight and feel about it of a novella. But the time for such considerations is past.

I have not read much in late years; I lack the patience. But of the younger writers I have read Cary. Thinking of my rivers, my headland and estuary, the bulk of my great grey priory above the salt marsh, I looked again not a week since at a remembered passage in his novel *To Be a Pilgrim*. Old Wilcher speaking. It has stayed in my mind:

'The English summer weighs upon me with its richness. I know why Robert ran away from so much history to the new lands where the weather is as stupid as the trees, chance dropped, are meaningless. Where earth is only new dirt, and corn, food for animals two and four-footed. I must go, too, for life's sake. This place is so doused in memory that only to breathe makes me dream like an opium eater. Like one who has taken a narcotic, I have lived among fantastic loves and purposes. The shape of a field, the turn of a lane, have had the power to move me as if they were my children, and

I had made them. I have wished immortal life for them, though they were even more transient appearances than human beings.'

I, too, have thought myself a pilgrim.

In the summer, dilapidated farmhouses in the Eastern Townships; in the winter, Montreal's cold-water flats. My mother's letters to me when I was young, how they amused yet rankled: 'living like a gypsy', 'a man of your age', 'not a stick of furniture to your name'. My early books returned. All so many years ago.

A blue night-light burns on my bedside table. Mary put it there in case I have need of the pills and bottles which crowd the table-top, Milk of Magnesia, sedatives, digitalis, the inhaler, the glycerine capsules.

Yes, I have thought myself a pilgrim, the books my milestones. But these recent weeks, the images that haunt my nights and days . . .

I have seen the holy places though I never knew it. I have travelled on, not knowing all my life that the mecca of my pilgrimage had been reached so young, and that all after was the homeward journey.

Fortnell House.

The curve of the weed-grown drive, the rank laurels, the plaster-fallen crumbling portico. Lower windows blind and boarded.

I read once in a travel book of an African tribe, the Dogon, famed for their masks and ancestor figures. They live, if I remember aright, south of Timbuctu under the curve of the Niger. Their masks and carvings are a part of their burial rites; the carvings offer a fixed abode for spirits liberated by death. The figures are placed in caves and fissures where the termites soon attack the wood and the weather erodes.

I have seen such weathered figures in museums.

I stare at my wrist as it lies along the aluminum arm of the chair, the blue veins. The left side of the wrist might be the river Avon and its estuary, the right side the sea. And then my fist, the bulge of the headland.

Away from the Southbourne beach, away from the sand, the bathers, and the beach games onto the five miles of crunching pebbles towards Hengistbury Head. Scavenging, I followed the line of sea-wrack, the tangles and heaps of seaware, kelp, and bladderwrack. In my knapsack I carried sandwiches, pill-boxes for rare shells, and a hammer.

Sometimes among the tarred rope and driftwood branches, the broken crates, the cracked crab shells and hollowed bodies of birds, were great baulks of timber covered with goose barnacles stinking in the sun. Scattered above and below the seaweed were the shells, limpet, mussel, periwinkle, whelk and cockle, painted top and piddock. Razor shells. The white shields of cuttlefish, whelks' egg cases like coarse sponge, mermaids' purses.

At low tide, the expanse of firm wet sand would shine in the sun, the silver smoothness broken only by the casts of lugworms.

The halfway point of my journey was marked by The Rocks. I always thought of them as a fossilized monster, the bulk of its body on the beach, its lower vertebrae and tail disappearing into the sea. The rocks in the sea were in a straight line, water between them, smaller and smaller, and almost invariably on the last black rock stood a cormorant.

I always liked the cormorant's solitary state. As I climbed up the rocks, it would usually void in a flash of white and fly off low over the water. My favourite birds were ravens; they nested on the Headland strutting on the turf near the dangerous cliff edge. Cormorant in Latin means 'sea raven'. I liked the sound of that; it might have been a name for Vikings.

I climbed among the rocks looking in the rock pools where small green crabs scuttled and squishy sea anemones closed their flowered mouths at a touch. I usually rested in the shadow of the rocks and used my hammer on the larger pebbles, often those with a yellowish area of discolouration; they broke more easily. I sometimes found inside the fossils of sea-urchins. I dug, too, at the cliff face dreaming of finding the imprint of some great fish.

Two or three miles past The Rocks I scrambled up where the cliff dipped to perhaps twenty feet before beginning its great rise to the Headland. At this point the Double Dykes met the cliff edge. The Dykes ran across the wrist of land to the estuary on the other side. They were Iron Age earthworks designed to cut the Headland off from attack by land, built presumably by the people whose barrows still rose above the turf and heather high up on the hill. They were perhaps twelve or fifteen feet high from their ditch, still a struggle up slippery turf to gain the other side.

They must have been much higher 2000 years ago but were eroded now by time and rabbits; they formed a huge warren and the fresh sandy diggings were visible everywhere. The land beyond the Dykes was low on the estuary side and rose to 180 feet at the point of the Headland. On the estuary side there were woods and pools and marsh and then, as the land rose, short turf, bracken, and heather.

At the far end of the Dykes, the estuary end, stood the keeper's cottage. Mr Taylor was of uncertain temper and had a collie with one eye, and ferrets, and an adder just over three feet long pickled in alcohol. On his good days he showed me the adder or gave me owl pellets; once he let me help with the ferrets.

Before going along the curve of the estuary into the woods, it was part of my ritual to climb the height of the land and sit beside the larger of the two burial mounds to eat my sandwiches. The headland behind the Dykes had been a camp for many peoples. Before the legions arrived, some British king or chieftain had even established a mint here. Later, the Vikings, penetrating up the Avon and Stour, had used the headland as a base camp. Although I knew that the larger barrow was of the Iron Age or even earlier I preferred to connect it with Hengist and Horsa, legendary leaders of the first Anglo-Saxon settlers in Britain. According to Bede, Hengist and his son Aesc landed and eventually reigned in far-away Kent. But for me, Hengistbury Head was Hengist's fort and I imagined inside the larger mound the war-leader's huge skeleton lying with his accoutrements. An axe and shield, a sword, spears and his horned helmet. I knew that he was huge because I had read in the encyclopedia that Hengist was probably a personal name meaning 'stallion'. I gave alliterative names to his weapons.

'Bone-Biter' was one, I seem to remember.

I always poured a trickle of lemonade, wishing I had wine.

This was my Valley of the Kings.

Sitting by the burial mound I looked out over the estuary. It curved in at both sides where it met the sea, a narrow run of water between two spits of beach, the salmon run, and then white breakers beyond. On the far side of the estuary mouth was the village of Mudeford, eight or nine houses, one painted black. It was called, simply, The Black House, and in the eighteenth century had been a meeting place for smugglers. It had once been an inn, I believe, but now served teas to summer visitors.

I used to imagine moonless nights, a lugger standing off, the rowing boats grating up the shingle. The brandy, wine, and lace were taken by the winding paths across the saltings to Christchurch where it was rumoured they were hidden in a false tomb in the Priory graveyard.

Across the estuary sailed and tackled the white yachts like toys but at Mudeford the fishermen netted the salmon run or put out to sea with lobster pots. Although the run was less than fifty yards across there was no way of getting over and Mudeford could only be approached from the Christchurch side. I used to walk to Christchurch sometimes and then set out for Mudeford at low tide across the saltings, jumping from tussock to tussock, always getting plastered with mud. The knowledge of the paths was lost or they had eroded with the shifting tides. Sometimes I imagined myself a smuggler, sometimes a revenuer, but after I got the cutlass with its brass guard and Tower of London stamp near the hilt from Fortnell House I was always an excise man.

Behind Mr Taylor's thatched cottage, on a triangular patch of land between the back of the house and a shed, there grew teazles. After the death of the purple flowers, the brown, spiky teazles stood tall and dry in the autumn. Every autumn I cut teazles for my mother. They stood in the Chinese dragon vase in the hall.

I often wondered if they were chance-sewn behind the house so thickly or if for centuries the cottage people had grown them specially to card and comb the wool from sheep they grazed on the Headland.

I can still remember the maps I used to draw marking the cottage and the teazle patch, the burial mounds and Dykes, the wood, the estuary and salmon run, The Black House, dotted lines marking the smugglers' routes across the saltings, Christchurch Priory and the river Avon in its tidal reaches to Wick Ferry, the nesting sites of the ravens.

I can see those childish maps now as clearly as I see the petunias by my chair or the willow in the next-door garden. I can remember the names I gave to various areas: 'The Heron-Sedge', 'Badger's Sett', 'Lily-Pad Pond', 'Honeysuckle Valley'.

Dear God. I can smell the honeysuckle!

A pair of Monarchs chasing each other about the leaves of the apple tree; the lawn is strewn with fresh windfalls. The sun is higher now. The Monarchs will not find milkweed in this garden. Will you, my beauties? No weeds here for you. Robert doesn't like weeds. Roots them out. Weed-killer and trowel.

Were it my garden, I would sow it thick with milkweed so that you would always grace me with your presence.

The windfalls surprise me; Robert will doubtless gather them this evening. He has an oblong wooden basket of woven strips, cotton gloves, a pair of secateurs. He does not know that such a basket is called a 'trug'.

I hug the word to myself.

Earlier, Mary brought me lemonade. My bladder will not hold liquid as it once did. I have to suffer the indignity of struggling from this reclining chair like a wounded thing to go indoors to the lavatory. She's still vacuuming, now upstairs. It is cool and dim in the bathroom. I urinate without control and when I have finished and zipped up my trousers, I can feel a dribble of urine wetting my underpants.

I wonder if my room smells, if I smell? I often remarked it in old people when I was younger. I can remember still the smell of my grandmother. Thank God I will never know. I can, at least, still bathe without assistance though she insists I do not lock the door. Some I remember smelled medicinal, some of mothballs, some just a mustiness. I have not shaved today. I must remember to shave before evening for the young man is coming to ask me questions.

The cushion for the small of my back.

The Monarchs have disappeared in search of ground less disciplined.

I have always disliked Wordsworth. Once, I must admit, I thought I disliked him for his bathos, his lugubrious tone. But now I know that it is because he could not do justice to the truth; no philosophical cast of mind can do justice to particularity.

I am uncomfortable with abstraction, his *or* mine.

I stood one morning in the fierce heat by the Lily-pad Pond. Two frogs were croaking and then stopped. A dragonfly hovered and darted, blue sheen of its wings. Then I, too, heard it. The continuous slither of a snake moving through dead grass and sedge at the pond's edge. I knew, being by water, that it would be a grass snake. I stood rooted, staring at the yellow flags where the faint sound seemed to be coming from.

I had caught grass snakes and adders by the dozen, yet for unknown reasons felt upon me again that awful sense of intrusion, that feeling of holy terror. I stood waiting to see the snake curve into the water and swim sinuous through the lily pads, its head reared. But nothing happened. The snake did not move again. I stepped away backwards from the margin of the pond, placing my feet silently until I was at a distance to turn and walk down-hill towards the wider sky and the open light of the estuary.

Again.

In the valley of the honeysuckle it was full noon; the bordering wood was dim. As I stepped into the wood's overgrown darkness, over a fallen tree and brushing aside some saplings, the air suddenly moved and above my head was a great shape. I never knew what it was. I was afraid to turn. I felt my hair ruffle in its wind.

A holiday in Dorset in my tenth year in the Purbeck Hills outside the haven of Poole. The cottage was called 'Four Winds', I remember, and in the garden stood a sundial. I remember the collection of Marble Whites and variants I was netting. I went out every day with net and cyanide jar, happy to wander for hours along the cliff path and across fields.

The fields were separated by dry-stone walls and where stones had fallen I pulled them up from the gripping turf in search of slow worms. I carried the slow worms inside my shirt and kept them in a large box in the cottage garden.

One day I prised up a large stone by its corner. The earth beneath was black. A few white threads of roots. Three bright red ants. And there lay the largest slow worm I had ever seen. It was over twelve inches long, strangely dark on its back, almost black, and fat. It was as fat as two of my fingers together. It started to move. Its belly was fawn. I was filled with terror. It start-ed to burrow into the grass roots surrounding the oblong of black earth, the length of its body slowly disappearing.

The sky was blue, the wind blowing over the grass from the sea. I knew I had seen the slow worm king. Filled with an enormous guilt, I ran from the place my heart pounding, the killing-jar thumping against my back in the knapsack. I ran for three fields before the terror quieted and I remember then sitting on a pile of rocks emptying out the limp, closed Marble Whites from the cyanide jar; I remember the greenish veins of the underside of their wings as they lay scattered on the grasses.

Mary has brought me a tuna sandwich and a peeled apple cut into slices and has moved my chair back into the sun. She is still wearing a headscarf ready to attack another part of the house. As I eat the sandwich, I crave for all the things I am forbidden—cucumber, strong cheese, radishes, tomatoes in vine-gar. Pork. Especially pork. I cannot abide this blandness. Like an old circus lion with worn down teeth.

Mounting the centre box, cuffing at the trainer.

Words on paper. Words on paper.

With my chair in this position I can see her through the kitchen window. The hair pulled back, framed in the scarf, the shape of her face seems to change; she has, surprisingly, my looks about her.

I always wanted to own a piece of land so that the children could grow up in the country or visit me in a place they could make their own. True, we lived in a variety of rural slums during the summers but the children were always too young to begin to learn and appropriate things and place. It was only in the city I could hawk my largely unwanted talents. Hand to mouth for so many years as the books and dry times bore on, the struggle to make ends meet thwarted me. And by the time I could have afforded land, the time and the children were gone.

I have spent so many hours dreaming of that place. A stream running over rocks sweeping into deep, silent trout pools. Honeysuckle in the evenings. Near the house, clumps of brambles which in the late summer would be heavy with blackberries. A barn filled with hay for the children to run and jump in, sunlight filtering in through broken boards, swimming down in shafts of dust-motes.

I can hear their voices calling.

Would they, too, have made maps with magical names?

Once I felt bitter.

A memory of Mrs Rosen fills my mind. She is sitting on a park bench holding a grey poodle on her lap and gazing across the baseball field.

I worked for Mr Rosen for over five years. I taught English in the mornings in his private school trying to drill the rudiments into dense and wealthy heads and toiled over my typewriter in the afternoons and on into the early evening.

He is now long dead.

Rosen College Preparatory High School occupied five rooms on the floor above the Chateau Bar-B-Q Restaurant and Take-Out Service. There were three classrooms, the Library, the supplies locker, and the Office. The staff was all part-time and so in my five years I came to know only the morning shift—Geography, Mathematics and Science. At recess, the four of us would huddle in the supplies locker and make coffee.

Mr Kapoor was a reserved and melancholy hypochondriac from New Delhi who habitually wore black suits and shoes, a white shirt, and striped college tie. His only concession to summer was that he wore the gleaming shoes without socks. I remember his telling me one day that peahens became fertilized by raising their tail feathers during a rain storm; he held earnestly to this, telling me that it was indeed so because his grandmother had told him, she having seen it with her own eyes in Delhi. He taught science in all grades.

Mr Gingley was a retired accountant who taught Mathematics and wore a curiously pink hearing-aid which was shaped like a fat human ear.

Mr Helwig Syllm, the Geography teacher, was an ex-masseur.

Mrs Rosen, who drew salaries as secretary, teacher, and School Nurse, would sometimes grip one by the arm in the hall and hiss:

'Don't foment. My husband can fire anyone. *Anyone.*'

Exercising my dog one morning some three years or more after Mr Rosen's death and some five years after I'd left the school, I saw his widow in the park. Bundled in an astrakhan coat against the weak spring sunshine, she was holding a grey poodle on her lap and gazing across the baseball field. Queenie, who was in heat, pulled towards her but I did not recognize her until I had passed and she did not notice me. I kept Queenie busy on the far side of the park and, throwing sticks for that ungainly dog, I suddenly felt loss, an absurd diminishment.

I wonder if this coming March I will be sitting across the desk from Mr Vogel? When I first went to see him he was just a sprig but is now a portly middle-aged man. Even then, he made me feel a little like a truant youth before the principal. He shakes his head over the mysteries, his spectacles glint as he reproves me for lack of receipts. His fingers chatter over his adding machine.

His manner is dry; his inventions are fantastical.

'And now,' he always says, 'we come to Entertainment.'

Flashing a glance of severe probity.

'A very *grey* area.'

I do not want to be seen laughing aloud in the garden. I stifle the laughter and cough into my handkerchief.

Will Mr Vogel and I invent my taxes this coming March?

Only the cartons of papers for Queen's await my attention; my other papers are in order. My will is drawn up, insurance policies in force, assigns of copyright assigned. I should not pretend any longer. I remember the papers in that outer room of Fortnell House, a scullery perhaps. I do not want my papers abandoned in that way, stored in the damp to rot. But if I do not put them in order perhaps they will be consigned to some air-conditioned but equal oblivion. Tomorrow, after the young man, I must start to sort them, the manuscripts, the journals, the letters from dead friends.

The doors had been nailed up.

That outer room in the rear of Fortnell House whose iron window bars we forced with a branch must have been a scullery or pantry. It was stone-flagged and whitewashed, green mould growing down the walls and on some of the damp papers. After the awful noise of screws being wrenched and wood splintering, we stood in the cold room listening.

Stacked in boxes were bundles of letters, newspapers, parchment deeds with red seals, account books, admiralty charts and municipal records. The papers littered the floor, too, in sodden mounds where other boys had emptied boxes searching for more exciting things.

I stuffed my shirt.

I took bundles of parchment deeds, indentures, wills and leases, documents written in faded Latin.

THIS INDENTURE *made the second day of May in the seventeenth year of our Sovereign Lord George the Third by the Grace of God of Great Britain France and Ireland King Defender of the Faith and so forth and in the Year of Our Lord . . .*

I remember, too, the half-leather ledger of the clerk of the Christchurch magistrate's court. The dates ran from 1863–65. The handwriting was a faded sepia copperplate, the name of the defendant in one column, the offence in a second, the fine in a third.

For bastardy, the commonest charge, the fine was five shillings.

The cover was, yes, mottled pink and white. The end papers were marbled. The leather spine was mildewed. The front lower corner was bruised, the cardboard raised and puffy with damp.

I can feel it in my hands.

The salmon fishers who netted the run between Mudeford and Hengistbury Head—the hours I have sat watching the two rowing boats laying the cork-bobbing net across the incoming tide. Mostly they came up empty, the net piling slack and easy. Perhaps twice a day the net would strain, a flash of roiling silver, and then the great fish hauled in over the side to be clubbed in the boat bottom.

The name for a bludgeon used to kill fish is a 'priest'. How I hug these words to myself, savouring them. 'Priest' was not a local usage; I have seen it in print. It is not recorded in the *Shorter Oxford*.

One of Mr Taylor's ferrets was brown, the other albino. I swung a stake with him one day on the Double Dykes despatching rabbits as they bolted into the nets pegged over their holes. The albino ferret eventually reappeared masked in blood. The ferrets frightened me; Mr Taylor handled them with gauntlets. Some of the dead rabbits were wet underneath with trickles of thick bright yellow urine which stood on the fur.

Over the two stone bridges and beyond Christchurch, along the New Forest road towards the Cat and Fiddle inn, we cycled sometimes on our new Raleigh All-Steel bicycles to Summerfield. The Summerfield Estate stretched for miles over heath, farmland and woods. We visited the roadside rookery where in late spring we gathered the shiny twelve-bore cartridge cases that the gamekeeper had scattered blasting into the nests from underneath. Beyond lay the heath where adders basked and kestrels circled the sky. We visited the hornets' nests in the trees in the dead wood and the pools where the palmated newts bred and we walked down the stream-bed to attach leeches to our legs. And always, past the cottages and the wheat fields and pasture, we headed down for the woods and coverts.

The gamekeeper was our invisible enemy; he was rumoured to have shot a boy in the behind. The raucous calls of pheasants held us in strained silence; rootling blackbirds froze us.

We trespassed into the heart of the wood where in a clearing we would stare at the gamekeeper's gibbet—a dead, grey tree hung with the corpses of rats, crows, owls, stoats and weasels, hawks and shapeless things. Some of the bodies would be fresh, others rotted to a slime. There in the still heat of the afternoon we stared. Over the bodies in a gauze of sound crawled the iridescent flies.

Children are, I think, drawn towards death and dying. I remember the ambivalence of a young girl of eight or nine to a litter of puppies at suck, the blind mouths and puddling forepaws at the swollen dugs—she, too, it seemed to me, sensed a relationship between herself and the bitch. I remember it vividly. The daughter of a friend. I seem to remember attempting a story once on that but as with so many of my stories, I could find no adequate structure.

The cutlass was about three feet long and slightly curved. The guard was brass and the Tower of London armoury mark was stamped on the blade near the hilt. The hilt was bound in blackened silver wire. I got the cutlass from one of the older boys—I forget his name—in exchange for six Christmas annuals and a William and Mary shilling. It was from him, too, that I learned the secret of Fortnell House.

I went there first on my own. The house was an eighteenth century mansion on the outskirts of Christchurch. It was invisible from the road; large padlocked gates marked the entrance to the drive. On the gate-pillars weathered heraldic beasts stood holding shields. The details of the quartering within the shields were little more than lumps and hollows. I think the beasts were griffins but time and the weather had so eroded the soft grey stone that the outlines of the carving were indistinct.

I climbed the iron spears of the railings and forced my way through the rank laurels onto the drive. The wood and the drive were overgrown and dark; the gravel had reverted to grass and weeds. The bottom windows of the house were blind and boarded; the front door was padlocked. Pink willowherb and weeds sprouted from the guttering. Some of the second storey windows were broken.

Around the back of the house were extensive grounds and a spinney, the lawns and terraces overgrown, the garden statuary tumbled. The windows were boarded and the doors nailed shut. I tried the doors with my shoulder. Inside, according to report, upstairs, room after room was filled with swords and spears and armour, guns, statues, strange machines, old tools, pictures, books—a treasury. The silence and the rank growth frightened me.

To one side of the house at the back, next to the coach house, stood three wooden sheds, their doors smashed open to the weather. Two were empty except for a rusted lawnmower and an anchor but in the third I found a broken mahogany cabinet full of shallow drawers. It had contained a collection of mineral specimens many of which were scattered about the floor. I filled my pockets with strange and glittering stones. In a corner of the shed were stacks of plates and dishes; many had been smashed. I found intact two large willow-pattern plates, meat chargers. The blue was soft and deep. I told my parents I had traded something for them.

Fortnell House had been built in the seventeen-twenties. The last Fortnell, Sir Charles, had left the house and his collections to the town of

Christchurch as a museum. The town had accepted the gift but was disin-
clined or unable to raise the money to refurbish the building and install a
curator.

Sir Charles had served for many years in India, the Middle East and
Africa. He was one of that vanished breed like Burton, Speke and
Layard—romantic amateurs who were gentlemen, scholars, linguists and
adventurers. Fortnell House became the repository of collections of miner-
als, fossils, books, weapons, tribal regalia, paintings and carvings. On his
retirement, Sir Charles had devoted his energies to Christchurch and the
county collecting local records, books, memorabilia and the evidences of
the prehistoric past.

It has become the fashion to decry such men as wealthy plunderers but
we shall not see their like again. My youngest grandson, he of Adidas
College, has called me fascist and them racist. I forbear to point out that his
precious victims of oppression and colonialism despoiled their ancestral
tombs for gold and used the monuments of their past for target practice. My
heart does not bleed for the Egyptians; I do not weep for the Greeks.

It is, I suppose, natural to clash with those younger, natural this conser-
vatism as one grows older; one has learned how easily things break.

What will the young man say to me this evening? And what can I say to
him? It is difficult to talk to these young college men whose minds no longer
move in pictures. Had he been here this morning I could, like some Zen
sage, have pointed to the Monarchs about the apple leaves and preserved
my silence.

Particular life. Particular life.

All else is tricks of the trade or inexpressible.

I have often wondered, I wonder still, what became of those willow-pattern plates I stole from Fortnell House. I brought them to Canada with me
when I was a young man and they survived endless moves and hung on an
endless variety of kitchen walls. They disappeared when June and I were
divorced. She was quite capable of breaking them to spite me. Or, more likely, selling them. She had little aesthetic sense. She would have called them
dust-gatherers or eyesores—some such thin-lipped epithet. So do they now
hang on some Westmount wall or decorate an expensive restaurant?

I liked to be able to glance at them while I was eating; I used to like running my fingertips over that glaze. It comforted me. That deep lead glaze,
the softness of the blue—one did not need to check pottery marks to know
such richness was eighteenth-century work.

I remember reading that Wedgwood used to tour the benches inspecting
work. When he found an imperfect piece he smashed it with a hammer and
wrote on the bench with chalk: *This will not do for Josiah Wedgwood.* I have
always liked that story. We would have understood each other, Josiah and I.

As the years passed, I thought more often, and with greater bitterness, of
those two large plates than I did of June. She is now the dimmest of memories. Strange that I cannot recall her features or her body; strange that she

was Mary's mother. Alison, too, has receded now so far that I must concentrate to see her features, strain to hear her voice. She sends me Christmas cards from Florida.

Far clearer and more immediate is Patricia Hopkins. I see the scene like an enlarged detail from a great canvas. We are hidden in the laurel bushes in her garden; it is gloomy there though light hints on the glossy leaves. In the far distance the sunshine sparkles on the greenhouse. In the immediate background is a weed-grown tennis court along whose nearest edge the wire netting sags in a great belly. Patricia's knickers are round her knees. I am staring at the smooth cleft mound of her vagina. I am nine and she is eight.

Better remembered than the bodies of two wives.

I have always detested photographs. There was an article in Robert's *Time* magazine about that fellow Land and his Polaroid cameras. He called photography 'the most basic form of creativity'. So obscenely wrong.

But I must not get excited.

My third visit to Fortnell House was my last.

We got in through the bars of the scullery window and both lingered, turning over the sodden papers and documents that littered the floor unwilling to go further into the dark house. Eventually we crept along a short passage into the kitchen.

One wall was taken up by a vast black range, another by two long sinks. In the middle of the room was a long wooden table. On the wall above the door that led out of the kitchen was a glass case of dials. Inside the dials were numbers and beneath the case hung two rows of jangly bells on coiled strips of metal—a device, we decided, for summoning servants to the different rooms.

A passage led from the kitchen through two doors to the hall. The hall was dark and echoey. On the walls hung the dim shapes of mounted heads and antlers. All the doors off the hall were closed. The staircase was uncarpeted. We started up it towards the first landing.

A few thin rays of light came through chinks in the boards that covered the landing window. A line of light ran up the handrail of the bannisters. We spoke in whispers and walked on the outside edges of the stairs.

A board creaked; a shoe cap knocked hollow on a riser.

It was just as my hand was turning on the huge carved acorn of the newel post on the landing that a door opened below and a man came out. He was a black shape with the light of the room behind him, shelf after shelf of books. He called us down and demanded our names and addresses. He was cataloguing the library. He was sick of boys breaking in and was giving our names to the police. He fumbled the front door open and ordered us out.

Secure in our aliases, we walked away down the drive.

Now, in my dreams, I have returned.

Nightly I brave the weathered griffins, the rank laurels; nightly I climb those uncarpeted stairs; nightly my hand grasps the great carved acorn of the newel post. But my dream does not continue.

Perhaps one night I will not awaken in the blue dark to turn and stare at the blue night-light on the bedside table. Perhaps one night soon—I have that feeling—I will round the dark acorn and reach the rooms above.

The sun has long since passed over the house and I am sitting in the shade. Soon Robert will return from his office and change into his gardening clothes; he will gather the windfalls in his oblong wooden basket. Soon the garage will sound as my grandson, returning from his college, roars his motorbike into the narrow space; soon the kitchen will be full of noise. Then Mary will call me for dinner. I should go and shave. But I will sit a little longer in the sunshine. Here between the moored houseboats where I can watch the turn of the quicksilver dace. Here by the piles of the bridge where in the refracted sunlight swim the golden-barred and red-finned perch.

∿

True Trash

The waitresses are basking in the sun like a herd of skinned seals, their pinky-brown bodies shining with oil. They have their bathing suits on because it's the afternoon. In the early dawn and the dusk they sometimes go skinny-dipping, which makes this itchy crouching in the mosquito-infested bushes across from their small private dock a great deal more worthwhile.

Donny has the binoculars, which are not his own but Monty's. Monty's dad gave them to him for bird-watching but Monty isn't interested in birds. He's found a better use for the binoculars: he rents them out to the other boys, five minutes maximum, a nickel a look or else a chocolate bar from the tuck shop, though he prefers the money. He doesn't eat the chocolate bars; he resells them, black market, for twice their original price; but the total supply on the island is limited, so he can get away with it.

Donny has already seen everything worth seeing, but he lingers on with the binoculars anyway, despite the hoarse whispers and the proddings from those next in line. He wants to get his money's worth.

'Would you look at that,' he says, in what he hopes is a tantalizing voice. 'Slobber, slobber.' There's a stick poking into his stomach, right on a fresh mosquito bite, but he can't move it without taking one hand off the binoculars. He knows about flank attacks.

'Lessee,' says Ritchie, tugging at his elbow.

'Piss off,' says Donny. He shifts the binoculars, taking in a slippery bared haunch, a red-polka-dotted breast, a long falling strand of bleach-blond hair: Ronette the tartiest, Ronette the most forbidden. When there are lectures from the masters at St Jude's during the winter about the dangers of consorting with the town girls, it's those like Ronette they have in mind: the ones who stand in line at the town's only movie theatre, chewing gum and wearing their boyfriends' leather jackets, their ruminating mouths glistening and deep red like mushed-up raspberries. If you whistle at them or even look, they stare right through you.

Ronette has everything but the stare. Unlike the others, she has been known to smile. Every day Donny and his friends make bets over whether they will get her at their table. When she leans over to clear the plates, they try to look down the front of her sedate but V-necked uniform. They angle towards her, breathing her in: she smells of hair spray, nail polish, something artificial and too sweet. Cheap, Donny's mother would say. It's an enticing word. Most of the things in his life are expensive, and not very interesting.

Ronette changes position on the dock. Now she's lying on her stomach, chin propped on her hands, her breasts pulled down by gravity. She has a real cleavage, not like some of them. But he can see her collar-bone and some chest ribs, above the top of her suit. Despite the breasts, she's skinny, scrawny; she has little stick arms and a thin, sucked-in face. She has a missing side tooth, you can see it when she smiles, and this bothers him. He knows he's supposed to feel lust for her, but this is not what he feels.

The waitresses know they're being looked at: they can see the bushes jiggling. The boys are only twelve or thirteen, fourteen at most, small fry. If it was counsellors, the waitresses would giggle more, preen more, arch their backs. Or some of them would. As it is, they go on with their afternoon break as if no one is there. They rub oil on one another's backs, toast themselves evenly, turning lazily this way and that and causing Ritchie, who now has the binoculars, to groan in a way that is supposed to madden the other boys, and does. Small punches are dealt out, mutterings of 'Jerk' and 'Asshole'. 'Drool, drool,' says Ritchie, grinning from ear to ear.

The waitresses are reading out loud. They are taking turns: their voices float across the water, punctuated by occasional snorts and barks of laughter. Donny would like to know what they're reading with such absorption, such relish, but it would be dangerous for him to admit it. It's their bodies that count. Who cares what they read?

'Time's up, shitface,' he whispers to Ritchie.

'Shitface yourself,' says Ritchie. The bushes thrash.

What the waitresses are reading is a *True Romance* magazine. Tricia has a whole stash of them, stowed under her mattress, and Sandy and Pat have each contributed a couple of others. Every one of these magazines has a woman on the cover, with her dress pulled down over one shoulder or a cigarette in her mouth or some other evidence of a messy life. Usually these women are in tears. Their colours are odd: sleazy, dirt-permeated, like the hand-tinted photos in the five-and-ten. Knee-between-the-legs colours. They have none of the cheerful primaries and clean, toothy smiles of the movie magazines: these are not success stories. True Trash, Hilary calls them. Joanne calls them Moan-o-dramas.

Right now it's Joanne reading. She reads in a serious, histrionic voice, like someone on the radio; she's been in a play, at school. *Our Town*. She's got her sunglasses perched on the end of her nose, like a teacher. For extra hilarity she's thrown in a fake English accent.

The story is about a girl who lives with her divorced mother in a cramped, run-down apartment above a shoe store. Her name is Marleen. She has a part-time job in the store, after school and on Saturdays, and two of the shoe clerks are chasing around after her. One is dependable and boring and wants them to get married. The other one, whose name is Dirk, rides a motorcycle and has a knowing, audacious grin that turns Marleen's knees to jelly. The mother slaves over Marleen's wardrobe, on her sewing machine—she makes a meagre living doing dressmaking for rich ladies who sneer at her, so the wardrobe comes out all right—and she nags Marleen about choosing the right man and not making a terrible mistake, the way she did. The girl herself has planned to go to trade school and learn hospital management, but lack of money makes this impossible. She is in her last year of high school and her grades are slipping, because she is discouraged and also she can't decide between the two shoe clerks. Now the mother is on her case about the slipping grades as well.

'Oh God,' says Hilary. She is doing her nails, with a metal file rather than an emery board. She disapproves of emery boards. 'Someone please give her a double Scotch.'

'Maybe she should murder the mother, collect the insurance, and get the hell out of there,' says Sandy.

'Have you heard one word about any insurance?' says Joanne, peering over the tops of her glasses.

'You could put some in,' says Pat.

'Maybe she should try out both of them, to see which one's the best,' says Liz brazenly.

'We know which one's the best,' says Tricia. 'Listen, with a name like *Dirk*! How can you miss?'

'They're both creeps,' says Stephanie.

'If she does that, she'll be a Fallen Woman, capital F, capital W,' says Joanne. 'She'd have to Repent, capital R.'

The others hoot. Repentance! The girls in the stories make such fools of themselves. They are so weak. They fall helplessly in love with the wrong men, they give in, they are jilted. Then they cry.

'Wait,' says Joanne. 'Here comes the big night.' She reads on, breathily. '*My mother had gone out to deliver a cocktail dress to one of her customers. I was all alone in our shabby apartment.*'

'Pant, pant,' says Liz.

'No, that comes later. *I was all alone in our shabby apartment. The evening was hot and stifling. I knew I should be studying, but I could not concentrate. I took a shower to cool off. Then, on impulse, I decided to try on the graduation formal my mother had spent so many late-night hours making for me.*'

'That's right, pour on the guilt,' says Hilary with satisfaction. 'If it was me I'd axe the mother.'

'*It was a dream of pink—*'

'A dream of pink what?' says Tricia.

'A dream of pink, period, and shut up. *I looked at myself in the full-length mirror in my mother's tiny bedroom. The dress was just right for me. It fitted my ripe but slender body to perfection. I looked different in it, older, beautiful, like a girl used to every luxury. Like a princess. I smiled at myself. I was transformed.*

'*I had just undone the hooks at the back, meaning to take the dress off and hang it up again, when I heard footsteps on the stairs. Too late I remembered that I'd forgotten to lock the door on the inside, after my mother's departure. I rushed to the door, holding up my dress—it could be a burglar, or worse! But instead it was Dirk.*'

'Dirk the jerk,' says Alex, from underneath her towel.

'Go back to sleep,' says Liz.

Joanne drops her voice, does a drawl. ' "*Thought I'd come up and keep you company,*" ' he said mischievously. "*I saw your mom go out.*" *He knew I was alone! I was blushing and shivering. I could hear the blood pounding in my veins. I couldn't speak. Every instinct warned me against him—every instinct but those of my body, and my heart.*'

'So what else is there?' says Sandy. 'You can't have a mental instinct.'

'You want to read this?' says Joanne. 'Then shush. *I held the frothy pink lace in front of me like a shield. "Hey, you look great in that," Dirk said. His voice was rough and tender. "But you'd look even greater out of it." I was frightened of him. His eyes were burning, determined. He looked like an animal stalking its prey.*'

'Pretty steamy,' says Hilary.

'What kind of animal?' says Sandy.

'A weasel,' says Stephanie.

'A skunk,' says Tricia.

'Shh,' says Liz.

'*I backed away from him,*' Joanne reads. '*I had never seen him look that way before. Now I was pressed against the wall and he was crushing me in his arms. I felt the dress slipping down . . .*'

'So much for all that sewing,' says Pat.

'*. . . and his hand was on my breast, his hard mouth was seeking mine. I knew he was the wrong man for me but I could no longer resist. My whole body was crying out to his.*'

'What did it say?'

'It said, *Hey, body, over here!*'

'Shh.'

'*I felt myself lifted. He was carrying me to the sofa. Then I felt the length of his hard, sinewy body pressing against mine. Feebly I tried to push his hands away, but I didn't really want to. And then*—dot dot dot—*we were One*, capital O, exclamation mark.'

There was a moment of silence. Then the waitresses laugh. Their laughter is outraged, disbelieving. *One.* Just like that. There has to be more to it.

'The dress is a wreck,' says Joanne in her ordinary voice. 'Now the mother comes home.'

'Not today, she doesn't,' says Hilary briskly. 'We've only got ten more minutes. I'm going for a swim, get some of this oil off me.' She stands up, clips back her honey-blonde hair, stretches her tanned athlete's body, and does a perfect swan-dive off the end of the dock.

'Who's got the soap?' says Stephanie.

Ronette has not said anything during the story. When the others have laughed, she has only smiled. She's smiling now. Hers is an off-centre smile, puzzled, a little apologetic.

'Yeah, but,' she says to Joanne, 'why is it funny?'

The waitresses stand at their stations around the dining hall, hands clasped in front of them, heads bowed. Their royal-blue uniforms come down almost to the tops of their white socks, worn with white bucks or white-and-black saddle shoes or white sneakers. Over their uniforms they wear plain white aprons. The rustic log sleeping cabins at Camp Adanaqui don't have electric lights, the toilets are outhouses, the boys wash their own clothes, not even in sinks but in the lake; but there are waitresses, with uniforms and aprons. Roughing it builds a boy's character, but only certain kinds of roughing it.

Mr B. is saying grace. He owns the camp, and is a master at St Jude's as well, during the winters. He has a leathery, handsome face, the grey, tailored hair of a Bay Street lawyer, and the eyes of a hawk: he sees all, but pounces only sometimes. Today he's wearing a white V-necked tennis sweater. He could be drinking a gin and tonic, but is not.

Behind him on the wall, above his head, there's a weathered plank with a motto painted on it in black Gothic lettering: *As the Twig is Bent.* A piece of bleached driftwood ornaments each end of the plank, and beneath it are two crossed paddles and a gigantic pike's head in profile, its mouth open to show its needle teeth, its one glass eye fixed in a ferocious maniac's glare.

To Mr B.'s left is the end window, and beyond it is Georgian Bay, blue as amnesia, stretching to infinity. Rising out of it like the backs of whales, like rounded knees, like the calves and thighs of enormous floating women, are several islands of pink rock, scraped and rounded and fissured by glaciers and lapping water and endless weather, a few jack pines clinging to the larger ones, their twisted roots digging into the cracks. It was through these archipelagos that the waitresses were ferried here, twenty miles out from shore, by the same cumbersome mahogany inboard launch that brings the mail and the groceries and everything else to the island. Brings, and takes away. But the waitresses will not be shipped back to the mainland until the end of summer: it's too far for a day off, and they would never be allowed to stay away overnight. So here they are, for the duration. They are the only women on the island, except for Mrs B. and Miss Fisk, the dietitian. But those two are old and don't count.

There are nine waitresses. There are always nine. Only the names and faces change, thinks Donny, who has been going to this camp ever since he was eight. When he was eight he paid no attention to the waitresses except when he felt homesick. Then he would think of excuses to go past the kitchen window when they were washing the dishes. There they would be, safely aproned, safely behind glass: nine mothers. He does not think of them as mothers any more.

Ronette is doing his table tonight. From between his half-closed eyelids Donny watches her thin averted face. He can see one earring, a little gold hoop. It goes right through her ear. Only Italians and cheap girls have pierced ears, says his mother. It would hurt to have a hole put through your ear. It would take bravery. He wonders what the inside of Ronette's room looks like, what other cheap, intriguing things she's got in there. About someone like Hilary he doesn't have to wonder, because he already knows: the clean bedspread, the rows of shoes in their shoe-trees, the comb and brush and manicure set laid out on the dresser like implements in a surgery.

Behind Ronette's bowed head there's the skin of a rattlesnake, a big one, nailed to the wall. That's what you have to watch out for around here: rattlesnakes. Also poison ivy, thunderstorms, and drowning. A whole war canoe full of kids drowned last year, but they were from another camp. There's been some talk of making everyone wear sissy life-jackets; the mothers want it. Donny would like a rattlesnake skin of his own, to nail up over his bed; but even if he caught the snake himself, strangled it with his bare hands, bit its head off, he'd never be allowed to keep the skin.

Mr B. winds up the grace and sits down, and the campers begin again their three-times-daily ritual of bread-grabbing, face-stuffing, under-the-table kicking, whispered cursing. Ronette comes from the kitchen with a platter: macaroni and cheese. 'There you go, boys,' she says, with her good-natured, lopsided smile.

'Thank you kindly, ma'am,' says Darce the counsellor, with fraudulent charm. Darce has a reputation as a make-out artist; Donny knows he's after Ronette. This makes him feel sad. Sad, and too young. He would like to get out of his own body for a while; he'd like to be somebody else.

The waitresses are doing the dishes. Two to scrape, one to wash, one to rinse in the scalding-hot rinsing sink, three to dry. The other two sweep the floors and wipe off the tables. Later, the number of dryers will vary because of days off—they'll choose to take their days off in twos, so they can double-date with the counsellors—but today all are here. It's early in the season, things are still fluid, the territories are not yet staked out.

While they work they sing. They're missing the ocean of music in which they float during the winter. Pat and Liz have both brought their portables, though you can't pick up much radio out here, it's too far from shore. There's a record player in the counsellors' rec hall, but the records are out of date. Patti Page, The Singing Rage. 'How Much Is That Doggie in the Window.' 'The Tennessee Waltz.' Who waltzes any more?

' "Wake up, little Susie," ' trills Sandy. The Everly Brothers are popular this summer; or they were, on the mainland, when they left.

' "What're we gonna tell your mama, what're we gonna tell your pa," '
sing the others. Joanne can improvise the alto harmony, which makes everything sound less screechy.

Hilary, Stephanie, and Alex don't sing this one. They go to a private
school, all girls, and are better at rounds, like 'Fire's Burning' and 'White
Coral Bells'. They are good at tennis though, and sailing, skills that have
passed the others by.

It's odd that Hilary and the other two are here at all, waitressing at Camp
Adanaqui; it's not as if they need the money. (Not like me, thinks Joanne,
who haunts the mail desk every noon to see if she got her scholarship.) But
it's the doing of their mothers. According to Alex, the three mothers band-
ed together and jumped Mrs B. at a charity function, and twisted her arm.
Naturally Mrs B. would attend the same functions as the mothers: they've
seen her, sunglasses pushed up on her forehead, a tall drink in her hand,
entertaining on the veranda of Mr B.'s white hilltop house, which is well
away from the camp proper. They've seen the guests, in their spotless, well-
pressed sailing clothes. They've heard the laughter, the voices, husky and
casual. *Oh God don't tell me.* Like Hilary.

'We were kidnapped,' says Alex. 'They thought it was time we met some
boys.'

Joanne can see it for Alex, who is chubby and awkward, and for
Stephanie, who is built like a boy and walks like one; but Hilary? Hilary is
classic. Hilary is like a shampoo ad. Hilary is perfect. She ought to be sought
after. Oddly, here she is not.

Ronette is scraping, and drops a plate. 'Shoot,' she says. 'What a stunned
broad.' Nobody bawls her out or even teases her as they would anyone else.
She is a favourite with them, though it's hard to put your finger on why. It
isn't just that she's easygoing: so is Liz, so is Pat. She has some mysterious,
extra status. For instance, everyone else has a nickname: Hilary is Hil,
Stephanie is Steph, Alex is Al; Joanne is Jo, Tricia is Trish, Sandy is San. Pat
and Liz, who cannot be contracted any further, have become Pet and
Lizard. Only Ronette has been accorded the dignity of her full, improbable
name.

In some ways she is more grown-up than the rest of them. But it isn't
because she knows more things. She knows fewer things; she often has trouble making her way through the vocabularies of the others, especially the
offhand slang of the private-school trio. 'I don't get that,' is what she says,
and the others take a delight in explaining, as if she's a foreigner, a cherished visitor from some other country. She goes to movies and watches television like the rest of them but she has few opinions about what she has
seen. The most she will say is 'Crap' or 'He's not bad.' Though friendly, she
is cautious about expressing approval in words. 'Fair' is her best compliment. When the others talk about what they've read or what subjects they
will take next year at university, she is silent.

But she knows other things, hidden things. Secrets. And these other things are older, and on some level more important. More fundamental. Closer to the bone.

Or so thinks Joanne, who has a bad habit of novelizing.

Outside the window Darce and Perry stroll by, herding a group of campers. Joanne recognizes a few of them: Donny, Monty. It's hard to remember the campers by name. They're just a crowd of indistinguishable, usually grimy young boys who have to be fed three times a day, whose crusts and crumbs and rinds have to be cleaned up afterwards. The counsellors call them Grubbies.

But some stand out. Donny is tall for his age, all elbows and spindly knees, with huge deep-blue eyes; even when he's swearing—they all swear during meals, furtively but also loudly enough so that the waitresses can hear them—it's more like a meditation, or more like a question, as if he's trying the words out, tasting them. Monty on the other hand is like a miniature forty-five-year-old: his shoulders already have a businessman's slump, his paunch is fully formed. He walks with a pompous little strut. Joanne thinks he's hilarious.

Right now he's carrying a broom with five rolls of toilet paper threaded onto the handle. All the boys are: they're on Bog Duty, sweeping out the outhouses, replacing the paper. Joanne wonders what they do with the used sanitary napkins in the brown paper bag in the waitresses' private outhouse. She can imagine the remarks.

'Company . . . halt!' shouts Darce. The group shambles to a stop in front of the window. 'Present . . . arms!' The brooms are raised, the ends of the toilet-paper rolls fluttering in the breeze like flags. The girls laugh and wave.

Monty's salute is half-hearted: this is well beneath his dignity. He may rent out his binoculars—that story is all over camp, by now—but he has no interest in using them himself. He has made that known. *Not on these girls*, he says, implying higher tastes.

Darce himself gives a comic salute, then marches his bunch away. The singing in the kitchen has stopped; the topic among the waitresses is now the counsellors. Darce is the best, the most admired, the most desirable. His teeth are the whitest, his hair the blondest, his grin the sexiest. In the counsellors' rec hall, where they go every night after the dishes are done, after they've changed out of their blue uniforms into their jeans and pullovers, after the campers have been inserted into their beds for the night, he has flirted with each one of them in turn. So who was he really saluting?

'It was me,' says Pat, joking. 'Don't I wish.'

'Dream on,' says Liz.

'It was Hil,' says Stephanie loyally. But Joanne knows it wasn't. It wasn't her, either. It was Ronette. They all suspect it. None of them says it.

'Perry likes Jo,' says Sandy.

'Does not,' says Joanne. She has given out that she has a boyfriend already and is therefore exempt from these contests. Half of this is true: she has a boyfriend. This summer he has a job as a salad chef on the Canadian National, running back and forth across the continent. She pictures him standing at the back of the train, on the caboose, smoking a cigarette between bouts of salad-making, watching the country slide away behind him. He writes her letters, in blue ball-point pen, on lined paper. *My first night on the Prairies,* he writes. *It's magnificent—all that land and sky. The sunsets are unbelievable.* Then there's a line across the page and a new date, and he gets to the Rockies. Joanne resents it a little that he raves on about places she's never been. It seems to her a kind of male showing-off: he's footloose. He closes with *Wish you were here* and several X's and O's. This seems too formal, like a letter to your mother. Like a peck on the cheek.

She put the first letter under her pillow, but woke up with blue smears on her face and the pillowcase both. Now she keeps the letters in her suitcase under the bed. She's having trouble remembering what he looks like. An image flits past, his face close up, at night, in the front seat of his father's car. The rustle of cloth. The smell of smoke.

Miss Fisk bumbles into the kitchen. She's short, plump, flustered; what she wears, always, is a hairnet over her grey bun, worn wool slippers—there's something wrong with her toes—and a faded blue knee-length sweater-coat, no matter how hot it is. She thinks of this summer job as her vacation. Occasionally she can be seen bobbing in the water in a droopy-chested bathing suit and a white rubber cap with the earflaps up. She never gets her head wet, so why she wears the cap is anyone's guess.

'Well, girls. Almost done?' She never calls the waitresses by name. To their faces they are *girls*, behind their backs *My girls*. They are her excuse for everything that goes wrong: *One of the girls must have done it.* She also functions as a sort of chaperon: her cabin is on the pathway that leads to theirs, and she has radar ears, like a bat.

I will never be that old, thinks Joanne. I will die before I'm thirty. She knows this absolutely. It's a tragic but satisfactory thought. If necessary, if some wasting disease refused to carry her off, she'll do it herself, with pills. She is not at all unhappy but she intends to be, later. It seems required.

This is no country for old men, she recites to herself. One of the poems she memorized, though it wasn't on the final exam. Change that to old women.

When they're all in their pyjamas, ready for bed, Joanne offers to read them the rest of the True Trash story. But everyone is too tired, so she reads it herself, with her flashlight, after the one feeble bulb has been switched off. She has a compulsion about getting to the ends of things. Sometimes she reads books backwards.

Needless to say, Marleen gets knocked up and Dirk takes off on his motorcycle when he finds out. *I'm not the settling-down type, baby. See ya round.*

Vroom. The mother practically has a nervous breakdown, because she made the same mistake when young and blew her chances and now look at her. Marleen cries and regrets, and even prays. But luckily the other shoe clerk, the boring one, still wants to marry her. So that's what happens. The mother forgives her, and Marleen herself learns the true value of quiet devotion. Her life isn't exciting maybe, but it's a good life, in the trailer park, the three of them. The baby is adorable. They buy a dog. It's an Irish setter, and chases sticks in the twilight while the baby laughs. This is how the story ends, with the dog.

Joanne stuffs the magazine down between her narrow little bed and the wall. She's almost crying. She will never have a dog like that, or a baby either. She doesn't want them, and anyway how would she have time, considering everything she has to get done? She has a long, though vague, agenda. Nevertheless she feels deprived.

Between two oval hills of pink granite there's a small crescent of beach. The boys, wearing their bathing suits (as they never do on canoe trips but only around the camp where they might be seen by girls), are doing their laundry, standing up to their knees and swabbing their wet T-shirts and underpants with yellow bars of Sunlight soap. This only happens when they run out of clothes, or when the stench of dirty socks in the cabin becomes too overpowering. Darce the counsellor is supervising, stretched out on a rock, taking the sun on his already tanned torso and smoking a fag. It's forbidden to smoke in front of the campers but he knows this bunch won't tell. To be on the safe side he's furtive about it, holding the cigarette down close to the rock and sneaking quick puffs.

Something hits Donny in the side of the head. It's Ritchie's wet underpants, squashed into a ball. Donny throws them back and soon there's an underpants war. Monty refuses to join in, so he becomes the common target. 'Sod off!' he yells.

'Cut it out, you pinheads,' Darce says. But he isn't really paying attention: he's seen something else, a flash of blue uniform, up among the trees. The waitresses aren't supposed to be over here on this side of the island. They're supposed to be on their own dock, having their afternoon break.

Darce is up among the trees now, one arm braced against a trunk. A conversation is going on; there are murmurs. Donny knows it's Ronette, he can tell by the shape, by the colour of the hair. And here he is, with his washboard ribs exposed, his hairless chest, throwing underpants around like a kid. He's disgusted with himself.

Monty, outnumbered but not wanting to admit defeat, says he needs to take a crap and disappears along the path to the outhouse. By now Darce is nowhere in sight. Donny captures Monty's laundry, which is already finished and wrung out and spread neatly on the hot rock to dry. He starts tossing it up into a jack pine, piece by piece. The others, delighted, help him. By the time Monty gets back, the tree is festooned with Monty's underpants and the other boys are innocently rinsing.

They're on one of the pink granite islands, the four of them: Joanne and Ronette, Perry and Darce. It's a double date. The two canoes have been pulled half out of the water and roped to the obligatory jack pines, the fire has done its main burning and is dying down to coals. The western sky is still peach-toned and luminous, the soft ripe juicy moon is rising, the evening air is warm and sweet, the waves wash gently against the rocks. It's the Summer Issue, thinks Joanne. *Lazy Daze. Tanning Tips. Shipboard Romance.*

Joanne is toasting a marshmallow. She has a special way of doing it: she holds it close to the coals but no so close that it catches fire, just close enough so that it swells up like a pillow and browns gently. Then she pulls off the toasted skin and eats it, and toasted the white inside part the same way, peeling it down to the core. She licks marshmallow goo off her fingers and stares pensively into the shifting red glow of the coal bed. All of this is a way of ignoring or pretending to ignore what is really going on.

There ought to be a tear drop, painted and static, on her cheek. There ought to be a caption: *Heartbreak.* On the spread-out groundsheet right behind her, his knee touching her back, is Perry, cheesed off with her because she won't neck with him. Off behind the rocks, out of the dim circle of firelight, are Ronette and Darce. It's the third week in July and by now they're a couple, everyone knows it. In the rec hall she wears his sweatshirt with the St Jude's crest; she smiles more these days, and even laughs when the other girls tease her about him. During this teasing Hilary does not join in. Ronette's face seems rounder, healthier, its angles smoothed out as if by a hand. She is less watchful, less diffident. She ought to have a caption too, thinks Joanne. *Was I Too Easy?*

There are rustlings from the darkness, small murmurings, breathing noises. It's like a movie theatre on Saturday night. Group grope. *The young in one another's arms.* Possibly, thinks Joanne, they will disturb a rattlesnake.

Perry puts a hand, tentatively, on her shoulder. 'Want me to toast you a marshmallow?' she says to him politely. The frosty freeze. Perry is no consolation prize. He merely irritates her, with his peeling sunburnt skin and begging spaniel's eyes. Her so-called real boyfriend is no help either, whizzing on his train tracks back and forth across the prairies, writing his by-now infrequent inky letters, the image of his face all but obliterated, as if it's been soaked in water.

Nor is it Darce she wants, not really. What she wants is what Ronette has: the power to give herself up, without reservation and without commentary. It's that languor, that leaning back. Voluptuous mindlessness. Everything Joanne herself does is surrounded by quotation marks.

'Marshmallows. Geez,' says Perry, in a doleful, cheated voice. All that paddling, and what for? Why the hell did she come along, if not to make out?

Joanne feels guilty of a lapse of manners. Would it hurt so much to kiss him?

Yes. It would.

Donny and Monty are on a canoe trip, somewhere within the tangled bush of the mainland. Camp Adanaqui is known for its tripping. For five days they and the others, twelve boys in all, have been paddling across lake after lake, hauling the gear over wave-rounded boulders or through the suck and stench of the moose-meadows at the portage entrances, grunting uphill with the packs and canoes, slapping the mosquitoes off their legs. Monty has blisters, on both his feet and his hands. Donny isn't too sad about that. He himself has a festering sliver. Maybe he will get blood-poisoning, become delirious, collapse and die on a portage, among the rocks and pine needles. That will serve someone right. Someone ought to be made to pay for the pain he's feeling.

The counsellors are Darce and Perry. During the days they crack the whip; at night they relax, backs against a rock or tree, smoking and supervising while the boys light the fire, carry the water, cook the Kraft Dinners. They both have smooth large muscles which ripple under their tans, they both—by now—have stubbly beards. When everyone goes swimming Donny sneaks covert, envious looks at their groins. They make him feel spindly, and infantile in his own desires.

Right now it's night. Perry and Darce are still up, talking in low voices, poking the embers of the dying fire. The boys are supposed to be asleep. There are tents in case of rain, but nobody's suggested putting them up since the day before yesterday. The smell of grime and sweaty feet and wood smoke is getting too potent at close quarters; the sleeping bags are high as cheese. It's better to be outside, rolled up in the bag, a groundsheet handy in case of a deluge, head under a turned-over canoe.

Monty is the only one who has voted for a tent. The bugs are getting him; he says he's allergic. He hates canoe trips and makes no secret of it. When he's older, he says, and can finally get his hands on the family boodle, he's going to buy the place from Mr B. and close it down. 'Generations of boys unborn will thank me,' he says. 'They'll give me a medal.' Sometimes Donny almost likes him. He's so blatant about wanting to be filthy rich. No hypocrisy about him, not like some of the other millionaire offshoots, who pretend they want to be scientists or something else that's not paid much.

Now Monty is twisting around, scratching his bites. 'Hey Finley,' he whispers.

'Go to sleep,' says Donny.

'I bet they've got a flask.'

'What?'

'I bet they're drinking. I smelled it on Perry's breath yesterday.'

'So?' says Donny.

'So,' says Monty. 'It's against the rules. Maybe we can get something out of them.'

Donny has to hand it to him. He certainly knows the angles. At the very least they might be able to share the wealth.

The two of them inch out of their sleeping bags and circle around behind the fire, keeping low. Their practice while spying on the waitresses stands them in good stead. They crouch behind a bushy spruce, watching for lifted elbows or the outlines of bottles, their ears straining.

But what they hear isn't about booze. Instead it's about Ronette. Darce is talking about her as if she's a piece of meat. From what he's implying she lets him do anything he wants. 'Summer sausage' is what he calls her. This is an expression Donny has never heard before, and ordinarily he would think it was hilarious.

Monty sniggers under his breath and pokes Donny in the ribs with his elbow. Does he know how much it hurts, is he rubbing it in? *Donny loves Ronette.* The ultimate grade six insult, to be accused of loving someone. Donny feels as if it's he himself who's been smeared with words, who's had his face rubbed in them. He knows Monty will repeat this conversation to the other boys. He will say Darce has been porking Ronette. Right now Donny detests this word, with its conjuring of two heaving pigs, or two dead but animate uncooked Sunday roasts; although just yesterday he used it himself, and found it funny enough.

He can hardly charge out of the bushes and punch Darce in the nose. Not only would he look ridiculous, he'd get flattened.

He does the only thing he can think of. Next morning, when they're breaking camp, he pinches Monty's binoculars and sinks them in the lake.

Monty guesses, and accuses him. Some sort of pride keeps Donny from denying it. Neither can he say why he did it. When they get back to the island there's an unpleasant conversation with Mr B. in the dining hall. Or not a conversation: Mr B. talks, Donny is silent. He does not look at Mr B. but at the pike's head on the wall, with its goggling voyeur's eye.

The next time the mahogany inboard goes back into town, Donny is in it. His parents are not pleased.

It's the end of summer. The campers have already left, though some of the counsellors and all of the waitresses are still here. Tomorrow they'll go down to the main dock, climb into the slow launch, thread their way among the pink islands, heading towards winter.

It's Joanne's half-day off so she isn't in the dining hall, washing the dishes with the others. She's in the cabin, packing up. Her duffle bag is finished, propped like an enormous canvas wiener against her bed; now she's doing her small suitcase. Her pay-cheque is already tucked inside: two hundred dollars, which is a lot of money.

Ronette comes into the cabin, still in her uniform, shutting the screen door quietly behind her. She sits down on Joanne's bed and lights a cigarette. Joanne is standing there with her folded-up flannelette pyjamas, alert: something's going on. Lately, Ronette has returned to her previous taciturn self; her smiles have become rare. In the counsellors' rec hall, Darce is again playing the field. He's been circling around Hilary, who's pretending—out of consideration for Ronette—not to notice. Maybe, now, Joanne will get to hear what caused the big split. So far Ronette has not said anything about it.

Ronette looks up at Joanne, through her long yellow bangs. Looking up like that makes her seem younger, despite the red lipstick. 'I'm in trouble,' she says.

'What sort of trouble?' says Joanne. Ronette smiles sadly, blows out smoke. Now she looks old. 'You know. Trouble.'

'Oh,' says Joanne. She sits down beside Ronette, hugging the flannelette pyjamas. She feels cold. It must be Darce. *Caught in that sensual music.* Now he will have to marry her. Or something. 'What're you going to do?'

'I don't know,' says Ronette. 'Don't tell, okay? Don't tell the others.'

'Aren't you going to tell *him?*' says Joanne. She can't imagine doing that, herself. She can't imagine any of it.

'Tell who?' Ronette says.

'Darce.'

Ronette blows out more smoke. 'Darce,' she says. 'Mr Chickenshit. It's not *his.*'

Joan is astounded, and relieved. But also annoyed with herself: what's gone past her, what has she missed? 'It's not? Then whose is it?'

But Ronette has apparently changed her mind about confiding. 'That's for me to know and you to find out,' she says, with a small attempt at a laugh.

'Well,' says Joanne. Her hands are clammy, as if it's her that's in trouble. She wants to be helpful, but has no idea how. 'Maybe you could—I don't know.' She doesn't know. An abortion? That is a dark and mysterious word, connected with the States. You have to go away. It costs a lot of money. A home for unwed mothers, followed by adoption? Loss washes through her. She foresees Ronette, bloated beyond recognition, as if she's drowned—a sacrifice, captured by her own body, offered up to it. Truncated in some way, disgraced. Unfree. There is something nun-like about this condition. She is in awe. 'I guess you could get rid of it, one way or another,' she says; which is not at all what she feels. *Whatever is begotten, born, and dies.*

'Are you kidding?' says Ronette, with something like contempt. 'Hell, not me.' She throws her cigarette on the floor, grinds it out with her heel. 'I'm keeping it. Don't worry, my mom will help me out.'

'Yeah,' says Joanne. Now she has caught her breath; now she's beginning to wonder why Ronette has dumped all this on her, especially since she isn't willing to tell the whole thing. She's beginning to feel cheated, imposed upon. So who's the guy, so which one of them? She shuffles through the faces of the counsellors, trying to remember hints, traces of guilt, but finds nothing.

'Anyways,' says Ronette, 'I won't have to go back to school. Thank the Lord for small mercies, like they say.'

Joanne hears bravado, and desolation. She reaches out a hand, gives Ronette's arm a small squeeze. 'Good luck,' she says. It comes out sounding like something you'd say before a race or an exam, or a war. It sounds stupid.

Ronette grins. The gap in her teeth shows, at the side. 'Same to you,' she says.

Eleven years later Donny is walking along Yorkville Avenue, in Toronto, in the summer heat. He's no longer Donny. At some point, which even he can't remember exactly, he has changed into Don. He's wearing sandals, and a white Indian-style shirt over his cut-off jeans. He has longish hair and a beard. The beard has come out yellow, whereas the hair is brown. He likes the effect: WASP Jesus or Hollywood Viking, depending on his mood. He has a string of wooden beads around his neck.

This is how he dresses on Saturdays, to go to Yorkville; to go there and just hang around, with the crowds of others who are doing the same. Sometimes he gets high, on the pot that circulates as freely as cigarettes did once. He thinks he should be enjoying this experience more than he actually does.

During the rest of the week he has a job in his father's law office. He can get away with the beard there, just barely, as long as he balances it with a suit. (But even the older guys are growing their sideburns and wearing coloured shirts, and using words like 'creative' more than they used to.) He doesn't tell the people he meets in Yorkville about this job, just as he doesn't tell the law office about his friends' acid trips. He's leading a double life. It feels precarious, and brave.

Suddenly, across the street, he sees Joanne. He hasn't even thought about her for a long time, but it's her all right. She isn't wearing the tie-dyed or flowing-shift uniform of the Yorkville girls; instead she's dressed in a brisk, businesslike white mini-skirt, with matching suit-jacket top. She's swinging a briefcase, striding along as if she has a purpose. This makes her stand out: the accepted walk here is a saunter.

Donny wonders whether he should run across the street, intercept her, reveal what he thinks of as his true but secret identity. Now all he can see is her back. In a minute she'll be gone.

'Joanne,' he calls. She doesn't hear him. He dodges between cars, catches up to her, touches her elbow. 'Don Finley,' he says. He's conscious of himself standing there, grinning like a fool. Luckily and a little disappointingly, she recognizes him at once.

'Donny!' she says. 'My God, you've grown!'

'I'm taller than you,' he says, like a kid, an idiot.

'You were then,' she says, smiling. 'I mean you've grown *up*.'

'So have you,' says Donny, and they find themselves laughing, almost like equals. Three years, four years between them. It was a large difference then. Now it's nothing.

So, thinks Joanne, Donny is no longer Donny. That must mean Ritchie is now Richard. As for Monty, he has become initials only, and a millionaire. True, he inherited some of it, but he's used it to advantage; Joanne has tuned in on his exploits now and then, in the business papers. And he got married to Hilary, three years ago. Imagine that. She saw that in the paper too.

They go for coffee and sit drinking it at one of the new, daring, outside tables, under a large, brightly painted wooden parrot. There's an intimacy between them, as if they are old friends. Donny asks Joanne what she's doing. 'I live by my wits,' she says. 'I freelance.' At the moment she's writing ad copy. Her face is thinner, she's lost that adolescent roundness; her once nondescript hair has been shaped into a stylish cap. Good enough legs, too. You have to have good legs to wear a mini. So many women look stumpy in them, hams in cloth, their legs bulging out the bottom like loaves of white bread. Joanne's legs are out of sight under the table, but Donny finds himself dwelling on them as he never did when they were clearly visible, all the way up, on the waitresses' dock. He'd skimmed over those legs then, skimmed over Joanne altogether. It was Ronette who had held his attention. He is more of a connoisseur, by now.

'We used to spy on you,' he says. 'We used to watch you skinny-dipping.' In fact they'd never managed to see much. The girls had held their towels around their bodies until the last minute, and anyway it was dusk. There would be a blur of white, some shrieking and splashing. The great thing would have been pubic hair. Several boys claimed sightings, but Donny had felt they were lying. Or was that just envy?

'Did you?' says Joanne absently. Then, 'I know. We could see the bushes waving around. We thought it was so cute.'

Donny feels himself blushing. He's glad he has the beard; it conceals things. 'It wasn't cute,' he says. 'Actually we were pretty vicious.' He's remembering the word *pork*. 'Do you ever see the others?'

'Not any more,' says Joanne. 'I used to see a few of them, at university. Hilary and Alex. Pat sometimes.'

'What about Ronette?' he says, which is the only thing he really wants to ask.

'I used to see Darce,' says Joanne, as if she hasn't heard him.

Used to see is an exaggeration. She saw him once.

It was in the winter, a February. He phoned her, at *The Varsity* office: that was how he knew where to find her, he'd seen her name in the campus paper. By that time Joanne scarcely remembered him. The summer she'd been a waitress was three years, light-years, away. The railroad-chef boyfriend was long gone; nobody so innocent had replaced him. She no longer wore white bucks, no longer sang songs. She wore turtlenecks and drank beer and a lot of coffee, and wrote cynical exposés of such things as the campus dining facilities. She'd given up on the idea of dying young, however. By this time it seemed overly romantic.

What Darce wanted was to go out with her. Specifically, he wanted her to go to a fraternity party with him. Joanne was so taken aback that she said yes, even though fraternities were in political disfavour among the people she travelled with now. It was something she would have to do on the sly, and she did. She had to borrow a dress from her room-mate, however. The thing was a semi-formal, and she had not deigned to go to a semi-formal since high school.

She had last seen Darce with sun-bleached hair and a deep glowing tan. Now, in his winter skin, he looked wan and malnourished. Also, he no longer flirted with everyone. He didn't even flirt with Joanne. Instead he introduced her to a few other couples, danced her perfunctorily around the floor, and proceeded to get very drunk on a mixture of grape juice and straight alcohol that the fraternity brothers called Purple Jesus. He told her he'd been engaged to Hilary for over six months, but she'd just ditched him. She wouldn't even say why. He said he'd asked Joanne out because she was the kind of girl you could talk to, he knew she would understand. After that he threw up a lot of Purple Jesus, first onto her dress, then—when she'd led him outside, to the veranda—onto a snowdrift. The colour scheme was amazing.

Joanne got some coffee into him and hitched a lift back to the residence, where she had to climb up the icy fire escape and in at a window because it was after hours.

Joanne was hurt. All she was for him was a big flapping ear. Also she was irritated. The dress she'd borrowed was pale blue, and the Purple Jesus would not come out with just water. Darce called the next day to apologize—St Jude's at least taught manners, of a sort—and Joanne stuck him with the cleaning bill. Even so there was a faint residual stain.

While they were dancing, before he started to slur and reel, she said, 'Do you ever hear from Ronette?' She still had the narrative habit, she still wanted to know the ends of stories. But he'd looked at her in complete bewilderment.

'Who?' he said. It wasn't a put-down, he really didn't remember. She found this blank in his memory offensive. She herself might forget a name, a face even. But a body? A body that has been so close to your own, that had generated those murmurings, those rustlings in the darkness, that aching pain—it was an affront to bodies, her own included.

After the interview with Mr B. and the stuffed pike's head, Donny walks down to the small beach where they do their laundry. The rest of his cabin is out sailing, but he's free now of camp routine, he's been discharged. A dishonourable discharge. After seven summers of being under orders here he can do what he wants. He has no idea what this might be.

He sits on a bulge of pink rock, feet on the sand. A lizard goes across the rock, near his hand, not fast. It hasn't spotted him. Its tail is blue and will come off if grabbed. Skinks, they're called. Once he would have taken joy from this knowledge. The waves wash in, wash out, the familiar heartbeat. He closes his eyes and hears only a machine. Possibly he is very angry, or sad. He hardly knows.

Ronette is there without warning. She must have come down the path behind him, through the trees. She's still in her uniform, although it isn't close to dinner. It's only late afternoon, when the waitresses usually leave their dock to go and change.

Ronette sits down beside him, takes out her cigarettes from some hidden pocket under her apron. 'Want a cig?' she says.

Donny takes one and says 'Thank you.' Not *thanks*, not wordlessly like leather-jacketed men in movies, but 'Thank you,' like a good boy from St Jude's, like a suck. He lets her light it. What else can he do? She's got the matches. Gingerly he inhales. He doesn't smoke much really, and is afraid of coughing.

'I heard they kicked you out,' Ronette says. 'That's really tough.'

'It's okay,' says Donny. 'I don't care.' He can't tell her why, how noble he's been. He hopes he won't cry.

'I heard you tossed Monty's binoculars,' she says. 'In the lake.'

Donny can only nod. He glances at her. She's smiling; he can see the heartbreaking space at the side of her mouth: the missing tooth. She thinks he's funny.

'Well, I'm with you,' she says. 'He's a little creep.'

'It wasn't because of him,' says Donny, overcome by the need to confess, or to be taken seriously. 'It was because of Darce.' He turns, and for the first time looks her straight in the eyes. They are so green. Now his hands are shaking. He drops the cigarette into the sand. They'll find the butt tomorrow, after he's gone. After he's gone, leaving Ronette behind, at the mercy of other people's words. 'It was because of you. What they were saying about you. Darce was.'

Ronette isn't smiling any more. 'Such as what?' she says.

'Never mind,' says Donny. 'You don't want to know.'

'I know anyhow,' Ronette says. 'That shit.' She sounds resigned rather than angry. She stands up, puts both her hands behind her back. It takes Donny a moment to realize she's untying her apron. When she's got it off she takes him by the hand, pulls gently. He allows himself to be led around the hill of rock, out of sight of anything but the water. She sits down, lies down, smiles as she reaches up, arranges his hands. Her blue uniform unbuttons down the front. Donny can't believe this is happening, to him, in full daylight. It's like sleepwalking, it's like running too fast, it's like nothing else.

'Want another coffee?' Joanne says. She nods to the waitress. Donny hasn't heard her.

'She was really nice to me,' he is saying. 'Ronette. You know, when Mr B. turfed me out. That meant a lot to me at the time.' He's feeling guilty, because he never wrote her. He didn't know where she lived, but he didn't take any steps to find out. Also, he couldn't keep himself from thinking: *They're right. She's a slut.* Part of him had been profoundly shocked by what she'd done. He hadn't been ready for it.

Joanne is looking at him with her mouth slightly open, as if he's a talking dog, a talking stone. He fingers his beard nervously, wondering what he's said wrong, or given away.

Joanne has just seen the end of the story, or one end of one story. Or at least a missing piece. So that's why Ronette wouldn't tell: it was Donny. She'd been protecting him; or maybe she'd been protecting herself. A fourteen-year-old boy. Ludicrous.

Ludicrous then, possible now. You can do anything now and it won't cause a shock. Just a shrug. Everything is *cool.* A line has been drawn and on the other side of it is the past, both darker and more brightly intense than the present.

She looks across the line and sees the nine waitresses in their bathing suits, in the clear blazing sunlight, laughing on the dock, herself among them; and off in the shadowy rustling bushes of the shoreline, sex lurking dangerously. It had been dangerous, then. It had been sin. Forbidden, secret, sullying. *Sick with desire.* Three dots had expressed it perfectly, because there had been no ordinary words for it.

On the other hand there had been marriage, which meant wifely checked aprons, play-pens, a sugary safety.

But nothing has turned out that way. Sex has been domesticated, stripped of the promised mystery, added to the category of the merely expected. It's just what is done, mundane as hockey. It's celibacy these days that would raise eyebrows.

And what has become of Ronette, after all, left behind in the past, dappled by its chiaroscuro, stained and haloed by it, stuck with other people's adjectives? What is she doing, now that everyone else is following in her footsteps? More practically: did she have the baby, or not? Keep it or not? Donny, sitting sweetly across the table from her, is in all probability the father of a ten-year-old child, and he knows nothing about it at all.

Should she tell him? The melodrama tempts her, the idea of a revelation, a sensation, a neat ending.

But it would not be an ending, it would only be the beginning of something else. In any case, the story itself seems to her outmoded. It's an archaic story, a folk-tale, a mosaic artefact. It's a story that would never happen now.

W.D. VALGARDSON
(1939)

∽

God is Not a Fish Inspector

Although Emma made no noise as she descended, Fusi Bergman knew his daughter was watching him from the bottom of the stairs.

'God will punish you,' she promised in a low, intense voice.

'Render unto Caesar what is Caesar's,' he snapped. 'God's not a fish inspector. He doesn't work for the government.'

By the light of the front ring of the kitchen stove, he had been drinking a cup of coffee mixed half and half with whisky. Now, he shifted in his captain's chair so as to partly face the stairs. Though he was unable to make out more than the white blur of Emma's nightgown, after living with her for 48 years he knew exactly how she would look if he turned on the light.

She was tall and big boned with the square, pugnacious face of a bulldog. Every inch of her head would be crammed with metal curlers and her angular body hidden by a plain white cotton shift that hung from her broad shoulders like a tent. Whenever she was angry with him, she always stood rigid and white lipped, her hands clenched at her sides.

'You prevaricate,' she warned. 'You will not be able to prevaricate at the gates of Heaven.'

He drained his cup, sighed, and pulled on his jacket. As he opened the door, Fusi said, 'He made fish to catch. There is no place in the Bible where it says you can't catch fish when you are three score and ten.'

'You'll be the ruin of us,' she hissed as he closed the door on her.

She was aggressive and overbearing, but he knew her too well to be impressed. Behind her forcefulness, there was always that trace of self-pity nurtured in plain women who go unmarried until they think they have been passed by. Even if they eventually found a husband, the self-pity returned to change their determination into a whine. Still, he was glad to have the door between them.

This morning, as every morning, he had wakened at three. Years before, he had trained himself to get up at that time and now, in spite of his age, he never woke more than five minutes after the hour. He was proud of his early rising for he felt it showed he was not, like many of his contemporaries, relentlessly sliding into the endless blur of senility. Each morning, because he had become reconciled to the idea of dying, he felt, on the instant of his awakening, a spontaneous sense of amazement at being alive. The thought never lasted longer than the brief time between sleep and consciousness, but the good feeling lingered throughout the day.

When Fusi stepped outside, the air was cold and damp. The moon that hung low in the west was pale and fragile and very small. Fifty feet from the house, the breakwater that ran along the rear of his property loomed like the purple spine of some great beast guarding the land from a lake which seemed, in the darkness, to go on forever.

Holding his breath to still the noise of his own breathing, Fusi listened for a cough or the scuff of gravel that would mean someone was close by, watching and waiting, but the only sound was the muted rubbing of his skiff against the piling to which it was moored. Half a mile away where the land was lower, rows of gas boats roped five abreast lined the docks. The short, stubby boats with their high cabins, the grey surface of the docks and the dark water were all tinged purple from the mercury lamps. At the harbour mouth, high on a thin spire, a red light burned like a distant star.

Behind him, he heard the door open and, for a moment, he was afraid Emma might begin to shout, or worse still, turn on the back-door light and alert his enemies, but she did neither. Above all things, Emma was afraid of scandal, and would do anything to avoid causing an unsavoury rumour to be attached to her own or her husband's name.

Her husband, John Smith, was as bland and inconsequential as his name. Moon faced with wide blue eyes and a small mouth above which sat a carefully trimmed moustache, he was a head shorter than Emma and a good 50 pounds ligher. Six years before, he had been transferred to the Eddyville branch of the Bank of Montreal. His transfer from Calgary to a small town in Manitoba was the bank's way of letting him know that there would be no more promotions. He would stay in Eddyville until he retired.

A year after he arrived, Emma had married him and instead of her moving out, he had moved in. For the last two years, under Emma's prodding, John had been taking a correspondence course in theology so that when he no longer worked at the bank he could be a full-time preacher.

On the evenings when he wasn't balancing the bank's books, he laboured over the multiple-choice questions in the Famous Preacher's course that he received each month from the One True and Only Word of God Church in Mobile, Alabama. Because of a freak in the atmosphere one night while she had been fiddling with the radio, Emma had heard a gospel hour advertising the course and, although neither she nor John had ever been south of Minneapolis and had never heard of the One True and Only Word of God Church before, she took it as a sign and immediately enrolled her husband in it. It cost $500.

John's notes urged him not to wait to answer His Call but to begin ministering to the needy at once for the Judgment Day was always imminent. In anticipation of the end of the world and his need for a congregation once he retired, he and Emma had become zealous missionaries, cramming their

Volkswagen with a movie projector, a record-player, films, trays of slides, religious records for every occasion, posters and pamphlets, all bought or rented from the One True and Only Word of God Church. Since the townspeople were obstinately Lutheran, and since John did not want to give offence to any of his bank's customers, he and Emma hunted converts along the grey dirt roads that led past tumble-down farmhouses, the inhabitants of which were never likely to enter a bank.

Fusi did not turn to face his daughter but hurried away because he knew he had no more than an hour and a half until dawn. His legs were fine as he crossed the yard, but by the time he had mounted the steps that led over the breakwater, then climbed down fifteen feet to the shore, he left knee has begun to throb.

Holding his leg rigid to ease the pain, he waded out, loosened the ropes and heaved himself away from the shore. As soon as the boat was in deep water, he took his seat, and set both oars in the oar-locks he had carefully muffled with strips from an old shirt.

For a moment, he rested his hands on his knees, the oars rising like too-small wings from a cumbersome body, then he straightened his arms, dipped the oars cleanly into the water and in one smooth motion pulled his hands toward his chest. The first few strokes were even and graceful but then as a speck of pain like a grain of sand formed in his shoulder, the sweep of his left oar became shorter than his right. Each time he leaned against the oars, the pain grew until it was, in his mind, a bent shingle-nail twisted and turned in his shoulder socket.

With the exertion, a ball of gas formed in his stomach, making him uncomfortable. As quickly as a balloon being blown up, it expanded until his lungs and heart were cramped and he couldn't draw in a full breath. Although the air over the lake was cool, sweat ran from his hairline.

At his two-hundredth stroke, he shipped his left oar and pulled a coil of rope with a large hook from under the seat. After checking to see that it was securely tied through the gunwale, he dropped the rope overboard and once more began to row. Normally, he would have had a buoy made from a slender tamarack pole, a block of wood and some lead weights to mark his net, but he no longer had a fishing licence so his net had to be sunk below the surface where it could not be seen by the fish inspectors.

Five more strokes of the oars and the rope went taut. He lifted both oars into the skiff, then, standing in the bow, began to pull. The boat responded sluggishly but gradually it turned and the cork line that lay hidden under two feet of water broke the surface. He grasped the net, freed the hook and began to collect the mesh until the lead line appeared. For once he had been lucky and the hook had caught the net close to one end so there was no need to backtrack.

Hand over hand he pulled, being careful not to let the corks and leads bang against the bow, for on the open water sound carried clearly for miles. In the first two fathoms there was a freshly caught pickerel. As he pulled it toward him, it beat the water with its tail, making light, slapping sounds. His fingers were cramped, but Fusi managed to catch the fish around its soft middle and, with his other hand, work the mesh free of the gills.

It was then that the pain in his knee forced him to sit. Working from the seat was awkward and cost him precious time, but he had no choice, for the pain had begun to inch up the bone toward his crotch.

He wiped his forehead with his hand and cursed his infirmity. When he was twenty, he had thought nothing of rowing five miles from the shore to lift five and six gangs of nets and then, nearly knee deep in fish, row home again. Now, he reflected bitterly, a quarter of a mile and one net were nearly beyond him. Externally, he had changed very little over the years. He was still tall and thin, his arms and legs corded with muscle. His belly was hard. His long face, with its pointed jaw, showed his age the most. That and his hands. His face was lined until it seemed there was nowhere the skin was smooth. His hands were scarred and heavily veined. His hair was grey but it was still thick.

While others were amazed at his condition, he was afraid of the changes that had taken place inside him. It was this invisible deterioration that was gradually shrinking the limits of his endurance.

Even in the darkness, he could see the distant steeple of the Lutheran church and the square bulk of the old folk's home that was directly across from his house. Emma, he thought grimly, would not be satisfied until he was safely trapped in one or carried out of the other.

He hated the old folk's home. He hated the three storeys of pale yellow brick with their small, close-set windows. He hated the concrete porch with its five round pillars and the large white buckets of red geraniums. When he saw the men poking at the flowers like a bunch of old women, he pulled his blinds.

The local people who worked in the home were good to the inmates, tenants they called them, but there was no way a man could be a man in there. No whisky. Going to bed at ten. Getting up at eight. Bells for breakfast, coffee and dinner. Bells for everything. He was surprised that they didn't have bells for going to the toilet. Someone watching over you every minute of every day. It was as if, having earned the right to be an adult, you had suddenly, in some inexplicable way, lost it again.

The porch was the worst part of the building. Long and narrow and lined with yellow and red rocking-chairs, it sat ten feet above the ground and the steps were so steep that even those who could get around all right were afraid to try them. Fusi had lived across from the old folk's home for 40 years and he had seen old people, all interchangeable as time erased their identities, shuffling and bickering their way to their deaths. Now, most of those who came out to sleep in the sun and to watch the world with glittering, jealous eyes, were people he had known.

He would have none of it. He was not afraid of dying, but he was determined that it would be in his own home. His licence had been taken from him because of his age, but he did not stop. One net was not thirty, but it was one, and a quarter-mile from shore was not five miles, but it was a quarter-mile.

He didn't shuffle and he didn't have to be fed or have a rubber diaper pinned around him each day. If anything, he had become more cunning for, time and again, the inspectors had come and destroyed the illegal nets of other fishermen, even catching and sending them to court to be fined, but they hadn't caught him for four years. Every day of the fishing season, he pitted his wits against theirs and won. At time, they had come close, but their searches had never turned up anything and, once, to his delight, when he was on the verge of being found with freshly caught fish on him, he hid them under a hole in the breakwater and then sat on the edge of the boat, talked about old times, and shared the inspectors' coffee. The memory still brought back a feeling of pleasure and excitement.

As his mind strayed over past events, he drew the boat along the net in fits and starts for his shoulder would not take the strain of steady pulling. Another good-sized fish hung limp as he pulled it to him, but then as he slipped the mesh from its head, it gave a violent shake and flew from his hands. Too stiff and slow to lunge for it, he could do nothing but watch the white flash of its belly before it struck the water and disappeared.

He paused to knead the backs of his hands, then began again. Before he was finished, his breath roared in his ears like the lake in a storm, but there were four more pickerel. With a sigh that was nearly a cry of pain, he let the net drop. Immediately, pulled down by the heavy, rusted anchors at each end, it disappeared. People were like that, he thought. One moment they were here, then they were gone and it was as if they had never been.

Behind the town, the horizon was a pale, hard grey. The silhouette of rooftops and trees might have been cut from a child's purple construction paper.

The urgent need to reach the shore before the sky became any lighter drove Fusi, for he knew that if the inspectors saw him on the water they would catch him as easily as a child. They would take his fish and net, which he did not really mind, for there were more fish in the lake and more nets in his shed, but he couldn't afford to lose his boat. His savings were not enough to buy another.

He put out the oars, only to be unable to close the fingers of his left hand. When he tried to bend his fingers around the handle, his whole arm began to tremble. Unable to do anything else, he leaned forward and pressing his fingers flat to the seat, he began to relentlessly knead them. Alternately, he prayed and cursed, trying with words to delay the sun.

'A few minutes,' he whispered through clenched teeth. 'Just a few minutes more.' But even as he watched, the horizon turned red, then yellow and a sliver of the sun's rim rose above the houses.

Unable to wait any longer, he grabbed his left hand in his right and forced his fingers around the oar, then braced himself and began to row.

Instead of cutting the water cleanly, the left oar skimmed over the surface, twisting the handle in his grip. He tried again, not letting either oar go deep. The skiff moved sluggishly ahead.

Once again, the balloon in his chest swelled and threatened to gag him, making his gorge rise, but he did not dare stop. Again and again, the left oar skipped across the surface so that the bow swung back and forth like a wounded and dying animal trying to shake away its pain. Behind him, the orange sun inched above the sharp angles of the roofs.

When the bow slid across the sand, he dropped the oars, letting them trail in the water. He grasped the gunwale, but as he climbed out, his left leg collapsed and he slid to his knees. Cold water filled his boots and soaked the legs of his trousers. Resting his head against the boat, he breathed noisily through his mouth. He remained there until gradually his breathing eased and the pain in his chest closed like a night flower touched by daylight. When he could stand, he tied the boat to one of the black pilings that was left from a breakwater that had long since been smashed and carried away.

As he collected his catch, he noticed the green fisheries department truck on the dock. He had been right. They were there. Crouching behind his boat, he waited to see if anyone was watching him. It seemed like a miracle that they had not already seen him, but he knew that they had not for if they had, their launch would have raced out of the harbour and swept down upon him.

Bending close to the sand, he limped into the deep shadow at the foot of the breakwater. They might, he knew, be waiting for him at the top of the ladder but if they were, there was nothing he could do about it. He climbed the ladder and, hearing and seeing nothing, he rested near the top so that when he climbed into sight, he wouldn't need to sit down.

No one was in the yard. The block was empty. With a sigh of relief, he crossed to the small shed where he kept his equipment and hefted the fish onto the shelf that was nailed to one wall. He filleted his catch with care, leaving none of the translucent flesh on the back-bone or skin. Then, because they were pickerel, he scooped out the cheeks, which he set aside with the roe for his breakfast.

As he carried the offal across the backyard in a bucket, the line of gulls that gathered every morning on the breakwater broke into flight and began to circle overhead. Swinging back the bucket, he flung the guts and heads and skin into the air and the gulls darted down to snatch the red entrails and irridescent heads. In a thrumming of white and grey wings, those who hadn't caught anything descended to the sand to fight for what remained.

Relieved at being rid of the evidence of his fishing—if anyone asked where he got the fillets he would say he had bought them and the other fishermen would lie for him—Fusi squatted and wiped his hands clean on the wet grass.

There was no sign of movement in the house. The blinds were still drawn and the high, narrow house with its steep roof and faded red-brick siding looked deserted. The yard was flat and bare except for the dead trunk of an elm, which was stripped bare of its bark and wind polished to the colour of bone.

He returned to the shed and wrapped the fillets in a sheet of brown waxed paper, then put the roe and the cheeks into the bucket. Neither Emma nor John were up when he came in and washed the bucket and his food, but as he started cooking, Emma appeared in a quilted housecoat covered with large, purple tulips. Her head was a tangle of metal.

'Are you satisfied?' she asked, her voice trembling. 'I've had no sleep since you left.'

Without turning from the stove, he said, 'Leave. Nobody's making you stay.'

Indignantly, she answered, 'And who would look after you?'

He grimaced and turned over the roe so they would be golden brown on all sides. For two weeks around Christmas he had been sick with the flu and she never let him forget it.

'Honour thy father and mother that thy days may be long upon this earth.'

He snorted out loud. What she really wanted to be sure of was that she got the house.

'You don't have to be like this,' she said, starting to talk to him as if he was a child. 'I only want you to stop because I care about you. All those people who live across the street, they don't. . . .'

'I'm not one of them,' he barked.

'You're 70 years old. . . .'

'And I still fish,' he replied angrily, cutting her off. 'And I still row a boat and lift my nets. That's more than your husband can do and he's just 50.' He jerked his breakfast off the stove. Because he knew it would annoy her, he began to eat out of the pan.

'I'm 70,' he continued between bites, 'and I beat the entire fisheries department. They catch men half my age, but they haven't caught me. Not for four years. And I fish right under their noses.' He laughed with glee and laced his coffee with a finger of whisky.

Emma, her lips clamped shut and her hands clenched in fury, marched back up the stairs. In half an hour both she and John came down for their breakfast. Under Emma's glare, John cleared his throat and said, 'Emma, that is we, think—' He stopped and fiddled with the knot of his tie. He always wore light grey ties and a light grey suit. 'If you don't quit breaking the law, something will have to be done.' He stopped and looked beseechingly at his wife, but she narrowed her eyes until little folds of flesh formed beneath them. 'Perhaps something like putting you in custody so you'll be saved from yourself.'

Fusi was so shocked that for once he could think of nothing to say. Encouraged by his silence, John said, 'It will be for your own good.'

Before either of them realized what he was up to, Fusi leaned sideways and emptied his cup into his son-in-law's lap.

The coffee was hot. John flung himself backward with a screech, but the back legs of his chair caught on a crack in the linoleum and he tipped over with a crash. In the confusion Fusi stalked upstairs.

In a moment he flung an armload of clothes down. When his daughter rushed to the bottom of the stairs, Fusi flung another armload of clothes at her.

'This is my house,' he bellowed. 'You're not running it yet.'

Emma began grabbing clothes and laying them flat so they wouldn't wrinkle. John, both hands clenched between his legs, hobbled over to stare.

Fusi descended the stairs and they parted to let him by. At the counter, he picked up the package of fish and turning toward them, said, 'I want you out of here when I get back or I'll go out on the lake and get caught and tell everyone that you put me up to it.'

His fury was so great that once he was outside he had to lean against the house while a spasm of trembling swept over him. When he was composed, he rounded the corner. At one side of the old folk's home there was an enclosed fire escape that curled to the ground like a piece of intestine. He headed for the kitchen door under it.

Fusi had kept on his rubber boats, dark slacks and red turtle-neck sweater, and because he knew that behind the curtains, eyes were watching his every move, he tried to hide the stiffness of his left leg.

Although it was early, Rosie Melysyn was already at work. She always came first, never missing a day. She was a large, good natured widow with grey hair.

'How are you today, Mr Bergman?' she asked.

'Fine,' he replied. 'I'm feeling great.' He held out the brown paper package. 'I thought some of the old people might like some fish.' Although he had brought fish for the last four years, he always said the same thing.

Rosie dusted off her hands, took the package and placed it on the counter.

'I'll see someone gets it,' she assured him. 'Help yourself to some coffee.'

As he took the pot from the stove, she asked, 'No trouble with the inspectors?'

He always waited for her to ask that. He grinned delightedly, the pain of the morning already becoming a memory. 'No trouble. They'll never catch me. I'm up too early. I saw them hanging about, but it didn't do them any good.'

'Jimmy Henderson died last night,' Rosie offered.

'Jimmy Henderson,' Fusi repeated. They had been friends, but he felt no particular sense of loss. Jimmy had been in the home for three years. 'I'm not surprised. He wasn't more than 68 but he had given up. You give up, you're going to die. You believe in yourself and you can keep right on going.'

Rosie started mixing oatmeal and water.

'You know,' he said to her broad back, 'I was with Jimmy the first time he got paid. He cut four cords of wood for 60¢ and spent it on hootch. He kept running up and down the street and flapping his arms, trying to fly. When he passed out, we hid him in the hayloft of the stable so his old man couldn't find him.'

Rosie tried to imagine Jimmy Henderson attempting to fly and failed. To her, he was a bent man with a sad face who had to use a walker to get to the dining room. What she remembered about him best was coming on him unexpectedly and finding him silently crying. He had not seen her and she had quietly backed away.

Fusi was lingering because after he left, there was a long day ahead of him. He would have the house to himself and after checking the vacated room to see that nothing of his had been taken, he would tie his boat properly, sleep for three hours, then eat lunch. In the afternoon he would make a trip to the docks to see what the inspectors were up to and collect information about their movements.

The back door opened with a swish and he felt a cool draft. Both he and Rosie turned to look. He was shocked to see that instead of being one of the kitchen help, it was Emma. She shut the door and glanced at them both, then at the package of fish.

'What do you want?' he demanded.

'I called the inspectors,' she replied, 'to tell them you're not responsible for yourself. I told them about the net.'

He gave a start, but then was relieved when he remembered they had to actually catch him fishing before they could take the skiff. 'So what?' he asked, confident once more.

Quietly, she replied, 'You don't have to worry about being caught. They've known about your fishing all along.'

Suddenly frightened by her calm certainty, his voice rose as he said, 'That's not true.'

'They don't care,' she repeated. 'Inspector McKenzie was the name of one I talked to. He said you couldn't do any harm with one net. They've been watching you every morning just in case you should get into trouble and need help.'

Emma stood there, not moving, her head tipped back, her eyes benevolent.

He turned to Rosie. 'She's lying, isn't she? That's not true. They wouldn't do that?'

'Of course, she lying.' Rosie assured him.

He would have rushed outside but Emma was standing in his way. Since he could not get past her, he fled through the swinging doors that led to the dining-room.

As the doors shut. Rosie turned on Emma and said, 'You shouldn't have done that.' She picked up the package of fish with its carefully folded wrapping. In the artificial light, the package glowed like a piece of amber. She held it cupped in the hollows of her hands. 'You had no right.'

Emma seemed to grow larger and her eyes shone.

'The Lord's work be done,' she said, her right hand partly raised as if she were preparing to give a benediction.

CLARK BLAISE

(1940)

~

A Class of New Canadians

Norman Dyer hurried down Sherbrooke Street, collar turned against the snow. 'Superb!' he muttered, passing a basement gallery next to a French bookstore. Bleached and tanned women in furs dashed from hotel lobbies into waiting cabs. Even the neon clutter of the side streets and the honks of slithering taxis seemed remote tonight through the peaceful snow. *Superb*, he thought again, waiting for a light and backing from a slushy curb: a word reserved for wines, cigars, and delicate sauces; he was feeling superb this evening. After eighteen months in Montreal, he still found himself freshly impressed by everything he saw. He was proud of himself for having steered his life north, even for jobs that were menial by standards he could have demanded. Great just being here no matter what they paid, looking at these buildings, these faces, and hearing all the languages. He was learning to be insulted by simple bad taste, wherever he encountered it.

Since leaving graduate school and coming to Montreal, he had sampled every ethnic restaurant downtown and in the old city, plus a few Levantine places out in Outremont. He had worked on conversational French and mastered much of the local dialect, done reviews for local papers, translated French-Canadian poets for Toronto quarterlies, and tweaked his colleagues for not sympathizing enough with Quebec separatism. He attended French performances of plays he had ignored in English, and kept a small but elegant apartment near a colony of *émigré* Russians just off Park Avenue. Since coming to Montreal he'd witnessed a hold-up, watched a murder, and seen several riots. When stopped on the street for directions, he would answer in French or accented English. To live this well and travel each long academic summer, he held two jobs. He had no intention of returning to the States. In fact, he had begun to think of himself as a semi-permanent, semi-political exile.

Now, stopped again a few blocks farther, he studied the window of Holt-Renfrew's exclusive men's shop. Incredible, he thought, the authority of simple good taste. Double-breasted chalk-striped suits he would never dare to buy. Knitted sweaters, and fifty-dollar shoes. One tanned mannequin was decked out in a brash checkered sportscoat with a burgundy vest and dashing ascot. Not a price tag under three hundred dollars. Unlike food, drink, cinema, and literature, clothing had never really involved him. Some day, he now realized, it would. Dyer's clothes, thus far, had all been bought in a chain department store. He was a walking violation of American law, clad shoes to scarf in Egyptian cottons, Polish leathers, and woollens from the People's Republic of China.

He had no time for dinner tonight; this was Wednesday, a day of lectures at one university, and then an evening course in English as a Foreign Language at McGill, beginning at six. He would eat afterwards.

Besides the money, he had kept this second job because it flattered him. There was to Dyer something fiercely elemental, almost existential, about teaching both his language and his literature in a foreign country—like Joyce in Trieste, Isherwood and Nabokov in Berlin, Beckett in Paris. Also it was necessary for his students. It was the first time in his life that he had done something socially useful. What difference did it make that the job was beneath him, a recent Ph.D., while most of his colleagues in the evening school at McGill were idle housewives and bachelor civil servants? It didn't matter, even, that this job was a perversion of all the sentiments he held as a progressive young teacher. He was a god two evenings a week, sometimes suffering and fatigued, but nevertheless an omniscient, benevolent god. His students were silent, ignorant, and dedicated to learning English. No discussions, no demonstrations, no dialogue.

I love them, he thought. They need me.

He entered the room, pocketed his cap and ear muffs, and dropped his briefcase on the podium. Two girls smiled good evening.

They love me, he thought, taking off his boots and hanging up his coat; I'm not like their English-speaking bosses.

I love myself, he thought with amazement even while conducting a drill on word order. I love myself for tramping down Sherbrooke Street in zero weather just to help them with noun clauses. I love myself standing behind this podium and showing Gilles Carrier and Claude Veilleux the difference between the past continuous and the simple past; or the sultry Armenian girl with the bewitching half-glasses that 'put on' is not the same as 'take on'; or telling that dashing Mr Miguel Mayor, late of Madrid, that simple futurity can be expressed in four different ways, at least.

This is what mastery is like, he thought. Being superb in one's chosen field, not merely in one's mother tongue. A respected performer in the lecture halls of the major universities, equipped by twenty years' research in the remotest libraries, and slowly giving it back to those who must have it. Dishing it out suavely, even wittily. Being a legend. Being loved and a little feared.

'Yes, Mrs David?'

A *sabra*: freckled, reddish hair, looking like a British model, speaks with a nifty British accent, and loves me.

'No,' he smiled, 'I *were* is not correct except in the present subjunctive, which you haven't studied yet.'

The first hour's bell rang. The students closed their books for the intermission. Dyer put his away, then noticed a page of his Faulkner lecture from the afternoon class. *Absalom, Absalom!* his favourite.

'Can anyone here tell me what the *impregnable citadel of his passive rectitude* means?'

'What, sir?' asked Mr Vassilopoulos, ready to copy.

'What about *the presbyterian and lugubrious effluvium of his passive vindictiveness?*' A few girls giggled. 'O.K.,' said Dyer, 'take your break.'

In the halls of McGill they broke into the usual groups. French Canadians and South Americans into two large circles, then the Greeks, Germans, Spanish, and French into smaller groups. The patterns interested Dyer. Madrid Spaniards and Parisian French always spoke English with their New World co-linguals. The Middle Europeans spoke German together, not Russian, preferring one occupier to the other. Two Israeli men went off alone. Dyer decided to join them for the break.

Not *sabras*, Dyer concluded, not like Mrs David. The shorter one, dark and wavy-haired, held his cigarette like a violin bow. The other, Mr Weinrot, was tall and pot-bellied, with a ruddy face and thick stubby fingers. Something about him suggested truck-driving, perhaps of beer, maybe in Germany. Neither one, he decided, could supply the name of a good Israeli restaurant.

'This is really hard, you know?' said Weinrot.

'Why?'

'I think it's because I'm not speaking much of English at my job.'

'French?' asked Dyer.

'French? Pah! All the time Hebrew, sometimes German, sometimes little Polish. Crazy thing, eh? How long you think they let me speak Hebrew if I'm working in America?'

'Depends on where you're working,' he said.

'Hell, I'm working for the Canadian government, what you think? Plant I work in—I'm engineer, see—makes boilers for the turbines going up North. Look. When I'm leaving Israel I go first to Italy. Right away-bamm I'm working in Italy I'm speaking Italian like a native. Passing for a native.'

'A native Jew,' said his dark-haired friend.

'Listen to him. So in Rome they think I'm from Tyrol—that's still native, eh? So I speak Russian and German and Italian like a Jew. My Hebrew is bad, I admit it, but it's a lousy language anyway. Nobody likes it. French I understand but English I'm talking like a bum. Arabic I know five dialects. Danish fluent. So what's the matter I can't learn English?'

'It'll come, don't worry,' Dyer smiled. *Don't worry, my son;* he wanted to pat him on the arm. 'Anyway, that's what makes Canada so appealing. Here they don't force you.'

'What's this *appealing?* Means nice? Look, my friend, keep it, eh? Two years in a country I don't learn the language means it isn't a country.'

'Come on,' said Dyer. 'Neither does forcing you.'

'Let me tell you a story why I come to Canada. Then you tell me if I was wrong, O.K.?'

'Certainly,' said Dyer, flattered.

In Italy, Weinrot told him, he had lost his job to a Communist union. He left Italy for Denmark and opened up an Israeli restaurant with five other friends. Then the six Israelis decided to rent a bigger apartment downtown near the restaurant. They found a perfect nine-room place for two thousand kroner a month, not bad shared six ways. Next day the landlord told them the deal was off. 'You tell me why,' Weinrot demanded.

No Jews? Dyer wondered. 'He wanted more rent,' he finally said.

'More—you kidding? More we expected. *Less* we didn't expect. A couple with eight kids is showing up after we're gone and the law in Denmark says a man has a right to a room for each kid plus a hundred kroner knocked off the rent for each kid. What you think of that? So a guy who comes in *after* us gets a nine-room place for a thousand kroner *less*. Law says no way a bachelor can get a place ahead of a family, and bachelors pay twice as much.'

Dyer waited, then asked, 'So?'

'So, I make up my mind the world is full of communismus, just like Israel. So I take out applications next day for Australia, South Africa, U.S.A., and Canada. Canada says come right away, so I go. Should have waited for South Africa.'

'How could you?' Dyer cried. 'What's wrong with you anyway? South Africa is fascist. Australia is racist.'

The bell rang, and the Israelis, with Dyer, began walking to the room.

'What I was wondering, then,' said Mr Weinrot, ignoring Dyer's outburst, 'was if my English is good enough to be working in the United States. You're American, aren't you?'

It was a question Dyer had often avoided in Europe, but had rarely been asked in Montreal. 'Yes,' he admitted, 'your English is probably good enough for the States or South Africa, whichever one wants you first.'

He hurried ahead to the room, feeling that he had let Montreal down. He wanted to turn and shout to Weinrot and to all the others that Montreal was the greatest city on the continent, if only they knew it as well as he did. If they'd just break out of their little ghettos.

At the door, the Armenian girl with the half-glasses caught his arm. She was standing with Mrs David and Miss Parizeau, a jolly French-Canadian girl that Dyer had been thinking of asking out.

'Please, sir,' she said, looking at him over the tops of her tiny glasses, 'what I was asking earlier—*put on*—I heard on the television. A man said *You are putting me on* and everybody laughed. I think it was supposed to be funny but *put on* we learned means get dressed, no?'

'Ah—*don't put me on,*' Dyer laughed.

'I yaven't erd it neither,' said Miss Parizeau.

'To put some*body* on means to make a fool of him. To put some*thing* on is to wear it. O.K.?' He gave examples.

'Ah, now I know,' said Miss Parizeau. 'Like bullshitting somebody. Is it the same?'

'Ah, yes,' he said, smiling. French-Canadians were like children learning the language. 'Your example isn't considered polite. 'Put on' is very common now in the States.'

'Then maybe,' said Miss Parizeau, 'we'll ave it ere in twenty years.'

The Armenian giggled.

'No—I've heard it here just as often,' Dyer protested, but the girls had already entered the room.

He began the second hour with a smile which slowly soured as he thought of the Israelis. America's anti-communism was bad enough, but it was worse hearing it echoed by immigrants, by Jews, here in Montreal. Wasn't there a psychological type who chose Canada over South Africa? Or was it just a matter of visa and slow adjustment? Did Johannesburg lose its Greeks, and Melbourne its Italians, the way Dyer's students were always leaving Montreal?

And after class when Dyer was again feeling content and thinking of approaching one of the Israelis for a restaurant tip, there came the flood of small requests: should Mrs Papadopoulos go into a more advanced course; could Mr Perez miss a week for an interview in Toronto; could Mr Giguère, who spoke English perfectly, have a harder book; Mr. Coté an easier one?

Then as he packed his briefcase in the empty room, Miguel Mayor, the vain and impeccable Spaniard, came forward from the hallway.

'Sir,' he began, walking stiffly, ready to bow or salute. He wore a loud grey checkered sportscoat this evening, blue shirt, and matching ascot-handkerchief, slightly mauve. He must have shaved just before class, Dyer noticed, for two fresh daubs of antiseptic cream stood out on his jaw, just under his earlobe.

'I have been wanting to ask *you* something, as a matter of fact,' said Dyer. 'Do you know any good Spanish restaurants I might try tonight?'

'There are not any good Spanish restaurants in Montreal,' he said. He stepped closer. 'Sir?'

'What's on your mind, then?'

'Please—have you the time to look on a letter for me?'

He laid the letter on the podium.

'Look *over* a letter,' said Dyer. 'What is it for'

'I have applied,' he began, stopping to emphasize the present perfect construction, 'for a job in Cleveland, Ohio, and I want to know if my letter will be good. Will an American, I mean—'

'Why are you going there?'

'It is a good job.'

'But Cleveland—'

'They have a blackman mayor, I have read. But the job is not in Cleveland.'

'Let me see it.'

Most honourable Sir: I humbly beg consideration for a position in your grand company . . .

'Who are you writing this to?'

'The president,' said Miguel Mayor.

I am once a student of Dr Ramiro Gutierrez of the Hydraulic Institute of Sevilla, Spain . . .

'Does the president know this Ramiro Gutierrez?'

'Oh, everybody is knowing him,' Miguel Mayor assured, 'he is the most famous expert in all Spain.'

'Did he recommend this company to you?'

'No—I have said in my letter, if you look—'

An ancient student of Dr Gutierrez, Salvador del Este, is actually a boiler expert who is being employed like supervisor is formerly a friend of mine . . .

'Is he still your friend?'

Whenever you say come to my city Miguel Mayor for talking I will be coming. I am working in Montreal since two years and am now wanting more money than I am getting here now . . .

'Well . . . ' Dyer sighed.

'Sir—what I want from you is knowing in good English how to interview me by this man. The letters in Spanish are not the same to English ones, you know?'

I remain humbly at your orders . . .

'Why do you want to leave Montreal?'

'It's time for a change.'

'Have you ever been to Cleveland?'

'I am one summer in California. Very beautiful there and hot like my country. Montreal is big port just like Barcelona. Everybody mixed together and having no money. It is just a place to land, no?'

'Montreal? Don't be silly.'

'I thought I come here and learn good English but where I work I get by in Spanish and French. It's hard, you know?' he smiled. Then he took a few steps back and gave his cuffs a gentle tug, exposing a set of jade cufflinks.

Dyer looked at the letter again and calculated how long he would be correcting it, then up at his student. How old is he? My age? Thirty? Is he married? Where do the Spanish live in Montreal? He looks so prosperous, so confident, like a male model off a page of *Playboy*. For an instant Dyer felt that his student was mocking him, somehow pitting his astounding confidence and wardrobe, sharp chin and matador's bearing against Dyer's command of English and mastery of the side streets, bistros, and ethnic restaurants. Mayor's letter was painful, yet he remained somehow competent. He would pass his interview, if he got one. What would he care about America, and the odiousness he'd soon be supporting? It was as though a superstructure of exploitation had been revealed, and Dyer felt himself abused by the very people he wanted so much to help. It had to end someplace.

He scratched out the second 'humbly' from the letter, then folded the sheet of foolscap. 'Get it typed right away,' he said. 'Good luck.'

'Thank you, sir,' said his student, with a bow. Dyer watched the letter disappear in the inner pocket of the checkered sportscoat. Then the folding of the cashmere scarf, the draping of the camel's hair coat about the shoulders, the easing of the fur hat down to the rims of his ears. The meticulous filling of the pigskin gloves. Mayor's patent leather galoshes glistened.

'Good evening, sir,' he said.

'*Buenas noches,*' Dyer replied.

He hurried now, back down Sherbrooke Street to his daytime office where he could deposit his books. Montreal on a winter night was still mysterious, still magical. Snow blurred the arc lights. The wind was dying. Every second car was now a taxi, crowned with an orange crescent. Slushy curbs had hardened. The window of Holt-Renfrew's was still attractive. The legless dummies invited a final stare. He stood longer than he had earlier, in front of the sporty mannequin with a burgundy waistcoat, the mauve and blue ensemble, the jade cufflinks.

Good evening, sir, he could almost hear. The ascot, the shirt, the complete outfit, had leaped off the back of Miguel Mayor. He pictured how he must have entered the store with three hundred dollars and a prepared speech, and walked out again with everything off the torso's back.

I want that.

What, sir?

That.

The coat, sir?

Yes.

Very well, sir.

And *that.*

Which, sir?

All that.

'Absurd man!' Dyer whispered. There had been a moment of fear, as though the naked body would leap from the window, and legless, chase him down Sherbrooke Street. But the moment was passing. Dyer realized now that it was comic, even touching. Miguel Mayor had simply tried too hard, too fast, and it would be good for him to stay in Montreal until he deserved those clothes, that touching vanity and confidence. With one last look at the window, he turned sharply, before the clothes could speak again.

CYNTHIA FLOOD
(1940)

The Meaning of the Marriage

Mrs Perren marries my grandfather on a Tuesday afternoon, late, so providing a wedding meal is unnecessary. The guests simply drink tea and eat pound cake. On the Tuesday morning, Mrs Perren comes with her sister to inspect my grandfather's house. (I don't know where he is.) They find everything very clean. The oak floors shine, as do the thin high windows. Mrs Perren's sister is enthusiastic about a man who keeps house so. (My grandfather is a saddler.) The two women see the bedroom prepared for the motherless little girl, my mother, who is now to leave her grandparents' house and come to live with her father, because he will again have a wife.

The sisters end their tour in the kitchen. Glass-fronted cupboards go right up to the ceiling, so Mrs Perren stands on a chair to inspect the topmost shelves. From her altitude she sees out to the back yard, where a nasty box-headed tomcat rolls about in the sun-dappled shade of the maple. She sends the sister out with a broom. Then the two leave my grandfather's house to go along to the village dressmaker.

During the many fittings of her wedding dress, the bride has been narrowly inspected, for she is not local; this unknown woman is to replace my dead grandmother and to 'take on' my mother, aged five. Mrs Perren's wedding garment is of mauve silk, for she has been a widow long enough to finish with black and dove-grey in their turn. The dress is the bride's 'best' for some time after the ceremony; it moves then through a sequence of annual demotions which lead to temporary burial in the rag bag, but thence it rises to magnificent resurrection in the crazy quilt on the spare room bed. Mrs Perren was a notable quilter.

Of the rite I know only that it was Methodist, though Mrs Perren, I believe, adhered to a harder covenant. I don't know if my mother was at the wedding, to carry flowers for her new step-mother. At the little reception, did she chatter and clown to get the attention she was accustomed to? How did my grandfather feel on his wedding night? He was after all a veteran. His first wife had died after childbirth, taking twin girls with her to the grave, and his second, my grandmother, proved no more durable. A beautiful twenty-six, she fell victim to the same 'childbed fever' as her predecessor . . . but her offspring survived.

Looking at my grandmother's photograph, taken in the year of her marriage and death, made me feel strange when I turned twenty-six. Years later I told my mother so. For her, she said, the strangest time had been when she herself was fifty-two. These jumping years unnerve me. Two days after my first daughter's birth, my body's temperature rose. I lay cold and sweating, could not eat, wept feebly on the nurse when she arrived at last. *Chills, headache, malaise, and anorexia are common.* In no time flat I was out of the ward, into isolation, on antibiotics. *Treatment consists of debridement by curettage and administration of penicillin*; I don't remember being debrided. The baby ran a fever too. Nobody named the poison in us.

Could my grandmother's family bring themselves to attend the wedding? My great-grandmother did make the pound cake for the occasion. I know, because over the years Mrs Perren was repeatedly plaintive to her new husband and his little girl about its impropriety: 'A fruit-cake would have been seemlier.' Perhaps Mrs Perren felt that the rite hadn't really 'taken'. How did my great-grandmother feel as she mixed the butter and sugar and flour, a pound of each? And did she and my great-grandfather witness the wedding that featured the same bridegroom as in their daughter's ceremony and was held in the same church? There also my grandmother's funeral had been conducted, with, as my mother always says, 'the entire village in tears'. This is a direct quotation from my great-grandparents, who told and retold to my mother the terrible story of their daughter's death. The narrative shaped the ends of their lives. My great-grandparents also told my mother, repeatedly, that their dead daughter was a joyful woman. My mother still repeats this to me. Her voice lingers with the phrasing. 'My mother made everyone laugh with her,' she says. The pound cake suggests that my great-grandmother tried to wish the marriage well (not perhaps so well as to merit candied fruit).

That is all I have for the story's opening.

Next comes a story set in the same polished kitchen that Mrs Perren and her sister saw on the wedding morning. (I never heard a thing else about that sister.)

My mother is now nine, and wears a green checked dress. Her dark hair shines and her eyes are hazel like mine, like her dead mother's. Her cheeks are hot. In her hands is a small box, dark blue leather. The clasp is stiff, my mother's fingers determined, and the opening lid reveals a set of miniature ivory-handled cutlery. Oh perfect, she sees, for raspberries on leaf plates with girlfriends in the back yard, for imaginary cat-banquets with the strays watching lickerishly from the lower branches of the maple . . . The little things exactly fit her hands. (My mother now looks with disbelief at her arthritic digits.)

Who has given her this present? Its extravagance suggests grandparents. My mother has never said. I don't think she cares. The cutlery's fate is far more important than its provenance. My step-grandmother snatches the box away. She throws it into the wood stove. With the toasting fork, she rams the gift well down into the flames. 'Sinful waste,' says Mrs Perren, 'and for a wicked girl like you.' Burning leather smells dreadful.

Why didn't my grandfather stop her? He isn't there, in the story.

Then did my mother tell him, crying, when he came home from work? Why didn't he do something then? Or later?

Mrs Perren did not approve of pets—I believe she was originally a farm woman—and so my mother played with the neighbours' cats and dogs, and with strays. Mrs Perren said they were all 'dirty beasts'. One such was the box-headed tomcat, which turned out to have been a female rolling about desirously in heat; Tipsy's kittens caused the first full confrontation between step-mother and step-daughter. Yet my mother has always been vague about this story, never releasing details about how 'she got rid of them'. When—rare—she talks about her step-mother, she usually tells about the poison.

This story begins in an act of straightforward evil: Some person or persons unknown leave gobbets of raw meat daubed with strychnine up and down the village lanes. Dying cats and dogs writhe and yowl and froth. Now thirteen years old, my mother is frantic to hold the dying animals, stroke, comfort. Not unreasonably (in her narrative, my mother is always careful so to characterize the action), my step-grandmother refuses permission.

What Mrs Perren does instead is to walk my mother out to the back lane and hold her there, forcibly, to watch one of the cats complete its death. She does this to convey to my mother the meaning of the expression 'tortures of the damned', for, as Mrs Perren says to the thirteen-year-old girl, 'You do not know yet that you are wicked, and it is my business to teach you.'

I can never bear this part, and break in. 'But your father, why didn't he do something so she wouldn't be so mean to you?'

The answer never satisfies. 'Well,' my mother says mildly, '*she* was looking after me, you know. I was her job. And everybody said I was very spoiled. My grandparents—they were broken-hearted, you see. I looked exactly like my mother. My step-mother probably told my father I was difficult. I suppose I was. And he was a quiet man.'

A twenty-year gap comes between this story and the next.

My mother, thirty-three years old and now really a mother, drives out from Toronto to the village with her little son, my older brother. She drives out on a pretty spring day to visit my step-grandmother. Why?

Mrs Perren is a widow again. My grandfather died when my mother was twenty-six.

Why does my mother, fully-orphaned now, make this journey?

I still think of Mrs Perren as Mrs Perren; she doesn't feel like a relative. Recently, it came to me that I don't even know her first name. She must have come *from somewhere* when she and her sister walked up to that thin clean house on that Tuesday. What happened to Mr Perren? Why were there no little Perrens? Why did she remarry, at forty? My grandfather presumably sought the stability of husband-hood and of having a mother-substitute for his child; losing *this* wife to puerperal fever was unlikely. If age was one of Mrs Perren's charms, what were those of a middle-aged saddler with two dead wives and a young wilful child? What were her options?

My mother drives out to see her step-mother.

All I know of my step-grandmother, this woman who has so influenced my own life and my brother's, lies in these stories and questions. I tack them together into the rough shape of Mrs Perren's ignorance and hate; as a dress for the tale, they suffice. But *he* is missing. The man is missing—my grandfather. Where is he? I do not know one single story about him. The space where he should be is a blatant absence that magnetizes me.

My mother tells me about my *great*-grandfather, about a time when he goes to England, I don't know why. While there, he makes a purchase for my great-grandmother and her five sisters: beautiful silk. (Every decent woman must have her good black dress.) To get the goods past Canadian customs, my great-grandfather wraps the gleaming yardage around his waist and so passes, unscathed though bulky, under authority's eye. This story, pleasingly, takes the edge off the intimidating probity of my forebears. I like to imagine my great-grandfather in his stateroom as the ship pulls in to Quebec, breathing heavily, winding the stuff round and round himself and pinning it firmly at his sides. Further back, I like to see him in the English shop—in London? in a textile city of the Midlands?—looking at the black shining rivers of fabric. 'Yes, this is good. Rachel will like this.'

Those sisters—my great-great-aunts, are they?—I know stores about them too. One has a daughter, Sarah, who dithers in her selection of a husband until my great-great-aunt loses patience and declares, 'Sarah! you will go round and round a bush and choose a crooked stick at last!' I even know that Sarah's marriage in fact turns out well. And I know that another great-great-aunt, designated to teach my mother tatting, finally takes away from her the small circle of grubby botched work and issues the verdict: 'Some are not born to tat.'

But I have not even a little story like these about my grandfather.

Mrs Perren did not like the story about the smuggled silk. (In what context did she hear it?) My mother says simply, 'My step-mother disapproved.' Of the purchase itself? Of the deceit? Yet she used strips of that silk to edge the splendid crazy quilt she created for the spare room in my grandfather's house. How did the scraps get to Mrs Perren? Perhaps my great-grandmother and great-great-aunts sent them along as a compliment, intended to soften; competent needlewomen themselves, they recognized, but did not possess, the talent required to conceive such an extraordinary bedcovering as my mother describes. To follow a pattern—log-cabin or wedding ring or Texas star—is one thing; to create *ex nihilo*, quite another. Buying material would be dreadful waste. No. The quilt-maker must use whatever has come to her rag bag through the years, and thence generate a design that exploits those random colours and textures, displays them to their utmost brilliance. Thus she is midwife to a metamorphosis. In her quilt, the scraps and bits and tatters fuse and then explode into a shapely galaxy of shattered stained glass.

Perhaps my great-grandmother and my great-great-aunts hoped, through this gift, to win influence over Mrs Perren, to move her towards a gentler treatment of my mother. They must have mourned to see the little girl, beloved both for her resemblance to the dead and for her own living sweetness and dearness, unhappily exiled in that mother-loveless dwelling. But perhaps I'm just making up that supposition; perhaps none of them even knew how my mother felt—my mother, another scrap sent from house to house. Did she ever speak of her misery, then? I don't know—but for those women I can imagine possibilities, scenes, expressions. My grandfather's face I cannot see.

So now my mother is thirty-three. Her visit to Mrs Perren may be intended to say, 'You taught me I was evil. You did all you could to stop me from living my life, yet I have won. I am educated, a trained teacher. I have travelled. I am married, pretty, happy. I have borne a beautiful healthy son.' The subtext is clear: 'None of this is true of you, step-mother.' Yet that is not the story she tells of the visit.

She only told me the full story once, when I was young. Now my mother wants me to tell her how the story ends.

During the visit, my brother is noisily vigorous, running about the neat back yard and stomping in the kitchen and wanting to throw his ball in the livingroom.

Mrs Perren says to my mother, 'Take him away.'

My mother is angry, but she does not leave. Instead she leads my brother upstairs, to show him mummy's room when she was a little girl. Mrs Perren does not go upstairs any more (arthritis), has not for some years; a bed has been placed for her in the dining room. So she sits, alone again, in the chair by the window. How does she pass the time today, any day? She can no longer quilt. No novels—devil's work. Perhaps Mrs. Perren reads the Bible, looks out the window and disapproves of passersby.

I can imagine thus about my step-grandmother, my great-grandfather, my great-great-aunts. I cannot imagine about my grandfather, because my imagination requires a toehold on the known world, and I know no stories about him.

Up the stairs go my mother and my brother, in the story, and as they climb they smell the musty acrid odour of stale cat excrement, stronger and stronger, nearer and nearer. In the spare room, a branch, from the maple tree beloved in my mother's youth, has pierced the window. The wind has shaken out big shards of glass, the tree has kept on growing, and now a convenient cat-bridge leads to shelter and relative warmth. Right now, as my mother and brother enter the room, they find two animals dozing on the quilt. Silk and velveteen and grosgrain and muslin and polished cotton and gingham and corduroy and chintz, triangles and rhomboids and squares in all the colours—all are smeared, all stained, rumpled. Cat fur lies thick. A drift floats, airborne, as one cat rushes out the broken window into safe leafiness. The other purrs under my delighted brother's pats. The floor is littered, sticky, with feces. The down pillows drip urine. My mother goes quickly into the other rooms on this upper floor. The cats have been everywhere.

My mother no longer remembers what she did next. In her memory, she can only find what she thought of doing.

One choice is to tell Mrs Perren, perhaps even to help her make arrangements for pruning, glazing, cleaning. (My mother wonders if undiluted Javex would work.)

The other choice is to say nothing, to leave her step-mother stewing in her stink. My mother worries about getting my brother's co-operation, so he will not cry excitedly to Mrs Perren, 'Kitties pee on floor!' Surely, she thinks, the coming summer heat will eventually let the old nose know. Or some other visitor will come. (She herself never went to that house again.)

My mother asks me now, 'Which did I do?' But I don't remember. Nor does my brother. Neither of us can tell her what she wants to know.

I wish I could tell her, but for me as a child that story had little to do with the solitary woman waiting downstairs or the sharp resentful voice saying, 'Take him away.' I did not care, either, about the reeking sodden floorboards in the spare room, the precious quilt ruined, the golden double featherstitching frayed. No. What I loved was the branch to the spare room, the branch where the cats ran back and forth in the moony night and through the green leaves of the day. Perhaps if that branch were sturdy, the window-hole big enough, a child might travel thus and hide in the heart of the tree, with the furry cats purring and snoozing and stretching their lithe long selves?

For me, this cat-story was just one of many from Before Me, stories told and retold by my mother and my brother, like the one about Slippers the calico, who in her first pregnancy follows my mother from room to room, sleeps on her lap and on her bed. Her labour begins as my mother prepares for a dinnerparty; my brother strokes and soothes the cat as my mother finishes dressing, takes up her cloak. (This wonderful garment is purple velvet, cast-off church curtains. How has my agnostic mother come by this fabric? The purple is limp, the nap gone in parts, but my mother takes scrim and shapes a high dramatic collar to show off her high-piled hair.)

Slippers struggles up and follows my mother, mewing, one scarcely-born kitten left behind in the basket and another's nose sticking out of her vagina. My brother retrieves the cat, but Slippers writhes and yowls and my brother, fearful, drops her. She runs after my mother and half-way down the stairs delivers her second kitten. My mother stops. She gathers cat and kitten into her cloak. She brings them back to the basket in her bedroom. My brother has to go downstairs and tell my father, waiting impatiently in the livingroom with the fire going out, that she isn't coming. She settles down with Slippers, and the kittens are born in peace. When all are safely curled by their mother, she does go to the party, where she makes a fine story out of the event and my father almost forgives her.

And another story is of the cat Johnny-come-lately, of a winter's dusk, thick snow falling, my brother by the livingroom window gazing, half-dreaming with the white movement of the flakes. A red car comes along—an uncommon colour in 1930s Toronto—and stops by our house. My brother calls, 'Mum, come look at the red car.' The moment she appears at the window, the car opens, a black kitten is flung out, and the car flees scarlet down the street, with rooster tails of snow and exhaust whirling behind it. Johnny, who lived with our family for years, was the first animal whose death I grieved.

My mother wants me to tell her the ending of the story about the visit so she will know whether she did right or wrong. Did she obey duty or desire? Which was which? Without the memory, she cannot judge herself.

I want other knowledge. I want to know why my mother forgot my grandfather. She has never in my presence pronounced the term *Dad,* never used the words, 'I remember when my father . . .' No snapshot or painting is extant. No letters survive, account books, diaries. No stories. But a beautiful joyous woman married him; she must have had her reasons, and I wish I knew what they were.

Did my mother feel such abandonment that when she grew up she simply obliterated him from the stones of memory? Did she unilaterally declare herself fatherless as well as motherless? Her mother was always dead, a person who existed only in stories, none told by her father. None of his words have survived. Nor has he. At this point in the story, I have said every single thing I know about him.

I'll try to imagine. Let us suppose that after my mother's birth my grandfather sits by my grandmother's bedside, looking down at her lovely face, seeing with delight his living daughter. Likely he goes away then, to tell family and friends, perhaps to thank his God for the safe deliverance this time, to sleep at night and wake joyful in the morning. But by then the dirt, the poison, is thick in her blood. She feels unwell. The doctor comes. The milk stops. The baby cries. The smells begin. *The patient is toxic and febrile, the lochia is foul-smelling, and the uterus is tender. . . .* The young woman lies quietly. *Chills, headache, malaise, and anorexia are common. Pallor, tachycardia, and leukocytosis are the rule.* This rule holds. So as she dies my grandmother does not scream and writhe and froth like the cat, but slowly dazes and drifts, descending into a poisoned stupor *(Hemolytic anemia may develop. . . . With severe hemolysis and coexistent toxicity, acute renal failure is to be expected)* and so to her death. The mortality rate is then about fifty percent. But then there was neither debridement nor penicillin, so that rate did not apply.

The father sends the child off to live with her grandparents. What else to do? My great-grandparents love the baby, painfully. They live nearby. He cannot be a saddler and care for an infant on his own. Paid help is not possible. So for five years the little girl lives thus. Then—inexplicably, to such a young child—comes the alleged reunion, which is in truth a meeting with a cold bitter woman who resents her step-daughter even before they meet, who burns her present and makes her witness the agony of the cat.

In his third marriage, how came my grandfather to make such an error in judgement?

In my fifteenth summer, our plump tabby cat Mitzi with the extra toes dies on the operating table as she is being spayed. My mother collapses with grief, self-blame, rage at herself and my father for having determined that this cat should not kitten. 'She mewed all the way in the car,' my mother shouts, weeping, her sweating face contorted. 'She didn't want to go. I made her. Because I was bigger and stronger. I took her to her death.' My mother falls on the sofa and shoves her head into the cushions and hits the sofa arm repeatedly. My father and I look at each other. I start to leave the room. 'You can't run away from this,' he says, gripping my arm hard. 'Come back to her.'

Somehow the afternoon comes to its end. My mother does not make any dinner, and this is very difficult for me because my father likes no cooking but hers. Early in the evening, she goes up to the spare room in the attic and closes the door. She stays there overnight. We hear her crying from time to time, and shoving at the stiff window; finally it surrenders to her strength, with a harsh scraping rattle of glass against wood. In the spare room are stored non-working lamps, moth-nibbled blankets, magazines that my brother will sort through some day. The bed is not made up. Faded chenille covers its lunar surface. The heart of the house beats in the wrong place that night, and, though the spare room is next to mine, I gain no comfort from my mother's nearness. Thinking of her there disturbs me still.

S A N D R A   B I R D S E L L
(1942)

~~~

Flowers for Weddings and Funerals

My Omah supplies flowers for weddings and funerals. In winter, the flowers come from the greenhouse she keeps warm with a woodstove as long as she can; and then the potted begonias and asters are moved to the house and line the shelves in front of the large triple-pane window she had installed when Opah died so that she could carry on the tradition of flowers for weddings and for funerals. She has no telephone. Telephones are the devil's temptation to gossip and God admonishes widows to beware of that exact thing.

And so I am the messenger. I bring requests to her, riding my bicycle along the dirt road to her cottage that stands watermarked beneath its whitewash because it so foolishly nestles too close to the Red River.

A dozen or two glads please, the note says. The bride has chosen coral for the colour of her wedding and Omah adds a few white ones because she says that white is important at a wedding. She does not charge for this service. It is unthinkable to her to ask for money to do this thing which she loves.

She has studied carefully the long rows of blossoms to find perfect ones with just the correct number of buds near the top, and laid them gently on newspaper. She straightens and absently brushes perspiration from her brow. She frowns at the plum tree in the corner of the garden where the flies hover in the heat waves. Their buzzing sounds and the thick humid air makes me feel lazy. But she never seems to notice the heat, and works tirelessly.

'In Russia,' she says as she once more bends to her task, 'we made jam. Wild plum jam to put into fruit pockets and platz.' Her hands, brown and earth-stained, feel for the proper place to cut into the last gladiolus stalk.

She gathers the stalks into the crook of her arm, coral and white gladioli, large icy-looking petals that are beaded with tears. Babies' tears, she told me long ago. Each convex drop holds a perfectly shaped baby. The children of the world who cry out to be born are the dew of the earth.

For a long time afterward, I imagined I could hear the garden crying and when I told her this, she said it was true. All of creation cries and groans, you just cannot hear it. But God does.

Poor God. I squint at the sun because she has also said He is Light and I have grown accustomed to the thought that the sun is His eye. To have to face that every day. To have to look down and see a perpetually twisting, writhing, crying creation. The trees have arms uplifted, beseeching. Today I am not sure I can believe it, the way everything hangs limp and silent in the heat.

I follow her back to the house, thinking that perhaps tonight, after the wedding, there will be one less dewdrop in the morning.

'What now is a plum tree but a blessing to the red ants and flies only?' She mutters to herself and shakes dust from her feet before she enters the house. When she speaks her own language, her voice rises and falls like a butterfly on the wind as she smooths over the gutteral sounds. Unlike my mother, who does not grow gladioli or speak the language of her youth freely, but with square, harsh sounds, Omah makes a sonatina.

While I wait for her to come from the house, I search the ground beneath the tree to find out what offends her so greatly. I can see red ants crawling over sticky, pink pulp, studying the dynamics of moving one rotting plum.

'In Russia, we at gophers and some people ate babies.' I recall her words as I pedal back towards the town. The glads are in a pail of water inside my wire basket. Cool spikelets of flowers seemingly spread across my chest. Here I come. Here comes the bride, big, fat and wide. Where is the groom? Home washing diapers because the baby came too soon.

Laurence's version of that song reminds me that he is waiting for me at the river.

'Jesus Christ, wild plums, that's just what I need,' Laurence says and begins pacing up and down across the baked river bank. His feet lift clay tiles as he paces and I squat waiting, feeling the nylon line between my fingers, waiting for something other than the river's current to tug there at the end of it.

I am intrigued by the patterns the sun has baked into the river bank. Octagonal shapes spread down to the willows. How this happens, I don't know. But it reminds me of a picture I have seen in Omah's Bible or geography book, something old and ancient like the tile floor in a pharaoh's garden. It is recreated here by the sun on the banks of the Red River.

'What do you need plums for?'

'Can't you see,' he says. 'Wild plums are perfect to make wine.'

I wonder at the tone of his voice when it is just the two of us fishing. He has told me two bobbers today instead of one and the depth of the stick must be screwed down into the muck just so. Only he can do it. And I never question as I would want to because I am grateful to him for the world he has opened up to me. If anyone should come and join us here, Laurence would silently gather his line in, wind it around the stick with precise movements that are meant to show his annoyance, but really are a cover for his sense of not belonging. He would move further down the bank or walk up the hill to the road and his bike. He would turn his back on me, the only friend he has.

I have loved you since grade three, my eyes keep telling him. You, with your lice crawling about your thickly matted hair. My father, being the town's barber, would know, Laurence. But I defied him and played with you anyway.

It is of no consequence to Laurence that daily our friendship drives wedges into my life. He stops pacing and stands in front of me, hands raised up like a preacher's hands.

'Wild plums make damned good wine. My old man has a recipe.'

I turn over a clay tile and watch an earthworm scramble to bury itself, so that my smile will not show and twist down inside him.

Laurence's father works up north cutting timber. He would know about wild plum wine. Laurence's mother cooks at the hotel because his father seldom sends money home. Laurence's brother is in the navy and has a tattoo on his arm. I envy Laurence for the way he can take his time rolling cigarettes, never having to worry about someone who might sneak up and look over his shoulder. I find it hard to understand his kind of freedom. He will have the space and time to make his wine at leisure.

'Come with me.' I give him my hand.

Omah bends over in the garden. Her only concession to the summer's heat has been to roll her nylon stockings to her ankles. They circle her legs in neat coils. Her instep is swollen, mottled blue with broken blood vessels. She gathers tomatoes in her apron.

Laurence hesitates. He stands away from us with his arms folded across his chest as though he were bracing himself against extreme cold.

'His mother could use the plums,' I tell Omah. Her eyes brighten and her tanned wrinkles spread outwards from her smile. She half-runs like a goose to her house with her apron bulging red fruit.

'See,' I say to Laurence, 'I told you she wouldn't mind.'

When Omah returns with pails for picking, Laurence's arms hang down by his sides.

'You tell your Mama,' she says to Laurence, 'that it takes one cup of sugar to one cup of juice for the jelly.' Her English is broken and she looks like any peasant standing in her bedroom slippers. She has hidden her beautiful white hair beneath a kerchief.

She's not what you think, I want to tell Laurence and erase that slight bit of derision from his mouth. Did you know that in their village they were once very wealthy? My grandfather was a teacher. Not just a teacher, but he could have been a professor here at a university.

But our heads are different. Laurence would not be impressed. He has never asked me about myself. We are friends on his territory only.

I beg Laurence silently not to swear in front of her. Her freckled hands pluck fruit joyfully.

'In the old country, we didn't waste fruit. Not like here where people let it fall to the ground and then go to the store and buy what they could have made for themselves. And much better too.'

Laurence has sniffed out my uneasiness. 'I like homemade jelly,' he says. 'My mother makes good crabapple jelly.'

She studies him with renewed interest. When we each have a pail full of the dust-covered fruit, she tops it with a cabbage and several of the largest unblemished tomatoes I have ever seen.

'Give my regards to your Mama,' she says, as though some bond has been established because this woman makes her own jelly.

We leave her standing at the edge of the road shielding her eyes against the setting sun. She waves and I am so proud that I want to tell Laurence about the apple that is named for her. She had experimented with crabapple trees for years and in recognition of her work, the experimental farm has given a new apple tree her name.

'What does she mean, give her regards?' Laurence asks and my intentions are lost in the explanation.

When we are well down the road and the pails begin to get heavy, we stop to rest. I sit beside the road and chew the tender end of a foxtail.

Laurence chooses the largest of the tomatoes carefully, and then, his arm a wide arc, he smashes it against a telephone pole.

I watch red juice dripping against the splintered grey wood. The sun is dying. It paints the water tower shades of gold. The killdeers call to each other as they pass as silhouettes above the road. The crickets in the ditch speak to me of Omah's greenhouse where they hide behind earthenware pots.

What does Laurence know of hauling pails of water from the river, bending and trailing moisture, row upon row? What does he know of coaxing seedlings to grow or babies crying from dewdrops beneath the eye of God?

I turn from him and walk with my face reflecting the fired sky and my dust-coated bare feet raising puffs of anger in the fine warm silt.

'Hey, where are you going,' Laurence calls my retreating back. 'Wait a minute. What did I do?'

The fleeing birds fill the silence with their cries and the night breezes begin to swoop down onto our heads.

She sits across from me, Bible open on the grey arborite, cleaning her wireframed glasses with a tiny linen handkerchief that she has prettied with blue cross-stitch flowers. She places them back on her nose and continues to read while I dunk pastry in tea and suck noisily to keep from concentrating.

'And so,' she concludes, 'God called His people to be separated from the heathen.'

I can see children from the window, three of them, scooting down the hill to the river and I try not to think of Laurence. I haven't been with him since the day on the road, but I've seen him. He is not alone anymore. He has friends now, kids who are strange to me. They are the same ones who make me feel stupid about the way I run at recess so that I can be pitcher when we play scrub. I envy the easy way they can laugh at everything.

'Well, if it isn't Sparky,' he said, giving me a new name and I liked it. Then he also gave me a showy kiss for them to see and laugh. I pushed against his chest and smelled something sticky like jam, but faintly sour at the same time. He was wearing a new jacket and had hammered silver studs into the back of it that spelled his name out across his shoulders. Gone is the mousy step of my Laurence.

Omah closes the book. The sun reflects off her glasses into my eyes. 'And so,' she says, 'it is very clear. When God calls us to be separate, we must respond. With adulthood comes a responsibility.'

There is so much blood and death in what she says that I feel as though I am choking. I can smell sulphur from smoking mountains and dust rising from feet that circle a golden calf. With the teaching of these stories, changing from pleasant fairy tales of faraway lands to this joyless search for meaning, her house has become a snare.

She pushes sugar cubes into my pocket. 'You are a fine child,' she says, 'to visit your Omah. God will reward you in heaven.'

The following Saturday, I walk a different way to her house, the way that brings me past the hotel, and I can see them as I pass by the window, pressed together all in one booth. They greet me as though they knew I would come. I squeeze in beside Laurence and listen with amazement to their fast-moving conversation. The jukebox swells with forbidden music. I can feel its beat in Laurence's thigh.

I laugh at things I don't understand and try not to think of my Omah who will have weak tea and sugar cookies set out on her white cloth. Her stained fingers will turn pages, contemplating what lesson to point out.

'I'm glad you're here,' Laurence says, his lips speaking the old way to me. When he joins the conversation that leaps and jumps without direction from one person to another, his voice is changed. But he has taken my hand in his and covered it beneath the table. He laughs and spreads his plum breath across my face.

I can see Omah bending in the garden cutting flowers for weddings and funerals. I can see her rising to search the way I take and she will not find me there.

MATT COHEN
(1942)

⌒

Trotsky's First Confessions

Love is like a revolution: the monotonous routine of life is smashed.
Ivan Turgenev

Lately you hear on television that depression is a chemical condition. You
are invited to imagine the victim in question, whether yourself or some
famous historical figure like Napoleon or Virginia Woolf, as an empty silhouette filled with clouds of skewed molecules. For such a situation, a
micro-galactic misunderstanding, Sigmund Freud is of no use. Even his
famous couch—let us not speak of those of his successors—was apparently the
scene of quackeries and depravities best resolved by the courts. What does
this say about the erotic collapse of the middle class when faced by the monstrous success of its capitalist offspring? No one knows. Inflammatory questions are no longer permitted. If you want to ask something do so politely
and in terms of a survey. The answer will be a pill administered in the comfort of your own home or outpatient clinic. This pill, through processes kept
secret by the drug companies, will realign your nasty neurons or supply you
with those artificial hormones whose random absence need no longer ruin
your life or make you a burden to your family and friends. The next day the
sun rises on an entirely different person. A positive thinker whose pleasure
receptors are now primed to quiver and trill with the first chirp of a bird or
the feeling of toes sliding into a pair of clean socks. Experts say, for example, that under more auspicious chemical circumstances Virginia Woolf
would have had the sense to reject a life built on prose without punctuation,
and instead run a very successful restaurant, specializing in Bloomsburies,
the fruit tart from which the melancholic literary circle eventually took its
name.

Virginia Woolf, it hardly needs saying, is dead. There is something honest about being dead, just as being alive is necessarily evasive.

This necessary evasion is what makes beginning so difficult. Talk about
not having a leg to stand on. It's that old stork dilemma that cracked Lenin's
brain and brought us Stalin, my downfall, etc. Or perhaps it is a matter of
cultural disjunction. Lately I am a fanatic on the subject because I have been
preparing a little paper on Walter Benjamin—an obscure literary critic who

killed himself under circumstances with which I can identify, and whose greatest ambition was to present the public with a book composed entirely of quotation. One of his own: 'Quotations in my works are like robbers by the roadside who make an armed attack and relieve an idler of his convictions.'

If this is going to be Benjamin's attitude I might do better returning to Virginia Woolf, who was more a case of dysfunction that disjunction. In an earlier paper, also presented to the faculty association, I attempted to lay out a sort of schema regarding problems that rhymed. It wasn't very well received. We live in an era when—despite all the new big words—ideas are less important than biography.

In fact I have 'real-life' connections with Virginia Woolf. It all began many years ago. Even at the time I felt as though I were in the opening scenes of a movie. There I was, at the wheel of a rented car. Following a series of improbably events, events which do not require recounting, I was touring the south of England with a temporary companion.

As might be expected, it was a literary tour, long on quotations and short on convictions. At a certain point the highlight was a walk along the seawall that figures in a very famous spy novel. While reading the novel it had come to me that I would have been useless as a British spy because I look ridiculous in damp tweeds and trenchcoats. Also, my father never taught me how to wear a hat. But strolling along the wall, I imagined myself not in the novel, but as the novelist himself. This was a curious sensation. Suddenly, rather than being a humble and useless intellectual of the male sex, I was promoted to being a rich and famous writer, not only a popular icon but an astute and worldly man who had peered under the skirts of the Cold War and found a fortune.

Why, I asked myself, could I not do the same? As salt spray from the English Channel blew across my face, I had an image of myself pacing this wall for hours at a time, trailed by admiring secretaries taking notes while I dictated the complex Faustian story of a man who sold his soul because he didn't believe it existed. Until—perhaps at this point I would have a couple of shots of single malt—the time came, etc.

I was still half believing that I would one day return to the seawall—my Berlin Wall—to figure out the details of this masterpiece, when we came upon what seemed to be an interesting house conspicuously located on a promontory looking out to the sea. It had a sign advertising apartments to let.

We were in search of a life to believe in. Unfortunately, this was a chronic problem for me, and my temporary companions—intelligent, caring persons with both feet on the ground—always become infected by my own uncertainty. Thus begins a cycle that had already become predictable by the time of my first encounter with Virginia Woolf.

I admit, of course, that I should be able to write about my past in a more measured way. Though he had his own problems, T.S. Eliot proclaimed 'maturity of language may naturally be expected to accompany maturity of mind'. But who can wait? As with myself and my temporary companion, once you have bashed the brass lion against the door, it's too late to turn back.

The owner of the interesting house—a self-contented but anxious man—answered and surveyed our Canadian faces for signs of money. I had already learned that to the English our faces appear as barren New Worlds with a geography composed of television sports and credit cards. Therefore I said, 'The rent is no problem.' A few moments later we were in an apartment with a striking view of the sea. It had new wall-to-wall broadloom, a 'kitchenette', and a frigid little bathroom with two electric heaters. The main attraction was the view. 'This is where Virginia Woolf wrote *To The Lighthouse*,' the proprietor announced.

We looked reverently out the window. Battered gently by waves and dappled by the sun was a lighthouse. I turned back to the owner, who nodded complacently. Once again I went to inspect the kitchenette. The stove where she baked her pies had been replaced by a hotplate.

'I love Virginia Woolf,' said my companion. I knew she was seeing herself sitting at a desk looking out the window at the waves and writing the book she needed to write.

According to the dictionary at hand, 'disjunction' is 'the state of being disjoined'. I once knew someone with this problem, my best friend. She was named Rebecca Thomas but it should have been Rebecca/Thomas.

Walter Benjamin's disjunction sprang from the fact, he believed, that he was a German Jew—two mutually exclusive realities, each closed to him because he was poisoned by the other. At one point he wanted to become, an ambition he knew was preposterous, Germany's 'foremost literary critic'. On the other hand he considered accepting a monthly salary to study Hebrew; although he had no interest in the subject, he was desperate for a stipend.

Apropos of my own equivalents to these problems, I once asked R/T, 'Why is my life always farcical?'

Rebecca smiled sympathetically, but Thomas answered: 'Don't worry, it's not a universal condition.'

By writing a Ph.D. thesis on the Bloomsburies, followed by several learned articles published in worthy journals, R/T had become a professor of English literature. My occupation—'Perfect for a schizophrenic,' R/T pronounced, although in my opinion she was never fully able to refute the chemical hypothesis—was the same.

Perhaps R/T should be presented in her full biographical splendour: the little squibs at the end of her articles always read: 'Rebecca Thomas was born in Regina. She received her BA from the University of Alberta in

Edmonton, then was a Woodrow Wilson Scholar at the University of Michigan. Her doctoral thesis, *Linguistic Recipes of the Bloomsbury Group* was published by the University of Chicago Press.' I could add that she had thick black hair, strong squarish hands, a mouth which sometimes twitched like Marcello Mastroianni trying to decide between Sophia Loren and an ice cream cone. Bright warm eyes, an elegant neck. When I first met her she also had a husband, a science fiction fanatic who drifted off into the hyperspace of computer games, then ran away to Vancouver with their babysitter.

R/T and I became friends. As first we just knew that we were people safe to talk to at those faculty parties it was best to attend for political reasons. She made the occasional remark about my 'temporary companions', perhaps just to let me know she wasn't going to be one, and I observed initial attempts to find a successor for her departed husband.

We began to write each other memos. For example:

> Professor Trotsky: It has come to my attention that during the past several weeks you have been avoiding self-improvement regarding your attire. Please report for lunch tomorrow at noon so that these and other failings can be discussed.

Or:

> My dear Leon: You may be interested to know that I overheard your neo-revisionist tendencies being discussed over lunch at the Student Union. Apparently you have been making a fetish of wearing your ice pick. For your own sake I advise you to renounce personalist masochism in favour of collective silence.

Early on R/T (as I addressed her in memos) and I decided to attend each other's lectures for a few months and give each other 'honest' appraisals of each other's classroom behaviour. This could have been professionalism at its highest, the gloomy conviction that no one else is listening, or just one of the strange ways we found to amuse each other.

More recently, we resumed the habit. It was amazing for me to hear R/T again after such a gap. It seemed to me—or perhaps the years have made me a better listener—that her own linguistic recipes had changed. She was more subtle, more complex, she spoke with assurance and conviction. The edgy unsure young woman who seemed to be describing something she sensed but couldn't quite see, was now offering broadcasts from the very centre of her personal cosmology.

But although Rebecca had evolved, Thomas was unchanged. Last fall, for example, not long after the first essays had been assigned, Rebecca was manoeuvring into position at the lectern, all wound up for a discourse on the literary-sexual politics of Virginia's relationship with her publisher-husband Leonard, when a student raised her hand. She wanted to know something about the allowable length of footnotes. Rebecca answered her question and then, as often happens when Rebecca gets distracted, Thomas stepped in.

'I was thinking,' he said and looked out the window. The students, who recognized the tone of voice even if they hadn't made the diagnosis, followed Thomas's gaze. It was a day in that monochromatic zone between fall and winter. Dark grey clouds turning black in the late afternoon. Cold rain streaming from an adjoining slate roof and making the smoky grit on the windows streak down the glass.

'Suppose I were to die in Toronto. Not now, of course. Don't be alarmed. But I was thinking that somewhere out there must be the men who will dig my grave. The trees that will be sacrificed for my coffin. The mourners who will watch the coffin slide into the earth . . .'

Thomas's voice became so gloomy that the students began to shift about uneasily. Not wanting to criticize directly, I sent a memo:

> R/T: Excellent lecture but heavy on the melodrama. I liked the idea of your future mourners scattered across the city, unbeknownst to each other, waiting for the event of your funeral to bring them together. Even your pompous claim that your entry in 'Who's Who' is just the dry run for your obituary. But the little darlings are still frightened of death. So am I. If you have a fatal illness and have been hesitating to inform me, leave a message on my machine.

When I returned to my apartment the little red light on my answering machine was flashing. 'Not fatal but terminal.' Rebecca's voice. Then Thomas: 'Never speak of this again.'

Those who wander in the literary alleyways of the past may recall a recent biography of T.S. Eliot, the poet and critic. When I was a young would-be poet, Eliot was a more than minor god. I memorized many of his poems, along with various weighty epigrams like the one cited above, and would recite them to myself—or aloud—whenever I was drunk, lonely, or otherwise sensed a void that required decoration. Perhaps that is another reason that my companions have always been temporary. But my worship went much further. Eliot, a banker then editor, was noted for his meticulous appearance and personal habits. To make my hair blond, like his, I rubbed it with hydrogen peroxide and then spent a sunny afternoon walking the streets of Toronto. In the same vein I would part it in the middle. When I received my first teaching assistantship, I went so far as to purchase a three-piece suit and wire-rimmed frames to encase my thick lenses.

I appeared in front of my class, convinced I was the young Tom incarnate; later than morning I was told I looked like Trotsky without the beard.

To go back to the recent biography: Eliot had his own cosmetic moments, but at the time of my three-piece suit I was ignorant of the best. This happened near the end of his first marriage, a bizarre relationship which made Eliot very unhappy. Although Eliot prided himself on bearing the burden of his apparently insane wife with great fortitude, Virginia Woolf once wrote to a friend that to emphasize his silent struggle, Eliot had taken to wearing green make-up, which enhanced his unhappy ghostly pallor.

Imagine T.S. Eliot and Virginia Woolf, legendary giants whose colossal shadows surely extend beyond any future a professor of literature could possibly imagine. There they are, in some Parnassian moment of the gilded past, drinking tea and exchanging a few *bon mots*. Eliot's hair is perfectly parted in the middle and he speaks with built-in punctuation. Virginia Woolf is sporting a 1920s version of a long tie-dyed shirt, and drawing sketches of her lighthouse on the tablecloth. As she looks up at Eliot the sun emerges, an unexpected shaft of light illuminates his right cheek, she sees greenish powder clinging to his pores.

I am writing this in R/T's apartment, sitting at R/T's desk. Before the movers arrive, I will have finished; meanwhile, the relevant documents are at hand. R/T's medical reports, various of her articles and research notes. From one of the files drifts a memo never sent:

> Trotsky: Enough of your political diatribes! Even the beginning
> practitioner will agree that cultural impersonation is the disease
> of our times! I accept your invitation for late afternoon 'drinks'
> (your use of the plural will be discussed in a separate document)
> on the impossible condition that you appear as your authentic
> self!

Why did she reject this memo? What did she send me instead? Did we ever meet, that afternoon? Certainly not our 'authentic selves', whoever they might have been. Like those who so fascinated us, R/T and I were cultural transvestites; the only state to which we could claim real citizenship was that of the disjoined. Like Eliot, obviously, the American with his British banker's suit, his perfectly cut cloak of modernist free verse. 'Henry James with anorexia' as R/T once termed him. Or Walter Benjamin, neither German nor Jew. His most attractive option, as he saw it, was to go to Paris and become an expert on the politics of Baudelaire. Unfortunately the French were only able to read his studies of Baudelaire long after his death, a suicide brought on by the fact that the French he so admired had refused him the papers he required to escape the German police by crossing into Spain. That Benjamin, whose entire work is founded on the limitations of biography, should die for the lack of a visa is another of those events for which reasoned language fails me, thought Eliot promised that 'we may expect the language to approach maturity at the moment when men have a critical sense of the past, a confidence in the present, and no conscious doubt of the future'. As R/T once said about the book of a valued colleague, with this kind of load the Great Wall could have been built in a week.

This year spring is slow. *April is the cruellest month.* Overnight the temperature fell below freezing and this morning there was a new thin scattering of snow on the grass. A white dusting over the cars parked along the street. When I stepped out to buy a paper I saw a bird pecking angrily at the frozen ground. It shook its head at me, fluttered to the fence, looked up to the sky to let me know he was suing God for this fracture of the bird-God weather bargain.

I had been dreaming about my own cultural disjunction, or at least about the trip between those two cultures which are supposedly mine. In the dream I was standing on deck with my grandparents, Jewish-Russian refugees who came over by boat just after the turn of the century. Their departure was not a glittering Nabokovian tragedy of lost estates and multi-lingual nannies. They were happy to have escaped, and they were young, dressed in black and white like their pictures. My grandmother leaned over the rail, her kerchief snapping back in the wind and her long triangular nose poking towards the Atlantic coast. Her eyes so black, the skin around them white and smooth. By the time I met her that skin had turned soft and mottled. She would look at me affectionately but also as though I were absolutely unexpected, some strange kind of pet my parents had mistakenly invented when they were alone in their room at night.

I was snuggled beside my grandmother at the rail, her arm was around me and she smelled like baking bread. She pulled me in close against her. I was in love with her. Her smell, the clean salt wind from the sea, the lush piney shoreline drawing closer.

Then she turned me around. Behind us, a squalid city filled the sky with its smoke. Suddenly we were tramping down its muddy streets. My grandmother led us into a dirty alleyway. It was filled with garbage. Old crones peered into our faces, a dog jumped at the hamper my grandmother was carrying, then sprang back when she kicked it.

We went in the back door of a rotting wood house, up narrow twisting stairs to the apartment of her grandparents. The grandparents of my grandmother. A low-ceilinged room with a dining table and a couch on which my great-great-grandfather lay. The heavy rhythm of his breathing. Drawn over him was a thick quilt. His bearded face was turned eagerly towards me, though he did not speak.

About this and other such dreams I have no one to ask. I myself am sliding through middle age—no one alive can remember my great-great-grandparents. No one can care. Let them die and be buried in their stale European breath. Their dead dreams that lived on the edge of crumbled empires whose name no one remembers.

Why mourn over these immigrants and their ancestors? They were always unwelcome wherever they went. They were always lying somewhere, sick,

watching their children or grandchildren go out the door in search of some
new haven, some new hope that would turn out to be false.

At certain times—in their ghettos, on their boats, walking the streets at
night in their new land—they must have looked at the sky, seen that the stars
had maintained their same configurations even though the land beneath
their boots had changed. Glad to escape, happy to arrive, living in the midst
of their self-made islands. Watching their children and their grandchildren
step off those islands. Playing the fatal game of cultural impersonation that
all of history had taught against. Looking as absurd in their adopted costumes as did Eliot in his green make-up and mascara.

We are in my mid-town, mid-rise, mid-price, mid-Toronto apartment. R/T is
lying on the floor, her feet just sufficiently apart that she can, while wearing
her high-heeled shoes, tap her toes together. 'You never wanted to have children with me,' she says. She is pronouncing her words carefully, which is
how I know she has mixed just the right amount of Scotch into her blood.

'I would have been a terrible father.'

'No. You would have been a good father.'

It is amazing how reassuring I find her words. It is as though I've been
given the seal of approval by the Canadian Standards Association. A fierce
and necessary gratitude towards R/T sweeps across my desert soul. I slide to
my knees and begin crawling towards her. The few times we've made
love—not unsympathetic episodes scattered through the years—it has always
been on the floor in this apartment, once in a cabin we rented together,
once in a car under circumstances that require much explanation but
ended with showers to get rid of the bits of potato chips we inadvertently
ground between the carpeting and our consenting skins.

I kneel above her. She is crying. I bend to kiss the tears from her cheeks.
This is a huge aberration. Between R/T and me, despite flare-ups of desire,
there has never been the slightest pretence of temporary companionship. 'I
don't want to have an affair with you,' she said when I first invited her up,
lifetimes ago. 'My intentions are honourable,' I'd protested. 'I don't believe
you, and you don't understand me,' she's replied. 'With me it's all or nothing and I *know* you won't understand that.'

Immediately I'd imagined R/T casting me in the role of stepfather to the
little brat she sometimes brought around the department, a spoiled fat-
faced beribboned girl who gave me knowing and precocious sneering looks
whenever she thought her mother wasn't looking.

She takes my face in her hands. 'You still don't understand,' she says.
Although I think I do; she means we should be in a lawn-surrounded house
somewhere, vibrating to the sound of running feet. I start to withdraw but
even drunk R/T is too fast for me, and soon we're rocking and rolling to
our own strange beat.

Afterwards, R/T insists I come into the bathroom with her and soap her
all over. This isn't the kind of intimacy I'm used to with her. I light candles

for modesty's sake, make a few embarrassed jokes about hot tubs. Once R/T is actually lying in the water, and one of the candles has gone out, I regain confidence. I'm kneeling beside her, rubbing the soap up and down her body in the golden light. She's barely visible beneath the water, though her breasts float and her nipples break the surface. 'Look at them,' R/T says, flushing, suddenly embarrassed herself and trying to push them down. 'Wait,' I say, and tear some petals from the flowers she brought me and use them to make small glowing hats that bob like tiny sails on the rippling surface of the water.

When depressed, Virginia Woolf dressed in flowers. Sceptics say this strategy must have failed—she did drown herself, after all. But legends are not made of scepticism, and everyone dies in the end.

Walter Benjamin was fascinated with Kafka, whom he regarded as a fellow specialist in the problem of being someone and on one at the same time. Benjamin wrote, 'On many occasions and often for strange reasons Kafka's figures clap their hands. Once the casual remark is made that these hands are "really steam hammers".' He also said of Kafka that 'he perceived what was to come without perceiving what exists in the present.' As always when he is writing about Kafka, one feels Benjamin is really writing about himself—for example, the above lines are from a letter Benjamin wrote in 1938, two years before his suicide. R/T in my bed. Not the night of the bath—that night we had the good fortune of perceiving the present without perceiving the future. But a few months later, when she was recovering from her second round of chemotherapy. The precocious sneering daughter had long since turned into a perfectly nice young woman, a graduate student with a big fellowship in biochemistry. R/T could not bear to bother her with the incessant cycles, remissions, collapses of her illness. 'She already went through enough with me and her father. I'll call her when I'm dying.'

Meanwhile R/T kept teaching, though it was so difficult for her to take care of herself that she eventually ended up in my apartment on a semi-permanent basis. At first it was just for a weekend—a change of beds, we joked.

That was winter. It snowed a lot, unusually, and if she was well enough I would often install R/T, covered by her favourite quilt, in my rocker-armchair by the window. With our lights out we could watch the snow beating in waves against the window. R/T would nurse a glass of sherry while I tried to drink enough Scotch to stay calm.

Often on those evenings, lights out and classical music in the background, we would pretend we were at a place we imagined, the Modernist Café, where we would see Eliot, Woolf, Benjamin, and Kafka sitting at their table, drinking drinks we would invent for them, making terrible puns we also supplied.

At the end of such a visit, when R/T had gone into her pre-midnight doze, I would walk over to her place and get her the various files and books she had requested. Of course she was always about to be well enough to move back. Twice a week I would change the milk in her refrigerator, replace the loaf of bread, take the rotten fruit from the bowl on her table and replenish it with bright fat oranges and gleaming red apples.

In the worst weather R/T would wear her coat while she was teaching. As always she insisted on delivering her lectures standing up. Thomas hardly ever appeared; when he did it was in response to a particularly hopeless question and he would snap back something brittle and bitter. Then Rebecca would shake her head and smile, as though this eruption were a gastric accident best ignored.

After her lectures, I would drive her home. Sweaty and shaking, entirely drained, she would let me help her from the car and upstairs to bed. Sometimes it would be hours before she could speak again.

At my insistence Julia started coming to visit us. 'You're like an old couple,' she said one night when I was seeing her to the door. And she gave me that old knowing smile—this time without the sneer—but how could I explain to her?

Beginning is difficult, ending has its own problems. Something about Rebecca, her mannish Thomas-like hands, the way she drank, she used her eyebrows for punctuation.

I would sleep on the couch and when I came in to see R/T in the morning her eyes would be bigger. This was in April, the cruellest month. Her students were used to me and it seemed the most natural thing in the world when one day, instead of taking my usual seat in the back, I moved up to the front. After I had finished the lecture R/T had prepared the week before, I told them the story of the lighthouse and said that if any one of them should ever go there, they might think about R/T. I might have liked to say something about the unconsidered perils of companionship, the temporary nature of things, the way we feel, you and I, when the evening is spread out against the sky, but I didn't. I read them my last memo and the reply R/T had left for me on my answering machine.

For a few moments there was silence. The sky was blue, the windows open; then you could hear the sound of spades biting into the raw earth, the slow uncertain shuffle of mourners gathering to remember.

ISABEL HUGGAN

(1943)

∿

Celia Behind Me

There was a little girl with large smooth cheeks and very thick glasses who lived up the street when I was in public school. Her name was Celia. It was far too rare and grown-up a name, so we always laughed at it. And we laughed at her because she was a chubby, diabetic child, made peevish by our teasing.

My mother always said, 'You must be nice to Celia, she won't live forever,' and even as early as seven I could see the unfairness of that position. Everybody died sooner or later, I'd die too, but that didn't mean everybody was nice to me or to each other. I already knew about mortality and was prepared to go to heaven with my two aunts who had died together in a car crash with their heads smashed like overripe melons. I overheard the bit about the melons when my mother was on the telephone, repeating that phrase and sobbing. I used to think about it often, repeating the words to myself as I did other things so that I got a nice rhythm: 'Their heads smashed like melons, like melons, like melons.' I imagined the pulpy insides of muskmelons and watermelons all over the road.

I often thought about the melons when I saw Celia because her head was so round and she seemed so bland and stupid and fruitlike. All rosy and vulnerable at the same time as being the most *awful* pain. She'd follow us home from school, whining if we walked faster than she did. Everybody always walked faster than Celia because her short little legs wouldn't keep up. And she was bundled in long stockings and heavy underwear, summer and winter, so that even her clothes held her back from our sturdy, leaping pace over and under hedges and across backyards and, when it was dry, or when it was frozen, down the stream bed and through the drainage pipe beneath the bridge on Church Street.

Celia, by the year I turned nine in December, had failed once and was behind us in school, which was a relief because at least in class there wasn't someone telling you to be nice to Celia. But she'd always be in the playground at recess, her pleading eyes magnified behind those ugly lenses so that you couldn't look at her when you told her she couldn't play skipping unless she was an ender. 'Because you can't skip worth a fart,' we'd whisper in her ear. 'Fart, fart, fart,' and watch her round pink face crumple as she stood there, turning, turning, turning the rope over and over.

As the fall turned to winter, the five of us who lived on Brubacher Street and went back and forth to school together got meaner and meaner to Celia. And, after the brief diversions of Christmas, we returned with a vengeance to our running and hiding and scaring games that kept Celia in a state of terror all the way home.

My mother said, one day when I'd come into the kitchen and she'd just turned away from the window so I could see she'd been watching us coming down the street, 'You'll be sorry, Elizabeth. I see how you're treating that poor child, and it makes me sick. You wait, young lady. Some day you'll see how it feels yourself. Now you be nice to her, d'you hear?'

'But it's not just me,' I protested. 'I'm nicer to her than anybody else, and I don't see why I have to be. She's nobody special, she's just a pain. She's really dumb and she can't do anything. Why can't I just play with the other kids like everybody else?'

'You just remember I'm watching,' she said, ignoring every word I'd said. 'And if I see one more snowball thrown in her direction, by you or by anybody else, I'm coming right out there and spanking you in front of them all. Now you remember that.'

I knew my mother, and knew this was no idle threat. The awesome responsibility of now making sure the other kids stopped snowballing Celia made me weep with rage and despair, and I was locked in my room after supper to 'think things over'.

I thought things over. I hated Celia with a dreadful and absolute passion. Her round guileless face floated in the air above me as I finally fell asleep, taunting me: 'You have to be nice to me because I'm going to die.'

I did as my mother bid me, out of fear and the thought of the shame that a public spanking would bring. I imagined my mother could see much farther up the street than she really could, and it prevented me from throwing snowballs or teasing Celia for the last four blocks of our homeward journey. And then came the stomach-wrenching task of making the others quit.

'You'd better stop,' I'd say. 'If my mother sees you she's going to thrash us all.'

Terror of terrors that they wouldn't be sufficiently scared of her strap-wielding hand; gut-knotting fear that they'd find out or guess what she'd really said and throw millions of snowballs just for the joy of seeing me whipped, pants down in the snowbank, screaming. I visualized that scene all winter, and felt a shock of relief when March brought such a cold spell that the snow was too crisp for packing. It meant a temporary safety for Celia, and respite for me. For I knew, deep in my wretched heart, that were it not for Celia I was next in line for humiliation. I was kind of chunky and wore glasses too, and had sucked my thumb so openly in kindergarten that 'Sucky' had stuck with me all the way to Grade 3 where I now balanced at a hazardous point, nearly accepted by the amorphous Other Kids and always at the brink of being laughed at, ignored or teased. I cried very easily, and prayed during those years—not to become pretty or smart or popular, all aims too far out of my or God's reach, but simply to be strong enough not to cry when I got called Sucky.

During that cold snap, we were all bundled up by our mothers as much as poor Celia ever was. Our comings and goings were hampered by layers of flannel bloomers and undershirts and ribbed stockings and itchy wool against us no matter which way we turned; mitts, sweaters, scarves and hats, heavy and wet-smelling when the snot from our dripping noses mixed with the melting snow on our collars and we wiped, in frigid resignation, our sore red faces with rough sleeves knobbed over with icy pellets.

Trudging, turgid little beasts we were, making our way along slippery streets, breaking the crusts on those few front yards we'd not yet stepped all over in glee to hear the glorious snapping sound of boot through hard snow. Celia, her glasses steamed up even worse than mine, would scuffle and trip a few yards behind us, and I walked along wishing that some time I'd look back and she wouldn't be there. But she always was, and I was always conscious of the abiding hatred that had built up during the winter, in conflict with other emotions that gave me no peace at all. I felt pity, and a rising urge within me to cry as hard as I could so that Celia would cry too, and somehow realize how bad she made me feel, and ask my forgiveness.

It was the last day before the thaw when the tension broke, like northern lights exploding in the frozen air. We were all a little wingy after days of switching between the extremes of bitter cold outdoors and the heat of our homes and school. Thermostats had been turned up in a desperate attempt to combat the arctic air, so that we children suffered scratchy, tingly torment in our faces, hands and feet as the blood in our bodies roared in confusion, first freezing, then boiling. At school we had to go outside at recess—only an act of God would have ever prevented recess, the teachers had to have their cigarettes and tea—and in bad weather we huddled in a shed where the bicycles and the janitor's outdoor equipment was stored.

During the afternoon recess of the day I'm remembering, at the end of the shed where the girls stood, a sudden commotion broke out when Sandra, a rich big girl from Grade 4, brought forth a huge milk-chocolate bar from her pocket. It was brittle in the icy air, and snapped into little bits in its foil wrapper, to be divided among the chosen. I made my way cautiously to the fringe of her group, where many of my classmates were receiving their smidgens of sweet chocolate, letting it melt on their tongues like dark communion wafers. Behind me hung Celia, who had mistaken my earlier cries of 'Stop throwing snowballs at Celia!' for kindness. She'd been mooning behind me for days, it seemed to me, as I stepped a little farther forward to see that there were only a few pieces left. Happily, though, most mouths were full and the air hummed with the murmuring sound of chocolate being pressed between tongue and palate.

Made bold by cold and desire, I spoke up. 'Could I have a bit, Sandra?'

She turned to where Celia and I stood, holding the precious foil in her mittened hand. Wrapping it in a ball, she pushed it over at Celia. Act of kindness, act of spite, vicious bitch or richness seeking expiation? She gave the
chocolate to Celia and smiled at her. 'This last bit is for Celia,' she said to
me.

'But I can't eat it,' whispered Celia, her round red face aflame with the
sensation of being singled out for a gift. 'I've got di-a-beet-is.' The word. Said
so carefully. As if it were a talisman, a charm to protect her against our
rough healthiness.

I knew it was a trick. I knew she was watching me out of the corner of her
eye, that Sandra, but I was driven. 'Then could I have it, eh?' The duress
under which I acted prompted my chin to quiver and a tear to start down
my cheek before I could wipe it away.

'No, no, no!' jeered Sandra then. 'Suckybabies can't have sweets either.
Di-a-beet-ics and Suck-y-ba-bies can't eat chocolate. Give it back, you little
fart, Celia! That's the last time I ever give you anything!'

Wild, appreciative laughter from the chocolate-tongued mob, and they
turned their backs on us, Celia and me, and waited while Sandra crushed
the remaining bits into minuscule slivers. They had to take off their mitts
and lick their fingers to pick up the last fragments from the foil. I stood
there and prayed: 'Dear God and Jesus, I would please like very much not
to cry. Please help me. Amen.' And with that the clanging recess bell
clanked through the playground noise, and we all lined up, girls and boys
in straight, straight rows, to go inside.

After school there was the usual bunch of us walking home and, of
course, Celia trailing behind us. The cold of the past few days had been
making us hurry, taking the shortest routes on our way to steaming cups of
Ovaltine and cocoa. But this day we were all full of that peculiar energy that
swells up before a turn in the weather and, as one body, we turned down the
street that meant the long way home. Past the feed store where the
Mennonites tied their horses, out the back of the town hall parking-lot and
then down a ridge to the ice-covered stream and through the Church Street
culvert to come out in the unused field behind the Front Street stores; the
forbidden adventure we indulged in as a gesture of defiance against the
parental 'come right home'.

We slid down the snowy slope at the mouth of the pipe that seemed
immense then but was really only five feet in diameter. Part of its attraction
was the tremendous racket you could make by scraping a stick along the cor-
rugated sides as you went through. It was also long enough to echo very
nicely if you made good booming noises, and we occasionally titillated each
other by saying bad words at one end that grew as they bounced along the
pipe and became wonderfully shocking in their magnitude . . . poopy,
Poopy, POOpy, POOOOPy, POOOOPPYYY!

I was last because I had dropped my schoolbag in the snow and stopped
to brush it off. And when I looked up, down at the far end, where the white

plate of daylight lay stark in the darkness, the figures of my four friends were silhouetted as they emerged into the brightness. As I started making great sliding steps to catch up, I heard Celia behind me, and her plaintive, high voice: 'Elizabeth! Wait for me, okay? I'm scared to go through alone. Elizabeth?'

And of course I slid faster and faster, unable to stand the thought of being the only one in the culvert with Celia. Then we would come out together and we'd really be paired up. What if they always ran on ahead and left us to walk together? What would I ever do? And behind me I heard the rising call of Celia, who had ventured as far as a few yards into the pipe, calling my name to come back and walk with her. I got right to the end, when I heard another noise and looked up. There they all were, on the bridge looking down, and as soon as they saw my face began to chant, 'Better wait for Celia, Sucky. Better get Celia, Sucky.'

The sky was very pale and lifeless, and I looked up in the air at my breath curling in spirals and felt, I remember this very well, an exhilarating, clear-headed instant of understanding. And with that, raced back into the tunnel where Celia stood whimpering half-way along.

'You little fart!' I screamed at her, my voice breaking and tearing at the words. 'You little diabetic fart! I hate you! I hate you! Stop it, stop crying, I hate you! I could bash your head in I hate you so much, you fart, you fart! I'll smash your head like a melon! And it'll go in pieces all over and you'll die. You'll die, you diabetic. You're going to die!' Shaking her, shaking her and banging her against the cold, ribbed metal, crying and sobbing for grief and gasping with the exertion of pure hatred. And then there were the others, pulling at me, yanking me away, and in the moral tones of those who don't actually take part, warning me that they were going to tell, that Celia probably was going to die now, that I was really evil, they would tell what I said.

And there, slumped in a little heap was Celia, her round head in its furry bonnet all dirty at the back where it had hit against the pipe, and she was hiccupping with fear. And for a wild, terrible moment I thought I had killed her, that the movements and noises her body made were part of dying.

I ran.

I ran as fast as I could back out the way we had come, and all the way back to the schoolyard. I didn't think about where I was going, it simply seemed the only bulwark to turn to when I knew I couldn't go home. There were a few kids still in the yard but they were older and ignored me as I tried the handle of the side door and found it open. I'd never been in the school after hours, and was stricken with another kind of terror that it might be a strappable offence. But no one saw me, even the janitor was blessedly in another part of the building, so I was able to creep down to the girls' wash-room and quickly hide in one of the cubicles. Furtive, criminal, condemned.

I was so filled with horror I couldn't even cry. I just sat on the toilet seat, reading all the things that were written in pencil on the green, wooden walls. *G.R. loves M.H.* and *Y.F. hates W.S. for double double sure. Mr Becker wears ladies pants.* Thinking that I might die myself, die right here, and then it wouldn't matter if they told on me that I had killed Celia.

But the inevitable footsteps of retribution came down the stone steps before I had been there very long. I heard the janitor's voice explaining he hadn't seen any children come in and then my father's voice saying that the others were sure this is where Elizabeth would be. And they called my name, and then came in, and I guess saw my boots beneath the door because I suddenly thought it was too late to scrunch them up on the seat and my father was looking down at me and grabbing my arm, hurting it, pulling me, saying 'Get in the car, Elizabeth.'

Both my mother and my father spanked me that night. At first I tried not to cry, and tried to defend myself against their diatribe, tried to tell them when they asked, 'But whatever possessed you to do such a terrible thing?' But whatever I said seemed to make them more angry and they became so soured by their own shame that they slapped my stinging buttocks for personal revenge as much as for any rehabilitative purposes.

'I'll never be able to lift my head on this street again!' my mother cried, and it struck me then, as it still does now, as a marvellous turn of phrase. I thought about her head on the street as she hit me, and wondered what Celia's head looked like, and if I had dented it at all.

Celia hadn't died, of course. She'd been half-carried, half-dragged home by the heroic others, and given pills and attention and love, and the doctor had come to look at her head but she didn't have so much as a bruise. She had a dirty hat, and a bad case of hiccups all night, but she survived.

Celia forgave me, all too soon. Within weeks her mother allowed her to walk back and forth to school with me again. But, in all the years before she finally died at seventeen, I was never able to forgive her. She made me discover a darkness far more frightening than the echoing culvert, far more enduring than her smooth, pink face.

THOMAS KING
(1943)

〜

One Good Story, That One

Alright.

You know, I hear this story up north. Maybe Yellowknife, that one, some-where. I hear it maybe a long time. Old story this one. One hundred years, maybe more. Maybe not so long either, this story.

So.

You know, they come to my place. Summer place, pretty good place, that one. Those ones, they come with Napiao, my friend. Cool. On the river. Indians call him Ka-sin-ta, that river, like if you did nothing but stand in one place all day and maybe longer. Ka-sin-ta also call Na-po. Napiao knows that one, my friend. Whiteman call him Saint Merry, but I don't know what that mean. Maybe like Ka-sin-ta. Maybe not.

Napiao comes with those three. Whiteman, those.

No Indianman.

No Chinaman.

No Frenchman.

Too bad, those.

Sometimes the wind come along say hello. Pretty fast, that one. Blow some things down on the river, that Ka-sin-ta. Sometimes he comes up too, pretty high. Moves things around, that Ka-sin-ta.

Three men come to my summer place, also my friend Napiao. Pretty loud talkers, those ones. One is big. I tell him maybe looks like Big Joe. Maybe not.

Anyway.

They come and Napiao, too. Bring greetings, how are you, many nice things they bring to says. Three.

All white.

Too bad, those.

Ho, my friend says, real nice day. Here is some tobacco.

All those smile. Good teeth.

Your friend Napiao, they says, that one says you tell a good story, you tell us your good story.

They says, those ones.

I tell Napiao, sit down, rest, eat something. Those three like to stand.

Stand still. I think of Ka-sin-ta, as I told you. So I says to Napiao, Ka-sin-ta, in our language and he laugh. Those three laugh, too. Good teeth. Whiteman, white teeth.

I says to them, those ones stand pretty good. Napiao, my friend, says tell these a good story. Maybe not too long, he says. Those ones pretty young, go to sleep pretty quick. Anthropologist, you know. That one has a camera. Maybe.

Okay, I says, sit down.

These are good men, my friend says, those come a long ways from past Ta-pe-loo-za. Call him Blind Man Coulee, too. Ta-pe-loo-za means like a quiet place where the fish can rest, deep quiet place. Blind man maybe comes there later. To that place. Maybe fish.

Alright.

How about a story, that one says.

Sure, I says. Maybe about Jimmy runs the store near Two Bridges. His brother become dead and give Jimmy his car. But Jimmy never drives.

Napiao hold his hand up pretty soft. My friend says that good story, Jimmy and his car. These ones don't know Jimmy.

Okay, I says. Tell about Billy Frank and the dead-river pig. Funny story, that one, Billy Frank and the dead-river pig. Pretty big pig. Billy is real small, like Napiao, my friend. Hurt his back. Lost his truck.

Those ones like old stories, says my friend, maybe how the world was put together. Good Indian story like that, Napiao says. Those ones have tape recorders, he says.

Okay, I says.

Have some tea.

Stay awake.

Once upon a time.

Those stories start like that, pretty much, those ones, start on time. Anyway. There was nothing. Pretty hard to believe that, maybe.

You fellows keep listening, I says. Watch the floor. Be careful.

No water, no land, no stars, no moon. None of those things. Must have a sun someplace. Maybe not. Can't say. No Indians are there once upon a time. Lots of air. Only one person walk around. Call him god.

So.

They look around, and there is nothing. No grass. No fish. No trees. No mountains. No Indians, like I says. No whiteman, either. Those come later, maybe one hundred years. Maybe not. That one god walk around, but pretty soon they get tired. Maybe that one says, we will get some stars. So he does. And then he says, maybe we should get a moon. So, they get one of them, too.

Someone write all this down. I don't know. Lots of things left to get.

Me-a-loo, call her deer.

Pa-pe-po, call her elk.

Tsling-ta, call her Blue-flower-berry.

Ga-ling, call her moon.

So-see-ka, call her flint.

A-ma-po, call her dog.

Ba-ko-zao, call her grocery store.

Pe-to-pa-zasling, call her television.

Pretty long list of things to get, that. Too many, maybe those ones say, how many more that one needs for world. So. Pretty soon that one can fix up real nice place. Not too hot. Not too cold. Like here, we sit here. My summer place is like that one.

I call my summer place O-say-ta-he-to-peo-teh. Means cool sleeping place. Other place, they call her Evening's garden. Good time to fish, that. Evening. Cool, not so hot. That Evening's garden like here.

Two human beings that one puts there. Call the man Ah-damn. Call the woman, Evening. Same as garden.

Okay.

She looks around her garden. Pretty nice place, that one. Good tree. Good deer. Good rock. Good water. Good sky. Good wind. No grocery store, no television.

Ah-damn and Evening real happy, those ones. No clothes, those, you know. Ha, Ha, Ha, Ha. But they pretty dumb, then. New, you know.

Have some tea.

Stay awake.

Good part is soon here.

That woman, Evening, she is curious, nosy, that one. She walk around the garden and she look everywhere. Look under rock. Look in grass. Look in sky. Look in water. Look in tree.

So.

She find that tree, big one. Not like now, that tree. This one have lots of good things to eat. Have potato. Have pumpkin. Have corn. Have berries, all kind. Too many to say now.

This good tree also have some mee-so. Whiteman call them apples. This first woman look at the tree with the good things and she gets hungry. Make a meal in her head.

Leave that mee-so alone. Someone says that. Leave that mee-so alone. Leave that tree alone. The voice says that. Go away someplace else to eat!

That one, god. Hello, he's back.

Hey, says Evening, this is my garden.

You watch out, says that one, pretty loud voice. Sort of shout. Bad temper, that one. Maybe like Harley James. Bad temper, that one. Always shouting. Always with pulled-down mean look. Sometimes Harley come to town, drives his truck to town. Gets drunk. Drives back to that house. That one goes to town, get drunk, come home, that one, beat his wife. His wife leave. Goes back up north. Pretty mean one, that one. You boys know Harley James? Nobody there to beat up, now. Likes to shout, that one. Maybe you want to hear about Billy Frank and the dead-river pig?

Boy, my friend says, I can taste the mee-so. These boys pretty excited about those mee-so, I think.

Okay, I says.

Keep your eyes open, look around.

Evening, that one says, look pretty good, these. So she eat one, that mee-so. Boy, not bad, real juicy, that one. She is generous, Evening, good woman, that one. Brings mee-so to Ah-damn. I think he is busy then, writing things down. All the animals' names he writes somewhere, I don't know. Pretty boring that.

Deer come by, says Me-a-loo.

Elk come by, says Pa-pe-o.

Blue-flower-berry come by, says Tsling-ta.

Ah-damn not so smart like Evening, that one thinks Blue-flower-berry is animal, maybe.

Dog come by, says A-ma-po.

Raven come by, says Ne-co-ta.

Coyote come by, says Klee-qua.

Snail come by, says E-too.

Squirrel come by, says Qay-tha.

Owl come by, says Ba-tee-po-tah.

Weasel come by, says So-tha-nee-so.

Rabbit come by, says Klaaa-coo.

Flint come by, says So-see-ka.

Fish come by, says Laa-po.

Crayfish come by, says Tling.

Beaver come by, says Khan-yah-da.

Boy, all worn out. All those animals come by. Coyote come by maybe four, maybe eight times. Gets dressed up, fool around.

Says Piisto-pa.

Says Ho-ta-go.

Says Woho-i-kee.

Says Caw-ho-ha.

Ha, ha, ha, ha.

Tricky one, that coyote. Walks in circles. Sneaky.

That Ah-damn not so smart. Like Harley James, whiteman, those. Evening, she be Indian woman, I guess.

Evening come back. Hey, she says, what are all these coyote tracks come around in a circle. Not so smart, Ah-damn, pretty hungry though. Here, says Evening, mee-so, real juicy. So they do. Ah-damn, that one eat three mee-so. Ah-damn, says Evening, I better get some more mee-so.

Pretty soon that one, god, come by. He is pretty mad. You ate my mee-so, he says.

Don't be upset, says Evening, that one, first woman. Many more mee-so back there. Calm down, watch some television, she says.

But they are upset and that one says that Evening and Ah-damn better leave that good place, garden, Evening's garden, go somewhere else. Just like Indian today.

Evening says, okay, many good places around here. Ah-damn, that one wants to stay. But that fellow, god, whiteman I think, he says, you go too, you ate those mee-so, my mee-so.

Ah-damn is unhappy. He cry three times, ho, ho, ho. I only ate one, he says.

No, says that god fellow. I see everything. I see you eat three of my mee-so.

I only ate two, says Ah-damn but pretty quick that one throw him out.

Ha!

Throw him out on his back, right on those rocks. Ouch, ouch, ouch, that one says. Evening, she have to come back and fix him up before he is any good again. Alright.

There is also a Ju-poo-pea, whiteman call him snake. Don't know what kind. Big white one maybe, I hear, maybe black, something else. I forgot this part. He lives in tree with mee-so. That one try to get friendly with Evening so she stick a mee-so in his mouth, that one. Crawl back into tree. Have trouble talking, hissss, hissss, hissss, hissss. Maybe he is still there. Like that dead-river pig and Billy Frank lose his truck.

So.

Evening and Ah-damn leave. Everybody else leave, too. That tree leave, too. Just god and Ju-poo-pea together.

Ah-damn and Evening come out here. Have a bunch of kids.

So.

That's all. It is ended.

Boy, my friend says, better get some more tea. One good story, that one, my friend, Napiao says.

Those men push their tape recorders, fix their cameras. All of those ones smile. Nod their head around. Look out window. Shake my hand. Make happy noises. Say goodbyes, see you later. Leave pretty quick.

We watch them go. My friend, Napiao, put the pot on for some tea. I clean up all the coyote tracks on the floor.

BONNIE BURNARD
(1945)

Deer Heart

The embossed invitation to lunch with the visiting Queen hadn't come as a big surprise. At forty-one, she found herself included on some far-off proto-col list, the result of serving on a minor provincial board or two, the result of middle age.

She wouldn't have made the trip on her own; two hundred miles across the prairie, it wasn't worth it. She'd read the invitation immediately as a chance to be with her daughter, not the Queen, to be off with her on a long drive in the car, contained, remote, private. When she'd asked her daughter to join her at the luncheon the girl had turned down her stereo, briefly, and said, 'What Queen?'

She was aware of orchestrating these spaces in time with each of the kids, she'd been doing it religiously since their father's departure. She would have named it instinct rather than wisdom. And they were good, the kids were fine; there was no bed-wetting, no nail chewing, there were no night-mares, at least none severe enough to throw them from their beds and send them to her own in a cold sweat. If they did have nightmares, the quiet kind, they were still able to stand up in the morning with a smile, forgetful.

Her own acceptance, after nearly two years, took an unexpected form. She'd started files. One file contained the actual separation agreement, which listed all five of their names in full capitals, in bold type, the format generic and formal, applicable to any family; with the agreement she kept her list of the modest assets, the things that had to be valued against the day of final division. Another file held the information supplied by her govern-ment, little booklets on this aspect of family breakdown, supportive statistics on that. And the notification that she would be taxed differently, now that she was alone. In the third file she kept the letters. It was the thickest of the three, although its growth had slowed.

When the mailman began to leave these letters, casually tucked in with the usual bills and junk, she'd been dumbfounded. She'd sat on the couch with her morning coffee after the kids had gone to school, unsealing, unfolding, reading one word after another, recognizing the intent of the words as they arranged themselves into paragraphs of affection. A few of the letters contained almost honourable confessions of steamy fantasies, which apparently had been alive in the world for years, right under her nose. The words *fond of* and *hesitate* appeared more than once.

These men were in her circle, there was no reason to expect they would ever leave it.And they were, to a man, firmly and comfortably attached to women they would be wise to choose all over again, in spite of waists and enthusiasms as thick and diminished as her own. She disallowed all but one of the fantasies with laughter and common sense and a profound appreciation for the nerve behind the confessions.

Her short-lived defence, the time she gave in, had been what she called her net-gain theory. She tried to explain that any increased contentment for her would have to mean an equivalent loss for some other woman. She said that nothing new would be created. She said it was like chemistry. Her admirer had stood with his hands on her hips and told her it wasn't her job to measure and distribute; he'd told her to relax, to lighten up. And she did lighten up, for about an hour.

She kept the letters. If she was hit by a truck on the way to the Tom Boy, she would simply have to count on whoever went through her things to take care of them. The fireplace was just a few feet from her desk.

Her husband, her ex-husband, had found acceptable companionship, young companionship, young smooth-skinned fertile companionship, much more readily. A different life altogether.

When the big day came, she and the girl began the drive to the small prairie city where the Queen was to lunch with her subjects as she'd hoped, like an excursion. They stopped for gas and jujubes and two cans of Five Alive. They talked about school and the broad wheatland through which they were moving. She pointed out how bone dry it all was, told the girl how rain could change the colour of the landscape and how this in turn could change the economy of the province. She told her a little about the people who had to make a living from the parched land, most of the details only imagined. And she told her that when she was twelve she'd kept several scrapbooks with Queen Elizabeth II emblazoned on the cover, had filled them with this woman's life, her marriage and coronation, the magnificent christening gowns worn by her children, her scrappy younger sister, in love. She confessed all her young need for romance.

Then, without deliberation, she confessed how easily the romance had given way to tacky glamour, the Everly Brothers, James Dean, Brenda Lee. And how easily the glamour had been overtaken by Lightfoot, and Joni Mitchell, and Dylan. She tried to explain Dylan, what she'd absorbed from him, how he'd turned abstractions into something more useful, but without much success. She didn't confess to the next phase, the disdain, although she'd been happy to discover it at the time. She'd used it, while it lasted, without restraint. From this distance, of course, her young, mindless condescension looked merely cramped, and suspiciously safe. It looked like ordinary cowardice.

The girl took it all in, polite in the extreme, and asked the right questions, to please her. And then they were silent, cosy in the car, and she set the cruise control and began to dream a little. She was interrupted by some of the questions she hoped might find their opportunity on this drive. There was a boy. Of course there was a boy.

'Why can't he talk to me normally? I haven't changed,' and 'Why does he have to sneak looks at me all of a sudden?'

Old questions, easy to answer. She simply told the truth as she knew it, said the words out loud: *longing, confusion, afraid, dream.* She named the feeling a crush and said it was as common as house dust, which made the girl groan and giggle.

And then the girl asked, 'Were you pretty?'

'For a time,' she said, firmly. Shared, intimate laughter, women's laughter, the first between them. Her daughter's face open and soft.

When they arrived they had only to find the arena and it wasn't difficult. The city was more or less deserted except for the arena parking lot and the streets leading into it. She guessed maybe a couple of thousand people would be involved in this little affair. She parked the car and they cut across the parched, leaf-covered baseball diamond to the arena. Inside they found the washroom and freshened up together, the girl imitating her mother's moves, although with her own style. At the entrance to the huge high-beamed room, which would in a month or perhaps even sooner be transformed into a hockey rink, she found the invitation in her bag and handed it to a uniformed woman.

They waited only a few moments at their seats at the long table and then the orchestra, from the area of the penalty box, began 'God Save the Queen.' They stood up and in she came. In a hot pink wool coat and a trim little hot pink hat, visible to all, waving and nodding with a fixed, flat smile.

She regretted not wearing what she'd wanted to wear, her cherry red coat and her mother's fox stole, which she'd claimed and kept wrapped in tissue in a closet, an absurdity now with its cold glassy nose and the hooks sewn into the paws. She had no idea why she loved it and longed to wear it, somewhere, before she grew old. She had her mother's opal ring, which she sometimes wore, so it wasn't that, it wasn't just the need to keep her mother's things alive. There was a prayer, for the Queen, for the country, for rain, and then the heavy noise of two thousand chairs being scraped over the cold cement floor. Prairie people, in expensive suits and silk dresses and elegant felt hats sitting down to eat a roast beef dinner for lunch.

She talked superficially and politely to the people around them at their table, people she knew she would never see again, and her daughter listened and tried a couple of superficial lines of her own. 'Have you been looking forward to seeing the Queen?' she asked the elderly woman across from her.

They didn't get to shake hands with the Royals, which was an obvious and unexpected disappointment for the girl, but they heard the Queen speak, crisply about the settling of this land, about the native peoples, textbook talk. She was followed by government officials, unable to resist a go at the captive audience. And then the program began, children in coy little dance groups and choirs and a youth orchestra, and she could feel her daughter wanting to be up there on the stage, performing, taking the only chance she'd likely ever have to curtsy to someone. She wanted to tell her that there had never been anyone who'd made her want to curtsy. She often caught herself wanting to hand over fully developed attitudes, to save the girl time, and trouble.

A couple of hours later, when it was finally over, they were both more than ready to stand up from their hard chairs and leave the arena. After they crossed the ball field with hundreds of other subjects, and found the car, they decided to drive around the city a bit, explore, and, to the girl's way of thinking, they got lucky. There was a shopping mall, brand spanking new. They wandered together through a maze of sale signs and racks of last year's fashions and temporary counters filled with junk jewellery, where they found two pairs of gaudy, oversized, dirt-cheap earrings. The girl did not ask why you never saw tiaras in jewellery stores, which was something she had wondered herself when she was young. The prom queen, not her, not even a friend, had worn a tiara, so they must have been available then, some-where. Neither of them was hungry, they'd eaten everything served to them at the arena, including magnificent pumpkin tarts, but they sat down to a shared Diet Coke and watched everyone else who'd been at the luncheon wander around the mall. Then it was nearly five o'clock and she said they should get on the road. The girl had school in the morning, and the sitter might be getting worn down.

As they crossed the parking lot she said, 'She looks so fat on TV. But she's really not all that fat.' The girl laughed in complicity.

In the car, on a whim, because she wanted the day to hold more than the Queen, she dug out the road map and found the big dam, asked the girl if she was interested. 'Sure,' she said. 'Why not?' She told her that they would have to take smaller, older roads to see it and that it might take a little longer going home than coming, if they decided to venture off.

She was glad the girl was game, capable of handling all this distance between their position here in the east central part of this huge province and home. She knew next to nothing about the dam, but she'd seen lots of others and she could improvise if she had to. They could get some books on it when they got home. There might even be a school project on it some day.

It would take about an hour to get near it and then some determining which side roads to choose to get right up to the thing. She drove easily, there was no traffic left for the old highway, not with the dead-straight four-lane fifty miles to the west. She confidently anticipated the curves and set the cruise control again, relaxed. They cut through farmland and then into bush, far more bush than she'd ever seen in this province. The prairie ceased to be open and she began to wonder if making this side trip was wise. The sun that remained was behind the trees, blocked, and dusk, she knew, would be brief. She put the headlights on. There had been a time when she loved being in the car in the dark, like a space traveller, someone chosen, the blue-white dash lights crucial, reliable, contributing precise information, the darkness around her body a release. Some of her best moments had been in dark cars.

The girl was quiet beside her, thinking. About the Queen? About her new earrings, which pair she would allow her sister to borrow if she promised not to leave them somewhere, or trade with a friend? About the boy who could no longer talk to her, normally?

The deer appeared in the corner of her eye. It had every chance. It was thirty yards ahead of them, in the other lane. All it had to do was freeze. Or dive straight ahead, or veer left. Lots of choices. She threw her arm hard across her daughter's chest, forgetting that she was belted in,and she kept her steering as steady as she could with the grip of one firm hand. She braked deliberately, repeatedly; she did not slam the pedal to the floor. She locked her jaw. Just hold tight, she told the deer. Just close your eyes and hold tight. When it dove for the headlights she yelled 'Shit,' and brought her arm away from the girl's chest back to the wheel. And then it was over. She'd hit it.

Before she could say, Don't look, the girl did. 'I think you took its leg off,' she said. 'Why didn't you stop? Why did you have to hit it?'

She saw gain the right headlight coming into sudden, silent, irrevocable contact with the tawny hindquarter. The thump belonged to something else, seemed to come neither from the car nor from the deer.

'You killed a deer,' the girl said.

She pulled the car over to the side of the dark road and they sat there, waiting for her to do something. She put her hand on the door handle and unbuckled but she made no further move. Wherever it was, it was beyond her help. Her daughter looked back again.

'He's in the ditch. I think he's trying to climb out of the ditch.'

'I'm sorry,' she said. 'I couldn't go off the road to save him. We'd be the ones in the ditch if I'd tried. I'm really sorry.'

She pulled slowly back onto the road and, remembering her seat belt, buckled up. She took note of the reading on the odometer.

'Are we just going to go?' the girl asked.

'I'll have to find someone to kill it,' she said. 'We'll stop in the next town. That's all there is to do. I don't feel really good about this either.'

The girl sat in silence, pushed down into her seat.

Ten minutes later there was a town, a small group of houses clustered around one long main street, the only sign of life at the Sands Hotel. She pulled in and parked beside a blue half-ton.

'I'll just go in and talk to someone,' she said. 'You might as well wait here. It won't take long.'

She got out and walked to the front of the car. The fog lamp had been bent like a walleye and the glass on the headlight was broken but there was no blood. She'd broken bones, not skin. She noticed for the first time a symbol on the Volvo's grille, the Greek symbol for the male, the circle with the arrow pointing off northeast. She remembered the first time she'd seen it, when she was a girl watching 'Ben Casey' on television, wholeheartedly in love with him, with his dark face and his big arms, a precursor to the men she would really love, later. And now it was later than later, and here she was in a bleak prairie town with grey hair growing out of her head, an angry adolescent in her car and a mangled deer twelve kilometres behind her on the road.

Inside the hotel she went directly to the young blond bartender to explain what she'd done, but she'd known the instant she was in the bar which of them would be the one to go back and find the deer and finish it off. They were sitting in a large group around a table, watching her, eight or ten of them in green and brown and plaid, drinking beer and coffee. She knew she looked ridiculous to them in her high black boots and her long dark trenchcoat with the oversized shoulders, like something out of a bad war movie. Still, they waited in well-mannered silence for her to speak.

'Talk to him,' the kid at the bar said, pointing. She approached the table and a couple of them, the older ones, tipped their hats. One of these hat-tippers leaned back in his chair and asked, 'Pussycat, pussycat, where have you been?' and it took her a few stalled seconds to reply, 'I've been to London to visit the Queen.' He chuckled and saluted her with his coffee.

'I've hit a deer,' she said. 'About twelve kilometres back. I was wondering if someone could maybe take care of it.' She looked at the one she'd picked.

'North?' he asked.

'Yes,' she said. 'On number ten.'

'How bad?' he asked.

'I think I pretty well ruined his hindquarters,' she said.

'Your car,' he said. 'I meant your car.' There was no laughter.

'The car's all right,' she said. 'My insurance will likely cover it.'

'You should report it,' he said. 'You have to phone the wildlife people. Unless you want to pay the two-hundred deductible. You call and report it now, it's the deer's fault.'

'Is there a phone I could use?' she asked.

He led her out of the bar into a cold back room. The light was amber, muted, dusty. There was a stained sink in the corner and a battered leather couch along one wall, the rest of the room was filled with beer cases, stacked four high. There was a pay phone, and beside it, taped to the door-frame, a list of phone numbers. He put his own quarter in and dialled the number for her.

She took the phone and talked to a woman at an answering service who put her through to a man who was in some way official and she gave him all the information she could, the time and location, her registration and licence numbers, her apologies. She couldn't tell him how old the deer might have been.

While she stood there, reporting the incident, the man stayed on the arm of the couch, watching her. She became aware of her perfume and her long, wild hair.

When she was finished he got up and stood beside her.

'Someone hits a deer here about once a week,' he said. He reached behind her head and turned down the collar of her trenchcoat, slowly. She would not have been surprised if his mouth had grazed her forehead. 'I can check your car.'

'The car's okay,' she said. 'The engine didn't take any damage.'

'Whatever,' he said.

'My daughter's out there,' she said. 'She's pretty upset.'

He nodded. 'This kind of thing is hard on kids.'

Outside, he hunched down in the light from the hotel sign and ran his hand over the shattered glass. 'Looks like it was a young deer,' he said, standing up, stretching. He opened the car door for her and she climbed in behind the wheel. 'I've got my gun in the truck,' he said. 'I'll go back for it.'

'Thank you,' she said.

He tucked her coat around her legs and closed the door.

On the highway again, the girl listened to the explanation of the procedure. She sat in silence for a long time, her legs under her on the seat, trying, in spite of the seat belt, to curl up. When her mother turned on the radio, to some easy listening music, she started in.

'I don't see why she has to be there every weekend we go to Dad's,' the girl said. 'I don't see why we have to see her lying in bed in the morning. I think it's rude.'

'Where did this come from?' she asked. But she knew the answer. It came from a very young woman riding in a dark car through the bush with her mother.

'You could tell your Dad if it bothers you, her being there when you are. Or I could, if you want me to.'

'I already have,' the girl said. 'He just tells her. They don't care.'

'Your Dad cares,' she said. 'He's not himself. But he misses you. He's told me and I believe him.'

'She bought that nightshirt I wanted, the mauve one,' she said. 'She bought it for herself. And she doesn't get dressed till lunchtime.' She reached for the radio and punched in a rock station. 'She's everywhere you look.'

'That's why you changed your mind about the nightshirt?' she asked.

There was no answer.

The young lady in question had not shown any particular skill at the unenviable task of winning the affections of a middle-aged man's half-grown kids. Although she'd tried. One weekend she'd even done their wash, an effort to appease the mother who bitched about sending them off clean and getting them back, always, in disorder. When they got home they'd stood in the kitchen emptying their weekend bags, showing off their clean clothes.

In her pile, the girl discovered pink bikini panties not her own. She tossed them hard across the room to her sister, who screeched and pitched them like a live hand grenade to her defenceless brother, who cringed and ducked.

'She loves your Dad,' she said.

'Because you won't,' the girl said.

'I'll talk to him,' she offered.

'Don't bother,' the girl said. 'I'll just get a lecture about how everyone's got a right to be happy and all that crap.'

'It's not crap,' she said.

She wanted to be his wife again, just for a little while. She wanted to talk to him about what people, very young people, have a right to. She'd heard more than once, from her friends, from the inarticulate counsellor, from a British homemakers' magazine in her doctor's office, the theory that kids could withstand a lot. All you had to do was look around you, all these kids carrying right on. She bought into it herself, sometimes, taking pride in their hard-won stability, their distracted smiles. Good pluggers, all.

The girl stared out her window, watching the bush fly by. 'Don't ever expect me to say good morning to some boyfriend of yours.'

'No,' she said. 'I won't be expecting that.'

They drove on. She could think of nothing light and harmless to say, nothing would come.

'I saw this TV show,' she said, hesitating.

The girl waited.

'There was a woman standing in front of a mirror and she was very unhappy. It was just a dumb mini-series. Anyway, she was standing talking into this mirror, to someone behind her, and she said when she was a kid she'd been driving with her father in a car, at night, like we are, and it was winter, there was a lot of snow. And they saw a deer draped over a fence. It looked dead. She said she began to cry and her father told her it was all right. He told her that deer have a trick. When they're trapped like that they don't have to wait to die. They can make their hearts explode.'

'A trick,' the girl said.

'I think it would be fright,' she said. 'I think it would be a heart attack brought on by fright. That would be the real explanation. But it means that our deer could be out of its misery before that man even gets to it with his gun. It could have been dead before we left it.'

Even as she recited this she knew it was unlikely. She assumed the deer was back there, not far from the ditch, dying the hard way. It would watch him approach, hear the soft 'Easy now. Easy.'

And she knew that one of them would hold the deer forever in her mind, not dying, but fully alive in the bright shock of the headlights, and that the other would hold it just as long cold and wide-eyed, after the hunter.

⌒

For Puzzled in Wisconsin

Dear Allie: My husband has an intricate tattoo on his chest. I am very fond of it, and don't want to see it go with him when he dies.

I'm wondering if there is a way to have it taken off and preserved somehow at the time of his passing. Is this against the law? If not, who would look after this sort of thing, should it be possible: a taxidermist, the funeral director, or someone else?

My husband enjoys the best of health now, but I'd like to know what your answer is so that I can prepare myself.

—Puzzled in Wisconsin

My daughter reads me your letter, laughing.

'Do you believe this?' she says, in the voice she has for the tabloids at the checkout at Loblaws. 'Baby Born Repeating Message from Aliens!' 'I Saw My Husband Snatched by a Mermaid.'

'Do you believe this!' Not a question, of course, since for her the answer is obvious.

After she goes off to do her homework, I pick up the paper and read your letter through again, two or three times, until I can see you there at your kitchen table writing it. Beside you is a coffee mug and a pack of Player's Light. The mug says I ❤ my mutt and there's a picture on it of a dog like the one that's lying by the door watching you.

You're just about due for a perm and a rinse. Your hair's showing grey at the roots, greyer than mine, I think, but fine like mine and straggly. Faded blonde, like your skin, which is dry and washed-out looking under your blush and your blue eye shadow.

When your husband gets off work tonight—he's on afternoons this week—the letter will be in your purse, which is on the sideboard in the dining room. I can see you in the living room with your bathrobe on, watching 'Johnny Carson'. Your husband usually brings home a pizza or some Chinese and you both have a couple of beers. Then he'll start sucking on your earlobe or tickling your breasts. It's fun, not having to worry any more about the kids hearing. Your baby, Tommy, moved out on his own three months ago.

At this point, your husband pulls his T-shirt off. You like to run your tongue over his tattoo. Sometimes, that's all you do. Sometimes, that's just for starters.

Dear Puzzled: Ask the funeral director when the time comes. He (or she) will be able to answer your questions. In the meantime, perhaps someone who knows will see this and let me know if anything of the sort of has been done before, and, if so, how they handled it.

I, too, am puzzled.

Well, she didn't exactly bust her ass trying to find an answer, did she? *I, too, am puzzled.* When you read that out loud it sounds kind of snotty, as if she thinks this can't be serious. *When the time comes* . . . Oh, brilliant. When the time comes you'll have a million other things on your mind. The boys'll make fun of you, the undertaker will pat you on the arm and say: 'There, there, you're just upset.' It gets you upset, all right, just thinking about it.

Your husband just thinks you're weird. 'But what the hell,' he says, 'go ahead if you want to. They're already gonna take my eyes and my liver. Might as well have my tattoo, too.'

He doesn't know about the letter, of course. He never reads 'Dear Allie'. 'They just make that shit up,' he says, 'to sell papers.'

The summer I was eighteen, I worked as a waitress at the Bangor Lodge in Muskoka. Most of the other waitresses were girls like me, just finished high school, earning money for university in the fall, but the cooking staff were all local, from Bracebridge or Huntsville. They worked there every summer and on into the off-season after the rest of us left. Most of them were women my mother's age, except for the girl who did the salads and the bread baskets and stuff.

Gwen MacIntyre. She was my age, though she looked older. Short and busty with thick black hair and huge violet eyes. Like Liz Taylor, of course, and she emphasized that, piling her hair up in thick curls and wearing lots of dark eyeliner. On her it was okay, too. She really was beautiful, just as Liz herself *was* beautiful, temporarily, but perfectly, before she got all bloated and silly.

Usually the waitresses didn't hang around much with the kitchen staff, but Gwen and I soon found we had something in common. Our boyfriends both worked in Toronto. Gwen's boyfriend, Chuck, was a welder; my boyfriend, Jeff, was working at a paint factory for the summer.

'I suppose he's comin' up on the weekend, eh?' Gwen asked, though she didn't really put it as a question. It was just sort of assumed. She'd already told me that Chuck came up every Saturday.

'Probably not, actually.' I tried to sound casual, but I felt, somehow, apologetic. 'He doesn't have a car.'

'Well, why didn't you say so? He can drive up with Chuck and we can do something together. It'll be great.'

That night, Gwen phoned Chuck to tell him the plan.

'He'll pay half the gas,' she said, which is what we'd agreed she'd say, 'and he can get over to your place, easy. All you have to do is call him up and introduce yourself. Anna's gonna call him first, right after I hang up. She's really nice, honey. It'll be great. See you Saturday. Bye, hon.'

She always called him 'honey' or 'hon'. He called her 'babe'. I couldn't imagine Jeff calling me anything.

'Jesus, I don't even know the guy,' he kept saying. 'Why didn't you call me first.'

'If you don't want to come,' I said after a few minutes of this, 'don't bother.' And I hung up, hard.

We were using the phone in the little office just off the kitchen where the cook made up the orders and paid the delivery men. You had to reverse the charges. There'd been a minute at the start when I thought Jeff wasn't going to accept and, now that I'd hung up, I realized he couldn't call me back. Even if he bothered to find out, the only number listed for the lodge was the front desk. They didn't take personal calls for staff.

Gwen was in the kitchen putting the last of the dishes in the dishwasher, but she didn't try to hide the fact that she was listening. As soon as I banged the phone down, she came to the door with a coffee and my cigarettes.

'Don't worry,' she said, 'he'll show up.'

As it turned out, she was right. Jeff said he thought Chuck was a bit of an asshole, but he could stand it, so the summer was set. They both had to work Saturdays and, what with holiday traffic and all, they usually didn't get to the lodge before 9:30 or 10:00 P.M. By that time, we'd be pretty well finished. If I had a late table, Gwen'd help me set up for breakfast, though she wasn't supposed to.

Chuck had an old Ford pickup that his father had sold him for a dollar when he started working in Toronto. The passenger door was so rusted he'd had to weld it shut, so everyone piled in from the driver's side. By half past ten, we'd be heading out to a spot he knew about along the lake where there was a bit of a beach and no other cottages. We'd build a fire and sit around drinking beer and listening to Jeff's radio. After an hour or so, Chuck'd grab Gwen and say, 'C'mon, babe, come and say hello to your old man,' and they'd move off a ways into the little woods while Jeff and I stretched out by the fire.

The air was always hot and close and still. You could hear everything. Especially Chuck.

'Oh, babe!' he'd say. 'Oh, babe!' And then louder and louder. 'Oh babe, oh, Gwennie, oh-h, oh-h, babe!' then silence. Then it would start again.

Later, driving back to the lodge, I'd try to fit Chuck's face—which was broader and fair and sort of *eager*, I guess, but in the way a kid's face is eager, one front tooth chipped, the other missing—to the sounds I heard in the woods, but I never could. It was like it never happened. Jeff never even let on, but one night, just as he came inside me, he started whining in this forced, stupid whisper: 'Oh, babe, oh, babe.' I pushed him away and tried to stand up.

'Hey'—he held me—'c'mon. I was only fooling.'

'Yeah, I know.' I wanted to punch him, to hurt him in some way I knew I never could. I don't know why.

Jeff and I always used a safe, of course, but I knew for a fact, because she told me, that Gwen and Chuck never did. I wasn't surprised. There'd been lots of Gwens at my high school. I knew exactly what would happen.

By the end of August, Gwen was pregnant. Chuck was ecstatic. He even brought a bottle of champagne up the next weekend. He'd already found a bigger apartment. They planned to get married on the Labour Day weekend, though Gwen would go on working at the lodge until it closed in October. They could use the extra money.

Jeff and I used to talk about getting married, too, but it was just talk. He was going to Queen's, to med school, in the fall and he kept saying he wanted me to come there instead of going to Western. He talked about how a small apartment would be cheaper than residence.

Knowing what I know now, this would have meant my getting a part-time job to help with expenses, failing courses, getting pregnant and then finding out five years down the road that Jeff was in love with some night nurse and wanted a divorce. At the time, I just didn't like the way he kept kissing the back of my neck when I tried to talk about something I'd read or even about one of my customers.

'Is this what you really want to do?' I asked Gwen once.

She looked as if she thought I must be joking. 'Of course. Don't you?'

That was all she said. I thought it was because she was too stupid to want anything else. I guess I saw her as a victim of her own life, forced into it because she hadn't been smart enough to plan ahead. I never even considered then that she might see me in the same light.

Peter, the man I *did* marry, sixteen years ago, is an archivist at the university. When our daughter read him your letter, he laughed with her, but for different reasons. He can believe it all right, some people are probably like that, he just doesn't think it has anything to do with him. When they laugh, both Peter and our daughter, Jennifer, dip their heads slightly to the side at precisely the same angle, mouths wide open, showing the same even teeth.

That night in bed, I ask Peter, 'Is there anything like that of mine you'd want to save?'

'Like what?'

'You know, that "Dear Allie" letter Jennifer read about that tattoo.'

'Of course not; I'd never even think of it.'

'Well, think about it now. *If* you were going to do something like that, what would you want? Some of my stretch marks? The mole on my left breast?'

'I can't imagine it, Anna. Really, this is silly.'

He lies flat on his back, his hands at his sides, his eyes closed, his face set in the pained expression he wears for conversations like this—'What if's' speculations. When Jennifer and I sit in a restaurant making up stories about the people around us, he closes his eyes, just as he's doing now.

'Tightass. You never even try.'

'I just can't, Anna. You know that. I don't know what you want me to do.'

'I don't either.' I try to make it light, nonchalant. 'Night.' I kiss him lightly as I reach across him to turn off the lamp, then roll over as if to sleep. I don't want him to think I'm angry, it's just a silly game, after all.

I don't even want to *be* angry, dammit. It's not like he isn't imaginative. He is—about gifts, for example, and vacations. I don't think this other is something he can do anything about, and why should he? Once I asked him if he ever made up stories about the material at the archives, the people whose bits and pieces he sorts and labels.

'Of course not, Anna. I'd never get any work done.'

And I can see what he means. His job is to organize the known world, after all. It's up to someone else to explore the rest. Why should I hold it against him?

But I do. Just because I understand doesn't mean it doesn't poke at me, niggling and sore, like the pea under all those mattresses in the fairy story.

After a few minutes, I get up and slip on my bathrobe. Peter, who can sleep through anything, doesn't move, even his breathing stays slow and regular.

Downstairs, the house has that smooth, mirror-like quality that always makes me feel like a figure in someone else's dream. I grab a glass and the bourbon and go out on the deck at the back. It's hot tonight. All the houses are open, relaxed, letting go of their secrets. A toilet flushes, a baby cries, a man's voice coaxes a cat inside. 'Susie, c'mon now, Susie, come and see Daddy.' It's not very often that I sit here, late like this, with my feet on the railing, drinking bourbon. I wish I had a cigarette. I wish I could stay up all night, drinking and smoking.

The first time I ever drank bourbon was with Gwen and Chuck and Jeff at Chuck's parents' house. The boys had come up one Saturday, as usual, but just as they pulled in, it started to rain, hard. We didn't know what to do.

'Hop in,' Chuck said. 'We'll go see my folks. They won't mind.'

Chuck's parents, Roy and Joan, were sitting at the kitchen table when we came up to the back porch. Roy was an older version of Chuck with the same eager face, even the missing tooth. He was wearing a baggy pair of Bermuda shorts and a green T-shirt with ART'S ESSO in black across the chest. Joan was wearing shorts, too, white, with a white halter top and a man's plaid flannel shirt, open, over the whole thing. Her hair, which was dark brown (obviously, but gloriously dyed), was teased and piled into a high beehive. On her feet she had gold, high-heeled slippers.

They both jumped up as soon as they saw us.

'Hey there, Chuckie boy!' Roy shouted. 'C'mon in outta the rain.' He pulled chairs up around the table, while Joan brought over glasses and a forty-ouncer of bourbon.

'You're workin' with Gwen at the lodge then,' she said, handing me a drink and holding out her pack of cigarettes.

'Yeah, in the dining room, though. I'm a waitress.'

'Tips good?'

'Yeah, I guess so. I get about one hundred dollars a week.'

'Shit!' Joan exhaled smoke sharply. 'You hear that, Roy? One hundred lousy bucks a week in tips at Bangor. Cheapskates. What you don't have to put up with, eh?'

She laughed, but even her laugh had an edge to it, angry, as if she were personally involved.

I took another sip of my bourbon. I'd never drunk liquor straight before. I was beginning to like the way it stung my tongue, burned my whole mouth frozen all the way down. One hundred a week in tips had seemed like a lot to me, but now I could see what Joan meant. I thought about how people's voices sounded when they gave their order, how they always stopped talking to each other when I came up to the table.

We sat around drinking and smoking for what seemed like hours. Food kept appearing. Some doughnuts Joan had made fresh that morning, salami and cheese, crackers, homemade pickles.

All of a sudden Roy leaned back in his chair and pulled his T-shirt up almost to his neck.

'What do ya think about this baby here?' he asked.

Across his middle, from his belt line to just below his left nipple was a wide, jagged, white scar. He had a lot of hair, but it hadn't grown back over the scar, which was thicker in some places than others. It glistened and bulged in the yellow kitchen light, stretched taut over his gut as if the skin couldn't take much more.

'Quite a mess, eh?' He said. 'I used to be a guard at the Pen in Kingston, there. Had some trouble one night. One of the guys had a shank. Ripped me open in one swipe. Felt like he'd sliced my liver out. Next thing I know, I'm wakin' up in the hospital.'

He took another swig of bourbon and lit a cigarette off the one he had going. 'Turned out I lost a lot of blood, but that was about it. The guy missed every single vital organ. Can you believe it? Every single goddamn vital organ. The doctors said I was the luckiest sonofabitch they'd ever seen. I wanted to go right back as soon as the stitches were out, but Joan here, she said she couldn't take it, what with the kids and all, especially the nights. So I let 'er go. Ten years seniority, pension, the whole goddamn shot.'

He let go of his shirt so that it dropped slightly and wrinkled around his gut. Nobody said anything, but it wasn't from embarrassment or shock or anything like that. It was more as if we weren't expected to.

Whenever I have told this story—and I have, many times—I always tell about Roy and the scar, of course, but it's just part of it, part of the story about that summer and about Gwen and Chuck (neither of whom I ever saw again, after the season ended, though we promised we'd visit), and about drinking bourbon all night. I tell about going out to drive back to the lodge and see-ing the sky lightening over the trees and realizing that we'd been up all night, Gwen and me working all day Sunday, no sleep, hung-over and never giving it a thought. That's how the story ends when I've told it lately. How you can do it when you're young.

Not now though. So I haul myself off the deck, rinse the glass and tiptoe back upstairs. Peter doesn't wake up when I crawl into bed, but he says my name, out loud. 'Anna.' As if he were checking it off a list, some part of him still awake until everything's accounted for. He always does this and I always sort of like it, even though I'm still a little angry.

I'm just drifting off when I see something else. It's almost as if I'm watch-ing a movie of the six of us in that kitchen, sitting around the table and the camera moves in all of a sudden, so that what I can see now is a close-up of Joan's hand, reaching out to Roy's bare gut, caressing it so intimately I can't believe she's doing it in front of us. And then, with the tip of her index fin-ger, gently, very gently, she traces the scar, every turn and bulge, from Roy's nipple to his waist, as if to show us exactly what it's like.

As if his belly were a map, almost, and the scar was this road she was pointing out, wanting us to see where he'd been. And where'd she'd been, too. After he got out of the hospital, when he spent days just sitting there, staring, and she had to keep the kids quiet, not knowing what he was going to do next, what was going to happen to them. That was part of it. And more, that we could never know.

It's just for a minute that I see this, mind you, Joan's hand on Roy's scar like that. But it's what I would want to tell you, Puzzled in Wisconsin, if I ever had the chance, or knew how.

Douglas Glover
(1948)

～

Swain Corliss, Hero of Malcolm's Mills (now Oakland, Ontario), November 6, 1814

In the morning, the men rubbed their eyes and saw Kentucky cavalry and Indians mounted on stolen farm forses cresting the hill on the opposite side of the valley. The Kentuckians looked weary and calm, their hollow eyes slitted with analysis. We were another problem to be solved; they had been solving problems all the way from Fort Detroit, mostly by killing, maiming and burning, which were the usual methods.

The Indians were Cherokee and Kickapoo, with some Muncies thrown in. They had eagle-feather rosettes and long hair down the sides of their heads and paint on their faces, which looked feminine in that light. Some wore scalps hanging at their belts.

They came over the hill in a column, silent as the steam rising from their mounts, and stopped to chew plug tobacco or smoke clay pipes while they analyzed us. More Kentuckians coming on extended the line on either side of the track into the woods, dismounted, and started cook fires or fell asleep under their horses' bellies, with reins tied at the wrists.

General McArthur rode in with his staff, all dressed in blue, with brass buttons and dirty white facings. He spurred his mare to the front, where she shied and pranced and nearly fell on the steep downward incline. He gave a sign, and the Indians dismounted and walked down the road to push our pickets in. The Indians had an air of attending their eighty-seventh-or-so battle. They trudged down the dirt road bolt upright, with their muskets cradled, as though bored with the whole thing, as though they possessed some precise delineation of the zone of danger that bespoke a vast familiarity with death and dying.

The men who could count counted.

Somebody said, 'Oh, sweet Baby Jesus, if there's one, there must be a thousand.'

I should say that we had about four hundred—the 1st and 2nd Norfolk

Militia, some Oxfords and Lincolns, six instructors from the 41st Foot and some local farmers who had come up the day before for the society.

Colonel Bostwick (the men called him Smiling Jack) stood higher up on the ridge behind our line, watching the enemy across the valley with a spyglass, his red coat flapping at his thighs. He stood alone mostly. He had been shot in the leg at Frenchman's Creek and in the face at Nanticoke when he walked into the Dunham place and stumbled on Sutherland and Onstone's gang by accident. The wound on his face made him look as though he were smiling all the time, which was repellent and unnerved his troops in a fight.

Injun George, an old Chippeway who kept house in a hut above Troyer's Flats, was first up from the creek. He said he had seen a black snake in the water, which was bad luck. He said the Kickapoo had disappeared when he shot at them, which meant that they had learned the disappearing trick and had strong medicine. He himself had been trying to disappear for years with little success. Later, he shot a crow off the mill roof, which he said was probably one of the Kickapoos.

A troop of Kentuckians came down the hill with ammunition pouches and Pennsylvania long rifles and started taking pot shots at McCall's company hiding behind a barricade of elm logs strung across the road. We could not reply much for lack of powder, so the Kentuckians stood out in the open on the stream bank, smoking their white clay pipes and firing up at us. Others merely watched, or pissed down the hill, or washed their shirts and hung them out to dry, as though fighting and killing were just another domestic chore, like slopping pigs or putting up preserves.

Somebody said, 'They are just like us except that we are not in Kentucky lifting scalps and stealing horses and trying to take over the place.'

The balls sounded like pure-D evil thunking into the logs.

Someone else tried to raise a yell for King George, which fell flat, many men allowing as it was a mystery why King George had drawn his regulars across to the other side of the Grand River and burned the ferry scow so that they could not be here when the fighting started.

Thunk, thunk went the balls. A melancholy rain began to fall, running in muddy rivulets down the dirt track. Smoke from the Republican cook fires drifted down into the valley and hung over the mill race.

Colonel Bostwick caused some consternation coming down to be with his men, marching up and down just behind the line with that strange double grin on his face (his cheek tattooed with powder burns embedded in the skin) and an old officer's spontoon across his shoulders, exhorting us in a hoarse, excited mutter.

'Behold, ye infidels, ye armies of Gog and Magog, agents and familiars of Azazel. Smite, smite! O Lord, bless the children who go into battle in thy name. Remember, boys, the Hebrew kings did not scruple to saw their enemies with saws and harrow them with harrows of iron!'

Sergeant Major Collins of the 41st tried to make him lie down behind the snake fence, but the colonel shook him off, saying, 'The men must see me.'

The sergeant took a spent ball in the forehead and went down. The ball bounced off, but he was dead nonetheless, a black knot sprouting between his brows like a third eye.

A sharpshooter with a good Pennsylvania Dutch long rifle can hit a man at three hundred yards, which is twice as far as any weapon we could throw, let alone be accurate. So far we had only killed one crow, which might or might not have been an enemy Indian.

Edwin Barton said, 'I dreamt of Tamson Mabee all night. I threw her down in the hay last August, but she kept her hand over her hair pie and wouldn't let me. She ain't hardly fourteen. I'll bet I'm going to hell today.'

Somebody said, 'You ever done it with a squaw? A squaw'll lay quiet and not go all herky-jerky like a white woman. I prefer a squaw to a white woman any day.'

And somebody else said, 'I know a man over at Port Rowan who prefers hogs for the same reason.'

This was war and whisky talking.

We lay in the rain, dreaming of wives and lovers, seeking amnesty in the hot purity of lust—yes, some furtively masturbating in the rain with cold hands. Across the valley, the Kentuckians seemed like creatures of the autumn and of rain, their amphibian eyes slitty with analysis. Our officers, Salmon and Ryerson, said we held good ground, whatever that meant, that the American army at Niagara was already moving back across the river, that we had to stop McArthur from burning the mills of Norfolk so we could go on feeding King George's regulars.

Trapped in that valley, waiting for the demon cavalry to come whooping and shrieking across the swollen creek, we seemed to have entered some strange universe of curved space and strings of light. Rain fell in strings. Some of us were already dead, heroes of other wars and battles. We had been fighting since August 1812, when we went down the lake with Brock to the relief of Amherstburg. At times like these, we could foresee the mass extinction of the whole species, the world turned to a desert of glass.

Everything seemed familiar and inevitable. We had marched up from Culver's Tavern the day before. We had heard firing in the direction of Brant's Ford at dusk, and awakened to see Kentucky cavalry and Indians emerging from the forest road and smoke rising from barn fires behind them. Evidently, given their history, Kentuckians are born to arson and mayhem. Now they sniped with passionate precision (*thunk, thunk* went the balls), keeping us under cover while they moved troops down the steep bank.

Shielding our priming pans with our hats, we cursed the rain and passed the time calculating angles of assault. The mill pond, too deep except to swim, protected our left wing. That meant Salmon's boys would get hit first, thank goodness. Mrs Malcolm and her Negro servant were busy moving trunks and armoires out of the house in case of fire. No one paid them any mind. All at once, we heard shouts and war cries deep in the woods down-stream. Colonel Bostwick sent a scout, who returned a moment later to say McArthur's Indians had out-flanked us, crawling across a deadfall ford.

We stared at the clouds and saw fatherless youngsters weeping at the well, lonely widows sleeping with their hands tucked between their legs, and shadows moving with horrible wounds, arms or legs missing, brains dripping out their ears.

Someone said, 'I can't stand this no more,' stood up, and was shot in the spine, turning. He farted and lay on his face with his legs quivering. His legs shook like a snake with its back broken. The Kentuckians were throwing an amazing amount of hot lead our way.

The colonel smiled and shouted additional remarks against Azazel, then ordered McCall to stand at the elm-tree barricade while the rest retired. This was good news for us. We could get by without the mills of Norfolk; it was our bodies, our limbs, lungs, nerves and intestines we depended on for today and tomorrow.

McCall had Jo Kitchen, a noted pugilist, three of the Austin brothers, Edwin Barton and some others. We left them our powder and shot, which was ample for a few men. At the top of the valley, Swain Corliss turned back, cursing some of us who had begun to run. 'Save your horses first, boys, and, if you can, your women!' He was drunk. Many of us did not stop till we reached home, which is why they sometimes call this the Battle of the Foot Race.

Swain Corliss hailed from a family of violent Baptists with farms on the Boston Creek about three miles from Malcolm's. His brother Ashur had been wounded thirteen times in the war and had stood his ground at Lundy's Lane, which Swain had missed on account of ague. Swain did not much like his brother getting ahead of him like that.

He had a Brown Bess musket and a long-barrelled dragoon pistol his father had bought broken from an officer. He turned at the top of the hill and started down into the racket of lead and Indian shouts. Musket balls swarmed round McCall's company like bees, some stinging. Swain took up a position against a tree, guarding the flank, and started flinging lead back. Edwin Barton, shot through the thighs, loaded for him. Men kept getting up to leave, and Captain McCall would whack them over the shoulders with the flat of his sword.

Swain Corliss, pounding a rock into the barrel of his gun with a wooden mallet, kept saying, 'Boys, she may be rough, but she sure is regular.'

Bees stung him.

That night, his father dreaming, dreamed a bee stung him in the throat and knew. Swain Corliss was catching up to Ashur. He killed a Kentucky private coming over the creek on a cart horse. Then Swain Corliss shot the horse. Smoke emerged from the mill. Mrs Malcom ran around in a circle, fanning the smoke with a linen cloth. (*Thunk, thunk, buzz, buzz* went the balls.) Though we were running, we were with them. It was our boys fighting in the hollow. Colonel Bostwick sat on his race horse, Governor, at the top of the track.

The company gave ground, turning to fire every few yards. Martin Boughner tied a handkerchief to his ramrod and surrendered to an Indian. Swain Corliss tied up Edwin Barton's legs with his homespun shirt. Deaf from the guns, they had to shout.

'By the Jesus, Ned, I do believe it ain't hard to kill them when they stand around you like this.'

'I mind a whore I knew in Chappawa—'

'Ned, I wished you'd stop bleeding so freely. I think they have kilt you.'

'Yes.'

They were in another place, a region of black light and maximum density. On the road, sweating with shame in the cold, we heard the muskets dwindle and go out. We saw Swain Corliss, white-faced, slumped against an oak amongst the dead smouldering leaves, Edwin's head in his lap, without a weapon except for his bayonet, which he held across his chest as Kickapoo warriors came up one by one, reverently touching Swain's shoulders with their musket barrels.

The Kentuckians had lost one dead, eight wounded and a couple of borrowed horses. That day, they burned the mill and one downstream and sent out patrols to catch stragglers, which they did, and then released after making them promise on the Good Book not to shoot at another person from the United States. The Indians skinned and butchered Edwin Barton's body, Ned having no further use for it.

During the night, three miles away, James Corliss dreamed that a venomous bee had stung him in the throat. Rising from his bed, he told the family, 'Yonder, yer baby boy is dead or something.' Then James Corliss went out into the darkness, hitched his horse to a stoneboat, placed a feather tick, pillows and sheets upon it, and started for the scene of the battle.

MARGARET GIBSON

(1948)

∿

Making It

Sat. Nov. 11/74

Dear Bette,

Did you fumble your way up the long staircase with eyeless fingers (because you are so unused to your condition), did you make it to the softness of the bed where you will lie down accepting the darkness? Come and get me, come and get me. I accept this last defeat. The violins play. Or are you someone else today? Joan Crawford married to a lunatic, the leaves falling to the ground, dusting the surface. I know who you are but I will pretend I don't just to confuse anyone else who might read this letter. Maybe I should tear it up into tiny bits and swallow it so no one but me will ever know who you are. All that matters is that you know who you are. That is something I could never master. Alice in Wonderland—and who-o are you? Steel snowflakes fall up here, so far away from you in Carnival Country. Is God in the snowflakes? I am looking for a God. It seems a sensible thing to do now that I am going to have this baby. I must have something mysterious to believe in, not just concrete and glass and huge filing cabinets that touch the sky, so today I will say that God is in the snowflakes. Yesterday he was Caliban. Tomorrow if the snow is gone I will assume that God is dead—again. Perhaps he is always Caliban.

The public health nurse comes to visit me twice a week. Oh Robin, how proud you would be of me, I function. Yes, really. Mondays at two, Thursdays at 4.15. She comes to the door brushing snow from her black boots and her old blue coat (perhaps they're not paid too well for visiting people like me). Her briefcase full of my brains and the brains of others like me bulges under her arm. I smile and take her coat and tell her to please sit down.

Of course I no longer have to tell her to please sit down, she has been coming here for so long she just automatically sits in the red chair by the mantel-piece, her heavy thighs filling the chair as mine have never done. I go to the kitchen and make her coffee, no sugar but a little cream. We sit by the electric fire and she smiles and I smile and we drink our coffee over the open folder. 'And how are things going today, Liza?' She no longer calls me Miss, we are too intimate with the things in that open folder. I answer, quite well and the baby is moving a lot now. I do not tell her that God may be

Caliban or in the snowflakes, she would tell my psychiatrist immediately. And so much depends on these weekly checks. They say it's because I am alone and have a history of mental illness (why not say insanity—crazed, burnt-out skull? No, only mental illness). They say that's why they come and check on me but it is really to see if I am acting crazy and then they could take the baby away from me but I will not let that happen, Robin. As long as I *function* they are powerless. I keep this flat on the top floor of the farmhouse spotless so the nurse can't write listless and sloppy on her report and I make sure the coffee is always hot but not too hot so that it might seem that I am trying to scald her. There are so many things one learns about functioning. She stays for an hour each time, the folder spread open across her heavy legs, sometimes making notations. We talk of chemo-therapy and my decorations for the nursery. I have manoeuvred her into the conversations of the general. I am safe. She tells me as she leaves that I am doing very well and I smile again (but not a very large smile—I do not want to be put down as manic) and I say good-bye and see you next time. Oh, I am clever. I can see her now getting on the Scarborough bus, knocking the snow from her boots, clutching her briefcase full of brains, pleased with my progress. Hugo is fine and I—I am surviving. Make lots of money out there in Carnival Country and write soon, yours is the only mail I get except for coupons. The snow is in a deep blanket now. I would like to run outside and lie in the snow and make an angel but I am afraid I would just lie there and lie there letting the frozen sheet cover me and then it would all be over and no one would find me for days and days.

Love, Liza

PS. Has the Great Divider got you yet?

Love, love Liza

Wed. Nov. 15/74

Dear Liza,
I read your letter twice, as usual. I have to read all your letters twice in spite of the fact that I lived with you a few years. Maybe I don't know you any better than anyone else does, it may be just a vanity I allow myself. I am booked at Caesar's for the next three weeks and then on to San Francisco where I will send you an address where you can reach me. There is not much left to my life but my career and your letters. I hardly ever see the days any more and there is just enough time to have a drink in a salute to Judy on the other side of that rainbow and then it is off to rehearsals and more rehearsals. You would not like it out here in LA. This is no place to dream and you are so addicted to dreaming. It suits me fine for I have no need of dreams, no time to dream. I must concentrate on one thing—making it is what it is all about and that is what I intend to do, make it. I have added Shirley Bassey, Ella

Fitzgerald and several other black performers to my act. They seem to be going over well. When I got into this business I swore I would be the best female impersonator ever, beyond comparison, and I have five years to make it in and if I don't I will probably be rattling those beads in John Rechy's book. But make it I must.

I don't know why you would search for God in a snowflake. I think it is most unoriginal of you, but to say that God is Caliban, that's my Liza. You never did tell me who the father of the baby is. Why did he leave you like that in that old farm house? Perhaps I am the only one who could tolerate your craziness but I could never have been what you wanted me to be. I did not choose what I am any more than you did but it was a pleasant dream that you entertained, you and I touching, maybe I am guilty of entertaining it too. We saw each other in various stages of undress, you in your nightgown, you in the bath soaking a scarred arm, me in the shower, and yet we never touched. It is a hard fact of our lives that such a thing would have been impossible and yet I know you were never glad when one of my lovers left me, you were always sad for me, perhaps sadder than I myself was. You collect lame things Liza, just like your awful cat, Hugo. I have never seen such an ugly cat but you caress him as if he came from an Egyptian tomb. I am writing this in my dressing-room, which is littered with jars of make-up and cream and wigs and gowns and plastic coffee cups with cigarette butts floating in them. It is not much different from those dressing-rooms at the gay bars up in Toronto, although it is larger. What would Miss Carr say if she knew you carried on correspondence with me, a homosexual, a female impersonator (what was that awful book—*The Twilight People?*) You had better keep quiet on that score, she may think you are imagining pathos where there is none. Keep taking your medication and who is the Great Divider?

Love, Robin

Dear Robin,
Marvin came to visit me last Monday. For a moment when I heard the door I thought it was Miss Carr come very early. No one but her ever comes here. It was so early, though, I decided it couldn't be Miss Carr and so I put on a different face than the one that warms Miss Carr with my coffee and my health. It was nine a.m. when he knocked on the door. I knew it was Marvin as soon as I started down the stairs. I could see his black hair sticking up like wild grass and weeds. He was crouching inside the screen door away from the wind in a thin black coat and he had no boots, still being the ghetto Jew, a part he likes very much. He had a mickey of rye in a brown paper bag. He said that he had come to talk to me about his camps and his latest communiqués from Mao because no one else would listen, not even his psychiatrist. I felt very sorry for him. It is so important to Marvin to have someone to listen to his newest plans for these world-wide concentration camps. At first, at the hospital when I was there with him everyone listened, what a find for

psychiatry! Concentration camps with rose gardens and communion with Mao. But now no one takes him seriously any longer—he has talked about it too much—and so they released him from the hospital on maintenance care even though I know that Marvin is going to kill someone some day. It's in those beads you were talking about.

We sat in the kitchen. I moved the heater in (God, this place gets cold in the winter) and Marvin and I poured rye into our coffee. He was, as usual, wearing eye-liner to make his eyes look more Oriental. Under his greasy wild black hair and low forehead his eyes looked like two black marbles, glass. He was wearing a short-sleeved blue shirt and blue jeans with Superman written on them in magic marker. I looked at his arms, I am always surprised not to see a number there like his parents have and all the people who work in his father's textile factory. He said that Hugo would look better stuffed and put his hands around Hugo's throat but Hugo is clever and escaped his grasp. He wanted me to go into Toronto with him and since it only takes half an hour by bus I said all right. I put on my brown corduroy maternity pants and a long-sleeved red top to keep warm since I can no longer do my coat up. We had one more shot of rye in our coffee and left.

On the bus Marvin put up his protective invisible shield and he began to talk about the camps and the messages from Mao. No one can hear through the protective invisible shield. He told me that Mao said he would be Superman of the world by 1976 (Marvin that is) and told Marvin how pleased he was with his ideas for the camps. Mao also thinks that Marvin would be very helpful in the border dispute between Russia and China. Marvin has it all figured out. He is going to put the Chinese into the camps. I asked him how he would get so many millions of people in and he said he would pretend the camps were full of capitalists on display like a zoo and the Chinese would be free to visit and throw stones at the capitalists and puncture their ear drums with chopsticks and that they would all come as they haven't much else to do. Of course Marvin is still going to have his gardens leading to the massive camps, with roses and daisies, and the Chinese would think it quite nice until they found that the gardens were actually part of the camps and meant to trap them. The point of it all, Marvin said, is that if all the Russians and Chinese are in camps there would be no border dispute. Marvin says that Mao does not like the Chinese people much anyway even though Mao is Chinese. Marvin suspects that he might have been baptized a Catholic with a little bit of holy water and a prayer. Capitalists, Russians, Chinese are all going to be in the camps, very few people are going to escape, Marvin said.

I was wondering why the insides of buses always look like winter even when it is not winter. I think it is the yellow light that does that. Marvin has promised me that the baby and I will not be put in a camp once he becomes Superman. Marvin is very fond of me in his own neuter way. I asked him if he had ever read Nietzsche and he said no and I believe him. Marvin showed me some writings in his note book, messages from Mao but I could not understand the languages. I know it is Marvin's own secret language. He said of course I couldn't understand it because it was in code. People on the bus were looking at us. What a strange pair, me with my stomach ballooning out, Marvin with his eye make-up, and I don't believe that the protective shield does a proper job. I do not deny its existence. If Marvin believes it exists then it exists. A is not really absolute.

We had a coke in a restaurant near the textile factory and Marvin drank half a bottle of vinegar to show me his superhuman powers and then we went over to the factory. Nothing has changed, everyone is sitting or standing exactly where they were when I was last there eight months or was it more ago? Row on row of numbered arms like the numbered pieces of a puzzle. That puzzle is what made Marvin. While Marvin was stealing money from the Coke machine his father asked me if I would like a cigarette. I took one and he lit it. I thought of the numbers scorched into his skin. 'Liza,' he said, 'you're a good girl, a smart girl. Tell me, I do not understand, why is Marvin like this, so—so strange?'

'I don't know,' I said even though I did know. It is because of the puzzle of seared flesh.

'We taught him right from wrong, we were gentle, if our pain has been passed on to him it is because of our heritage. Life is pain. Pain is life. Someone said that once. It is true Liza. We did not do it consciously.' Look around you, I thought.

'They let him out of the hospital,' I said.

'Yes, yes, that is true but he has no friends, he has never had any friends but you.' I looked around at the women bent over their sewing machines, the men at the cutting machines, all I could see were numbers.

'Does Marvin ever talk to you?' I asked.

'No,' he said softly, 'no, never.' Marvin had managed to steal the money from the Coke machine and was coming toward us ready to leave. 'Do you think Marvin is getting better? Isn't that why they let him out of the hospital?'

'Yes,' I said, 'yes, that's why.'

'Why did you take me to your father's factory? Why do you go?' I asked him on the bus ride back.

'To see how much more splendid my camps will be than theirs,' he said. Lest we forget, I thought but said nothing.

'They have ovens at the hospital,' Marvin said. I had heard this before. 'They put lobotomies in them,' and he smiled.

'I know Marvin, I know about that already.' I suppose I hurt his feelings by being so short with him, he really does like to talk about the ovens at the hospital but I had heard it many times before. I was thinking about Catholic schoolgirls who wear blue ribbons on their slips in honour of the Virgin's purity. I thought Marvin should wear one. He is really so pure, like a child, but no one can see that but me. I left Marvin in an empty park. He said he was getting another communiqué from Mao and had to concentrate. I was glad for it. I did not want Marvin to try and strangle Hugo again.

Marvin asks about you. He remembers you very well. Remember when he and I escaped the hospital once and came to the apartment for a drink and later Marvin, very drunk, kissed for the first and last time. Marvin who admires perfection so much, Marvin encased in his ragged, bony body remembers your physical grace, your hair, blonde like an archangel's and your green eyes and how you danced that night jumping high into the air, touching the ceiling with your fingertips. Oh, how Marvin remembers you and I'm sure he hopes you have kind thoughts of him, which you don't but I do not tell him to the contrary. He is easily hurt.

What should I name the baby? Everything must be labelled but I do not want to name it Christ or Flower or any of those names that are so in vogue, meant to be prophetic but succeeding merely in being cute in a boring way. Hugo just looks like Hugo, large and bruised, he was easy to name but a baby lacks substance, is thin and vapour-like in my mind. What do I call it? If you can think of any names that are not too cute or clever please write them down and send them to me. The Great Divider lives in the void, burnishing our bones.

Love, Liza

Tues. Dec. 12/74

Dear Liza,

Sorry to be so late in replying but I have been very busy with rehearsals and more rehearsals. I barely have time left in the late afternoon to salute Judy with a drink. Enclosed are some publicity shots and newspaper clippings of Tallulah and Friends. I'm sorry you have been receiving nothing but coupons in your mail for three weeks. I am writing this from my hotel room in San Francisco. Tallulah, Peggy, Mae, Shirley and Ella have all gone over very well in this town. See enclosed reviews.

My life is really not any more exciting than your, Liza, despite publicity and hotels and room service. My lover for the evening just left half an hour ago. I will probably not see him again. His name was Eric (was already, just half an hour later). I met him in a bar with my managers after the last show. He was very flattering in the bar and insisted on buying me a drink and said over and over again how much he loved the show and how talented I was, and so to bed (remember that dreadful movie we saw once?—it was raining and I picked you up from the hospital and we went to that cheap film where you burnt me with a cigarette, by accident you said). He was disappointed. It didn't go very well. He wanted to sleep with one of the girls. Peggy maybe or bourbon-voiced Tallulah but I had nothing to offer him but Robin. He said—why can't you be real? I said I am being real. And he said, like shit and put his clothes on and left. Only you know that I am real or when I am real. It is ironic, isn't it, that it takes a crazy Liza to know reality from fiction. Raining here, God, what a night. Cigarette ashes on the sheets.

I don't have unkind thoughts about Marvin, I just think he is dangerous and you yourself said you know some day he is going to kill someone. Why make yourself the victim of his fantasies? Remember Ken? He is now a she. He scrimped and saved for seven years and finally got the operation in New York. He was never really the type to be gay anyway. He will make a much better woman, not that I want an operation like that, I am not happy being what I am—a fag, a queer etc., etc. Whatever name you use it all comes down to the same thing, futility. At least I have this career and it is going well. I could not be a woman, homosexuality is branded into me like the scars on your arm or the numbers on the people in Marvin's father's textile factory. It is the only thing I know to be. I am not the fine physical specimen you remember, I have been drinking too much and it is going to fat and so I must get off the bottle and lose weight again. Why don't you tell me who the Great Divider is and who the father of your child is?

Love, Robin

Fri. Dec. 15/74

Dear Tallulah and Company,
Wiped the sleep from my eyes and there was your letter in the mail box. Remember once at the apartment on O'Connor I had just gotten up and was in the kitchen making coffee and you came in and said sleepy seeds and wiped my eyes as if I were a child? It is a pleasant memory that I have captured in a two-dimensional frame, unchanging. Time passes but the memories captured in the frames do not diminish. There is another memory caught in that two dimensional frame—I see three things clearly—you are standing in the doorway of our apartment, drunk, your head is thrown back in a laugh that is really a scream because someone from New York has called you a disease, the bare electric light bulb makes your face pale and cavernous and you stand under it, your head thrown back, laughing. There are memories best forgotten but it is there, ever present on the two-dimensional frame within my cranium.

Thank you for the cheque but I don't really need it, Family Benefits pays the rent and buys the food but now with your cheque I can buy something nice for Hugo (a catnip mouse?) and some things for the baby. The baby exits somewhere beyond me, it seems to be a separate entity, the balloon in front of me has nothing to do with it. I would like to believe that it came from under a cabbage plant or that the stork left it in my mailbox and that nothing ever happened but since God is Caliban it cannot be that way and remains a big balloon before me. I am sorry that Eric did not think you real but he is no great loss, anyway that doesn't know the fine line between reality and fantasy is a fool. Remember that one night you put on huge furry mittens and pretended you were a gorilla eating pillows and throwing fruit and papers all over the living-room and then charging after me—I was Fay Wray and you were King Kong and I was laughing but I was frightened too, that is understanding reality. I never told anyone that you were a gorilla. I know that it would embarrass you, you want everyone to think that the only humour in you is cynical and that you are light years removed from jumping on chairs and couches with your arms swinging low making gorilla sounds. Who would I tell anyway. Miss Carr? Marvin? Neither of them would understand it and how bright and real you were being a gorilla. The father of this baby is not as real as your gorilla. Wouldn't it be better for us if we went through life having a series of affairs that meant nothing to us and after each one lay alone and safe and chaste on clean pillows, absent of cigarette ashes? Caring is what ruins us.

I went to the doctor's yesterday afternoon. I hate sitting in that waiting room with all those other swollen women. They all look at each other and smile, their smiles saying—we are one, we are one, we have those swollen bellies in common. I never smile back. I am not one of them. It is as if they all have some secret and no one will tell me what it is. So secretive and separate from men, the urine specimen in little aspirin bottles tucked safely away in their purses with their compacts and their hairpins, the support stockings and the back aches. I am a heathen. I never wear support stockings and go barefoot throught the flat. Sometimes I forget my urine specimen on purpose.

Dr Johnston beamed down at me and said everything was going very smoothly and afterward we sat in his office, he too is curator of my brain. You'd be proud, Robin. I *function* there too. He tapped his pipe ashtray and asked me how did I feel and how was I getting on with Miss Carr and that the latest report from my psychiatrist was very good. They are all fools, I've been going to psychiatrists since before I even knew how to spell psychiatrist and it is so easy to fool them all but I could never fool you, Robin. He told me not to smoke so much and then he released me back out into the waiting room again, the swollen women giving me secretive smiles. I hate their conspiracy over the misshapen bellies. They are all children with a grown-up secret tucked inside their stomachs. Children playing a grown-up game. I never wanted to grow up and know all the terrible things that I know but I am 23 and I've known so many dark and terrible things for so long, sometimes I cover my eyes so that I can't hear any more. You would never do anything like that Robin, if anyone looks hell straight in the eye it is you.

I went to Anne's after the doctor's. I did not want to go but it had been so long—a year I think and for some reason she phoned me and insisted so much over the phone that I come and see her that I finally relented. She is living in a very small but expensive apartment near Yonge Street. She said to me when she first saw me, you're so big, and touched my stomach with her palm. I recoiled. We drank vodka and orange juice and she talked on and on about furniture, about suede couches and fur carpets and marble tables and how I just must get some new furniture for my apartment when she knows very well that I can just make the rent and buy food with my cheques. Anne says that you are merely acting out your sickness through your nightclub act like the way Fellini puts his sickness on the screen. I said I did not think that was so and she smiled over her two-dollar glass and said I had always idolized you too much and that you should have seen a shrink (her words) long ago but that it was far too late for you now. I said then—my legs are still better than yours even though I'm pregnant and she said—you never could concentrate on any one subject for long, could you Liza and gave me a horrible smile. You're full of crap, I said and smiled and put on my coat and left Anne in her 230-dollar-a-month apartment. I don't know why she dislikes you so. I remember once she made you cry. It was a strange cry, like laughter, just like your laughter had been a scream and I put my arms around you and you pressed your golden head against my small breasts and there was laughter from the other room. We didn't come out of the bathroom for a long time and when we did come out you were smiling and you began to dance in front of Anne, a ritualistic dance and it frightened her, which is what you meant to do. When she told you to stop you smiled and said—why darling I'm just dancing for you, for you my darling. Aren't you entertained by it all? You were magnificent in your hate. Incandescent.

The Great Divider is bone-splitting. Have a drink of bourbon for me, Tallulah and don't push any wheelchairs down the staircase. Write soon. I have coupons for Maxim coffee, and Puss and Boots cat food, and for Downy fabric softener but I don't have you.

Love, Liza

Tues. Dec. 19/74

Dear Liza,
How sweet of you dau-ling to remember how I transfixed all those lovely, lovely people in *The Little Foxes*. Clever girl! Remember that tape we made of *Whatever Happened To Baby Jane?* I have it still, your laughter whirling out from the tape at the most dramatic moments in the movie. We played all the parts through the night right down to Victor Buono's and into the early morning and drunk with wearinss we began to dance and I painted a blue flower on your breast. You were laughing and danced in the open window much to the delight of the two male occupants across from us. Your psychiatrist would never believe how carefree you could be or that I was a gorilla—what crazy secrets we have!

I saw the most beautiful man last night. I was Peggy singing 'Is That All There Is,' and sitting in the front at a table a little over to the left was the beautiful man with three companions, two women and another man. I sang the song straight to their table and afterward he took a rose from the vase on the table and threw it on stage. I will never know if he was gay or not, he left directly after the show with his companions. Women are no guarantee that a guy is straight—look at all the places you and I went together (what did you call us—Gazelle and Pan) and we lived together for three years but if I am straight then my mother was a transvestite (maybe she was, who knows—I never saw her, just a bundle of joy left on someone's doorstep in a makeup bag). Enough about that. The less I can remember of dear old Uncle Rodney the better.

You and I are monks. Every night I drive back to the hotel in the half dusk of morning from my last show and I enter my hotel room alone. There is no trace of humanness anywhere. I pour myself a drink, sitting on the sterile bed that the maid has made up and then I take a shower to wash off the sweat and the makeup, put on my bathrobe and sit once again thinking what shall I do now. I listen a while to the piped-in music and I think—I could die tonight in this hotel room with the blue carpeting and sterile bed and disposable bath mats and the music would play on and on and no one would miss me or know that I was dead, except maybe you, Liza and my managers who want their cut. A twenty-pound-overweight fag found dead in a terrycloth bathrobe with 'Jesus Christ Superstar' playing on and on in the room like you and your snow angel. When I get too old (40) a large bottle of barbiturates will take care of it all. Unlike Peggy I am ready for that final disappointment or will be when the wrinkles begin to spread like a fine cobweb across my face.

Why did you go to see Anne? It was very stupid of you. You know her only pleasure in life is making other people uncomfortable and miserable. She should write a book on all her opinions on Life and and People and bore herself to death in the process. Keep away from her. She owns all that expensive furniture and apartment simply because she would disappear without them. Fade away. Have another drink, Tallulah. Morning is coming, heavy and warm. God, Liza I get so tired sometimes with it all but making it is what it's all about or I will be just one of the faceless legions of fags—no future and a past etched in the worry lines on my brow. You have them too, though not as bad as mine. When your face is in repose I cannot see them at all. Is this what it's all about? Jars of cream and makeup and hot lights and coffee cups with cigarette butts in them and singing and singing and talking and talking until your voice is scratchy—making it. You would say that I am trying to get in touch with my humanness but it is nothing so complicated. I don't want to die an old fag alone, without lovers, without a certain amount of respect, I want to say—I made it once, me. I made it. Don't you want to make it Liza? I am tired of being always less than good in the world's eyes. So tired. I should have another drink in a salute to Judy on the other side of that rainbow, my final salute for this long day. Remember, one day we will all be on the other side of that rainbow with Judy.

PS. If it's a girl name her Vanessa because you look like Vanessa Redgrave, if it's a boy name him Michael. Why does the Great Divider burnish our bones? Is it just our bones or everybody's?

Love, Robin

Sun. Dec. 24/74

Dear Robin,

I hate to hear you sounding so discouraged over everything. You told me that making it is what it's all about and even if that means sterile hotel rooms with disposable bath mats and loneliness you must hang in there. I think it's because it is the Christmas season, Christmas here tomorrow, and Christmas has never been one of our better times. We did have a couple of nice Christmases though. The year we stole a Christmas tree from the cemetery, remember how we raced between the graves, you clutching an axe, anxiety the hand-maiden only adding to our excitement, danger close at hand. We must have been in the cemetery for a couple of hours sawing and cutting at the tree and our fingers were frozen and finally we got the tree into the car only to see a police cruiser barrelling down on us and we jumped into the car and you drove like a crazy man until we finally lost the cruiser. We hadn't laughed so much in a long time. Oh, I know there have been the bad Christmases too without any presents or a tree and you and I sitting in the empty living-room trying to be casual and flip about the whole thing, but just hang onto the good Christmases.

The other nice Christmas was when we stayed up all night packing in antcipation of the move to a larger apartment, I was feeling good on my pills and whisky and you were feeling good just on the whisky. We found so many old photos, you as a young adolescent, me as a child of four with my dog but that night the past did not bother us, it was good to exchange those photos and old letters back and forth. That was a good Christmas even if we didn't have a tree because we were so close to each other with our old memories. Don't go out on me now, we have something, you have your career and I have this baby—baby Vanessa or baby Michael. I won't have to be alone anymore. I have been alone since you left for LA, over a year ago. No one else could live with me. No one else would lie on the bed with me and help me push back the bone-crushers with the palms of their hands using all their strength as you did for me that one night. I know you couldn't see Them but you knew that They were crushing me and so you helped push Them away. I think They must have been afraid of you. I would know if you were dead. I would be hollowed out. Then the Great Divider would get me for sure.

Marvin has run away from home. His father phoned me last night to see if I knew where he was. I don't know where he is but I know that he has run away from home so he can kill somebody without having to face the Talmud in the living-room bookcase afterwards. If only people had listened to Marvin, had listened to his endless plans for the camps and about his being Superman. It's the ones that don't talk that they keep locked up in hospitals, like me. There was a man, Graham, in the first hospital I was sent to, the place you called the Southern Plantation because of the huge dripping green trees. It had thick stone walls and barred windows that look fragile for all the work that was put into their construction. Graham didn't speak much. He had been there ten years the year I arrived. Graham had raped two little girls but he said he was only helping them fix their bicycle chains and that is all he would ever say about it to anyone. I used to talk to him sometimes in OT. Day after day Graham would make little ships, tiny ships to go into bottles with sails and bows and tiny windows, he worked for hours on his perfect little ships, talking to them as if they were his children. The other thing Graham was doing was studying psychiatry but mostly he worked on his ships. Once he said to me—I was only fixing their bicycle chains—and then stopped abruptly. I looked at his beautiful hands, long and pale and slender, that made beautiful miniature ships. I could not imagine bicycle grease on them but I could imagine those hands around a small, pale throat. Graham said, 'But it does. No one will believe me, not even my mother. Isn't this ship beautiful? You know last night I dreamt of you. I dreamt of your pelvis bones, tiny like a child's.' He smiled and I thought how pure his hands looked working on the tiny mast, how delicate and pure. Graham never said much more after that, maybe if he had talked on and on like Marvin . . . Graham could wear a blue ribbon on his pale fingers.

What will Marvin do away from home? He has no money and it's bitter cold out and he has been gone since yesterday wandering around in his thin black coat, without boots. Perhaps if he is set on killing someone he will not feel the cold or maybe his invisible protective shield will keep him warm. Don't worry, Robin, it will not be me who is his victim, he is fond of me and a little afraid of me.

The father of this baby is nothing, he has less substance than the frost on the windowpane. He was a taxi-cab driver who drove me to my psychiatrist's once and asked afterward if he could come up and see me. I said all right. Like you and Eric he did not think me real. I did not like him at all. He drew grotesque half faces on pieces of paper, faces of bilious yellow and green, something out of a nightmare. He would come here with a cheap bottle of wine and all through the few evenings we spent together he would ask me if I was on acid. I was not real to him and I didn't like him for the half faces littering the kitchen table. He was thin, emaciated, with a face like a mad saint and one night we went to bed because I was alone and didn't care and you were gone. We only went to bed a few times and then I had had enough of his green and yellow faces and his sweaty body and I told him I didn't want to see him again. He began to cry and I hated him even more and then he picked up a chair and said he was going to put it through the window and use the broken glass to slash his wrists if I didn't change my mind. 'I love you,' he said. 'Don't bleed on my floor,' and I turned away and lit a cigarette. 'I'll do it! I'll do it!' He reminded me a bit of Rasputin, only without the glory and the power. 'If you do you'll have to clean up the blood.' He began to wail and Hugo attacked his foot (Hugo doesn't like excessive noise) and finally, still weeping, he left and I have never seen him or his yellow cab again. I think that he will die soon. He had a cough that could rival Camille's. He does not know about the baby and that's the way I want it, and it's better that way. He couldn't even help financially. I went to his place once, it was two rooms and smelt of old soup and damp mattresses. I do not even remember his name. Hugo and I are very glad he's gone. Hugo hated him and so did I.

The baby is my future. I will prove something to the Great Divider and then he won't be able to get me any more than he already has. The Great Divider is what made you and me. He is bone splitting. He is what kept us away and apart from other people. You could not divide the he-she in your being and I—I could not stop the bone splitting, dividing into nightmares and hallucinations and breathing floors. Somewhere in the void you and I met, walking and wounded and collapsed into each other's arms but we cannot give in to him now, to his pile of bones, split asunder, he would be the winner if we gave in, right now we hang on by the edge of our teeth. The baby will have me a few steps removed from the Great Divider and so will your career. I will no longer hear his laughter rippling just beneath the surface of my skin. Don't you see, the Great Divider is Defeat, the Defeat we were born with and now we have a chance to out-distance him and we must. You're right, making it is what it's all about. The baby's nursery is all set up with the money you sent me, a white bassinet and animals and little sleepers and shirts and a little going-to-school outfit and a chest of drawers. Soon, soon, I will be making it too.

Love, love Liza

Wed. Dec. 27/74

Dear Liza

The mail arrived this morning just as I was about to hit the bed and I've been thinking all morning. It seems silly that we two should live alone when we really don't have to. I have enough money to get you and the baby a ticket to LA and my career is going better and better. We could share an apartment here. It wouldn't be much trouble to get a three-bedroom, a room for each of us and I know I don't know the first thing about being a father but maybe I could be like an uncle to the baby and I know how to make people laugh. You could bring Hugo too, of course. It may be a crazy idea but I don't see why it couldn't work out. If you think I would be a bad influence on the baby write and let me know, I would understand, after all being homosexual and everything . . . Write soon,

Love, Robin

PS. I understand about the Great Divider now. He is really the God who made us human wrecks in such a gleeful fashion. Don't worry, the Great Divider won't get us into his void and burnish our split bones for all eternity, as you said we both have something to live for. And really I will understand if you don't want to come to LA. What kind of father would I be anyway. I bought a teddy bear for the baby and I will either keep it here or send it on, depending on your answer—it seems to me that children should not have to sleep alone too. The bear's name is Satchmo, who I have just recently added to my act.

Mon. Jan. 1/75

Dear Robin,

Yes, yes, yes. The baby, Vanessa or Michael is due in two more weeks. I am huge with it. Maybe you could be a gorilla for the baby. It will be easy to give up my apartment as I have no lease. See you soon. The Great Divider is conquered.

Love, love Liza

Sat. Jan. 6/75

Dear Liza,

Am back in LA frantically searching for a three-room apartment with a decent view and a nice, bright room for a nursery and a good kitchen. You used to make the most terrific chili. I saw the most beautiful man the other day and he offered to buy a drink but I said no—there is no time for that right now. I also bought the baby a Winnie the Pooh record. I don't know if kids like that sort of thing but the man in the record shop assured me they did. I never had any Winnie the Pooh records or anything like that so I don't really know, my foster parents weren't exactly generous. What is a layette? I was talking to a stripper I know and she said, well, of course the kid will need a layette and since I didn't want to appear stupid in front of a dumb, shooting-up-with-speed stripper, I didn't ask her what it was. So busy, we have cheated the Great Divider. See you soon.

Love, Robin

Thurs. Jan 11/75

Dear Robin,

A layette is clothing for the baby like a white gown and booties. Vanessa was born dead.

Love, Liza

Dear Liza,

KATHERINE GOVIER
(1948)

∽

Sociology

On the porch Ellen stood without looking behind her, like a pack horse at a crossing where she'd stopped many times before. Alec came up the steps: she heard the clinking as his hands sorted the keys from the change in his pocket. Then she heard a low, drawling voice.

'You folks stay right where you are, and this gun ain't going off. You keep right on looking at that door.'

She supposed it was time this happened. Their house was in what you called a transition area: you couldn't afford to buy there any more, but you weren't supposed to live there yet. Ellen enjoyed living there, however. She was morbidly fascinated by the differences in circumstances between themselves and the next-door neighbour who sat on his steps after dark and raised Newfoundland fishing songs to the sky. It fit with her view of the world, which was that as close as your hand were people who were not as lucky as you and therefore would like to kill you.

The man with the gun came up the stairs. He found Alec's wallet and took it. He took Ellen's purse. He asked for Alec's watch. The watch was gold with a gold band; it had been his father's, awarded for the forty years' work in the factory in Quebec. Having died two months after retirement, his father had never worn it. When Alec reached 21 without a cigarette, his mother added the gold band and gave it to her only son. Wordlessly, Alec snapped it off his wrist and handed it over. Ellen groaned. Then the gunman got greedy.

'Your jewellery too,' he said. He took a handful of Ellen's hair and pulled it back to see if she was wearing earrings. She wasn't. She had only a couple of rings, her wedding band and one other, which was a pearl she'd gotten for her sixteenth birthday. Earlier that month the pearl had become tight, and she had switched it to a smaller finger. Now she pulled and got it off. The wedding ring was hopeless.

'I can't get it off,' she said to the mugger. 'My fingers are swollen because I'm pregnant.'

She looked him in the eye as she said the word pregnant. She felt she had never been in such danger; she had to enunciate the point of greatest risk. She was testing. It had been her fantasy during these last months that she would run into one of those maniacs who shot pregnant women in the belly or cut them open with a knife.

But the mugger looked back at her with a disinterested rage. Perhaps he would shoot her finger off and get the ring that way. It was still early in the evening, however, and a man was walking by only fifteen feet away, so the mugger just snarled and ran off.

Ellen and Alec attended pre-natal classes in a boys' gymnasium in Cabbagetown. Alongside nine other pregnant women Ellen lay on the gym floor on a blanket brought from home and practised breathing patterns to prepare herself for labour. Her head on the pink and blue flowered pillow-case from their bedroom, she raised her hips and lowered them again; the water balloon that was her stomach went up and down. Then she got on hands and knees and Alec rolled tennis balls on her back as she humped it up and down like a dog trying to vomit. The idea was to make the birth natural.

They kept this up for six consecutive Thursdays. On the whole Ellen was disappointed in the classes. It was not the material so much as the other people. She'd thought their common predicament would promote instant friendship, but it had not. This was not for lack of effort on the part of the instructor, Riva, who used the word 'share' frequently. By the end they would develop a limited closeness, like that of people stuck together in a train which was liable to go off the tracks. But where they came from, where they would go afterward would not be mentioned.

Ellen tried to pin down some information. She learned that Gloria and Ted were born-agains. She divined that Miriam was at least forty and was not married to the man she came with. She explained them to Alec, who disapproved of her curiosity. The only ones she could not explain were Robert and June.

June was tall with blonde hair and moved hesitantly, but gracefully. Her eyes were cloudy blue. Sometimes the irises darted back and forth as if panicked, but Ellen did not believe she saw anything at all, not even light and shadow, because of the way she held her head. The way she held her head was the best part about her. Her carriage was like that of a large and elegant bird, her head alert and still as if she were listening for an alarm. Her seeing-eye dog lay at her feet, so devoted that he made the husband look like a redundancy. Robert was thickset, pimply, and sullen, and he watched June all the time.

June gave what the rest withheld; she laughed, she talked her fear. Ellen remembered best the day she sat on her metal stacking chair like an oracle, transparent eyelids showing the darting of sightless eyes. 'I can't believe it's me who's pregnant,' she said. 'I suppose because I've never seen myself.'

But isn't that what it's like, Ellen thought.

On the last night of class they watched a film of natural childbirth. Someone had brought popcorn, and they stared at the screen, silently passing the bucket. In the dark room Ellen could hear Robert's nasal voice very softly telling June what was being shown. 'The baby is coming out of the mother's body,' he said. Ellen and Alec both cried. Ellen thought that most of the other people in the class did too. She didn't know for sure though because when the lights went up, she didn't want to look too closely at their faces.

Riva packed the projector, and the women and their supporters made ready to leave. Swollen feet pushed back into bulging shoes, knees poked out to ten and two o'clock as legs strained to lift the immobile trunks. Stomachs first, they walked; the hard, heavy egg shapes pushing flesh away from the centre up to chest, arms, puffing the cheeks. Eyes red from strain, the ten making each other seem more grotesque than ever, the women made ready to go alone into the perilous future.

In the hospital, Ellen forgot all about her childbirth training and began screaming for an anaesthetic. The baby was two weeks late and labour was being induced by a drug. 'This baby must like you a lot,' said the doctor, turning up the dose again. 'He doesn't want to be born.' When he came, he wasn't breathing, so the nurse grabbed him and ran down the hall. 'My mother always said the cord around the neck meant they're lucky,' said Alec. Ellen lay draped in green sheets, being stitched up by the doctor. She felt robbed, raped, aching, and empty. She told Alec it was just like being mugged, and they both began to laugh.

'Tell that to Riva,' he said.

'But I don't feel bad. I feel—purified.'

'Anyone who feels purified after a mugging has a bad case,' said Alec.

In two hours they brought Alain back, cleaned up and swathed in a little white flannel blanket with a toque over his head to keep in the heat. Ellen began to think of the others in the class and how it would be for them. 'I wonder what the odds are in ten births,' she said, holding her son.

The party was at their place. There had been an RSVP on the invitation, but by the evening before, Ellen had only heard from seven of the ten couples. They were bringing potluck, and she wanted to know how many paper plates to get. She found the class list with the telephone numbers.

The first thing she discovered was that Miriam's phone had been disconnected. Ellen began to feel superstitious. The idea of losing track of one of the group, of not knowing about one of Alain's peers, startled her. She called information and found Miriam's new listing. When she reached it, it turned out she had a new baby boy, and everything was perfectly all right.

Ellen's confidence returned. She decided to call the others she hadn't heard from. The Uruguayan woman had a girl, but Ellen didn't understand any of the details because of the language problem. She hung up and dialled June. The telephone rang seven times, and no one answered.

That was odd; there was always someone home when you have a new baby. She waited until after dinner and then tried again. This time Robert answered. Ellen felt irritated by the sound of his voice; that was when she realized how much she wanted to speak to June. But she said who she was to Robert and asked if they were coming to the party.

Robert cleared a rasp from his throat. Then he sucked in air. 'I might as well be straight with you,' he said. 'We lost our baby.'

'Oh my God,' said Ellen. 'I'm so sorry. I'm so sorry to intrude.'

'We got the invitation,' he said, continuing as if she hadn't spoken, 'and we thought about coming. June wanted to, but I didn't.'

Ellen was silent. 'But anyway,' he said, 'it's kind of you to call.'

'Oh no, no I shouldn't have. I had no idea.'

'June didn't want to tell people. She wanted them to just find out,' he said, 'naturally.' Oh of course it would be natural, thought Ellen, and at whose expense? She was ready to cry with embarrassment. She was dying to know what happened too, but she couldn't ask. 'I am very sorry to intrude,' she said again, more firmly. 'It's a terrible thing.'

'Yes,' said Robert.

Then no one said anything. Robert started the conversation again with greater energy. 'But that doesn't stop me from asking about your baby.'

'We had a little boy,' Ellen said, 'and he's just fine.' She didn't tell Robert about the fright they'd had when Alain didn't breathe. It didn't seem proper to have complaints when you had a live son.

'Congratulations,' said Robert. 'Your baby will bring you a lifetime of happiness.' His tone was mean, humble but punishing. Ellen wanted to tell him that their lifetimes would never be so exclusive as he imagined, especially not now, but she didn't.

It was only as she told Alec that Ellen got mad. 'Riva knew; she could have spared me that call; why didn't she tell me?'

'Maybe sparing you wasn't her concern,' said Alec. He had not been in favour of holding this reunion. The incident only confirmed his belief that coming close to strangers was asking for trouble. But he was sympathetic. He stood in the kitchen, holding Alain very tightly against his chest, and comforted his wife.

At noon the next day the new parents began to come up the narrow sidewalk. It was funny how nine babies looked like a mob. The oldest was three months, the youngest three weeks. Two of them had great swirls of black hair, but most were bald like Alain. One baby, born by Caesarian to the born-agains, had an angelic, calm face, but most were pinched and worried, unused to life on the outside. All through the house babies bounced on shoulders, slept on laps, sat propped in their infant seats. Now that it was all over, the parents could talk. They told birth stories about the heroism of wives, the callousness of physicians. Those whose babies slept through the night gloated over those whose babies didn't. It turned out one man was a lawyer like Alec and even had an office in the same block. One couple had a live-in already, and about half the women were going back to work.

Ellen got the sociology she wanted all along, and she was happy. Word had gone around about June, and everyone agreed it was better she hadn't come because it would have put such a damper on the party. The story was that she'd been two weeks overdue and had to go in for tests. At her second test the doctor told her the baby was dead. The worst part, all agreed, must have been having to carry the dead baby for another week. Finally June went through a difficult labour. There was nothing wrong with the baby that anyone could see.

When they told the story the women's eyes connected and their lips pressed down. It was as if a train had crashed and the person in the next seat had been crushed. They could not help but feel relief, lucky to have been missed. But with luck came fear that luck would not last, and the long, hard oval of dread that had quickened in Ellen along with her offspring was born.

Ellen wanted a picture of the babies together. They put Alain out first, in the corner of the couch, propped on his blanket. Others followed with Lila, Andrew, Evelyn, Adam, Ashley, Orin, Jackson, and William, nine prizes all in a row. Their heads bobbed down or dropped to the side; their mouths were open in round O's of astonishment. They fell asleep, leaning on their neighbour or they struck out with spastic hands and hit his face without knowing.

The parents had their cameras ready. They began to shoot pictures, laughing all the while. The line of babies was the funniest thing people had seen in ages. No one had imagined how funny it would be. The babies were startled. They looked not at each other but at the roomful of hysterical adults. One toppled, and the one next to him fell over onto him. Then the whole line began to collapse. Strange creatures with faces like cabbages and changing goblin shapes, tightly rolled in blankets or drooping into puddles of chin and stomach, they could have come from an alien star. The parents laughed, with relief at their babies' safe landing, and wonder at who they might be. The flashbulbs kept popping as the nine silly little bodies toppled and began to run together into a heap, until one of them, Evelyn, Ellen thinks it was, began to cry.

BARBARA GOWDY
(1950)

〜

We So Seldom Look on Love

When you die, and your earthly self begins turning into your disintegrated self, you radiate an intense current of energy. There is always energy given off when a thing turns into its opposite, when love, for instance, turns into hate. There are always sparks at those extreme points. But life turning into death is the most extreme of extreme points. So just after you die, the sparks are really stupendous. Really magical and explosive.

I've seen cadavers shining like stars. I'm the only person I've ever heard of who has. Almost everyone senses something, though, some vitality. That's why you get resistance to the idea of cremation or organ donation. 'I want to be in one piece,' people say. Even Matt, who claimed there was no soul and no afterlife, wrote a P.S. on his suicide note that he be buried intact.

As if it would have made any difference to his energy emission. No matter what you do—slice open the flesh, dissect everything, burn everything—you're in the path of a power way beyond your little interferences.

I grew up in a nice, normal, happy family outside a small town in New Jersey. My parents and my brother are still living there. My dad owned a flower store. Now my brother owns it. My brother is three years older than I am, a serious, remote man. But loyal. When I made the headlines he phoned to say that if I needed money for a lawyer, he would give it to me. I was really touched. Especially as he was standing up to Carol, his wife. She got on the extension and screamed, 'You're sick! You should be put away!'

She'd been wanting to tell me that since we were thirteen years old.

I had an animal cemetery back then. Our house was beside a woods and we had three outdoor cats, great hunters who tended to leave their kills in one piece. Whenever I found a body, usually a mouse or a bird, I took it into my bedroom and hid it until midnight. I didn't know anything about the ritual significance of the midnight hour. My burials took place then because that's when I woke up. It no longer happens, but I was such a sensitive child that I think I must have been aroused by the energy given off as day clicked over into the dead of night and, simultaneously, as the dead of night clicked over into the next day.

In any case, I'd be wide awake. I'd get up and go to the bathroom to wrap the body in toilet paper. I felt compelled to be so careful, so respectful. I whispered a chant. At each step of the burial I chanted, 'I shroud the body, shroud the body, shroud little sparrow with broken wing.' Or 'I lower the body, lower the body . . .' And so on.

Climbing out the bathroom window was accompanied by: 'I enter the night, enter the night . . .' At my cemetery I set the body down on a special flat rock and took my pyjamas off. I was behaving out of pure inclination. I dug up four or five graves and unwrapped the animals from their shrouds. The rotting smell was crucial. So was the cool air. Normally I'd be so keyed up at this point that I'd burst into a dance.

I used to dance for dead men, too. Before I climbed on top of them, I'd dance all around the prep room. When I told Matt about this he said that I was shaking my personality out of my body so that the sensation of participating in the cadaver's energy eruption would be intensified. 'You're trying to imitate the disintegration process,' he said.

Maybe—on an unconscious level. But what I was aware of was the heat, the heat of my danced-out body, which I cooled by lying on top of the cadaver. As a child I'd gently wipe my skin with two of the animals I'd just unwrapped. When I was covered all over with their scent, I put them, aside, unwrapped the new corpse and did the same with it. I called this the Anointment. I can't describe how it felt. The high, high rapture. The electricity that shot through me.

The rest, wrapping the bodies back up and burying them, was pretty much what you'd expect.

It astonishes me now to think how naïve I was. I thought I had discovered something that certain other people, if they weren't afraid to give it a try, would find just as fantastic as I did. It was a dark and forbidden thing, yes, but so was sex. I really had no idea that I was jumping across a vast behavioural gulf. In fact, I couldn't see that I was doing anything wrong. I still can't, and I'm including what happened with Matt. Carol said I should have ben put away, but I'm not bad-looking, so if offering my body to dead men is a crime, I'd like to know who the victim is.

Carol has always been jealous of me. She's fat and has a wandering eye. Her eye gives her a dreamy, distracted quality that I fell for (as I suppose my brother would eventually do) one day at a friend's thirteenth birthday party. It was the beginning of the summer holidays, and I was yearning for a kindred spirit, someone to share my secret life with. I saw Carol standing alone, looking everywhere at once, and I chose her.

I knew to take it easy, though. I knew not to push anything. We'd search for dead animals and birds, we'd chant and swaddle the bodies, dig graves, make popsicle-stick crosses. All by daylight. At midnight I'd go out and dig up the grave and conduct a proper burial.

There must have been some chipmunk sickness that summer. Carol and I found an incredible number of chipmunks, and a lot of them had no blood on them, no sign of cat. One day we found a chipmunk that evacuated a string of foetuses when I picked it up. The foetuses were still alive, but there was no saving them, so I took them into the house and flushed them down the toilet.

A mighty force was coming from the mother chipmunk. It was as if, along with her own energy, she was discharging all the energy of her dead brood. When Carol and I began to dance for her, we both went a little crazy. We stripped down to our underwear, screamed, spun in circles, threw dirt up into the air. Carol has always denied it, but she took off her bra and began whipping trees with it. I'm sure the sight of her doing this is what inspired me to take off my undershirt and underpants and to perform the Anointment.

Carol stopped dancing. I looked at her, and the expression on her face stopped me dancing, too. I looked down at the chipmunk in my hand. It was bloody. There were streaks of blood all over my body. I was horrified. I thought I'd squeezed the chipmunk too hard.

But what had happened was, I'd begun my period. I figured this out a few minutes after Carol ran off. I wrapped the chipmunk in its shroud and buried it. Then I got dressed and lay down on the grass. A little while later my mother appeared over em.

'Carol's mother phoned,' she said. 'Carol is very upset. She says you made her perform some disgusting witchcraft dance. You made her take her clothes off, and you attacked her with a bloody chipmunk.'

'That's a lie,' I said. 'I'm menstruating.'

After my mother had fixed me up with a sanitary napkin, she told me she didn't think I should play with Carol any more. 'There's a screw loose in there somewhere,' she said.

I had no intention of playing with Carol any more, but I cried at what seemed like a cruel loss. I think I knew that it was all loneliness from that moment on. Even though I was only thirteen, I was cutting any lines that still drifted out toward normal eroticism. Bosom friends, crushes, pyjama-party intimacy. I was cutting all those lines off.

A month or so after becoming a woman I developed a craving to perform autopsies. I resisted doing it for almost a year, though. I was frightened. Violating the intactness of the animal seemed sacrilegious and dangerous. Also unimaginable—I couldn't imagine what would happen.

Nothing. Nothing would happen, as I found out. I've read that necrophiles are frightened of getting hurt by normal sexual relationships, and maybe there's some truth in that (although my heart's been broken plenty of times by cadavers, and not once by a living man), but I think that my attraction to cadavers isn't driven by fear, it's driven by excitement, and that one of the most exciting things about a cadaver is how dedicated it is to dying. Its will is all directed to a single intention, like a huge wave heading for shore, and you can ride along on the wave if you want to, because no matter what you do, because with you or without you, that wave is going to hit the beach.

I felt this impetus the first time I worked up enough nerve to cut open a mouse. Like everyone else, I balked a little at slicing into the flesh, and I was repelled for a few seconds when I saw the insides. But something drove me to go through these compunctions. It was as if I were acting solely on instinct and curiosity, and anything I did was all right, provided it didn't kill me.

After the first few times, I started sticking my tongue into the incision. I don't know why. I thought about it, I did it, and I kept on doing it. One day I removed the organs and cleaned them with water, then put them back in, and I kept on doing that, too. Again, I couldn't tell you why except to say that any provocative thought, if you act upon it, seems to set you on a trajectory.

By the time I was sixteen I wanted human corpses. Men. (That way I'm straight.) I got my chauffeur's licence, but I had to wait until I was finished high school before Mr Wallis would hire me as a hearse driver at the funeral home.

Mr. Wallis knew me because he bought bereavement flowers at my father's store. Now *there* was a weird man. He would take a trocar, which is the big needle you use to draw out a cadaver's fluids, and he would push it into the penises of dead men to make them look semi-erect, and then he'd sodomize them. I caught him at it once, and he tried to tell me he'd been urinating in the hopper. I pretended to believe him. I was upset, though, because I knew that dead men were just dead flesh to him,. One minute he'd be locked up with a young male corpse, having his way with him, and the next he'd be embalming him as if nothing had happened, and making sick jokes about him, pretending to find evidence of rampant homosexuality—colons stalagmited with dried semen, and so on.

None of this joking ever happened in front of me. I heard about it from the crazy old man who did the mopping up. He was also a necrophile, I'm almost certain, but no longer active. He called dead women Madonnas. He rhapsodized about the beautiful Madonnas he'd had the privilege of seeing in the 1940s, about how much more womanly and feminine the Madonnas were twenty years before.

I just listened. I never let on what I was feeling, and I don't think anyone suspected. Necrophiles aren't supposed to be blond and pretty, let alone female. When I'd been working at the funeral home for about a year, a committee from the town council tried to get me to enter the Milk Marketer's Beauty Pageant. They knew about my job, and they knew I was studying embalming at night, but I told people I was preparing myself for medical school, and I guess the council believed me.

For fifteen years, ever since Matt died, people have been asking me how a woman makes love to a corpse.

Matt was the only person who figured it out. He was a medical student, so he knew that if you apply pressure to the chest of certain fresh corpses, they purge blood out of their mouths.

Matt was smart. I wish I could have loved him with more than sisterly love. He was tall and thin. My type. We met at the doughnut shop across from the medical library, got to talking, and liked each other immediately, an unusual experience for both of us. After about an hour I knew he loved me and that his love was unconditional. When I told him where I worked and what I was studying, he asked why.

'Because I'm a necrophile,' I said.

He lifted his head and stared at me. He had eyes like high-resolution monitors. Almost too vivid. Normally I don't like looking people in the eye, but I found myself staring back. I could see that he believed me.

'I've never told anyone else,' I said.

'With men or women?' he asked.

'Men. Young men.'

'How?'

'Cunnilingus.'

'Fresh corpses?'

'If I can get them.'

'What do you do, climb on top of them?'

'Yes.'

'You're turned on by blood.'

'It's a lubricant,' I said. 'It's colourful. Stimulating. It's the ultimate bodily fluid.'

'Yes,' he said, nodding. 'When you think about it. Sperm propagates life. But blood sustains it. Blood is primary.'

He kept asking questions, and I answered as truthfully as I could. Having confessed what I was, I felt driven to testing his intellectual rigour and the strength of his love at first sight. Throwing rocks at him without any expectation that he'd stay standing. He did, though. He caught the whole arsenal and asked for more. It began to excite me.

We went back to his place. He had a basement apartment in an old rundown building. There were books in orange-crate shelves, in piles on the floor, all over the bed. On the wall above his desk was a poster of Doris Day in the movie *Tea for Two*. Matt said she looked like me.

'Do you want to dance first?' he asked, heading for his record player. I'd told him about how I danced before climbing on corpses.

'No.'

He swept the books off the bed. Then he undressed me. He had an erection until I told him I was a virgin. 'Don't worry,' he said, sliding his head down my stomach. 'Lie still.'

The next morning he phoned me at work. I was hungover and blue from the night before. After leaving his place I'd gone straight to the funeral home and made love to an autopsy case. Then I'd got drunk in a seedy country-and-western bar and debated going back to the funeral home and suctioning out my own blood until I lost consciousness.

It had finally hit me that I was incapable of falling in love with a man who wasn't dead. I kept thinking, 'I'm not normal.' I'd never faced this before. Obviously, making love to corpses isn't normal, but while I was still a virgin I must have been assuming that I could give it up any time I liked. Get married, have babies. I must have been banking on a future that I didn't even want let alone have access to.

Matt was phoning to get me to come around again after work.

'I don't know,' I said.

'You had a good time. Didn't you?'

'Sure, I guess.'

'I think you're fascinating,' he said.

I sighed.

'Please,' he said. 'Please.'

A few nights later I went to his apartment. From then on we started to meet every Tuesday and Thursday evening after my embalming class, and as soon as I left his place, if I knew there was a corpse in the mortuary—any male corpse, young or old—I went straight there and climbed in a basement window.

Entering the prep room, especially at night when there was nobody else around, was like diving into a lake. Sudden cold and silence, and the sensation of penetrating a new element where the rules of other elements don't apply. Being with Matt was like lying on the beach of the lake. Matt had warm, dry skin. His apartment was overheated and noisy. I lay on Matt's bed and soaked him up, but only to make the moment when I entered the prep room even more overpowering.

If the cadaver was freshly embalmed, I could usually smell him from the basement. The smell is like a hospital and old cheese. For me, it's the smell of danger and permission, it used to key me up like amphetamine, so that by the time I reached the prep room, tremors were running up and down my legs. I locked the door behind me and broke into a wild dance, tearing my clothes off, spinning around, pulling at my hair. I'm not sure what this was all about, whether or not I was trying to take part in the chaos of the corpse's disintegration, as Matt suggested. Maybe I was prostrating myself, I don't know.

Once the dancing was over, I was always very calm, almost entranced. I drew back the sheet. This was the most exquisite moment. I felt as if I were being blasted by white light. Almost blinded, I climbed onto the table and straddled the corpse. I ran my hands over his skin. My hands and the insides of my thighs burned as if I were touching dry ice. After a few minutes I lay down and pulled the sheet up over my head. I began to kiss his mouth. By now he might be drooling blood. A corpse's blood is thick, cool and sweet. My head roared.

I was no longer depressed. Far from it, I felt better, more confident, than I had ever felt in my life. I had discovered myself to be irredeemably abnormal. I could either slit my throat or surrender—wholeheartedly now—to my obsession. I surrendered. And what happened was that obsession began to storm through me, as if I were a tunnel. I became the medium of obsession as well as both ends of it. With Matt, when we made love, I was the receiving end, I was the cadaver. When I left him and went to the funeral home, I was the lover. Through me Matt's love poured into the cadavers at the funeral home, and through me the cadavers filled Matt with explosive energy.

He quickly got addicted to this energy. The minute I arrived at his apartment, he had to hear every detail about the last corpse I'd been with. For a month so I had him pegged as a latent homosexual necrophile voyeur, but then I began to see that it wasn't the corpses themselves that excited him, it was my passion for them. It was the power that went into that passion and that came back, doubled, for his pleasure. He kept asking, 'How did you feel? Why do you think you felt that way?' And then, because the source of all this power disturbed him, he'd try to prove that my feelings were delusory.

'A corpse shows simultaneous extremes of character,' I told him. 'Wisdom and innocence, happiness and grief, and so on.'

'Therefore all corpses are alike,' he said. 'Once you've had one you've had them all.'

'No, no. They're all different. Each corpse contains his own extremes. Each corpse is only as wise and as innocent as the living person could have been.'

He said, 'You're drafting personalities onto corpses in order to have power over them.'

'In that case,' I said, 'I'm pretty imaginative, since I've never met two corpses who were alike.'

'You *could* be that imaginative,' he argued. 'Schizophrenics are capable of manufacturing dozens of complex personalities.'

I didn't mind these attacks. There was no malice in them, and there was no way they could touch me, either. It was as if I were luxuriously pouring my heart out to a very clever, very concerned, very tormented analyst. I fet sorry for him. I understood his twisted desire to turn me into somebody else (somebody who might love him). I used to fall madly in love with cadavers and then cry because they were dead. The difference between Matt and me was that I had become philosophical. I was all right.

I thought that he was, too. He was in pain, yes, but he seemed confident that what he was going through was temporary and not unnatural. 'I am excessively curious,' he said. 'My fascination is any curious man's fascination with the unusual.' He said that by feeding his lust through mine, he would eventually saturate it, then turn it into disgust.

I told him to go ahead, give it a try. So he began to scour the newspapers for my cadavers' obituaries and to go to their funerals and memorial services. He made charts of my preferences and the frequency of my morgue encounters. He followed me to the morgue at night and waited outside so that he could get a replay while I was still in an erotic haze. He sniffed my skin. He pulled me over to streetlights and examined the blood on my face and hands.

I suppose I shouldn't have encouraged him. I can't really say why I did, except that in the beginning I saw his obsession as the outer edge of my own obsession, a place I didn't have to visit as long as he was there. And then later, and despite his increasingly erratic behaviour, I started to have doubts about an obsession that could come on so suddenly and that could come through me.

One night he announced that he might as well face it, he was going to have to make love to corpses, male corpses. The idea nauseated him, he said, but he said that secretly, deep down, unknown even to himself, making love to male corpses was clearly the target of his desire. I blew up. I told him that necrophilia wasn't something you forced yourself to do. You longed to do it, you needed to do it. You were born to do it.

He wasn't listening. He was glued to the dresser mirror. In the last weeks of his life he stared at himself in the mirror without the least self-consciousness. He focused on his face, even though what was going on from the neck down was the arresting part. He had begun to wear incredibly weird outfits. Velvet capes, pantaloons, high-heeled red boots. When we made love, he kept these outfits on. He stared into my eyes, riveted (it later occurred to me) by his own reflection.

Matt committed suicide, there was never any doubt about that. As for the necrophilia, it wasn't a crime, not fifteen years ago. So even though I was caught in the act, naked and straddling an unmistakably dead body, even though the newspaper found out about it and made it front-page news, there was nothing the police could charge me with.

In spite of which I made a full confession. It was crucial to me that the official report contain more than the detective's bleak observations. I wanted two things on record: one, that Matt was ravished by a reverential expert; two, that his cadaver blasted the energy of a star.

'Did this energy blast happen before or after he died?' the detective asked.

'After,' I said, adding quickly that I couldn't have foreseen such a blast. The one tricky area was why I hadn't stopped the suicide. Why I hadn't talked, or cut, Matt down.

I lied. I said that as soon as I entered Matt's room, he kicked away the ladder. Nobody could prove otherwise. But I've often wondered how much time actually passed between when I opened the door and when his neck broke. In crises, a minute isn't a minute. There's the same chaos you get at the instant of death, with time and form breaking free, and everything magnifying and coming apart.

Matt must have been in a state of crisis for days, maybe weeks before he died. All that staring into mirrors, thinking, 'Is this my face?' Watching as his face separated into its infinitesimal particles and reassembled into a strange new face. The night before he died, he had a mask on. A Dracula mask, but he wasn't joking. He wanted to wear the mask while I made love to him as if he were a cadaver. NO way, I said. The whole point, I reminded him, was that *I* played the cadaver. He begged me, and I laughed because of the mask and with relief. If he wanted to turn the game around, then it was over between us, and I was suddenly aware of how much I liked that idea.

The next night he phoned me at my parents' and said, 'I love you,' then hung up.

I don't know how I knew, but I did. A gun, I thought. Men always use guns. And then I thought, no, poison, cyanide. He was a medical student and had access to drugs. When I arrived at his apartment, the door was open. Across from the door, taped to the wall, was a note: 'DEAD PERSON IN BEDROOM.'

But he wasn't dead. He was standing on a step-ladder. He was naked. An impressively knotted noose, attached to a pipe that ran across the ceiling, was looped around his neck.

He smiled tenderly. 'I knew you'd come,' he said.

'So why the note?' I demanded.

'Pull away the ladder,' he crooned. 'My beloved.'

'Come on. This is stupid. Get down.' I went up to him and punched his leg.

'All you have to do,' he said, 'is pull away the ladder.'

His eyes were even darker and more expressive than usual. His cheekbones appeared to be highlighted. (I discovered minutes later he had makeup on.) I glanced around the room for a chair or table that I could bring over and stand on. I was going to take the noose off him myself.

'If you leave,' he said, 'if you take a step back, if you do anything other than pull away the ladder, I'll kick it away.'

'I love you,' I said. 'Okay?'

'No, you don't,' he said.

'I do!' To sound like I meant it I stared at his legs and imagined them lifeless. 'I do!'

'No, you don't,' he said softly. 'But' he said, 'you will.'

I was gripping the ladder. I remember thinking that if I held tight to the ladder, he wouldn't be able to kick it away. I was gripping the ladder, and then it was by the wall, tipped over. I have no memory of transition between these two events. There was a loud crack, and gushing water. Matt dropped gracefully, like a girl fainting. Water poured on him from the broken pipe. There was a smell of excrement. I dragged him by the noose.

In the living room I pulled him onto the green shag carpet. I took my clothes off. I knelt over him. I kissed the blood at the corner of his mouth.

True obsession depends on the object's absolute unresponsiveness. When I used to fall for a particular cadaver, I would feel as if I were a hollow instrument, a bell or a flute. I'd empty out. *I* would clear out (it was involuntary) until I was an instrument for the cadaver to swell into and be amplified. As the object of Matt's obsession how could I be other than impassive, while he was alive?

He was playing with fire, playing with me. Not just because I couldn't love him, but because I was irradiated. The whole time that I was involved with Matt, I was making love to corpses, absorbing their energy, blazing it back out. Since that energy came from the act of life alchemizing into death, there's a possibility that it was alchemical itself. Even if it wasn't I'm sure it gave Matt the impression that I had the power to change him in some huge and dangerous way.

I now believe that his addiction to my energy was really a craving for such a transformation. In fact, I think that all desire is desire for transformation, and that all transformation—all movement, all process—happens because life turns into death.

I am still a necrophile, occasionally, and recklessly. I have found no replacement for the torrid serenity of a cadaver.

GUY VANDERHAEGHE
(1951)

〜

Dancing Bear

The old man lay sleeping on the taut red rubber sheet as if he were some specimen mounted and pinned there to dry. His housekeeper, the widowed Mrs Hax, paused in the doorway and then walked heavily to the bedside window, where she abruptly freed the blind and sent it up, whirring and clattering.

She studied the sky. Far away, to the east, and high above the bursting green of the elms that lined the street, greasy black clouds rolled languidly, their swollen underbellies lit by the occasional shudder of lightning that popped in the distance. After each flash she counted aloud to herself until she heard the faint, muttering accompaniment of thunder. Finally satisfied, she turned away from the window to find Dieter Bethge awake and watching her cautiously from his bed.

'It's going to rain,' she said, moving about the room and grunting softly as she stooped to gather up his clothes and pile them on a chair.

'Oh?' he answered, feigning some kind of interest. He picked a flake of dried skin from his leg and lifted it tenderly to the light like a jeweller, intently examining its whorled grain and yellow translucence.

Sighing, Mrs Hax smoothed the creases of his carelessly discarded trousers with a soft, fat palm and draped them over the back of a chair. The old bugger made more work that a whole tribe of kids.

She glanced over her shoulder and saw him fingering the bit of skin between thumb and forefinger. 'Leave that be,' she said curtly. 'It's time we were up. Quit dawdling.'

He looked up, his pale blue eyes surprised. 'What?'

'Time to get up.'

'No', he said. 'Not yet.'

'It's reveille. No malingering. Won't have it,' she said, fixing an unconvincing smile on her broad face. 'Come on now, up and at 'em. We've slept long enough.'

'That rubber thing kept me awake last night,' he said plaintively. 'Every time I move it squeaks and pulls at my skin. There's no give to it.'

'Complainers' noses fall off,' Mrs Hax said absent-mindedly as she held a shirt up to her own wrinkled nose. She sniffed. It wasn't exactly fresh but she decided it would do, and tossed it back on the chair.

The old man felt his face burn with humiliation, as it did whenever he was thwarted or ignored. 'I want that damn thing off my bed!' he yelled. 'This is my bed! This is my house! Get it off!'

Mrs Hax truculently folded her arms across her large loose breasts and stared down at him. For a moment he met her gaze defiantly, but then he averted his eyes and his trembling jaw confirmed his confusion.

'I am not moved by childish tempers,' she announced. 'You haven't learned that yet?' Mrs Hax paused. 'It's about time you did. One thing about Mrs Hax,' she declared in a piping falsetto that betrayed her anger, 'is that when someone pushes her, she pushes back twice as hard. I am ruthless.' She assumed a stance that she imagined to be an illustration of ruthlessness, her flaccid arms akimbo. A burlesque of violence. 'So let me make this per- fectly, crystal clear. That rubber sheet is staying on that bed until you forget your lazy, dirty habits and stop them accidents. A grown man,' she said dis- paragingly, shaking her head. 'I just got sick and tired of hauling one mat- tress off the bed to dry and hauling another one on. Just remember I'm not getting any younger either. I'm not up to heavy work like that. So if you want that rubber thing off, you try and remember not to pee the bed.'

The old man turned on his side and hid his face.

'No sulking allowed,' she said sternly. 'Breakfast is ready and I have plen- ty to do today. I can't keep it waiting forever.'

Dieter turned on to his back and fixed his eyes on the ceiling. Mrs Hax shook her head in exasperation. It was going to be one of those days. What went on in the old bastard's head, if anything? What made him so peculiar, so difficult at times like these?

She walked over to the bed and took him firmly by the wrist. 'Upsy-daisy!' she cried brightly, planting her feet solidly apart and jerking him upright. She skidded him to the edge of the bed, the rubber sheet whining a muffled complaint, and his hands, in startled protest and ineffectual rebellion, paw- ing at the front of her dress. Mrs Hax propped him upright while his head wobbled feebly from side to side and his tongue flickered angrily, darting and questing like a snake's.

'There,' she said, patting his hand, 'that's better. Now let's let bygones be bygones. A fresh start. I'll say, "Good morning, Mr Bethge!" and you answer, "Good morning, Mrs Hax!" '

He gave no sign of agreement. Mrs Hax hopefully cocked her head to one side and, like some huge, querulous bird, chirped, 'Good morning, Mr Bethge!' The old man stubbornly disregarded her, smiling sweetly and vacantly into space.

'Well,' she said, patting her dress down around her wide hips and heavy haunches, 'it's no skin off my teeth, mister.'

She stumped to the door, stopped and looked back. The old man sat perched precariously on the edge of the bed, his white hair ruffled, tufted and crested like some angry heron. A pale shadow fell across the lower half of his face and threw his eyes into relief, so that they shone with the dull, glazed intensity of the most devout of worshippers.

Mrs Hax often saw him like this, mute and still, lost in reverie; and she liked to suppose that, somehow, he was moved by a dim apprehension of mortality and loss. Perhaps he was even overcome with memories of his wife, and felt the same vast yearning she felt for her own dead Albert.

She mustered a smile and offered it. 'Five minutes, dear,' she said, and then closed the door softly behind her.

Bethge made no response. He was thinking—trying to pry those memories out of the soft beds into which they had so comfortably settled, sinking deeper and deeper under the weight of all the years, growing more somnolent and lazy, less easily stirred from sleep. He could no longer make his head crackle with the sudden, decisive leap of quick thought hurtling from synapse to synapse. Instead, memories had now to be pricked and prodded, and sometimes, if he was lucky, they came in revelatory flashes. Yet it was only old, old thoughts and things that came to him. Only they had any real clarity—and the sharpness to wound.

And now it was something about a bear. What?

Bethge, with a jerky, tremulous movement, swiped at the spittle on his chin with the back of his hand. In his agitation he crossed and recrossed his thin legs, the marbly, polished legs of a very old man.

Bear? He rubbed the bridge of his nose; somehow, it was important. He began to rock himself gently, his long, curving nose slicing like a scythe, back and forth, reaping the dim air of his stale little room. And as he swayed, it all began to come to him, and he began to run, swiftly, surely, silently back into time.

In the dark barn that smells of brittle straw, and sharply of horse dung, the knife is making little greedy, tearing noises. It is not sharp enough. Then he hears the hoarse, dragging whisper of steel on whetstone. Although he is afraid that the bear his father is skinning may suddenly rear to life, he climbs over the wall of the box stall and steps into the manger and crouches down. He is only five, so the manger is a nice, tight, comforting fit.

What a bear! A killer, a marauder who had left two sows tangled in their guts with single blows from his needle-sharp claws.

The smell of the bear makes him think of gun metal—oily, smoky. Each hair bristles like polished black wire, and when the sun catches the pelt it shines vividly, electrically blue.

The curved blade of the knife, now sharpened, slices through the bear's fat like butter, relentlessly peeling back the coat and exposing long, flat, pink muscles. As his father's busy, bloody hands work, Dieter feels a growing uneasiness. The strong hands tug and tear, wrestling with the heavy, inert body as if they are frantically searching for something. Like clay under a sculptor's hand, the bear begins to change. Each stroke of the knife renders him less bear-like and more like something else. Dieter senses this and crouches lower in the manger in anticipation.

His father begins to raise the skin off the back, his forearms hidden as the knife moles upward toward the neck. At last he grunts and stands. Reaches for the axe. In two sharp, snapping blows the head is severed from the trunk and the grinning mask flung into a corner. He gathers up the skin and carries it out to salt it and peg it down in the yard. Dieter hears the chickens clamouring to pick it clean.

He stares down into the pit of the shadowy stall. This is no bear. Stripped of its rich, glossy fur, naked, it is no bear. Two arms, two legs, a raw pink skin. A man. Under all that lank, black hair a man was hiding, lurking in disguise.

He feels the spiralling terror of an unwilling accomplice to murder. He begins to cry and call for his father, who suddenly appears in the doorway covered in grease and blood, a murderer.

From far away, he heard someone call him. 'Mr Bethge! Mr Bethge!' The last syllable of his name was drawn out and held like a note, so that it quivered in the air and urged him on with its stridency.

He realized he had been crying, that his eyes are filled with those unexpected tears that came so suddenly they constantly surprised and embarrassed him.

For a bear? But this wasn't all of it. There had been another bear; he was sure of it. A bear who had lived in shame and impotence.

He edged himself off the bed and painfully on to his knobbed, arthritic feet. Breakfast.

At breakfast they quarrel in the dreary, passionless manner of master and charge. He wants what she has, bacon and eggs. He tells her he hates porridge.

'Look,' Mrs Hax said, 'I can't give you bacon and eggs. Doctor's orders.'

'What doctor?'

'The doctor we saw last month. You remember.'

'No.' It was true. He couldn't remember any doctor.

'Yes you do. Come on now. We took a ride downtown in a cab. Remember now?'

'No.'

'And we stopped by Woolworth's and bought a big bag of that sticky candy you like so much. Remember?'

'No.'

'That's fine,' she said irritably. 'You don't want to remember, there's nothing I can do. It doesn't matter, because you're not getting bacon and eggs.'

'I don't want porridge,' he said tiredly.

'Eat it.'

'Give me some corn flakes.'

'Look at my plate,' she said, pointing with her knife. 'I'm not getting cold grease scum all over everything. Fight, fight. When do I get a moment's peace to eat?'

'I want corn flakes,' he said with a little self-satisfied tuck to the corners of his mouth.

'You can't have corn flakes,' she said. 'Corn flakes bung you up. That's why you eat hot cereal—to keep you regular. Just like stewed prunes. Now, which you want,' she asked slyly, 'Sunny Boy or stewed prunes?'

'I want corn flakes.' He smiled up happily at the ceiling.

'Like a stuck record.' She folded her hands on the table and leaned conspiratorially toward him. 'You don't even care if you eat or not, do you? You're just trying to get under my skin, aren't you?'

'I want corn flakes,' he said definitely and happily.

'I could kill that man,' she told her plate. 'Just kill him.' Then, abruptly, she asked. 'Where's your glasses? No, not there, in the other pocket. Okay, put them on. Now take a good long look at that porridge.'

The old man peered down intently into his bowl.

'That's fine. Take it easy. It's not a goddamn wishing-well. You see them little brown specks?'

He nodded.

'That's what this whole fight's about? Something as tiny as that? You know what this is. It's flax. And flax keeps you regular. So eat it.'

'I'm not eating it. What do I want with flax?' he asked quizzically.

'Sure you're crazy,' she said. 'Crazy like a fox.'

'I want some coffee.'

Mrs Hax slammed down her fork and knife, snatched up his cup, and marched to the kitchen counter. While she poured the coffee, Bethge's hand crept across the table and stole several strips of bacon from her plate. He crammed these clumsily into his mouth, leaving a grease shine on his chin.

Mrs Hax set his cup down in front of him. 'Be careful,' she said. 'Don't spill.'

Bethge giggled. In a glance, Mrs Hax took in his grease-daubed chin and her plate. 'Well, well, look at the cat who swallowed the canary. Grinning from ear-lobe to ear-lobe with a pound of feathers bristling from his trap.'

'So?' he said defiantly.

'You think I enjoy the idea of you pawing through my food?' Mrs Hax carried her plate to the garbage and scraped it with a flourish. 'Given all your dirty little habits, who's to know where your hands have been?' she asked, smiling wickedly. 'But go ahead and laugh. Because he who laughs last, laughs best. Chew this around for a bit and see how she tastes. You're not getting one single, solitary cigarette today, my friend.'

Startled, he demanded his cigarettes.

'We're singing a different tune now, aren't we?' She paused. 'N-O spells no. Put that in your pipe and smoke it.'

'You give them. They're mine.'

'Not since you set the chesterfield on fire. Not since then. Your son told me I was to give them out one at a time so's I could watch you and avoid "regrettable accidents". Thank God, there's some sense in the family. How he came by it I'm sure I don't know.'

The old man hoisted himself out of his chair. 'Don't you dare talk to me like that. I want my cigarettes—and I want them now.'

Mrs Hax crossed her arms and set her jaw. 'No.'

'You're fired!' he shouted. 'Get out!' He flapped his arms awkwardly in an attempt to startle her into motion.

'Oho!' she said, rubbing her large red hands together in delight, 'fired am I? On whose say-so? Them that hires is them that fires. He who pays the piper calls the tune. And you don't do neither. Not a bit. Your son hired me, and your son pays me. I don't budge a step unless I get the word straight from the horse's mouth.'

'Get out!'

'Save your breath.'

He is beaten and he knows it. This large, stubborn woman cannot, will not, be moved.

'I want to talk to my son.'

'If you got information you feel your son should have, write him a letter.'

He knows this would never do. He would forget, she would steal the letter, conveniently forget to mail it. Justice demands immediate action. The iron is hot and fit for striking. He feels the ground beneath his feet is treacherous; he cannot become confused, or be led astray. One thing at a time. He must talk to his son.

'Get him on the telephone.'

'Your son, if you remember,' Mrs Hax said, 'got a little upset about all those long-distance calls—collect. And his words to me were, "Mrs Hax, I think it best if my father phone only on important matters, at your discretion." At my discretion, mind you. And my discretion informs me that this isn't one of those times. I've got a responsibility to my employer.'

'I'll phone him myself.'

'That I've got to see.'

'I will.'

'Yes, like the last time. Half the time you can't remember the city John lives in, let alone his street. The last time you tried to phone him you got the operator so balled up you would have been talking to a Chinaman in Shanghai if I hadn't stepped in and saved your bacon.'

'I'll phone. I can do it.'

'Sure you will. Where does John live?'

'I know.'

'Uh-huh, then tell me. Where does he live?'

'I know.'

'Jesus, he could be living in the basement and you wouldn't realize it.'

This makes him cry. He realizes she is right. But minutes ago he had known where his son lived. How could he have forgotten? In the sudden twistings and turnings of the conversation he has lost his way, and now he hears himself making a wretched, disgusting noise; but he cannot stop.

Mrs Hax feels she has gone too far. She goes over to him and puts an arm around his shoulders. 'Now see what's happened. You went and got yourself all upset over a silly old bowl of porridge. Doctor says you have to watch that with your blood pressure. It's no laughing matter.' She boosts him out of his chair. 'I think you better lie down on the chesterfield for a bit.'

Mrs Hax led him into the living-room and made him comfortable on the chesterfield. She wondered how an old bugger like him could make so much water; if he wasn't peeing, he was crying.

'You want a Kleenex?' she asked.

He shook his head and, ashamed, covered his face with his forearm.

'No harm in crying,' she said bleakly. 'We all do some time.'

'Leave me be.'

'I suppose it's best,' she sighed. 'I'll be in the kitchen clearing up if you need me.'

Dieter lay on the chesterfield trying to stifle his tears. It was not an easy job because even the sound of Mrs Hax unconcernedly clacking the breakfast dishes reminded him of her monstrous carelessness with everything. His plates, his feelings. He filled with anger at the notion that he would never be nimble enough to evade her commands, or even her wishes. That he cannot outwit her or even flee her.

The living-room gradually darkens as the low, scudding rain clouds blot out the sun. He wishes it were a fine sunny day. The kind of day which tricks you into believing you are young and carefree as you once were. Like in Rumania before his family emigrated. Market days almost always felt that way. People bathed in sun and noise, their wits honed to a fine edge for trading and bartering. Every kind of people. The Jews with their curling sidelocks, the timid Italian tenant farmers, the Rumanians, and people like himself, German colonists. Even a gypsy or two. Then you had a sense of life, of living. Every good thing the earth offers or man's hand fashions could be found there. Gaily painted wagons, piles of potatoes with the wet clay still clinging to them; chickens, ducks and geese; tethered pigs tugging their back legs and squealing; horses with hooves as black and shining as basalt, and eyes as large and liquid-purple as plums.

Nothing but a sheet of sky above and good smells below: pickled herring and leather, paprika and the faint scent of little, hard, sweet apples.

Innocence. Innocence. But then again, on the other hand—yes, well, sometimes cruelty too. Right in the market.

A stranger arrived with a dancing bear once. Yes, the other bear, the one he had forgotten. He led him by a ring through the nose. When a crowd gathered, the man unsnapped the chain from the bear's nose and began to play a violin. It was a sad, languorous tune. For a moment, the bear tossed his head from side to side and snuffled in the dirt. This, for him, was a kind of freedom.

But the man spoke to him sharply. The bear lifted his head and then mournfully raised himself up on to his hind legs. His arms opened in a wide, charitable manner, as if he were offering an embrace. His mouth grinned, exposing black-speckled gums and sharp teeth. He danced, slowly, ponderously, tiredly.

The music changed tempo. It became gay and lively. The bear began to prance unsteadily; the hot sun beat down on him. A long, glittering thread of saliva fell from his panting mouth on the cinnamon-coloured fur of his chest.

Dieter, fascinated, tugged and pushed himself through the crowd. The bear hopped heavily from leg to leg. It was pathetic and comic. The pink tip of his penis jiggled up and down in the long hair of his loins. There was a wave of confused sniggering.

The trainer played faster and faster. The bear pirouetted wildly. He whirled and whirled, raising a small cloud of dust. The crowd began to clap. The bear spun and spun, his head lolling from side to side, his body tense with the effort of maintaining his human posture. And then he lost his balance and fell, blindly, with a bone-wrenching thump, onto his back.

The scraping of the violin bow stopped. The bear turned lazily on to his feet and bit savagely at his fleas.

'Up, Bruno!'

The bear whined and sat down. People began to laugh; some hooted and insulted the bear's master. He flourished the bear's nose lead and shouted, but the bear refused to budge. In the end, however, he could do nothing except attempt to save face; he bowed deeply, signifying an end to the performance. A few coins, a very few, bounced and bounded at his feet. He scooped them up quickly, as if he were afraid they might be reclaimed.

The audience began to disperse. Some hurried away to protect their wares. But Dieter had nothing to protect and nowhere to go, and so he stayed.

The sight of so many fleeing backs seemed to pique the bear. He got to his feet and began, once again, to dance. He mocked them. Or so it seemed. Of course, there was no music, but the bear danced much more daintily and elegantly than before, to a tune only he could perceive. And he grinned hugely, sardonically.

But the trainer reached up, caught his nose ring and yanked him down on all fours. He swore and cursed, and the bear breathed high, squeaking protests, feigning innocence.

This was unacceptable. This was rebellion. This was treason to the man who fed him, cared for him, taught him.

'Hairy bastard. Play the fool, will you,' the stranger muttered, wrenching and twisting the nose ring while the bear squealed with pain. The man punched his head, kicked him in the belly, shook him by the ears. 'Traitor. Ingrate.'

Dieter held his breath. His mind's eye had seen the bear suddenly strike, revenge himself. Yet nothing happened. Nothing; except the bear was beaten and battered, humiliated, even spat upon.

What shame he felt witnessing such an indignity, such complete indifference to the rightful pride of the bear. Such flouting of the respect owed him for his size and his power. Couldn't the man realize what he did? Diester wanted to shout out the secret. To warn him that appearances deceive. That a bear is a man in masquerade. Perhaps even a judge, but at the very least a brother.

But he couldn't. He ran away instead.

The house is still. He hears her footsteps, knows that she is watching him from the doorway. As always, she is judging him, calculating her words and responses, planning. Her plots deny him even the illusion of freedom. He decides he will not turn to look at her. But perhaps she knows this will be his reaction? Petulant, childish.

'I want to be left in peace.' He surprises himself. This giving voice to thought without weighing the consequences is dangerous.

But she doesn't catch it. 'What?'

'I don't chew my words twice,' he says.

She comes to the side of the chesterfield. 'Feeling better now?'

'Yes.'

'Truth?'

He nods.

'Now mind, you got to be sure. I'm going down to the store. You need the bathroom?'

'No.'

'All right then. I'll just be a few minutes. That's all. You'll be okay?'

He is trying to think. All this talk, these interruptions, annoy him. He burns with impatience. 'Fine. That's fine. Good.' Suddenly, he feels happy. He can steal a little peace. He'll do it.

'I must be careful,' he tell himself aloud. How do these things slip out?

But Mrs Hax doesn't understand. 'With your blood pressure, I should say so.'

His luck, his good fortune, make him feel strong and cunning. Following her to the front door, he almost pities this fat woman. He watches her start down the street. It is lined with old and substantial homes, most of them painted modestly white, and their yards flourish tall, rough-barked elms. On this street, Mrs Hax, in her fluorescent orange rain slicker, appears ridiculous and inappropriate. Like a bird of paradise in an English garden. He waits until he loses sight of her at the first turning of the street.

He hurries to his business. His hands fumble with the chain on the front door; at last it is fastened. His excitement leaves him breathless, but he shuffles to the back door and draws the bolt. Safe. Mrs Hax is banished, exiled.

At first he thinks the noise is caused by the blood pulsing in his temples. But it fades to an insistent, whispering rush. Dieter goes to the window to look out. The rain is falling in a gleaming, thick curtain that obscures the outlines of the nearest house; striking the roadway, it throws up fine silvery plumes of spray. He decides to wait for Mrs Hax at the front door. He stands there and smells the coco matting, the dust and rubber boots. Somehow, he has forgotten they smell this way, a scent that can be peculiarly comforting when you are dry and warm, with a cold rain slashing against the windows.

And here is Mrs Hax trotting stiff-legged up the street with a shredding brown-paper bag huddled to her body. She flees up the walk, past the beaten and dripping caraganas, and around back to the kitchen door. He hears her bumping and rattling it.

Here she comes again, and scurrying along, head bent purposefully, rain glancing off her plastic cap. But as she begins to climb the front steps he withdraws and hides himself in the coat closet. Her key rasps in the chamber, the spring lock snaps free. The door opens several inches but then meets the resistance of the chain, and sticks. She grumbles and curses; some fat, disembodied fingers curl through the gap and pluck at the chain. For a moment he is tempted to slam the door shut on those fingers, but he resists the impulse. The fingers are replaced by a slice of face, an eye and a mouth.

'Mr Bethge! Mr Bethge! Open up!'

Bethge stumbles out of the closet and lays his face along the door jamb, eye to eye with Mrs Hax. They stare at each other. At last she breaks the spell.

'Well, open this door,' she says irritably. 'I feel like a drowned cat.'

'Go away. You're not wanted here.'

'What!'

'Go away.'

Her one eye winks suspiciously. 'You do know who I am? This is Mrs Hax, your housekeeper. Open up.'

'I know who you are. I don't want any part of you. So go away.'

She shows him the soggy paper bag. 'I brought you a Jersey Milk.'

'Pass it through.'

Her one eye opens wide in blue disbelief. 'You open this door.'

'No.'

'It's the cigarettes, I suppose? All right, I give up. You can have your damn cigarettes.'

'Go away.'

'I'm losing my patience,' she says, lowering her voice; 'now open this door, you senile old fart.'

'Old fart yourself. Old fat fart.'

'You wait until I get in there. There'll be hell to pay.'

He realizes his legs are tired from standing. There is a nagging pain in the small of his back. 'I've got to go now,' he says. 'Goodbye,' and he closes the door in her face.

He is suddenly very light-headed and tired, but nevertheless exultant. He decides he will have a nap. But the woman has begun to hammer at the door.

'Stop it,' he shouts. He makes his way to his bedroom on unsteady legs; in fact, one is trailing and he must support himself by leaning against the wall. What is this?

The bedroom lies in half-light, but he can see the red rubber sheet. It must go. He tugs at it and it resists him like some living thing, like a limpet clinging to a rock. His leg crumples, his mouth falls open in surprise as he falls. He lands loosely like a bundle of sticks, his legs and arms splayed wide, but feels nothing but a prickling sensation in his bladder. No pain, nothing. There are shadows everywhere in the room, they seem to float, and hover, and quiver. He realizes the front of his pants is wet. He tries to get up, but the strength ebbs out of his limbs and is replaced by a sensation of dizzying heaviness. He decides he will rest a minute and then get up.

But he doesn't. He sleeps.

Mrs Hax waited under the eaves for the rain to abate. It fell for an hour with sodden fury, and then began to slacken into a dispirited drizzle. When it did, she picked her way carefully through the puddles in the garden to where the hoe lay. With it, she broke a basement window and methodically trimmed the glass out of the frame. Then she settled herself onto her haunches and, gasping, wriggled into the opening. She closed her eyes, committed her injuries in advance to Bethge's head, and then let herself drop. She landed on one leg, which buckled, and sent her headlong against the gas furnace, which set every heat vent and duct in the building vibrating with a deep, atonal ringing. Uninjured, she picked herself up from the floor. Her dignity bruised, her authority wounded, she began to edge her way through the basement clutter toward the stairs.

Dieter Bethge woke with a start. Some noise had broken into his dream. It had been a good and happy dream. The dancing bear had been performing for him under no compulsion, a gift freely given. It had been a perfect, graceful dance, performed without a hint of the foppishness or studied concentration that mars the dance of humans. As the bear had danced he had seemed to grow, as if fed by the pure, clear notes of the music. He had grown larger and larger, but Dieter had watched this with a feeling of great peace rather than alarm.

The sun glinted on his cinnamon fur and burnished his coat with red, winking light. And when the music stopped, the bear had opened his arms very wide in a gesture of friendship and welcome. His mouth had opened as if he were about to speak. And that was exactly what Dieter had expected all along. That the bear would confide in him the truth, and prove that under the shagginess that belied it, there was something that only Dieter had recognized.

But then something had broken the spell of the dream.

He was confused. Where was he? His hand reached out and touched something smooth and hard and resisting. He gave a startled grunt. This was wrong. His mind slipped backward and forward, easily and smoothly, from dream to the sharp, troubling present.

He tried to get up. He rose, trembling, swayed, felt the floor shift, and fell, striking his head on a chest of drawers. His mouth filled with something warm and salty. He could hear something moving in the house, then the sound was lost in the tumult of the blood singing in his veins. His pulse beat dimly in his eyelids, his ears, his neck and fingertips.

He managed to struggle to his feet and beat his way into the roar of the shadows which slipped by like surf, and out into the hallway.

And then he saw a form in the muted light, patiently waiting. It was the bear.

'Bear?' he asked, shuffling forward, trailing his leg.

The bear said something he did not understand. He was waiting.

Dieter lifted his arms for the expected embrace, the embrace that should fold him onto the fragrant, brilliant fur; but, curiously, one arm would not rise. It dangled limply like a rag. Dieter felt something strike the side of his face—a numbing blow. His left eyelid fell like a shutter. He tried to speak but his tongue felt swollen and could only batter noiselessly against his teeth. He felt himself fall but the bear reached out and caught him in the warm embrace he desired above all.

And so, Dieter Bethge, dead of a stroke, fell gently, gently, like a leaf, into the waiting arms of Mrs Hax.

∽

The Ghost of Firozsha Baag

I always believed in ghosts. When I was little I saw them in my father's small field in Goa. That was very long ago, before I came to Bombay to work as ayah.

Father also saw them, mostly by the well, drawing water. He would come in and tell us, the *bhoot* is thirsty again. But it never scared us. Most people in our village had seen ghosts. Everyone believed in them.

Not like in Firozsha Baag. First time I saw a ghost here and people found out, how much fun they made of me. Calling me crazy, saying it is time for old ayah to go back to Goa, back to her *muluk*, she is seeing things.

Two years ago on Christmas Eve I first saw the *bhoot*. No, it was really Christmas Day. At ten o'clock on Christmas Eve I went to Cooperage Stadium for midnight mass. Every year all of us Catholic ayahs from Firozsha Baag go for mass. But this time I came home alone, the others went somewhere with their boyfriends. Must have been about two o'clock in the morning. Lift in B Block was out of order, so I started up slowly. Thinking how easy to climb three floors when I was younger, even with a full bazaar-bag.

After reaching first floor I stopped to rest. My breath was coming fast-fast. Fast-fast, like it does nowadays when I grind curry *masala* on the stone. Jaakaylee, my *bai* calls out, Jaakaylee, is *masala* ready? Thinks a sixty-three-year-old ayah can make *masala* as quick as she used to when she was fifteen. Yes, fifteen. The day after my fourteenth birthday I came by bus from Goa to Bombay. All day and night I rode the bus. I still remember when my father took me to bus station in Panjim. Now it is called Panaji. Joseph Uncle, who was mechanic in Mazagaon, met me at Bombay Central Station. So crowded it was, people running all around, shouting, screaming, and coolies with big-big trunks on their heads. Never will I forget that first day in Bombay. I just stood in one place, not knowing what to do, till Joseph Uncle saw me. Now it has been forty-nine years in this house as ayah, believe or don't believe. Forty-nine years in Firozsha Baag's B Block and they still don't say my name right. Is it so difficult to say Jacqueline? But they always say Jaakaylee. Or worse, Jaakayl.

All the fault is of old *bai* who died ten years ago. She was in charge till her son brought a wife, the new *bai* of the house. Old *bai* took English words and made them Parsi words. Easy chair was *igeechur*, French beans was *ferach eech*, and Jacqueline became Jaakaylee. Later I found out that all old Parsis did this, it was like they made up their own private language.

So then new *bai* called me Jaakaylee also, and children do the same. I don't care about it now. If someone asks me my name I saw Jaakaylee. And I talk Parsi-Gujarati all the time instead of Konkani, even with other ayahs. Sometimes also little bits of English.

But I was saying. My breath was fast-fast when I reached first floor and stopped for rest. And then I noticed someone, looked like in a white gown. Like a man, but I could not see the face, just body shape. *Kaun hai?* I asked in Hindi. Believe or don't believe, he vanished. Completely! I shook my head and started for second floor. Carefully, holding the railing, because the steps are so old, all slanting and crooked.

Then same thing happened. At the top of second floor he was waiting. And when I said, *kya hai?* believe or don't believe, he vanished again! Now I knew it must be a *bhoot*. I knew he would be on third floor also, and I was right. But I was not scared or anything.

I reached the third floor entrance and found my bedding which I had put outside before leaving. After midnight mass I always sleep outside, by the stairs, because *bai* and *seth* must not be woken up at two A.M., and they never give me a key. No ayah gets key to a flat. It is something I have learned, like I learned forty-nine years ago that life as ayah means living close to floor. All work I do, I do on floors, like grinding *masala*, cutting vegetables, cleaning rice. Food also is eaten sitting on floor, after serving them at dining-table. And my bedding is rolled out at night in kitchen-passage, on floor. No cot for me. Nowadays, my weight is much more than it used to be, and is getting very difficult to get up from floor. But I am managing.

So Christmas morning at two o'clock I opened my bedding and spread out my *saterunjee* by the stairs. Then stopped. The *bhoot* had vanished, and I was not scared or anything. But my father used to say some ghosts play mischief. The ghost of our field never did, he only took water from our well, but if this ghost of the stairs played mischief he might roll me downstairs, who was to say. So I thought about it and rang the doorbell.

After many, many rings *bai* opened, looking very mean. Mostly she looks okay, and when she dresses in nice sari for a wedding or something, and puts on all bangles and necklace, she looks really pretty, I must say. But now she looked so mean. Like she was going to bite somebody. Same kind of look she has every morning when she has just woken up, but this was much worse and meaner because it was so early in the morning. She was very angry, said I was going crazy, there was no ghost or anything, I was just telling lies not to sleep outside.

Then *seth* also woke up. He started laughing, saying he did not want any ghost to roll me downstairs because who would make *chai* in the morning. He was not angry, his mood was good. They went back to their room, and I knew why he was feeling happy when crrr-crr crrr-crr sound of their bed started coming in the dark.

When he was little I sang Konkani songs for him. *Mogacha Mary* and *Hanv Saiba*. Big man now, he's forgotten them and so have I. Forgetting my name, my language, my songs. But complaining I'm not, don't make mistake. I'm telling you, to have a job I was very lucky because in Goa there was nothing to do. From Panjim to Bombay on the bus I cried, leaving behind my brothers and sisters and parents, and all my village friends. But I knew leaving was best thing. My father had eleven children and very small field. Coming to Bombay was only thing to do. Even schooling I got first year, at night. Then *bai* said I must stop because who would serve dinner when *seth* came home from work, and who would carry away dirty dishes? But that was not the real reason. She thought I stole her eggs. There were six eggs yesterday evening, she would say, only five this morning, what happened to one? She used to think I took it with me to school to give to someone.

I was saying, it was very lucky for me to become ayah in Parsi house, and never will I forget that. Especially because I'm Goan Catholic and very dark skin colour. Parsis prefer Manglorean Catholics, they have light skin colour. For themselves also Parsis like light skin, and when Parsi baby is born that is the first and most important thing. If it is fair they say, O now nice light skin just like parents. But if it is dark skin they say, *arré* what is this *ayah no chhokro*, ayah's child.

All this doing was more in olden days, mostly among very rich *bais* and *seths*. They thought they were like British only, ruling India side by side. But don't make mistake, not just rich Parsis. Even all Marathi people in low class Tar Gully made fun of me when I went to buy grocery from *bunya*. Blackie, blackie, they would call out. Nowadays it does not happen because very dark skin colour is common in Bombay, so many people from south are coming here, Tamils and Keralites, with their funny *illay illay poe poe* language. Now people more used to different colours.

But still not to ghosts. Everybody in B Block found out about the *bhoot* of the stairs. They made so much fun of me all the time, children and grown-up people also.

And believe or don't believe, that *was* a ghost of mischief. Because just before Easter he came back. Not on the stairs this time but right in my bed. I'm telling you, he was sitting on my chest and bouncing up and down, and I couldn't push him off, so weak I was feeling (I'm a proper Catholic, I was fasting), couldn't even scream or anything (not because I was scared—he was choking me). Then someone woke up to go to WC and put on a light in the passage where I sleep. Only then did the rascal *bhoot* jump off and vanish.

This time I did not tell anyone. Already they were making so much fun of me. Children in Firozsha Baag would shout, ayah *bhoot!* ayah *bhoot!* every time they saw me. And a new Hindi film had come out, *Bhoot Bungla*, about a haunted house, so they would say, like the man on the radio, in a loud voice: SEE TODAY, at APSARA CINEMA, R.K. Anand's NEW fillum *Bhooot Bungla*, starring JAAKAYLEE of BLOCK B! Just like that! O they made a lot of fun of me, but I did not care, I knew what I had seen.

Jaakaylee, bai *calls out, is it ready yet? She wants to check curry* masala. *Too thick, she always says, grind it again, make it smoother. And she is right, I leave it thick purposely. Before, when I did it fine, she used to send me back anyway. O it pains in my old shoulders, grinding this* masala, *but they will never buy the automatic machine. Very rich people, my* bai-seth. *He is a chartered accountant. He has a nice motorcar, just like A Block priest, and like the one Dr Mody used to drive, which has not moved from the compound since the day he died.* Bai *says they should buy it from Mrs Mody, she wants it to go shopping. But a* masala *machine they will not buy. Jaakaylee must keep on doing it till her arms fall out from shoulders.*

How much teasing everyone was doing to me about the *bhoot.* It became a great game among boys, pretending to be ghosts. One who started it all was Dr Mody's son, from third floor of C Block. One day they call Pesi *paad-maroo* because he makes dirty wind all the time. Good thing he is in boarding school now. That family came to Firozsha Baag only few years ago, he was doctor for animals, a really nice man. But what a terrible boy. Must have been so shameful for Dr Mody. Such a kind man, what a shock everybody got when he died. But I'm telling you, that boy did a bad thing one night.

Vera and Dolly, the two fashionable sisters from C Block's first floor, went to nightshow at Eros Cinema, and Pesi knew. After nightshow was over, tock-tock they came in their high-heel shoes. It was when mini-skirts had just come out, and that is what they were wearing. Very *esskey-messkey,* so short I don't know how their *mai-baap* allowed it. They said their daughters were going foreign for studies, so maybe this kind of dressing was practice for over there. Anyway, they started up, the stairs were very dark. Then Pesi, wearing a white bedsheet and waiting under the staircase, jumped out shouting *bowe ré.* Vera and Dolly screamed so loudly, I'm telling you, and they started running.

Then Pesi did a really shameful thing. God knows where he got the idea from. Inside his sheet he had a torch, and he took it out and shined up into the girls' mini-skirts. Yes! He ran after them with his big torch shining in their skirts. And when Vera and Dolly reached the top they tripped and fell. That shameless boy just stood there with his light shining between their legs, seeing undies and everything, I'm telling you.

He ran away when all neighbours started opening their doors to see what is the matter, because everyone heard them screaming. All the men had good time with Vera and Dolly, pretending to be like concerned grown-up people, saying, it is all right, dears, don't worry, dears, just some bad boy, not a real ghost. And all the time petting-squeezing them as if to comfort them! Sheeh, these men!

Next day Pesi was telling his friends about it, how he shone the torch up their skirts and how they fell, and everything he saw. That boy, sheeh, terrible.

Afterwards, parents in Firozsha Baag made a very strict rule that no one plays the fool about ghosts because it can cause serious accident if sometime some old person is made scared and falls downstairs and breaks a bone or something or has heart attack. So there was no more ghost games and no more making fun of me. But I'm telling you, the *bhoot* kept coming every Friday night.

Curry is boiling nicely, smells very tasty. Bai *tells me don't forget about curry, don't burn the dinner. How many times have I burned the dinner in forty-nine years, I should ask her. Believe or don't believe, not one time.*

Yes, the *bhoot* came but he did not bounce any more upon my chest. Sometimes he just sat next to the bedding, other times he lay down beside me with his head on my chest, and if I tried to push him away he would hold me tighter. Or would try to put his hand up my gown or down from the neck. But I sleep with buttons up to my collar, so it was difficult for the rascal. O what a ghost of mischief he was! Reminded me of Cajetan back in Panjim always trying to do same thing with girls at the cinema or beach. His parents' house was not far from church of St Cajetan for whom he was named, but this boy was no saint, I'm telling you.

Calunqute and Anjuna beaches in those days were very quiet and beautiful. It was before foreigners all started coming, and no hippie-bippie business with *charas* and *ganja*, and no big-big hotels or nothing. Cajetan said to me once, let us go and see the fishermen. And we went, and started to wade a little, up to ankles, and Cajetan said let us go more. He rolled up his pants over the knees and I pulled up my skirt, and we went in deeper. Then a big wave made everything wet. We ran out and sat on the beach for my skirt to dry.

Us two were only ones there, fishermen were still out in boats. Sitting on the sand he made all funny eyes at me, like Hindi film hero, and put his hand on my thigh. I told him to stop or I would tell my father who would give him a solid pasting and throw him in the well where the *bhoot* would take care of him. But he didn't stop. Not till the fishermen came. Sheeh, what a boy that was.

Back to kitchen. To make good curry needs lots of stirring while boiling.

I'm telling you, that Cajetan! Once, it was feast of St Francis Xavier, and the body was to be in a glass case at Church of Bom Jesus. Once every ten years is this very big event for Catholics. They were not going to do it any more because, believe or don't believe, many years back some poor crazy woman took a bite from the toe of St Francis Xavier. But then they changed their minds. Poor St Francis, it is not his luck to have a whole body—one day, Pope asked for a bone from the right arm, for people in Rome to see, and never sent it back; that is where it is till today.

But I was saying about Cajetan. All boys and girls from my village were going to Bom Jesus by bus. In church it was so crowded, and a long long line to walk by St Francis Xavier's glass case. Capitan was standing behind my friend Lily, he had finished his fun with me, now it was Lily's turn. And I'm telling you, he kept bumping her and letting his hand touch her body like it was by accident in the crowd. Sheeh, even in church that boy could not behave.

And the ghost reminded me of Cajetan, whom I have not seen since I came to Bombay—what did I say, forty-nine years ago. Once a week the ghost came, and always on Friday. On Fridays I eat fish, so I started thinking, maybe he likes the smell of fish. Then I just ate vegetarian, and yet he came. For almost a whole year the ghost slept with me, every Friday night, and Christmas was not far away.

And still no one knew about it, how he came to my bed, lay down with me, tried to touch me. There was one thing I was feeling so terrible about—even to Father D'Silva at Byculla Church I had not told anything for the whole year. Every time in confession I would keep completely quiet about it. But now Christmas was coming and I was feeling very bad, so first Sunday in December I told Father D'Silva everything and then I was feeling much better. Father D'Silva said I was blameless because it was not my wish to have the *bhoot* sleeping with me. But he gave three Hail Marys, and said eating fish again was okay if I wanted.

So on Friday of that week I had fish curry-rice and went to bed. And believe or don't believe, the *bhoot* did not come. After midnight, first I thought maybe he is late, maybe he has somewhere else to go. Then the clock in *bai*'s room went three times and I was really worried. Was he going to come in early morning while I was making tea? That would be terrible.

But he did not come. Why, I wondered. If he came to the bedding of a fat and ugly ayah all this time, now what was the matter? I could not understand. But then I said to myself, what are you thinking, Jaakaylee, where is your head, do you really want the ghost to come sleep with you and touch you so shamefully?

After drinking my tea that morning I knew what had happened. The ghost did not come because of my confession. He was ashamed now. Because Father D'Silva knew about what he had been doing to me in the darkness every Friday night.

Next Friday night also there was no ghost. Now I was completely sure my confession had got rid of him and his shameless habits. But in a few days it would be Christmas Eve and time for midnight mass. I thought, maybe if he is ashamed to come into my bed, he could wait for me on the stairs like last year.

Time to cook rice now, time for seth *to come home. Best quality Basmati rice we use, always, makes such a lovely fragrance while cooking, so tasty.*

For midnight mass I left my bedding outside, and when I returned it was two A.M. But for worrying there was no reason. No ghost on any floor this time. I opened the bedding by the stairs, thinking about Cajetan, how scared he was when I said I would tell my father about his touching me. Did not ask me to go anywhere after that, no beaches, no cinema. Now same thing with the ghost. How scared men are of fathers.

And next morning *bai* opened the door, saying, good thing ghost took a holiday this year, if you had woken us again I would have killed you. I laughed a little and said Merry Christmas, *bai,* and she said same to me.

When *seth* woke up he also made a little joke. If they only knew that in one week they would say I had been right. Yes, on New Year's Day they would start believing, when there was really no ghost. Never has been since the day I told Father D'Silva in confession. But I was not going to tell them they were mistaken, after such fun they made of me. Let them feel sorry now for saying Jaakaylee was crazy.

Bai and *Seth* were going to New Year's Eve dance, somewhere in Bandra, for first time since children were born. She used to say they were too small to leave alone with ayah, but that year he kept saying please, now children were bigger. So she agreed. She kept telling me what to do and gave telephone number to call in case of emergency. Such fuss she made, I'm telling you, when they left for Bandra I was so nervous.

I said special prayer that nothing goes wrong, that children would eat dinner properly, not spill anything, go to bed without crying or trouble. If *bai* found out she would say, what did I tell you, children cannot be left with ayah. And then she would give poor *seth* hell for it. He gets a lot anyway.

Everything went right and children went to sleep. I opened my bedding, but I was going to wait till they came home. Spreading out the *saterunjee,* I saw a tear in the white bedsheet used for covering—maybe from all pulling and pushing with the ghost—and was going to repair it next morning. I put off the light and lay down just to rest.

Then cockroach sounds started. I lay quietly in the dark, first to decide where it was. If you put a light on they stop singing and then you don't know where to look. So I listened carefully. It was coming from the gas stove table. I put on the light now and took my *chappal.* There were two of them, sitting next to cylinder. I lifted my *chappal,* very slowly and quietly, then phut! phut! Must say I am expert at cockroach-killing. The poison which *seth* puts out is really not doing much good, my *chappal* is much better.

I picked up the two dead ones and threw them outside, in Baag's backyard. Two cockroaches would make nice little snack for some rat in the yard, I thought. Then I lay down again after switching off light.

Clock in *bai-seth*'s room went twelve times. They would all be giving kiss now and saying Happy New Year. When I was little in Panjim, my parents, before all the money went, always gave a party on New Year's Eve. I lay on my bedding, thinking of those days. It is so strange that so much of your life you can remember if you think quietly in the darkness.

Must not forget rice on stove. With rice, especially Basmati, one minute more or one minute less, one spoon extra water or less water, and it will spoil, it will not be light and every grain separate.

So there I was in the darkness remembering my father and mother, Panjim and Cajetan, nice beaches and boats. Suddenly it was very sad, so I got up and put a light on. In *bai-seth*'s room their clock said two o'clock. I wished they would come home soon. I checked children's room, they were sleeping.

Back to my passage I went, and started mending the torn sheet. Sewing, thinking about my mother, how hard she used to work, how she would repair clothes for my brothers and sisters. Not only sewing to mend but also to alter. When my big brother's pants would not fit, she would open out the waist and undo trouser cuffs to make longer legs. Then when he grew so big that even with alterations it did not fit, she sewed same pants again, making a smaller waist, shorter legs, so little brother could wear. How much work my mother did, sometimes even helping my father outside in the small field, especially if he was visiting a *taverna* the night before.

But sewing and remembering brought me more sadness. I put away the needle and thread and went outside by the stairs. There is a little balcony there. It was so nice and dark and quiet, I just stood there. Then it became a little chilly. I wondered if the ghost was coming again. My father used to say that whenever a ghost is around it feels chilly, it is a sign. He said he always did in the field when the *bhoot* came to the well.

There was no ghost or anything so I must be chilly, I thought, because it is so early morning. I went in and brought my white bedsheet. Shivering a little, I put it over my head, covering up my ears. There was a full moon, and it looked so good. In Panjim sometimes we used to go to the each at night when there was a full moon, and father would tell us about when he was little, and the old days when Portuguese ruled Goa, and about grandfather, who had been to Portugal in a big ship.

Then I saw *bai-seth*'s car come in the compound. I leaned over the balcony, thinking to wave if they looked up, let them know I had not gone to sleep. Then I thought, no, it is better if I go in quietly before they see me, or *bai* might get angry and say, what are you doing outside in middle of night, leaving children alone inside. But she looked up suddenly. I thought, O my Jesus, she has already seen me.

And then she screamed. I'm telling you, she screamed so loudly I almost fell down faint. It was not angry screaming, it was frightened screaming, *bhoot! bhoot!* and I understood. I quickly went inside and lay down on my bedding.

It took some time for them to come up because she sat inside the car and locked all doors. Would not come out until he climbed upstairs, put on every staircase light to make sure the ghost was gone, and then went back for her.

She came in the house at last and straight to my passage, shaking me, saying wake up, Jaakaylee, wake up! I pretended to be sleeping deeply, then turned around and said, Happy New Year, *bai*, everything is okay, children are okay.

She said, yes yes, but the *bhoot* is on the stairs! I saw him, the one you saw last year at Christmas, he is back, I saw him with my own eyes!

I wanted so much to laugh, but I just said, don't be afraid, *bai*, he will not do any harm, he is not a ghost of mischief, he must have just lost his way.

Then she said, Jaakaylee, you were telling the truth and I was angry with you. I will tell everybody in B Block you were right, there really is a *bhoot*.

I said *bai*, let it be now, everyone has forgotten about it, and no one will believe anyway. But she said, when *I* tell them, they will believe.

And after that many people in Firozsha Baag started to believe in the ghost. One was *dustoorji* in A Block. He came one day and taught *bai* a prayer, *saykasté saykasté sataan*, to say it every time she was on the stairs. He told her, because you have seen a *bhoot* on the balcony by the stairs, it is better to have a special Parsi prayer ceremony there so he does not come again and cause any trouble. He said, many years ago, near Marine Lines where Hindus have their funerals and burn bodies, a *bhoot* walked at midnight in the middle of the road, scaring motorists and causing many accidents. Hindu priests said prayers to make him stop. But no use. *Bhoot* kept walking at midnight, motorists kept having accidents. So Hindu priests called me to do a *jashan*, they knew Parsi priest has most powerful prayers of all. And after I did a *jashan* right in the middle of the road, everything was all right.

Bai listened to all this talk of *dustoorji* from A Block, then said she would check with *seth* and let him know if they wanted a balcony *jashan*. Now *seth* says yes to everything, so he told her, sure sure, let *dustoorji* do it. It will be fun to see the exkoriseesum, he said, some big English word like that.

Dustoorji was pleased, and he checked his Parsi calendar for a good day. On that morning I had to wash the whole balcony floor specially, then *dustoorji* came, spread a white sheet, and put all prayer items on it, a silver thing in which he made fire with sandalwood and *loban*, a big silver dish, a *lotta* full of water, flowers, and some fruit.

When it was time to start saying prayers *dustoorji* told me to go inside. Later, *bai* told me that was because Parsi prayers are so powerful, only a Parsi can listen to them. Everyone else can be badly damaged inside their soul if they listen.

So *jashan* was done and *dustoorji* went home with all his prayer things. But when people in Firozsha Baag who did not believe in the ghost heard about prayer ceremony, they began talking and mocking.

Some said Jaakaylee's *bai* has gone crazy, first the ayah was seeing things, and now she has made her *bai* go mad. *Bai* will not talk to those people in the Baag. She is really angry, says she does not want friends who think she is crazy. She hopes *jashan* was not very powerful, so the ghost can come again. She wants everyone to see him and know the truth like her.

Busy eating, bai-seth *are. Curry is hot, they are blowing whoosh-whoosh on their tongues but still eating, they love it hot. Secret of good curry is not only what spices to put, but also what goes in first, what goes in second, and third, and so on. And never cook curry with lid on pot, always leave it open, stir it often, stir it to urge the flavours to come out.*

So *bai* is hoping the ghost will come again. She keeps asking me about ghosts, what they do, why they come. She thinks because I saw the ghost first in Firozsha Baag, it must be my specialty or something. Especially since I am from village—she says village people know more about such things than city people. So I tell her about the *bhoot* we used to see in the small field, and what my father said when he saw the *bhoot* near the well. *Bai* enjoys it, even asks me to sit with her at table, bring my separate mug, and pours a cup for me, listening to my ghost-talk. She does not treat me like servant all the time.

One night she came to my passage when I was saying my rosary and sat down with me on the bedding. I could not believe it, I stopped my rosary. She said, Jaakaylee, what is it Catholics say when they touch their head and stomach and both sides of chest? So I told her, Father, Son and Holy Ghost. Right right! she said, I remember it now, when I went to St Anne's High School there were many Catholic girls and they used to say it always before and after class prayer, yes, Holy Ghost. Jaakaylee, you don't think this is that Holy Ghost you pray to, do you? And I said, no *bai,* that Holy Ghost has a different meaning, it is not like the *bhoot* you and I saw.

Yesterday she said, Jaakaylee, will you help me with something? All morning she was looking restless, so I said, yes *bai.* She left the table and came back with her big scissors and the flat cane *soopra* I use for winnowing rice and wheat. She said, my granny showed me a little magic once, she told me to keep it for important things only. The *bhoot* is, so I am going to use it. If you help me. It needs two Parsis, but I'll do it with you.

I just sat quietly, a little worried, wondering what she was up to now. First, she covered her head with a white *mathoobanoo,* and gave me one for mine, she said to put it over my head like a scarf. Then, the two points of scissors she poked through one side of *soopra,* really tight, so it could hang from the scissors. On two chairs we sat face to face. She made me balance one ring of scissors on my finger, and she balanced the other ring on hers. And we sat like that, with *soopra* hanging from scissors between us, our heads covered with white cloth. Believe or don't believe, it looked funny and scary at the same time. When *soopra* became still and stopped swinging around she said, now close your eyes and don't think of anything, just keep your hand steady. So I closed my eyes, wondering if *seth* knew what was going on.

Then she started to speak, in a voice I had never heard before. It seemed to come from very far away, very soft, all scary. My hair was standing, I felt chilly, as if a *bhoot* was about to come. This is what she said: if the ghost is going to appear again, then *soopra* must turn.

Nothing happened. But I'm telling you, I was so afraid I just kept my eyes shut tight, like she told me to do. I wanted to see nothing which I was not supposed to see. All this was something completely new for me. Even in my village, where everyone knew so much about ghosts, magic with *soopra* and scissors was unknown.

Then *bai* spoke once more, in that same scary voice: if the ghost is going to appear again, upstairs or downstairs, on balcony or inside the house, this year or next year, in daylight or in darkness, for good purpose or for bad purpose, then *soopra* must surely turn.

Believe or don't believe, this time it started to turn. I could feel the ring of the scissors moving on my finger. I screamed and pulled away my hand, there was a loud crash, and *bai* also screamed.

Slowly I opened my eyes. Everything was on the floor, scissors were broken, and I said to *bai*, I'm very sorry I was so frightened, *bai*, and for breaking your big scissors, you can take it from my pay.

She said, you scared me with your scream, Jaakaylee, but it is all right now, nothing to be scared about, I'm here with you. All the worry was gone from her face. She took off her *mathoobanoo* and patted my shoulder, picked up the broken scissors and *soopra*, and took it back to the kitchen.

Bai was looking very pleased. She came back and said to me, don't worry about broken scissors, come, bring your mug, I'm making tea for both of us, forget about *soopra* and ghost for now. So I removed my *mathoobanoo* and went with her.

Jaakaylee, O Jaakaylee, she is calling from dining-room. They must want more curry. Good thing I took some out for my dinner, they will finish the whole pot. Whenever I make Goan curry, nothing is left over. At the end seth always takes a piece of bread and rubs it round and round in the pot, wiping every little bit. They always joke, Jaakaylee, no need today for washing pot, all cleaned out. Yes, it is one thing I really enjoy, cooking my Goan curry, stirring and stirring, taking the aroma as it boils and cooks, stirring it again and again, watching it bubbling and steaming, stirring and stirring till it is ready to eat.

Sans Souci

Rough grass asserted itself everywhere, keeping the earth damp and muddy. It inched its way closer and closer to doorsteps and walls until some hand, it was usually hers, ripped it from its tendrilled roots. But it soon grew back again. It kept the woman in a protracted battle with its creeping mossyness. She ripping it out; shaking the roots of earth. It grew again the minute she turned her back. The house, like the others running up and down the hill, could barely be seen from the struggling road, covered as it was by lush immortelle trees with coarse vine spread among them so that they looked like women with great bushy hair, embracing.

In Sans Souci, the place was called, they said that the people were as rough as the grass.

She may have looked that way but it was from walking the hills and tearing out the grass which grew until she was afraid of it covering her. It hung like tattered clothing from her hips, her breasts, her whole large body. Even when her arms were lifted to carry water to the small shack, she felt weighed down by the bush. Great green patches of leaves, bougainvillea, almond, karili vine fastened her ankles to her wrists. She kept her eyes to the floor of the land. Her look tracing, piercing the bush and marking her steps to the water, to the tub, to the fire, to the road, to the land. The woman turning into a tree, though she was not even old yet. As time went on she felt her back harden like a crab's, like the bark of a tree, like its hard brown meat. A man would come often, but it was difficult to know. When she saw him coming, she would never know him until he said her name, 'Claudine'. Then she would remember him vaguely. A bee near her ear, her hand brushing it away. Sometimes she let the bush grow as tall as it wanted. It overwhelmed her. Reaching at her each new spore or shoot burdened her. Then someone would pass by and not see the house and say that she was minding snakes. Then she would cut it down.

She climbed the hill often when the bush was low around the house. Then she went for water, or so it seemed because she carried a pot. Reaching the top, her feet caking with mud, she would sit on the ground near the edge of the cliff. Then she would look down into the sea and rehearse her falling—a free fall, a dive into the sea. How fast the sea would come toward her—probably not—the cliff was not vertical enough. Her body would hit tufts of grass before reaching the bottom. She could not push off far enough to fall into the water. Musing on whether it would work or not she would lie down on the ground, confused. Spread out, the pot beneath her head, she would be faced by the sky. Then her eyes would close, tired of the blue of the sky zooming in and out at her gaze, and she would be asleep. She never woke up suddenly. Always slowly, as if someone else was there moving in on her sleep. Even when it rained a strong rain which pushed her into the ground or when she slept till the sky turned purple.

Her children knew where she was. They would come up the hill when they did not see her or go to their grandmother's. She never woke up suddenly here, even when the three of them screamed her name—'Claudine!' The boy with his glum face turning cloudier and the girl and the little boy looking hungry.

Three of them. In the beginning she had bathed them and oiled their skins in coconut and dressed them in the wildest and brightest of colours and played with them and shown them off to the other inhabitants of the place. Then they were not good to play with any more. They cried and felt her hands. They cried for the roughness of her hands and the slap. If he was there he would either say 'don't hit them' or 'why don't you hit those children?' His ambiguity caused her to hesitate before each decision on punishment. Then she decided not to touch the children, since either instruction he gave, he gave in an angry and distant voice and for her the two had to be separate thoughts, clear opposites. So after a time the children did not get bathed and dressed and after a time they did not get beaten either.

The people around spoke well of him, described his physical attributes which were in the main two cheloidal scars on his chin and face. When he came he told them of his escapades on the bigger island. Like the time he met the famous criminal Weapon and he and Weapon spent the night drinking and touring the whore houses and the gambling dens and Weapon stuck a knife into the palm of a man who touched his drink. He brought new fashions to the place. The wearing of a gold ring on his little finger and the growing of an elegant nail to set it off. The men, they retold his stories until he came with new ones. They wore copper rings on their little fingers.

If she wasn't careful they would come into the house and tell her what to do again. The shacks up and down the hill were arranged like spiders crawling towards her. One strong rain and they'd be inside of her house which was not at the bottom of the hill so there was no real reason to think that it would actually happen. Looking at them, the other people, they made gestures towards her as they did to each other, to everyone else. They brought her things and she gave them things and they never noticed, nor did she, that she was not her mother's child nor her sister's sister nor an inhabitant of the place, but the woman turning into a tree. They had pressed her with their eyes and their talk and their complicit winks first into a hibiscus switch then into a shrub and now this . . . a tree.

He didn't live there. The dirt path beside the house ran arbitrarily up the hill. Whenever he came he broke a switch with which to scare the children. This was his idea of being fatherly. Coming through the path, he made his stern face up to greet the children and the woman. He came and went and the people in the place expected him to come for her and made excuses when he did not. They expected her to be his. They assumed this as they assumed the path up the hill, the steady rain in March. He is a man, you're a woman, that's how it is.

Those times, not like the first, he would sit on her bed—a piece of wood, his face blunt in the air, dense and unmoving, he had no memory, almost like the first, his breathing and his sweat smelling the same furry thickness as before. Like something which had walked for miles with rain falling and insects biting and the bush and trees slapping some green and murky scent onto its body, a scent rough from years of instinct, and horrible. Now he grew his fingernails and splashed himself with cheap scent but sometimes when he lifted his arm she recalled and forgot quickly. And sometimes she saw his face as before. Always, in and out of seeing him and not seeing him; or wondering who he was and disbelieving when she knew.

Those times he would sit on her bed and tell her about a piece of land which his maternal grandmother had left him. He was just waiting for the day that they built the road across Sans Souci and that was the day that he was going to be a rich man. Because it was good agricultural land and only a road was holding it back. He went on about how he would work the land and how he was really a man of the earth. She listened even though she knew that his mouth was full of nonsense. He had said that for the last many years.

How many . . . was he the same as the first . . . somehow she had come to be with him. Not if he was the first, not him.

His hands with their long fingernails, the elegant long nail on the right finger could never dig into the soil. She listened to him even though she knew that he was lying. But he really wasn't lying to deceive her. He liked to hear himself. He liked to think that he sounded like a man of ideas, like a man going somewhere. Mostly he repeated some phrase which he heard in a popular reggae song about having the heights of jah-jah or something he had heard at the occasional north-american evangelist meeting. He had woven these two into a thousand more convolutions than they already were and only he could understand them. He, the other men in the place and Claudine who couldn't really understand either but liked the sound of him. The sound confused her, it was different, not like the pig squealing that sorrowful squealing as it hung in front of the knife nor its empty sound as it hung for days . . . years . . . its white belly bloodless when it hung with no one seeing it. None around except the air of the yard folding and sealing pockets of flesh, dying. The sound covered an afternoon or so for her above the chorus of the pig's squeal at once mournful and brief in its urgency. The startling incidence of its death mixed with commonplaceness and routine. She liked to have him sit with her as if they were husband and wife.

II

She had met uncle Ranni on the Carenage, she never thought that he would ever get old, he used to be quick and smooth, with golden rings on his fingers. Each time he smiled or laughed that challenging sweet laugh of his the sun would catch the glint of his rings and throw it onto his teeth so that they looked yellow. He would throw his head way back revealing the gold nugget on his thick chain. He was a small man really but you would never know, looking at him when he laughed.

Then even when he talked of killing a man he laughed that sweet laugh, only his eyes were different.

They cut across your face for the briefest of moments like the knife that he intended to use. Once he even threatened to kill his father and his father believed him and slapped his face and never spoke with him again. She poured everything out to him now hoping he would kill the man this time.

Everything about Prime's exhortations and his lies. It came out of her mouth and she didn't know who was saying it. Uncle Ranni's laugh only changed slightly. No one in the family ever really believed that he'd ever kill anyone but no one ever dared not to believe either. Something about his laugh said that he'd never kill a man if he didn't have to and if he did, it would be personal. With a knife or a machete, never with a gun, but close so that the dying man would know who had killed him and why. She'd caught a glimpse of him once, under a tamarind tree, talking about cutting a man's head off and the eyes of the head open, as it lay apart from its body in the dirt. He had told it and the men around, kicking the dust with their toes, had laughed, weakly. Claudine told him everything, even some things that she only thought happened, but happened. These didn't make the case against Prime any worse, they just made her story more lyrical—inspiring the challenging laugh from Ranni. 'This man don't know who your uncle is, or what?' This only made her say more, Prime had lied to her and left her with three children to feed.

The new child, the fourth, moved in her like the first, it felt green and angry. Her flesh all around it, forced to hang there protecting this green and angry thing. It reached into her throat sending up bubbles and making her dizzy all the time. It was not that she hated it, she only wanted to be without it. Out, out, out, out, never to have happened. She wanted to be before it, to never know or have known about it. He had said that the land was in her name, he had even shown her papers which said so and now he had run off, taken a boat to St Croix. 'St Croix? it don't have a place that man can hide; he don't know me,' uncle Ranni said. Claudine got more and more

frightened and more and more excited as she talked the story. It would
serve Prime right to have uncle Ranni chop him up with a knife, she would
like to see it herself. Uncle Ranni was old now. Sixty-four, but when he
laughed like that she could see his mouth still full of his white teeth. It surprised her.

Her mother's brother—he had looked at her once back then as if she had
made it happen. Looked at her as if she were a woman and contemptible,
but it passed quickly like his other looks.

She'd only been talking to an old man about her trouble. She had not
been paying attention. His old face had lit up briefly with that look and his
teeth were as white as when he was young. His skin was tight and black as
she remembered it years ago. He seemed to laugh out of a real joy. She
remembered liking to hear him laugh and see his white teeth against his
beautiful skin. He would spit afterward as if there was something too sweet
in his mouth. Now when she'd first seen him on the Carenage she had seen
an old man with grey eyelashes and a slight stubble of grey on parts of his
skin and face. She had told him everything in a surge of relief and nostal-
gia, never expecting him to do anything but it was he, uncle Ranni, she had
told. She almost regretted saying anything but she needed to say it to someone.

The look across her face as before, cutting her eyes away, cutting her lips,
her head, slicing her, isolating sections of her for scrutiny and inevitable
judgment. Her hand reached to touch her face, to settle it, dishevelled as it
was, to settle it on her empty chest. All that she had said was eaten up by the
old man's face, and thrown at her in a transient lacerating look which he
gave back. Her eyes sniffed the quickly sealed cut and turned, fell on a
wrecked boat in the Carenage.

A little boy jumped off the end not submerged in the water. The glum-
faced boy at home came to her. She hurriedly made excuses to uncle Ranni
about having to go and ran with a kind of urgency toward the tied-up boat
to Cast Island. Disappearing into its confusion of provisions, vegetables and
goats. She did what she always had to do. She pretended to live in the present. She looked at the awful sky. She made its insistent blueness define the
extent of what she could see. Before meeting uncle Ranni she had walked
along pretending that the boat was not there; that she did not have to go;
wishing she could keep walking; that the Carenage would stretch out into
the ocean, that the water of the ocean was a broad floor and the horizon a
shelf which divided and forgot. An end to things completely. Where she did
not exist. The line of her eyes' furthest look burned her face into the sunset of yellow, descending. The red appearing behind her eyelids, rubbing
the line with her head. She had wished that the water between the jetty and
the lapping boat was wider and fit to drink so that she could drink deeply,
become like sand, change places with the bottom of the ocean, sitting in its
fat-legged deepness and its immutable width.

III

After the abortion, she went to Mama's Bar, even though she was in pain and even though she knew that she should lie down. Mama's was a wooden house turned into a restaurant and bar and Mama was a huge woman who had an excellent figure. Mama dominated the bar; she never shouted; she raised her eyebrows lazily when challenged. There were other women in the bar, regulars, who imitated Mam's walk and Mama's eyelids but deferred to Mama and faded, when Mama was in the bar. Mama always sat with her back to the door, which proved just how dangerous she was.

The walls of the bar, at unaccounted intervals, had psychedelic posters in fluorescent oranges and blues. One of them was of an aztec-like mountain— dry, mud brown, cracked, strewn with human bones. Nothing stood on it except bones of feet and ribs and skulls. It would be a foreboding picture if it weren't so glossy. Instead it looked sickly and distant. It was printed by someone in California and one of Mama's visitors had bought it at a head shop in San Diego. Mama though that it was high art and placed it so that people entering the bar could see it immediately.

Claudine walked down the steps to the bar, closed her eyes anticipating the poster then opened them too soon and felt her stomach reach for her throat.

Mama's eyes watched her walk to the counter, ask for a rum, down it and turning to leave bump into the man with the limp. A foamy bit of saliva hung onto the stubble on his face. He grabbed Claudine to save himself from falling and then they began dancing to Mama's crackling stereo.

They danced until lunch time, until the saliva from the limping man's face stretched onto the shoulder of Claudine's dress. Mama had not moved either. She controlled all of it with her eyes and when they told Claudine to leave, she sat the man with the limp onto a stool and left. Going somewhere, averting her stare from the mountain strewn with human bones.

IV

She went to the address on the piece of paper someone had given her—29 Ponces Road. When she got to the street there was no number on any of the houses. She didn't know the woman's name. It was best in these situations not to know anyone's name or to ask anyone where. She walked up and down the street looking at the houses. Some were back from the curb and faced the next street over so there was no way of telling. Maybe something about the house would tell her—what does a house where a woman does that look like, she asked herself—she walked up and down the street thinking that maybe it was this one with the blue veranda or that one with the dog tied to a post. No, she couldn't tell. Maybe this was a sign or something. She gave up, suddenly frightened that it may be just a sign—holy mary mother of god—and bent her head walking very fast up the street for the last time.

She passed a house with nine or ten children in the yard. Most of them were chasing after a half-dressed little boy. They were screaming and pointing at something he was chewing. She hadn't seen the woman on the wooden veranda until one of the children ran towards her saying something breathless and pointing to the woman on the veranda. Then she saw her as the woman on the veranda reached out into the yard and hit a flying child. It didn't seem as if she wanted to hit this one in particular or any one in particular. The group of children gave a common flinch (accustomed to these random attacks on their chasing and rushing around), then continued after the boy. Faced with finally doing this Claudine didn't know anymore. She hesitated, looked at the woman's face for some assurance. But nothing. The woman looked unconcerned waiting for her, and then turning and walking into the ramshackle house, her back expecting Claudine to follow. Claudine walked toward the yard not wanting to stand in the street. Now she moved because of the smallest reasons, now she was trapped by even tinier steps, by tinier reasons. She moved so that her feet would follow each other, so that she could get away from the road, so that she could make the distance to the house, so that it would be over. Nothing had come from the woman's face, no sign of any opinion. Claudine had seen her face, less familiar than a stranger's. Later when she tried she would never remember the face, only as a disquieting and unresolved meeting. Like waking in between sleep and catching a figure, a movement in the room.

V

He had raped her. That is how her first child was born. He had grabbed her and forced her into his little room and covered her mouth so that his mother would not hear her screaming. She had bitten the flesh on his hand until there was blood and still he had exploded her insides, broken her. His face was dense against her crying. He did it as if she was not there, not herself, not how she knew herself. Anyone would have seen that he was killing her but his dense face told her that he saw nothing. She was thirteen, she felt like the hogs that were strung on the limbs of trees and slit from the genitals to the throat. That is how her first child was born. With blood streaming down her legs and feeling broken and his standing up and saying 'Nothing is wrong, go home and don't tell anyone.' And when she ran through the bush crying that she would tell her mother and stood at the stand pipe to wash the blood off her dress and to cool the pain between her thighs, she knew she could tell no one.

Up the hill to the top overlooking the water, she wanted to dive into the sea. The water would hit her face, it would rush past her ears quickly it would wash her limbs and everything would be as before and this would not have happened—a free fall, a dive into the sea. Her body would hit the tuft of grass before reaching the bottom and it would hurt even more. She could not push off far enough to fall into the water.

She said nothing. She became sick and puffy. And her stepfather told her mother that she was pregnant and she begged her mother not to believe him, it was a lie, and her mother sent her to the doctor and told her not to come back home if it was true. When the doctor explained the rape, he said 'Someone put a baby in your belly.' And she could not go home. And when it was dark that night and she was alone on the road because everyone—her aunt first and then her grandmother had said 'go home', she saw her mother on the road coming down with a torchlight. Her mother, rakish and holding her skirt coming toward her. Both of them alone on the road. And she walked behind her all the way home silent, as her mother cursed and told her that she'd still have to do all the work and maybe more. Every day until the birth her mother swore and took care of her.

He denied it when the child was coming and she screamed it was 'you, you, you!' loud and tearing so that the whole village could hear, that it was he. He kept quiet after that and his mother bore his shame by feeding her and asking her 'How're things?'

From then, everyone explained the rape by saying that she was his woman. In fact they did not even say it, they did not have to. Only they made her feel as if she was carrying his body around. In their looking at her and their smiles which moved to one side of the cheek and with their eyelids, uncommonly demurring, or round and wide and gazing she came into the gaze of all of them no longer a child, much less a child who had been raped, now—a man's body. All she remembered was his face as if he saw nothing when he saw her and his unusual body resembling the man who slaughtered pigs for the village—so gnarled and horrible, the way he moved. Closing her eyes he seemed like a tamarind tree—sour and unclimbable—her arms could not move, pinned by his knotted hands and she could not breathe, her breathing took up all the time and she wanted to scream, not breathe—more screaming than breathing.

That is how her first child with him was born. Much as she tried her screaming did not get past the bush and the trees even though she tried to force it through the blades of grass and the coarse vines. Upon every movement of the bush her thin and piercing voice grabbed for the light between but the grass would move the other way making the notes which got through dissonant and unconnected, not like the sound of a killing.

~

Transfigurations

On the way to Régine's, Angèle waves to the trucks that thunder up the highway from the ferries at Yarmouth or Digby, on to Maritime cities and towns about which she knows less than she does about Beirut, Bombay, Ethiopia—places she's seen at least on the evening news, and in colour. She waves to the potato-faced, genially obscene men behind the wheels, and they hoot horns back to her; on a good day she might get half a dozen blasts in the quarter mile between her house and the Salon. Half a dozen blasts: as good as angel trumpets, crashing cymbals, movie choirs. Assessing her breasts and thighs and bum: finding them good, as if the trucks were an enormous mobile mirror lining the highway, imaging only her—seventeen, single, a year out of school: Angèle à Omer à Calixte Deveau.

The door into Régine's Salon has a knotted cord with bells ringing each customer in, announcing to Régine that their hour has come—the hour spent in company with plastic combs and pins, pink and turquoise hairnets, glass jars full of a heavy lucent amber syrup (disinfectant) and a circumambient chemical cloud, soothing as the names of the creams and sprays which seed it—Karesse, Silkspun, Désirée. Into this room the rouged or sallow-skinned, the wrinkled or acne-ravaged, the fleshy or shrivelled come to be transformed into the images of their desiring. On the plywood coffee table between the rows of dryers are the magazines which Angèle, each morning, racks up the way an attendant in a pool hall racks up balls and cues. *People, Us, Look, Life, Cosmopolitan* and *Family Circle.* Magazines which promise Pearl and Rita, Adèle, Aline, Annette, the shade of hair, the heel of shoe to complete the miracle Régine's fingers and the whirr of her dryers will begin; fix it even better than the can of spray Régine waves like an enchanter's wand over the newborn hairdos of her customers.

It is eight forty-five; Régine is still upstairs sipping tepid coffee and watching a talk show. The Salon is in the basement of the A-frame she and her husband constructed from a kit the year they moved down from Chéticamp. Angèle never sees much of Régine's Joe—he's employed by the Department of Highways to hold up an orange sign marked SLOW on the road they have been building for the last twelve years between Weymouth and Annapolis. Régine drinks her coffee out of a cup as brightly blue as a baby's eyes:

Angèle knows this because, when things downstairs are slow, Régine sends her up to load the breakfast plates into the dishwasher. Angèle takes special care of, even holds up to her lips as if to kiss, the azure cup which has R E G I N E and a little crown with silver balls on its tips stamped into the blue—the same kind of crown printed on Régine's business cards and on the sign outside the shop:

> Régine's Beauty Salon/Salon Aesthétique
> Cuts, Perms, Electrolysis, Manicure, Etc.
> Come to Us for All You're Beauty Needs

Us was Régine herself, though a new customer might assume the term embraced both underlings: Angèle, and Eric Saulnier who had been hired a full two years before Angèle, which made the girl only an apprentice's apprentice. Eric had been to Montréal, and went every July down to a beach in Maine where, he told Angèle, people were cultivated enough to have other ideas of Heaven than farting down the beach on mechanized tricycles, or pumping video games at the Social Club. Eric lived with his grandmother in an unpainted frame house across the road from Régine's. He dressed beautifully from the catalogue, had a long moustache the colour of toffee, and was the gentlest of them all with the old ladies who came in for a tint and a poodle perm, though they'd barely a hundred hairs left on their puckered scalps. At first Angèle had sworn she couldn't bear to touch them, until Eric had shown her how, if she pretended it was dough and not skin she were kneading, she'd forget herself and actually begin to enjoy the work.

Eric comes in just before Régine leaves the television set upstairs—she never turns it off, liking the muffled crash of commercials and soaps and news to ground the spiky jabber from the AM radio. It plays a chocolate-box assortment of tunes at least one of which every customer from eighty-eight-year-old Madame Wagner to eight-year-old Shanda Comeau can croon to as the neutralizer's being squirted on or the hairnet knotted tighter. When Eric comes in late like this Angèle always turns up the radio so that Régine won't hear the bells and dock him a quarter of an hour's salary. He is supposed to be there early to check over the books and begin call-ups for the next day's appointments, though what he likes doing best when there's no one but Angèle and himself around is to rearrange the giant combs which Régine has hooked up over the wallpaper for decoration. She has collected them on her travels. Régine has been to nearly every state in the Union, even Hawaii, so there are combs in the shape of pineapples, teepees, sharks, lobsters, ten-gallon hats, southern belles, cobs of corn and even the President and First Lady. Eric rearranges the combs in shifting patterns, so that each is a knot in the ribbon of a story he whispers to Angèle when the clients are under the dryers and Régine busy combing out a wedding hairdo in the swivel chair. Stories to which Angèle listens in a coconut-cream abstraction: stories of escape, of finding your true heart's desire—stories better than those in the Harlequins she buys at the Kwikway store on the way home from Régine's.

Régine is a pair of purple-bloated feet in plastic thongs; legs thick and sturdy as the concrete pillars holding up the porch of the A-frame; a nurse's uniform dyed moss green to match the ferns in the wallpaper; a face flat and ashy as the highway over which her husband slows the cars. But most of all, Régine is hair. Hair like meringue on a lemon pie; hair like cotton candy whirled into a sunset cloud around the cone; hair that each week takes on a different shade and tone—frosted here, darkened there, frizzed at the nape, moussed at the crown, spooled down before her ears or rolled in waves like barbells held up by straining rhinestone-studded combs. Each Monday Régine descends the stairs to her salon, while Eric and Angèle, mute witnesses of an apparition part celestial, part demonic, stare in tribute.

Régine walks over to the table on which the appointment books are kept, cocks an eye at today's page, flicks an artificial fingernail at the rayon roses in the crystal vase which she insists be filled halfway up with water, and then thumps over to the swivel-chair. Tests it with a spin or two, stills it before the mirror, lights a menthol cigarette and waits for the first of her customers. When she arrives—the doctor's wife, who's been up to a funeral in Halifax and needs a quick comb-out—Régine does not so much surrender as release her chair. Leaving her cigarette to unravel into smoke in the ashtray Eric has deftly placed beside the combs, she greets the doctor's wife by her first name (for the crown on her business card extends to her social niche and manner) and allows Angèle to tie a vinyl apron round the client's neck. Upon Angèle's retreat, Régine moves in with comb and brush: a general to a chaotic battlefield.

And it begins. In and out the golden oldies on the radio, over the rumblings from the television set upstairs, through the clickings of combs and scissors and the rustling of end papers, the squish of shampoo and fumes of permanent solution. All the length of St Alphonse Bay and beyond—south to Pubnico and north to Chéticamp; across the Bay of Fundy to Moncton and Memramcook; down the Happy Valley to Halifax and back. Each shampoo'd head full of news or questions offered to Régine like pearls on a platter—who did how did why did what. Steve à Louis who married Charline à Hector who went back to her bed in her mother's house saying Steve couldn't get it up any higher than the nap on the hall carpet. But then Steve had been having it off with Delima before and after the wedding, Delima in the trailer down by the fishplant, Delima who's had three already and is starting her fourth—not off Steve but that little shit of a Landry whose wife most likely wouldn't last out the year. Had It so bad they'd taken her out of Sidmouth hospital to Halifax, where no one could come to visit—all the more convenient for him, the bastard. So why do we all lie down and spread our legs and take it? Who knows, who needs it? You listen now, Angèle, you be smart—steer clear of the buggers, don't you melt any butter for 'em, not yet. Plenty of time for that. But it's no use, you'll end up just like the rest of us.

Just watch out for them smart-asses back from the oil rigs—good for nothing but whoring and drinking and belching through Mass, every damn one of 'em. Present company excepted, that means you, Eric—

Eric works through it all as if the words are bubbles in the lather he's working up on this scalp or rinsing out of those eyes. He opens his mouth only to compliment Doreen on having finally found a scarf to match the extraordinary deep blue of her eyes, or to assure Ginette that if the solution were left on a fraction of a moment longer the curls would be just that much tighter—exactly like the picture in the magazine, though the model hadn't Ginette's wonderfully thick hair, and such a gorgeous colour—he wouldn't have her dye a hair of it, honestly he wouldn't. Eric earns as much in tips as he does in salary at Régine's.

Each week he comes to work in a new shirt, with rolled or button-down or detachable collar; in new trousers with or without cuffs, pleats at the waist or else so low across the hips that Angèle finds herself waiting for the pants to drop as he darts back and forth between the chairs or bends under the dryers to make sure some client isn't having her curls scorched. Waiting and wondering if he knows how they talk about him when he's off on holiday in Maine and Régine elaborates with grossly fluent gestures just what kind of beach it is; the sort of customers it attracts. They would start in then on the absent Eric, plucking and clawing and ripping until it made Angèle think of the huge crows she saw along the highway, jabbing beaks into the green garbage bags, scattering shreds of rotting meat and bashed-in tins inside the ditch. Until Eric came back, his skin toffee-coloured like his moustache, and eight or ten new words—he called it Boston slang—he'd drop into his conversation as showily as sugar cubes into tea. He would not need to rearrange the combs or tell her stories for a long time, then—at least till the first storms came in autumn, the wind and rain that battered down even his memories of the summer.

Angèle is given the job of washing hair: lathering the shampoo that smells fizzily of strawberries or peaches or lime, playing waterfall with the hose attachment at the sink, towelling gently, leading the ladies like blind children from the sink and patting them into their chairs; taking a long, thick comb out of the glass jar and dragging it through the drenched clumps of hair. As soon as each new head is washed and combed she calls out to Eric, or sometimes, if it is a special customer, to Régine herself, who takes up the rollers, scrabbling in the tray for the different sizes and colours of plastic, scrolling and twisting the hair, shoving in pins like bayonets. And while the dryers whirl Angèle takes the broom and sweeps curls, split ends and ratty pony tails into the soft, dense, dull mat that she will scoop into a garbage bag and place in the shed out back where the crows and dogs will not get at it.

Most of the time she waits for something important to do, wishing she could have a cigarette—but Régine doesn't like to see young girls smoking—and watching the women under the dryer, the fluorescent salon lights and torrid heat puffing up the faces, revealing pouchy bags of chins, deltas of wrinkles around mouths and eyes like little metal bits screwed in too tight. Their bodies soft and swollen as the garbage bags full of their hair, for the women sag in the chairs, relaxing as much as pincer curlers and abrading heat permit. Relax in the limbo between that first desperate hope of beauty and the ultimate despair, once they have paid Régine and rushed to their own bathroom mirrors, that all the lilac and azure curlers, the snowy mousses and dizzy-scented sprays have not this time, or any other time, transfigured them into the heart of their desire. They are still what they were—women whose invariable story Angèle has read and reread in the ads placed in the *French Shore Shopper.* 'For sale: wedding dress, size 5-6, excellent condition'—'For sale, child's crib and high chair, sturdy make'—'For sale, woman's fun-fur coat, mature size'—and finally, 'Words aren't enough to thank our friends for their kindness shown in Mom's last illness. We'll never forget your help in this difficult time.'

Watching the rows of hopelessly hoping faces, Angèle knows in every pliant bone, in every glinting hair of her sweet-skinned, seventeen-year-old body that she will never, ever look like these old women under the dryers—never let herself tell or be told such a story. For she is saving not so much herself, as that one perfect picture of desire which none of these women know, not even Régine. You had only to find the true picture and you would have no need of nets and curlers and dizzying heat; you could be like Christ on the high mountain, shining as snow, if you kept it always, like a gold locket over your heart, no matter what was happening, no matter what Régine and her customers told you would happen, had to happen to you—

it is summer and she is walking along a path that leads up from the highway into a grove of trees whose leaves are new-green still, without a blotch or tear or hole, and he holds her hand, is tracing her palm with his finger the way Régine traces a scalp with her comb—delicately, yet so precisely the skin tingles and reddens to the touch. His eyes are blue as Régine's coffee cup. He wears trousers pleated like Eric's and tells stories like Eric, but always about her, how she is so beautiful that no one can possibly find words to tell, that the truck drivers from off the ferries at Yarmouth and Digby see her walking along the highway and hoot their horns the whole Trans-Canada long for love of her, telling how she is more shiningsweetsnowybeautiful than the models on TV or videos or glossy magazines. That her hair is like gold, no, is auburn and rippling down her small shoulders, over her breasts and hips to her toes that are small, pink as shells half-hidden in the sand. Her hair a cape, a cloak all over her so that she needs no clothes, only her hair and the skin all cool and shadowy beneath. His hands, gentle, finely shaped, and she shakes her long, bright hair, she is somehow under the water of her hair, watching his hands like lovely, lazy fish, parting the waves and coming to her . . . . Air full of angel choirs, clouds pink, moss-green and lilac, pillows of new-cut grass, as they lie down together

Her face flushed as that of the customer she leads from the dryer to the swivel chair where Régine waits, arms raised, comb quivering while Eric undoes the rollers as carefully as if he's pulling a bandage from a wound. And Régine rakes a fistful of hair rinsed the blind-blue of fading forget-me-nots; makes it into a tumbling froth above the eyes of the woman who has waited her whole life for this transfiguration to take place. Door ringing open and open, Angèle washing hair, towelling it dry, sweeping up soft, dun-coloured mounds into green garbage bags while Eric fishes for tips and tells his stories. Wanting, waiting, wanting.

∿

Red Plaid Shirt

RED PLAID SHIRT that your mother bought you one summer in Banff. It is 100% Pure Virgin Wool, itchy but flattering against your pale skin, your black hair. You got it in a store called Western Outfitters, of the sort indigenous to the region, which stocked only *real* (as opposed to designer) blue jeans, Stetson hats, and $300 hand-tooled cowboy boots with very pointy toes. There was a saddle and a stuffed deer-head in the window.

Outside, the majestic mountains were sitting all around, magnanimously letting their pictures be taken by ten thousand tourists wielding Japanese cameras and eating ice-cream cones. You had tricked your mother into leaving her camera in the car so she wouldn't embarrass you, who lived there and were supposed to be taking the scenery for granted by now.

You liked the red plaid shirt so much that she bought you two more just like it, one green, the other chocolate brown. But these two stayed shirts, never acquiring any particular significance, eventually getting left unceremoniously behind in a Salvation Army drop-box in a grocery store parking lot somewhere along the way.

The red plaid shirt reminded you of your mother's gardening shirt, which was also plaid and which you rescued one winter when she was going to throw it away because the elbows were out. You picture her kneeling in the side garden where she grew only flowers, bleeding hearts, roses, peonies, poppies, and a small patch of strawberries. You picture her hair in a bright babushka, her hands in the black earth with her shirt-sleeves rolled up past the elbow. The honeysuckle hedge bloomed fragrantly behind her and the sweet peas curled interminably up the white trellis. You are sorry now for the way you always sulked and whined when she asked you to help, for the way you hated the dirt under your nails and the sweat running into your eyes, the sweat dripping down her shirt-front between her small breasts. You kept her old shirt in a bag in your closet for years, with a leather patch half-sewn onto the left sleeve, but now you can't find it.

You were wearing the red plaid shirt the night you met Daniel in the tavern where he was drinking beer with his buddies from the highway construction crew. You ended up living with him for the next five years. He was always calling it your 'magic shirt', teasing you, saying how it was the shirt that made him fall in love with you in the first place. You would tease him back, saying how you'd better hang onto it then, in case you had to use it on somebody else. You've even worn it in that spirit a few times since, but the magic seems to have seeped out of it and you are hardly surprised.

You've gained a little weight since then or the shirt has shrunk, so you can't wear it any more, but you can't throw or give it away either.

> RED: *crimson carmine cochineal cinnebar sanguine scarlet red ruby rouge my birthstone red and blood-red brick-red beet-red bleeding hearts Queen of fire god of war Mars the colour of magic my magic the colour of iron flowers and fruit the colour of meat dripping lobster cracking claws lips nipples blisters blood my blood and all power.*

BLUE COTTON SWEATSHIRT that says 'Why Be Normal?' in a circle on the front. This is your comfort shirt, fleecy on the inside, soft from many washings, and three sizes too big so you can tuck your hands up inside the sleeves when they're shaking or cold. You like to sit on the couch with the curtains closed, wearing your comfort shirt, eating comfort food: vanilla ice-cream, macaroni and cheese, white rice with butter and salt, white toast with CheezWhiz and peanut-butter. Sometimes you even sleep in it.

This is the shirt you wore when you had the abortion three days before Christmas. They told you to be there at nine in the morning and then you didn't get into the operation room until nearly twelve-thirty. So you wore it in the waiting room with the other women also waiting, and the weight you had already gained was hidden beneath it while you pretended to read *Better Homes and Gardens* and they wouldn't let you smoke. After you came to, you put the shirt back on and waited in another waiting room for your friend, Alice, to come and pick you up because they said you weren't capable yet of going home alone. One of the other women was waiting there too, for her boyfriend who was always late, and when he finally got there, first she yelled at him briefly, and then they decided to go to McDonald's for a hamburger. At home, Alice pours you tea from the porcelain pot into white china cups like precious opaque stones.

None of this has diminished, as you feared it might, the comfort this shirt can give you when you need it. Alice always puts her arms around you whenever she sees you wearing it now. She has one just like it, only pink.

> BLUE: *azure aqua turquoise delft and navy-blue royal-blue cool cerulean peacock-blue ultramarine cobalt-blue Prussian-blue cyan the sky and electric a space the colour of the firmament and sapphire sleeping silence the sea the blues my lover plays the saxophone cool blue he plays the blues.*

PALE GREY TURTLENECK that you bought when you were seeing Dwight, who said one night for no apparent reason that grey is a mystical colour. You took this judgement to heart because Dwight was more likely to talk about hockey or carburetors and you were pleasantly surprised to discover that he might also think about other things. You spotted the turtleneck the very next day on sale at Maggie's for $9.99.

You took to wearing it on Sundays because that was the day Dwight was most likely to wander in, unannounced, on his way to or from somewhere else. You wore it while you just happened to put a bottle of good white wine into the fridge to chill and a chicken, a roast, or a pan of spinach lasagna into the oven to cook slowly just in case he showed up hungry. You suppose now that this was pathetic, but at the time you were thinking of yourself as patient and him as worth waiting for.

Three Sundays in a row you ended up passed out on the couch, the wine bottle empty on the coffee table, and supper dried out, and a black-and-white movie with violin music flickering on the TV. In the coloured morning, the pattern of the upholstery was imprinted on your cheek and your whole head was hurting. When Dwight finally did show up, it was a Wednesday and you were wearing your orange flannelette nightie with all the buttons gone and a rip down the front, because it was three in the morning, he was drunk, and you had been in bed for hours. He just laughed and took you in his arms when you told him to get lost. Until you said you were seeing someone else, which was a lie, but one that you both wanted to believe because it was an easy answer that let both of you gingerly off the hook.

You keep meaning to wear that turtleneck again sometime because you know it's juvenile to think it's a jinx, but then you keep forgetting to iron it.

Finally, you get tough and wear it, wrinkled, grocery-shopping one Saturday afternoon. You careen through the aisles like a crazed hamster, dodging toddlers, old ladies, and other carts, scooping up vegetables with both hands, eating an apple you haven't paid for, leaving the core in the dairy section. But nothing happens and no one notices your turtleneck: the colour or the wrinkles.

Sure enough, Dwight calls the next day, Sunday, at five o'clock. You say you can't talk now, you're just cooking supper: prime rib, wild rice, broccoli with Hollandaise. You have no trouble at all hanging quietly up on him while pouring the wine into the crystal goblet before setting the table for one with the Royal Albert china your mother left you in her will.

> GREY: *oyster pewter slate dull lead dove-grey pearl-grey brain my brains silver or simple gone into the mystic a cool grey day overcast with clouds ashes concrete the aftermath of airplanes gun-metal-grey granite and gossamer whales elephants cats in the country the colour of questions the best camouflage the opaque elegance an oyster.*

WHITE EMBROIDERED BLOUSE that you bought for $80 to wear with your red-flowered skirt to a Christmas party with Peter, who was working as a pizza cook until he could afford to play his sax full-time. You also bought a silken red belt with gold beads and tassels, a pair of red earrings with dragons on them, and ribbed red stockings which are too small but you wanted them anyway. This striking outfit involves you and Alice in a whole day of trudging around downtown in a snowstorm, holding accessories up in front of mirrors like talismans.

You spend an hour in the bathroom getting ready, drinking white wine, plucking your eyebrows, dancing like a dervish, and smiling seductively at yourself. Peter calls to say he has to work late but he'll meet you there at midnight.

By the time he arrives, you are having a complex anatomical conversation with an intern named Fernando, who has spilled a glass of red wine down the front of your blouse. He is going to be a plastic surgeon. Your blouse is soaking in the bathtub and you are wearing only your white lace camisole. Fernando is feeding you green grapes and little squares of cheese, complimenting you on your cheekbones, and falling in love with your smooth forehead. You are having the time of your life and it's funny how you notice for the first time that Peter has an inferior bone structure.

> WHITE: *ivory alabaster magnolia milk the moon is full and chalk-white pure-white snow-white moonstone limestone rime and clay marble may seashells and my bones are china bones precious porcelain lace white magic white feather the immaculate conception of white lies wax white wine is a virtue.*

YELLOW EVENING GOWN that you bought for your New Year's Eve date with Fernando. It has a plunging neckline and a dropped sash which flatteringly accentuates your hips. You wear it with black hoop earrings, black lace stockings with seams, and black high-heels that Alice forced you to buy even though they hurt your toes and you are so unco-ordinated that you expect you will have to spend the entire evening sitting down with your legs crossed, calves nicely flexed.

You spend an hour in the bathroom getting ready, drinking pink champagne, applying blusher with a fat brush according to a diagram in a women's magazine that shows you how to make the most of your face. You practise holding your chin up so it doesn't sag and look double. Alice french-braids your hair and teaches you how to waltz like a lady. Fernando calls to say he has to work late but he'll meet you there before midnight.

You go to the club with Alice instead. They seat you at a tiny table for two so that when you sit down, your knees touch hers. You are in the middle of a room full of candles, fresh flowers, lounge music, and well-groomed couples staring feverishly into each other's eyes. The meal is sumptuous: green salad, a whole lobster, home-made pasta, fresh asparagus, and warm buns wrapped in white linen in a wicker basket. You eat everything and then you get the hell out of there, leaving a message for Fernando.

You go down the street to a bar you know where they will let you in without a ticket even though it's New Year's Eve. In the lobby you meet Fernando in a tuxedo with his arm around a short homely woman in black who, when you ask, 'Who the hell are you?', says, 'His wife.' In your black high-heels you are taller than both of them and you know your gown is gorgeous. When the wife says, 'And who the hell are *you*?', you point a long finger at Fernando's nose and say, 'Ask him.' You stomp away with your chin up and your dropped sash swaying.

Out of sight, you take off your high-heels and walk home through the park and the snow with them in your hands, dangling. Alice follows in a cab. By the time you get there, your black lace stockings are in shreds and your feet are cut and you are laughing and crying, mostly laughing.

> YELLOW: *jonquil jasmine daffodil lemon and honey-coloured corn-coloured cornsilk canary crocus the egg yolk in the morning the colour of mustard bananas brass cadmium yellow is the colour of craving craven chicken cats' eyes I am faint-hearted weak-kneed lily-livered or the sun lucid luminous means caution or yield.*

BLACK LEATHER JACKET that you bought when you were seeing Ivan, who rode a red Harley Davidson low-rider with a suicide shift, his black beard blowing in the wind. The jacket has rows of diagonal pleats at the yoke and a red leather collar and cuffs.

Ivan used to take you on weekend runs with his buddies and their old ladies to little bars in other towns where they were afraid of you: especially of Ivan's best friend, Spy, who had been hurt in a bike accident two years before and now his hands hung off his wrists at odd angles and he could not speak, could only make gutteral growls, write obscene notes to the waitress on a serviette, and laugh at her like a madman, his eyes rolling back in his head, and you could see what was left of his tongue.

You would come riding up in a noisy pack with bugs in your teeth, dropping your black helmets like bowling balls on the floor, eating greasy burgers and pickled eggs, drinking draft beer by the jug, the foam running down your chin. Your legs, after the long ride, felt like a wishbone waiting to be sprung. If no one would rent you a room, you slept on picnic tables in the campground, the bikes pulled in around you like wagons, a case of beer and one sleeping bag between ten of you. In the early morning, there was dew on your jacket and your legs were numb with the weight of Ivan's head on them.

You never did get around to telling your mother you were dating a biker (she thought you said 'baker') which was just as well since Ivan eventually got tired, sold his bike, and moved back to Manitoba to live with his mother who was dying. He got a job in a hardware store and soon married his high school sweetheart, Betty, who was a dental hygienist. Spy was killed on the highway, drove his bike into the back of a tanker truck in broad daylight: there was nothing left of him.

You wear your leather jacket now when you need to feel tough. You wear it with your tight blue jeans and your cowboy boots. You strut slowly with your hands in your pockets. Your boots click on the concrete and you are a different person. You can handle anything and no one had better get in your way. You will take on the world if you have to. You will die young and in flames if you have to.

> BLACK: *ebon sable charcoal jet lamp-black blue-black bruises in a night sky ink-black soot-black the colour of my hair and burning rubber dirt the colour of infinite space speeding blackball blacklist black sheep blackberries ravens eat crow black as the ace of spades and black is black I want my baby back before midnight yes of course midnight that old black dog behind me.*

BROWN CASHMERE SWEATER that you were wearing the night you told Daniel you were leaving him. It was that week between Christmas and New Year's which is always a wasteland. Everyone was digging up recipes called Turkey-Grape Salad, Turkey Soufflé, and Turkey-Almond-Noodle Bake. You kept vacuuming up tinsel and pine needles, putting away presents one at a time from under the tree. You and Daniel sat at the kitchen table all afternoon, drinking hot rum toddies, munching on crackers and garlic sausage, playing Trivial Pursuit, asking each other questions like:

What's the most mountainous country in Europe?

Which is more tender, the left or right leg of a chicken?

What race of warriors burned off their right breasts in Greek legend?

Daniel was a poor loser and he thought that Europe was a country, maybe somewhere near Spain.

This night you have just come from a party at his friend Harold's house. You are sitting on the new couch, a loveseat, blue with white flowers, which was Daniel's Christmas present to you, and you can't help thinking of the year your father got your mother a coffee percolator when all she wanted was something personal: earrings, a necklace, a scarf for God's sake. She spent most of the day locked in their bedroom, crying noisily, coming out every hour or so to baste the turkey, white-lipped, tucking more Kleenex up her sleeve. You were on her side this time and wondered how your father, who you had always secretly loved the most, could be so insensitive. It was the changing of the guard, your allegience shifting like sand from one to the other.

You were sitting on the new couch eating cold pizza and trying to figure out why you didn't have a good time at the party. Daniel was accusing you alternately of looking down on his friends or sleeping with them. He is wearing the black leather vest you bought him for Christmas and he says you are a cheapskate.

When you tell him you are leaving (which is a decision you made months ago but it took you this long to figure out how you were going to manage it and it has nothing to do with the party, the couch, or the season), Daniel grips you by the shoulders and bangs your head against the wall until the picture hung there falls off. It is a photograph of the mountains on a pink spring morning, the ridges like ribs, the runoff like incisions or veins. There is glass flying everywhere in slices into your face, into your hands pressed over your eyes, and the front of your sweater is spotted and matted with blood.

On the way to the hospital, he says he will kill you if you tell them what he did to you. You promise him anything, you promise him that you will love him forever and that you will never leave.

The nurse takes you into the examining room. Daniel waits in the waiting room, reading magazines, buys a chocolate bar from the vending machine, then a Coke and a bag of ripple chips. You tell the nurse what happened and the police take him away in handcuffs with their guns drawn. In the car on the way to the station, he tells them he only did it because he loves you. The officer who takes down your report tells you this and he just keeps shaking his head and patting your arm. The police photographer takes pictures of your face, your broken fingers, your left breast which has purple bruises all over it where he grabbed it and twisted and twisted.

By the time you get to the women's shelter, it is morning and the blood on your sweater has dried, doesn't show. There is no way of knowing. There, the other women hold you, brush your hair, bring you coffee and cream and mushroom soup. The woman with the broken cheekbone has two canaries in a gold cage that she carries with her everywhere like a lamp. She shows you how the doors are steel, six inches thick, and the windows are bullet-proof. She shows you where you will sleep, in a room on the third floor with six other women, some of them lying now fully-dressed on their little iron cots with their hands behind their heads, staring at the ceiling as if it were full of stars or clouds that drift slowing westward in the shape of camels, horses, or bears. She shows you how the canaries will sit on your finger if you hold very still and pretend you are a tree or a roof or another bird.

> BROWN: *ochre cinnamon coffee copper caramel the colour of my Christmas cake chocolate mocha walnut chestnuts raw sienna my suntan burnt umber burning toast fried fricasseed sautéed grilled I baste the turkey the colour of stupid cows smart horses brown bears brown shirt brown sugar apple brown betty brunette the colour of thought and sepia the colour of old photographs the old earth and wood.*

GREEN SATIN QUILTED JACKET in the Oriental style with mandarin collar and four red frogs down the front. This jacket is older than you are. It belonged to your mother, who bought it when she was the same age you are now. In the black-and-white photos from that time, the jacket is grey but shiny and your mother is pale but smooth-skinned, smiling with her hand on her hip or your father's thigh.

You were always pestering her to let you wear it to play dress-up, with her red high-heels and that white hat with the feathers and the little veil that covered your whole face. You wanted to wear it to a Hallowe'en party at school where all the other girls would be witches, ghosts, or princesses and you would be the only mandarin, with your eyes, you imagined, painted up slanty and two sticks through the bun in your hair. But she would never let you. She would just keep on cooking supper, bringing carrots, potatoes, cabbages up from the root cellar, taking peas, beans, broccoli out of the freezer in labelled dated parcels, humming, looking out through the slats of the Venetian blind at the black garden and the leafless rose bushes. Each year, at least one of them would be winter-killed no matter how hard she had tried to protect them. And she would dig it up in the spring by the dead roots and the thorns would get tangled in her hair, leave long bloody scratches all down her arms. And the green jacket stayed where it was, in the cedar chest with the hand-made lace doilies, her grey linen wedding suit, and the picture of your father as a small boy with blond ringlets.

After the funeral, you go through her clothes while your father is outside shovelling snow. You lay them out in piles on the bed: one for the Salvation Army, one for the second-hand store, one for yourself because your father wants you to take something home with you. You will take the green satin jacket, also a white mohair cardigan with multi-coloured squares on the front, a black-and-white striped shirt you sent her for her birthday last year that she never wore, an imitation pearl necklace for Alice, and a dozen unopened packages of pantyhose. There is a fourth pile for your father's friend Jack's new wife, Frances, whom your mother never liked, but your father says Jack and Frances have fallen on hard times on the farm since Jack got the emphysema, and Frances will be glad of some new clothes.

Jack and Frances drop by the next day with your Aunt Jeanne. You serve tea and the shortbread cookies Aunt Jeanne has brought. She makes them just the way your mother did, whipped, with a sliver of maraschino cherry on top. Jack, looking weather-beaten or embarrassed, sits on the edge of the couch with his baseball cap in his lap and marvels at how grown-up you've got to be. Frances is genuinely grateful for the two green garbage bags of clothes, which you carry out to the truck for her.

After they leave you reminisce fondly with your father and Aunt Jeanne about taking the toboggan out to Jack's farm when you were small, tying it to the back of the car, your father driving slowly down the country lane, towing you on your stomach, clutching the front of the toboggan which curled like a wooden wave. You tell him for the first time how frightened you were of the black tires spinning the snow into your face, and he says he had no idea, he thought you were having fun. This was when Jack's first wife, Winnifred, was still alive. Your Aunt Jeanne, who knows everything, tells you that when Winnifred was killed in that car accident, it was Jack, driving drunk, who caused it. And now when he gets drunk, he beats Frances up, locks her out of the house in her bare feet, and she has to sleep in the barn, in the hay with the horses.

You are leaving in the morning. Aunt Jeanne helps you pack. You are anxious to get home but worried about leaving your father alone. Aunt Jeanne says she'll watch out for him.

The green satin jacket hangs in your front hall closet now, between your black leather jacket and your raincoat. You can still small the cedar from the chest and the satin is always cool on your cheek like clean sheets or glass.

One day you think you will wear it downtown, where you are meeting a new man for lunch. You study yourself in the full-length mirror on the back of the bathroom door and you decide it makes you look like a different person: someone unconventional, unusual, and unconcerned. This new man, who you met recently at an outdoor jazz festival, is a free spirit who eats health food, plays the dulcimer, paints well, writes well, sings well, and has just completed an independent study of eastern religions. He doesn't smoke, drink, or do drugs. He is pure and peaceful, perfect. He is teaching you how to garden, how to turn the black soil, how to plant the seeds, how to water them, weed them, watch them turn into lettuce, carrots, peas, beans, radishes, and pumpkins, how to get the kinks out of your back by stretching your brown arms right up to the sun. You haven't even told Alice about him yet because he is too good to be true. He is bound to love this green jacket, and you in it too.

You get in your car, drive down the block, go back inside because you forgot your cigarettes, and you leave the green jacket on the back of a kitchen chair because who are you trying to kid? More than anything, you want to be transparent. More than anything, you want to hold his hands across the table and then you will tell him you love him and it will all come true.

GREEN: *viridian verdigris chlorophyll grass leafy jade mossy verdant apple-green pea-green lime-green sage-green sea-green bottle-green emeralds avocadoes olives all leaves the colour of Venus hope and jealousy the colour of mould mildew envy poison and pain and snakes the colour of everything that grows in my garden fertile nourishing sturdy sane and strong.*

LINDA SVENDSEN
(1954)

White Shoulders

My oldest sister's name is Irene de Haan and she has never hurt anybody. She lives with cancer, in remission, and she has stayed married to the same undemonstrative Belgian Canadian, a brake specialist, going on thirty years. In the family's crumbling domestic empire, Irene and Peter's union has been, quietly, and despite tragedy, what our mother calls the lone success.

Back in the late summer of 1984, before Irene was admitted into hospital for removal of her left breast, I flew home from New York to Vancouver to be with her. We hadn't seen each other for four years, and since I didn't start teaching ESL night classes until mid-September, I was free, at loose ends, unlike the rest of her family. Over the past months, Peter had used up vacation and personal days shuttling her to numerous tests, but finally had to get back to work. He still had a mortgage. Their only child, Jill, who'd just turned seventeen, was entering her last year of high school. Until junior high, she'd been one of those unnaturally well-rounded kids—taking classes in the high dive, water ballet, drawing, and drama, and boy-hunting in the mall on Saturdays with a posse of dizzy friends. Then, Irene said, overnight she became unathletic, withdrawn, and bookish: an academic drone. At any rate, for Jill and Pete's sake, Irene didn't intend to allow her illness to interfere with their life. She wanted everything to proceed as normally as possible. As who wouldn't.

In a way, and this will sound callous, the timing had worked out. Earlier that summer, my ex-husband had been offered a temporary teaching position across the country, and after a long dinner at our old Szechuan dive, I'd agreed to temporarily revise our custody arrangement. With his new-found bounty, Bill would rent a California town house for nine months and royally support the kids. 'Dine and Disney,' he'd said.

I'd blessed this, but then missed them. I found myself dead asleep in the middle of the day in Jane's lower bunk, or tuning in late afternoon to my six-year-old son's, and Bill's, obsession, *People's Court*. My arms ached when I saw other women holding sticky hands, pulling frenzied children along behind them in the August dog days. So I flew west. To be a mother again, I'd jokingly told Irene over the phone. To serve that very need.

Peter was late meeting me at the airport. We gave each other a minimal hug, and then he shouldered my bags and walked ahead out into the rain. The Datsun was double-parked, hazards flashing, with a homemade sign taped on the rear window that said STUD. DRIVER. 'Jill,' he said, loading the trunk. 'Irene's been teaching her so she can pick up the groceries. Help out for a change.' I got in, he turned on easy-listening, and we headed north towards the grey mountains.

Irene had been in love with him since I was a child; he'd been orphaned in Belgium during World War II, which moved both Irene and our mother. He'd also reminded us of Emile, the Frenchman in *South Pacific*, because he was greying, autocratic, and seemed misunderstood. But the European charm had gradually worn thin; over the years, I'd been startled by Peter's racism and petty tyranny. I'd often wished that the young Irene had been fondled off her two feet by a breadwinner more tender, more local. Nobody else in the family agreed and Mum even hinted that I'd become bitter since the demise of my own marriage.

'So how is she?' I finally asked Peter.

'She's got a cold,' he said, 'worrying herself sick. And other than that, it's hard to say.' His tone was markedly guarded. He said prospects were poor; the lump was large and she had the fast-growing, speedy sort of cancer. 'But she thinks the Paki quack will get it when he cuts,' he said.

I sat with that. 'And how's Jill?'

'Grouchy,' he said. 'Bitchy.' This gave me pause, and it seemed to have the same effect on him.

We pulled into the garage of the brick house they'd lived in since Jill's birth, and he waved me on while he handled the luggage. The house seemed smaller now, tucked under tall Douglas firs and fringed with baskets of acutely pink geraniums and baby's breath. The back door was open, so I walked in; the master bedroom door was ajar, but I knocked first. She wasn't there. Jill called, 'Aunt Adele?' and I headed back down the hall to the guestroom, and stuck my head in.

A wan version of my sister rested on a water bed in the dark. When I plunked down I made a tiny wave. Irene almost smiled. She was thin as a fine chain; in my embrace, her flesh barely did the favour of keeping her bones company. Her blondish hair was quite short, and she looked ordinary, like a middle-aged matron who probably worked at a bank and kept a no-fail punch recipe filed away. I had to hold her, barely, close again. Behind us, the closet was full of her convervative garments—flannel, floral—and I understood that this was her room now. She slept here alone. She didn't frolic with Peter any more, have sex.

'Don't cling,' Irene said slowly, but with her old warmth. 'Don't get melodramatic. I'm not dying. It's just a cold.'

'Aunt Adele,' Jill said.

I turned around; I'd forgotten my niece was even there, and she was sitting right on the bed, wedged against a bolster. We kissed hello with loud smooch effects—our ritual—and while she kept a hand on Irene's shoulder, she stuttered answers to my questions about school and her summer. Irene kept an eye on a mute TV—the U.S. Open—although she didn't have much interest in tennis; I sensed, really, that she didn't have any extra energy available for banter. This was conservation, not rudeness.

Jill looked different. In fact, the change in her appearance and demeanour exceeded the ordinary drama of puberty; she seemed to be another girl—sly, unsure, and unable to look in the eye. She wore silver wire glasses, no makeup, jeans with an oversize kelly-green sweatshirt, and many extra pounds. Her soft strawcoloured hair was pulled back with a swan barrette, the swan's eye downcast. When she passed Irene a glass of water and a pill, Irene managed to swallow, then passed it back, and Jill drank, too. To me, it seemed she took great care, twisting the glass in her hand, to sip from the very spot her mother's lips had touched.

Peter came in, sat down on Jill's side of the bed, and stretched both arms around to raise the back of his shirt. He bared red, hairless skin, and said, 'Scratch.'

'But I'm watching tennis,' Jill said softly.

'But you're my daughter,' he said. 'And I have an itch.'

Peter looked at Irene and she gave Jill a sharp nudge. 'Do your poor dad,' she said. 'You don't even have to get up.'

'But aren't I watching something?' Jill said. She glanced around, searching for an ally.

'*Vrouw,*' Peter spoke up. 'This girl, she doesn't do anything except mope, eat, mope, eat.'

Jill's shoulders sagged slightly, as if all air had suddenly abandoned her body, and then she slowly got up. 'I'll see you after, Aunt Adele,' she whispered, and I said, 'Yes, sure,' and then she walked out.

Irene looked dismally at Peter; he made a perverse sort of face—skewing his lips south. Then she reached over and started to scratch his bare back. It was an effort. 'Be patient with her, Peter,' she said. 'She's worried about the surgery.'

'She's worried you won't be around to wait on her,' Peter said, then instructed, 'Go a little higher.' Irene's fingers crept obediently up. 'Tell Adele what Jill said.'

Irene shook her head. 'I don't remember.'

Peter turned to me. 'When Irene told her about the cancer, she said, "Don't die on me, Mum, or I'll kill you." And she said this so serious. Can you imagine?' Peter laughed uninhibitedly, and then Irene joined in, too, although her quiet accompaniment was forced. There wasn't any recollected pleasure in her eyes at all; rather, it seemed as if she didn't want Peter to laugh alone, to appear as odd as he did. 'Don't die or I'll kill you,' Peter said.

Irene had always been private about her marriage. If there were disagreements with Peter, and there had been—I'd once dropped in unannounced and witnessed a string of Christmas lights whip against the fireplace and shatter—they were never rebroadcast to the rest of the family; if she was ever discouraged or lonely, she didn't confide in anyone, unless she kept a journal or spoke to her God. She had never said a word against the man.

The night before Irene's surgery, after many earnest wishes and ugly flowers had been delivered, she asked me to stay late with her at Lion's Gate Hospital. The room had emptied. Peter had absconded with Jill—and she'd gone reluctantly, asking to stay until I left—and our mother, who'd been so nervous and sad that an intern had fed her Valium from his pocket. 'why is this happening to her?' Mum said to him. 'To my only happy child.'

Irene, leashed to an IV, raised herself to the edge of the bed and looked out at the parking lot and that kind Pacific twilight. 'That Jill,' Irene said. She allowed her head to fall, arms crossed in front of her. 'She should lift a finger for her father.'

'Well,' I said, watching my step, aware she needed peace, 'Peter's not exactly the most easygoing.'

'No,' she said weakly.

We sat for a long time, Irene in her white gown, me beside her in my orange-and-avocado track suit, until I began to think I'd been too tough on Peter and had distressed her. Then she spoke. 'Sometimes I wish I'd learned more Dutch,' she said neutrally. 'When I met Peter, we married not speaking the same language, really. And that made a difference.'

She didn't expect a comment—she raised her head and stared out the half-open window—but I was too shocked to respond anyway. I'd never heard her remotely suggest that her and Peter's marriage had been less than a living storybook. 'You don't like him, do you?' she said. 'You don't care for his Belgian manner.'

I didn't answer; it didn't need to be said aloud. I turned away. 'I'm probably not the woman who can best judge these things,' I said.

Out in the hall, a female patient talked on the phone. Irene and I both listened. 'I left it in the top drawer,' she said wearily. 'No. The *bedroom*.' There was a pause. 'The desk in the hall, try that.' Another pause. 'Then ask Susan where she put it, because I'm tired of this and I need it.' I turned as she hung the phone up and saw her check to see if money had tumbled back. The hospital was quiet again. Irene did not move, but she was shaking; I found it difficult to watch this and reached out and took her hand.

'What is it?' I said. 'Irene.'

She told me she was scared. Not for herself, but for Peter. That when she had first explained to him about the cancer, he hadn't spoken to her for three weeks. Or touched her. Or kissed her. He'd slept in the guestroom, until she'd offered to move there. And he'd been after Jill to butter his toast, change the sheets, iron his pants. Irene had speculated about this, she said, until she'd realized he was acting this way because of what had happened to him when he was little. In Belgium. Bruges, the war. He had only confided in her once. He'd said all the women he'd ever loved had left him. His mother killed, his sister. 'And now me,' Irene said. 'The big C which leads to the big D. If I move on, I leave two children. And I've told Jill they have to stick together.'

I got off the bed. 'But, Irene,' I said, 'she's not on earth to please her father. Who can be unreasonable. In my opinion.'

By this time, a medical team was touring the room. The junior member paused by Irene and said, 'Give me your vein.'

'In a minute,' she said to him, 'please,' and he left. There were dark areas, the colour of new bruises, under her eyes. 'I want you to promise me something.'

'Yes.'

'If I die,' she said, 'and I'm not going to, but if I do, I don't want Jill to live with you in New York. Because that's what she wants to do. I want her to stay with Peter. Even if she runs to you, send her back.'

'I can't promise that,' I said. 'Because you're not going to go anywhere.'

She looked at me. Pale, fragile. She was my oldest sister, who'd always been zealous about the silver lining in that cloud; and now it seemed she might be dying, in her forties—too soon—and she needed to believe I could relieve her of this burden. So I nodded, *Yes*.

When I got back, by cab, to Irene and Peter's that night, the house was dark. I groped up the back steps, ascending through a hovering scent of honeysuckle, stepped inside, and turned on the kitchen light. The TV was going—some ultra-loud camera commercial—in the living room. Nobody was watching. 'Jill?' I said. 'Peter?'

I wandered down the long hall, snapping on switches: Irene's sickroom, the upstairs bathroom, the master bedroom, Peter's domain. I did a double-take; he was there. Naked, lying on top of the bed, his still hand holding his penis—as if to keep it warm and safe—the head shining. The blades of the ceiling fan cut in slow circles above him. His eyes were vague and didn't turn my way; he was staring up. 'Oh sorry,' I whispered, 'God, sorry,' and flicked the light off again.

I headed back to the living room and sat, for a few seconds. When I'd collected myself, I went to find Jill. She wasn't in her downstairs room, which seemed typically adolescent in decor—Boy George poster, socks multiplying in a corner—until I spotted a quote from Rilke, in careful purple handwriting, taped for her long mirror: 'Beauty is only the first touch of terror we can still bear.'

I finally spotted the light under the basement bathroom door.

'Jill,' I said. 'It's me.'

'I'm in the bathroom,' she said.

'I know,' I said. 'I want to talk.'

She unlocked the door and let me in. She looked tense and peculiar; it looked as if she'd just thrown water on her face. She was still dressed in her clothes from the hospital—from the day before, the kelly-green sweat job—and she'd obviously been sitting on the edge of the tub, writing. There was a Papermate, a pad of yellow legal paper. The top sheet was covered with verses of tiny backward-slanting words. There was also last night's pot of Kraft Dinner on the sink.

'You're all locked in,' I said.

She didn't comment, and when the silence stretched on too long I said, 'Homework?' and pointed to the legal pad.

'No,' she said. Then she gave me a look and said, 'Poem.'

'Oh,' I said, and I *was* surprised. 'Do you ever show them? Or it?'

'No,' she said. 'They're not very good.' She sat back down on the tub. 'But maybe I'd show you, Aunt Adele.'

'Good,' I said. 'Not that I'm a judge.' I told her Irene was tucked in and that she was in a better, more positive frame of mind. More like herself. This seemed to relax Jill so much, I marched the lie a step further. 'Once your mum is out of the woods,' I said, 'your father may lighten up.'

'That day will never come,' she said.

'Never say never,' I said. I gave her a hug—she was so much bigger than my daughter, but I embraced her the same way I had Jane since she was born: a hand and a held kiss on the top of the head.

She hugged me back. 'Maybe I'll come live with you, Auntie A.'

'Maybe,' I said, mindful of Irene's wishes. 'You and everybody,' and saw the disappointment on her streaked face. So I added, 'Everything will be all right. Wait and see. She'll be all right.'

And Irene was. They claimed they'd got it, and ten days later she came home, earlier than expected. When Peter, Jill, and I were gathered around her in the sickroom, Irene started cracking jokes about her future prosthetic fitting. 'How about the Dolly Parton, hon?' she said to Peter. 'Then I'd be a handful.'

I was surprised to see Peter envelop her in his arm; I hadn't ever seen him offer an affectionate gesture. He told her he didn't care what size boob she bought, because breasts were for the hungry babies—not so much for the husband. 'I have these,' he said. 'These are mine. These big white shoulders.' And he rested his head against her shoulder and looked placidly at Jill; he was heavy, but Irene used her other arm to bolster herself, hold him up, and she closed her eyes in what seemed to be joy. Jill came and sat by me.

Irene took it easy the next few days; I stuck by, as did Jill, when she ventured in after school. I was shocked that there weren't more calls, or cards, or visitors except for Mum, and I realized my sister's life was actually very narrow, or extremely focused: family came first. Even Jill didn't seem to have any friends at all; the phone never rang for her.

Then Irene suddenly started to push herself—she prepared a complicated deep-fried Belgian dish; in the afternoon, she sat with Jill, in the Datsun, while Jill practiced parallel parking in front of the house and lobbied for a mother-daughter trip to lovely downtown Brooklyn for Christmas. And then, after a long nap and little dinner, Irene insisted on attending the open house at Jill's school.

We were sitting listening to the band rehearse, a *Flashdance* medley, when I became aware of Irene's body heat—she was on my right—and asked if she might not want to head home. She was burning up. 'Let me get through this,' she said. Then Jill, on my other side, suddenly said in a small tight voice, 'Mum.' She was staring her mother's blouse, where a bright stitch of scarlet had shown up. Irene had bled through her dressing. Irene looked down. 'Oh,' she said. 'Peter.'

On the tear to the hospital, Peter said he'd sue Irene's stupid 'Paki bugger' doctor. He also said he should take his stupid wife to court for loss of sex. He should get a divorce for no-nookie. For supporting a one-tit wonder. And on and on.

Irene wasn't in shape to respond; I doubt she would have anyway.

Beside me in the back seat, Jill turned to stare out the window; she was white, sitting on her hands.

I found my voice. 'I don't think we need to hear this right now, Peter,' I said.

'Oh, Adele,' Irene said warningly. Disappointed.

He pulled over, smoothly, into a bus zone. Some of the people waiting for the bus weren't pleased. Peter turned and faced me, his finger punctuating. 'This is my wife, my daughter, my Datsun.' He paused. 'I can say what the hell I want. And you're welcome to walk.' He reached over and opened my door.

The two women at the bus shelter hurried away, correctly sensing an incident.

'I'm going with Aunt—' Jill was barely audible.

'No,' said Irene. 'You stay here.'

I sat there, paralyzed. I wanted to get out, but didn't want to leave Irene and Jill alone with him; Irene was very ill, Jill seemed defenceless. 'Look,' I said to Peter, 'forget I said anything. Let's just get Irene there, okay?'

He pulled the door shut, then turned front, checked me in the rearview one last time—cold, intimidating—and headed off again. Jill was crying silently. The insides of her glasses were smeared; I shifted over beside her and she linked her arm through mine tight, tight. Up front, Irene did not move.

They said it was an infection which had spread to the chest wall, requiring antibiotics and hospital admission. They were also going to perform more tests.

Peter took off with Jill, saying that they both had to get up in the morning.

Before I left Irene, she spoke to me privately, in a curtained cubicle in Emergency, and asked if I could stay at our mother's for the last few days of my visit; Irene didn't want to hurt me, but she thought it would be better, for all concerned, if I cleared out.

And then she went on; her fever was high, but she was lucid and fighting hard to stay that way. Could I keep quiet about this to our mother? And stop gushing about the East to Jill, going on about the Statue of Liberty and the view of the water from the window in the crown? And worry a little more about my own lost children and less about her daughter? And try to be more understanding of her husband, who sometimes wasn't able to exercise control over his emotions? Irene said Peter needed more love, more time; more of her, God willing. After that, she couldn't speak. And, frankly, neither could I.

I gave in to everything she asked. Jill and Peter dropped in together during the evening to see her; I visited Irene, with Mum, during the day when Peter was at work. Our conversations were banal and strained—they didn't seem to do either of us much good. After I left her one afternoon, I didn't know where I was going and ended up at my father's grave. I just sat there, on top of it, on the lap of the stone.

The day before my New York flight, I borrowed my mother's car to pick up a prescription for her at the mall. I was window-shopping my way back to the parking lot, when I saw somebody resembling my niece sitting on a bench outside a sporting goods store. At first, the girl seemed too dishevelled, too dirty-looking, actually, to be Jill, but as I approached, it became clear it was her. She wasn't doing anything. She sat there, draped in her mother's London Fog raincoat, her hands resting on her thickish thighs, clicking a barrette open, closed, open, closed. It was ten in the morning; she should have been at school. In English. For a moment, it crossed my mind that she might be on drugs: this was a relief; it would explain everything. But I didn't think she was. I was going to go over and simply say, *Yo, Jill, let's do tea*, and then I remembered my sister's frightening talk with me at the hospital and thought, *Fuck it. Butt out, Adele*, and walked the long way round. I turned my back.

One sultry Saturday morning, in late September—after I'd been back in Brooklyn for a few weeks—I was up on the roof preparing the first lessons for classes, when the super brought a handful of mail up. He'd been delivering it personally to tenants since the box had been ripped out of the entrance wall. It was the usual stuff and a thin white business envelope from Canada. From Jill. I opened it: *Dearlingest* (sic) *Aunt Adele, These are my only copies. Love, your only niece, Jill. P.S. I'm going to get a job and come see you at Easter.*

There were two. The poems were carefully written, each neat on their single page, with the script leaning left, as if blown by a stiff breeze. 'Black Milk' was about three deaths: before her beloved husband leaves for war, a nursing mother shares a bottle of old wine with him, saved from their wedding day, and unknowingly poisons her child and then herself. Dying, she rocks her dying child in her arms, but her last conscious thought is for her husband at the front. Jill had misspelled wedding; she'd put *weeding*.

'Belgium' described a young girl ice skating across a frozen lake—Jill had been to Belgium with her parents two times—fleeing an unnamed pursuer. During each quick, desperate glide, the ice melts beneath her until, at the end, she is underwater: 'In the deep cold / Face to face / Look, he comes now / My Father / My Maker.' The girl wakes up; it was a bad dream. And then her earthly father appears in her bed and, 'He makes night / Come again / All night,' by covering her eyes with his large, heavy hand.

I read these, and read them again, and I wept. I looked out, past the steeples and the tar roofs, where I thought I saw the heat rising, toward the green of Prospect Park, and held the poems in my lap, flat under my two hands. I didn't know what to do; I didn't know what to do right away; I thought I should wait until I knew clearly what to say and whom to say it to.

In late October, Mum phoned, crying, and said that Irene's cancer had not been caught by the mastectomy. Stray cells had been detected in other areas of her body. Chemotherapy was advised. Irene had switched doctors; she was seeing a naturopath. She was paying big money for an American miracle gum, among other things.

Mum also said that Jill had disappeared for thirty-two hours. Irene claimed that Jill had been upset because of a grade—a C in Phys Ed. Mum didn't believe it was really that; she thought Irene's condition was disturbing Jill, but hadn't said that to Irene.

She didn't volunteer any information about the other member of Irene's family and I did not ask.

In November, Bill came east for a visit and brought the children, as scheduled; he also brought a woman named Cheryl Oak. The day before Thanksgiving, the two of them were invited to a dinner party, and I took Graham and Jane, taller and both painfully shy with me, to Central Park. It was a crisp, windy night. We watched the gi-normous balloons being blown up for the Macy's parade and bought roasted chestnuts, not to eat, but to warm the palms of our hands. I walked them back to their hotel and delivered them to the quiet, intelligent person who would probably become their stepmother, and be good to them, as she'd obviously been for Bill. Later, back in Brooklyn, I was still awake—wondering how another woman had succeeded with my husband and, now, my own little ones—when Irene phoned at 3 a.m. She told me Jill was dead. 'There's been an accident,' she said.

A few days later, my mother and stepfather picked me up at the Vancouver airport on a warm, cloudy morning. On the way to the funeral, they tried to tell me, between them—between breakdowns—what had happened. She had died of hypothermia; the impact of hitting the water had most likely rendered her unconscious. She probably hadn't been aware of drowning, but she'd done that, too. She'd driven the Datsun to Stanley

Park—she'd told Irene she was going to the library—left the key in the ignition, walked not quite to the middle of the bridge, and hoisted herself over
the railing. There was one eye-witness: a guy who worked in a video store.
He'd kept saying, 'It was like a movie, I saw this little dumpling girl just
throw herself off.'

The chapel was half-empty, and the director mumbled that that was
unusual when a teenager passed on. Irene had not known, and neither had
Mum, where to reach Joyce, our middle sister, who was missing as usual; Ray,
our older brother, gave a short eulogy. He stated that he didn't believe in
any God, but Irene did, and he was glad for that this day. He also guessed
that when any child takes her own life, the whole family must wonder why,
and probably do that forever. The face of my sister was not to be borne.
Then we all sang 'The Water Is Wide', which Jill had once performed in an
elementary-school talent show. She'd won Honourable Mention.

After the congregation dispersed, Peter remained on his knees, his head
in his hands, while Irene approached the casket. Jill wore a pale pink dress
and her other glasses, and her hair was pinned back, as usual, with a barrette—this time, a dove. Irene bent and kissed her on the mouth, on the forehead, then tugged at Jill's lace collar, adjusting it just so. It was the eternal
mother's gesture, that finishing touch, before your daughter sails out the
door on her big date.

I drank to excess at the reception; we all did, and needed to. Irene and I
did not exchange a word; we just held each other for a long minute. From
a distance, and that distance was necessary, I heard Peter talking about
Belgium and memories of his childhood. On his fifth birthday, his sister,
Kristin, had sent him a pencil from Paris, a new one, unsharpened, and he
had used it until the lead was gone and it was so short he could barely hold
it between his fingers. On the morning his mother was shot, in cold blood,
he'd been dressing in the dark. The last thing she had said, to the Germans,
was 'Don't hurt my little boy.' This was when Mum and I saw Irene go to him
and take his hand. She led him down the hall to his bedroom and closed the
door behind them. 'Thank God,' Mum said. 'Thank God, they have each
other. Thank God, she has him.'

And for that moment, I forget about the despair that had prompted Jill
to do what she did, and my own responsibility and silence, because I was
alive and full of needs, sickness, and dreams myself. I thought, *No, I will never
tell my sister what I suspect, because life is short and very hard,* and I thought, *Yes,
a bad marriage is better than none,* and I thought, *Adele, let the sun go down on
your anger, because it will not bring her back,* and I turned to my mother. 'Yes,' I
said. 'Thank God.'

NEIL BISSOONDATH
(1955)

Digging Up the Mountains

1.

Hari Beharry lived a comfortable life, until, citing the usual reasons of
national security, the government declared a State of Emergency.

'National security, my ass,' Hari mumbled. 'Protecting their own backsides, is all.'

His wife, anguished, said, 'Things really bad, hon.'

'*Things really bad, hon,*' Hari mimicked her. He sucked his teeth. 'Looking
after their own backsides.'

'The milk gone sour and the honey turn sugary.' She gave a wry little
smile.

Hari sucked his teeth once more. 'Don't give me none of that stupid nonsense. "Land a milk and honey", my ass.'

'You used to call it that.'

'That was a long time ago.'

'Rangee used to blame it on independence. He used to blame the British
for—'

'I know what Rangee used to say. It ain't get him very far, eh? Shut up
about Rangee, anyway. I don't want to talk about him.'

'Again? Still? Faizal? They tried to help you.'

'Why you like to talk about dead people so much?' he demanded irritably.

'Because you don't. You ain't mentioned their names once in the last two
weeks.'

'Why should I?'

'Because you might be next.'

'Don't talk nonsense.'

'Because *we* might be next, me and the children.'

'Shut up, woman!'

Hari stalked angrily out to the back porch. The evening air, cooled by the
higher ground which made the area so desirable to those who could afford
it, tempered the heat of the day. The bulk of the mountains, cutting jagged
against the inky sky, allowed only the faintest glow of the last of the sunset.

In those mountains, Hari had once found comfort. His childhood had been spent in the shadow of their bulk and it was through them, through their brooding permanence, that he developed an attachment to this island, an attachment his father had admitted only in later life when, as strength ebbed and distances grew larger, inherited images of mythic India dipped into darkness.

The island, however, was no longer that in which his father had lived. Its simplicity, its unsophistication, had vanished over the years and had been replaced by the cynical politics of corruption that plagued all the urchin nations scrambling in the larger world. Independence—written ever since with a capital I, small i being considered a spelling mistake at best, treason at worst—had promised the world. It had failed to deliver, and the island, in its isolation, blamed the world.

Hari's father had died on Independence night and Hari had sought consolation in the mountains. He'd received it that night and continued to receive it many nights after. Now things had changed: the mountains spoke only of threat. He didn't know if he could trust them anymore.

The emergency legislation had shut his stores. Hari was idle, and the sudden idleness made him irritable. If only he had someone with whom he could discuss the situation, someone who would make him privy to state secrets, as his old friends used to do. But the government had changed, his friends were no longer ministers, and the new ministers were not his friends. He could no longer say, 'Eh, eh, you know what the Minister of National Security tell me yesterday?' The former Minister of National Security was in prison, put there by the new Minister for State Security. No one was left to show Hari the scheme of things; he was left to grapple alone, his wife useless, whining, demanding escape.

The darkness of the evening deepened. Hari felt a constriction in his throat. In the sky the first stars appeared. Hari reached into his back pocket and took out a large grey revolver. Its squared bulk fit nicely into his hand, its weight intimated power. He raised his arm with deliberation, keeping the elbow locked, and fired a shot at the sky. His arm, still locked, moved rapidly down and left; he fired another shot, at the mountains. The reports mingled and echoed away into the depths of the hidden gully.

'Come, you bastards, just try and come.'

Only the barking of the German Shepherds answered him.

2.

It had started—when? Five, six, seven months before? He couldn't be sure. So much had happened, and in so short a time, event superseding grasp, comprehension exhausted. And it had all begun, quietly, with rumour: a whisper that had rapidly bred of itself, engendering others, each wilder, more speculative, and, so, more frightening than the last; rumour of trouble in the Ferdinand Pale, the shanty area to the east of the town.

Hari had dismissed the rumours: 'Trouble, my ass. Shoot two or three of them and bam!—no more trouble.'

But it hadn't worked out that way. The police had shot several people and had arrested dozens more, yet the rumours and the troubles persisted.

Hari had obtained a pistol from his friend, the Minister of National Security.

Hari said to the minister, 'To protect the shops, you know, boy.'

And to his wife, Hari said, 'Let them come here. This is my land and my house. Let them come. It's bullet in their backside.'

But no backsides presented themselves. Occasionally Hari would go out to the back porch and brandish his pistol: 'Let them see what they walking into,' he would say to his children who stood in the doorway staring wide-eyed at him. And to the darkness he would say, 'Come, come and try.'

Unexpectedly, the rumours dried up. Tension abated and fears were packed away. Life resumed. Hari called in the contractor, and gardeners—dark, sullen men of the Pale—started putting the yard in order, tugging out rocks and stones and laying out the drainage, preparing the ground for the topsoil.

Hari spent much of his free time overseeing this activity. Constantly followed by the children, he stalked around the yard nodding and murmuring and giving the occasional order, his tall rubber boots sinking deep into the convulsed earth. Slowly, at intervals less frequent that promised by the contractor, trucks arrived with loads of topsoil. Hari railed at the contractor: 'But at this rate, man, it going to take five years to cover the whole yard!' The contractor, a fat man with red, wet eyes and a shirt that strained at the buttons, replied with exasperation: 'But what I going to do, boss? The boys don't want to work, half of them ain't even show their face around the office since the little trouble in the Pale.' The soil that did arrive was dumped into one corner of the yard under Hari's direction. He had it furrowed and combed, and had holes dug for the small grove of shade trees he would plant.

He started thinking about giving the place a name, like a ranch: Middlemarch, Rancho Rico, Golden Bough. He tossed the names about in his mind, playing with them, trying to picture how each would look on the personal stationery he was having printed up. He asked his wife's opinion. She suggested Bombay Alley. He stomped away, angry.

Twice he beat his son for playing with the gardeners' tools. 'Look here, boy,' he said, 'I have enough troubles without you giving me more.'

Still, the progress of the lawn pleased Hari. The contractor managed to hire additional men; trucks dumped their loads of topsoil at regular intervals. In less than a month, there swept from the base of the house to the base of the wrought-iron fence neatly raked stretches of an opulent brown. Hari, pleased, decided to order the grass.

He was on the phone arguing with the contractor about the price of the grass—it would mean sending three men and a truck to the country to dig up clumps of shoots; the contractor wanted more money than Hari was offering—when the music on the radio was interrupted by the announcement of a sudden call to elections. Hari understood immediately: the government, taking advantage of the apathy that followed the troubles, hoped to catch the opposition, such as it was, off-balance. Hari told the contractor he would call him back.

He poured himself a large whisky and listened to the Prime Minister's deep, bored voice as he spoke of a renewed mandate, of the confidence of the people. Hari thought the use of the island accent a little overdone. Did this election switch from Oxford drawl to island lilt really fool those at whom it was aimed? Did they really believe him to be one of them?

He dialled the number of his friend, the Minister of National Security: 'Since when all-you care about mandate, boy? Is a new word you pick up in New York, or what?' Hari laughed. 'Or maybe the Americans want a little reassurance before they hand over the loan cheque?' Hari laughed again, and his friend laughed with him.

But things went wrong. It was not a matter of political miscalculation; it was simply the plight of the small country: nothing went as planned, the foreseen never came into sight, and possibilities were quickly exhausted. The government lost. The opposition, on the verge of illegality only weeks before, took power.

Hari was untroubled. Life continued. He had, through it all, remained a financial contributor to both parties; and he liked the new Prime Minister, the scion of an old, respected island family that, adapting itself to the times, often publicly decried its slave-owning roots. The new Prime Minister considered himself a man truly of the people, for in him flowed the blood of master and slave alike.

The Americans handed over the cheque. The Prime Minister, serious and handsome, with a sallow island whiteness, went on television: '. . . the land of milk and honey . . . new loans from the World Bank . . . stimulation of industry and agriculture . . . a socialist economy . . .' This became known as the Milk and Honey speech. It was printed in pamphlet form and distributed to all the schools in the island. It was reported on the BBC World Service news.

The rumours started once more about a month later: trouble in the Ferdinand Pale. There were reports of shootings. Death threats were made against the new Prime Minister. Hari, without knowing why, sensed the hand of his friend, the former Minister of National Security. Pamphlets began appearing in the streets, accusing several businessmen of collusion with 'imperialists'. Hari's name cropped up time and time again. Letters—typed askew on good-quality paper, words often misspelt—began arriving at the house. Occasionally the phone would ring in the middle of the night, giving Hari the fearful vision of sudden death in the family. But always the same voice with the lazy island drawl would say in a conversational tone: 'Damned exploitationist . . . Yankee slave . . .'

Hari complained to the police. The sergeant was apologetic: there was nothing they could do, their hands were full with the Ferdinand Pale.

The letters, less accusatory, more threatening, continued; the phone calls increased to three and four a night. Hari bought a whistle and blasted it into the phone. The next night the caller returned the favour. Hari's wife said, 'You ask for that, you damn fool.'

Hari complained directly to the Minister for State Security. He was called in; the minister wanted to see him.

Hari had never met the minister, and the new title, more sinister, less British, worried him. Before he entered the cream-coloured colonial building on Parliament Square, Hari noticed that his shirt was sticking to his back with perspiration. He wished he could dash back home to change it.

The minister was cordial. A big black man with a puffy face and clipped beard, he explained that his men were investigating the threats—a man of Mr Beharry's standing deserved 'the full attention of the security forces'—but that it was a slow process, it would take time. 'Processes,' the minister said, and Hari noticed he seemed to smack his lips when he pronounced the word, as if relishing it, 'processes take a long time, they are established by law, there's paperwork. You understand?'

Hari nodded. He thought: How can I trust this man? The minister used to be what was called a 'fighter for social justice'. He had studied in the United States and Canada, until he was expelled from Canada for his part in the destruction of the computer centre at Sir George Williams College in Montreal. He had returned to the island as a hero. The papers had said he'd struck a blow for freedom and racial equality. In Hari's circle he'd been considered a common criminal; the former Minister of National Security had said at a party, 'We have a cell reserved for that one.' Now here he was, Minister for State Security, growing pudgy, wearing a suit.

The minister offered a drink.

Hari asked for Scotch. 'Straight.'

'Imported or local?'

'Imported.' Then he changed his mind. 'Local.'

The minister buzzed his secretary. 'Pour us some whisky, Charlene. Local for Mr Beharry, imported for me.' The minister smiled. He said to Hari, 'I never drink the local stuff, disagrees with my stomach.'

Hari said, 'Too bad. It's good.' And he knew instantly that he was grovelling.

The minister swung his chair around and stood up. A big man, he towered over Hari. 'Mr Beharry, you are a well-known man here in our happy little island. You are an *important* man. You own a chain of stores, the Good Look Boutiques, not so? You are a rich man, you have a nice family. In short, Mr Beharry, you have a stake in this island.' He paused as the secretary came in with the drinks. As Hari took his glass, he noticed a tremble in his hand, and he was aware that the minister too had noticed it. The minister smiled, raised his glass briefly at Hari, and sipped at the whisky. Then he continued: 'It is because of all this, Mr Beharry, that I want you to trust me. I am responsible for the security of this island. Trust between people like us is vital. And that is why, right now, I am going to reveal to you a state secret: in a few days we are going to ask everybody to turn in their guns, you included. It's the best way we know how to clean up the island. This violence must stop.'

Hari's palm became sweaty on the glass. He said, 'But is my gun, there's no law—'

'The law will be pushed through Parliament tomorrow. No one can stop us, you know that.'

Hari, suddenly emboldened by the minister's smugness, said, 'You know better than me. I never went to university.'

The minister, unchastened, said, 'That's right, Mr Beharry.'

Then they drank their Scotch and talked soccer. Hari knew nothing about soccer. The minister talked. Hari listened.

A few days later, Hari turned in his gun. Before handing it over at the police station, he jammed a piece of wood down the barrel.

The letters and phone calls were still coming. Hari threw the letters out unopened and put the telephone into a drawer. His wife, constantly worried, asked him, 'How we going to defend ourselves now, hon?'

Hari said, 'Don't worry.'

That night, he went to his parents' old house, locked up and deserted. He hadn't been there in months. The place hadn't changed: the furniture was where it had always been, his parents' clothes still hung in the closets. Dust lay everywhere. Thieves, assuming the house contained nothing, had never bothered to break in. The air was musty, the familiar smells of childhood gone forever. Those smells, of food frying, of milk boiling, of his mother's perfumes and powders, had lingered several months after his mother's death and given Hari a haunted feeling. It was because of them that he'd stayed away so long, leaving the house and its ghosts to their own devices.

He went into his parents' bedroom. The bed had never been stripped and the sheets, now discoloured by dust, lay as they had been thrown by the undertakers who'd taken his mother's body away. He wondered if the impression left by the body in its attitude of death could still be seen. He rejected the thought as morbid but couldn't help taking a look: he saw only dusty, rumpled sheets.

Ignoring the dust, he lowered himself to the floor and felt around under the bed with his hand. He found what he was looking for: a rectangular wooden box the size of a cookie can. He opened it and took out a large grey revolver, the kind worn by American officers during the war. His father had bought it off an American soldier stationed on the island in 1945. After so many years of lying around, of being considered a toy, it would finally find a use.

Hari slipped the revolver into his pocket—it was bigger and heavier than the one he'd turned in and didn't fit as snugly into his pocket—and left the house. He didn't bother to lock the door.

Later that same night, Rangee, Hari's closest friend, telephoned. Hari was in bed, the revolver on the headboard just above him; and the ring of the telephone, startling in the semi-darkness, caused him to reach first for the revolver.

Rangee said, 'Listen, Hari, things really bad in the Pale, but watch out. Is not the Ferdinand Pale you have to fear, is the other pale.'

Before Hari could ask what he was talking about, the phone went dead. Hari assumed it was another of the frequent malfunctions of the telephone system.

Rangee was found the next day, shot twice in the head, the receiver still clutched in his hand. The police said it had been a robber: Rangee's watch and wallet were missing. Nothing else in his house had been touched.

Hari returned from the morgue. So many had already left, gone to lands unfamiliar beyond the seas, that he took Rangee's death as just another departure. He froze Rangee in his mind, as he'd done with the others. He was determined never to mention them again; they were like a challenge to him. He sat at the kitchen table, his son and daughter, large-eyed, across from him, and cleaned and oiled the American's revolver. It needed little work: the mechanism clicked sharply, precisely, the magazine full. Hari marvelled at American ingenuity.

About a week after Rangee's death—later, Hari would have difficulty separating events: which came first? which second?—Faizal, another friend and business partner, came to see Hari. Faizal had connections in the army and liked to show off his knowledge of things military. Once, after a dinner party, Hari had told his wife, 'Faizal went on and on. I feel as if I just finish planning the whole D-Day invasion.'

Seated in the darkened black porch, glass poised between restless fingers, Faizal appeared nervous. He talked about the weather, about business, about the Ferdinand Pale. His eyes, agitated, traced the bulky silhouette of the mountains against the star-strewn sky. He related the story of the Battle of Britain and explained the usefulness of the Dieppe raid.

Hari felt that Faizal was trying to say something important but that he had to work up the courage. He didn't push him.

Faizal left without saying anything. Despite all the alcohol he had consumed, he left as nervous as he'd arrived. Hari assumed he was just upset over Rangee's death, and he was thankful that Faizal had said nothing about it.

Faizal was shot three days later. He'd received two bullets in the head; his watch and wallet were missing. The police concluded it was another case of robbery.

Hari, steeled, said, 'Damn strange robbers. All they take is watches and wallets when they could empty the house.'

The night after Faizal's death, one of Hari's stores was destroyed by fire. The fire department, an hour late in responding to the call, said it was arson. Then the fire marshal changed his mind: the final report spoke of old wiring and electrical shorts.

It was after this that Hari obtained two German Shepherds and started firing his warning shots into the evening sky.

The troubles in the Ferdinand Pale erupted into riots. Two policemen were killed. The government declared a State of Emergency and sent the army into the streets. Hari said, 'Faizal would have been thrilled.' It was the last time he mentioned Faizal's name. Members of the former government, including Hari's friend the former Minister of National Security, were arrested, for agitation, for treason. Stores and schools were closed, the airport and ports cordoned off.

It was only after watching the Prime Minister announce the Emergency on television that the meaning of Rangee's strange last words clicked in Hari's mind. The announcement had included news of an offer, at once accepted, of fraternal aid from Cuba. The Prime Minister, exhausted, had looked very, very pale.

3.

The day after the Emergency proclamation, the labourers didn't turn up, as was to be expected. Hari, restless, walked around the yard pretending to inspect the progress of the lawn. There had been problems obtaining the grass. The contractor, once more, complained of the workmen, their laziness, drunkenness. But Hari guessed at the real problem: whatever was seething in the Pale had seized them. Only one load of grass had been delivered, and the soil was beginning to harden in spots, to bind to itself.

Hari, feeling the heaviness of the revolver in his back pocket, let his eyes roam over the few rows of grass that had been planted, scraggly little shoots not quite in straight lines. Looking at them he found it difficult to picture the thick, carpet-like lawn he'd envisaged. His eyes moved on, past the ugliness of incomplete lawn, past several piles of wood left over from the construction of the house and not yet carted away, to the deep gully where his wife, if she got the chance, would start to plant her nursery, to the wall of forest, dank and steamy, to the mountains beyond, a great distance away yet ever present, like a dead loved one.

Just let them try to take it away. Let them try!

'Hari,' his wife called from the kitchen window, 'we need milk, you better go to the plaza.'

'For sour milk?'

'We need milk, Hari.' She sounded tired. Her anxiety had distilled to fatigue. She had given up dreams of a nursery; she wanted only flight—to Toronto, Vancouver, Miami.

He looked at her and said, 'This is my island. My father born here, I born here, you born here, our children born here. Nobody can make me leave, nobody can take it away.'

'All right, Hari. But we still need milk.'

His son came to the door. He was so small that Hari, when drunk, doubted his parentage. His son said, 'I want chocolate milk.'

His daughter, plump, more like Hari, echoed, 'I want chocolate milk too.'

Hari sucked his teeth and brushed roughly past them into the house. He snatched up the car keys from the kitchen counter and started to remove the revolver from his pocket. Then he paused and let it fall back, an ungainly lump in his trousers. It was a calculated risk: what if the police stopped him? They could shoot him and announce that Mr Hari Beharry, well-known businessman, had died of a heart attack during a road-block search; an illegal revolver had been the source of his anxiety. Bullet holes? If the government said he'd died of a heart attack, he'd died of a heart attack. Hari had lived here too long, been too close to the former government, to delude himself. He knew the way of the island: nowhere was truth more relative.

It occurred to him only afterwards that they might have simply shot him, then claimed he had shot first. But this was too simple, the island didn't seek simplicity. With the obvious evidence, it would have been smarter to claim a heart attack: it was more brazen, it would be admired.

He braked at the driveway and glanced into the rearview mirror: the house, white, brilliant in the sun, the windows and doors of mahogany lending a touch of simple elegance, filled the glass. His wife had surprised him with her suggestion of mahogany: he hadn't thought her capable of such taste. With all the trimmings, he'd ended up sinking over a hundred thousand dollars into the house. It was the investment of a lifetime and one that would have caused his father both pride and anguish: pride that the family could spend so vast a sum on a house, anguish that they would. It was in this house that Hari planned to entertain his grandchildren and their children, to this house that he would welcome future Beharry hordes, from this house that he would be buried. The house spoke of generations.

But now, as he drove along the serpentine road, verges broken and nibbled by wild grass, his dreams all managed to elude him. Those scenes of future familial joy that he had for so long caressed had, almost frighteningly, become like a second, parallel, life. And now they had gone out of reach: he could no longer conjure up a future and what did come to him, in little snippets, like wayward pieces of film negative, caused him to shudder.

It wasn't yet ten o'clock but the sun was already high, radiating a merciless heat. Hari could fee the mounting degrees pressing down on him from the car roof. He could see waves rising like insubstantial cobras from the asphalt paving; he dripped with perspiration. The wind rushing in through the window did little to relieve his discomfort. He wiped away a drop of perspiration that had settled in the deep cleft between his nose and upper lip and shifted in his seat, trying to get used to the feel of the revolver under him.

The plaza was only a short distance away but already Hari could sense the change of atmosphere. At the house the heat was manageable. It suggested comfort, security; it was like the heat of the womb. Outside, away from the house, under the blue of a sky so expansive, so untrammelled that it seemed to expose him, to strip him, the heat became tangible, held menace, was suggestive of physical threat. It conjured not a desire for beach and sea but an awareness of the lack of cover, a sense of nothing to hide behind. The familiar of the outside world had undergone an irrevocable transformation.

The revolver, he realized with a twinge of disappointment, gave no comfort. He used to be able to picture himself blazing away at blurry figures, but his image had been the result of too many paperback westerns. The blurry figures had unexpectedly taken on more substance. What had once seemed epic now seemed absurd.

He drove past several empty lots, wild grass punctuated occasionally by the rusting hulks of abandoned cars. In the distance, on both sides, beyond the land that had been cleared for an aborted agricultural scheme (money had disappeared, as had the minister responsible), he could see the indistinct line of forest, recalling a smudged, green watercolour: government land, guerrilla land. And far away to the left, beyond and above forest, the mountains, sturdy, mottled green, irregularly irrigated by vertical streams of white smoke: signs, some said, of guerrilla camps, signs, others said, of the immemorial bush fires.

At last the plaza came into sight, low stucco buildings with teak panelling and light fixtures imported from Switzerland. The fixtures were broken and in several places were marked only by the forlorn ends of electrical wire. The teak had been scratched and gouged, some pieces ripped from the wall for a bonfire that had been lit at the entrance to the bookstore. The stucco, unrecognizable, had been defaced by slogans, both sexual and political, and crude paintings and election posters and askew copies of the Emergency proclamation, unglued corners hanging limply in the hot air.

In front of the barricaded shops, in the shadow of the overhang, lounged a line of black youths, wool caps pulled down tightly over their heads, impenetrable sunglasses masking their eyes.

Hari couldn't separate his fear from his quick anger.

'We need milk, must have milk, chocolate milk,' he muttered, vexed, as he pulled into the parking lot. He could hear their voices, his wife, his son, his daughter, and they were like mockery, demanding and insistent, ignorant of his problems and worries.

He pulled carefully into a parking space, stopping neatly in the middle equidistant from the white lines on either side of the car. An unnecessary vanity, the lot was deserted. He sucked his teeth with irritation and tugged the keys out of the ignition. With the engine dead, an anticlimactic silence fell over the plaza. None of the youths moved and Hari couldn't tell whether they were looking at him. He wished he knew.

He opened the door—it squeaked a little, disturbing the quiet like a fingernail scraping a blackboard—and put one leg out onto the scorching asphalt. Heat waves tickled up his pant leg, sending a spasm through him. Faintly, from the shadow of the overhang, came the sound of a radio, disturbingly gay, the music local, proud, threatening.

Hari let his foot rest on the asphalt and sat still, trying to discern where the music was coming from. As he looked around, it occurred to him that the milk store would be closed, everything was closed by the Emergency; it was a wasted trip. He noted, as if from a distance, a curious lack of emotion within him: it was as if all feeling had dried up.

'Wha' you doin' here, boss?'

The voice startled Hari. Four black faces were at his door, sunglasses scrutinizing him. He could see his reflection in the black lenses, his strained face eight times, each a caricature of himself.

He heard his voice reply, 'I come to get milk, *bredda*. For the children. You know. They need milk. They just small.' He wondered if the men were hot under those wool caps, but they were part of the uniform.

'Look like you out of luck, boss. The milk store close.' He was the leader, the others deferred to him.

'Yeah, I just remember that myself.'

Another of the men said, 'You better get out of the car, boss.'

Hari didn't move.

The leader said, 'My friend like your car, boss.'

Hari didn't hear him. He was wondering if the leader had bought his pink dashiki at his store.

Hari said, 'You buy that dashiki at the Good Look Boutique?'

One of the men said, 'What business that is of yours?'

Hari said, 'I own the Good Look.'

Fingering the dashiki, the leader said, 'I know that, boss. And no. My wife make the dashiki for me. You like it? How much you'd sell that for, boss?'

Hari's heart sank.

'Get out of the car.'

'Look, all-you know who I am?'

'Yes, Boss Beharry, we know you. Get out of the car.'

'What you want, *bredda*?'

'Get out. I not going to ask you again.'

Hari stumbled out. The men crowded in. Hari reached for the revolver, levelled it at the leader, and pulled the trigger. The hammer clicked emptily. Hari's vision fogged; the world went into a tilt: he had drained the clip at the sky and mountains.

The leader said, 'Well, well, boss. So the Americans supplying you with guns now, eh?' He knocked the revolver from Hari's hand with an easy, fluid blow.

'What you want, *bredda?*'

'The keys.'

Hari gave the car keys to the leader. Hari noticed he was wearing a large silver ring marked U.S. Air Force Academy, the kind advertised in comic books.

'The money.'

'Money?' A sudden presence of mind gripped Hari. The heat scorched his skin, the asphalt solidified beneath his feet, the world righted itself.

Hari said, 'Give me room, *bredda*, I'll give you the money.' He reached into his pocket and pulled out a thick wad of bills. With a quick movement of the wrist, he flung it high and away. The bills scattered like confetti.

The leader looked perplexed. No one moved. Then suddenly everyone was running, the youths from the shadow of the overhang to the money, the robbers from the car to the money. Only the leader remained; Hari pushed him, hard. The man stumbled and fell. Hari started to run.

At the corner of the farthest building, he looked quickly back. No one was following him. The leader, standing casually by the car, was dusting himself off and smoothing the creases in his pink dashiki. It was a strangely domestic sight.

Hari had just finished watering the little patch of lawn when the police came to return his car. All the windows had been smashed into tiny crystal diamonds. Glittering in the sunlight, they littered the seats and floor like so many water droplets. The body had been badly dented in several places and the paint maliciously gouged with an icepick. Hari could make out the letters CA but only deep gouges followed, as if the vandal had gotten into a sudden rage. This, more than anything, frightened Hari: it was an elegant, hieroglyphic statement.

'We find it on a back road,' the policeman said, cocking his military-style helmet to one side. In the old days Hari might have pulled him up for sloppiness; now he said nothing. 'We didn't find no money. The keys was in the ignition.'

Hari said, 'You didn't find the—' He stopped short, remembering he had had the revolver illegally.

The policeman said, 'What?'

Hari said, 'Nothing. The men. You know.'

The policeman said, 'No, nothing. We'll call if we find anything.'

Hari took the keys and thanked him. The policeman turned and walked away, up the driveway into a waiting jeep. Four men were sitting in the back of the jeep; they all wore police uniforms and sported impenetrable sunglasses.

As the jeep pulled away, one of the men waved at Hari.

Hari waved back.

A second man raised his arm; in his hand fluttered a pink dashiki. The man shouted, 'Thanks, boss.'

Hari pulled the children inside and bolted the door.

That evening the Minister for State Security telephoned. He said, 'Mr Beharry, I hear you are leaving our happy little island. That's too bad.'

Hari said, 'Well, I—'

The minister said, 'Are you going to visit your American friends?'

Hari said nothing.

The minister said, 'You know if you are out of the island for more than six months, your property reverts to the people, who are its rightful owners.'

Hari put the phone down.

Flight had become necessary, and it would be a penniless flight. The government controlled the flow of money. Friends had been caught smuggling; some had had their life savings confiscated. He could leave with nothing. It was the price for years of opulent celebrity in a little place going wrong.

His wife, stabbing at her eyes with a tissue, said, 'At least we not dead.'

Hari said, 'We're not?'

He went out into the back yard. The sun was beginning to set behind the mountains and random dark clouds diffused the light into a harsh yellowness. It would probably rain tomorrow.

Hari went to the tool shed and got a fork. The earth around the patch of lawn was loose and damp. The grass shoots had not yet begun to root; they popped out easily under the probing prongs. In a few minutes, the work was done. Hari looked up. The sun had already sunk behind the mountains: Hari wished he could dig them up too.

C AROLINE A DDERSON
(1963)

~

The Chmarnyk

In 1906, after scorching the Dakota sky, an asteroid fell to earth and struck and killed a dog. Only a mutt, but Baba said, 'Omen.' It was her dog. They crossed the border into safety, into Canada. But the next spring was strange in Manitoba, alternating spells of heat and cold. One bright day Mama went to town, stood before a shop window admiring yard goods, swaddled infant in her arms. From the eaves above a long glimmering icicle gave up its hold, dropped like a shining spear. The baby was impaled.

These misfortunes occurred before I was born. I learned them from tongues, in awe, as warnings. My brother Teo said, 'Every great change is wrought in the sky.'

Grieving, they fled Manitoba, just another cursed place. Open wagon, mattresses baled, copper pots clanking. Around the neck of the wall-eyed horse two things: cardboard picture of the Sacred Heart; cotton strip torn from Baba's knickers. Every morning as she knotted the cloth, she whispered in the twitching ear, 'As drawers over buttocks, cover those evil eyes!' Thus protected, that old horse carried them right across Saskatchewan. In Alberta it fell down dead.

So they had to put voice to what they had feared all along: the land wasn't cursed, they were. More exactly, Papa. A reasonable man most of the time, he had these spells, these ups and downs. Up, he could throw off his clothes and tread a circular path around the house knee-deep through snow. Or he would claim to be speaking English when, in fact, he was speaking in tongues. 'English, the language of Angels!' but no one understood him. Down, he lay on the hearth, deathly mute, Baba spoon-feeding him, Teo and Mama saying the rosary. I was just a baby when he died.

But this is a story about Teo, dead so many years. I remember him stocky and energetic, his streaky blond hair. If they had stayed in Galicia, he would have been a *chmarnyk*, a rain-man. In the Bible, Pharaoh had a dream that seven gaunt cows came out of the river to feed on cattails. He dreamed of seven ears of corn on a single stalk, withered and blighted by east wind. But Teo never relied on the auguries of sleep. He could read the sky.

'Rain on Easter Day and the whole summer is wet. If you see stars in the morning from one to three, the price of wheat rises.'

He told me this in a field still bound by old snow. He had stood out there the whole night and I was calling him to Easter Mass, 1929. 'What'll it be this year then, smartie?'

'Drought.' He pronounced the word like he was already thirsty. 'Little sister, listen. The sky is only as high as the horizon is far.'

'Well, la-di-da.'

Teo was nineteen, I twelve, and the skin of my own dry lips cracked as I echoed: 'drought'. All that spring, smoke rose straight out of chimneys and every evening the sky flared. 'That's dust in the air already. That's dry weather,' he said.

Always reading, he got an idea about the cattail. 'Ten times more edible tubers per acre than a crop of potatoes.'

'Just before a storm,' he said, 'you can see the farthest.'

Since the price of wheat was not going to rise, Teo sold our farm and bought the store in town. There I learned our other names: 'bohunk' and 'garlic-eater'. People didn't like owing us money, but the fact that they did never stopped them writing in the newspaper that we couldn't be loyal subjects of the British Empire. That we would never learn to put saucers under our cups. I refused to wear my embroidered blouses and sometimes even turned to the wall the cardboard picture of the Sacred Heart. It embarrassed me the way Our Saviour bared his sweet breast, as if he didn't care what people thought of him.

Teo was unperturbed. There was work to be done and I could be his little helper. At Mud Lake, by then half receded, ringed by white alkali scum, he asked me to remove my clothes. Covering my breasts with spread-open hands, I waded in, then clung to a snag slippery with algae while Teo, on shore, named clouds.

'Cumulus. Cumulus. Cumulus.'

'Why me?' I shouted.

'Needs a virgin,' he called. 'A smooth thigh.'

I came out festooned with leeches—arms, legs, shoulder even. He chose the halest one and burned the rest off with his cigarette. All the way home I wore that guzzling leech sheltered in a wet handkerchief. Like a doting mother I nursed it. Then we put it in a Mason jar with water and a little stick.

'Leech barometer,' Teo said. 'Fair weather when the leech stays in the water. Unless the leech is dead.'

The next year Mud Lake had disappeared. Rising out of what once was water—a secret charnel-house. Old glowing buffalo bones.

Already farms were being seized. Some families had been paying us in chits since 1929. To one farmer Teo made a gift—an idea expressed to hide the giving. 'If he wanted, a man might collect and sell those bones as fertilizer.' We saw the farmer working every day. On first sight of the bones his horse had spooked. Now it had to be blindfolded—led like a reluctant bride through the sweltering town, an antimacassar the veil on its head. It strained with the cart, load white and rattling. Vertebrae fell in puffs of dust on the road, provoking feud amongst the forsaken dogs.

I never knew there could be so much death in one place or that the labour of removing it could be so gruelling. Finally, all the bones in a dry heap at the train station, ready to be loaded. Women could go down and have their photograph taken with a huge skull in their lap. Boys swung at each other with the leg bones.

Strangest railway robbery anybody had ever heard of. Overnight it all vanished. Not even a tooth left on the platform. The exhausted farmer lost his remuneration. After that he posted himself in front of the store warning those who entered that Teo was not as stupid as he looked. Declaring revenge was a man's right when he thirsted for justice. He spat so often on our window I made a routine of cleaning it off. The pattern of saliva on the dusty glass was like cloudburst.

It was so dry in the Palliser Triangle dunes of dust stopped the trains. We tucked rags around doors and window sills, blew black when we blew into our handkerchiefs. In Galicia, Teo would have been a *chmarnyk*, a rain-man. He took me with him, driving where roads were passable, farm to farm. Waiting in the car, I watched him point at the sky. Children circled, staring in at me. They thumbed their noses and wrote 'garlic' in the dust on the windscreen. I kept my gaze on Teo as he exhorted skeletal-faced farmers to send their wives and daughters into the fields. Send them into the fields on Sunday morning and have them urinate, for a woman's urine has power to cause rain.

Brandishing brooms, they drove him off their porches. They kicked him in the seat of the pants.

'Why are we doing this?' I cried. His every good deed bred animosity.

Teo said, 'They didn't know Our Saviour either.' To give me faith, he made a drop of water appear at the end of his nose, glistening like a glass rosary bead. 'That's without even trying,' he said.

Nobody went into the fields, of course. Just Mama and Baba. And me, squatting, skirts hoisted. I saw my urine pool in the dust, ground too parched to drink. High in a tree a crow was watching me. It shouted down that rain comes at a cost, and even then might not come for good.

In the Bible, Pharaoh dreamed of seven gaunt cows. By 1932, I must have seen seven hundred so much worse than gaunt. Angular with starvation or dead and bloated, legs straight up in the air.

'Ten times more edible tubers per acre in a crop of cattails than a crop of potatoes!'

'Who told you that?'

'And the fluff! That's good insulation! Mattress stuffing, quilt batting! From the stalks, wallboard and paper! The leaves—baskets, clothing!'

I laughed. Who would wear a cattail? 'How come nobody ever thought of this before, smartie?'

'Lots nobody ever thought of! Every great change is wrought in the sky! God made the cattail!' His tongue raced, arms circled in the air.

But the big idea was cheap cattle feed, deliverance from famine. Teo the Deliverer. 'Is a cow going to eat a cattail root?' I wanted to know.

'Cows eating pieces of tractors! Cows eating gate latches!' Hardware disease.

And the next morning he drove away from the Palliser Triangle, northward, looking for a cattail slough. I waited. Baba sucked on her bare gums all day, as if that way she could wet her throat. Mama—always the same stories. 'Dakota. 1906. A good doggie.' She raised her fist in the air, swept it down with a loud smack into her outstretched palm. Weeping, she mimed the baby in her arms. That lance of ice, it dropped right out of heaven.

Then this, another sorrow: how Papa died. As a child I thought he'd been plucked from the plough and raptured straight on high. Mama used to tell how she had clutched his ankle and dangled in mid-air trying to hold him back. Nothing could be further from the truth. He threw himself on a pitch-fork. So much blood, it was like when they killed a pig. This she confessed in the back room of the store as I sat on a lard pail. Suicide triples a curse.

On a red background I appliquéd a cattail. The words: THE EVERYTHING PLANT. For batting I planned to use the brown and gold pollen of the cattail flower. We were going to string it across the back of the car when we, brother and sister, did our tour of the drought towns, made our presentation at the feed stores. We were going to sleep under it at night. I was Teo's little helper.

In the corner of every eye, a plug of dust. I was afraid of crying, of someone licking the water off my face.

I urinated again in the field.

There were no clouds to name.

Now they said we were worse than Jews, almost as bad as Chinamen. I had never seen either. On the counter they scattered handfuls of raisins, railing, 'Stones! Stones!' as if they actually paid us. What could we do about fly-infested flour, rancid bacon, the desiccated mouse in the sugar? When the cash register opened, chits flew out like a hundred moths. On all these accusing faces the dirty lines were a map of the roads Teo had gone away on.

Now we wanted Teo to take us away. Baba said she could smell hatred. It smelled like gunpowder.

In Galicia, Mama said, Drought is a beautiful woman. She persuades a young peasant to carry her on his back. Wherever he goes crops wither and die, ponds evaporate, birds, songs stuck in their throats, drop out of trees. Horrified, he struggles to loosen the cinch of her legs round his waist, her grappling hands at his neck. In the end, to be rid of his burden, he leaps from a bridge. Drought dries up the river instantly and, crashing on the rocks below, our young peasant breaks open his head.

Finally, a package. Inside, a big tuberous finger, hairy and gnarled. We marvelled it was still wet.

'What is it?' Mama asked.

'A cattail root.'

When Baba touched it, she started to cry. What did it mean? Would Teo come for us? Alive, it was holding the rain. That night, to keep it moist, I brought it to bed and put it inside me.

To cure fever, drink whisky with ground garlic. Eat bread wrapped in cobwebs. But I did not think it was fever. Overnight my hair had curled like vetch tendrils and my head throbbed where a horse had kicked me seven years before. Beside my bed, the leech barometer. So many years in the jar, I had thought the leech was dead. Now it shimmied out of the water and halfway up the stick.

Mama said, looking over the town, 'Smoke from all these chimneys curling down.' When I would not take the bread and whisky, she pulled my hair.

Just before a storm, you can see the farthest. We saw you coming miles away. Dust-maker, you were weaving all over the road, horn pressed. By the time we got Baba down the stairs and into the street, a crowd had gathered round the car. You were standing on the hood, almost naked, wet skirt of cattail leaves pasted to your thighs.

Mama gasped, 'Teo has his father's curse.'

The sere voice of a crow: *rain costs.*

And I was part to blame. I had given my innocence to a cattail root while you held its power.

From the beating part of your chest, your brow, water had begun to trickle, ribboning downward, the sheen of moisture all across you. Motionless, arms open, fingers spread and dripping—you were sowing rain. We were sweating too, the day dry and searing, but soon you were dissolving, hair saturated, nostrils and eyes streaming culverts. Then you turned, spun round and spattered the silent crowd. Turned again, kept spinning, faster. Whirling, whirling on the slippery hood, you drenched and astounded us, became a living fountain. And then, amazing! A nimbus, seven-coloured, shimmering all around you.

In Galicia, when thunder sounds, prostrate yourself to save your soul. That day thunder discharged, a firearm, reverberating. Mama and Baba dropped to the ground. A dark curtain was drawn across the Palliser Triangle. Black geyser sky.

You bowed forward and vomited a river.

The crowd fell back. They had never seen a *chmarnyk.*

After Teo made it rain, the whole town was filled with steam, water evaporating off the streets and the wet backs of the men who carried Teo's body away. Dogs staggered out of cover to drink from temporary puddles. And in all the fields, green shoots reared, only to wither later in the reborn drought.

They carried Teo's body away and wouldn't let us see him. 'Struck by lightning,' they said. How could we argue? I was only fifteen and neither Mama nor Baba could speak English. The moment he was taken, we had been rolling on the ground. But I remember clearly the presence of that farmer, the one robbed of his charnel-house, his smile like lightning. The English word 'shotgun' never had a place on my tongue.

Years later Teo came to Mama in a dream. In the dream he had a hole in his chest big enough to climb into, gory as the Sacred Heart. 'I have seen the face of Our Saviour,' he told her. 'He lets me spit off the clouds.'

As for me, two things at least I know. The cattail root holds more than water. Every great change is wrought in the sky.

Biographical Notes

CAROLINE ADDERSON (b. 1963) was born in Edmonton, Alberta, and now lives in Vancouver, where she teaches at Vancouver Community College. She has written a feature-length film and a radio play for Morningside, but has been most active as a writer of short stories. She has twice won prizes for fiction in the CBC literary competition, and was published in The Journey Prize Anthology 5. Her first story collection, *Bad Imaginings* (1993), was published by The Porcupine's Quill, and was nominated for the Commonwealth Writers Prize and the Governor General's award. She won the Ethel Wilson fiction award in 1994.

Adderson's story 'The Chmarnyk' is from *Bad Imaginings*.

SANDRA BIRDSELL (b. 1942) grew up in rural Manitoba and now lives in Winnipeg. She began publishing her short stories in 'little magazines'—particularly those in western Canada, such as *Grain, Capilano Review, NeWest Review,* and *Prairie Fire*—and has been an active member of the Manitoba Writers' Guild for a number of years. Her first collection, *Night Travellers* (1982), consists of a series of linked stories set in the fictitious Manitoba town of Agassiz. *Ladies of the House* (1984), her second book, contains stories of rural Manitoba and others that explore the often gritty working-class life of Winnipeg. She has published two novels, *The Missing Child* (1987) and *The Chrome Suite* (1992).

Sandra Birdsell has written film scripts for the National Film Board, including dramatizations of her own work, and plays for Winnipeg theatres. She won a National Magazine Award for fiction, and in 1984 received the Gerald Lampert Award, administered by the League of Canadian Poets and given in alternate years for poetry and prose fiction. 'Flowers for Weddings and Funerals' is reprinted from *Night Travellers*.

NEIL BISSOONDATH was born in 1955 in Trinidad and now lives in Montreal. He comes from a literary family. His grandfather, Seepersad Naipaul, was a journalist on the *Trinidad Guardian* for most of his working life and published a collection of short stories in Trinidad in 1943. Two of his sons became well-known writers: V.S. Naipaul and Shiva Naipaul, who died suddenly at the age of forty in 1985.

Bissoondath immigrated to Canada in 1973, partly on the advice of his uncle, V.S. Naipaul. He studied French at York University, Toronto, and afterwards taught in a language school in that city. He has published two collections of short stories, *Digging Up the Mountains* (1985)—the title story has been reprinted here—and *On the Eve of Uncertain Tomorrows* (1990), and two novels, *A Casual Brutality* (1988) and *The Innocence of Age* (1993). In 1994 he published a controversial work of non-fiction, *Selling Illusions: The Cult of Multiculturalism in Canada.*

CLARK BLAISE (b. 1940) was born in North Dakota of a French-Canadian father and an English-Canadian mother. In a recent book, *Resident Alien* (1986), a collection of short stories and autobiographical sketches, he wrote: 'I lived my childhood in the deep, segregated South, my adolescence in Pittsburgh, my manhood in Montreal, and have started my middle age somewhere in middle America.' Along the way, like a number of Canadian writers, he studied at the Writer's Workshop at the University of Iowa, and he has taught at several universities in the United States and at Concordia in Montreal and York University in Toronto.

Blaise's books include *A North American Education* (1973), from which 'A Class of New Canadians' was taken, and *Tribal Justice* (1974), both collections of short stories. His novel *Lunar Attractions* (1979) won the *Books in Canada* Award for the best first novel of the year, and a second novel, *Lusts,* was published in 1983. Blaise and his wife, the Indian-born writer Bharati Mukherjee, collaborated on an unusual travel book about a visit to India, *Days and Nights in Calcutta* (1977).

Another short-story collection, *Man and His World,* was published in 1992 and *I Had a Father,* a 'post-modern autobiography', in 1993. Blaise now heads the International Writing Program at the University of Iowa.

GEORGE BOWERING (b. 1935) was born and raised in the Okanagan Valley in the interior of British Columbia, and became an RCAF aerial photographer after finishing high school. He then studied at the University of British Columbia and later taught at the University of Calgary and at Sir George Williams College (now Concordia University) in Montreal. At UBC Bowering became one of the editors of the 'little magazine' *Tish,* which was influenced by the Black Mountain school of contemporary American poets. He now teaches at Simon Fraser University.

Bowering, who has written poetry, fiction, and criticism, won a Governor General's Award for poetry in 1968 for two books, *Rocky Mountain Foot* and *The Gangs of Kosmos.* In 1980 his *Burning Water,* a novel about George Vancouver's search for the Northwest Passage, won him a Governor General's Award for fiction. He has edited short-story collections ranging from *Great Canadian Sports Stories* (1979) to the experimental *Fiction of Contemporary Canada* (1980). His many books of poetry include *Selected Poems: Particular Accidents* (1980) and a collection of long poems, *West*

444 $ **Biographical Notes**

Window (1982). He has also written a critical study of his fellow poet Al Purdy (1970) and the lively and opinionated *The Mask in Place: Essays on Fiction in North America* (1983).

Two recent novels are *Caprice* (1988) and *Shoot!* (1994), a story about the McLean Gang, three brothers of mixed Scottish and Salish blood and their companion Alex Hare, who terrorized the interior of British Columbia in the late 1800s.

DIONNE BRAND (b. 1953) was born in Trinidad and now lives in Toronto, where she studied at the University of Toronto and OISE. She is best known as a writer of poetry that has been published in a number of literary magazines and anthologies, including the *Penguin Book of Caribbean Verse*. Her most recent collection, *No Language Is Neutral* (1990), was published by Coach House Press. Dionne Brand's short stories have been published in *Fireweed* and the anthologies *Stories by Canadian Women* and *From Ink Lake*. Her collection *Sans Souci and Other Stories* was published in 1988 by Williams-Wallace. She is also the author of *No Burden to Carry: Black Working Women in Ontario 1920s-1950s* (1991) and *Bread Out of Stone* (1994), a personal account by a black woman who is also a writer and an activist trying to come to terms with life in Canada. Dionne Brand has been writer-in-residence at the Halifax City Regional Library and the University of Toronto.

BONNIE BURNARD (b. 1945) was born in southwestern Ontario and recently returned to live in that part of Canada. In the interval she lived for a number of years in Regina, Saskatchewan, where she was active in the literary community. She was fiction editor for *Grain* magazine from 1982 to 1986. In 1983 four of her stories appeared in *Coming Attractions*, an annual anthology in which Oberon Press introduced new fiction writers. Other stories were published in literary magazines, broadcast on CBC radio, and dramatized for television. Burnard's short-story collection, *Women of Influence* (1988), was named the best first-published book in the Caribbean-Canadian region for the 1989 Commonwealth Writers' Prize, and partly as a result of that award she has given readings not only throughout Canada but also in the US, England, Europe, South Africa, and Australia. 'Deer Heart' is from *Casino & Other Stories*, published in 1994, which was one of the five finalists for the first Giller Prize that year.

BARRY CALLAGHAN, the son of Morley Callaghan, was born in 1937 in Toronto, where he still lives, and educated at St Michael's College, University of Toronto. Since the mid-1960s he has taught contemporary literature at Atkinson College, York University. He has had a parallel and very active career in journalism as a writer and commentator on radio and television and as a contributor to such magazines as *Toronto Life* and *Saturday Night*. For a half-dozen years in the late 1960s he edited and wrote extensively for a lively, wide-ranging, and frequently controversial weekly book page in the Toronto *Telegram* (which no longer exists). He is publisher and editor of the literary quarterly *Exile*, and under the imprint Exile Editions also publishes books, with an emphasis on imaginative literature and the visual arts. (A recent publication of Exile Editions was *A Passage Back Home*, mentioned in the biographical note about Austin Clarke.)

Barry Callaghan's stories have appeared in *Saturday Night*, *Exile*, *The Ontario Review*, and frequently in the English magazine *Punch*. Notable for their literary sophistication and for the sympathy with which he writes about gamblers, whores, gays, and other non-conformists, they have been collected in *The Black Queen Stories* (1983), from which the title story is reprinted here. Callaghan is also a poet, the author of a complex and ambitious long poem, *The Hogg Poems and Drawings* (1978), and of *As Close as We Came*, a collection that appeared in 1983. He edited an anthology of Canadian love poems in English and French, *Lords of Winter and of Love* (1983), and gathered together *The Lost and Found Stories of Morley Callaghan* (1985). He has also edited a major anthology, *Alchemists in Winter: Canadian Poetry in French and English* (1986). His most recent novel, *When Things Get Worst*, was published in 1993.

MORLEY CALLAGHAN (1903-90) was born in Toronto, where he lived for most of his life. Educated at St Michael's College, University of Toronto, and in law at Osgoode Hall, he was called to the bar but never practised law. While he was a student he worked during the summers on the Toronto *Daily Star*, where he met Ernest Hemingway. Callaghan's first novel, *Strange Fugitive* (1928), and his first collection of short stories, *A Native Argosy* (1929), were both published by Scribner's in New York. In 1929 Callaghan and his wife Loretto went to Paris, where his stories had been appearing in the 'little magazines'. There he met Hemingway again, Scott Fitzgerald, James Joyce, Ford Madox Ford, and other expatriate writers and artists. He later described this period of his life in the memoir *That Summer in Paris* (1963).

After returning to Toronto, Callaghan continued to publish his novels and short stories throughout the 1930s. Novels from the period include *A Broken Journey* (1932), *Such Is My Beloved* (1934), and *More Joy in Heaven* (1937). His short stories appeared in such magazines as *The New Yorker*, *Atlantic Monthly*, and *Esquire*, and in a second collection, *Now That April's Here* (1936). This prolific period came to an end in the late 1930s, and during the Second World War Callaghan was chairman of the CBC radio program *Of Things to Come* and was later a regular panelist on the radio program *Now I Ask You* and a frequent guest on the TV series Fighting Words.

In 1951 Callaghan returned to fiction with one of his major novels, *The Loved and The Lost*, and in 1959 more than fifty of his short stories were gathered together in *Morley Callaghan's Stories*. 'All the Years of Her Life' has been reprinted from that book. Novels that have appeared since the 1950s include *A Passion in Rome* (1961), *Close to the Sun Again* (1977), and *A Time for Judas* (1983). Two dozen stories from the 1930s and 1940s not previous-ly published in a book were collected in *The Lost and Found Stories of Morley Callaghan* (1985). Among the many awards Callaghan won are a Governor General's Award for *The Loved and the Lost*, and in 1970 the Molson Prize and the Royal Bank Award.

AUSTIN CLARKE (b. 1932) was born and brought up in Barbados, and moved to Canada in 1955 to study at the University of Toronto. In 1959-60 he was a reporter in Timmins and Kirkland Lake, Ontario, and then worked as a freelance broadcaster for the CBC. He taught creative writing at Yale, Duke, and other American universities in the late 1960s and early 1970s. For a time he was general manager of the Caribbean Broadcasting Corporation in Barbados. He now lives in Toronto, where he served for some years on the Ontario Film Review Board.

Clarke's first book, *Survivors of the Crossing*, a novel about life in Barbados, appeared in 1963. Three years later he published *The Meeting Point*, the first novel in a trilogy about the lives of Caribbean immigrants in Toronto: the next two books were *Storm of Fortune* (1971) and *The Bigger Light* (1975). He has also written a political novel, *The Prime Minister* (1977), set in a develop-ing nation, and the first volume of an autobiography, *Growing Up Stupid Under the Union Jack* (1980). Clarke's short stories—set in Barbados, Canada, and the United States—were collected in *When He Was Free and Young and He Used to Wear Silks* (1971 Canada; 1973 US)—'Griff!' was included in that book—and *Nine Men Who Laughed* (1986) in the Penguin Short Fiction series. In 1994 Clarke published *A Passage Back Home* (Exile Editions), a reminis-cence of his friend the Trinidad-born writer Samuel Selvon, who died earli-er that year.

MATT COHEN (b. 1942), was born in Kingston, Ontario, and grew up in Ottawa. He now lives in Toronto. He studied at the University of Toronto and was briefly a lecturer in the department of religion at McMaster University in Hamilton, Ontario. He gave that up to write full time. His first novel, *Korsoniloff*, was published in 1969. Two years later he published a sec-ond novel, *Johnny Crackle Sings*, which uses the Ottawa Valley as its setting. Cohen owns a farm north of Kingston, and beginning with *The Disinherited* (1974) he published four novels set in the fictional Ontario community of Salem, concluding with *Flowers of Darkness* in 1981.

In addition to his novels, Matt Cohen has been active as a writer of short stories, an editor of anthologies, and an occasional translator. The story included here, 'Trotsky's First Confessions', is from his most recent collec-tion, *Lives of the Mind Slaves: Selected Stories* (1994), published by Porcupine's Quill, Erin, Ontario.

MARIAN ENGEL (1933-85) was born in Toronto but grew up in smaller Ontario cities—Sarnia, Galt, Hamilton—and various aspects of the province later played important roles in her fiction. Educated at McMaster and McGill Universities, she studied French literature in Provence and taught for a while in Cyprus. She married, and later divorced, the writer and broadcaster Howard Engel. The first chairperson of the Writers' Union, she worked until her death towards improving the situation of her fellow writers in Canada.

Marian Engel wrote radio scripts, journalism, two books for children, and published two collections of short stories, *Inside the Easter Egg* (1975) and *The Tattooed Woman*, which appeared posthumously in 1985. Most of her fiction–the bulk of which consists of seven novels published between 1968 and 1981–reflects her life as a writer and a working mother. Her novels include *No Clouds of Glory* (later re-issued as *Sara Bastard's Notebook*); *The Honeyman Festival; Bear*, which achieved both a scandalous and an admiring critical reception (it won a Governor General's Award); and *The Glassy Sea* and *Lunatic Villas*.

'Share and Share Alike', reprinted here, appears in *The Tattooed Woman* in the Penguin Short Fiction series.

TIMOTHY FINDLEY was born in Toronto in 1930. The city of his birth, two world wars, the ugly history of fascism in the twentieth century, the lives of such public figures as Ezra Pound and the Duke and Duchess of Windsor are all obsessions with which his fictions try to come to terms.

Before becoming a writer, Findley had a promising career as an actor. He played summer stock in Ontario and worked in the Stratford (Ontario) Shakespearean Festival in its first season in 1953. Then, for three years, he acted in Europe, England, and the United States, and was encouraged by, among others, Ruth Gordon and Thornton Wilder. Throughout his later career as a writer of fiction he has continued to write scripts for CBC radio and television, and plays, and has also occasionally acted.

Findley's first short stories were published or broadcast when he was in his twenties; two novels, *The Last of The Crazy People* and *The Butterfly Plague*, were published in the late 1960s. *The Wars* (1977) won a Governor General's Award, and it was followed by three major works of fiction all published in the 1980s: *Famous Last Words, Not Wanted on the Voyage*, and *The Telling of Lies*. Findley's short stories have been collected in *Dinner Along the Amazon* (1984) and *Stones* (1988). In 1990 Findley published *Inside Memory*, a selection of journal entries and memoirs covering his career in the theatre, as a novelist, and as an activist on artistic issues in Canada. His most recent novel is *The Piano Man's Daughter* (1995).

'The Duel in Cluny Park' was first published in the PEN-Canada Supplement of *Toronto Life* (August 1989).

CYNTHIA FLOOD (b. 1940) lives in Vancouver, where she teaches English at Langara College. For the past two decades she has been active in the women's movement and in left-wing politics. Her short stories have been published in several anthologies and a number of literary journals, including *Fireweed, Queen's Quarterly, Room of One's Own,* and *Wascana Review.* Her story 'My Father Took a Cake to France', first published in *The Malahat Review,* won the $10,000 Journey Prize and was included in the second edition of *The Journey Prize Anthology* (1980), published by McClelland & Stewart. Two collections of Cynthia Flood's short stories have been published, both by Talonbooks in Vancouver: *The Animal In Their Elements* (1987) and *My Father Took a Cake to France* (1992), from which 'The Meaning of the Marriage' has been chosen.

MAVIS GALLANT (b. 1922) was born in Montreal and educated in seventeen different public, private, and convent schools in Canada and the United States. She worked briefly for the National Film Board and then on the Montreal *Standard* (a weekly newspaper that was a competitor of the Toronto *Star Weekly;* both papers are now gone). She left Montreal in 1950 and has lived in Paris ever since, but makes frequent visits to Canada. She was writer-in-residence at the University of Toronto in 1983-4.

Gallant has published two novels—*Green Water, Green Sky* (1959) and *A Fairly Good Time* (1970)—and numerous collections of short stories (almost all of which first appeared in *The New Yorker,* to which she began contributing in 1951). These include *The Other Paris* (1956), *My Heart Is Broken* (1959), The *Pegnitz Junction* (1973), and *Home Truths* (1981), which won a Governor General's Award. (An American edition of this collection of her Canadian stories was published in 1985 to highly favourable reviews.) More recent collections include *Overhead in a Balloon: Stories of Paris* (1985) and *Across The Bridge* (1993). *The Muslim Wife and Other Stories,* selected and with an Afterword by Mordecai Richler, appeared in the New Canadian Library in 1995.

Mavis Gallant has also written distinguished non-fiction. *The New Yorker* published (in September 1968) her two-part account of the student riots in Paris in the spring of 1968—'The Events in May: A Paris Notebook'—and a long essay that served as the introduction to *The Affair of Gabrielle Russier* (1971), about a thirty-year-old teacher of languages in Mar-seilles who had a love affair with a sixteen-year-old male student and later killed herself. Both works appear in *Paris Notebooks: Essays and Reviews* (1986).

'Scarves, Beads, Sandals' was included in the 70th Anniversary double issue of *The New Yorker* for February 20 & 27, 1995.

HUGH GARNER was born in 1913 in Batley, Yorkshire, and died in Toronto in 1979. In 1919 Garner's father moved his family from England to Toronto, where he soon deserted them, leaving the mother to raise four children in the Cabbagetown area of the city. Garner later described this part of Toronto as 'a sociological phenomenon, the largest Anglo-Saxon slum in North America'. His novel *Cabbagetown,* published in a badly cut paperback edition in 1950, eventually appeared in its original length in 1968.

Garner, who left school at sixteen, worked during the Depression at unskilled jobs and rode freight trains across North America. He joined the Abraham Lincoln Battalion of the International Brigade and fought for the Loyalists in the Spanish Civil War. During the Second World War he served in the Canadian Navy on convoy duty in the Atlantic. The novel *Storm Below* (1949) is based on his naval experiences. At the end of the war Garner became a full-time writer. Among his many books are the novels *The Silence on the Shore* (1962) and *The Intruders* (1976), both set in Toronto, and an autobiography, *One Damn Thing After Another* (1973). He won a Governor General's Award in 1963 for *Hugh Garner's Best Stories*. Garner also wrote three police novels—*Sin Sniper* (1970), *Death in Don Mills* (1975), and *Murder Has Your Number* (1978)—all set in Toronto.

Garner's most successful stories are realistic studies of outsiders in Canadian society. He has written about alcoholics, an itinerant evangelist, a displaced person trying to make a fresh start at the end of the Second World War by working in the tobacco fields on the north shore of Lake Erie, and a dispossessed Indian family trying to survive on the fringes of white society in Northern Ontario—in 'One, Two, Three Little Indians'.

MARGARET GIBSON (b. 1948) lives in Toronto. She has published three short-story collections: *The Butterfly Ward* (1976), *Considering her Condition* (1978), and *Sweet Poison* (1993). *The Butterfly Ward* was co-winner of the Toronto Book Award for 1977. 'Ada' one of the stories in this book, was filmed as a CBC-TV drama, directed by Claude Jutra. The story 'Making It' was the basis for the film *Outrageous!* starring Craig Russell.

The Butterfly Ward, from which 'Making It' was reprinted, was reissued in the Oberon Library series in 1994 by HarperCollins.

DOUGLAS GLOVER (b. 1948), who grew up on a tobacco farm in Southwestern Ontario, is a graduate of the University of Edinburgh and the University of Iowa Writers' Workshop. He has published articles and short stories in Canada and the US, and has taught creative-writing courses in both countries. He is the author of three novels, most recently *The Life and Times of Captain N.* (1993), and three collections of short stories. 'Swain Corliss, Hero of Malcolm's Mills (now Oakland, Ontario), November 6. 1814' is from *A Guide to Animal Behaviour* (1991), published by Goose Lane Editions, Fredericton, New Brunswick. Glover lives near Saratoga Springs, New York.

KATHERINE GOVIER (b. 1948) was born in Edmonton and studied at the University of Alberta, where she was encouraged as a young writer by Rudy Wiebe and Dorothy Livesay. She now lives in Toronto, where she has taught a creative-writing course at York University and is active in national writers' organizations. She has written articles and reviews for the Toronto *Globe & Mail*, the Toronto *Star*, *Saturday Night* and *Toronto Life*, and has won several national journalism awards. She has published four novels, *Random Descent* (1979), *Going Through the Motions* (1982), *Between Men* (1987), and *Hearts of Flame* (1991). Her short stories have been published in Canada and abroad, and in her collections: *Fables of Brunswick Avenue* (1985) in the Penguin Short Fiction series, *Before and After* (1989), and *The Immaculate Conception Photograph Gallery* (1994). 'Sociology' is from *Fables of Brunswick Avenue.*

BARBARA GOWDY (b. 1950) grew up in Toronto. She worked for the publishing house Lester & Orpen Dennys, and has been an interviewer for the TV Ontario arts program *Imprint.* She is the author of the novels *Falling Angels* (1989) and *Mister Sandman* (1995). A film version of *Falling Angels* is underway in Germany.

Barbara Gowdy's short stories have appeared in *Story, Descant, Canadian Fiction Magazine,* and other literary journals, and were published in *We So Seldom Look on Love* (1992) by Somerville House.

HUGH HOOD (b. 1928) grew up in Toronto and received his Ph.D. from the University of Toronto in 1955. He taught for a few years in the United States, then joined the English department at the Université de Montréal, where he has remained since 1961.

Hood has published short stories, novels, memoirs, journalism, and sports biographies. He has produced half-a-dozen collections of short stories, including *Flying a Red Kite* (1962); *Around the Mountain: Scenes from Montreal Life* (1967); *The Fruit Man, the Meat Man and the Manager* (1971), from which 'Getting to Williamstown' was taken; *Dark Glasses* (1976); and *August Nights* (1985). Hood's other interests include painting, film, and the theatre; his first novel, *White Figure, White Ground* (1964), was about a painter. In 1975 he published *The Swing in the Garden,* the first of the projected twelve novels in his *New Age* series, which explores Canadian society and the city of Toronto at various stages in its history. The series is to be completed at the end of this decade, which will also be the end of the century. Two of Hugh Hood's recent books are *Trusting the Tale* (1983), a collection of essays, and *You'll Catch Your Death* (1992), a book of stories.

ISABEL HUGGAN (b. 1943) lived in Ottawa until 1987. Since that time she and her husband and daughter have lived in Kenya, southern France, and, recently, the Philippines. She contributed an essay 'Notes from the Philippines' to *Writing Away, the PEN Canada Travel Anthology* (1994), edited by Constance Rooke and published by McClelland & Stewart.

Isabel Huggan has published two short-story collections: *The Elizabeth Stories* (1984), from which 'Celia Behind Me' was taken, and *You Never Know* (1993).

JANICE KULYK KEEFER, born in Toronto in 1953, has been able to combine an academic career with an impressive range of literary activities. She received her doctorate in modern English literature from the University of Sussex. She taught at the Université Sainte-Anne in Nova Scotia, where she lived for several years, and now teaches at the University of Guelph. She has published a collection of poetry, *White of the Lesser Angels* (1986), and a novel, *Constellations* (1989), but Keefer is best known for her short stories. They have been collected in *The Paris-Napoli Express* (1986), *Transfigurations* (1988), and *Travelling Ladies* (1990). The title story from *Transfigurations* is reprinted here.

Janice Kulyk Keefer won the first prize for fiction in both the 1985 and the 1986 CBC Literary Competition. She is also the author of two critical works, *Under Eastern Eyes* (1987), a study of Maritime fiction, which was nominated for a Governor General's Award, and *Reading Mavis Gallant* (1989).

THOMAS KING (b. 1943) is the son of a Cherokee father and a mother who is of Greek and German descent. He taught Native Studies for ten years at the University of Lethbridge in Alberta and more recently was Chair of American Indian Studies at the University of Minnesota in Minneapolis. In addition to teaching, King has written radio and TV dramas. He spent the year 1993-4 in Toronto as Story Editor for *The Four Directions*, a CBC-TV drama series by and about native people. He is the author of two novels, *Green Grass, Running Water* (1993) and *Medicine River* (1990), and of a children's book, *A Coyote Columbus Story* (1992). 'One Good Story, That One' was first published in *The Malahat Review* and is the title story of a collection published in 1993 by HarperCollins.

W.P. KINSELLA was born in 1935 in Edmonton, Alberta. He worked as a civil servant, a life-insurance salesman, a cab driver, and as the manager of a pizza parlour before enrolling in the creative-writing department at the University of Victoria in Victoria, British Columbia. Later he attended the Writer's Workshop at the University of Iowa. He taught for several years at the University of Calgary, and now lives as a full-time writer in White Rock, BC. Kinsella has written four books of Indian stories, beginning with *Dance Me Outside* (1977). In 1980 he published a collection of baseball stories, *Shoeless Joe Jackson Comes to Iowa*, and in 1982 a novel, Shoeless Joe, which won the Houghton Mifflin Literary Fellowship and the *Books in Canada* First Novel Award. *Brother Frank's Gospel Hour* (1994) is a recent short-story collection and *The Winter Helen Dropped By* (1995) is a novel.

In 'Shoeless Joe' and his other baseball stories Kinsella makes exuberant use of the traditions, myths, and present-day issues that enliven a sport that has attracted so many fiction writers in Canada and the United States. (Kinsella's Shoeless Joe inspired the popular film *Field of Dreams* starring Kevin Costner.) The same high spirits inform his stories about the people of the Indian reserve near Hobbema in southern Alberta. A film version of *Dance Me Outside* was released in 1995; its Executive Producer was Norman Jewison, and it was directed by Bruce McDonald.

MARGARET LAURENCE (1926-87) was born in Neepawa, Manitoba, which became the model for 'Manawaka', the prairie town in her fiction. Her parents died when she was young and she was brought up by her aunt. After graduating from United College in Winnipeg in 1947, she worked as a reporter for the Winnipeg *Citizen* and in the same year married Jack Laurence, a civil engineer. From 1950 to 1957 they lived in Africa, first in Somalia and then in Ghana just before its independence. After separating from her husband in 1962, Laurence spent ten years in England. She lived for many years in Lakefield, Ontario, where she died.

Laurence's African experience was fruitful for her as a writer: in 1960 she published an African novel, *This Side Jordan*; in 1962 a collection of African stories, *The Tomorrow-Tamer*; and a year later a memoir of her life in Somalia, *The Prophet's Camel Bell*. Meanwhile she was beginning her series of four Manawaka novels: *The Stone Angel* (1961), *A Jest of God* (1966), *The Fire-Dwellers* (1966), and *The Diviners* (1974). Interspersed with her fiction were several books for children and a collection of magazine articles, *Heart of a Stranger* (1976). Laurence received many honorary degrees, literary prizes, and awards, and served as chancellor of Trent University in Peterborough, Ontario, beginning in 1980.

Many of Margaret Laurence's stories and novels have been dramatized for radio and television, and one of her children's books, *The Olden Days Coat* (1979), which was produced for television by Atlantis Films in Toronto, has been shown regularly in the Christmas season. Laurence's Manawaka stories were published in *A Bird in the House* (1970); 'Mask of the Bear' is from that collection.

NORMAN LEVINE (b. 1923). In *Canada Made Me*, Norman Levine described how he grew up in the Jewish community in Ottawa's Lower Town. He served in the RCAF during the Second World War and afterwards studied at McGill University. He went to England in the late 1940s and lived there—for much of the time in St Ives, Cornwall–until his return to Canada in 1980, where he lived for a time in Toronto. He is now living in France.

Levine published a collection of poetry, *The Tight-Rope Walker*, in 1950 and a war novel. *The Angled Road*, two years later. In the mid-1950s he began work on a book that would combine autobiographical material with an investigation of Canadian society from the underside in the manner of Henry Miller and George Orwell. That book became *Canada Made Me*, published in England and the United States in 1958; but because of its disenchanted view of life in this country, there was no Canadian edition until 1979.

Levine published a second novel, *From a Seaside Town*, in 1970; but he is best known, as a writer of fiction, for his short stories. Among his collections are *One Way Ticket* (1961), *I Don't Want to Know Anyone Too Well* (1971), *Thin Ice* (1979), and *Champagne Barn* (1984). Many of his stories have been broadcast by the CBC and the BBC, and have been translated and published throughout Europe. His German translators were the distinguished novelist Heinrich Böll and his wife. In recent years three collections of his stories have appeared in The Netherlands.

'Something Happened Here' is the title story of a collection first published by Penguin in 1991.

ALISTAIR MACLEOD (b. 1936) was born in Inverness County, Cape Breton, Nova Scotia, and for many years has taught English and creative writing at the University of Windsor in Windsor, Ontario. His short stories have been published in *The Fiddlehead, The Tamarack Review,* and the annual *Best American Short Stories*; 'As Birds Bring Forth the Sun' first appeared in the Vancouver literary magazine *Event.* Two collections of his stories have been published: *The Lost Salt Gift of Blood* in 1976 and *As Birds Bring Forth the Sun & Other Stories* in 1986.

Alistair MacLeod is currently working on a novel, *No Great Mischief If They Fail.*

JOYCE MARSHALL (b. 1913) was born in Montreal and educated at McGill University; but she has made her career as a writer, editor, and translator in Toronto. Her first novel, *Presently Tomorrow* (1946), was set in the Eastern Townships of Quebec in the early 1930s, and a second novel, *Lovers and Strangers* (1957), took place in Toronto in the late 1940s.

Two collections of Joyce Marshall's short stories have been published: *A Private Place* in 1975, and in 1993 *Any Time At All and Other Stories,* selected with an Afterword by Timothy Findley (New Canadian Library). 'The Old Woman' was included in both books.

Joyce Marshall is also a distinguished translator from the French. Among her translations are *Word from New France: The Selected Letters of Marie de l'Incarnation,* for which she wrote an important historical introduction, and *No Passport: A Discovery of Canada,* by the late Quebec travel writer Eugène Cloutier. Her translations of three books by Gabrielle Roy—*The Road Past Altamont, Windflower,* and *Enchanted Summer*—involved her in a close collaboration with that author; she was awarded the Canada Council Translation Prize in 1976 for her translation of *Enchanted Summer.*

JOHN METCALF (b. 1938) was born in Carlisle, England, and educated at the University of Bristol. In 1961 he settled in Montreal, where he taught for a while in the high-school system. He has also taught at Loyola College and McGill University, and has been writer-in-residence at several universities in other parts of the country. He now lives in Ottawa. Metcalf's books include a satirical novel about the teaching profession, *Going Down Slow* (1972); *Girl in Gingham* (1978), which consists of two novellas; *General Ludd* (1980), a satire of university life about a poet-in-residence; and the short-story collections *The Lady Who Sold Furniture* (1970); *The Teeth of My Father* (1975), in which 'The Years in Exile' appeared; and *Adult Entertainment* (1990).

Metcalf has been active as a critic, anthologist and editor. With Clark Blaise he edited the short-story annuals published by Oberon Press, *New Canadian Stories* and *Best Canadian Stories*. He edited the anthology *Canadian Classics* (1993), with J.R. (Tim) Struthers, and in recent years he has worked with a number of new writers whose first story collections have been published by the literary press The Porcupine's Quill.

ROHINTON MISTRY was born in 1952 in Bombay and immigrated to Canada in 1975. He began writing stories in 1983 while studying at the University of Toronto. In 1985 he won *Canadian Fiction Magazine*'s Annual Contributor's Prize, and *Tales from Firozsha Baag*, a collection of short stories, was published in 1987. 'The Ghost of Firozsha Baag' is from that book.

Mistry's first novel, *Such a Long Journey* (1991), was shortlisted for the Booker Prize, won a Governor General's Award in Canada, the 1991 Commonwealth Writers Prize for Best Book of the Year, and the Smith Books/*Books in Canada* First Novel Award. He is the 1995 winner of the Canada-Australia Literary Prize. Mistry's books have been published in the UK and the USA, and in translation in Germany, Japan, Sweden, Norway, and Denmark. A new novel, *A Fine Balance*, is forthcoming.

ALICE MUNRO (b. 1931) lives in Clinton in southwestern Ontario, not far from Lake Huron and from another southwestern Ontario town, Wingham, where she was born and grew up. She attended the University of Western Ontario in London, and then lived for a number of years in Vancouver and Victoria, British Columbia, where her first husband owned a bookstore.

Munro began writing stories while she was at university. Her early stories were published in *Chatelaine, The Canadian Forum, The Montrealer*, and *The Tamarack Review*. Her first collection, *Dance of the Happy Shades* (1968), appeared in 1968 and won a Governor General's Award; her first novel, *Lives of Girls and Women* (1971), won the Canadian Bookseller's Award in 1972. Six more collections of stories have been published: *Something I've Been Meaning to Tell You* (1974), *Who Do You Think You Are?* (1978), *The Moons of Jupiter* (1982), *The Progress of Love* (1986), *Friend of My Youth* (1990), and *Open Secrets* (1994). *Who Do You Think You Are?* won a Governor General's Award and was a runner-up for the Booker Prize in the UK. Most of her recent stories first appeared in *The New Yorker*, though two long stories, and a memoir of her father, were published in the New York literary quarterly *Grand Street*. 'The Jack Randa Hotel' is from her most recent collection, *Open Secrets*.

Several of Munro's stories have been dramatized for television; one of them, 'Boys and Girls', a production by Atlantis Films, Toronto, won an Academy Award in 1984.

THOMAS RADDALL (1903-94), whose father was an instructor in the British Army, was born while the family lived in married quarters at Hythe, England. His father was posted to Halifax in 1913, and Thomas Raddall's life has been associated with Nova Scotia ever since. He did not attend university, but served as a wireless operator on coastal stations and at sea. He then qualified as a bookkeeper, took a job with a lumber company, and soon began to write.

Raddall's many books display a wide range of interests. His historical novels include *His Majesty's Yankees* (1942), *Roger Sudden* (1944), and *Pride's Fancy* (1946). *The Nymph and the Lamp* (1950) is his major work of contemporary fiction. His non-fiction books include *Halifax, Warden of the North* (1948) and an interesting and candid autobiography, *In My Time* (1976).

Raddall began his writing career by publishing stories in *Blackwood's* and other magazines. Between 1939 and 1959 five collections of his short fiction appeared, including *The Pied Piper of Dipper Creek and Other Stories* (1939), which won a Governor General's Award; the 1959 collection for the New Canadian Library, *At the Tide's Turn and Other Stories*, is a selection from the earlier books. 'The Wedding Gift' is an attractive example of Raddall's treatment of historical material in the short-story form.

JAMES REANEY (b. 1926) grew up on a farm near Stratford, Ontario, and now lives in London, where he taught in the English department at the University of Western Ontario from 1960 until his retirement. He studied at the University of Toronto and from 1949 to 1956 taught at the University of Manitoba. As a writer of poetry, drama, fiction, and criticism—and through the magazine *Alphabet*, which he founded in 1960 and edited for ten years—he has made both the workaday and the mythic world of Southwestern Ontario the focus of his imaginative concerns.

Reaney's first book of poems, *The Red Heart* (1949), which won a Governor General's Award, was written while he was a student at the University of Toronto. *A Suite of Nettles* (1958) and *Twelve Letters to a Small Town* (1962) also won Governor General's Awards. Three other collections—*Poems* (1972), *Selected Shorter Poems* (1975), and *Selected Longer Poems* (1976)—were edited by Germaine Warkentin, whose extensive introductions provide important information about the poet.

Reaney was an established poet when he began a second career writing for the theatre. His early plays were published in *The Killdeer and Other Plays* (1962). John Hirsch staged *Colours in the Dark* at the Stratford Festival in 1967. Reaney's major dramatic work is *The Donnellys*, a trilogy about an Irish immigrant family massacred in Lucan, Ontario (not far from London), in 1880. These plays were first staged at Toronto's Tarragon Theatre between 1973 and 1975, and later toured Canada, from Vancouver to Halifax. 'The Bully', one of Reaney's few short stories, became widely known after it was broadcast in 1950, then anthologized. In 1994 his dramatic version of *Alice Through the Looking Glass* was staged at the Stratford Festival.

LEON ROOKE was born in 1934 in North Carolina and educated there. He served in the US Army in Alaska from 1958 to 1960, and taught English and creative writing in several American universities before moving to Victoria, BC, in 1969. In 1981 he won the Canada-Australia literary prize, and in 1984-5 he was writer-in-residence at the University of Toronto. With the writer John Metcalf he edited two volumes of *The New Press Anthology*, lively collections of short fiction by Canadian writers.

Rooke has contributed many stories to literary magazines in Canada and the United States, and since 1968 has published almost a dozen books—both novels and short-story collections. His novels include *Fat Woman* (1980) and *Shakespeare's Dog* (1983), which won a Governor General's Award. Among his short-story collections are *The Broad Back of the Angel* (1977), *The Birth Control King of the Upper Volta* (1982), *Sing Me No Love Songs, I'll Say You No Prayers* (1984), *A Bolt of White Cloth* (also 1984), and *Who Do You Love?* (1992). Critics have described Rooke as a 'post-realistic' and a 'post-modernist' writer. Imaginative titles are a Leon Rooke trademark. His fiction is notable for its portraits of strong, exuberant women and often for its humour, as in 'The Woman Who Talked to Horses', reprinted here from *Sing Me No Love Songs*.

SINCLAIR ROSS (b. 1908) was born on a homestead near Prince Albert, Saskatchewan. After finishing high school he worked as a bank clerk, first in a succession of small towns in Saskatchewan, then in Winnipeg, and finally in Montreal until his retirement in 1968. He now lives in Vancouver.

Ross's first novel, *As For Me and My House*, attracted only modest attention when it was published in 1941, but later came to be regarded as a central work in the development of Canadian fiction. He published three later novels: *The Well* (1958), *Whir of Gold* (1970), and *Sawbones Memorial* (1974).

Beginning in 1934 Ross published almost twenty short stories, most of which first appeared in the magazine *Queen's Quarterly*, published at Queen's University in Kingston, Ontario. They have been reprinted in two collections: *The Lamp at Noon and Other Stories* (1968, with an introduction by Margaret Laurence) and *The Race and Other Stories* (1982). Like *As For Me and My House*, many of Ross's stories explore the grim realities of life on isolated farms and in small villages during the drought and Depression years on the Canadian prairies.

JANE RULE (b. 1931) was born in Plainfield, New Jersey, and grew up in various parts of the American mid-west and in California. She attended Mills College in California and did graduate work at University College, London. In 1956 she moved to Vancouver, and taught from time to time at the University of British Columbia. Since 1976 she has lived on Galiano Island, BC.

Jane Rule has published four novels. Her first, *Desert of the Heart* (1964), which is set in Reno, Nevada, and explores a developing lesbian relationship, became the basis for the film *Desert Hearts*, released in 1986 to good reviews and substantial audiences in the larger cities of Canada and the

United States. She has published three collections of short stories: *Themes for Diverse Instruments* (1975), *Outlander* (1981), and *Inward Passage* (1985), from which 'The End of Summer' is reprinted here. Rule is also the author of *Lesbian Images* (1975)—which discusses such writers as Radclyffe Hall, Colette, and Vita Sackville West—and of a more recent essay collection, *Hot-Eyed Moderate* (1985). Best known for her writings on lesbian themes, she also deals frequently with children and family life in her fiction.

DIANE SCHOEMPERLEN(b. 1954) was born in Thunder Bay, Ontario. She graduated from Lakehead University there and lived for the next ten years in Canmore, Alberta, working at various jobs, including bank-teller and avalanche researcher. She now lives in Kingston, Ontario.

Schoemperlen has published four books of short fiction: *Double Exposures* (1984), *Frogs and Other Stories* (1986), *Hockey Night in Canada* (1987), and *The Man of My Dreams* (1990). *Frogs and Other Stories* won the Writers' Guild of Alberta Award for Excellence in Short Fiction in 1986, and the title story from *Hockey Night in Canada* has been made into a 30-minute television play.

Her first novel, *In the Language of Love* (1994), was published by HarperCollins. It will be published in the US in 1996 by Viking Penguin, and in Sweden. 'Red Plaid Shirt' was first published in *Saturday Night* and is included in *The Man of My Dreams*.

CAROL SHIELDS (b. 1935) was born in Oak Park, Illinois, and was educated in Indiana and at the University of Ottawa. She is married to Douglas Shields, a professor of civil engineering, and they have five children. She has taught at the Universities of Ottawa, British Columbia, and Manitoba, and lives in Winnipeg.

Shields has had a wide-ranging literary career. Beginning in the early 1970s she has published poetry, short stories, literary criticism—her MA thesis, later published as a monograph, was about Susanna Moodie—and novels, and has written plays for radio and the stage. Her first novel, *Small Ceremonies* (1976), won the Canadian Authors' Association Award for the best novel of the year. Among her other novels are *The Box Garden* (1977), *Happenstance* (1980), *A Fairly Conventional Woman* (1982), *Swann: A Mystery* (1987), and *The Republic of Love* (1992). Carol Shields Issues of the magazines *Room of One's Own* and *Prairie Fire* were published in 1989 and 1995 respectively. She was given the Marian Engel Award in 1990.

Between 1993 and 1995 Carol Shields' most recent novel, *The Stone Dairies*—which was published in Canada, the UK, and then the US—received a magnificent series of honours: the short list for the Booker Prize in the UK, the Governor General's Award in Canada, and the Pulitzer Prize for fiction in the US.

Her short stories have been collected in *Various Miracles* (1985) and *The Orange Fish* (1989), which contains 'Milk Bread Beer Ice', first published in *Saturday Night*.

LINDA SVENDSEN (b. 1948) was born and raised in Vancouver. She studied at the University of British Columbia, Columbia University, Stanford University (where she was a Stegner Fellow), and Radcliffe College. Her stories have been published in *The Atlantic, Saturday Night, Canadian Fiction Magazine,* and *Vanity Fair,* and in her first collection, *Marine Life* (HarperCollins, 1992), which contains 'White Shoulders'. She now lives in Vancouver, where she teaches creative writing at the University of British Columbia.

AUDREY THOMAS was born in 1935 in Binghamton, New York, and educated at Smith College in the US and St Andrews University in Scotland. She and her ex-husband immigrated to Canada in 1959, though in the mid-sixties she lived for three years in Ghana, where her husband was teaching at the time. The United States, Canada, and West Africa have all provided settings for her fiction. In recent years she has combined her own writing with periods of teaching at the University of Victoria and the University of British Columbia. In the academic year 1985-6 she was writer-in-residence at the Centre of Canadian Studies in the University of Edinburgh, in the annual exchange program of Canadian and Scottish writers that is supported by the Canadian Council and the Scottish Arts Council. Recently she taught creative writing at Concordia University in Montreal.

Thomas's first book was a collection of short stories, *Ten Green Bottles* (1967). Her other fiction includes novels (*Mrs Blood; Blown Figures*), two related novellas published in one volume (*Munchmeyer* and *Prospero on the Island*), and two more collections of stories, *Real Mothers* and *Two in the Bush and Other Stories,* both published in 1981. A novel, *Graven Images,* was published in 1993.

A collection of recent stories, *Goodbye Harold, Good Luck,* was published in the Penguin Short Fiction series in 1986. Volume 10, Numbers 3 & 4 of the Vancouver literary quarterly *Room of One's Own* (March 1986) is an Audrey Thomas Issue that includes a substantial interview with the author, new fiction, comments by fellow writers and critics, and a select bibliography.

Audrey Thomas's story in this anthology, 'Bear Country', was first published in the June 1991 issue of *Saturday Night* magazine.

W.D. VALGARDSON (b. 1939) grew up in Gimli, a town in the Interlake District of Manitoba not far from Winnipeg, whose inhabitants are mostly of Icelandic descent. He was educated at United College in Winnipeg, the University of Manitoba, and the University of Iowa, where—like W.P. Kinsella, Clark Blaise, and other Canadian writers—he was enrolled in the university's influential Writer's Workshop. Valgardson has published four collections of stories: *Bloodflowers* (1973); *God is Not a Fish Inspector* (1975), of which the title story is reprinted here; *Red Dust* (1978); and *What Can't Be Changed Shouldn't Be Mourned* (1990). He has also published two books of poetry, *In the Gutting Shed* (1976) and *The Carpenter of Dreams* (1986), and a novel, *Gentle Sinners*, which won the *Books in Canada* First Novel Award for 1980.

Gentle Sinners and several of Valgardson's short stories have been filmed for television, and he himself has written plays for CBC Radio. In May 1995 *Thor*, written by Valgardson and illustrated by Ange Zhang, won the annual Mr Christie Book Award for the best English-language book for children of 7 and under.

GUY VANDERHAEGHE (b. 1951) was born in Esterhazy, Sask. He studied history at the University of Saskatchewan, where he wrote an MA thesis about the novelist John Buchan. He has worked as a teacher, archivist, and researcher, and is now a full-time writer living in Saskatoon.

Vanderhaeghe began writing short stories in the late 1970s, influenced—as the critic David Staines has noted—by such prairie novelists as Margaret Laurence, Sinclair Ross, and Robert Kroetsch. Other major influences have been Alice Munro and certain writers from the American South for their treatment of small-town life. Vanderhaeghe's stories were published widely in Canadian literary magazines, and in 1980 his story 'The Watcher' won the Annual Contributor's Prize awarded by *Canadian Fiction Magazine*. Twelve of his stories appeared in the collection *Man Descending* (1982), which won a Governor General's Award. *The Trouble with Heroes*, a second collection of stories, was published in 1983. A novel, *Homesick*, was published in 1989 and won the City of Toronto Book Award. 'The Dancing Bear' is from *Man Descending*.

BRONWEN WALLACE (1945-89) was born in Kingston, Ontario, and lived most of her life there. Her poetry and short stories were published in a number of literary magazines and anthologies. She won a National Magazine Award, the Pat Lowther Award, and the Du Maurier Award for poetry. Her poems were collected in two books, *Common Magic* and *The Stubborn Particulars of Grace*. The story 'Puzzled in Wisconsin' is from her one collection of short fiction, *People You'd Trust Your Life To*, published posthumously in 1990.

RUDY WIEBE (b. 1930) was born near Fairholme, Saskatchewan, of parents who came to Canada from the Soviet Union. He attended a Mennonite high school in Coaldale, Alberta, and the University of Alberta in Edmonton, where he later taught English and creative writing. He has published numerous novels and has edited half-a-dozen short-story anthologies. Two of his novels, *Peace Shall Destroy Many* (1962) and *The Blue Mountains of China* (1970), portray the Mennonite experience in the New World. *First and Vital Candle* (1966) is about Indian and Eskimo life in the Canadian North. Both *The Temptations of Big Bear* (1973), which won a Governor General's Award, and *The Scorched-Wood People* (1977) deal with the nineteenth-century rebellions of the Indians and Métis in the Canadian Northwest. In 1994 Wiebe published *A Discovery of Strangers*, a novel that explores the encounter between John Franklin's first expedition in search of a route through the Arctic and the Yellowknife Indians.

Wiebe's stories have been collected in *Where Is the Voice Coming From?* (1974), of which the title story is reprinted here, and *The Angel of the Tar Sands and Other Stories* (1982), which also won a Governor General's Award. *River of Stone*, a collection of short fiction and memoirs, was published in 1995. Wiebe has edited *Stories from Western Canada* (1972), *Stories from Pacific and Arctic Canada* (1974, with Andreas Schroeder), and *More Stories from Western Canada* (1980, with Aritha Van Herk).

ETHEL WILSON (1888-1980), born in Port Elizabeth, South Africa, was orphaned at the age of ten and was sent to live with her grandmother in Vancouver. She was educated in boarding schools in England and Vancouver, and taught in the Vancouver school system from 1907 until 1920. In 1921 she married Dr Wallace Wilson, who had a distinguished medical career, including a term as president of the Canadian Medical Association.

Ethel Wilson began writing in her fifties; her first novel, *Hetty Dorval*, was not published until 1947. Her other long fiction includes the novel *The Innocent Traveller* (1949); two novellas published in one volume as *The Equations of Love* (1952); and two further novels, *Swamp Angel* (1954) and *Love and Salt Water* (1956). The setting for most of Ethel Wilson's fiction is Canada's West Coast, but she and her husband travelled a good deal, and the story in this collection has its origins in a trip to Egypt. Her sensibility, intelligence, and unique style made her an example for such younger women writers as Margaret Laurence, Jane Rule, and Alice Munro (all represented in this book).

Index

~